A TREASURY OF GREAT MYSTERIES

VOLUME 1

AGATHA CHRISTIE

ERLE STANLEY GARDNER

EDGAR WALLACE

GEORGES SIMENON

PATRICK QUENTIN

A TREASURY OF

MARY ROBERTS RINEHART

JOHN DICKSON CARR

ELLERY QUEEN

MARGERY ALLINGHAM

WILLIAM IRISH

ERIC AMBLER

RAYMOND CHANDLER

DOROTHY L. SAYERS

LESLIE CHARTERIS

NGAIO MARSH

REX STOUT

CRAIG RICE & STUART PALMER

CARTER DICKSON

DAPHNE du MAURIER

GREAT MYSTERIES

edited by HOWARD HAYCRAFT
and JOHN BEECROFT

SIMON AND SCHUSTER, NEW YORK

Library of Congress Catalog Card Number 57–6099

Printed in the United States of America

INTRODUCTION

ONE OF THE MOST distinguished literary figures of our time, Mr. Somerset Maugham, once declared that the reason so many modern readers have turned to mystery fiction is that here, and here alone, they can be sure of a novel which tells a story. A striking proof of Mr. Maugham's assertion occurred in London during the great blitz of 1940 when (as reported by the New York *Times*) "raid" libraries were set up nightly at the entrances to the underground shelters to supply, by popular demand, mystery stories and nothing else.

Mr. Maugham might well have added that some of the best writing and most careful craftsmanship of our age goes into the construction of the mystery story. Certainly the form has not lacked for discriminating followers. Among the heads of state (to take just one category) who have turned to mystery reading for relaxation and stimulation in difficult days may be named, among many, Presidents Woodrow Wilson and Franklin D. Roosevelt, Prime Minister Stanley Baldwin, and General George C. Marshall. In fact, the first eminent mystery fan was no less a person than Abraham Lincoln. In an early biography, published in 1860, William Dean Howells wrote that Lincoln "suffers no year to pass without a perusal" of Edgar Allan Poe's tales of detection. Small wonder that those of us with lesser burdens have found similar solace and satisfaction in the fictional pursuit of crime.

Today, of course, the mystery story is infinitely more varied than it was in Lincoln's or even Woodrow Wilson's time. Today people read mystery stories for a diversity of reasons. Some read them for the intellectual challenge of the puzzles they present; others for the vicarious pleasures of the chase. Certain thoughtful critics have suggested that mystery reading is a healthy substitute for the crimes we have all yearned to commit at one time or another. Others believe with equal conviction that the vast popularity of the *genre* lies in the fact that, in a disorderly world, it represents one of the few fixed points of order and morality, where justice may be counted on to emerge triumphant. No doubt there is truth in both assumptions. Be that as it may, it can safely be asserted that everybody who reads mysteries today does so for one common and primary reason—they are good entertainment.

In the present collection your editors have attempted to bring together the most enjoyable examples of all types of the modern mystery. To the best of our knowledge no previous mystery anthology has assembled so much material in a single collection, and no previous collection has combined novels, novelettes, and shorter matter to the same extent. We hope you will like the freshness of this approach, as well as the material itself, much of which is appearing in book form for the first time, or (especially the longer selections) has not been obtainable for some years.

It should be said promptly that this collection makes no pretense of being either "historical" or "definitive." Rather, the editors have simply tried to find and present the most entertaining examples they could of modern mystery writing (by modern meaning the last quarter century, give or take a few years). Coincidentally—though this was not a part of the planning of the work—all the authors represented save one, are alive and active, at press time. Our only regret is that there are so many fine writers and stories we did not have room to include. In this connection we are well aware that every reader or critic would have chosen differently in some respect—but that is an occupational hazard every anthologist must cheerfully assume.

Here, then, are stories of detection and of fear; of puzzles resolved and of perils escaped. American mysteries, English mysteries, and one French mystery. Deductive masterpieces and gay sleuthing adventures. Serious stories, tender stories, humorous stories. Hardboiled mysteries, softboiled mysteries —and just plain mysteries. If they have a common denominator, we like to think it is quality—each in its own special category or type.

We have greatly enjoyed putting these volumes together. We hope you will like them too.

In addition to the formal acknowledgments which follow, we wish to express our special gratitude to Mr. Milton Runyon of Doubleday & Company, Inc. and Miss Lee Wright of Simon and Schuster for their advice and encouragement at all stages of the editorial work.

HOWARD HAYCRAFT

CONTENTS

VOLUME 1

MURDER IN THE CALAIS COACH

by Agatha Christie

PART ONE *The Facts*

CHAPTER ONE

AN IMPORTANT PASSENGER ON THE TAURUS EXPRESS

IT WAS five o'clock on a winter's morning in Syria. Alongside the platform at Aleppo stood the train grandly designated in railway guides as the Taurus Express. It consisted of a kitchen and dining-car, a sleeping-car and two local coaches.

By the step leading up into the sleeping-car stood a young French lieutenant, resplendent in uniform, conversing with a small man muffled up to the ears of whom nothing was visible but a pink-tipped nose and the two points of an upward-curled moustache.

It was freezingly cold, and this job of seeing off a distinguished stranger was not one to be envied, but Lieutenant Dubosc performed his part manfully. Graceful phrases fell from his lips in polished French. Not that he knew what it was all about. There had been rumours, of course, as there always were in such cases. The General's—*his* General's—temper had grown worse and worse. And then there had come this Belgian stranger—all the way from England, it seemed. There had been a week—a week of curious tensity. And then certain things had happened. A very distinguished officer had committed suicide, another had suddenly resigned, anxious faces had suddenly lost their anxiety, certain military precautions were relaxed. And the General, Lieutenant Dubosc's own particular General, had suddenly looked ten years younger.

Dubosc had overheard part of a conversation between him and the stranger. "You have saved us, *mon cher*," said the General emotionally, his great white moustache trembling as he spoke. "You have saved the honour of the French Army—you have averted much bloodshed! How can I thank you for acceding to my request? To have come so far—"

To which the stranger (by name M. Hercule Poirot) had made a fitting reply including the phrase—"But indeed, do I not remember that once you saved my life?" And then the General had made another fitting reply to that, disclaiming any merit for that past service; and with more mention of France, of

Belgium, of glory, of honour and of such kindred things they had embraced each other heartily and the conversation had ended.

As to what it had all been about, Lieutenant Dubosc was still in the dark, but to him had been delegated the duty of seeing off M. Poirot by the Taurus Express, and he was carrying it out with all the zeal and ardour befitting a young officer with a promising career ahead of him.

"To-day is Sunday," said Lieutenant Dubosc. "To-morrow, Monday evening, you will be in Stamboul."

It was not the first time he had made this observation. Conversations on the platform, before the departure of a train, are apt to be somewhat repetitive in character.

"That is so," agreed M. Poirot.

"And you intend to remain there a few days, I think?"

"*Mais oui*. Stamboul, it is a city I have never visited. It would be a pity to pass through—*comme ça*." He snapped his fingers descriptively. "Nothing presses—I shall remain there as a tourist for a few days."

"La Sainte Sophie, it is very fine," said Lieutenant Dubosc, who had never seen it.

A cold wind came whistling down the platform. Both men shivered. Lieutenant Dubosc managed to cast a surreptitious glance at his watch. Five minutes to five—only five minutes more!

Fancying that the other man had noticed his glance, he hastened once more into speech.

"There are few people travelling this time of year," he said, glancing up at the windows of the sleeping-car above them.

"That is so," agreed M. Poirot.

"Let us hope you will not be snowed up in the Taurus!"

"That happens?"

"It has occurred, yes. Not this year, as yet."

"Let us hope, then," said M. Poirot. "The weather reports from Europe, they are bad."

"Very bad. In the Balkans there is much snow."

"In Germany, too, I have heard."

"*Eh bien*," said Lieutenant Dubosc hastily as another pause seemed to be about to occur. "To-morrow evening at seven-forty you will be in Constantinople."

"Yes," said M. Poirot, and went on desperately, "La Sainte Sophie, I have heard it is very fine."

"Magnificent, I believe."

Above their heads the blinds of one of the sleeping-car compartments was pushed aside and a young woman looked out.

Mary Debenham had had little sleep since she left Baghdad on the preceding Thursday. Neither in the train to Kirkuk, nor in the Rest House at Mosul, nor last night on the train had she slept properly. Now, weary of lying wakeful in the hot stuffiness of her overheated compartment, she got up and peered out.

This must be Aleppo. Nothing to see, of course. Just a long, poorly lighted platform with loud, furious altercations in Arabic going on somewhere. Two men below her window were talking French. One was a French officer, the other was a little man with enormous moustaches. She smiled faintly. She had never seen anyone quite so heavily muffled up. It must be very cold outside. That was why they heated the train so terribly. She tried to force the window down lower, but it would not go.

The Wagon Lit conductor had come up to the two men. The train was about to depart, he said. Monsieur had better mount. The little man removed his hat. What an egg-shaped head he had! In spite of her preoccupations Mary Debenham smiled. A ridiculous-looking little man. The sort of little man one could never take seriously.

Lieutenant Dubosc was saying his parting speech. He had thought it out beforehand and had kept it till the last minute. It was a very beautiful, polished speech.

Not to be outdone, M. Poirot replied in kind. . . .

"*En voiture, Monsieur,*" said the Wagon Lit conductor.

With an air of infinite reluctance M. Poirot climbed aboard the train. The conductor climbed after him. M. Poirot waved his hand. Lieutenant Dubosc came to the salute. The train, with a terrific jerk, moved slowly forward.

"*Enfin!*" murmured M. Hercule Poirot.

"*Brrrrrrrr,*" said Lieutenant Dubosc, realising to the full how cold he was.

"*Voilà, Monsieur!*" The conductor displayed to Poirot with a dramatic gesture the beauty of his sleeping compartment and the neat arrangement of his luggage. "The little valise of Monsieur, I have put it *here.*"

His outstretched hand was suggestive. Hercule Poirot placed in it a folded note.

"*Merci, Monsieur.*" The conductor became brisk and business-like. "I have the tickets of Monsieur. I will also take the passport, please. Monsieur breaks his journey in Stamboul, I understand?"

M. Poirot assented. "There are not many people travelling, I imagine?" he said.

"No, Monsieur. I have only two other passengers—both English. A Colonel from India and a young English lady from Baghdad. Monsieur requires anything?"

Monsieur demanded a small bottle of Perrier.

Five o'clock in the morning is an awkward time to board a train. There were still two hours before dawn. Conscious of an inadequate night's sleep, and of a delicate mission successfully accomplished, M. Poirot curled up in a corner and fell asleep.

When he awoke it was half-past nine and he sallied forth to the restaurant car in search of hot coffee.

There was only one occupant at the moment, obviously the young English lady referred to by the conductor. She was tall, slim and dark—perhaps twenty-eight years of age. There was a kind of cool efficiency in the way she was eating her breakfast and in the way she called to the attendant to bring her more coffee which bespoke a knowledge of the world and of travelling. She wore a dark-coloured travelling dress of some thin material eminently suitable for the heated atmosphere of the train.

M. Hercule Poirot, having nothing better to do, amused himself by studying her without appearing to do so.

She was, he judged, the kind of young woman who could take care of herself with perfect ease wherever she went. She had poise and efficiency. He rather liked the severe regularity of her features and the delicate pallor of her skin. He liked the burnished black head with its neat waves of hair, and her eyes—cool, impersonal and grey. But she was, he decided, just a little too efficient to be what he called "*jolie femme.*"

Presently another person entered the restaurant car. This was a tall man of between forty and fifty, lean of figure, brown of skin, with hair slightly grizzled round the temples.

"The Colonel from India," said Poirot to himself.

The newcomer gave a little bow to the girl. "Morning, Miss Debenham."

"Good morning, Colonel Arbuthnot."

The Colonel was standing with a hand on the chair opposite her.

"Any objections?" he asked.

"Of course not. Sit down."

"Well, you know, breakfast isn't always a chatty meal."

"I should hope not. But I don't bite."

The Colonel sat down. "Boy," he called in peremptory fashion.

He gave an order for eggs and coffee.

His eyes rested for a moment on Hercule Poirot, but they passed on indifferently. Poirot, reading the English mind correctly, knew that he had said to himself: "Only some damned foreigner."

True to their nationality, the two English people were not chatty. They exchanged a few brief remarks and presently the girl rose and went back to her compartment.

At lunch time the other two again shared a table and again they both completely ignored the third passenger. Their conversation was more animated than at breakfast. Colonel Arbuthnot talked of the Punjab and occasionally asked the girl a few questions about Baghdad where, it became clear, she had been in a post as governess. In the course of conversation they discovered some mutual friends, which had the immediate effect of making them more friendly and less stiff. They discussed old Tommy Somebody and old Reggie Someone Else. The Colonel inquired whether she was going straight through to England or whether she was stopping in Stamboul.

"No, I'm going straight on."

"Isn't that rather a pity?"

"I came out this way two years ago and spent three days in Stamboul then."

"Oh! I see. Well, I may say I'm very glad you are going right through, because I am."

He made a kind of clumsy little bow, flushing a little as he did so.

"He is susceptible, our Colonel," thought Hercule Poirot to himself with some amusement. "The train, it is as dangerous as a sea voyage!"

Miss Debenham said evenly that that would be very nice. Her manner was slightly repressive.

The Colonel, Hercule Poirot noticed, accompanied her back to her compartment. Later they passed through the magnificent scenery of the Taurus. As they looked down towards the Cilician Gates, standing in the corridor side by side, a sigh came suddenly from the girl. Poirot was standing near them and heard her murmur:

"It's so beautiful! I wish—I wish—"

"Yes?"

"I wish I could enjoy it!"

Arbuthnot did not answer. The square line of his jaw seemed a little sterner and grimmer.

"I wish to Heaven you were out of all this," he said.

"Hush, please. Hush."

"Oh! it's all right." He shot a slightly annoyed glance in Poirot's direction. Then he went on: "But I don't like the idea of your being a governess—at the beck and call of tyrannical mothers and their tiresome brats."

She laughed with just a hint of uncontrol in the sound.

"Oh! you mustn't think that. The downtrodden governess is quite an exploded myth. I can assure you that it's the parents who are afraid of being bullied by *me*."

They said no more. Arbuthnot was, perhaps, ashamed of his outburst.

"Rather an odd little comedy that I watch here," said Poirot to himself thoughtfully.

He was to remember that thought of his later.

They arrived at Konya that night about half-past eleven. The two English travellers got out to stretch their legs, pacing up and down the snowy platform.

M. Poirot was content to watch the teeming activity of the station through a window pane. After about ten minutes, however, he decided that a breath of air would not perhaps be a bad thing after all. He made careful preparations, wrapping himself in several coats and mufflers and encasing his neat boots in goloshes. Thus attired, he descended gingerly to the platform and began to pace its length. He walked out beyond the engine.

It was the voices which gave him the clue to the two indistinct figures standing in the shadow of a traffic van. Arbuthnot was speaking.

"Mary—"

The girl interrupted him.

"Not now. Not now. When it's all over. When it's behind us—*then*—"

Discreetly M. Poirot turned away. He wondered. . . .

He would hardly have recognised the cool, efficient voice of Miss Debenham. . . .

"Curious," he said to himself.

The next day he wondered whether, perhaps, they had quarrelled. They spoke little to each other. The girl, he thought, looked anxious. There were dark circles under her eyes.

It was about half-past two in the afternoon when the train came to a halt. Heads were poked out of windows. A little knot of men were clustered by the side of the line looking and pointing at something under the dining-car.

Poirot leaned out and spoke to the Wagon Lit conductor who was hurrying past. The man answered, and Poirot drew back his head and, turning, almost collided with Mary Debenham who was standing just behind him.

"What is the matter?" she asked rather breathlessly in French. "Why are we stopping?"

"It is nothing, Mademoiselle. It is something that has caught fire under the dining-car. Nothing serious. It is put out. They are now repairing the damage. There is no danger, I assure you."

She made a little abrupt gesture, as though she were waving the idea of danger aside as something completely unimportant.

"Yes, yes, I understand that. But the *time!*"

"The time?"

"Yes, this will delay us."

"It is possible—yes," agreed Poirot.

"But we can't afford delay! This train is due in at 6.55, and one has to cross the Bosphorus and catch the Simplon Orient Express on the other side at nine o'clock. If there is an hour or two of delay we shall miss the connection."

"It is possible, yes," he admitted.

He looked at her curiously. The hand that held the window bar was not quite steady; her lips, too, were trembling.

"Does it matter to you very much, Mademoiselle?" he asked.

"Yes. Yes, it does. I—I *must* catch that train."

She turned away from him and went down the corridor to join Colonel Arbuthnot.

Her anxiety, however, was needless. Ten minutes later the train started again. It arrived at Haydapassar only five minutes late, having made up time on the journey.

The Bosphorus was rough and M. Poirot did not enjoy the crossing. He was separated from his travelling companions on the boat and did not see them again.

On arrival at the Galata Bridge he drove straight to the Tokatlian Hotel.

CHAPTER TWO

THE TOKATLIAN HOTEL

AT THE TOKATLIAN, Hercule Poirot asked for a room with bath. Then he stepped over to the concierge's desk and inquired for letters.

There were three waiting for him and a telegram. His eyebrows rose a little at the sight of the telegram. It was unexpected.

He opened it in his usual neat, unhurried fashion. The printed words stood out clearly.

> *Development you predicted in Kassner case has come unexpectedly. Please return immediately.*

"*Voilà ce qui est embêtant,*" muttered Poirot vexedly. He glanced up at the clock. "I shall have to go on to-night," he said to the concierge. "At what time does the Simplon Orient leave?"

"At nine o'clock, Monsieur."

"Can you get me a sleeper?"

"Assuredly, Monsieur. There is no difficulty this time of year. The trains are almost empty. First-class or second?"

"First."

"*Très bien, Monsieur.* How far are you going?"

"To London."

"*Bien, Monsieur.* I will get you a ticket to London and reserve your sleeping-car accommodation in the Stamboul-Calais coach."

Poirot glanced at the clock again. It was ten minutes to eight. "I have time to dine?"

"But assuredly, Monsieur."

The little Belgian nodded. He went over and cancelled his room order and crossed the hall to the restaurant.

As he was giving his order to the waiter, a hand was placed on his shoulder.

"Ah, *mon vieux,* but this is an unexpected pleasure!" said a voice behind him.

The speaker was a short stout elderly man, his hair cut *en brosse.* He was smiling delightedly.

Poirot sprang up.

"M. Bouc!"

"M. Poirot!"

M. Bouc was a Belgian, a director of the Compagnie Internationale des Wagons Lits, and his acquaintance with the former star of the Belgian police force dated back many years.

"You find yourself far from home, *mon cher,*" said M. Bouc.

"A little affair in Syria."

"Ah! and you return home—when?"

"To-night."

"Splendid! I, too. That is to say, I go as far as Lausanne, where I have affairs. You travel on the Simplon Orient, I presume?"

"Yes. I have just asked them to get me a sleeper. It was my intention to remain here some days, but I have received a telegram recalling me to England on important business."

"Ah!" sighed M. Bouc. "*Les affaires—les affaires!* But you, you are at the top of the tree nowadays, *mon vieux!*"

"Some little success I have had, perhaps." Hercule Poirot tried to look modest but failed signally.

M. Bouc laughed.

"We will meet later," he said.

Hercule Poirot addressed himself to the task of keeping his moustaches out of the soup.

That difficult task accomplished, he glanced round him whilst waiting for the next course. There were only about half a dozen people in the restaurant, and of those half dozen there were only two that interested Hercule Poirot.

These two sat at a table not far away. The younger was a likeable-looking young man of thirty, clearly an American. It was, however, not he but his companion who had attracted the little detective's attention.

He was a man perhaps of between sixty and seventy. From a little distance he had the bland aspect of a philanthropist. His slightly bald head, his domed forehead, the smiling mouth that displayed a very white set of false teeth—all seemed to speak of a benevolent personality. Only the eyes belied this assumption. They were small, deep-set and crafty. Not only that. As the man, making some remark to his young companion, glanced across the room, his gaze stopped on Poirot for a moment and just for that second there was a strange malevolence, an unnatural tensity in the glance.

Then he rose.

"Pay the bill, Hector," he said.

His voice was slightly husky in tone. It had a queer, soft, dangerous quality.

When Poirot rejoined his friend in the lounge, the other two men were just leaving the hotel. Their luggage was being brought down. The younger was supervising the process. Presently he opened the glass door and said:

"Quite ready now, Mr. Ratchett."

The elder man grunted an assent and passed out.

"*Eh bien,*" said Poirot. "What do you think of those two?"

"They are Americans," said M. Bouc.

"Assuredly they are Americans. I meant what did you think of their personalities?"

"The young man seemed quite agreeable."

"And the other?"

"To tell you the truth, my friend, I did not care for him. He produced on me an unpleasant impression. And you?"

Hercule Poirot was a moment in replying.

"When he passed me in the restaurant," he said at last, "I had a curious impression. It was as though a wild animal—an animal savage, but savage! you understand—had passed me by."

"And yet he looked altogether of the most respectable."

"*Précisément!* The body—the cage—is everything of the most respectable—but through the bars, the wild animal looks out."

"You are fanciful, *mon vieux*," said M. Bouc.

"It may be so. But I could not rid myself of the impression that evil had passed me by very close."

"That respectable American gentleman?"

"That respectable American gentleman."

"Well," said M. Bouc cheerfully, "it may be so. There is much evil in the world."

At that moment the door opened and the concierge came towards them. He looked concerned and apologetic.

"It is extraordinary, Monsieur," he said to Poirot. "There is not one first-class sleeping berth to be had on the train."

"*Comment?*" cried M. Bouc. "At this time of year? Ah, without doubt there is some party of journalists—of politicians—?"

"I don't know, sir," said the concierge, turning to him respectfully. "But that's how it is."

"Well, well." M. Bouc turned to Poirot. "Have no fear, my friend. We will arrange something. There is always one compartment, the No. 16, which is not engaged. The conductor sees to that!" He smiled, then glanced up at the clock. "Come," he said, "it is time we started."

At the station M. Bouc was greeted with respectful empressement by the brown-uniformed Wagon Lit conductor.

"Good evening, Monsieur. Your compartment is the No. 1."

He called to the porters and they wheeled their load half-way along the carriage on which the tin plates proclaimed its destination:

ISTANBUL TRIESTE CALAIS

"You are full up to-night, I hear?"

"It is incredible, Monsieur. All the world elects to travel to-night!"

"All the same you must find room for this gentleman here. He is a friend of mine. He can have the No. 16."

"It is taken, Monsieur."

"What? The No. 16?"

A glance of understanding passed between them, and the conductor smiled. He was a tall sallow man of middle age.

"But yes, Monsieur. As I told you, we are full—full—everywhere."

"But what passes itself?" demanded M. Bouc angrily. "There is a conference somewhere? It is a party?"

"No, Monsieur. It is only chance. It just happens that many people have elected to travel to-night."

M. Bouc made a clicking sound of annoyance.

"At Belgrade," he said, "there will be the slip coach from Athens. There will also be the Bucharest-Paris coach. But we do not reach Belgrade until to-morrow evening. The problem is for to-night. There is no second-class berth free?"

"There *is* a second-class berth, Monsieur—"

"Well, then—"

"But it is a lady's berth. There is already a German woman in the compartment—a lady's-maid."

"Là-là, that is awkward," said M. Bouc.

"Do not distress yourself, my friend," said Poirot. "I must travel in an ordinary carriage."

"Not at all. Not at all." He turned once more to the conductor. "Everyone has arrived?"

"It is true," said the man, "that there is one passenger who has not yet arrived." He spoke slowly, with hesitation.

"But speak then!"

"No. 7 berth—a second-class. The gentleman has not yet come, and it is four minutes to nine."

"Who is it?"

"An Englishman," the conductor consulted his list. "A M. Harris."

"A name of good omen," said Poirot. "I read my Dickens. M. Harris he will not arrive."

"Put Monsieur's luggage in No. 7," said M. Bouc. "If this M. Harris arrives we will tell him that he is too late—that berths cannot be retained so long— we will arrange the matter one way or another. What do I care for a M. Harris?"

"As Monsieur pleases," said the conductor. He spoke to Poirot's porter, directing him where to go. Then he stood aside from the steps to let Poirot enter the train.

"*Tout à fait au bout, Monsieur,*" he called. "The end compartment but one."

Poirot passed along the corridor, a somewhat slow progress, since most of the people travelling were standing outside their carriages.

His polite "Pardons" were uttered with the regularity of clockwork. At last he reached the compartment indicated. Inside it, reaching up to a suitcase, was the tall young American of the Tokatlian.

He frowned as Poirot entered.

"Excuse me," he said. "I think you've made a mistake." Then, laboriously in French: "*Je crois que vous avez un erreur.*"

Poirot replied in English. "You are Mr. Harris?"

"No, my name is MacQueen. I—"

But at that moment the voice of the Wagon Lit conductor spoke from over Poirot's shoulder—an apologetic, rather breathless voice.

"There is no other berth on the train, Monsieur. The gentleman has to come in here."

He was hauling up the corridor window as he spoke and began to lift in Poirot's luggage.

Poirot noticed the apology in his tone with some amusement. Doubtless the man had been promised a good tip if he could keep the compartment for the sole use of the other traveller. However, even the most munificent of tips lose their effect when a Director of the Company is on board and issues his orders.

The conductor emerged from the compartment, having swung the suitcases up onto the racks.

"Voilà, Monsieur," he said. "All is arranged. Yours is the upper berth, the No. 7. We start in one minute."

He hurried off down the corridor. Poirot re-entered the compartment.

"A phenomenon I have seldom seen," he said cheerfully. "A Wagon Lit conductor himself puts up the luggage! It is unheard of!"

His fellow traveller smiled. He had evidently got over his annoyance—had probably decided that it was no good to take the matter otherwise than philosophically. "The train's remarkably full," he said.

A whistle blew, there was a long melancholy cry from the engine. Both men stepped out into the corridor.

Outside a voice shouted, "En voiture!"

"We're off," said MacQueen.

But they were not quite off. The whistle blew again.

"I say, sir," said the young man suddenly. "If you'd rather have the lower berth—easier and all that—well, that's all right by me."

A likeable young fellow.

"No, no," protested Poirot. "I would not deprive you—"

"That's all right—"

"You are too amiable—"

Polite protests on both sides.

"It is for one night only," explained Poirot. "At Belgrade—"

"Oh! I see. You're getting out at Belgrade—"

"Not exactly. You see—"

There was a sudden jerk. Both men swung round to the window, looking out at the long lighted platform as it slid slowly past them.

The Orient Express had started on its three-day journey across Europe.

CHAPTER THREE

POIROT REFUSES A CASE

M. HERCULE POIROT was a little late in entering the luncheon-car on the following day. He had risen early, had breakfasted almost alone, and had spent the morning going over the notes of the case that was recalling him to London. He had seen little of his travelling companion.

M. Bouc, who was already seated, gesticulated a greeting and summoned his friend to the empty place opposite him. Poirot sat down and soon found himself in the favoured position of being at the table which was served first and with the choicest morsels. The food, too, was unusually good.

It was not till they were eating a delicate cream cheese that M. Bouc allowed his attention to wander to matters other than nourishment. He was at the stage of a meal when one becomes philosophic.

"Ah!" he sighed. "If I had but the pen of a Balzac! I would depict this scene." He waved a hand.

"It is an idea, that," said Poirot.

"Ah, you agree? It has not been done, I think? And yet—it lends itself to romance, my friend. All around us are people, of all classes, of all nationalities, of all ages. For three days these people, these strangers to one another, are brought together. They sleep and eat under one roof, they cannot get away from each other. At the end of three days they part, they go their several ways, never perhaps to see each other again."

"And yet," said Poirot, "suppose an accident—"

"Ah, no, my friend—"

"From your point of view it would be regrettable, I agree. But nevertheless let us just for one moment suppose it. Then, perhaps, all these here are linked together—by death."

"Some more wine," said M. Bouc, hastily pouring it out. "You are morbid, *mon cher*. It is, perhaps, the digestion."

"It is true," agreed Poirot, "that the food in Syria was not perhaps quite suited to my stomach."

He sipped his wine. Then, leaning back, he ran his eye thoughtfully round the dining-car. There were thirteen people seated there and, as M. Bouc had said, of all classes and nationalities. He began to study them.

At the table opposite them were three men. They were, he guessed, single travellers graded and placed there by the unerring judgment of the restaurant attendants. A big swarthy Italian was picking his teeth with gusto. Opposite him a spare neat Englishman had the expressionless disapproving face of the well-trained servant. Next to the Englishman was a big American in a loud suit—possibly a commercial traveller.

"You've got to put it over *big*," he was saying in a loud, nasal voice.

The Italian removed his toothpick to gesticulate with it freely.

"Sure," he said. "That whatta I say alla de time."

The Englishman looked out of the window and coughed.

Poirot's eye passed on.

At a small table, sitting very upright, was one of the ugliest old ladies he had ever seen. It was an ugliness of distinction—it fascinated rather than repelled. She sat very upright. Round her neck was a collar of very large pearls which, improbable though it seemed, were real. Her hands were covered with rings. Her sable coat was pushed back on her shoulders. A very small and expensive black toque was hideously unbecoming to the yellow, toad-like face beneath it.

She was speaking now to the restaurant attendant in a clear, courteous, but completely autocratic tone.

"You will be sufficiently amiable to place in my compartment a bottle of mineral water and a large glass of orange juice. You will arrange that I shall have chicken cooked without sauces for dinner this evening—also some boiled fish."

The attendant replied respectfully that it should be done.

She gave a slight gracious nod of the head and rose. Her glance caught Poirot's and swept over him with the nonchalance of the uninterested aristocrat.

"That is Princess Dragomiroff," said M. Bouc in a low tone. "She is a Russian. Her husband realised all his money before the Revolution and invested it abroad. She is extremely rich. A cosmopolitan."

Poirot nodded. He had heard of Princess Dragomiroff.

"She is a personality," said M. Bouc. "Ugly as sin but she makes herself felt. You agree?"

Poirot agreed.

At another of the large tables Mary Debenham was sitting with two other women. One of them was tall and middle-aged, in a plaid blouse and tweed skirt. She had a mass of faded yellow hair unbecomingly arranged in a large bun, wore glasses, and had a long mild amiable face rather like a sheep. She was listening to the third woman, a stout, pleasant-faced, elderly person who was talking in a slow clear monotone which showed no signs of pausing for breath or coming to a stop.

"—and so my daughter said, 'Why,' she said, 'you just can't apply American methods in this country. It's natural to the folks here to be indolent,' she said. 'They just haven't got any hustle in them—' But all the same you'd be surprised to know what our college there is doing. They've got a fine staff of teachers. I guess there's nothing like education. We've got to apply our Western ideals and teach the East to recognise them. My daughter says—"

The train plunged into a tunnel. The calm, monotonous voice was drowned.

At the next table, a small one, sat Colonel Arbuthnot—alone. His gaze was fixed upon the back of Mary Debenham's head. They were not sitting together. Yet it could easily have been managed. Why?

Perhaps, Poirot thought, Mary Debenham had demurred. A governess learns to be careful. Appearances are important. A girl with her living to get has to be discreet.

His glance shifted to the other side of the carriage. At the far end, against the wall, was a middle-aged woman dressed in black with a broad, expressionless face. German or Scandinavian, he thought. Probably the German lady's-maid.

Beyond her were a couple leaning forward and talking animatedly together. The man wore English clothes of loose tweed, but he was not English. Though only the back of his head was visible to Poirot, the shape of it and the set of the shoulders betrayed him. A big man, well made. He turned his head suddenly and Poirot saw his profile. A very handsome man of thirty-odd with a big fair moustache.

The woman opposite him was a mere girl—twenty at a guess. A tight-fitting little black coat and skirt, white satin blouse, small chic black toque perched at the fashionable outrageous angle. She had a beautiful foreign-looking face, dead white skin, large brown eyes, jet black hair. She was smoking a cigarette in a long holder. Her manicured hands had deep red nails. She wore one large emerald set in platinum. There was coquetry in her glance and voice.

"*Elle est jolie—et chic*," murmured Poirot. "Husband and wife—eh?"

M. Bouc nodded. "Hungarian Embassy, I believe," he said. "A handsome couple."

There were only two more lunchers—Poirot's fellow traveller MacQueen and his employer Mr. Ratchett. The latter sat facing Poirot, and for the second time Poirot studied that unprepossessing face, noting the false benevolence of the brow and the small, cruel eyes.

Doubtless M. Bouc saw a change in his friend's expression.

"It is at your wild animal you look?" he asked.

Poirot nodded.

As his coffee was brought to him, M. Bouc rose to his feet. Having started before Poirot he had finished some time ago.

"I return to my compartment," he said. "Come along presently and converse with me."

"With pleasure."

Poirot sipped his coffee and ordered a liqueur. The attendant was passing from table to table with his box of money, accepting payment for bills. The elderly American lady's voice rose shrill and plaintive.

"My daughter said: 'Take a book of food tickets and you'll have no trouble —no trouble at all.' Now, that isn't so. Seems they have to have a ten per cent tip, and then there's that bottle of mineral water—and a queer sort of water too. They didn't have any Evian or Vichy, which seems queer to me."

"It is—they must—how do you say?—serve the water of the country," explained the sheep-faced lady.

"Well, it seems queer to me." She looked distastefully at the heap of small change on the table in front of her. "Look at all this peculiar stuff he's given me. Dinars or something. Just a lot of rubbish, it looks like! My daughter said—"

Mary Debenham pushed back her chair and left with a slight bow to the other two. Colonel Arbuthnot got up and followed her. Gathering up her despised money the American woman followed suit, followed by the other one like a sheep. The Hungarians had already departed. The restaurant car was empty save for Poirot and Ratchett and MacQueen.

Ratchett spoke to his companion, who got up and left the car. Then he rose himself, but instead of following MacQueen he dropped unexpectedly into the seat opposite Poirot.

"Can you oblige me with a light?" he said. His voice was soft—faintly nasal. "My name is Ratchett."

Poirot bowed slightly. He slipped his hand into his pocket and produced a matchbox which he handed to the other man, who took it but did not strike a light.

"I think," he went on, "that I have the pleasure of speaking to Mr. Hercule Poirot. Is that so?"

Poirot bowed again. "You have been correctly informed, Monsieur."

The detective was conscious of those strange shrewd eyes summing him up before the other spoke again.

"In my country," he said, "we come to the point quickly. Mr. Poirot, I want you to take on a job for me."

Hercule Poirot's eyebrows went up a trifle.

"My *clientèle*, Monsieur, is limited nowadays. I undertake very few cases."

"Why, naturally, I understand that. But this, Mr. Poirot, means big money." He repeated again in his soft, persuasive voice, "Big money."

Hercule Poirot was silent a minute or two. Then he said: "What is it you wish me to do for you, Monsieur—er—Ratchett?"

"Mr. Poirot, I am a rich man—a very rich man. Men in that position have enemies. I have an enemy."

"Only one enemy?"

"Just what do you mean by that question?" asked Ratchett sharply.

"Monsieur, in my experience when a man is in a position to have, as you say, enemies, then it does not usually resolve itself into one enemy only."

Ratchett seemed relieved by Poirot's answer. He said quickly:

"Why, yes, I appreciate that point. Enemy or enemies—it doesn't matter. What does matter is my safety."

"Safety?"

"My life has been threatened, Mr. Poirot. Now I'm a man who can take pretty good care of himself." From the pocket of his coat his hand brought a small automatic into sight for a moment. He continued grimly. "I don't think I'm the kind of man to be caught napping. But, as I look at it, I might as well make assurance doubly sure. I fancy you're the man for my money, Mr. Poirot. And remember—*big* money."

Poirot looked at him thoughtfully for some minutes. His face was completely expressionless. The other could have had no clue as to what thoughts were passing in that mind.

"I regret, Monsieur," he said at length, "that I cannot oblige you."

The other looked at him shrewdly. "Name your figure, then," he said.

Poirot shook his head.

"You do not understand, Monsieur. I have been very fortunate in my profession. I have made enough money to satisfy both my needs and my caprices. I take now only such cases as—interest me."

"You've got a pretty good nerve," said Ratchett. "Will twenty thousand dollars tempt you?"

"It will not."

"If you're holding out for more, you won't get it. I know what a thing's worth to me."

"I, also, M. Ratchett."

"What's wrong with my proposition?"

Poirot rose. "If you will forgive me for being personal—I do not like your face, M. Ratchett," he said.

And with that he left the restaurant car.

CHAPTER FOUR

A CRY IN THE NIGHT

THE SIMPLON ORIENT EXPRESS arrived at Belgrade at a quarter to nine that evening. It was not due to depart again until 9.15, so Poirot descended to the platform. He did not, however, remain there long. The cold was bitter, and though the platform itself was protected, heavy snow was falling outside. He returned to his compartment. The conductor, who was on the platform stamping his feet and waving his arms to keep warm, spoke to him.

"Your valises have been moved, Monsieur. To the compartment No. 1, the compartment of M. Bouc."

"But where is Monsieur Bouc, then?"

"He has moved into the coach from Athens which has just been put on."

Poirot went in search of his friend. M. Bouc waved his protestations aside.

"It is nothing. It is nothing. It is more convenient like this. You are going through to England, so it is better that you should stay in the through coach to Calais. Me, I am very well here. It is most peaceful. This coach is empty save for myself and one little Greek doctor. Ah! my friend, what a night! They say there has not been so much snow for years. Let us hope we shall not be held up. I am not too happy about it, I can tell you."

At 9.15 punctually the train pulled out of the station, and shortly afterwards Poirot got up, said good night to his friend, and made his way along the corridor back into his own coach which was in front next to the dining-car.

On this, the second day of the journey, barriers were breaking down. Colonel Arbuthnot was standing at the door of his compartment talking to MacQueen. When MacQueen saw Poirot he broke off something he was saying. He looked very much surprised.

"Why," he cried, "I thought you'd left us. You said you were getting off at Belgrade."

"You misunderstood me," said Poirot, smiling. "I remember now, the train started from Stamboul just as we were talking about it."

"But, man, your baggage. It's gone."

"It has been moved into another compartment, that is all."

"Oh! I see."

He resumed his conversation with Arbuthnot, and Poirot passed on down the corridor.

Two doors from his own compartment, the elderly American, Mrs. Hubbard, was standing talking to the sheep-like lady, who was a Swede. Mrs. Hubbard was pressing a magazine on the other.

"No, do take it, my dear," she said. "I've got plenty of other things to read. My, isn't the cold something frightful?" She nodded amicably to Poirot.

"You are most kind," said the Swedish lady.

"Not at all. I hope you'll sleep well and that your head will be better in the morning."

"It is the cold only. I make now myself a cup of tea."

"Have you got some aspirin? Are you sure now? I've got plenty. Well, good night, my dear."

She turned to Poirot conversationally as the other woman departed.

"Poor creature, she's a Swede. As far as I can make out she's a kind of missionary. A teaching one. A nice creature, but doesn't talk much English. She was *most* interested in what I told her about my daughter."

Poirot, by now, knew all about Mrs. Hubbard's daughter. Everyone on the train who could understand English did! How she and her husband were on the staff of a big American college in Smyrna, and how this was Mrs. Hubbard's first journey to the East, and what she thought of the Turks and their slipshod ways and the condition of their roads.

The door next to them opened and the thin pale man-servant stepped out. Inside, Poirot caught a glimpse of Mr. Ratchett sitting up in bed. He saw Poirot and his face changed, darkening with anger. Then the door was shut.

Mrs. Hubbard drew Poirot a little aside.

"You know, I'm dead scared of that man. Oh! not the valet—the other. His master. Master, indeed! There's something *wrong* about that man. My daughter always says I'm very intuitive. 'When Mamma gets a hunch, she's dead right,' that's what my daughter says. And I've got a hunch about that man. He's next door to me and I don't like it. I put my grips against the communicating door last night. I thought I heard him trying the handle. Do you know, I shouldn't be a bit surprised if that man turned out to be a murderer—one of these train robbers you read about. I daresay I'm foolish, but there it is. I'm absolutely scared to death of the man! My daughter said I'd have an easy journey, but somehow I don't feel happy about it. It may be foolish, but I feel as if anything might happen—anything at all. And how that nice young fellow can bear to be his secretary, I can't think."

Colonel Arbuthnot and MacQueen were coming towards them down the corridor.

"Come into my carriage," MacQueen was saying. "It isn't made up for the night yet. Now what I want to get right about your policy in India is this—"

The two men passed and went on down the corridor to MacQueen's carriage.

Mrs. Hubbard said good night to Poirot. "I guess I'll go right to bed and read," she said. "Good night."

"Good night, Madame."

Poirot passed into his own compartment, which was the next one beyond Ratchett's. He undressed and got into bed, read for about half an hour and then turned out the light.

He awoke some hours later, awoke with a start. He knew what it was that had wakened him—a loud groan, almost a cry, somewhere close at hand. At the same moment the ting of a bell sounded sharply.

Poirot sat up and switched on the light. He noticed that the train was at a standstill—presumably at a station.

That cry had startled him. He remembered that it was Ratchett who had the next compartment. He got out of bed and opened the door just as the Wagon Lit conductor came hurrying along the corridor and knocked on Ratchett's door. Poirot kept his door open a crack and watched. The conductor tapped a second time. A bell rang and a light showed over another door farther down. The conductor glanced over his shoulder. At the same moment a voice from within the next compartment called out: *"Ce n'est rien. Je me suis trompé."*

"Bien, Monsieur." The conductor scurried off again, to knock at the door where the light was showing.

Poirot returned to bed, his mind relieved, and switched off the light. He glanced at his watch. It was just twenty-three minutes to one.

CHAPTER FIVE

THE CRIME

HE FOUND IT difficult to go to sleep again at once. For one thing he missed the motion of the train. If it *was* a station outside, it was curiously quiet. By contrast the noises on the train seemed unusually loud. He could hear Ratchett moving about next door—a click as he pulled down the washbasin, the sound of the tap running, a splashing noise, then another click as the basin shut to again. Footsteps passed up the corridor outside, the shuffling footsteps of someone in bedroom slippers.

Hercule Poirot lay awake staring at the ceiling. Why was the station outside so silent? His throat felt dry. He had forgotten to ask for his usual bottle of mineral water. He looked at his watch again. Just after a quarter past one. He would ring for the conductor and ask for some mineral water. His finger went out to the bell, but he paused as in the stillness he heard a ting. The man couldn't answer every bell at once.

Ting. . . . Ting. . . . Ting. . . .

It sounded again and again. Where was the man? Somebody was getting impatient.

Ti-i-i-ing!

Whoever it was, was keeping a finger solidly on the push-button.

Suddenly with a rush, his footsteps echoing up the aisle, the man came. He knocked at a door not far from Poirot's own.

Then came voices—the conductor's, deferential, apologetic; and a woman's, insistent and voluble.

Mrs. Hubbard!

Poirot smiled to himself.

The altercation—if it was one—went on for some time. Its proportions were ninety per cent of Mrs. Hubbard's to a soothing ten per cent of the conductor's. Finally the matter seemed to be adjusted. Poirot heard distinctly a *"Bonne nuit, Madame,"* and a closing door.

He pressed his own finger on the bell.

The conductor arrived promptly. He looked hot and worried.

"De l'eau minérale, s'il vous plaît."

"Bien, Monsieur." Perhaps a twinkle in Poirot's eye led him to unburden himself. *"La dame américaine—"*

"Yes?"

He wiped his forehead. "Imagine to yourself the time I have had with her! She insists—but *insists*—that there is a man in her compartment! Figure to yourself, Monsieur. In a space of this size." He swept a hand round. "Where would he conceal himself? I argue with her. I point out that it is impossible. She insists. She woke up, and there was a man there. And how, I ask, did he get out and leave the door bolted behind him? But she will not listen to reason. As though there were not enough to worry us already. This snow—"

"Snow?"

"But yes, Monsieur. Monsieur has not noticed? The train has stopped. We have run into a snowdrift. Heaven knows how long we shall be here. I remember once being snowed up for seven days."

"Where are we?"

"Between Vincovci and Brod."

"Là-là," said Poirot vexedly.

The man withdrew and returned with the water.

"Bon soir, Monsieur."

Poirot drank a glass of water and composed himself to sleep.

He was just dropping off when something again woke him. This time it was as though something heavy had fallen with a thud against the door.

He sprang up, opened it and looked out. Nothing. But to his right, some distance down the corridor, a woman wrapped in a scarlet kimono was retreating from him. At the other end, sitting on his little seat, the conductor was entering up figures on large sheets of paper. Everything was deathly quiet.

"Decidedly I suffer from the nerves," said Poirot and retired to bed again. This time he slept till morning.

When he awoke the train was still at a standstill. He raised a blind and looked out. Heavy banks of snow surrounded the train.

He glanced at his watch and saw that it was past nine o'clock.

At a quarter to ten, neat, spruce and dandified as ever, he made his way to the restaurant car, where a chorus of woe was going on.

Any barriers there might have been between the passengers had now quite broken down. All were united by a common misfortune. Mrs. Hubbard was loudest in her lamentations.

"My daughter said it would be the easiest way in the world. Just sit in the train until I got to Parrus. And now we may be here for days and days," she wailed. "And my boat sails day after to-morrow. How am I going to catch it now? Why, I can't even wire to cancel my passage. I'm just too mad to talk about it!"

The Italian said that he had urgent business himself in Milan. The large American said that that was "too bad, Ma'am," and soothingly expressed a hope that the train might make up time.

"My sister—her children wait me," said the Swedish lady, and wept. "I get no word to them. What they think? They will say bad things have happen to me."

"How long shall we be here?" demanded Mary Debenham. "Doesn't anybody *know?*"

Her voice sounded impatient, but Poirot noted that there were no signs of that almost feverish anxiety which she had displayed during the check to the Taurus Express.

Mrs. Hubbard was off again.

"There isn't anybody knows a thing on this train. And nobody's trying to *do* anything. Just a pack of useless foreigners. Why, if this were at home, there'd be someone at least *trying* to do something!"

Arbuthnot turned to Poirot and spoke in careful British French.

"*Vous êtes un directeur de la ligne, je crois, Monsieur. Vous pouvez nous dire—*"

Smiling, Poirot corrected him.

"No, no," he said in English. "It is not I. You confound me with my friend, M. Bouc."

"Oh! I'm sorry."

"Not at all. It is most natural. I am now in the compartment that he had formerly."

M. Bouc was not present in the restaurant car. Poirot looked about to notice who else was absent.

Princess Dragomiroff was missing, and the Hungarian couple. Also Ratchette, his valet, and the German lady's-maid.

The Swedish lady wiped her eyes.

"I am foolish," she said. "I am bad to cry. All is for the best, whatever happen."

This Christian spirit, however, was far from being shared.

"That's all very well," said MacQueen restlessly. "We may be here for days."

"What *is* this country anyway?" demanded Mrs. Hubbard tearfully.

On being told it was Jugo-Slavia, she said: "Oh! one of these Balkan things. What can you expect?"

"You are the only patient one, Mademoiselle," said Poirot to Miss Debenham.

She shrugged her shoulders slightly. "What can one do?"

"You are a philosopher, Mademoiselle."

"That implies a detached attitude. I think my attitude is more selfish. I have learned to save myself useless emotion."

She was speaking more to herself than to him. She was not even looking at him. Her gaze went past him, out of the window to where the snow lay in heavy masses.

"You are a strong character, Mademoiselle," said Poirot gently. "You are, I think, the strongest character amongst us."

"Oh! no. No, indeed. I know one far, far stronger than I am.

"And that is—?"

She seemed suddenly to come to herself, to realise that she was talking to a stranger and foreigner, with whom, until this morning, she had exchanged only half a dozen sentences.

She laughed, a polite but estranging laugh.

"Well—that old lady, for instance. You have probably noticed her. A very ugly old lady but rather fascinating. She has only to lift a little finger and ask for something in a polite voice—and the whole train runs."

"It runs also for my friend M. Bouc," said Poirot. "But that is because he is a director of the line, not because he has a strong character."

Mary Debenham smiled.

The morning wore away. Several people, Poirot amongst them, remained in the dining-car. The communal life was felt, at the moment, to pass the time better. He heard a good deal more about Mrs. Hubbard's daughter, and he heard the lifelong habits of Mr. Hubbard, deceased, from his rising in the morning and commencing breakfast with a cereal to his final rest at night in the bed-socks that Mrs. Hubbard herself had been in the habit of knitting for him.

It was when he was listening to a confused account of the missionary aims of the Swedish lady that one of the Wagon Lit conductors came into the car and stood at his elbow.

"*Pardon, Monsieur.*"

"Yes?"

"The compliments of M. Bouc, and he would be glad if you would be so kind as to come to him for a few minutes."

Poirot rose, uttered excuses to the Swedish lady and followed the man out of the dining-car. It was not his own conductor, but a big fair man.

He followed his guide down the corridor of his own carriage and along

the corridor of the next one. The man tapped at a door, then stood aside
to let Poirot enter.

The compartment was not M. Bouc's own. It was a second-class one—
chosen presumably because of its slightly larger size. It certainly gave the impression of being crowded.

M. Bouc himself was sitting on the small seat in the opposite corner. In
the corner next the window, facing him, was a small dark man looking out
at the snow. Standing up and quite preventing Poirot from advancing any
farther were a big man in blue uniform (the *chef de train*) and his own
Wagon Lit conductor.

"Ah! my good friend," cried M. Bouc. "Come in. We have need of you."

The little man in the window shifted along the seat, and Poirot squeezed
past the other two men and sat down facing his friend.

The expression on M. Bouc's face gave him, as he would have expressed
it, furiously to think. It was clear that something out of the common had
happened.

"What has occurred?" he asked.

"You may well ask that. First this snow—this stoppage. And now—"

He paused—and a sort of strangled gasp came from the Wagon Lit conductor.

"And now what?"

"*And now a passenger lies dead in his berth—stabbed.*"

M. Bouc spoke with a kind of calm desperation.

"A passenger? Which passenger?"

"An American. A man called—called—" He consulted some notes in front
of him. "Ratchett. That is right—Ratchett?"

"Yes, Monsieur," the Wagon Lit man gulped.

Poirot looked at him. He was as white as chalk.

"You had better let that man sit down," he said. "He may faint otherwise."

The *chef de train* moved slightly and the Wagon Lit man sank down in
the corner and buried his face in his hands.

"*Brr!*" said Poirot. "This is serious!"

"Certainly it is serious. To begin with, a murder—that in itself is a calamity
of the first water. But not only that, the circumstances are unusual. Here we
are, brought to a standstill. We may be here for hours—and not only hours—
days! Another circumstance—passing through most countries we have the police of that country on the train. But in Jugo-Slavia, no. You comprehend?"

"It is a position of great difficulty," said Poirot.

"There is worse to come. Dr. Constantine—I forgot, I have not introduced
you. Dr. Constantine, M. Poirot."

The little dark man bowed, and Poirot returned the bow.

"Dr. Constantine is of the opinion that death occurred at about 1 A.M."

"It is difficult to speak exactly in these matters," said the doctor, "but I
think I can say definitely that death occurred between midnight and two in
the morning."

"When was this M. Ratchett last seen alive?" asked Poirot.

"He is known to have been alive at about twenty minutes to one, when he spoke to the conductor," said M. Bouc.

"That is quite correct," said Poirot. "I myself heard what passed. That is the last thing known?"

"Yes."

Poirot turned toward the doctor, who continued.

"The window of M. Ratchett's compartment was found wide open, leading one to suppose that the murderer escaped that way. But in my opinion that open window is a blind. Anyone departing that way would have left distinct traces in the snow. There were none."

"The crime was discovered—when?" asked Poirot.

"Michel!"

The Wagon Lit conductor sat up. His face still looked pale and frightened.

"Tell this gentleman exactly what occurred," ordered M. Bouc.

The man spoke somewhat jerkily.

"The valet of this M. Ratchett, he tapped several times at the door this morning. There was no answer. Then, half an hour ago, the restaurant car attendant came. He wanted to know if Monsieur was taking *déjeuner*. It was eleven o'clock, you comprehend.

"I open the door for him with my key. But there is a chain, too, and that is fastened. There is no answer and it is very still in there, and cold—but cold. With the window open and snow drifting in. I thought the gentleman had had a fit, perhaps. I got the *chef de train*. We broke the chain and went in. He was— Ah! *c'était terrible!*"

He buried his face in his hands again.

"The door was locked and chained on the inside," said Poirot thoughtfully. "It was not suicide—eh?"

The Greek doctor gave a sardonic laugh. "Does a man who commits suicide stab himself in ten—twelve—fifteen places?" he asked.

Poirot's eyes opened. "That is great ferocity," he said.

"It is a woman," said the *chef de train*, speaking for the first time. "Depend upon it, it was a woman. Only a woman would stab like that."

Dr. Constantine screwed up his face thoughtfully.

"She must have been a very strong woman," he said. "It is not my desire to speak technically—that is only confusing; but I can assure you that one or two of the blows were delivered with such force as to drive them through hard belts of bone and muscle."

"It was clearly not a scientific crime," said Poirot.

"It was most unscientific," returned Dr. Constantine. "The blows seem to have been delivered haphazard and at random. Some have glanced off, doing hardly any damage. It is as though somebody had shut his eyes and then in a frenzy struck blindly again and again."

"*C'est une femme*," said the *chef de train* again. "Women are like that.

When they are enraged they have great strength." He nodded so sagely that everyone suspected a personal experience of his own.

"I have, perhaps, something to contribute to your store of knowledge," said Poirot. "M. Ratchett spoke to me yesterday. He told me, as far as I was able to understand him, that he was in danger of his life."

" 'Bumped off'—that is the American expression, is it not?" asked M. Bouc. "Then it is not a woman. It is a 'gangster' or a 'gunman.' "

The *chef de train* looked pained at seeing his theory come to nought.

"If so," said Poirot, "it seems to have been done very amateurishly." His tone expressed professional disapproval.

"There is a large American on the train," said M. Bouc, pursuing his idea. "A common-looking man with terrible clothes. He chews the gum, which I believe is not done in good circles. You know whom I mean?"

The Wagon Lit conductor to whom he had appealed nodded.

"*Oui, Monsieur,* the No. 16. But it cannot have been he. I should have seen him enter or leave the compartment."

"You might not. You might not. But we will go into that presently. The question is, what to do?" He looked at Poirot.

Poirot looked back at him.

"Come, my friend," said M. Bouc. "You comprehend what I am about to ask of you. I know your powers. Take command of this investigation! No, no, do not refuse. See, to us it is serious—I speak for the Compagnie Internationale des Wagons Lits. By the time the Jugo-Slavian police arrive, how simple if we can present them with the solution! Otherwise delays, annoyances, a million and one inconveniences. Perhaps, who knows, serious annoyance to innocent persons. Instead—*you* solve the mystery! We say, 'A murder has occurred—*this* is the criminal!' "

"And suppose I do not solve it?"

"Ah, *mon cher!*" M. Bouc's voice became positively caressing. "I know your reputation. I know something of your methods. This is the ideal case for you. To look up the antecedents of all these people, to discover their *bona fides*—all that takes time and endless inconvenience. But have I not heard you say often that to solve a case a man has only to lie back in his chair and think? Do that. Interview the passengers on the train, view the body, examine what clues there are, and then—well, I have faith in you! I am assured that it is no idle boast of yours. Lie back and think—use (as I have heard you say so often) the little grey cells of the mind—and you will *know!*"

He leaned forward, looking affectionately at the detective.

"Your faith touches me, my friend," said Poirot emotionally. "As you say, this cannot be a difficult case. I myself last night—but we will not speak of that now. In truth, this problem intrigues me. I was reflecting, not half an hour ago, that many hours of boredom lay ahead whilst we are stuck here. And now—a problem lies ready to my hand."

"You accept then?" said M. Bouc eagerly.

"*C'est entendu.* You place the matter in my hands."

"Good—we are all at your service."

"To begin with, I should like a plan of the Istanbul-Calais coach, with a note of the people who occupied the several compartments, and I should also like to see their passports and their tickets."

"Michel will get you those."

The Wagon Lit conductor left the compartment.

"What other passengers are there on the train?" asked Poirot.

"In this coach Dr. Constantine and I are the only travellers. In the coach from Bucharest is an old gentleman with a lame leg. He is well known to the conductor. Beyond that are the ordinary carriages, but these do not concern us, since they were locked after dinner had been served last night. Forward of the Istanbul-Calais coach there is only the dining-car."

"Then it seems," said Poirot slowly, "as though we must look for our murderer in the Istanbul-Calais coach." He turned to the doctor. "That is what you were hinting, I think?"

The Greek nodded. "At half an hour after midnight we ran into the snowdrift. No one can have left the train since then."

M. Bouc said solemnly, *The murderer is with us—on the train now. . . .*"

CHAPTER SIX

A WOMAN

"FIRST OF ALL," said Poirot, "I should like a word or two with young Mr. MacQueen. He may be able to give us valuable information."

"Certainly," said M. Bouc. He turned to the *chef de train*. "Get Mr. Mac-Queen to come here."

The *chef de train* left the carriage.

The conductor returned with a bundle of passports and tickets. M. Bouc took them from him.

"Thank you, Michel. It would be best now, I think, if you were to go back to your post. We will take your evidence formally later."

"Very good, Monsieur," and Michel in his turn left the carriage.

"After we have seen young MacQueen," said Poirot, "perhaps M. *le docteur* will come with me to the dead man's carriage."

"Certainly."

"After we have finished there—"

But at this moment the *chef de train* returned with Hector MacQueen.

M. Bouc rose. "We are a little cramped here," he said pleasantly. "Take my seat, Mr. MacQueen. M. Poirot will sit opposite you—so."

He turned to the *chef de train*. "Clear all the people out of the restaurant car," he said, "and let it be left free for M. Poirot. You will conduct your interviews there, *mon cher?*"

"It would be the most convenient, yes," agreed Poirot.

MacQueen had stood looking from one to the other, not quite following the rapid flow of French.

"*Qu'est-ce qu'il y a?*" he began laboriously. "*Pourquoi—?*"

With a vigorous gesture Poirot motioned him to the seat in the corner. He took it and began once more.

"*Pourquoi—?*" Then checking himself and relapsing into his own tongue: "What's up on the train? Has anything happened?"

He looked from one man to another.

Poirot nodded. "Exactly. Something has happened. Prepare yourself for a shock. *Your employer, M. Ratchett, is dead!*"

MacQueen's mouth pursed itself into a whistle. Except that his eyes grew a shade brighter, he showed no signs of shock or distress.

"So they got him after all," he said.

"What exactly do you mean by that phrase, Mr. MacQueen?"

MacQueen hesitated.

"You are assuming," said Poirot, "that M. Ratchett was murdered?"

"Wasn't he?" This time MacQueen did show surprise. "Why, yes," he said slowly. "That's just what I did think. Do you mean he just died in his sleep? Why, the old man was as tough as—as tough—"

He stopped, at a loss for a simile.

"No, no," said Poirot. "Your assumption was quite right. M. Ratchett was murdered. Stabbed. But I should like to know why you were so sure it *was* murder, and not just—death."

MacQueen hesitated. "I must get this clear," he said. "Who exactly are you? And where do you come in?"

"I represent the Compagnie Internationale des Wagons Lits." Poirot paused, then added, "I am a detective. My name is Hercule Poirot."

If he expected an effect he did not get one. MacQueen said merely, "Oh! yes?" and waited for him to go on.

"You know the name, perhaps?"

"Why, it does seem kind of familiar. Only I always thought it was a woman's dressmaker."

Hercule Poirot looked at him with distaste. "It is incredible!" he said.

"What's incredible?"

"Nothing. Let us advance with the matter in hand. I want you to tell me, M. MacQueen, all that you know about the dead man. You were not related to him?"

"No. I am—was—his secretary."

"For how long have you held that post?"

"Just over a year."

"Please give me all the information you can."

"Well, I met Mr. Ratchett just over a year ago when I was in Persia—"

Poirot interrupted.

"What were you doing there?"

"I had come over from New York to look into an oil concession. I don't suppose you want to hear all about that. My friends and I had been let in rather badly over it. Mr. Ratchett was in the same hotel. He had just had a row with his secretary. He offered me the job and I took it. I was at a loose end and glad to find a well-paid job ready made, as it were."

"And since then?"

"We've travelled about. Mr. Ratchett wanted to see the world. He was hampered by knowing no languages. I acted more as a courier than as a secretary. It was a pleasant life."

"Now tell me as much as you can about your employer."

The young man shrugged his shoulders. A perplexed expression passed over his face.

"That's not so easy."

"What was his full name?"

"Samuel Edward Ratchett."

"He was an American citizen?"

"Yes."

"What part of America did he come from?"

"I don't know."

"Well, tell me what you do know."

"The actual truth is, Mr. Poirot, that I know nothing at all! Mr. Ratchett never spoke of himself or of his life in America."

"Why do you think that was?"

"I don't know. I imagined that he might be ashamed of his beginnings. Some men are."

"Does that strike you as a satisfactory solution?"

"Frankly, it doesn't."

"Has he any relatives?"

"He never mentioned any."

Poirot pressed the point.

"You must have formed *some* theory, Mr. MacQueen."

"Well, yes, I did. For one thing, I don't believe Ratchett was his real name. I think he left America definitely in order to escape someone or something. I think he was successful—until a few weeks ago."

"And then?"

"He began to get letters—threatening letters."

"Did you see them?"

"Yes. It was my business to attend to his correspondence. The first letter came a fortnight ago."

"Were these letters destroyed?"

"No, I think I've got a couple still in my files—one I know Ratchett tore up in a rage. Shall I get them for you?"

"If you would be so good."

MacQueen left the compartment. He returned a few minutes later and laid down two sheets of rather dirty notepaper before Poirot.

The first letter ran as follows:

Thought you'd double-cross us and get away with it, did you? Not on your life. We're out to GET *you, Ratchett, and we* WILL *get you!*

There was no signature.

With no comment beyond raised eyebrows, Poirot picked up the second letter.

We're going to take you for a ride, Ratchett. Some time soon. We're going to GET *you—see?*

Poirot laid the letter down.

"The style is monotonous!" he said. "More so than the handwriting."

MacQueen stared at him.

"You would not observe," said Poirot pleasantly. "It requires the eye of one used to such things. This letter was not written by one person, M. MacQueen. Two or more persons wrote it—each writing one letter of a word at a time. Also, the letters are printed. That makes the task of identifying the handwriting much more difficult." He paused, then said: "Did you know that M. Ratchett had applied for help to me?"

"To *you?*"

MacQueen's astonished tone told Poirot quite certainly that the young man had not known of it.

The detective nodded. "Yes. He was alarmed. Tell me, how did he act when he received the first letter?"

MacQueen hesitated.

"It's difficult to say. He—he—passed it off with a laugh in that quiet way of his. But somehow—" he gave a slight shiver—"I felt that there was a good deal going on underneath the quietness."

Poirot nodded. Then he asked an unexpected question.

"Mr. MacQueen, will you tell me, quite honestly, exactly how you regarded your employer? Did you like him?"

Hector MacQueen took a moment or two before replying.

"No," he said at last. "I did not."

"Why?"

"I can't exactly say. He was always quite pleasant in his manner." He paused, then said: "I'll tell you the truth, Mr. Poirot. I disliked and distrusted him. He was, I am sure, a cruel and dangerous man. I must admit, though, that I have no reasons to advance for my opinion."

"Thank you, Mr. MacQueen. One further question: when did you last see Mr. Ratchett alive?"

"Last evening about—" he thought for a minute—"ten o'clock, I should say. I went into his compartment to take down some memoranda from him."

"On what subject?"

"Some tiles and antique pottery that he bought in Persia. What had been delivered was not what he had purchased. There has been a long, vexatious correspondence on the subject."

"And that was the last time Mr. Ratchett was seen alive?"

"Yes, I suppose so."

"Do you know when Mr. Ratchett received the last threatening letter?"

"On the morning of the day we left Constantinople."

"There is one more question I must ask you, Mr. MacQueen. Were you on good terms with your employer?"

The young man's eyes twinkled suddenly.

"This is where I'm supposed to go all goosefleshy down the back. In the words of a best seller, 'You've nothing on me.' Ratchett and I were on perfectly good terms."

"Perhaps, Mr. MacQueen, you will give me your full name and your address in America."

MacQueen gave his name—Hector Willard MacQueen—and an address in New York.

Poirot leaned back against the cushions.

"That is all for the present, Mr. MacQueen," he said. "I should be obliged if you would keep the matter of Mr. Ratchett's death to yourself for a little time."

"His valet, Masterman, will have to know."

"He probably knows already," said Poirot drily. "If so, try to get him to hold his tongue."

"That oughtn't to be difficult. He's a Britisher and, as he calls it, he 'keeps to himself.' He has a low opinion of Americans, and no opinion at all of any other nationality."

"Thank you, Mr. MacQueen."

The American left the carriage.

"Well?" demanded M. Bouc. "You believe what he says, this young man?"

"He seems honest and straightforward. He did not pretend to any affection for his employer, as he probably would have done had he been involved in any way. It is true, Mr. Ratchett did not tell him that he had tried to enlist my services and failed, but I do not think that that is really a suspicious circumstance. I fancy Mr. Ratchett was a gentleman who kept his own counsel on every possible occasion."

"So you pronounce one person at least innocent of the crime," said M. Bouc jovially.

Poirot cast on him a look of reproach.

"Me, I suspect everybody till the last minute," he said. "All the same, I must admit that I cannot see this sober, long-headed MacQueen losing his head and stabbing his victim twelve or fourteen times. It is not in accord with his psychology—not at all."

"No," said M. Bouc thoughtfully. "That is the act of a man driven almost crazy with a frenzied hate—it suggests rather the Latin temperament. Or else it suggests, as our friend the *chef de train* insisted—a woman."

CHAPTER SEVEN

THE BODY

FOLLOWED BY Dr. Constantine, Poirot made his way to the next coach and to the compartment occupied by the murdered man. The conductor came and unlocked the door for them with his key.

The two men passed inside. Poirot turned inquiringly to his companion.

"How much has been disarranged in this compartment?"

"Nothing has been touched. I was careful not to move the body in making my examination."

Poirot nodded. He looked round him.

The first thing that struck the senses was the intense cold. The window was pushed down as far as it would go, and the blind was drawn up.

"*Brrr*," observed Poirot.

The other smiled appreciatively.

"I did not like to close it," he said.

Poirot examined the window carefully.

"You are right," he announced. "Nobody left the carriage this way. Possibly the open window was intended to suggest that somebody did; but if so, the snow has defeated the murderer's intention."

He examined the frame of the window carefully. Taking a small case from his pocket he blew a little powder over the frame.

"No fingerprints at all," he said. "That means it has been wiped. Well, if there had been fingerprints they would have told us very little. They would have been those of Mr. Ratchett or his valet or the conductor. Criminals do not make mistakes of that kind nowadays.

"And that being so," he added cheerfully, "we might as well shut the window. Positively it is the cold storage in here!"

He suited the action to the word and then turned his attention for the first time to the motionless figure lying in the bunk.

Ratchett lay on his back. His pyjama jacket, stained with rusty patches, had been unbuttoned and thrown back.

"I had to see the nature of the wounds, you see," explained the doctor.

Poirot nodded. He bent over the body. Finally he straightened himself with a slight grimace.

"It is not pretty," he said. "Someone must have stood there and stabbed him again and again. How many wounds are there exactly?"

"I make it twelve. One or two are so slight as to be practically scratches. On the other hand, at least three would be capable of causing death."

Something in the doctor's tone caught Poirot's attention. He looked at him sharply. The little Greek was standing staring down at the body with a puzzled frown.

"Something strikes you as odd, does it not?" he asked gently. "Speak, my friend. There is something here that puzzles you?"

"You are right," acknowledged the other.

"What is it?"

"You see these two wounds—here and here—" He pointed. "They are deep. Each cut must have severed blood vessels—and yet the edges do not gape. They have not bled as one would have expected."

"Which suggests?"

"That the man was already dead—some little time dead—when they were delivered. But that is surely absurd."

"It would seem so," said Poirot thoughtfully. "Unless our murderer figured to himself that he had not accomplished his job properly and came back to make quite sure—but that is manifestly absurd! Anything else?"

"Well, just one thing."

"And that?"

"You see this wound here—under the right arm—near the right shoulder. Take this pencil of mine. Could you deliver such a blow?"

Poirot poised his hand.

"*Précisément*," he said. "I see. With the *right* hand it is exceedingly difficult, almost impossible. One would have to strike backhanded, as it were. But if the blow were struck with the *left* hand—"

"Exactly, M. Poirot. That blow was almost certainly struck with the *left* hand."

"So that our murderer is left-handed? No, it is more difficult than that, is it not?"

"As you say, M. Poirot. Some of these other blows are just as obviously right-handed."

"Two people. We are back at two people again," murmured the detective. He asked abruptly: "Was the electric light on?"

"It is difficult to say. You see, it is turned off by the conductor every morning about ten o'clock."

"The switches will tell us," said Poirot.

He examined the switch of the top light and also the roll-back bed-head light. The former was turned off. The latter was closed.

"*Eh bien,*" he said thoughtfully. "We have here a hypothesis of the First and the Second Murderer, as the great Shakespeare would put it. The First Murderer stabbed his victim and left the compartment, turning off the light. The Second Murderer came in in the dark, did not see that his or her work had been done, and stabbed at least twice at a dead body. *Que pensez-vous de ça?*"

"Magnificent!" said the little doctor with enthusiasm.

The other's eyes twinkled.

"You think so? I am glad. It sounded to me a little like the nonsense."

"What other explanation can there be?"

"That is just what I am asking myself. Have we here a coincidence, or what? Are there any other inconsistencies, such as would point to two people being concerned?"

"I think I can say yes. Some of these blows, as I have already said, point to a weakness—a lack of strength or a lack of determination. They are feeble, glancing blows. But this one here—and this one—" Again he pointed. "Great strength was needed for those blows. They have penetrated the muscle."

"They were, in your opinion, delivered by a man?"

"Most certainly."

"They could not have been delivered by a woman?"

"A young, vigorous, athletic woman might have struck them, especially if she were in the grip of a strong emotion; but it is in my opinion highly unlikely."

Poirot was silent a moment or two.

The other asked anxiously, "You understand my point?"

"Perfectly," said Poirot. "The matter begins to clear itself up wonderfully! The murderer was a man of great strength—he was feeble—it was a woman—it was a right-handed person—it was a left-handed person. Ah! *c'est rigolo, tout ça!*" He spoke with sudden anger. "And the victim—what does he do in all this? Does he cry out? Does he struggle? Does he defend himself?"

He slipped his hand under the pillow and drew out the automatic pistol which Ratchett had shown him the day before.

"Fully loaded, you see," he said.

They looked round them. Ratchett's day clothing was hanging from the hooks on the wall. On the small table formed by the lid of the wash basin were various objects. False teeth in a glass of water. Another glass, empty. A bottle of mineral water. A large flask. An ash-tray containing the butt of a cigar and some charred fragments of paper; also two burnt matches.

The doctor picked up the empty glass and sniffed it.

"Here is the explanation of the victim's inertia," he said quietly.

"Drugged?"

"Yes."

Poirot nodded. He picked up the two matches and scrutinised them carefully.

"You have a clue then?" demanded the little doctor eagerly.

"Those two matches are of different shapes," said Poirot. "One is flatter than the other. You see?"

"It is the kind you get on the train," said the doctor. "In paper covers."

Poirot was feeling in the pockets of Ratchett's clothing. Presently he pulled out a box of matches. He compared them carefully with the burnt ones.

"The rounder one is a match struck by Mr. Ratchett," he said. "Let us see if he had also the flatter kind."

But a further search showed no other matches.

Poirot's eyes were darting about the compartment. They were bright and sharp like a bird's. One felt that nothing could escape their scrutiny.

With a little exclamation he bent and picked up something from the floor.

It was a small square of cambric, very dainty. In the corner was an embroidered initial—H.

"A woman's handkerchief," said the doctor. "Our friend the *chef de train* was right. There is a woman concerned in this."

"And most conveniently she leaves her handkerchief behind!" said Poirot. "Exactly as it happens in the books and on the films—and to make things even easier for us, it is marked with an initial."

"What a stroke of luck for us!" exclaimed the doctor.

"Is it not?" said Poirot.

Something in his tone surprised the doctor, but before he could ask for elucidation Poirot had made another dive onto the floor.

This time he held out on the palm of his hand—a pipe-cleaner.

"It is perhaps the property of Mr. Ratchett?" suggested the doctor.

"There was no pipe in any of his pockets, and no tobacco or tobacco pouch."

"Then it is a clue."

"Oh! decidedly. And again dropped most conveniently. A masculine clue, this time, you note! One cannot complain of having no clues in this case. There are clues here in abundance. By the way, what have you done with the weapon?"

"There was no sign of any weapon. The murderer must have taken it away with him."

"I wonder why," mused Poirot.

"Ah!" The doctor had been delicately exploring the pyjama pockets of the dead man.

"I overlooked this," he said. "I unbuttoned the jacket and threw it straight back."

From the breast pocket he brought out a gold watch. The case was dented savagely, and the hands pointed to a quarter past one.

"You see?" cried Constantine eagerly. "This gives us the hour of the crime. It agrees with my calculations. Between midnight and two in the morning is what I said, and probably about one o'clock, though it is difficult to be exact in these matters. *Eh bien,* here is confirmation. A quarter past one. That was the hour of the crime."

"It is possible, yes. It is certainly possible."

The doctor looked at him curiously. "You will pardon me, M. Poirot, but I do not quite understand you."

"I do not understand myself," said Poirot. "I understand nothing at all. And, as you perceive, it worries me."

He sighed and bent over the little table examining the charred fragment of paper. He murmured to himself, "What I need at this moment is an old-fashioned woman's hat-box."

Dr. Constantine was at a loss to know what to make of this singular remark. In any case Poirot gave him no time for questions. Opening the door into the corridor, he called for the conductor.

The man arrived at a run.

"How many women are there in this coach?"

The conductor counted on his fingers.

"One, two, three—six, Monsieur. The old American lady, a Swedish lady, the young English lady, the Countess Andrenyi, and Madame la Princesse Dragomiroff and her maid."

Poirot considered.

"They all have hat-boxes, yes?"

"Yes, Monsieur."

"Then bring me—let me see—yes, the Swedish lady's and that of the lady's-maid. Those two are the only hope. You will tell them it is a customs regulation—something—anything that occurs to you."

"That will be all right, Monsieur. Neither lady is in her compartment at the moment."

"Then be quick."

The conductor departed. He returned with the two hat-boxes. Poirot opened that of the maid, and tossed it aside. Then he opened the Swedish lady's and uttered an exclamation of satisfaction. Removing the hats carefully, he disclosed round humps of wire-netting.

"Ah, here is what we need! About fifteen years ago hat-boxes were made like this. You skewered through the hat with a hatpin on to this hump of wire-netting."

As he spoke he was skillfully removing two of the attached humps. Then he repacked the hat-box and told the conductor to return both boxes where they belonged.

When the door was shut once more he turned to his companion.

"See you, my dear doctor, me, I am not one to rely upon the expert procedure. It is the psychology I seek, not the fingerprint or the cigarette ash. But in this case I would welcome a little scientific assistance. This compartment is full of clues, but can I be sure that those clues are really what they seem to be?"

"I do not quite understand you, M. Poirot."

"Well, to give you an example—we find a woman's handkerchief. Did a woman drop it? Or did a man, committing the crime, say to himself: 'I will make this look like a woman's crime. I will stab my enemy an unnecessary number of times, making some of the blows feeble and ineffective, and I will drop this handkerchief where no one can miss it'? That is one possibility. Then there is another. Did a woman kill him, and did she deliberately drop a pipe-cleaner to make it look like a man's work? Or are we seriously to suppose that two people, a man and a woman, were separately concerned, and that each was so careless as to drop a clue to his or her identity? It is a little too much of a coincidence, that!"

"But where does the hat-box come in?" asked the doctor, still puzzled.

"Ah! I am coming to that. As I say, these clues—the watch stopped at a quarter past one, the handkerchief, the pipe-cleaner—they may be genuine, or they may be faked. As to that I cannot yet tell. But there is *one* clue here which—though again I may be wrong—I believe has *not* been faked.

I mean this flat match, M. *le docteur.* *I believe that that match was used by the murderer, not by Mr. Ratchett.* It was used to burn an incriminating paper of some kind. Possibly a note. If so, there was something in that note, some mistake, some error, that left a possible clue to the assailant. I am going to try to discover what that something was."

He went out of the compartment and returned a few moments later with a small spirit stove and a pair of curling-tongs.

"I use them for the moustaches," he said, referring to the latter.

The doctor watched him with great interest. Poirot flattened out the two humps of wire, and with great care wriggled the charred scrap of paper on to one of them. He clapped the other on top of it and then, holding both pieces together with the tongs, held the whole thing over the flame of the spiritlamp.

"It is a very makeshift affair, this," he said over his shoulder. "Let us hope that it will answer our purpose."

The doctor watched the proceedings attentively. The metal began to glow. Suddenly he saw faint indications of letters. Words formed themselves slowly —words of fire.

It was a very tiny scrap. Only three words and part of another showed.

—member little Daisy Armstrong

"Ah!" Poirot gave a sharp exclamation.

"It tells you something?" asked the doctor.

Poirot's eyes were shining. He laid down the tongs carefully.

"Yes," he said. "*I know the dead man's real name. I know why he had to leave America.*"

"What was his name?"

"Cassetti."

"Cassetti?" Constantine knitted his brows. "It brings back to me something. Some years ago. I cannot remember. . . . It was a case in America, was it not?"

"Yes," said Poirot. "A case in America."

Further than that Poirot was not disposed to be communicative. He looked round him as he went on:

"We will go into all that presently. Let us first make sure that we have seen all there is to be seen here."

Quickly and deftly he went once more through the pockets of the dead man's clothes but found nothing there of interest. He tried the communicating door which led through to the next compartment, but it was bolted on the other side.

"There is one thing that I do not understand," said Dr. Constantine. "If the murderer did not escape through the window, and if this communicating door was bolted on the other side, and if the door into the corridor was not only locked on the inside but chained, how then did the murderer leave the compartment?"

"That is what the audience says when a person bound hand and foot is shut into a cabinet—and disappears."

"You mean—?"

"I mean," explained Poirot, "that if the murderer intended us to believe that he had escaped by way of the window, he would naturally make it appear that the other two exits were impossible. Like the 'disappearing person' in the cabinet, it is a trick. It is our business to find out how the trick is done."

He locked the communicating door on their side—"in case," he said, "the excellent Mrs. Hubbard should take it into her head to acquire first-hand details of the crime to write to her daughter."

He looked round once more.

"There is nothing more to do here, I think. Let us rejoin M. Bouc."

CHAPTER EIGHT

THE ARMSTRONG KIDNAPPING CASE

THEY FOUND M. Bouc finishing an omelet.

"I thought it best to have lunch served immediately in the restaurant car," he said. "Afterwards it will be cleared and M. Poirot can conduct his examination of the passengers there. In the meantime I have ordered them to bring us three some food here."

"An excellent idea," said Poirot.

None of the three men was hungry, and the meal was soon eaten; but not till they were sipping their coffee did M. Bouc mention the subject that was occupying all their minds.

"*Eh bien?*" he asked.

"*Eh bien,* I have discovered the identity of the victim. I know why it was imperative he should leave America."

"Who was he?"

"Do you remember reading of the Armstrong baby? This is the man who murdered little Daisy Armstrong. Cassetti."

"I recall it now. A shocking affair—though I cannot remember the details."

"Colonel Armstrong was an Englishman—a V.C. He was half American, his mother having been a daughter of W. K. Van der Halt, the Wall Street millionaire. He married the daughter of Linda Arden, the most famous tragic American actress of her day. They lived in America and had one child—a girl whom they idolized. When she was three years old she was kidnapped, and an impossibly high sum demanded as the price of her return. I will not weary you with all the intricacies that followed. I will come to the moment when, after the parents had paid over the enormous sum of two hundred thousand dollars, the child's dead body was discovered; it had been dead for at least a fortnight. Public indignation rose to fever point. And there was worse to follow. Mrs. Armstrong was expecting another baby. Following the shock of the discovery, she gave birth prematurely to a dead child, and herself died. Her broken-hearted husband shot himself."

"*Mon Dieu*, what a tragedy. I remember now," said M. Bouc. "There was also another death, if I remember rightly?"

"Yes, an unfortunate French or Swiss nursemaid. The police were convinced that she had some knowledge of the crime. They refused to believe her hysterical denials. Finally, in a fit of despair the poor girl threw herself from a window and was killed. It was proved afterwards that she had been absolutely innocent of any complicity in the crime."

"It is not good to think of," said M. Bouc.

"About six months later, this man Cassetti was arrested as the head of the gang who had kidnapped the child. They had used the same methods in the past. If the police seemed likely to get on their trail, they killed their prisoner, hid the body, and continued to extract as much money as possible before the crime was discovered.

"Now, I will make clear to you this, my friend. Cassetti was the man! But by means of the enormous wealth he had piled up, and owing to the secret hold he had over various persons, he was acquitted on some technical inaccuracy. Notwithstanding that, he would have been lynched by the populace had he not been clever enough to give them the slip. It is now clear to me what happened. He changed his name and left America. Since then he has been a gentleman of leisure, travelling abroad and living on his *rentes*."

"*Ah! quel animal!*" M. Bouc's tone was redolent of heartfelt disgust. "I cannot regret that he is dead—not at all!"

"I agree with you."

"*Tout de même*, it is not necessary that he should be killed on the Orient Express. There are other places."

Poirot smiled a little. He realised that M. Bouc was biased in the matter.

"The question we have now to ask ourselves is this," he said. "Is this murder the work of some rival gang whom Cassetti had double-crossed in the past, or is it an act of private vengeance?"

He explained his discovery of the few words on the charred fragment of paper.

"If I am right in my assumption, then, the letter was burnt by the murderer. Why? Because it mentioned the name 'Armstrong,' which is the clue to the mystery."

"Are there any members of the Armstrong family living?"

"That, unfortunately, I do not know. I think I remember reading of a younger sister of Mrs. Armstrong's."

Poirot went on to relate the joint conclusions of himself and Dr. Constantine. M. Bouc brightened at the mention of the broken watch.

"That seems to give us the time of the crime very exactly."

"Yes," said Poirot. "It is very convenient."

There was an indescribable something in his tone that made both the other two look at him curiously.

"You say that you yourself heard Ratchett speak to the conductor at twenty minutes to one?" asked M. Bouc.

Poirot related just what had occurred.

"Well," said M. Bouc, "that proves at least that Cassetti—or Ratchett, as I shall continue to call him—was certainly alive at twenty minutes to one."

"Twenty-three minutes to one, to be precise."

"Then at twelve thirty-seven, to put it formally, Mr. Ratchett was alive. That is *one* fact, at least."

Poirot did not reply. He sat looking thoughtfully in front of him.

There was a tap on the door and the restaurant attendant entered.

"The restaurant car is free now, Monsieur," he said.

"We will go there," said M. Bouc, rising.

"I may accompany you?" asked Constantine.

"Certainly, my dear doctor. Unless M. Poirot has any objection?"

"Not at all. Not at all," said Poirot.

After a little politeness in the matter of precedence—"*Après vous, Monsieur*"—"*Mais non, après vous*"—they left the compartment.

CHAPTER ONE

THE EVIDENCE OF THE WAGON LIT CONDUCTOR

IN THE RESTAURANT CAR all was in readiness.

Poirot and M. Bouc sat together on one side of a table. The doctor sat across the aisle.

On the table in front of Poirot was a plan of the Istanbul-Calais coach with the names of the passengers marked in in red ink. The passports and tickets were in a pile at one side. There was writing paper, ink, pen and pencils.

"Excellent," said Poirot. "We can open our Court of Inquiry without more ado. First, I think, we should take the evidence of the Wagon Lit conductor. You probably know something about the man. What character has he? Is he a man on whose word you would place reliance?"

"I should say so, most assuredly. Pierre Michel has been employed by the company for over fifteen years. He is a Frenchman—lives near Calais. Thoroughly respectable and honest. Not, perhaps, remarkable for brains."

Poirot nodded comprehendingly. "Good," he said. "Let us see him."

Pierre Michel had recovered some of his assurance, but he was still extremely nervous.

"I hope Monsieur will not think that there has been any negligence on my part," he said anxiously, his eyes going from Poirot to M. Bouc. "It is a terrible thing that has happened. I hope Monsieur does not think that it reflects on me in any way?"

Having soothed the man's fears, Poirot began his questions. He first elicited Michel's name and address, his length of service, and the length of time he had been on this particular route. These particulars he already knew, but the routine questions served to put the man at his ease.

"And now," went on Poirot, "let us come to the events of last night. M. Ratchett retired to bed—when?"

"Almost immediately after dinner, Monsieur. Actually before we left Belgrade. So he did on the previous night. He had directed me to make up the bed while he was at dinner, and I did so."

"Did anybody go into his compartment afterwards?"

"His valet, Monsieur, and the young American gentleman, his secretary."

"Anyone else?"

"No, Monsieur, not that I know of."

"Good. And that is the last you saw or heard of him?"

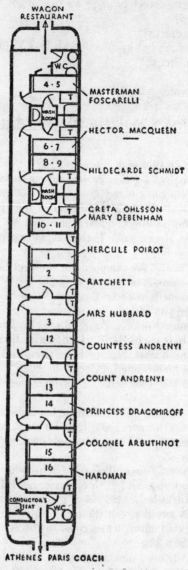

WAGON
RESTAURANT

TWC

4·5 — MASTERMAN
FOSCARELLI

WASH
ROOM

T — HECTOR MACQUEEN

6·7
8·9 — HILDEGARDE SCHMIDT

WASH
ROOM

T — GRETA OHLSSON
MARY DEBENHAM

10·11

T — HERCULE POIROT

1

2 — RATCHETT

T

T — MRS HUBBARD

3

12 — COUNTESS ANDRENYI

T

13 — COUNT ANDRENYI

14 — PRINCESS DRACOMIROFF

T

T — COLONEL ARBUTHNOT

15

16 — HARDMAN

T

CONDUCTOR'S
SEAT   WC

ATHENES PARIS COACH

PLAN OF THE CALAIS COACH

"No, Monsieur. You forget he rang his bell about twenty to one—soon after we had stopped."

"What happened exactly?"

"I knocked at the door, but he called out and said he had made a mistake."

"In English or in French?"

"In French."

"What were his words exactly?"

"*Ce n'est rien. Je me suis trompé.*"

"Quite right," said Poirot. "That is what I heard. And then you went away?"

"Yes, Monsieur."

"Did you go back to your seat?"

"No, Monsieur, I went first to answer another bell that had just rung."

"Now, Michel, I am going to ask you an important question. Where were you at a quarter past one?"

"I, Monsieur? I was at my little seat at the end—facing up the corridor."

"You are sure?"

"*Mais oui*—at least—"

"Yes?"

"I went into the next coach, the Athens coach, to speak to my colleague there. We spoke about the snow. That was at some time soon after one o'clock. I cannot say exactly."

"And you returned—when?"

"One of my bells rang, Monsieur—I remember—I told you. It was the American lady. She had rung several times."

"I recollect," said Poirot. "And after that?"

"After that, Monsieur? I answered your bell and brought you some mineral water. Then, about half an hour later, I made up the bed in one of the other compartments—that of the young American gentleman, Mr. Ratchett's secretary."

"Was Mr. MacQueen alone in his compartment when you went to make up his bed?"

"The English Colonel from No. 15 was with him. They had been sitting talking."

"What did the Colonel do when he left Mr. MacQueen?"

"He went back to his own compartment."

"No. 15—that is quite close to your seat, is it not?"

"Yes, Monsieur, it is the second compartment from that end of the corridor."

"His bed was already made up?"

"Yes, Monsieur. I had made it up while he was at dinner."

"What time was all this?"

"I could not say exactly, Monsieur. Not later than two o'clock certainly."

"And after that?"

"After that, Monsieur, I sat in my seat till morning."

"You did not go again into the Athens coach?"

"No, Monsieur."

"Perhaps you slept?"

"I do not think so, Monsieur. The train being at a standstill prevented me from dozing off as I usually do."

"Did you see any of the passengers moving up or down the corridor?"

The man reflected. "One of the ladies went to the toilet at the far end, I think."

"Which lady?"

"I do not know, Monsieur. It was far down the corridor and she had her back to me. She had on a kimono of scarlet with dragons on it."

Poirot nodded. "And after that?"

"Nothing, Monsieur, until the morning."

"You are sure?"

"Ah, pardon—you yourself, Monsieur, opened your door and looked out for a second."

"Good, my friend," said Poirot. "I wondered whether you would remember that. By the way, I was awakened by what sounded like something heavy falling against my door. Have you any idea what that could have been?"

The man stared at him. "There was nothing, Monsieur. Nothing, I am positive of it."

"Then I must have had the *cauchemar*," said Poirot philosophically.

"Unless," put in M. Bouc, "it was something in the compartment next door that you heard."

Poirot took no notice of the suggestion. Perhaps he did not wish to before the Wagon Lit conductor.

"Let us pass to another point," he said. "Supposing that last night an assassin joined the train. Is it quite certain that he could not have left it after committing the crime?"

Pierre Michel shook his head.

"Nor that he can be concealed on it somewhere?"

"It has been well searched," said M. Bouc. "Abandon that idea, my friend."

"Besides," said Michel, "no one could get on to the sleeping-car without my seeing them."

"When was the last stop?"

"Vincovci."

"What time was that?"

"We should have left there at 11.58, but owing to the weather we were twenty minutes late."

"Someone might have come along from the ordinary part of the train?"

"No, Monsieur. After the service of dinner, the door between the ordinary carriages and the sleeping-cars is locked."

"Did you yourself descend from the train at Vincovci?"

"Yes, Monsieur. I got down onto the platform as usual and stood by the step up into the train. The other conductors did the same."

"What about the forward door—the one near the restaurant car?"

"It is always fastened on the inside."

"It is not so fastened now."

The man looked surprised; then his face cleared. "Doubtless one of the passengers opened it to look out on the snow."

"Probably," said Poirot.

He tapped thoughtfully on the table for a minute or two.

"Monsieur does not blame me?" said the man timidly.

Poirot smiled on him kindly.

"You have had the evil chance, my friend," he said. "Ah! one other point while I remember it. You said that another bell rang just as you were knocking at M. Ratchett's door. In fact I heard it myself. Whose was it?"

"It was the bell of Madame la Princesse Dragomiroff. She desired me to summon her maid."

"And you did so?"

"Yes, Monsieur."

Poirot studied the plan in front of him thoughtfully. Then he inclined his head.

"That is all," he said, "for the moment."

"Thank you, Monsieur."

The man rose. He looked at M. Bouc.

"Do not distress yourself," said the latter kindly. "I cannot see that there has been any negligence on your part."

Gratified, Pierre Michel left the compartment.

CHAPTER TWO

THE EVIDENCE OF THE SECRETARY

FOR A MINUTE or two Poirot remained lost in thought.

"I think," he said at last, "that it would be well to have a further word with Mr. MacQueen, in view of what we now know."

The young American appeared promptly.

"Well," he said, "how are things going?"

"Not too badly. Since our last conversation, I have learnt something—the identity of Mr. Ratchett."

Hector MacQueen leaned forward interestedly. "Yes?" he said.

"'Ratchett,' as you suspected, was merely an alias. The man 'Ratchett' was Cassetti, who ran the celebrated kidnapping stunts—including the famous affair of little Daisy Armstrong."

An expression of utter astonishment appeared on MacQueen's face. Then it darkened. "The damned skunk!" he exclaimed.

"You had no idea of this, Mr. MacQueen?"

"No, sir," said the young American decidedly. "If I had, I'd have cut off my right hand before it had a chance to do secretarial work for him!"

"You feel strongly about the matter, Mr. MacQueen?"

"I have a particular reason for doing so. My father was the district attorney who handled the case, Mr. Poirot. I saw Mrs. Armstrong more than once—she was a lovely woman. So gentle and heartbroken." His face darkened. "If ever a man deserved what he got, Ratchett—or Cassetti—is the man. I'm rejoiced at his end. Such a man wasn't fit to live!"

"You almost feel as though you would have been willing to do the good deed yourself?"

"I do. I—" He paused, then added rather guiltily, "Seems I'm kind of incriminating myself."

"I should be more inclined to suspect you, Mr. MacQueen, if you displayed an inordinate sorrow at your employer's decease."

"I don't think I could do that even to save myself from the chair," said MacQueen grimly. Then he added: "If I'm not being unduly curious, just how did you figure this out? Cassetti's identity, I mean."

"By a fragment of a letter found in his compartment."

"But surely—I mean—that was rather careless of the old man?"

"That depends," said Poirot, "on the point of view."

The young man seemed to find this remark rather baffling. He stared at Poirot as though trying to make him out.

"The task before me," said Poirot, "is to make sure of the movements of every one on the train. No offence need be taken, you understand. It is only a matter of routine."

"Sure. Get right on with it and let me clear my character if I can."

"I need hardly ask you the number of your compartment," said Poirot, smiling, "since I shared it with you for a night. It is the second-class compartment Nos. 6 and 7, and after my departure you had it to yourself."

"That's right."

"Now, Mr. MacQueen, I want you to describe your movements last night from the time of leaving the dining-car."

"That's quite easy. I went back to my compartment, read a bit, got out on the platform at Belgrade, decided it was too cold, and got in again. I talked for a while to a young English lady who is in the compartment next to mine. Then I fell into conversation with that Englishman, Colonel Arbuthnot—as a matter of fact I think you passed us as we were talking. Then I went in to Mr. Ratchett and, as I told you, took down some memoranda of letters he wanted written. I said good night to him and left him. Colonel Arbuthnot was still standing in the corridor. His compartment was already made up for the night, so I suggested that he should come along to mine. I ordered a couple of drinks and we got right down to it. Discussed world politics and the Government of India and our own troubles with Prohibition and the Wall Street crisis. I don't as a rule cotton to Britishers—they're a stiff-necked lot—but I liked this one."

"Do you know what time it was when he left you?"

"Pretty late. Nearly two o'clock, I should say."

"You noticed that the train had stopped?"

"Oh, yes. We wondered a bit. Looked out and saw the snow lying very thick, but we didn't think it was serious."

"What happened when Colonel Arbuthnot finally said good night?"

"He went along to his compartment and I called to the conductor to make up my bed."

"Where were you whilst he was making it?"

"Standing just outside the door in the corridor smoking a cigarette."

"And then?"

"And then I went to bed and slept till morning."

"During the evening did you leave the train at all?"

"Arbuthnot and I thought we'd get out at—what was the name of the place?—Vincovci—to stretch our legs a bit. But it was bitterly cold—a blizzard on. We soon hopped back again."

"By which door did you leave the train?"

"By the one nearest to our compartment."

"The one next to the dining-car?"

"Yes."

"Do you remember if it was bolted?"

MacQueen considered.

"Why, yes, I seem to remember it was. At least there was a kind of bar that fitted across the handle. Is that what you mean?"

"Yes. On getting back into the train did you replace that bar?"

"Why, no—I don't think I did. I got in last. No, I don't seem to remember doing so." He added suddenly, "Is that an important point?"

"It may be. Now, I presume, Monsieur, that while you and Colonel Arbuthnot were sitting talking, the door of your compartment into the corridor was open?"

Hector MacQueen nodded.

"I want you, if you can, to tell me if anyone passed along that corridor *after* the train left Vincovci up to the time you parted company for the night."

MacQueen drew his brows together.

"I think the conductor passed along once," he said, "coming from the direction of the dining-car. And a woman passed the other way, going towards it."

"Which woman?"

"I couldn't say. I didn't really notice. You see I was arguing a point with Arbuthnot. I just seem to remember a glimpse of some scarlet silk affair passing the door. I didn't look, and anyway I wouldn't have seen the person's face. As you know, my carriage faces the dining-car end of the train, so a woman going along the corridor in that direction would have her back to me as soon as she'd passed."

Poirot nodded. "She was going to the toilet, I presume?"

"I suppose so."

"And you saw her return?"

"Well, no, now that you mention it, I didn't notice her returning, but I suppose she must have done so."

"One more question. Do you smoke a pipe, Mr. MacQueen?"

"No, sir, I do not."

Poirot paused a moment. "I think that is all at present. I should now like to see the valet of Mr. Ratchett. By the way, did both you and he always travel second-class?"

"He did. But I usually went first—if possible in the compartment adjoining Mr. Ratchett's. Then he had most of his baggage put in my compartment and yet could get at both it and me easily whenever he chose. But on this occasion all the first-class berths were booked except the one that he took."

"I comprehend. Thank you, Mr. MacQueen."

CHAPTER THREE

THE EVIDENCE OF THE VALET

THE AMERICAN was succeeded by the pale Englishman with the inexpressive face whom Poirot had already noticed on the day before. He stood waiting very correctly. Poirot motioned to him to sit down.

"You are, I understand, the valet of M. Ratchett."

"Yes, sir."

"Your name?"

"Edward Henry Masterman."

"Your age?"

"Thirty-nine."

"And your home address?"

"21 Friar Street, Clerkenwell."

"You have heard that your master has been murdered?"

"Yes, sir. A very shocking occurrence."

"Will you now tell me, please, at what hour you last saw M. Ratchett?"

The valet considered.

"It must have been about nine o'clock, sir, last night. That or a little after."

"Tell me in your own words exactly what happened."

"I went in to Mr. Ratchett as usual, sir, and attended to his wants."

"What were your duties exactly?"

"To fold or hang up his clothes, sir, put his dental plate in water and see that he had everything he wanted for the night."

"Was his manner much the same as usual?"

The valet considered a moment.

"Well, sir, I think he was upset."

"In what way—upset?"

"Over a letter he'd been reading. He asked me if it was I who had put it in his compartment. Of course I told him I hadn't done any such thing, but he swore at me and found fault with everything I did."

"Was that unusual?"

"Oh, no, sir. He lost his temper easily—as I say, it just depended what had happened to upset him."

"Did your master ever take a sleeping draught?"

Dr. Constantine leaned forward a little.

"Always when travelling by train, sir. He said he couldn't sleep otherwise."

"Do you know what drug he was in the habit of taking?"

"I couldn't say, I'm sure, sir. There was no name on the bottle—just 'The Sleeping Draught to be taken at bedtime.'"

"Did he take it last night?"

"Yes, sir. I poured it into a glass and put it on top of the toilet table ready for him."

"You didn't actually see him drink it?"

"No, sir."

"What happened next?"

"I asked if there was anything further, and also asked what time he would like to be called in the morning. He said he didn't want to be disturbed till he rang."

"Was that usual?"

"Quite usual, sir. When he was ready to get up he used to ring the bell for the conductor and then send him for me."

"Was he usually an early or a late riser?"

"It depended, sir, on his mood. Sometimes he'd get up for breakfast, sometimes he wouldn't get up till just on lunch time."

"So that you weren't alarmed when the morning wore on and no summons came?"

"No, sir."

"Did you know that your master had enemies?"

"Yes, sir." The man spoke quite unemotionally.

"How did you know?"

"I had heard him discussing some letters, sir, with Mr. MacQueen."

"Had you an affection for your employer, Masterman?"

Masterman's face became, if possible, even more inexpressive than it was normally.

"I should hardly like to say that, sir. He was a generous employer."

"But you didn't like him?"

"Shall we put it that I don't care very much for Americans, sir?"

"Have you ever been in America?"

"No, sir."

"Do you remember reading in the paper of the Armstrong kidnapping case?"

A little colour came into the man's cheeks.

"Yes, indeed, sir. A little baby girl, wasn't it? A very shocking affair."

"Did you know that your employer, Mr. Ratchett, was the principal instigator in that affair?"

"No, indeed, sir." The valet's tone held positive warmth and feeling for the first time. "I can hardly believe it, sir."

"Nevertheless, it is true. Now, to pass to your own movements last night. A matter of routine, you understand. What did you do after leaving your master?"

"I told Mr. MacQueen, sir, that the master wanted him. Then I went to my own compartment and read."

"Your compartment was—"

"The end second-class one, sir. Next to the dining-car."

Poirot was looking at his plan.

"I see—and you had which berth?"

"The lower one, sir."

"That is No. 4?"

"Yes, sir."

"Is there anyone in with you?"

"Yes, sir. A big Italian fellow."

"Does he speak English?"

"Well, a kind of English, sir." The valet's tone was deprecating. "He's been in America—Chicago, I understand."

"Do you and he talk together much?"

"No, sir. I prefer to read."

Poirot smiled. He could visualize the scene—the large, voluble Italian, and the snub direct administered by the gentleman's gentleman.

"And what, may I ask, are you reading?" he inquired.

"At present, sir, I am reading *Love's Captive*, by Mrs. Arabella Richardson."

"A good story?"

"I find it highly enjoyable, sir."

"Well, let us continue. You returned to your compartment and read *Love's Captive* till—when?"

"At about ten thirty, sir, this Italian wanted to go to bed. So the conductor came and made the beds up."

"And then you went to bed and to sleep?"

"I went to bed, sir, but I didn't sleep."

"Why didn't you sleep?"

"I had the toothache, sir."

"Oh, là-là—that is painful."

"Most painful, sir."

"Did you do anything for it?"

"I applied a little oil of cloves, sir, which relieved the pain a little, but I was still not able to get to sleep. I turned the light on above my head and continued to read—to take my mind off, as it were."

"And did you not go to sleep at all?"

"Yes, sir, I dropped off about four in the morning."

"And your companion?"

"The Italian fellow? Oh, he just snored."

"He did not leave the compartment at all during the night?"

"No, sir."

"Did you?"

"No, sir."

"Did you hear anything during the night?"

"I don't think so, sir. Nothing unusual, I mean. The train being at a stand-still made it all very quiet."

Poirot was silent a moment or two. Then he spoke.

"Well, I think there is very little more to be said. You cannot throw any light upon the tragedy?"

"I'm afraid not. I'm sorry, sir."

"As far as you know, was there any quarrel or bad blood between your master and Mr. MacQueen?"

"Oh! no, sir. Mr. MacQueen was a very pleasant gentleman."

"Where were you in service before you came to Mr. Ratchett?"

"With Sir Henry Tomlinson, sir, in Grosvenor Square."

"Why did you leave him?"

"He was going to East Africa, sir, and did not require my services any longer. But I am sure he will speak for me, sir. I was with him some years."

"And you have been with Mr. Ratchett—how long?"

"Just over nine months, sir."

"Thank you, Masterman. By the way, are you a pipe-smoker?"

"No, sir. I only smoke cigarettes—gaspers, sir."

"Thank you, that will do."

Poirot gave him a nod of dismissal.

The valet hesitated a moment.

"You'll excuse me, sir, but the elderly American lady is in what I might describe as a state, sir. She's saying she knows all about the murderer. She's in a very excitable condition, sir."

"In that case," said Poirot, smiling, "we had better see her next."

"Shall I tell her, sir? She's been demanding to see someone in authority for a long time. The conductor's been trying to pacify her."

"Send her to us, my friend," said Poirot. "We will listen to her story now."

CHAPTER FOUR

THE EVIDENCE OF THE AMERICAN LADY

MRS. HUBBARD arrived in the dining-car in such a state of breathless excitement that she was hardly able to articulate her words.

"Now just tell me this—who's in authority here? I've got some very important information, *very* important indeed, and I'm going to tell it to someone in authority just as soon as I can. If you gentlemen—"

Her wavering glance fluctuated between the three men. Poirot leaned forward.

"Tell it to me, Madame," he said. "But first, pray be seated."

Mrs. Hubbard plumped heavily down on to the seat opposite to him.

"What I've got to tell you is just this. There was a murder on the train last night, and the murderer was *right there in my compartment!*"

She paused to give dramatic emphasis to her words.

"You are sure of this, Madame?"

"Of course I'm sure! The idea! I know what I'm talking about. I'll tell you everything there is to tell. I'd gotten into bed and gone to sleep, and suddenly I woke up—everything was dark—and I knew there was a man in my compartment. I was just so scared I couldn't scream, if you know what I mean. I just lay there and thought, 'Mercy, I'm going to be killed!' I just can't describe to you how I felt. These nasty trains, I thought, and all the outrages I'd read of. And I thought, 'Well, anyway, he won't get my jewellery' —because, you see, I'd put that in a stocking and hidden it under my pillow —which isn't any too comfortable, by the way; kinda bumpy, if you know what I mean. But that's neither here nor there. Where was I?"

"You realised, Madame, that there was a man in your compartment."

"Yes, well, I just lay there with my eyes closed, and wondered what I'd do. And I thought, well, I'm just thankful that my daughter doesn't know the plight I'm in. And then, somehow, I got my wits about me and I felt about with my hand and I pressed the bell for the conductor. I pressed it and I pressed it, but nothing happened—and I can tell you, I thought my heart was going to stop beating. 'Mercy,' I said to myself, 'maybe they've murdered every single soul on the train.' It was at a standstill anyhow and there was a nasty quiet feel in the air. But I just went on pressing that bell and oh! the relief when I heard footsteps coming running down the corridor and a knock on the door! 'Come in,' I screamed, and I switched on the lights at the same time. And would you believe it, there wasn't a *soul* there!"

This seemed to Mrs. Hubbard to be a dramatic climax rather than an anticlimax.

"And what happened next, Madame?"

"Why, I told the man what had happened and he didn't seem to believe me. Seemed to imagine I'd dreamed the whole thing. I made him look under the seat, though he said there wasn't room for a man to squeeze himself in there. It was plain enough that the man had got away—but there *had* been a man there, and it just made me mad the way the conductor tried to soothe me down! I'm not one to imagine things, Mr.— I don't think I know your name?"

"Poirot, Madame; and this is M. Bouc, a director of the company, and Dr. Constantine."

Mrs. Hubbard murmured, "Pleased to meet you, I'm sure," to all three of them in an abstracted manner and then plunged once more into her recital.

"Now I'm just not going to pretend I was as bright as I might have been. I got it into my head that it was the man from next door—the poor fellow who's been killed. I told the conductor to look at the door between the compartments, and sure enough it wasn't bolted. Well, I soon saw to that. I told him to bolt it then and there, and after he'd gone out I got up and put a suitcase against it to make sure."

"What time was this, Mrs. Hubbard?"

"Well, I'm sure I can't tell you. I never looked to see. I was so upset."

"And what is your theory now?"

"Why, I should say it was just as plain as plain could be. The man in my compartment was the murderer. Who else could he be?"

"And you think he went back into the adjoining compartment?"

"How do I know where he went? I had my eyes tight shut."

"He might have slipped out through the door into the corridor."

"Well, I couldn't say. You see, I had my eyes tight shut."

Mrs. Hubbard sighed convulsively.

"Mercy, I was scared! If my daughter only knew—"

"You do not think, Madame, that what you heard was the noise of someone moving about next door—in the murdered man's compartment?"

"No, I do not, Mr.—what is it?—Poirot. The man was *right there in the same compartment with me*. And what's more I've got proof of it."

Triumphantly, she hauled a large handbag into view and proceeded to burrow in its interior.

She took out in turn two large clean handkerchiefs, a pair of horn-rimmed glasses, a bottle of aspirin, a packet of Glauber's Salts, a celluloid tube of bright green peppermints, a bunch of keys, a pair of scissors, a book of American Express cheques, a snapshot of an extraordinarily plain-looking child, some letters, five strings of pseudo-Oriental beads, and a small metal object —a button.

"You see this button? Well, it's not one of *my* buttons. It's not off anything I've got. I found it this morning when I got up."

As she placed it on the table, M. Bouc leaned forward and gave an exclamation. "But this is a button from the tunic of a Wagon Lit attendant!"

"There may be a natural explanation for that," said Poirot.

He turned gently to the lady.

"This button, Madame, may have dropped from the conductor's uniform, either when he searched your cabin or when he was making the bed up last night."

"I just don't know what's the matter with all you people. Seems as though you don't want to do anything but make objections. Now listen here. I was reading a magazine last night before I went to sleep. Before I turned the light out, I placed that magazine on a little case that was standing on the floor near the window. Have you got that?"

They assured her that they had.

"Very well then. The conductor looked under the seat from near the door, and then he came in and bolted the door between me and the next compartment, but he never went *near* the window. Well, this morning that button was lying right on top of the magazine. What do you call that, I should like to know?"

"That, Madame, I call evidence," said Poirot.

The answer seemed to appease the lady.

"It makes me madder than a hornet to be disbelieved," she explained.

"You have given us most interesting and valuable evidence," said Poirot soothingly. "Now may I ask you a few questions?"

"Why, certainly."

"How was it, since you were nervous of this man Ratchett, that you hadn't already bolted the door between the compartments?"

"I had," returned Mrs. Hubbard promptly.

"Oh, you had?"

"Well, as a matter of fact I asked that Swedish creature—a pleasant soul— if it was bolted, and she said it was."

"How was it you couldn't see for yourself?"

"Because I was in bed and my spongebag was hanging on the door-handle."

"What time was it when you asked her to do this for you?"

"Now let me think. It must have been round about half-past ten or a quarter to eleven. She'd come along to see if I had an aspirin. I told her where to find it and she got it out of my grip."

"You yourself were in bed?"

"Yes."

Suddenly she laughed. "Poor soul—she was so upset! You see, she'd opened the door of the next compartment by mistake."

"Mr. Ratchett's?"

"Yes. You know how difficult it is as you come along the train and all the doors are shut. She opened his by mistake. She was very distressed about it. He'd laughed, it seemed, and I guess he said something not quite nice. Poor thing, she certainly was upset. 'Oh! I make mistake,' she said. 'I ashamed make mistake. Not nice man,' she said. 'He say, "You too old."'"

Dr. Constantine sniggered, and Mrs. Hubbard immediately froze him with a glance.

"He wasn't a nice kind of man," she said, "to say a thing like that to a lady. It's not right to laugh at such things."

Dr. Constantine hastily apologised.

"Did you hear any noise from Mr. Ratchett's compartment after that?" asked Poirot.

"Well—not exactly."

"What do you mean by that, Madame?"

"Well—" She paused. "He snored."

"Ah!—he snored, did he?"

"Terribly. The night before, it kept me awake."

"You didn't hear him snore after you had had the scare about a man being in your compartment?"

"Why, Mr. Poirot, how could I? He was dead."

"Ah, yes, truly," said Poirot. He appeared confused.

"Do you remember the affair of the Armstrong kidnapping, Mrs. Hubbard?" he asked.

"Yes, indeed I do. And how the wretch that did it escaped scot-free! My, I'd have liked to get my hands on him."

"He has not escaped. He is dead. He died last night."

"You don't mean—?" Mrs. Hubbard half rose from her chair in excitement.

"But yes, I do. Ratchett was the man."

"Well! Well, to think of that! I must write and tell my daughter. Now, didn't I tell you last night that that man had an evil face? I was right, you see. My daughter always says: 'When Mamma's got a hunch you can bet your bottom dollar it's O.K.'"

"Were you acquainted with any of the Armstrong family, Mrs. Hubbard?"

"No. They moved in a very exclusive circle. But I've always heard that Mrs. Armstrong was a perfectly lovely woman and that her husband worshipped her."

"Well, Mrs. Hubbard, you have helped us very much—very much indeed. Perhaps you will give me your full name?"

"Why, certainly. Caroline Martha Hubbard."

"Will you write your address down here?"

Mrs. Hubbard did so, without ceasing to speak. "I just can't get over it. Cassetti—on this train. I had a hunch about that man, didn't I, Mr. Poirot?"

"Yes, indeed, Madame. By the way, have you a scarlet silk dressing-gown?"

"Mercy, what a funny question! Why, no. I've got two dressing-gowns with me—a pink flannel one that's kind of cosy for on board ship, and one my daughter gave me as a present—a kind of local affair in purple silk. But what in creation do you want to know about my dressing-gowns for?"

"Well, you see, Madame, someone in a scarlet kimono entered either your or Mr. Ratchett's compartment last night. It is, as you said just now, very difficult when all the doors are shut to know which compartment is which."

"Well, no one in a scarlet dressing-gown came into my compartment."

"Then she must have gone into Mr. Ratchett's."

Mrs. Hubbard pursed her lips together and said grimly: "That wouldn't surprise me any."

Poirot leaned forward. "So you heard a woman's voice next door?"

"I don't know how you guessed that, Mr. Poirot. I don't really. But—well—as a matter of fact, I did."

"But when I asked you just now if you heard anything next door, you only said you heard Mr. Ratchett snoring."

"Well, that was true enough. He did snore part of the time. As for the other—" Mrs. Hubbard got rather embarrassed. "It isn't a very nice thing to speak about."

"What time was it when you heard a woman's voice?"

"I can't tell you. I just woke up for a minute and heard a woman talking, and it was plain enough where she was. So I just thought, 'Well, *that's* the kind of man he is! I'm not surprised'—and then I went to sleep again. And I'm sure I should never have mentioned anything of the kind to three strange gentlemen if you hadn't dragged it out of me."

"Was it before the scare about the man in your compartment, or after?"

"Why, that's like what you said just now! He wouldn't have had a woman talking to him if he were dead, would he?"

"*Pardon.* You must think me very stupid, Madame."

"I guess even you get kinda muddled now and then. I just can't get over its being that monster Cassetti. What my daughter will say—"

Poirot managed adroitly to help the good lady to replace the contents of her handbag, and he then shepherded her towards the door.

At the last moment, he said:

"You have dropped your handkerchief, Madame."

Mrs. Hubbard looked at the little scrap of cambric he held out to her.

"That's not mine, Mr. Poirot. I've got mine right here."

"*Pardon.* I thought as it had the initial H on it—"

"Well, now, that's funny, but it's certainly not mine. Mine are marked C.M.H., and they're sensible things—not expensive Paris fallals. What good is a handkerchief like that to anybody's nose?"

None of the three men seemed to have an answer to this question and Mrs. Hubbard sailed out triumphantly.

CHAPTER FIVE

THE EVIDENCE OF THE SWEDISH LADY

M. BOUC WAS HANDLING the button that Mrs. Hubbard had left behind her.

"This button. I cannot understand it. Does it mean that after all, Pierre Michel is involved in some way?" he asked. He paused, then continued, as Poirot did not reply. "What have you to say, my friend?"

"That button, it suggests possibilities," said Poirot thoughtfully. "Let us interview next the Swedish lady before we discuss the evidence that we have heard."

He sorted through the pile of passports in front of him.

"Ah! here we are. Greta Ohlsson, age forty-nine."

M. Bouc gave directions to the restaurant attendant, and presently the lady with the yellowish grey bun of hair and the long, mild, sheep-like face was ushered in. She peered short-sightedly at Poirot through her glasses, but was quite calm.

It transpired that she understood and spoke French, so the conversation took place in that language. Poirot first asked her the questions to which he already knew the answers—her name, age, and address. He then asked her her occupation.

She was, she told him, matron in a missionary school near Stamboul. She was a trained nurse.

"You know, of course, of what took place last night, Mademoiselle?"

"Naturally. It is very dreadful. And the American lady tells me that the murderer was actually in her compartment."

"I hear, Mademoiselle, that you were the last person to see the murdered man alive?"

"I do not know. It may be so. I opened the door of his compartment by mistake. I was much ashamed. It was a most awkward mistake."

"You actually saw him?"

"Yes. He was reading a book. I apologised quickly and withdrew."

"Did he say anything to you?"

A slight flush showed on the worthy lady's cheek.

"He laughed and said a few words. I—I did not quite catch them."

"And what did you do after that, Mademoiselle?" asked Poirot, passing from the subject tactfully.

"I went in to the American lady, Mrs. Hubbard. I asked her for some aspirin and she gave it to me."

"Did she ask you whether the communicating door between her compartment and that of Mr. Ratchett was bolted?"

"Yes."

"And was it?"

"Yes."

"And after that?"

"After that I went back to my own compartment, took the aspirin, and lay down."

"What time was all this?"

"When I got into bed it was five minutes to eleven. I know because I looked at my watch before I wound it up."

"Did you go to sleep quickly?"

"Not very quickly. My head got better, but I lay awake some time."

"Had the train come to a stop before you went to sleep?"

"I do not think so. We stopped, I think, at a station just as I was getting drowsy."

"That would be Vincovci. Now your compartment, Mademoiselle, is this one?" He indicated it on the plan.

"That is so, yes."

"You had the upper or the lower berth?"

"The lower berth, No. 10."

"And you had a companion?"

"Yes, a young English lady. Very nice, very amiable. She had travelled from Baghdad."

"After the train left Vincovci, did she leave the compartment?"

"No, I am sure she did not."

"Why are you sure if you were asleep?"

"I sleep very lightly. I am used to waking at a sound. I am sure that if she had come down from the berth above I should have awakened."

"Did you yourself leave the compartment?"

"Not until this morning."

"Have you a scarlet silk kimono, Mademoiselle?"

"No, indeed. I have a good comfortable dressing-gown of Jaeger material."

"And the lady with you, Miss Debenham? What colour is her dressing-gown?"

"A pale mauve aba such as you buy in the East."

Poirot nodded. Then he asked in a friendly tone: "Why are you taking this journey? A holiday?"

"Yes, I am going home for a holiday. But first I am going to Lausanne to stay with a sister for a week or so."

"Perhaps you will be so amiable as to write me down the name and address of your sister?"

"With pleasure."

She took the paper and pencil he gave her and wrote down the name and address as requested.

"Have you ever been in America, Mademoiselle?"

"No. I very nearly went once. I was to go with an invalid lady, but the plan was canceled at the last moment. I much regretted this. They are very good, the Americans. They give much money to found schools and hospitals. And they are very practical."

"Do you remember hearing of the Armstrong kidnapping case?"

"No, what was that?"

Poirot explained.

Greta Ohlsson was indignant. Her yellow bun of hair quivered with her emotion.

"That there are in the world such evil men! It tries one's faith. The poor mother—my heart aches for her."

The amiable Swede departed, her kindly face flushed, her eyes suffused with tears.

Poirot was writing busily on a sheet of paper.

"What is it you write there, my friend?" asked M. Bouc.

"*Mon cher*, it is my habit to be neat and orderly. I make here a little chronological table of events."

He finished writing and passed the paper to M. Bouc.

> 9.15 Train leaves Belgrade.
> about 9.40 Valet leaves Ratchett with sleeping draught beside him.
> about 10.00 MacQueen leaves Ratchett.
> about 10.40 Greta Ohlsson sees Ratchett (last seen alive). N.B. He was awake reading a book.
> 0.10 Train leaves Vincovci (late).
> 0.30 Train runs into a snowdrift.

0.37 Ratchett's bell rings. Conductor answers it. Ratchett says: "*Ce n'est rien. Je me suis trompé.*"
about 1.17 Mrs. Hubbard thinks man is in her carriage. Rings for conductor.

M. Bouc nodded approval.

"That is very clear," he said.

"There is nothing there that strikes you as at all odd?"

"No, it seems all quite clear and aboveboard. It seems quite plain that the crime was committed at 1.15. The evidence of the watch shows us that, and Mrs. Hubbard's story fits in. For my mind, I will make a guess at the identity of the murderer. I say, my friend, that it is the big Italian. He comes from America—from Chicago—and remember an Italian's weapon is the knife, and he stabs not once but several times."

"That is true."

"Without a doubt, that is the solution of the mystery. Doubtless he and this Ratchett were in this kidnapping business together. Cassetti is an Italian name. In some way Ratchett did on him what they call the double-cross. The Italian tracks him down, sends him warning letters first, and finally revenges himself upon him in a brutal way. It is all quite simple."

Poirot shook his head doubtfully.

"It is hardly so simple as that, I fear," he murmured.

"Me, I am convinced it is the truth," said M. Bouc, becoming more and more enamoured of his theory.

"And what about the valet with the toothache who swears that the Italian never left the compartment?"

"That is the difficulty."

Poirot twinkled.

"Yes, it is annoying, that. Unlucky for your theory, and extremely lucky for our Italian friend that M. Ratchett's valet should have had the toothache."

"It will be explained," said M. Bouc with magnificent certainty.

Poirot shook his head again.

"No, it is hardly so simple as that," he murmured again.

CHAPTER SIX

THE EVIDENCE OF THE RUSSIAN PRINCESS

"LET US HEAR what Pierre Michel has to say about this button," he said. The Wagon Lit conductor was recalled. He looked at them inquiringly. M. Bouc cleared his throat.

"Michel," he said, "here is a button from your tunic. It was found in the

American lady's compartment. What have you to say for yourself about it?"

The conductor's hand went automatically to his tunic.

"I have lost no button, Monsieur," he said. "There must be some mistake."

"That is very odd."

"I cannot account for it, Monsieur." The man seemed astonished, but not in any way guilty or confused.

M. Bouc said meaningly: "Owing to the circumstances in which it was found, it seems fairly certain that this button was dropped by the man who was in Mrs. Hubbard's compartment last night when she rang the bell."

"But, Monsieur, there was no one there. The lady must have imagined it."

"She did not imagine it, Michel. The assassin of M. Ratchett passed that way—*and dropped that button.*"

As the significance of M. Bouc's words became plain to him, Pierre Michel flew into a violent state of agitation.

"It is not true, Monsieur; it is not true!" he cried. "You are accusing me of the crime. Me, I am innocent. I am absolutely innocent! Why should I want to kill a Monsieur whom I have never seen before?"

"Where were you when Mrs. Hubbard's bell rang?"

"I told you, Monsieur, in the next coach talking to my colleague."

"We will send for him."

"Do so, Monsieur, I implore you, do so."

The conductor of the next coach was summoned. He immediately confirmed Pierre Michel's statement. He added that the conductor from the Bucharest coach had also been there. The three of them had been discussing the situation caused by the snow. They had been talking some ten minutes when Michel fancied he heard a bell. As he opened the doors connecting the two coaches, they had all heard it plainly—a bell ringing repeatedly. Michel had run post-haste to answer it.

"So you see, Monsieur, I am not guilty," cried Michel anxiously.

"And this button from a Wagon Lit tunic, how do you explain it?"

"I cannot, Monsieur. It is a mystery to me. All my buttons are intact."

Both of the other conductors also declared that they had not lost a button; also that they had not been inside Mrs. Hubbard's compartment at any time.

"Calm yourself, Michel," said M. Bouc, "and cast your mind back to the moment when you ran to answer Mrs. Hubbard's bell. Did you meet anyone at all in the corridor?"

"No, Monsieur."

"Did you see anyone going away from you down the corridor in the other direction?"

"Again, no, Monsieur."

"Odd," said M. Bouc.

"Not so very," said Poirot. "It is a question of time. Mrs. Hubbard wakes to find someone in her compartment. For a minute or two she lies paralysed, her eyes shut. Probably it was then that the man slipped out into the corridor. Then she starts ringing the bell. But the conductor does not come at once. It is only the third or fourth peal that he hears. I should say myself that there was ample time—"

"For what? For what, *mon cher?* Remember, there are thick drifts of snow all round the train."

"There are two courses open to our mysterious assassin," said Poirot slowly. "He could retreat into either of the toilets or—he could disappear into one of the compartments."

"But they were all occupied."

"Yes."

"You mean that he could retreat into his *own* compartment?"

Poirot nodded.

"It fits—it fits," murmured M. Bouc. "During that ten minutes' absence of the conductor, the murderer comes from his own compartment, goes into Ratchett's, kills him, locks and chains the door on the inside, goes out through Mrs. Hubbard's compartment, and is back safely in his own compartment by the time the conductor arrives."

Poirot murmured: "It is not quite so simple as that, my friend. Our friend the doctor here will tell you so."

With a gesture M. Bouc signified that the three conductors might depart.

"We have still to see eight passengers," said Poirot. "Five first-class passengers—Princess Dragomiroff, Count and Countess Andrenyi, Colonel Arbuthnot, and Mr. Hardman. Three second-class passengers—Miss Debenham, Antonio Foscarelli, and the lady's-maid, Fräulein Schmidt."

"Whom will you see first—the Italian?"

"How you harp on your Italian! No, we will start at the top of the tree. Perhaps Madame la Princesse will be so good as to spare us a few moments of her time. Convey that message to her, Michel."

"*Oui, Monsieur,*" said the conductor, who was just leaving the car.

"Tell her we can wait on her in her compartment if she does not wish to put herself to the trouble of coming here," called M. Bouc.

But Princess Dragomiroff declined to take this course. She appeared in the dining-car, inclined her head slightly and sat down opposite Poirot.

Her small toad-like face looked even yellower than the day before. She was certainly ugly, and yet, like the toad, she had eyes like jewels, dark and imperious, revealing latent energy and an intellectual force that could be felt at once.

Her voice was deep, very distinct, with a slight grating quality in it.

She cut short a flowery phrase of apology from M. Bouc.

"You need not offer apologies, Messieurs. I understand a murder has taken place. Naturally you must interview all the passengers. I shall be glad to give you all the assistance in my power."

"You are most amiable, Madame," said Poirot.

"Not at all. It is a duty. What do you wish to know?"

"Your full Christian names and address, Madame. Perhaps you would prefer to write them yourself?"

Poirot proffered a sheet of paper and pencil, but the Princess waved them aside.

"You can write it," she said. "There is nothing difficult. Natalia Dragomiroff, 17 Avenue Kléber, Paris."

"You are travelling home from Constantinople, Madame?"

"Yes. I have been staying at the Austrian Embassy. My maid is with me."

"Would you be so good as to give me a brief account of your movements last night from dinner onwards?"

"Willingly. I directed the conductor to make up my bed whilst I was in the dining-car. I retired to bed immediately after dinner. I read until the hour of eleven, when I turned out my light. I was unable to sleep owing to certain rheumatic pains from which I suffer. At about a quarter to one I rang for my maid. She massaged me and then read aloud till I felt sleepy. I cannot say exactly when she left me. It may have been half an hour afterward, it may have been later."

"The train had stopped then?"

"The train had stopped."

"You heard nothing—nothing unusual during the time, Madame?"

"I heard nothing unusual."

"What is your maid's name?"

"Hildegarde Schmidt."

"She has been with you long?"

"Fifteen years."

"You consider her trustworthy?"

"Absolutely. Her people come from an estate of my late husband's in Germany."

"You have been in America, I presume, Madame?"

The abrupt change of subject made the old lady raise her eyebrows. "Many times."

"Were you at any time acquainted with a family of the name of Armstrong—a family in which a tragedy occurred?"

With some emotion in her voice the old lady said: "You speak of friends of mine, Monsieur."

"You knew Colonel Armstrong well, then?"

"I knew him slightly, but his wife, Sonia Armstrong, was my god-daughter. I was on terms of friendship with her mother, the actress, Linda Arden. Linda Arden was a great genius, one of the greatest tragic actresses in the world. As Lady Macbeth, as Magda, there was no one to touch her. I was not only an admirer of her art, I was a personal friend."

"She is dead?"

"No, no, she is alive, but she lives in complete retirement. Her health is very delicate, and she has to lie on a sofa most of the time."

"There was, I think, a second daughter?"

"Yes, much younger than Mrs. Armstrong."

"And she is alive?"

"Certainly."

"Where is she?"

The old woman bent an acute glance at him.

"I must ask you the reason for these questions. What have they to do with the matter in hand—the murder on this train?"

"They are connected in this way, Madame: the man who was murdered was the man responsible for the kidnapping and murder of Mrs. Armstrong's child."

"Ah!"

The straight brows came together. Princess Dragomiroff drew herself a little more erect.

"In my view, then, this murder is an entirely admirable happening! You will pardon my slightly biased point of view."

"It is most natural, Madame. And now to return to the question you did not answer. Where is the younger daughter of Linda Arden, the sister of Mrs. Armstrong?"

"I honestly cannot tell you, Monsieur. I have lost touch with the younger generation. I believe she married an Englishman some years ago and went to England, but at the moment I cannot recollect the name."

She paused a minute and then said:

"Is there anything further you want to ask me, gentlemen?"

"Only one thing, Madame, a somewhat personal question. The colour of your dressing-gown."

She raised her eyebrows slightly. "I must suppose you have a reason for such a question. My dressing-gown is of black satin."

"There is nothing more, Madame. I am much obliged to you for answering my questions so promptly."

She made a slight gesture with her heavily beringed hand. Then as she rose, and the others rose with her, she stopped.

"You will excuse me, Monsieur," she said, "but may I ask your name? Your face is somehow familiar to me."

"My name, Madame, is Hercule Poirot—at your service."

She was silent a minute, then: "Hercule Poirot," she said. "Yes. I remember now. This is Destiny."

She walked away, very erect, a little stiff in her movements.

"*Voilà une grande dame*," said M. Bouc. "What do you think of her, my friend?"

But Hercule Poirot merely shook his head.

"I am wondering," he said, "what she meant by Destiny."

CHAPTER SEVEN

THE EVIDENCE OF COUNT AND COUNTESS ANDRENYI

COUNT AND COUNTESS ANDRENYI were next summoned. The Count, however, entered the dining-car alone.

There was no doubt that he was a fine-looking man seen face to face. He was at least six feet in height, with broad shoulders and slender hips. He was dressed in very well-cut English tweeds and might have been taken for an Englishman had it not been for the length of his moustache and something in the line of the cheekbone.

"Well, Messieurs," he said, "what can I do for you?"

"You understand, Monsieur," said Poirot, "that in view of what has occurred I am obliged to put certain questions to all the passengers."

"Perfectly, perfectly," said the Count easily. "I quite understand your position. Not, I fear, that my wife and I can do much to assist you. We were asleep and heard nothing at all."

"Are you aware of the identity of the deceased, Monsieur?"

"I understood it was the big American—a man with a decidedly unpleasant face. He sat at that table at meal times." He indicated with a nod of his head the table at which Ratchett and MacQueen had sat.

"Yes, yes, Monsieur, you are perfectly correct. I meant—did you know the name of the man?"

"No." The Count looked thoroughly puzzled by Poirot's queries.

"If you want to know his name," he said, "surely it is on his passport?"

"The name on his passport is Ratchett," said Poirot. "But that, Monsieur, is not his real name. He is the man Cassetti, who was responsible for a celebrated kidnapping outrage in America."

He watched the Count closely as he spoke, but the latter seemed quite unaffected by this piece of news. He merely opened his eyes a little.

"Ah!" he said. "That certainly should throw light upon the matter. An extraordinary country, America."

"You have been there, perhaps, Monsieur le Comte?"

"I was in Washington for a year."

"You knew, perhaps, the Armstrong family?"

"Armstrong—Armstrong—it is difficult to recall. One met so many." He smiled, shrugged his shoulders. "But to come back to the matter in hand, gentlemen," he said. "What more can I do to assist you?"

"You retired to rest—when, Monsieur le Comte?"

Hercule Poirot's eyes stole to his plan. Count and Countess Andrenyi occupied compartments Nos. 12 and 13 adjoining.

"We had one compartment made up for the night whilst we were in the dining-car. On returning we sat in the other for a while—"

"Which number would that be?"

"No. 13. We played piquet together. At about eleven o'clock my wife retired for the night. The conductor made up my compartment and I also went to bed. I slept soundly until morning."

"Did you notice the stopping of the train?"

"I was not aware of it till this morning."

"And your wife?"

The Count smiled. "My wife always takes a sleeping draught when travelling by train. She took her usual dose of trional."

He paused. "I am sorry I am not able to assist you in any way."

Poirot passed him a sheet of paper and a pen.

"Thank you, Monsieur le Comte. It is a formality, but will you just let me have your name and address?"

The Count wrote slowly and carefully.

"It is just as well that I should write this for you," he said pleasantly. "The spelling of my country estate is a little difficult for those unacquainted with the language."

He passed the paper across to Poirot and rose.

"It will be quite unnecessary for my wife to come here," he said. "She can tell you nothing more than I have."

A little gleam came into Poirot's eye.

"Doubtless, doubtless," he said. "But all the same I think I should like to have just one little word with Madame la Comtesse."

"I assure you it is quite unnecessary." The Count's voice rang out authoritatively.

Poirot blinked gently at him.

"It will be a mere formality," he said. "But, you understand, it is necessary for my report."

"As you please."

The Count gave way grudgingly. He made a short foreign bow and left the dining-car.

Poirot reached out a hand to a passport. It set out the Count's names and titles. He passed on to the further information. "*Accompanied by*, wife; *Christian name*, Elena Maria; *maiden name*, Goldenberg; *age*, twenty." A spot of grease had been dropped on it at some time by a careless official.

"A diplomatic passport," said M. Bouc. "We must be careful, my friend, to give no offence. These people can have nothing to do with the murder."

"Be easy, *mon vieux*, I will be most tactful. A mere formality."

His voice dropped as the Countess Andrenyi entered the dining-car. She looked timid and extremely charming.

"You wish to see me, Messieurs?"

"A mere formality, Madame la Comtesse." Poirot rose gallantly, bowed her into the seat opposite him. "It is only to ask you if you saw or heard anything last night that may throw light upon this matter."

"Nothing at all, Monsieur. I was asleep."

"You did not hear, for instance, a commotion going on in the compartment next to yours? The American lady who occupies it had quite an attack of hysterics and rang for the conductor."

"I heard nothing, Monsieur. You see, I had taken a sleeping draught."

"Ah! I comprehend. Well, I need not detain you further." Then, as she rose swiftly—"Just one little minute. These particulars—your maiden name, age and so on—they are correct?"

"Quite correct, Monsieur."

"Perhaps you will sign this memorandum to that effect, then."

She signed quickly, in a graceful slanting handwriting—*Elena Andrenyi.*

"Did you accompany your husband to America, Madame?"

"No, Monsieur." She smiled, flushed a little. "We were not married then; we have been married only a year."

"Ah, yes, thank you, Madame. By the way, does your husband smoke?" She stared at him as she stood poised for departure.

"Yes."

"A pipe?"

"No. Cigarettes and cigars."

"Ah! Thank you."

She lingered, her eyes watching him curiously. Lovely eyes they were, dark and almond-shaped with very long black lashes that swept the exquisite pallor of her cheeks. Her lips, very scarlet in the foriegn fashion, were parted just a little. She looked exotic and beautiful.

"Why did you ask me that?"

"Madame," Poirot waved an airy hand, "detectives have to ask all sorts of questions. For instance, perhaps you will tell me the colour of your dressing-gown?"

She stared at him. Then she laughed. "It is corn-coloured chiffon. Is that really important?"

"Very important, Madame."

She asked curiously: "Are you really a detective, then?"

"At your service, Madame."

"I thought there were no detectives on the train when it passed through Jugo-Slavia—not until one got to Italy."

"I am not a Jugo-Slavian detective, Madame. I am an international detective."

"You belong to the League of Nations?"

"I belong to the world, Madame," said Poirot dramatically. He went on: "I work mainly in London. You speak English?" he added in that language.

"I speak a leetle, yes." Her accent was charming.

Poirot bowed once more.

"We will not detain you further, Madame. You see, it was not so very terrible."

She smiled, inclined her head and departed.

"*Elle est jolie femme,*" said M. Bouc appreciatively. He sighed. "Well, that did not advance us much."

"No," said Poirot. "Two people who saw nothing and heard nothing." "Shall we now see the Italian?"

Poirot did not reply for a moment. He was studying a grease spot on a Hungarian diplomatic passport.

CHAPTER EIGHT

THE EVIDENCE OF COLONEL ARBUTHNOT

POIROT ROUSED himself with a slight start. His eyes twinkled a little as they met the eager ones of M. Bouc.

"Ah! my dear old friend," he said, "you see I have become what they call the snob! The first class, I feel it should be attended to before the second class. Next, I think, we will interview the good-looking Colonel Arbuthnot."

Finding the Colonel's French to be of a severely limited description, Poirot conducted his interrogatory in English.

Arbuthnot's name, age, home address and exact military standing were all ascertained. Poirot proceeded:

"It is that you come home from India on what is called the leave—what we call *en permission?*"

Colonel Arbuthnot, uninterested in what a pack of foreigners called anything, replied with true British brevity, "Yes."

"But you do not come home on the P. & O. boat?"

"No."

"Why not?"

"I chose to come by the overland route for reasons of my own."

("And that," his manner seemed to say, "is one for you, you interfering little jackanapes.")

"You came straight through from India?"

The Colonel replied drily: "I stopped for one night to see Ur of the Chaldees, and for three days in Baghdad with the A.O.C., who happens to be an old friend of mine."

"You stopped three days in Baghdad. I understand that the young English lady, Miss Debenham, also comes from Baghdad. Perhaps you met her there?"

"No, I did not. I first met Miss Debenham when she and I shared the railway convoy car from Kirkuk to Nissibin."

Poirot leaned forward. He became persuasive and a little more foreign than he need have been.

"Monsieur, I am about to appeal to you. You and Miss Debenham are

the only two English people on the train. It is necessary that I should ask
you each your opinion of the other."

"Highly irregular," said Colonel Arbuthnot coldly.

"Not so. You see, this crime, it was most probably committed by a woman.
The man was stabbed no fewer than twelve times. Even the *chef de train*
said at once, 'It is a woman.' Well, then, what is my first task? To give all
the women travelling on the Istanbul-Calais coach what Americans call the
'once-over.' But to judge of an Englishwoman is difficult. They are very reserved, the English. So I appeal to you, Monsieur, in the interests of justice.
What sort of person is this Miss Debenham? What do you know about her?"

"Miss Debenham," said the Colonel with some warmth, "is a lady."

"Ah!" said Poirot with every appearance of being much gratified. "So you
do not think that she is likely to be implicated in this crime?"

"The idea is absurd," said Arbuthnot. "The man was a perfect stranger—
she had never seen him before."

"Did she tell you so?"

"She did. She commented at once upon his somewhat unpleasant appearance. If a woman *is* concerned, as you seem to think (to my mind without
any evidence but on a mere assumption), I can assure you that Miss
Debenham could not possibly be implicated."

"You feel warmly in the matter," said Poirot with a smile.

Colonel Arbuthnot gave him a cold stare. "I really don't know what you
mean," he said.

The stare seemed to abash Poirot. He dropped his eyes and began fiddling
with the papers in front of him.

"All this is by the way," he said. "Let us be practical and come to facts.
This crime, we have reason to believe, took place at a quarter past one last
night. It is part of the necessary routine to ask everyone on the train what
he or she was doing at that time."

"Quite so. At a quarter past one, to the best of my belief, I was talking
to the young American fellow—secretary to the dead man."

"Ah! were you in his compartment, or was he in yours?"

"I was in his."

"That is the young man of the name of MacQueen?"

"Yes."

"He was a friend or acquaintance of yours?"

"No, I never saw him before this journey. We fell into casual conversation
yesterday and both became interested. I don't as a rule like Americans—
haven't any use for 'em—"

Poirot smiled, remembering MacQueen's strictures on "Britishers."

"—but I liked this young fellow. He'd got hold of some tomfool idiotic
ideas about the situation in India. That's the worst of Americans—they're
so sentimental and idealistic. Well, he was interested in what I had to tell
him. I've had nearly thirty years' experience of the country. And I was interested in what he had to tell me about the working of Prohibition in America.

Then we got down to world politics in general. I was quite surprised to look at my watch and find it was a quarter to two."

"That is the time you broke up this conversation?"

"Yes."

"What did you do then?"

"Walked along to my own compartment and turned in."

"Your bed was made up ready?"

"Yes."

"That is the compartment—let me see—No. 15—the one next but one to the end away from the dining-car?"

"Yes."

"Where was the conductor when you went to your compartment?"

"Sitting at the end at a little table. As a matter of fact MacQueen called him just as I went in to my own compartment."

"Why did he call him?"

"To make up his bed, I suppose. The compartment hadn't been made up for the night."

"Now, Colonel Arbuthnot, I want you to think carefully. During the time you were talking to Mr. MacQueen, did anyone pass along the corridor outside the door?"

"A good many people, I should think. I wasn't paying attention."

"Ah! but I am referring to—let us say, the last hour and a half of your conversation. You got out at Vincovci, didn't you?"

"Yes, but only for about a minute. There was a blizzard on. The cold was something frightful. Made one quite thankful to get back to the fug, though as a rule I think the way these trains are overheated is something scandalous."

M. Bouc sighed. "It is very difficult to please everybody," he said. "The English they open everything—then others they come along and shut everything. It is very difficult."

Neither Poirot nor Colonel Arbuthnot paid any attention to him.

"Now, Monsieur, cast your mind back," said Poirot encouragingly. "It was cold outside. You have returned to the train. You sit down again, you smoke —perhaps a cigarette—perhaps a pipe—"

He paused for the fraction of a second.

"A pipe for me. MacQueen smoked cigarettes."

"The train starts again. You smoke your pipe. You discuss the state of Europe—of the world. It is late now. Most people have retired for the night. Does anyone pass the door? Think."

Arbuthnot frowned in the effort of remembrance.

"Difficult to say," he said. "You see I wasn't paying any attention."

"But you have the soldier's observation for detail. You notice without noticing, so to speak."

The Colonel thought again, but shook his head.

"I couldn't say. I don't remember anyone passing except the conductor. Wait a minute—and there was a woman, I think."

"You saw her? Was she old—young?"

"Didn't see her. Wasn't looking that way. Just a rustle and a sort of smell of scent."

"Scent? A *good* scent?"

"Well, rather fruity, if you know what I mean. I mean you'd smell it a hundred yards away. But mind you," the Colonel went on hastily, "this may have been earlier in the evening. You see, as you said just now, it was just one of those things you notice without noticing, so to speak. Some time that evening I said to myself—'Woman—scent—got it on pretty thick.' But *when* it was I can't be sure, except that—why, yes, it must have been after Vincovci."

"Why?"

"Because I remember—sniffing, you know—just when I was talking about the utter washout Stalin's Five Year Plan was turning out. I know the idea *woman* brought the idea of the position of women in Russia into my mind. And I know we hadn't got on to Russia until pretty near the end of our talk."

"You can't pin it down more definitely than that?"

"N-no. It must have been roughly within the last half-hour."

"It was after the train had stopped?"

The other nodded. "Yes, I'm almost sure it was."

"Well, we will pass from that. Have you ever been in America, Colonel Arbuthnot?"

"Never. Don't want to go."

"Did you ever know a Colonel Armstrong?"

"Armstrong—Armstrong—I've known two or three Armstrongs. There was Tommy Armstrong in the 60th—you don't mean him? And Selby Armstrong —he was killed on the Somme."

"I mean the Colonel Armstrong who married an American wife and whose only child was kidnapped and killed."

"Ah, yes, I remember reading about that—shocking affair. I don't think I actually ever came across the fellow, though of course I knew of him. Toby Armstrong. Nice fellow. Everybody liked him. He had a very distinguished career. Got the V.C."

"The man who was killed last night was the man responsible for the murder of Colonel Armstrong's child."

Arbuthnot's face grew rather grim. "Then in my opinion the swine deserved what he got. Though I would have preferred to see him properly hanged—or electrocuted, I suppose, over there."

"In fact, Colonel Arbuthnot, you prefer law and order to private vengeance?"

"Well, you can't go about having blood feuds and stabbing each other like Corsicans or the Mafia," said the Colonel. "Say what you like, trial by jury is a sound system."

Poirot looked at him thoughtfully for a minute or two.

"Yes," he said. "I am sure that would be your view. Well, Colonel

Arbuthnot, I do not think there is anything more I have to ask you. There is nothing you yourself can recall last night that in any way struck you—or shall we say strikes you now, looking back—as suspicious?"

Arbuthnot considered for a moment or two.

"No," he said. "Nothing at all. Unless—" he hesitated.

"But yes, continue, I pray of you."

"Well, it's nothing really," said the Colonel slowly. "But you said *anything.*"

"Yes, yes. Go on."

"Oh! it's nothing. A mere detail. But as I got back to my compartment I noticed that the door of the one beyond mine—the end one, you know—"

"Yes, No. 16."

"Well, the door of it was not quite closed. And the fellow inside peered out in a furtive sort of way. Then he pulled the door to quickly. Of course I know there's nothing in that—but it just struck me as a bit odd. I mean, it's quite usual to open a door and stick your head out if you want to see anything. But it was the furtive way he did it that caught my attention."

"Ye-es," said Poirot doubtfully.

"I told you there was nothing to it," said Arbuthnot, apologetically. "But you know what it is—early hours of the morning—everything very still. The thing had a sinister look—like a detective story. All nonsense really."

He rose. "Well, if you don't want me any more—"

"Thank you, Colonel Arbuthnot, there is nothing else."

The soldier hesitated for a minute. His first natural distaste for being questioned by "foreigners" had evaporated.

"About Miss Debenham," he said rather awkwardly. "You can take it from me that she's all right. She's a *pukka sahib.*"

Flushing a little, he withdrew.

"What," asked Dr. Constantine with interest, "does a *pukka sahib* mean?"

"It means," said Poirot, "that Miss Debenham's father and brothers were at the same kind of school as Colonel Arbuthnot was."

"Oh!" said Dr. Constantine, disappointed. "Then it has nothing to do with the crime at all."

"Exactly," said Poirot.

He fell into a reverie, beating a light tattoo on the table. Then he looked up.

"Colonel Arbuthnot smokes a pipe," he said. "In the compartment of Mr. Ratchett I found a pipe-cleaner. Mr. Ratchett smoked only cigars."

"You think—?"

"He is the only man so far who admits to smoking a pipe. And he knew of Colonel Armstrong—perhaps actually did know him, though he won't admit it."

"So you think it possible—?"

Poirot shook his head violently.

"That is just it—it is *im*possible—quite impossible—that an honourable, slightly stupid, upright Englishman should stab an enemy twelve times with a knife! Do you not feel, my friends, how impossible it is?"

"That is the psychology," said M. Bouc.

"And one must respect the psychology. This crime has a signature, and it is certainly not the signature of Colonel Arbuthnot. But now to our next interview."

This time M. Bouc did not mention the Italian. But he thought of him.

CHAPTER NINE

THE EVIDENCE OF MR. HARDMAN

THE LAST of the first-class passengers to be interviewed, Mr. Hardman, was the big flamboyant American who had shared a table with the Italian and the valet.

He wore a somewhat loud check suit, a pink shirt, and a flashy tie-pin, and was rolling something round his tongue as he entered the dining-car. He had a big, fleshy, coarse-featured face, with a good-humoured expression.

"Morning, gentlemen," he said. "What can I do for you?"

"You have heard of this murder, Mr.—er—Hardman?"

"Sure." He shifted the chewing gum deftly.

"We are of necessity interviewing all the passengers on the train."

"That's all right by me. Guess that's the only way to tackle the job."

Poirot consulted the passport lying in front of him.

"You are Cyrus Bethman Hardman, United States subject, forty-one years of age, travelling salesman for typewriting ribbons?"

"O.K. That's me."

"You are travelling from Stamboul to Paris?"

"That's so."

"Reason?"

"Business."

"Do you always travel first-class, Mr. Hardman?"

"Yes, sir. The firm pays my travelling expenses." He winked.

"Now, Mr. Hardman, we come to the events of last night."

The American nodded.

"What can you tell us about the matter?"

"Exactly nothing at all."

"Ah, that is a pity. Perhaps, Mr. Hardman, you will tell us exactly what you did last night from dinner onwards?"

For the first time the American did not seem ready with his reply. At last he said: "Excuse me, gentlemen, but just who are you? Put me wise."

"This is M. Bouc, a director of the Compagnie des Wagons Lits. This gentleman is the doctor who examined the body."

"And you yourself?"

"I am Hercule Poirot. I am engaged by the company to investigate this matter."

"I've heard of you," said Mr. Hardman. He reflected a minute or two longer. "Guess I'd better come clean."

"It will certainly be advisable for you to tell us all you know," said Poirot drily.

"You'd have said a mouthful if there was anything I *did* know. But I don't. I know nothing at all—just as I said. But I *ought* to know something. That's what makes me sore. I *ought* to."

"Please explain, Mr. Hardman."

Mr. Hardman sighed, removed the chewing gum, and dived into a pocket. At the same time his whole personality seemed to undergo a change. He became less of a stage character and more of a real person. The resonant nasal tones of his voice became modified.

"That passport's a bit of bluff," he said. "That's who I really am."

Poirot scrutinised the card flipped across to him. M. Bouc peered over his shoulder.

Mr. Cyrus B. Hardman

McNeil's Detective Agency
New York City

Poirot knew the name as that of one of the best-known and most reputable private detective agencies in New York.

"Now, Mr. Hardman," he said, "let us hear the meaning of this."

"Sure. Things came about this way. I'd come over to Europe trailing a couple of crooks—nothing to do with this business. The chase ended in Stamboul. I wired the Chief and got his instructions to return, and I would have been making my tracks back to little old New York when I got this."

He pushed across a letter.

THE TOKATLIAN HOTEL

Dear Sir:

You have been pointed out to me as an operative of the McNeil Detective Agency. Kindly report at my suite at four o'clock this afternoon.

S. E. RATCHETT.

"Eh bien?"

"I reported at the time stated, and Mr. Ratchett put me wise to the situation. He showed me a couple of letters he'd got."

"He was alarmed?"

"Pretended not to be, but he was rattled, all right. He put up a proposition to me. I was to travel by the same train as he did to Parrus and see that nobody got him. Well, gentlemen, I *did* travel by the same train, and in spite of me, somebody *did* get him. I certainly feel sore about it. It doesn't look any too good for me."

"Did he give you any indication of the line you were to take?"

"Sure. He had it all taped out. It was his idea that I should travel in the compartment alongside his. Well, that blew up right at the start. The only place I could get was berth No. 16, and I had a job getting that. I guess the conductor likes to keep that compartment up his sleeve. But that's neither here nor there. When I looked all round the situation, it seemed to me that No. 16 was a pretty good strategic position. There was only the dining-car in front of the Stamboul sleeping-car, and the door onto the platform at the front end was barred at night. The only way a thug could come was through the rear-end door to the platform, or along the train from the rear, and in either case he'd have to pass right by my compartment."

"You had no idea, I suppose, of the identity of the possible assailant?"

"Well, I knew what he looked like. Mr. Ratchett described him to me."

"What?"

All three men leaned forward eagerly.

Hardman went on.

"A small man—dark—with a womanish kind of voice. That's what the old man said. Said, too, that he didn't think it would be the first night out. More likely the second or third."

"He knew something," said M. Bouc.

"He certainly knew more than he told his secretary," commented Poirot thoughtfully. "Did he tell you anything about this enemy of his? Did he, for instance, say *why* his life was threatened?"

"No, he was kinda reticent about that part of it. Just said the fellow was out for his blood and meant to get it."

"A small man—dark—with a womanish voice," repeated Poirot thoughtfully. Then, fixing a sharp glance on Hardman, he asked: "You knew who he really was, of course?"

"Which, Mister?"

"Ratchett. You recognised him?"

"I don't get you."

"Ratchett was Cassetti, the Armstrong murderer."

Mr. Hardman gave vent to a prolonged whistle.

"That certainly is some surprise!" he said. "Yes, *sir!* No, I didn't recognise him. I was away out West when that case came on. I suppose I saw photos of him in the papers, but I wouldn't recognise my own mother when a newspaper photographer got through with her. Well, I don't doubt that a few people had it in for Cassetti all right."

"Do you know of anyone connected with the Armstrong case who answers to that description: small—dark—womanish voice?"

Hardman reflected a minute or two. "It's hard to say. Pretty nearly everyone connected with that case is dead."

"There was the girl who threw herself out of the window, remember."

"Sure. That's a good point, that. She was a foreigner of some kind. Maybe she had some Wop relations. But you've got to remember that there were other cases besides the Armstrong one. Cassetti had been running this kidnapping stunt for some time. You can't concentrate on that only."

"Ah, but we have reason to believe that this crime *is* connected with the Armstrong case."

Mr. Hardman cocked an inquiring eye. Poirot did not respond. The American shook his head.

"I can't call to mind anybody answering that description in the Armstrong case," he said slowly. "But of course I wasn't in it and didn't know much about it."

"Well, continue your narrative, Mr. Hardman."

"There's very little to tell. I got my sleep in the daytime and stayed awake on the watch at night. Nothing suspicious happened the first night. Last night was the same, as far as I was concerned. I had my door a little ajar and watched. No stranger passed."

"You are sure of that, Mr. Hardman?"

"I'm plumb certain. Nobody got on that train from outside, and nobody came along the train from the rear carriages. I'll take my oath on that."

"Could you see the conductor from your position?"

"Sure. He sits on that little seat almost flush with my door."

"Did he leave that seat at all after the train stopped at Vincovci?"

"That was the last station? Why, yes, he answered a couple of bells—that would be just after the train came to a halt for good. Then, after that, he went past me into the rear coach—was there about a quarter of an hour. There was a bell ringing like mad and he came back running. I stepped out into the corridor to see what it was all about—felt a mite nervous, you understand—but it was only the American dame. She was raising hell about something or other. I grinned. Then he went on to another compartment and came back and got a bottle of mineral water for someone. After that he settled down in his seat till he went up to the far end to make somebody's bed up. I don't think he stirred after that until about five o'clock this morning."

"Did he doze off at all?"

"That I can't say. He may have."

Poirot nodded. Automatically his hands straightened the papers on the table. He picked up the official card once more.

"Be so good as just to initial this," he said.

The other complied.

"There is no one, I suppose, who can confirm your story of your identity, Mr. Hardman?"

"On this train? Well, not exactly. Unless it might be young MacQueen. I know him well enough—I've seen him in his father's office in New York. But that's not to say he'll remember me from a crowd of other operatives. No, Mr. Poirot, you'll have to wait and cable New York when the snow lets up. But it's O.K. I'm not telling the tale. Well, so long, gentlemen. Pleased to have met you, Mr. Poirot."

Poirot proffered his cigarette case. "But perhaps you prefer a pipe?"

"Not me." He helped himself, then strode briskly off.

The three men looked at each other.

"You think he is genuine?" asked Dr. Constantine.

"Yes, yes. I know the type. Besides, it is a story that would be very easy to disprove."

"He has given us a piece of very interesting evidence," said M. Bouc.

"Yes, indeed."

"A small man—dark—with a high-pitched voice," said M. Bouc thoughtfully.

"A description which applies to no one on the train," said Poirot.

CHAPTER TEN

THE EVIDENCE OF THE ITALIAN

"AND NOW," said Poirot with a twinkle in his eye, "we will delight the heart of M. Bouc and see the Italian."

Antonio Foscarelli came into the dining-car with a swift, cat-like tread. His face beamed. It was a typical Italian face, sunny-looking and swarthy.

He spoke French well and fluently with only a slight accent.

"Your name is Antonio Foscarelli?"

"Yes, Monsieur."

"You are, I see, a naturalised American subject?"

The American grinned. "Yes, Monsieur. It is better for my business."

"You are an agent for Ford motor cars?"

"Yes, you see—"

A voluble exposition followed. At the end of it anything that the three men did not know about Foscarelli's business methods, his journeys, his income, and his opinion of the United States and most European countries seemed a negligible factor. This was not a man who had to have information dragged from him. It gushed out.

His good-natured, childish face beamed with satisfaction as, with a last eloquent gesture, he paused and wiped his forehead with a handkerchief.

"So you see," he said. "I do big business. I am up to date. I understand salesmanship!"

"You have been in the United States, then, for the last ten years on and off."

"Yes, Monsieur. Ah! well do I remember the day I first took the boat—to go to America, so far away! My mother, my little sister—"

Poirot cut short the flood of reminiscence.

"During your sojourn in the United States, did you ever come across the deceased?"

"Never. But I know the type. Oh! yes." He snapped his fingers expressively. "It is very respectable, very well-dressed, but underneath it is all wrong. Out of my experience I should say he was the big crook. I give you my opinion for what it is worth."

"Your opinion is quite right," said Poirot drily. "Ratchett was Cassetti, the kidnapper."

"What did I tell you? I have learned to be very acute—to read the face. It is necessary. Only in America do they teach you the proper way to sell. I—"

"You remember the Armstrong case?"

"I do not quite remember. The name, yes? It was a little girl, a baby, was it not?"

"Yes, a very tragic affair."

The Italian seemed the first person to demur to this view.

"Ah! well, these things they happen," he said philosophically, "in a great civilisation such as America—"

Poirot cut him short. "Did you ever come across any members of the Armstrong family?"

"No, I do not think so. It is difficult to say. I will give you some figures. Last year alone, I sold—"

"Monsieur, pray confine yourself to the point."

The Italian's hands flung themselves out in a gesture of apology. "A thousand pardons."

"Tell me, if you please, your exact movements last night from dinner onwards."

"With pleasure. I stay here as long as I can. It is more amusing. I talk to the American gentleman at my table. He sells typewriter ribbons. Then I go back to my compartment. It is empty. The miserable John Bull who shares it with me is away attending to his master. At last he comes back—very long face as usual. He will not talk—says yes and no. A miserable race, the English —not sympathetic. He sits in the corner, very stiff, reading a book. Then the conductor comes and makes our beds."

"Nos. 4 and 5," murmured Poirot.

"Exactly—the end compartment. Mine is the upper berth. I get up there. I smoke and read. The little Englishman has, I think, the toothache. He gets out a little bottle of stuff that smells very strong. He lies in bed and groans. Presently I sleep. Whenever I wake I hear him groaning."

"Do you know if he left the carriage at all during the night?"

"I do not think so. That, I should hear. The light from the corridor—one wakes up automatically thinking it is the customs examination at some frontier."

"Did he ever speak of his master? Ever express any animus against him?"

"I tell you he did not speak. He was not sympathetic. A fish."

"You smoke, you say—a pipe, cigarettes, cigar?"

"Cigarettes only."

Poirot proffered one, which he accepted.

"Have you ever been in Chicago?" inquired M. Bouc.

"Oh! yes—a fine city—but I know best New York, Cleveland, Detroit. You have been to the States? No? You should go. It—"

Poirot pushed a sheet of paper across to him.

"If you will sign this, and put your permanent address, please."

The Italian wrote with a flourish. Then he rose, his smile as engaging as ever.

"That is all? You do not require me further? Good day to you, Messieurs. I wish we could get out of the snow. I have an appointment in Milan." He shook his head sadly. "I shall lose the business." He departed.

Poirot looked at his friend.

"He has been a long time in America," said M. Bouc, "and he is an Italian, and Italians use the knife! And they are great liars! I do not like Italians."

"*Ça se voit*," said Poirot with a smile. "Well, it may be that you are right, but I will point out to you, my friend, that there is absolutely no evidence against the man."

"And what about the psychology? Do not Italians stab?"

"Assuredly," said Poirot. "Especially in the heat of a quarrel. But this—this is a different kind of crime. I have the little idea, my friend, that this is a crime very carefully planned and staged. It is a far-sighted, long-headed crime. It is not—how shall I express it?—a *Latin* crime. It is a crime that shows traces of a cool, resourceful, deliberate brain—I think an Anglo-Saxon brain."

He picked up the last two passports.

"Let us now," he said, "see Miss Mary Debenham."

CHAPTER ELEVEN

THE EVIDENCE OF MISS DEBENHAM

WHEN MARY DEBENHAM entered the dining-car she confirmed Poirot's previous estimate of her. She was very neatly dressed in a little black suit with a French grey shirt, and the smooth waves of her dark head were neat and unruffled. Her manner was as calm and unruffled as her hair.

She sat down opposite Poirot and M. Bouc and looked at them inquiringly.

"Your name is Mary Hermione Debenham and you are twenty-six years of age?" began Poirot.

"Yes."

"English?"

"Yes."

"Will you be so kind, Mademoiselle, as to write down your permanent address on this piece of paper?"

She complied. Her writing was clear and legible.

"And now, Mademoiselle, what have you to tell us of the affair last night?"

"I am afraid I have nothing to tell you. I went to bed and slept."

"Does it distress you very much, Mademoiselle, that a crime has been committed on this train?"

The question was clearly unexpected. Her grey eyes widened a little.

"I don't quite understand you?"

"It was a perfectly simple question that I asked you, Mademoiselle. I will repeat it. Are you very much distressed that a crime should have been committed on this train?"

"I have not really thought about it from that point of view. No, I cannot say that I am at all distressed."

"A crime—it is all in the day's work to you, eh?"

"It is naturally an unpleasant thing to have happen," said Mary Debenham quietly.

"You are very Anglo-Saxon, Mademoiselle. Vous n'éprouvez pas d'émotion."

She smiled a little. "I am afraid I cannot have hysterics to prove my sensibility. After all, people die every day."

"They die, yes. But murder is a little more rare."

"Oh! certainly."

"You were not acquainted with the dead man?"

"I saw him for the first time when lunching here yesterday."

"And how did he strike you?"

"I hardly noticed him."

"He did not impress you as an evil personality?"

She shrugged her shoulders slightly. "Really, I cannot say I thought about it."

Poirot looked at her keenly.

"You are, I think, a little bit contemptuous of the way I prosecute my inquiries," he said with a twinkle. "Not so, you think, would an English inquiry be conducted. There everything would be cut and dried—it would be all kept to the facts—a well-ordered business. But I, Mademoiselle, have my little originalities. I look first at my witness, I sum up his or her character, and I frame my questions accordingly. Just a little minute ago I am asking questions of a gentleman who wants to tell me all his ideas on every subject. Well, him I keep strictly to the point. I want him to answer yes or no. This

or that. And then you come. I see at once that you will be orderly and methodical. You will confine yourself to the matter in hand. Your answers will
be brief and to the point. And because, Mademoiselle, human nature is per-
verse, I ask of you quite different questions. I ask what you feel, what you
think. It does not please you, this method?"

"If you will forgive my saying so, it seems somewhat of a waste of time.
Whether or not I liked Mr. Ratchett's face does not seem likely to be helpful
in finding out who killed him."

"Do you know who the man Ratchett really was, Mademoiselle?"

She nodded. "Mrs. Hubbard has been telling everyone."

"And what do you think of the Armstrong affair?"

"It was quite abominable," said the girl crisply.

Poirot looked at her thoughtfully.

"You are travelling from Baghdad, I believe, Miss Debenham?"

"Yes."

"To London?"

"Yes."

"What have you been doing in Baghdad?"

"I have been acting as governess to two children."

"Are you returning to your post after your holiday?"

"I am not sure."

"Why is that?"

"Baghdad is rather out of things. I think I should prefer a post in London
if I can hear of a suitable one."

"I see. I thought, perhaps, you might be going to be married."

Miss Debenham did not reply. She raised her eyes and looked Poirot full
in the face. The glance said plainly: "You are impertinent."

"What is your opinion of the lady who shares your compartment—Miss
Ohlsson?"

"She seems a pleasant, simple creature."

"What colour is her dressing-gown?"

Mary Debenham stared. "A kind of brownish colour—natural wool."

"Ah! I may mention without indiscretion, I hope, that I noticed the
colour of your dressing-gown on the way from Aleppo to Stamboul. A pale
mauve, I believe."

"Yes, that is right."

"Have you any other dressing-gown, Mademoiselle? A scarlet dressing-gown,
for example?"

"No, that is not mine."

Poirot leant forward. He was like a cat pouncing on a mouse.

"Whose, then?"

The girl drew back a little, startled. "I don't know. What do you mean?"

"You do not say, 'No, I have no such thing.' You say, 'That is not mine.'
Meaning that such a thing *does* belong to someone else."

She nodded.

"Somebody else on this train?"

"Yes."

"Whose is it?"

"I told you just now: I don't know. I woke up this morning about five o'clock with the feeling that the train had been standing still for a long time. I opened the door and looked out into the corridor, thinking we might be at a station. I saw someone in a scarlet kimono some way down the corridor."

"And you don't know who it was? Was she fair, or dark, or grey-haired?"

"I can't say. She had on a shingle cap and I only saw the back of her head."

"And in build?"

"Tallish and slim, I should judge, but it's difficult to say. The kimono was embroidered with dragons."

"Yes, yes, that is right—dragons." He was silent a minute. He murmured to himself: "I cannot understand. I cannot understand. None of this makes sense."

Then, looking up, he said: "I need not keep you further, Mademoiselle."

"Oh!" She seemed rather taken aback but rose promptly.

In the doorway, however, she hesitated a minute and then came back.

"The Swedish lady—Miss Ohlsson, is it?—seems rather worried. She says you told her she was the last person to see this man alive. She thinks, I believe, that you suspect her on that account. Can't I tell her that she has made a mistake? Really, you know, she is the kind of creature who wouldn't hurt a fly." She smiled a little as she spoke.

"What time was it that she went to fetch the aspirin from Mrs. Hubbard?"

"Just after half-past ten."

"She was away—how long?"

"About five minutes."

"Did she leave the compartment again during the night?"

"No."

Poirot turned to the doctor. "Could Ratchett have been killed as early as that?"

The doctor shook his head.

"Then I think you can reassure your friend, Mademoiselle."

"Thank you." She smiled suddenly at him, a smile that invited sympathy. "She's like a sheep, you know. She gets anxious and bleats."

She turned and went out.

CHAPTER TWELVE

THE EVIDENCE OF THE GERMAN LADY'S-MAID

M. BOUC WAS LOOKING at his friend curiously.

"I do not quite understand you, *mon vieux*. You were trying to do—what?"

"I was searching for a flaw, my friend."

"A flaw?"

"Yes—in the armour of a young lady's self-possession. I wished to shake her *sang-froid*. Did I succeed? I do not know. But I know this: she did not expect me to tackle the matter as I did."

"You suspect her," said M. Bouc slowly. "But why? She seems a very charming young lady—the last person in the world to be mixed up in a crime of this kind."

"I agree," said Constantine. "She is cold. She has not emotions. She would not stab a man—she would sue him in the law courts."

Poirot sighed.

"You must, both of you, get rid of your obsession that this is an unpremeditated and sudden crime. As for the reasons why I suspect Miss Debenham, there are two. One is because of something that I overheard, and that you do not as yet know."

He retailed to them the curious interchange of phrases he had overheard on the journey from Aleppo.

"That is curious, certainly," said M. Bouc when he had finished. "It needs explaining. If it means what you suspect it means, then they are both of them in it together—she and the stiff Englishman."

Poirot nodded.

"And that is just what is not borne out by the facts," he said. "See you, if they were both in this together, what should we expect to find? That each of them would provide an alibi for the other. Is not that so? But no—that does not happen. Miss Debenham's alibi is provided by a Swedish woman whom she has never seen before, and Colonel Arbuthnot's alibi is vouched for by MacQueen, the dead man's secretary. No, that solution of the puzzle is too easy."

"You said there was another reason for your suspicions of her," M. Bouc reminded him.

Poirot smiled.

"Ah! but that is only psychological. I ask myself, is it possible for Miss Debenham to have planned this crime? Behind this business, I am convinced, there is a cool, intelligent, resourceful brain. Miss Debenham answers to that description."

M. Bouc shook his head. "I think you are wrong, my friend. I do not see that young English girl as a criminal."

"Ah! well," said Poirot, picking up the last passport. "To the final name on our list. Hildegarde Schmidt, lady's-maid."

Summoned by the attendant, Hildegarde Schmidt came into the restaurant car and stood waiting respectfully.

Poirot motioned her to sit down.

She did so, folding her hands and waiting placidly till he questioned her. She seemed a placid creature altogether—eminently respectable, perhaps not overintelligent.

Poirot's methods with Hildegarde Schmidt were a complete contrast to his handling of Mary Debenham.

He was at his kindest and most genial, setting the woman at her ease. Then, having got her to write down her name and address, he slid gently into his questions.

The interview took place in German.

"We want to know as much as possible about what happened last night," he said. "We know that you cannot give us much information bearing on the crime itself, but you may have seen or heard something that, while conveying nothing to you, may be valuable to us. You understand?"

She did not seem to. Her broad, kindly face remained set in its expression of placid stupidity as she answered:

"I do not know anything, Monsieur."

"Well, for instance you know that your mistress sent for you last night."

"That, yes."

"Do you remember the time?"

"I do not, Monsieur. I was asleep, you see, when the attendant came and told me."

"Yes, yes. Was it usual for you to be sent for in this way?"

"It was not unusual, Monsieur. The gracious lady often required attention at night. She did not sleep well."

"*Eh bien*, then, you received the summons and you got up. Did you put on a dressing-gown?"

"No, Monsieur, I put on a few clothes. I would not like to go in to her Excellency in my dressing-gown."

"And yet it is a very nice dressing-gown—scarlet, is it not?"

She stared at him. "It is a dark blue flannel dressing-gown, Monsieur."

"Ah! continue. A little pleasantry on my part, that is all. So you went along to Madame la Princesse. And what did you do when you got there?"

"I gave her massage, Monsieur, and then I read aloud. I do not read aloud very well, but her Excellency says that is all the better—so it sends her better to sleep. When she became sleepy, Monsieur, she told me to go, so I closed the book and I returned to my own compartment."

"Do you know what time that was?"

"No, Monsieur."

"Well, how long had you been with Madame la Princesse?"

"About half an hour, Monsieur."

"Good, continue."

"First, I fetched her Excellency an extra rug from my compartment. It was very cold in spite of the heating. I arranged the rug over her, and she wished me good night. I poured her out some mineral water. Then I turned out the light and left her."

"And then?"

"There is nothing more, Monsieur. I returned to my carriage and went to sleep."

"And you met no one in the corridor?"

"No, Monsieur."

"You did not, for instance, see a lady in a scarlet kimono with dragons on it?"

Her mild eyes bulged at him. "No, indeed, Monsieur. There was nobody about except the attendant. Everyone was asleep."

"But you did see the conductor?"

"Yes, Monsieur."

"What was he doing?"

"He came out of one of the compartments, Monsieur."

"What?" M. Bouc leaned forward. "Which one?"

Hildegarde Schmidt looked frightened again, and Poirot cast a reproachful glance at his friend.

"Naturally," he said. "The conductor often has to answer bells at night. Do you remember which compartment it was?"

"It was about the middle of the coach, Monsieur. Two or three doors from Madame la Princesse."

"Ah! tell us, if you please, exactly where this was and what happened?"

"He nearly ran into me, Monsieur. It was when I was returning from my compartment to that of the Princess with the rug."

"And he came out of a compartment and almost collided with you. In which direction was he going?"

"Towards me, Monsieur. He apologised and passed on down the corridor towards the dining-car. A bell began ringing, but I do not think he answered it." She paused and then said: "I do not understand. How is it—"

Poirot spoke reassuringly.

"It is just a question of time," he said. "All a matter of routine. This poor conductor, he seems to have had a busy night—first waking you and then answering bells."

"It was not the same conductor who woke me, Monsieur. It was another one."

"Ah! another one! Had you seen him before?"

"No, Monsieur."

"Ah!—do you think you would recognise him if you saw him?"

"I think so, Monsieur."

Poirot murmured something in M. Bouc's ear. The latter got up and went to the door to give an order.

Poirot was continuing his questions in an easy, friendly manner.

"Have you ever been to America, Fräulein Schmidt?"

"Never, Monsieur. It must be a fine country."

"You have heard, perhaps, who this man who was killed really was—that he was responsible for the death of a little child?"

"Yes, I have heard, Monsieur. It was abominable—wicked. The good God should not allow such things. We are not so wicked as that in Germany."

Tears had come into the woman's eyes. Her strong, motherly soul was moved.

"It was an abominable crime," said Poirot gravely.

He drew a scrap of cambric from his pocket and handed it to her.

"Is this your handkerchief, Fräulein Schmidt?"

There was a moment's silence as the woman examined it. She looked up after a minute. The colour had mounted a little in her face.

"Ah! no, indeed. It is not mine, Monsieur."

"It has the initial H, you see. That is why I thought it was yours."

"Ah! Monsieur, it is a lady's handkerchief, that. A very expensive handkerchief. Embroidered by hand. It comes from Paris, I should say."

"It is not yours and you do not know whose it is?"

"I? Oh! no, Monsieur."

Of the three listening, only Poirot caught the nuance of hesitation in the reply.

M. Bouc whispered in his ear. Poirot nodded and said to the woman:

"The three sleeping-car attendants are coming in. Will you be so kind as to tell me which is the one you met last night as you were going with the rug to the Princess?"

The three men entered. Pierre Michel, the big blond conductor of the Athens-Paris coach, and the stout burly conductor of the Bucharest one.

Hildegarde Schmidt looked at them and immediately shook her head.

"No, Monsieur," she said. "None of these is the man I saw last night."

"But these are the only conductors on the train. You must be mistaken."

"I am quite sure, Monsieur. These are all tall, big men. The one I saw was small and dark. He had a little moustache. His voice when he said 'Pardon' was weak, like a woman's. Indeed, I remember him very well, Monsieur."

CHAPTER THIRTEEN

SUMMARY OF THE PASSENGERS' EVIDENCE

"A SMALL DARK MAN with a womanish voice," said M. Bouc.

The three conductors and Hildegarde Schmidt had been dismissed.

M. Bouc made a despairing gesture. "But I understand nothing—but nothing of all this! The enemy that this Ratchett spoke of, he was then on the train after all? But where is he now? How can he have vanished into thin air? My head, it whirls. Say something, then, my friend, I implore you. Show me how the impossible can be possible!"

"It is a good phrase that," said Poirot. "The impossible cannot have happened, therefore the impossible must be possible in spite of appearances."

"Explain to me, then, quickly, what actually happened on the train last night."

"I am not a magician, *mon cher*. I am, like you, a very puzzled man. This affair advances in a very strange manner."

"It does not advance at all. It stays where it was."

Poirot shook his head. "No, that is not true. We are more advanced. We know certain things. We have heard the evidence of the passengers."

"And what has that told us? Nothing at all."

"I would not say that, my friend."

"I exaggerate, perhaps. The American Hardman, and the German maid —yes, they have added something to our knowledge. That is to say, they have made the whole business more unintelligible than it was."

"No, no, no," said Poirot soothingly.

M. Bouc turned upon him. "Speak, then, let us hear the wisdom of Hercule Poirot."

"Did I not tell you that I was, like you, a very puzzled man? But at least we can face our problem. We can arrange such facts as we have with order and method."

"Pray continue, Monsieur," said Dr. Constantine.

Poirot cleared his throat and straightened a piece of blotting-paper.

"Let us review the case as it stands at this moment. First, there are certain indisputable facts. This man, Ratchett or Cassetti, was stabbed in twelve places and died last night. That is fact one."

"I grant it you—I grant it, *mon vieux*," said M. Bouc with a gesture of irony.

Hercule Poirot was not at all put out. He continued calmly.

"I will pass over for the moment certain rather peculiar appearances which Dr. Constantine and I have already discussed together. I will come to them presently. The next fact of importance, to my mind, is the *time* of the crime."

"That, again, is one of the few things we do know," said M. Bouc. "The crime was committed at a quarter past one this morning. Everything goes to show that that was so."

"Not *everything*. You exaggerate. There is, certainly, a fair amount of evidence to support that view."

"I am glad you admit that at least."

Poirot went on calmly, unperturbed by the interruption.

"We have before us three possibilities.

"(1)—that the crime was committed, as you say, at a quarter past one. This is supported by the evidence of the watch, by the evidence of Mrs. Hubbard, and by the evidence of the German woman, Hildegarde Schmidt. It agrees with the evidence of Dr. Constantine.

"(2)—that the crime was committed *later*, and that the evidence of the watch was deliberately faked in order to mislead.

"(3)—that the crime was committed *earlier*, and the evidence faked for the same reason as above.

"Now if we accept possibility (1) as the most likely to have occurred, and the one supported by most evidence, we must also accept certain facts arising from it. If the crime was committed at a quarter past one, the murderer cannot have left the train, and the questions arise: Where is he? And *who* is he?

"To begin with, let us examine the evidence carefully. We first hear of the existence of this man—the small dark man with a womanish voice—from the man Hardman. He says that Ratchett told him of this person and employed him to watch out for the man. There is no *evidence* to support this; we have only Hardman's word for it. Let us next examine the question: Is Hardman the person he pretends to be—an operative of a New York detective agency?

"What to my mind is so interesting in this case is that we have none of the facilities afforded to the police. We cannot investigate the *bona fides* of any of these people. We have to rely solely on deduction. That, to me, makes the matter very much more interesting. There is no routine work. It is all a matter of the intellect. I ask myself: Can we accept Hardman's account of himself? I make my decision and I answer 'Yes.' I am of the opinion that we *can* accept Hardman's account of himself."

"You rely on the intuition? What the Americans call the 'hunch'?" asked Dr. Constantine.

"Not at all. I regard the probabilities. Hardman is travelling with a false passport—that will at once make him an object of suspicion. The first thing that the police will do when they do arrive upon the scene is to detain Hardman and cable as to whether his account of himself is true. In the case of many of the passengers, to establish their *bona fides* will be difficult; in most cases it will probably not be attempted, especially since there seems nothing in the way of suspicion attaching to them. But in Hardman's case it is simple. Either he is the person he represents himself to be, or he is not. Therefore I say that all will prove to be in order."

"You acquit him of suspicion?"

"Not at all. You misunderstand me. For all I know, any American detective might have his own private reasons for wishing to murder Ratchett. No, what I am saying is that I think we *can* accept Hardman's own account of *himself*. This story, then, that he tells of Ratchett's seeking him out and employing him is not unlikely, and is most probably—though not of course certainly—true. If we are going to accept it as true, we must see if there is any confirmation of it. We find it in rather an unlikely place—in the evidence of Hildegarde Schmidt. Her description of the man she saw in Wagon Lit uniform tallies exactly. Is there any further confirmation of these two stories? There is. There is the button that Mrs. Hubbard found in her compartment.

And there is also another corroborating statement which you may not have noticed."

"What is that?"

"The fact that both Colonel Arbuthnot and Hector MacQueen mention that the conductor passed their carriage. They attached no importance to the fact, but, Messieurs, *Pierre Michel has declared that he did not leave his seat except on certain specified occasions*—none of which would take him down to the far end of the coach past the compartment in which Arbuthnot and MacQueen were sitting.

"Therefore this story, the story of a small dark man with a womanish voice dressed in Wagon Lit uniform, rests on the testimony, direct or indirect, of four witnesses."

"One small point," said Dr. Constantine. "If Hildegarde Schmidt's story is true, how is it that the real conductor did not mention having seen her when he came to answer Mrs. Hubbard's bell?"

"That is explained, I think. When he arrived to answer Mrs. Hubbard, the maid was in with her mistress. When she finally returned to her own compartment, the conductor was in with Mrs. Hubbard."

M. Bouc had been waiting with difficulty until they had finished.

"Yes, yes, my friend," he said impatiently to Poirot. "But whilst I admire your caution, your method of advancing a step at a time, I submit that you have not yet touched the point at issue. We are all agreed that this person exists. The point is, *where did he go?*"

Poirot shook his head reprovingly.

"You are in error. You are inclined to put the cart before the horse. Before I ask myself, 'Where did this man vanish to?' I ask myself, 'Did such a man really exist?' Because, you see, if the man were an invention—a fabrication—how much easier to make him disappear! So I try to establish first that there really *is* such a flesh-and-blood person."

"And having arrived at the fact that there is—*eh bien*, where is he now?"

"There are only two answers to that, *mon cher*. Either he is still hidden on the train in a place of such extraordinary ingenuity that we cannot even think of it; or else he is, as one might say, *two persons*. That is, he is both himself—the man feared by M. Ratchett—and a passenger on the train so well disguised that M. Ratchett did not recognise him."

"It is an idea, that," said M. Bouc, his face lighting up. Then it clouded over again. "But there is one objection—"

Poirot took the words out of his mouth.

"The height of the man. It is that you would say? With the exception of M. Ratchett's valet, all the passengers are big men—the Italian, Colonel Arbuthnot, Hector MacQueen, Count Andrenyi. Well, that leaves us the valet —not a very likely supposition. But there is another possibility. Remember the 'womanish' voice. That gives us a choice of alternatives. The man may be disguised as a woman, or, alternatively, he may actually *be* a woman. A tall woman dressed in men's clothes would look small."

"But surely Ratchett would have known—"

"Perhaps he *did* know. Perhaps, already, this woman had attempted his life, wearing a man's clothes the better to accomplish her purpose. Ratchett may have guessed that she would use the same trick again, so he tells Hardman to look for a man. But he mentions, however, a womanish voice."

"It is a possibility," said M. Bouc. "But—"

"Listen, my friend, I think that I should now tell you of certain inconsistencies noticed by Dr. Constantine."

He retailed at length the conclusions that he and the doctor had arrived at together from the nature of the dead man's wounds. M. Bouc groaned and held his head again.

"I know," said Poirot sympathetically. "I know exactly how you feel. The head spins, does it not?"

"The whole thing is a fantasy!" cried M. Bouc.

"Exactly. It is absurd—improbable—it cannot be. So I myself have said. And yet, my friend, *there it is!* One cannot escape from the facts."

"It is madness!"

"Is it not? It is so mad, my friend, that sometimes I am haunted by the sensation that really it must be very simple. . . . But that is only one of my 'little ideas'!"

"Two murderers," groaned M. Bouc. "And on the Orient Express—"

The thought almost made him weep.

"And now let us make the fantasy more fantastic," said Poirot cheerfully. "Last night on the train, there are two mysterious strangers. There is the Wagon Lit attendant answering to the description given us by M. Hardman, and seen by Hildegarde Schmidt, Colonel Arbuthnot and M. MacQueen. There is also a woman in a red kimono—a tall slim woman, seen by Pierre Michel, Miss Debenham, M. MacQueen and myself (and smelt, I may say, by Colonel Arbuthnot!) Who was she? No one on the train admits to having a scarlet kimono. She, too, has vanished. Was she one and the same with the spurious Wagon Lit attendant? Or was she some quite distinct personality? Where are they, these two? And incidentally, where are the Wagon Lit uniform and the scarlet kimono?"

"Ah! that is something definite." M. Bouc sprang up eagerly. "We must search all the passengers' luggage. Yes, that will be something."

Poirot rose also. "I will make a prophecy," he said.

"You know where they are?"

"I have a little idea."

"Where, then?"

"You will find the scarlet kimono in the baggage of one of the men, and you, will find the uniform of the Wagon Lit conductor in the baggage of Hildegarde Schmidt."

"Hildegarde Schmidt? You think—"

"Not what you are thinking. I will put it like this. If Hildegarde Schmidt is guilty, the uniform may be found in her baggage. But if she is innocent, it *certainly* will be."

"But how—" began M. Bouc and stopped. "What is this noise that approaches?" he cried. "It resembles a locomotive in motion."

The noise drew nearer. It consisted of shrill cries and protests in a woman's voice. The door at the end of the dining-car burst open. Mrs. Hubbard burst in.

"It's too horrible!" she cried. "It's just too horrible. In my sponge-bag. My sponge-bag! A great knife—all over blood!"

And suddenly toppling forward, she fainted heavily on M. Bouc's shoulder.

CHAPTER FOURTEEN

THE EVIDENCE OF THE WEAPON

WITH MORE VIGOUR than chivalry, M. Bouc deposited the fainting lady with her head on the table. Dr. Constantine yelled for one of the restaurant attendants, who came at a run.

"Keep her head so," said the doctor. "If she revives give her a little cognac. You understand?"

Then he hurried off after the other two. His interest lay wholly in the crime—swooning middle-aged ladies did not interest him at all.

It is possible that Mrs. Hubbard revived rather more quickly by these methods than she might otherwise have done. A few minutes later she was sitting up, sipping cognac from a glass proffered by the attendant, and talking once more.

"I just can't tell you how terrible it was! I don't suppose anybody on this train can understand my feelings. I've always been very, very sensitive ever since I was a child. The mere sight of blood—*ugh!* Why, even now I get faint when I think about it!"

The attendant proffered the glass again. "*Encore un peu, Madame?*"

"D'you think I'd better? I'm a lifelong teetotaller. I never touch spirits or wine at any time. All my family are abstainers. Still, perhaps as this is only medicinal—"

She sipped once more.

In the meantime Poirot and M. Bouc, closely followed by Dr. Constantine, had hurried out of the restaurant car and along the corridor of the Stamboul coach towards Mrs. Hubbard's compartment.

Every traveller on the train seemed to be congregated outside the door. The conductor, a harassed look on his face, was keeping them back.

"*Mais il n'y a rien à voir,*" he said, and repeated the sentiment in several other languages.

"Let me pass if you please," said M. Bouc.

Squeezing his rotundity past the obstructing passengers he entered the compartment, Poirot close behind him.

"I am glad you have come, Monsieur," said the conductor with a sigh of relief. "Everyone has been trying to enter. The American lady—such screams as she gave—*ma foi*, I thought she too had been murdered! I came at a run, and there she was screaming like a mad woman; and she cried out that she must fetch you, and she departed screeching at the top of her voice and telling everybody whose carriage she passed what had occurred."

He added, with a gesture of the hand: "*It* is in there, Monsieur. I have not touched it."

Hanging on the handle of the door that gave access to the next compartment was a large-checked rubber sponge-bag. Below it on the floor, just where it had fallen from Mrs. Hubbard's hand, was a straight-bladed dagger—a cheap affair, sham Oriental, with an embossed hilt and a tapering blade. The blade was stained with patches of what looked like rust.

Poirot picked it up delicately.

"Yes," he murmured. "There is no mistake. Here is our missing weapon all right—eh, doctor?"

The doctor examined it.

"You need not be so careful," said Poirot. "There will be no fingerprints on it save those of Mrs. Hubbard."

Constantine's examination did not take long.

"It is the weapon all right," he said. "It would account for any of the wounds."

"I implore you, my friend, do not say that!"

The doctor looked astonished.

"Already we are heavily overburdened by coincidence. Two people decided to stab M. Ratchett last night. It is too much of a good thing that both of them should select the same weapon."

"As to that, the coincidence is not perhaps so great as it seems," said the doctor. "Thousands of these sham Eastern daggers are made and shipped to the bazaars of Constantinople."

"You console me a little, but only a little," said Poirot.

He looked thoughtfully at the door in front of him, then, lifting off the sponge-bag, he tried the handle. The door did not budge. About a foot above the handle was the door bolt. Poirot drew it back and tried again, but still the door remained fast.

"We locked it from the other side, you remember," said the doctor.

"That is true," said Poirot absently. He seemed to be thinking about something else. His brow was furrowed as though in perplexity.

"It agrees, does it not?" said M. Bouc. "The man passes through this carriage. As he shuts the communicating door behind him he feels the sponge-bag. A thought comes to him and he quickly slips the blood-stained knife inside. Then, all unwitting that he has awakened Mrs. Hubbard, he slips out through the other door into the corridor."

"As you say," murmured Poirot. "That is how it must have happened." But the puzzled look did not leave his face.

"But what is it?" demanded M. Bouc. "There is something, is there not, that does not satisfy you?"

Poirot darted a quick look at him.

"The same point does not strike you? No, evidently not. Well, it is a small matter."

The conductor looked into the carriage. "The American lady is coming back."

Dr. Constantine looked rather guilty. He had, he felt, treated Mrs. Hubbard rather cavalierly. But she had no reproaches for him. Her energies were concentrated on another matter.

"I'm going to say one thing right out," she said breathlessly as she arrived in the doorway. "I'm not going on any longer in this compartment! Why, I wouldn't sleep in it to-night if you paid me a million dollars."

"But, Madame—"

"I know what you are going to say, and I'm telling you right now that I won't do any such thing! Why, I'd rather sit up all night in the corridor." She began to cry. "Oh, if my daughter could only know—if she could see me now, why—"

Poirot interrupted firmly.

"You misunderstand, Madame. Your demand is most reasonable. Your baggage shall be changed at once to another compartment."

Mrs. Hubbard lowered her handkerchief. "Is that so? Oh! I feel better right away. But surely it's all full, unless one of the gentlemen—"

M. Bouc spoke.

"Your baggage, Madame, shall be moved out of this coach altogether. You shall have a compartment in the next coach, which was put on at Belgrade."

"Why, that's splendid. I'm not an extra nervous woman, but to sleep in that compartment next door to a dead man!" She shivered. "It would drive me plumb crazy."

"Michel," called M. Bouc. "Move this baggage into a vacant compartment in the Athens-Paris coach."

"Yes, Monsieur. The same one as this—the No. 3?"

"No," said Poirot before his friend could reply. "I think it would be better for Madame to have a different number altogether. The No. 12, for instance."

"*Bien, Monsieur.*"

The conductor seized the luggage. Mrs. Hubbard turned gratefully to Poirot.

"That's very kind and delicate of you. I appreciate it, I assure you."

"Do not mention it, Madame. We will come with you and see you comfortably installed."

Mrs. Hubbard was escorted by the three men to her new home. She looked round her happily. "This is fine."

"It suits you, Madame? It is, you see, exactly like the compartment you have left."

"That's so—only it faces the other way. But that doesn't matter, for these trains go first one way and then the other. I said to my daughter, 'I want a carriage facing the engine,' and she said, 'Why, Mamma, that'll be no good to you, for if you go to sleep one way, when you wake up, the train's going the other!' And it was quite true what she said. Why, last evening we went into Belgrade one way and out the other."

"At any rate, Madame, you are quite happy and contented now?"

"Well, no, I wouldn't say that. Here we are stuck in a snowdrift and nobody doing anything about it, and my boat sailing the day after to-morrow."

"Madame," said M. Bouc, "we are all in the same case—every one of us."

"Well, that's true," admitted Mrs. Hubbard. "But nobody else has had a murderer walking right through her compartment in the middle of the night."

"What still puzzles me, Madame," said Poirot, "is how the man got into your compartment if the communicating door was bolted as you say. You are sure that it *was* bolted?"

"Why, the Swedish lady tried it before my eyes."

"Let us just reconstruct that little scene. You were lying in your bunk—so—and you could not see for yourself, you say?"

"No, because of the sponge-bag. Oh! my, I shall have to get a new sponge-bag. It makes me feel sick at my stomach to look at this one."

Poirot picked up the sponge-bag and hung it on the handle of the communicating door into the next carriage.

"*Précisément.* I see," he said. "The bolt is just underneath the handle—the sponge-bag masks it. You could not see from where you were lying whether the bolt was turned or not."

"Why, that's just what I've been telling you!"

"And the Swedish lady, Miss Ohlsson, stood so, between you and the door. She tried it and told you it was bolted."

"That's so."

"All the same, Madame, she may have made an error. You see what I mean." Poirot seemed anxious to explain. "The bolt is just a projection of metal—so. When it is turned to the right, the door is locked. When it is left straight, the door is unlocked. Possibly she merely tried the door, and as it was locked on the other side she may have assumed that it was locked on your side."

"Well, I guess that would be rather stupid of her."

"Madame, the most kind, the most amiable, are not always the cleverest."

"That's so, of course."

"By the way, Madame, did you travel out to Smyrna this way?"

"No. I sailed right to Stamboul, and a friend of my daughter's, Mr. Johnson (a perfectly lovely man, I'd like to have you know him), met me and showed me all round Stamboul. But it was a very disappointing city—all tumbling down; and as for those mosques, and putting on those great shuffling things over your shoes—where was I?"

"You were saying that Mr. Johnson met you."

"That's so, and he saw me on board a French Messageries boat for Smyrna, and my daughter's husband was waiting right on the quay. What he'll say when he hears about all this! My daughter said this would be just the safest, easiest way imaginable. 'You just sit in your carriage,' she said, 'and you land right in Parris, and there the American Express will meet you.' And, oh, dear, what am I to do about cancelling my steamship passage? I ought to let them know. I can't possibly make it now. This is just too terrible—"

Mrs. Hubbard showed signs of tears once more.

Poirot, who had been fidgeting slightly, seized his opportunity.

"You have had a shock, Madame. The restaurant attendant shall be instructed to bring you along some tea and some biscuits."

"I don't know that I'm so set on tea," said Mrs. Hubbard tearfully. "That's more an English habit."

"Coffee, then, Madame. You need some stimulant."

"That cognac's made my head feel mighty funny. I think I would like some coffee."

"Excellent. You must revive your forces."

"My, what a funny expression!"

"But first, Madame, a little matter of routine. You permit that I make a search of your baggage?"

"What for?"

"We are about to commence a search of all the passengers' luggage. I do not want to remind you of an unpleasant experience, but your sponge-bag—remember."

"Mercy! Perhaps you'd better! I just couldn't bear to get any more surprises of that kind."

The examination was quickly over. Mrs. Hubbard was travelling with the minimum of luggage—a hat-box, a cheap suitcase, and a well-burdened travelling bag. The contents of all three were simple and straightforward, and the examination would not have taken more than a couple of minutes had not Mrs. Hubbard delayed matters by insisting on due attention being paid to photographs of "my daughter" and of two rather ugly children—"my daughter's children. Aren't they cunning?"

CHAPTER FIFTEEN

THE EVIDENCE OF THE PASSENGERS' LUGGAGE

HAVING DELIVERED himself of various polite insincerities, and having told Mrs. Hubbard that he would order coffee to be brought to her, Poirot was able to take his leave accompanied by his two friends.

"Well, we have made a start and drawn a blank," observed M. Bouc. "Whom shall we tackle next?"

"It would be simplest, I think, just to proceed along the train, carriage by carriage. That means that we start with No. 16—the amiable Mr. Hardman."

Mr. Hardman, who was smoking a cigar, welcomed them affably.

"Come right in, gentlemen. That is, if it's humanly possible. It's just a mite cramped in here for a party."

M. Bouc explained the object of their visit, and the big detective nodded comprehendingly.

"That's O.K. To tell the truth I've been wondering you didn't get down to it sooner. Here are my keys, gentlemen, and if you like to search my pockets too, why, you're welcome. Shall I reach the grips down for you?"

"The conductor will do that. Michel!"

The contents of Mr. Hardman's two "grips" were soon examined and passed. They contained, perhaps, an undue proportion of spirituous liquor. Mr. Hardman winked.

"It's not often they search your grips at the frontiers—not if you fix the conductor. I handed out a wad of Turkish notes right away, and there's been no trouble so far."

"And at Paris?"

Mr. Hardman winked again. "By the time I get to Paris," he said, "what's left over of this little lot will go into a bottle labelled hairwash."

"You are not a believer in Prohibition, Monsieur Hardman," said M. Bouc with a smile.

"Well," said Hardman, "I can't say Prohibition has ever worried me any."

"Ah!" said M. Bouc. "The speakeasy." He pronounced the word with care, savouring it. "Your American terms are so quaint, so expressive," he said.

"Me, I would much like to go to America," said Poirot.

"You'd learn a few go-ahead methods over there," said Hardman. "Europe needs waking up. She's half asleep."

"It is true that America is the country of progress," agreed Poirot. "There is much that I admire about Americans. Only—I am perhaps old-fashioned —but me, I find the American women less charming than my own country-women. The French or the Belgian girl, coquettish, charming—I think there is no one to touch her."

Hardman turned away to peer out at the snow for a minute.

"Perhaps you're right, M. Poirot," he said. "But I guess every nation likes its own girls best." He blinked as though the snow hurt his eyes.

"Kind of dazzling, isn't it?" he remarked. "Say, gentlemen, this business is getting on my nerves. Murder and the snow and all. And nothing *doing*. Just hanging about and killing time. I'd like to get busy after someone or something."

"The true Western spirit of hustle," said Poirot with a smile.

The conductor replaced the bags and they moved on to the next compartment. Colonel Arbuthnot was sitting in a corner smoking a pipe and reading a magazine.

Poirot explained their errand. The Colonel made no demur. He had two heavy leather suitcases.

"The rest of my kit has gone by long sea," he explained.

Like most Army men the Colonel was a neat packer. The examination of his baggage took only a few minutes. Poirot noted a packet of pipe-cleaners.

"You always use the same kind?" he asked.

"Usually. If I can get 'em."

"Ah!" Poirot nodded. These pipe-cleaners corresponded exactly with the one he had found on the floor of the dead man's compartment.

Dr. Constantine remarked as much when they were out in the corridor again.

"*Tout de même,*" murmured Poirot, "I can hardly believe it. It is not *dans son caractère,* and when you have said that, you have said everything."

The door of the next compartment was closed. It was that occupied by Princess Dragomiroff. They knocked on the door and the Princess's deep voice called "*Entrez!*"

M. Bouc was spokesman. He was very deferential and polite as he explained their errand.

The Princess listened to him in silence, her small toad-like face quite impassive.

"If it is necessary, Messieurs," she said quietly when he had finished, "that is all there is to it. My maid has the keys. She will attend to it with you."

"Does your maid always carry your keys, Madame?" asked Poirot.

"Certainly, Monsieur."

"And if, during the night at one of the frontiers, the customs officials should require a piece of luggage to be opened?"

The old lady shrugged her shoulders. "It is very unlikely. But in such a case, the conductor would fetch her."

"You trust her, then, implicitly, Madame?"

"I have told you so already," said the Princess quietly. "I do not employ people whom I do not trust."

"Yes," said Poirot thoughtfully. "Trust is indeed something in these days. It is perhaps better to have a homely woman whom one can trust than a more *chic* maid—for example, some smart Parisienne."

He saw the dark intelligent eyes come slowly round and fasten themselves upon his face. "What exactly are you implying, M. Poirot?"

"Nothing, Madame. I? Nothing."

"But yes. You think, do you not, that I should have a smart Frenchwoman to attend to my toilet?"

"It would be perhaps more usual, Madame."

She shook her head. "Schmidt is devoted to me." Her voice dwelt lingeringly on the words. "Devotion—*c'est impayable.*"

The German woman had arrived with the keys. The Princess spoke to her in her own language, telling her to open the valises and help the gentlemen in their search. She herself remained in the corridor looking out at the snow, and Poirot remained with her, leaving M. Bouc to the task of searching the luggage.

She regarded him with a grim smile.

"Well, Monsieur, do you not wish to see what my valises contain?"

He shook his head. "Madame, it is a formality, that is all."

"Are you so sure?"

"In your case, yes."

"And yet I knew and loved Sonia Armstrong. What do you think, then? That I would not soil my hands with killing such *canaille* as that man Cassetti? Well, perhaps you are right."

She was silent a minute or two. Then she said:

"With such a man as that, do you know what I should have liked to do? I should have liked to call to my servants: 'Flog this man to death and fling him out on the rubbish heap!' That is the way things were done when I was young, Monsieur."

Still he did not speak, just listened attentively.

She looked at him with a sudden impetuosity. "You do not say anything, M. Poirot. What is it that you are thinking, I wonder?"

He looked at her with a very direct glance. "I think, Madame, that your strength is in your will—not in your arm."

She glanced down at her thin, black-clad arms ending in those claw-like yellow hands with the rings on the fingers.

"It is true," she said. "I have no strength in these—none. I do not know whether I am sorry or glad."

Then she turned abruptly back towards her carriage where the maid was busily packing up the cases.

The Princess cut short M. Bouc's apologies.

"There is no need for you to apologise, Monsieur," she said. "A murder has been committed. Certain actions have to be performed. That is all there is to it."

"*Vous êtes bien aimable, Madame.*"

She inclined her head slightly as they departed.

The doors of the next two carriages were shut. M. Bouc paused and scratched his head.

"*Diable!*" he said. "This may be awkward. These are diplomatic passports. Their luggage is exempt."

"From customs examination, yes. But a murder is different."

"I know. All the same—we do not want to have complications."

"Do not distress yourself, my friend. The Count and Countess will be reasonable. See how amiable Princess Dragomiroff was about it."

"She is truly *grande dame*. These two are also of the same position, but the Count impressed me as a man of somewhat truculent disposition. He was not pleased when you insisted on questioning his wife. And this will annoy him still further. Suppose—eh?—we omit them. After all, they can have nothing to do with the matter. Why should I stir up needless trouble for myself?"

"I do not agree with you," said Poirot. "I feel sure that Count Andrenyi will be reasonable. At any rate let us make the attempt."

And before M. Bouc could reply, he rapped sharply on the door of No. 13. A voice from within cried *"Entrez!"*

The Count was sitting in the corner near the door reading a newspaper. The Countess was curled up in the opposite corner near the window. There was a pillow behind her head and she seemed to have been asleep.

"Pardon, Monsieur le Comte," began Poirot. "Pray forgive this intrusion. It is that we are making a search of all the baggage on the train. In most cases a mere formality. But it has to be done. M. Bouc suggests that, as you have a diplomatic passport, you might reasonably claim to be exempt from such a search."

The Count considered for a moment.

"Thank you," he said. "But I do not think that I care to have an exception made in my case. I should prefer that our baggage should be examined like that of the other passengers."

He turned to his wife. "You do not object, I hope, Elena?"

"Not at all," said the Countess without hesitation.

A rapid and somewhat perfunctory search followed. Poirot seemed to be trying to mask an embarrassment by making various small pointless remarks, such as:

"Here is a label all wet on your suitcase, Madame," as he lifted down a blue morocco case with initials on it and a coronet.

The Countess did not reply to this observation. She seemed, indeed, rather bored by the whole proceeding, remaining curled up in her corner and staring dreamily out through the window whilst the men searched her luggage in the compartment next door.

Poirot finished his search by opening the little cupboard above the wash-basin and taking a rapid glance at its contents—a sponge, face cream, powder and a small bottle labelled trional.

Then with polite remarks on either side, the search party withdrew.

Mrs. Hubbard's compartment, that of the dead man, and Poirot's own came next.

They now came to the second-class carriages. The first one, Nos. 10 and 11, was occupied by Mary Debenham, who was reading a book, and Greta Ohlsson, who was fast asleep but woke with a start at their entrance.

Poirot repeated his formula. The Swedish lady seemed agitated, Mary Debenham calmly indifferent. He addressed himself to the Swedish lady.

"If you permit, Mademoiselle, we will examine your baggage first, and then perhaps you would be so good as to see how the American lady is getting on. We have moved her into one of the carriages in the next coach, but she is still very much upset as the result of her discovery. I have ordered coffee to be sent to her, but I think she is of those to whom someone to talk to is a necessity of the first order."

The good lady was instantly sympathetic. She would go immediately. It must have been indeed a terrible shock to the nerves, and already the poor lady was upset by the journey and leaving her daughter.

Ah, yes, certainly she would go at once—her case was not locked—and she would take with her some sal ammoniac.

She bustled off. Her possessions were soon examined. They were meagre in the extreme. She had evidently not yet noticed the missing wires from the hat-box.

Miss Debenham had put her book down. She was watching Poirot. When he asked her, she handed over her keys. Then, as he lifted down a case and opened it, she said:

"Why did you send her away, M. Poirot?"

"I, Mademoiselle? Why, to minister to the American lady."

"An excellent pretext—but a pretext all the same."

"I don't understand you, Mademoiselle."

"I think you understand me very well." She smiled. "You wanted to get me alone. Wasn't that it?"

"You are putting words into my mouth, Mademoiselle."

"And ideas into your head? No, I don't think so. The ideas are already there. That is right, isn't it?"

"Mademoiselle, we have a proverb—"

"*Qui s'excuse s'accuse*—is that what you were going to say? You must give me the credit for a certain amount of observation and common sense. For some reason or other you have got it into your head that I know something about this sordid business—this murder of a man I never saw before."

"You are imagining things, Mademoiselle."

"No, I am not imagining things at all. But it seems to me that a lot of time is wasted by not speaking the truth—by beating about the bush instead of coming straight out with things."

"And you do not like the waste of time. No, you like to come straight to the point. You like the direct method. *Eh bien,* I will give it to you, the direct method. I will ask you the meaning of certain words that I overheard on the journey from Syria. I had got out of the train to do what the English call 'stretch the legs' at the station of Konya. Your voice and the Colonel's, Mademoiselle, they came to me out of the night. You said to him, '*Not now. Not now. When it's all over. When it's behind us.*' What did you mean by those words, Mademoiselle?"

She asked very quietly, "Do you think I meant—murder?"

"It is I who am asking you, Mademoiselle."

She sighed—was lost a minute in thought. Then, as though rousing herself, she said:

"Those words had a meaning, Monsieur, but not one that I can tell you. I can only give you my solemn word of honour that I had never set eyes on this man Ratchett in my life until I saw him on this train."

"And—you refuse to explain those words?"

"Yes, if you like to put it that way—I refuse. They had to do with—with a task I had undertaken."

"A task that is now ended?"

"What do you mean?"

"It is ended, is it not?"

"Why should you think so?"

"Listen, Mademoiselle, I will recall to you another incident. There was a delay to the train on the day we were to reach Stamboul. You were very agitated, Mademoiselle. You, so calm, so self-controlled. You lost that calm."

"I did not want to miss my connection."

"So you said. But, Mademoiselle, the Orient Express leaves Stamboul every day of the week. Even if you had missed the connection it would only have been a matter of twenty-four hours' delay."

Miss Debenham for the first time showed signs of losing her temper.

"You do not seem to realise that one may have friends awaiting one's arrival in London, and that a day's delay upsets arrangements and causes a lot of annoyance."

"Ah, it is like that? There are friends awaiting your arrival? You do not want to cause them inconvenience?"

"Naturally."

"And yet—it is curious—"

"What is curious?"

"On this train—again we have a delay. And this time a more serious delay, since there is no possibility of sending a telegram to your friends or of getting them on the long—the long—"

"Long distance? The telephone, you mean."

"Ah, yes, the portmanteau call, as you say in England."

Mary Debenham smiled a little in spite of herself. "Trunk call," she corrected. "Yes, as you say, it is extremely annoying not to be able to get any word through, either by telephone or by telegraph."

"And yet, Mademoiselle, *this* time your manner is quite different. You no longer betray the impatience. You are calm and philosophical."

Mary Debenham flushed and bit her lip. She no longer felt inclined to smile.

"You do not answer, Mademoiselle?"

"I am sorry. I did not know that there was anything to answer."

"Your change of attitude, Mademoiselle."

"Don't you think that you are making rather a fuss about nothing, M. Poirot?"

Poirot spread out his hands in an apologetic gesture.

"It is perhaps a fault with us detectives. We expect the behaviour to be always consistent. We do not allow for changes of mood."

Mary Debenham made no reply.

"You know Colonel Arbuthnot well, Mademoiselle?"

He fancied that she was relieved by the change of subject.

"I met him for the first time on this journey."

"Have you any reason to suspect that he may have known this man Ratchett?"

She shook her head decisively. "I am quite sure he didn't."

"Why are you sure?"

"By the way he spoke."

"And yet, Mademoiselle, we found a pipe-cleaner on the floor of the dead man's compartment. And Colonel Arbuthnot is the only man on the train who smokes a pipe."

He watched her narrowly, but she displayed neither surprise nor emotion, merely said:

"Nonsense. It's absurd. Colonel Arbuthnot is the last man in the world to be mixed up in a crime—especially a theatrical kind of crime like this."

It was so much what Poirot himself thought that he found himself on the point of agreeing with her. He said instead:

"I must remind you that you do not know him very well, Mademoiselle."

She shrugged her shoulders. "I know the type well enough."

He said very gently:

"You still refuse to tell me the meaning of those words: 'When it's behind us'?"

She replied coldly, "I have nothing more to say."

"It does not matter," said Hercule Poirot. "I shall find out."

He bowed and left the compartment, closing the door after him.

"Was that wise, my friend?" asked M. Bouc. "You have put her on her guard—and through her you have put the Colonel on his guard also."

"*Mon ami*, if you wish to catch a rabbit you put a ferret into the hole, and if the rabbit is there—he runs. That is all I have done."

They entered the compartment of Hildegarde Schmidt.

The woman was standing in readiness, her face respectful but unemotional.

Poirot took a quick glance through the contents of the small case on the seat. Then he motioned to the attendant to get down the bigger suitcase from the rack.

"The keys?" he said.

"It is not locked, Monsieur."

Poirot undid the hasps and lifted the lid.

"Aha!" he said, and turning to M. Bouc, "You remember what I said? Look here a little moment!"

On the top of the suitcase was a hastily rolled-up brown Wagon Lit uniform.

The stolidity of the German woman underwent a sudden change.

"*Ach!*" she cried. "That is not mine. I did not put it there. I have never looked in that case since we left Stamboul. Indeed, indeed, it is true!" She looked from one to another of the men pleadingly.

Poirot took her gently by the arm and soothed her.

"No, no, all is well. We believe you. Do not be agitated. I am as sure you did not hide the uniform there as I am sure that you are a good cook. See. You *are* a good cook, are you not?"

Bewildered, the woman smiled in spite of herself. "Yes, indeed, all my ladies have said so. I—"

She stopped, her mouth open, looking frightened again.

"No, no," said Poirot. "I assure you all is well. See, I will tell you how this happened. This man, the man you saw in Wagon Lit uniform, comes out of the dead man's compartment. He collides with you. That is bad luck for him. He has hoped that no one will see him. What to do next? He must get rid of his uniform. It is now not a safeguard, but a danger."

His glance went to M. Bouc and Dr. Constantine, who were listening attentively.

"There is the snow, you see. The snow which confuses all his plans. Where can he hide these clothes? All the compartments are full. No, he passes one whose door is open, showing it to be unoccupied. It must be the one belonging to the woman with whom he has just collided. He slips in, removes the uniform and jams it hurriedly into a suitcase on the rack. It may be some time before it is discovered."

"And then?" said M. Bouc.

"That we must discuss," said Poirot with a warning glance.

He held up the tunic. A button, the third down, was missing. Poirot slipped his hand into the pocket and took out a conductor's pass-key, used to unlock the doors of the compartments.

"Here is the explanation of how one man was able to pass through locked doors," said M. Bouc. "Your questions to Mrs. Hubbard were unnecessary. Locked or not locked, the man could easily get through the communicating door. After all, if a Wagon Lit uniform, why not a Wagon Lit key?"

"Why not indeed?" returned Poirot.

"We might have known it, really. You remember that Michel said that the door into the corridor of Mrs. Hubbard's compartment was locked when he came in answer to her bell."

"That is so, Monsieur," said the conductor. "That is why I thought the lady must have been dreaming."

"But now it is easy," continued M. Bouc. "Doubtless he meant to relock the communicating door also, but perhaps he heard some movement from the bed and it startled him."

"We have now," said Poirot, "only to find the scarlet kimono."

"True. And these last two compartments are occupied by men."

"We will search all the same."

"Oh! assuredly. Besides, I remember what you said."

Hector MacQueen acquiesced willingly in the search.

"I'd just as soon you did," he said with a rueful smile. "I feel I'm definitely the most suspicious character on the train. You've only got to find a will in which the old man left me all his money, and that'll just about fix things."

M. Bouc bent a suspicious glance upon him.

"That's only my fun," added MacQueen hastily. "He'd never have left me a cent, really. I was just useful to him—languages and so on. You're likely to be out of luck, you know, if you don't speak anything but good American. I'm no linguist myself, but I know what I call Shopping and Hotel—snappy bits in French and German and Italian."

His voice was a little louder than usual. It was as though he were slightly uneasy over the search in spite of his expressed willingness.

Poirot emerged. "Nothing," he said. "Not even a compromising bequest!"

MacQueen sighed. "Well, that's a load off my mind," he said humorously.

They moved on to the last compartment. The examination of the luggage of the big Italian and of the valet yielded no result.

The three men stood at the end of the coach looking at each other.

"What next?" said M. Bouc.

"We will go back to the dining-car," said Poirot. "We know now all that we can know. We have the evidence of the passengers, the evidence of their baggage, the evidence of our eyes. . . . We can expect no further help. It must be our part now to use our brains."

He felt in his pocket for his cigarette case. It was empty.

"I will join you in a moment," he said. "I shall need the cigarettes. This is a very difficult, a very curious, affair. Who wore that scarlet kimono? Where is it now? I wish I knew. There is something in this case—some factor—that escapes me! It is difficult because it has been *made* difficult. But we will discuss it. Pardon me a moment."

He went hurriedly along the corridor to his own compartment. He had, he knew, a further supply of cigarettes in one of his valises.

He got it down and snapped back the lock.

Then he sat back on his heels and stared.

Neatly folded on the top of the case was a thin scarlet silk kimono embroidered with dragons.

"So," he murmured. "It is like that. A defiance. Very well, I take it up."

WHICH OF THEM?

M. BOUC AND Dr. Constantine were talking together when Poirot entered the dining-car. M. Bouc was looking depressed.

"*Le voilà*," said the latter when he saw Poirot. Then he added, as his friend sat down, "If you solve this case, *mon cher*, I shall indeed believe in miracles!"

"It worries you, this case?"

"Naturally it worries me. I cannot make head or tail of it."

"I agree," said the doctor. He looked at Poirot with interest. "To be frank," he said, "I cannot see what you are going to do next."

"No?" said Poirot thoughtfully.

He took out his cigarette case and lit one of his tiny cigarettes. His eyes were dreamy.

"That, to me, is the interest of this case," he said. "We are cut off from all the normal routes of procedure. Are these people whose evidence we have taken speaking the truth, or lying? We have no means of finding out—except such means as we can devise ourselves. It is an exercise, this, of the brain."

"That is all very fine," said M. Bouc. "But what have you to go upon?"

"I told you just now. We have the evidence of the passengers and the evidence of our own eyes."

"Pretty evidence—that of the passengers! It told us just nothing at all."

Poirot shook his head.

"I do not agree, my friend. The evidence of the passengers gave us several points of interest."

"Indeed," said M. Bouc sceptically. "I did not observe it."

"That is because you did not listen."

"Well, tell me, what did I miss?"

"I will just take one instance—the first evidence we heard, that of the young MacQueen. He uttered, to my mind, one very significant phrase."

"About the letters?"

"No, not about the letters. As far as I can remember, his words were: '*We travelled about. Mr. Ratchett wanted to see the world. He was hampered by knowing no languages. I acted more as a courier than a secretary.*'"

He looked from the doctor's face to that of M. Bouc.

"What? You still do not see? That is inexcusable—for you had a second chance again just now when he said, '*You're likely to be out of luck if you don't speak anything but good American.*'"

"You mean—?" M. Bouc still looked puzzled.

"Ah, it is that you want it given to you in words of one syllable. Well, here it is! *M. Ratchett spoke no French*. Yet, when the conductor came in answer to his bell last night, it was a voice speaking in *French* that told him that it was a mistake and that he was not wanted. It was, moreover, a perfectly idiomatic phrase that was used, not one that a man knowing only a few words of French would have selected. '*Ce n'est rien. Je me suis trompé.*'"

"It is true," cried Constantine excitedly. "We should have seen that! I remember your laying stress on the words when you repeated them to us. Now I understand your reluctance to rely upon the evidence of the dented watch. Already, at twenty-three minutes to one, Ratchett was dead—"

"And it was his murderer speaking!" finished M. Bouc impressively.

Poirot raised a deprecating hand.

"Let us not go too fast. And do not let us assume more than we actually know. It is safe, I think, to say that at that time—twenty-three minutes to one—*some other person* was in Ratchett's compartment, and that that person either was French or could speak the French language fluently."

"You are very cautious, *mon vieux*."

"One should advance only a step at a time. We have no actual *evidence* that Ratchett was dead at that time."

"There is the cry that awakened you."

"Yes, that is true."

"In one way," said M. Bouc thoughtfully, "this discovery does not affect things very much. You heard someone moving about next door. That someone was not Ratchett, but the other man. Doubtless he is washing blood from his hands, clearing up after the crime, burning the incriminating letter. Then he waits till all is still, and, when he thinks it is safe and the coast is clear, he locks and chains Ratchett's door on the inside, unlocks the communicating door through into Mrs. Hubbard's compartment and slips out that way. In fact, it is exactly as we thought, *with the difference that Ratchett was killed about half an hour earlier* and the watch put on to a quarter past one to create an alibi."

"Not such a famous alibi," said Poirot. "The hands of the watch pointed to 1.15—the exact time when the intruder actually left the scene of the crime."

"True," said M. Bouc, a little confused. "What then does the watch convey to you?"

"If the hands were altered—I say *if*—then the time at which they were set *must* have a significance. The natural reaction would be to suspect anyone who had a reliable alibi for the time indicated—in this case, 1.15."

"Yes, yes," said the doctor. "That reasoning is good."

"We must also pay a little attention to the time the intruder *entered* the compartment. When had he an opportunity of doing so? Unless we are to assume the complicity of the real conductor, there was only one time when he could have done so—during the time the train stopped at Vincovci. After the train left Vincovci the conductor was sitting facing the corridor, and whereas any one of the passengers would pay little attention to a Wagon Lit attendant, the *one* person who *would* notice an impostor is the real conductor. But during the halt at Vincovci the conductor is out on the platform. The coast is clear."

"And by our former reasoning, it *must* be one of the passengers," said M. Bouc. "We come back to where we were. Which of them?"

Poirot smiled.

"I have made a list," he said. "If you like to see it, it will perhaps refresh your memory."

The doctor and M. Bouc pored over the list together. It was written out neatly in a methodical manner in the order in which the passengers had been interviewed.

HECTOR MACQUEEN, American subject, Berth No. 6, Second Class.
  Motive—Possibly arising out of association with dead man?
  Alibi—From midnight to 2 A.M. (Midnight to 1.30 vouched for by Col. Arbuthnot, and 1.15 to 2 vouched for by conductor.)
  Evidence against him—None.
  Suspicious circumstances—None.
CONDUCTOR PIERRE MICHEL, French subject.
  Motive—None.
  Alibi—From midnight to 2 A.M. (Seen by H. P. in corridor at same time as voice spoke from Ratchett's compartment at 12.37. From 1 A.M. to 1.16 vouched for by other two conductors.)
  Evidence against him—None.
  Suspicious circumstances—The Wagon Lit uniform found is a point in his favour since it seems to have been intended to throw suspicion on him.
EDWARD MASTERMAN, English subject, Berth No. 4, Second Class.
  Motive—Possibly arising out of connection with deceased, whose valet he was.
  Alibi—From midnight to 2 A.M. (Vouched for by Antonio Foscarelli.)
  Evidence against him or suspicious circumstances—None, except that he is the only man of the right height or size to have worn the Wagon Lit uniform. On the other hand, it is unlikely that he speaks French well.
MRS. HUBBARD, American subject, Berth No. 3, First Class.
  Motive—None.
  Alibi—From midnight to 2 A.M.—None.
  Evidence against her or suspicious circumstances—Story of man in her compartment is substantiated by the evidence of Hardman and that of the woman Schmidt.
GRETA OHLSSON, Swedish subject, Berth No. 10, Second Class.
  Motive—None.
  Alibi—From midnight to 2 A.M. (Vouched for by Mary Debenham.)
  Note:—Was last to see Ratchett alive.
PRINCESS DRAGOMIROFF, Naturalised French subject, Berth No. 14, First Class.
  Motive—Was intimately acquainted with Armstrong family, and godmother to Sonia Armstrong.
  Alibi—From midnight to 2 A.M. (Vouched for by conductor and maid.)
  Evidence against her or suspicious circumstances—None.
COUNT ANDRENYI, Hungarian subject, Diplomatic passport, Berth No. 13, First Class.
  Motive—None.
  Alibi—Midnight to 2 A.M. (Vouched for by conductor—this does not cover period from 1 to 1.15.)

COUNTESS ANDRENYI, As above, Berth 12.
  Motive—None.
  Alibi—Midnight to 2 A.M. Took trional and slept. (Vouched for by husband. Trional bottle in her cupboard.)
COLONEL ARBUTHNOT, British subject, Berth No. 15, First Class.
  Motive—None.
  Alibi—Midnight to 2 A.M. Talked with MacQueen till 1.30. Went to own compartment and did not leave it. (Substantiated by MacQueen and conductor.)
  Evidence against him or suspicious circumstances—Pipe-cleaner.
CYRUS HARDMAN, American subject, Berth No. 16.
  Motive—None known.
  Alibi—Midnight to 2 A.M. Did not leave compartment. (Substantiated by conductor except for period 1 to 1.15.)
  Evidence against him or suspicious circumstances—None.
ANTONIO FOSCARELLI, American subject (Italian by birth), Berth No. 5, Second Class.
  Motive—None known.
  Alibi—Midnight to 2 A.M. (Vouched for by Edward Masterman.)
  Evidence against him or suspicious circumstances—None, except that weapon used might be said to suit his temperament. (*Vide* M. Bouc.)
MARY DEBENHAM, British subject, Berth No. 11, Second Class.
  Motive—None.
  Alibi—Midnight to 2 A.M. (Vouched for by Greta Ohlsson.)
  Evidence against her or suspicious circumstances—Conversation overheard by H. P., and her refusal to explain it.
HILDEGARDE SCHMIDT, German subject, Berth No. 8, Second Class.
  Motive—None.
  Alibi—Midnight to 2 A.M. (Vouched for by conductor and her mistress.) Went to bed. Was aroused by conductor at 12.38 approx. and went to mistress.

NOTE:—The evidence of the passengers is supported by the statement of the conductor that no one entered or left Mr. Ratchett's compartment from midnight to 1 o'clock (when he himself went into the next coach) and from 1.15 to 2 o'clock.

"That document, you understand," said Poirot, "is a mere *précis* of the evidence we heard, arranged in that way for convenience."

With a grimace, M. Bouc handed it back. "It is not illuminating," he said.

"Perhaps you may find this more to your taste," said Poirot, with a slight smile as he handed him a second sheet of paper.

CHAPTER TWO

TEN QUESTIONS

ON THE PAPER was written:

THINGS NEEDING EXPLANATION

1. The handkerchief marked with the initial H. Whose is it?
2. The pipe-cleaner. Was it dropped by Colonel Arbuthnot? Or by someone else?
3. Who wore the scarlet kimono?
4. Who was the man or woman masquerading in Wagon Lit uniform?
5. Why do the hands of the watch point to 1.15?
6. Was the murder committed at that time?
7. Was it earlier?
8. Was it later?
9. Can we be sure that Ratchett was stabbed by more than one person?
10. What other explanation of his wounds can there be?

"Well, let us see what we can do," said M. Bouc, brightening a little at this challenge to his wits. "The handkerchief, to begin with. Let us by all means be orderly and methodical."

"Assuredly," said Poirot, nodding his head in a satisfied fashion.

M. Bouc continued somewhat didactically.

"The initial H is connected with three people—Mrs. Hubbard, Miss Debenham, whose second name is Hermione, and the maid Hildegarde Schmidt."

"Ah! And of those three?"

"It is difficult to say. But I *think* I should vote for Miss Debenham. For all one knows she may be called by her second name and not her first. Also there is already some suspicion attaching to her. That conversation you overheard, *mon cher*, was certainly a little curious, and so is her refusal to explain it."

"As for me, I plump for the American," said Dr. Constantine. "It is a very expensive handkerchief, that; and Americans, as all the world knows, do not care what they pay."

"So you both eliminate the maid?" asked Poirot.

"Yes. As she herself said, it is the handkerchief of a member of the upper classes."

"And the second question—the pipe-cleaner. Did Colonel Arbuthnot drop it, or somebody else?"

"That is more difficult. The English, they do not stab. You are right there. I incline to the view that someone else dropped the pipe-cleaner—and did so to incriminate the long-legged Englishman."

"As you said, M. Poirot," put in the doctor, "*two* clues is too much carelessness. I agree with M. Bouc. The handkerchief was a genuine oversight—hence none of the women will admit that it is hers. The pipe-cleaner is a faked clue. In support of that theory, you notice that Colonel Arbuthnot shows no embarrassment and admits freely to smoking a pipe and using that type of cleaner."

"You reason well," said Poirot.

"Question No. 3—Who wore the scarlet kimono?" went on M. Bouc. "As to that, I will confess I have not the slightest idea. Have you any views on the subject, Dr. Constantine?"

"None."

"Then we confess ourselves beaten there. The next question has, at any rate, possibilities. Who was the man or the woman masquerading in Wagon Lit uniform? Well, one can list with a certainty a number of people that it could *not* have been. Hardman, Colonel Arbuthnot, Foscarelli, Count Andrenyi and Hector MacQueen are all too tall. Mrs. Hubbard, Hildegarde Schmidt and Greta Ohlsson are too broad. That leaves the valet, Miss Debenham, Princess Dragomiroff and Countess Andrenyi—and none of them sounds likely! Greta Ohlsson in one case, and Antonio Foscarelli in the other, both swear that Miss Debenham and the valet never left their compartments. Hildegarde Schmidt swears that the Princess was in hers, and Count Andrenyi has told us that his wife took a sleeping draught. Therefore it seems impossible that it can be anybody—which is absurd!"

"As our old friend Euclid says," murmured Poirot.

"It must be one of those four," said Dr. Constantine. "Unless it is someone from outside who has found a hiding-place—and that we agreed was impossible."

M. Bouc had passed on to the next question on the list.

"No. 5—Why do the hands of the broken watch point to 1.15? I can see two explanations of that. Either it was done by the murderer to establish an alibi, and afterwards, when he meant to leave the compartment, he was prevented by hearing people moving about; or else—wait—I have an idea coming—"

The other two waited respectfully while M. Bouc struggled in mental agony.

"I have it," he said at last. "It was *not* the Wagon Lit murderer who tampered with the watch! It was the person we have called the Second Murderer —the left-handed person—in other words the woman in the scarlet kimono. She arrives later and moves back the hands of the watch in order to make an alibi for herself."

"Bravo," said Dr. Constantine. "It is well imagined, that."

"In fact," said Poirot, "she stabbed him in the dark, not realising that he was dead already, but somehow deduced that he had a watch in his pyjama pocket, took it out, put back the hands blindly, and gave it the requisite dent."

M. Bouc looked at him coldly. "Have you anything better to suggest, yourself?" he asked. "At the moment—no," admitted Poirot. "All the same," he went on, "I do not think you have either of you appreciated the most interesting point about that watch."

"Does question No. 6 deal with it?" asked the doctor. "To that question— Was the murder committed at that time, 1.15?—I answer *No*."

"I agree," said M. Bouc. " 'Was it earlier?' is the next question. I say—Yes! You, too, doctor?"

The doctor nodded. "Yes, but the question 'Was it later?' can also be answered in the affirmative. I agree with your theory, M. Bouc, and so, I think, does M. Poirot, although he does not wish to commit himself. The First Murderer came earlier than 1.15, but the Second Murderer came *after* 1.15. And as regards the question of left-handedness, ought we not to take steps to ascertain which of the passengers is left-handed?"

"I have not completely neglected that point," said Poirot. "You may have noticed that I made each passenger write either a signature or an address. That is not conclusive, because some people do certain actions with the right hand and others with the left. Some write right-handed, but play golf left-handed. Still, it is something. Every person questioned took the pen in his or her right hand—with the exception of Princess Dragomiroff, who refused to write."

"Princess Dragomiroff—impossible," said M. Bouc.

"I doubt if she would have had the strength to inflict that left-handed blow," said Dr. Constantine dubiously. "That particular wound had been inflicted with considerable force."

"More force than a woman could use?"

"No, I would not say that. But I think more force than an elderly woman could display, and Princess Dragomiroff's physique is particularly frail."

"It might be a question of the influence of mind over body," said Poirot. "Princess Dragomiroff has great personality and immense will-power. But let us pass from that for the moment."

"To questions Nos. 9 and 10? Can we be sure that Ratchett was stabbed by more than one person, and what other explanation of the wounds can there be? In my opinion, medically speaking, there can be *no other* explanation of those wounds. To suggest that one man struck first feebly and then with violence, first with the right hand and then with the left, and after an interval of perhaps half an hour inflicted fresh wounds on a dead body—well, it does not make sense."

"No," said Poirot. "It does not make sense. And you think that two murderers do make sense?"

"As you yourself have said, what other explanation can there be?"

Poirot stared straight ahead of him. "That is what I ask myself," he said. "That is what I never cease to ask myself."

He leaned back in his seat.

"From now on, it is all here." He tapped himself on the forehead. "We have thrashed it all out. The facts are all in front of us—neatly arranged with order and method. The passengers have sat here, one by one, giving their evidence. We know all that can be known—*from outside*. . . ."

He gave M. Bouc an affectionate smile.

"It has been a little joke between us, has it not—this business of sitting back and *thinking* out the truth? Well, I am about to put my theory into practice—here before your eyes. You two must do the same. Let us all three close our eyes and *think*. . . .

"One or more of those passengers killed Ratchett. *Which of them?*"

CHAPTER THREE

CERTAIN SUGGESTIVE POINTS

IT WAS quite a quarter of an hour before anyone spoke.

M. Bouc and Dr. Constantine had started by trying to obey Poirot's instructions. They had endeavoured to see through a maze of conflicting particulars to a clear and outstanding solution.

M. Bouc's thoughts had run something as follows:

"Assuredly I must think. But as far as that goes I have already thought. . . . Poirot obviously thinks that this English girl is mixed up in the matter. I cannot help feeling that that is most unlikely. . . . The English are extremely cold. Probably it is because they have no figures. . . . But that is not the point. It seems that the Italian could not have done it—a pity. I suppose the English valet is not lying when he said the other never left the compartment? But why should he? It is not easy to bribe the English; they are so unapproachable. The whole thing is most unfortunate. I wonder when we shall get out of this. There must be *some* rescue work in progress. They are so slow in these countries . . . it is hours before anyone thinks of doing anything. And the police of these countries, they will be most trying to deal with—puffed up with importance, touchy, on their dignity. They will make a grand affair of all this. It is not often that such a chance comes their way. It will be in all the newspapers. . . ."

And from there on, M. Bouc's thoughts went along a well-worn course which they had already traversed some hundred times.

Dr. Constantine's thoughts ran thus:

"He is queer, this little man. A genius? Or a crank? Will he solve this mystery? Impossible—I can see no way out of it. It is all too confusing. . . . Everyone is lying, perhaps. . . . But even then, that does not help one. If they are all lying, it is just as confusing as if they were speaking the truth. Odd about those wounds. I cannot understand it. . . . It would be easier to understand if he had been shot—after all, the term 'gunman' must mean that they shoot with a gun. A curious country, America. I should like to go there. It is so progressive. When I get home I must get hold of Demetrius Zagone—he has been to America, he has all the modern ideas. . . . I wonder what Zia is doing at this moment. If my wife ever finds out—"

His thoughts went on to entirely private matters. . . .

Hercule Poirot sat very still.

One might have thought he was asleep.

And then, suddenly, after a quarter of an hour's complete immobility his eyebrows began to move slowly up his forehead. A little sigh escaped him. He murmured beneath his breath.

"But after all, why not? And if so—why, if so, that would explain everything."

His eyes opened. They were green like a cat's. He said softly: *"Eh bien.* I have thought. And you?"

Lost in their reflections, both men started violently.

"I have thought also," said M. Bouc, just a shade guiltily. "But I have arrived at no conclusion. The elucidation of crime is your *métier,* not mine, my friend."

"I, too, have reflected with great earnestness," said the doctor, unblushingly recalling his thoughts from certain pornographic details. "I have thought of many possible theories, but not one that really satisfies me."

Poirot nodded amiably. His nod seemed to say:

"Quite right. That is the proper thing to say. You have given me the cue I expected."

He sat very upright, threw out his chest, caressed his moustache and spoke in the manner of a practised speaker addressing a public meeting.

"My friends, I have reviewed the facts in my mind, and have also gone over to myself the evidence of the passengers—with this result: I see, nebulously as yet, a certain explanation that would cover the facts as we know them. It is a very curious explanation, and I cannot be sure as yet that it is the true one. To find out definitely I shall have to make certain experiments.

"I would like first to mention certain points which appear to me suggestive. Let us start with a remark made to me by M. Bouc in this very place on the occasion of our first lunch together on the train. He commented on the fact that we were surrounded by people of all classes, of all ages, of all nationalities. That is a fact somewhat rare at this time of year. The Athens-Paris and the Bucharest-Paris coaches, for instance, are almost empty. Remember also, the passenger who failed to turn up. He is, I think, significant. Then there are some minor points that strike me as suggestive—for instance, the position of Mrs. Hubbard's sponge-bag, the name of Mrs. Armstrong's mother, the detective methods of M. Hardman, the suggestion of M. Mac-Queen that Ratchett himself destroyed the charred note we found, Princess Dragomiroff's Christian name, and a grease spot on a Hungarian passport."

The two men stared at him.

"Do they suggest anything to you, those points?" asked Poirot.

"Not a thing," said M. Bouc frankly.

"And M. *le docteur?"*

"I do not understand in the least what you are talking of."

M. Bouc, meanwhile, seizing upon the one tangible thing his friend had mentioned, was sorting through the passports. With a grunt he picked up that of Count and Countess Andrenyi and opened it.

"Is this what you mean? This dirty mark?"

"Yes. It is a fairly fresh grease spot. You notice where it occurs?"

"At the beginning of the description of the Count's wife—her Christian name, to be exact. But I confess that I still do not see the point."

"I am going to approach it from another angle. Let us go back to the handkerchief found at the scene of the crime. As we stated not long ago, three people are associated with the letter H: Mrs. Hubbard, Miss Debenham and the maid, Hildegarde Schmidt. Now let us regard that handkerchief from another point of view. It is, my friends, an extremely expensive handkerchief—an *objet de luxe*, hand-made, embroidered in Paris. Which of the passengers, apart from the initial, was likely to own such a handkerchief? Not Mrs. Hubbard, a worthy woman with no pretensions to reckless extravagance in dress. Not Miss Debenham—that class of Englishwoman has a dainty linen handkerchief, not an expensive wisp of cambric costing perhaps two hundred francs. And certainly not the maid. But there *are* two women on the train who would be likely to own such a handkerchief. Let us see if we can connect them in any way with the letter H. The two women I refer to are Princess Dragomiroff—"

"Whose Christian name is Natalia," put in M. Bouc ironically.

"Exactly. And her Christian name, as I said just now, is decidedly suggestive. The other woman is Countess Andrenyi. And at once something strikes us—"

"*You!*"

"*Me*, then. Her Christian name on her passport is disfigured by a blob of grease. Just an accident, anyone would say. But consider that Christian name. Elena. Suppose that, instead of Elena, it were *Helena*. That capital H could be turned into a Capital E and then run over the small e next to it quite easily—and then a spot of grease dropped to cover up the alteration."

"Helena!" cried M. Bouc. "It is an idea, that."

"Certainly it is an idea! I look about for any confirmation, however slight, of my idea—and I find it. One of the luggage labels on the Countess's baggage is slightly damp. It is one that happens to run over the first initial on top of the case. That label has been soaked off and put on again in a different place."

"You begin to convince me," said M. Bouc. "But the Countess Andrenyi —surely—"

"Ah, now, *mon vieux*, you must turn yourself round and approach an entirely different angle of the case. How was this murder intended to appear to everybody? Do not forget that the snow has upset all the murderer's original plan. Let us imagine, for a little minute, that there is no snow, that the train proceeded on its normal course. What, then, would have happened?

"The murder, let us say, would still have been discovered in all probability at the Italian frontier early this morning. Much of the same evidence would have been given to the Italian police. The threatening letters would have been produced by M. MacQueen; M. Hardman would have told his story; Mrs. Hubbard would have been eager to tell how a man passed through her compartment; the button would have been found. I imagine that two things only would have been different. The man would have passed through Mrs. Hubbard's compartment just before one o'clock—and the Wagon Lit uniform would have been found cast off in one of the toilets."

"You mean?"

"I mean that the murder was *planned to look like an outside job*. It would have been presumed that the assassin had left the train at Brod where it is timed to arrive at 0.58. Somebody would probably have passed a strange Wagon Lit conductor in the corridor. The uniform would be left in a conspicuous place so as to show clearly just how the trick had been played. No suspicion would have attached to the passengers. That, my friends, was how the affair was intended to appear to the outside world.

"But the accident to the train changes everything. Doubtless we have here the reason why the man remained in the compartment with his victim so long. He was waiting for the train to go on. But at last he realised that *the train was not going on*. Different plans would have to be made. The murderer would now be *known* to be still on the train."

"Yes, yes," said M. Bouc impatiently. "I see all that. But where does the handkerchief come in?"

"I am returning to it by a somewhat circuitous route. To begin with, you must realise that the threatening letters were in the nature of a blind. They might have been lifted bodily out of an indifferently written American crime novel. They are not *real*. They are, in fact, simply intended for the police. What we have to ask ourselves is: 'Did they deceive Ratchett?' On the face of it, the answer seems to be No. His instructions to Hardman seem to point to a definite 'private' enemy, of whose identity he was well aware. That is, if we accept Hardman's story as true. But Ratchett certainly received *one* letter of a very different character—the one containing a reference to the Armstrong baby, a fragment of which we found in his compartment. In case Ratchett had not realised it sooner, this was to make sure that he understood the reason of the threats against his life. That letter, as I have said all along, was *not* intended to be found. The murderer's first care was to destroy it. This, then, was the second hitch in his plans. The first was the snow, the second was our reconstruction of that fragment.

"That the note was destroyed so carefully can mean only one thing. *There must be on the train someone so intimately connected with the Armstrong family that the finding of that note would immediately direct suspicion upon that person.*

"Now we come to the other two clues that we found. I pass over the pipe-cleaner. We have already said a good deal about that. Let us pass on to the handkerchief. Taken at its simplest it is a clue which directly incriminates someone whose initial is H, and it was dropped there unwittingly by that person."

"Exactly," said Dr. Constantine. "She finds out that she has dropped the handkerchief and immediately takes steps to conceal her Christian name."

"How fast you go! You arrive at a conclusion much sooner than I would permit myself to do."

"Is there any other alternative?"

"Certainly there is. Suppose, for instance, that you have committed a crime and wish to cast the blame for it on someone else. Well, there is on the train a certain person connected intimately with the Armstrong family —a woman. Suppose, then, that you leave there a handkerchief belonging to that woman. She will be questioned, her connection with the Armstrong family will be brought out—*et voilà*: motive—*and* an incriminating article of evidence."

"But in such a case," objected the doctor, "the person indicated, being innocent, would not take steps to conceal her identity."

"Ah, really? That is what you think? That is, truly, the opinion of the police court. But I know human nature, my friend, and I tell you that, suddenly confronted with the possibility of being tried for murder, the most innocent person will lose his head and do the most absurd things. No, no, the grease spot and the changed label do not prove guilt—they only prove that the Countess Andrenyi is anxious for some reason to conceal her identity."

"What do you think her connection with the Armstrong family can be? She has never been in America, she says."

"Exactly, and she speaks English with a foreign accent, and she has a very foreign appearance which she exaggerates. But it should not be difficult to guess who she is. I mentioned just now the name of Mrs. Armstrong's mother. It was 'Linda Arden,' and she was a very celebrated actress—among other things a Shakespearean actress. Think of *As You Like It*, with the Forest of Arden and Rosalind. It was there she got the inspiration for her acting name. 'Linda Arden,' the name by which she was known all over the world, was not her real name. It may have been Goldenberg; it is quite likely that she had Central European blood in her veins—a strain of Jewish, perhaps. Many nationalities drift to America. I suggest to you, gentlemen, that that young sister of Mrs. Armstrong's, little more than a child at the time of the tragedy, was Helena Goldenberg, the younger daughter of Linda Arden, and that she married Count Andrenyi when he was an attaché in Washington."

"But Princess Dragomiroff says that the girl married an Englishman."

"Whose name she cannot remember! I ask you, my friends, is that really likely? Princess Dragomiroff loved Linda Arden as great ladies do love great artists. She was godmother to one of the actress's daughters. Would she forget so quickly the married name of the other daughter? It is not likely. No, I think we can safely say that Princess Dragomiroff was lying. She knew Helena was on the train, she had seen her. She realised at once, as soon as she heard who Ratchett really was, that Helena would be suspected. And so, when we question her as to the sister, she promptly lies—is vague, cannot remember, but 'thinks Helena married an Englishman'—a suggestion as far away from the truth as possible."

One of the restaurant attendants came through the door at the end and approached them. He addressed M. Bouc.

"The dinner, Monsieur, shall I serve it? It is ready some little time."

M. Bouc looked at Poirot. The latter nodded. "By all means, let dinner be served."

The attendant vanished through the doors at the other end. His bell could be heard ringing and his voice upraised:

"*Premier service. Le dîner est servi. Premier dîner*—First service."

CHAPTER FOUR

THE GREASE SPOT ON A HUNGARIAN PASSPORT

POIROT SHARED a table with M. Bouc and the doctor.

The company assembled in the restaurant car was a very subdued one. They spoke little. Even the loquacious Mrs. Hubbard was unnaturally quiet. She murmured as she sat:

"I don't feel as though I had the heart to eat anything," and then partook of everything offered her, encouraged by the Swedish lady who seemed to regard her as a special charge.

Before the meal was served, Poirot had caught the chief attendant by the sleeve and murmured something to him. Constantine made a pretty good guess as to what the instructions had been when he noticed that the Count and Countess Andrenyi were always served last and that at the end of the meal there was a delay in making out their bill. It therefore came about that the Count and Countess were the last left in the restaurant car.

When they rose at length and moved in the direction of the door, Poirot sprang up and followed them.

"Pardon, Madame, you have dropped your handkerchief."

He was holding out to her the tiny monogrammed square.

She took it, glanced at it, then handed it back to him.

"You are mistaken, Monsieur, that is not my handkerchief."

"Not your handkerchief? Are you sure?"

"Perfectly sure, Monsieur."

"And yet, Madame, it has your initial—the initial H."

The Count made a sudden movement. Poirot ignored him. His eyes were fixed on the Countess's face.

Looking steadily at him she replied:

"I do not understand, Monsieur. My initials are E. A."

"I think not. Your name is Helena—not Elena. Helena Goldenberg, the younger daughter of Linda Arden—Helena Goldenberg, the sister of Mrs. Armstrong."

There was a dead silence for a minute or two. Both the Count and the Countess had gone deadly white.

Poirot said in a gentler tone: "It is of no use denying. That is the truth, is it not?"

The Count burst out furiously, "I demand, Monsieur, by what right you—"

She interrupted him, putting up a small hand towards his mouth.

"No, Rudolph. Let me speak. It is useless to deny what this gentleman says. We had better sit down and talk the matter out."

Her voice had changed. It still had the southern richness of tone, but it had become suddenly more clear cut and incisive. It was, for the first time, a definitely American voice.

The Count was silenced. He obeyed the gesture of her hand and they both sat down opposite Poirot.

"Your statement, Monsieur, is quite true," said the Countess. "I am Helena Goldenberg, the younger sister of Mrs. Armstrong."

"You did not acquaint me with that fact this morning, Madame la Comtesse."

"No."

"In fact, all that your husband and you told me was a tissue of lies."

"Monsieur!" cried the Count angrily.

"Do not be angry, Rudolph. M. Poirot puts the fact rather brutally, but what he says is undeniable."

"I am glad you admit the fact so freely, Madame. Will you now tell me your reasons for that, and also for altering your Christian name on your passport?"

"That was my doing entirely," put in the Count.

Helena said quietly: "Surely, M. Poirot, you can guess my reason—our reason. This man who was killed is the man who murdered my baby niece, who killed my sister, who broke my brother-in-law's heart. Three of the people I loved best and who made up my home—my world!"

Her voice rang out passionately. She was a true daughter of that mother, the emotional force of whose acting had moved huge audiences to tears.

She went on more quietly.

"Of all the people on the train I alone had probably the best motive for killing him."

"And you did not kill him, Madame?"

"I swear to you, M. Poirot—and my husband knows and will swear also—that much as I may have been tempted to do so, I never lifted a hand against that man."

"I, too, gentlemen," said the Count. "I give you my word of honour that last night Helena never left her compartment. She took a sleeping draught exactly as I said. She is utterly and entirely innocent."

Poirot looked from one to the other of them.

"On my word of honour," repeated the Count.

Poirot shook his head slightly.

"And yet you took it upon yourself to alter the name in the passport?"

"Monsieur Poirot," the Count said earnestly and passionately, "consider my position. Do you think I could stand the thought of my wife dragged through a sordid police case? She was innocent, I knew it, but what she said was true—because of her connection with the Armstrong family she would have been immediately suspected. She would have been questioned—arrested, perhaps. Since some evil chance had taken us on the same train as this man Ratchett, there was, I felt sure, but one thing for it. I admit, Monsieur, that I lied to you—all, that is, save in one thing. My wife never left her compartment last night."

He spoke with an earnestness that it was hard to gainsay.

"I do not say that I disbelieve you, Monsieur," said Poirot slowly. "Your family is, I know, a proud and ancient one. It would be bitter indeed for you to have your wife dragged into an unpleasant police case. With that I can sympathise. But how then do you explain the presence of your wife's handkerchief actually in the dead man's compartment?"

"That handkerchief is not mine, Monsieur," said the Countess.

"In spite of the initial H?"

"In spite of the initial. I have handkerchiefs not unlike that, but not one that is exactly of that pattern. I know, of course, that I cannot hope to make you believe me, but I assure you that it is so. That handkerchief is not mine."

"It may have been placed there by someone in order to incriminate you?"

She smiled a little. "You are enticing me to admit that, after all, it is mine? But indeed, M. Poirot, it isn't." She spoke with great earnestness.

"Then why, if the handkerchief was not yours, did you alter the name in the passport?"

The Count answered this.

"Because we heard that a handkerchief had been found with the initial H on it. We talked the matter over together before we came to be interviewed. I pointed out to Helena that if it were seen that her Christian name began with an H she would immediately be subjected to much more rigorous questioning. And the thing was so simple—to alter Helena to Elena was easily done."

"You have, M. le Comte, the makings of a very fine criminal," remarked Poirot drily. "A great natural ingenuity, and an apparently remorseless determination to mislead justice."

"Oh, no, no." The girl leaned forward. "M. Poirot, he's explained to you how it was." She broke from French into English. "I was scared—absolutely dead scared, you understand. It had been so awful—that time—and to have it all raked up again. And to be suspected and perhaps thrown into prison. I was just scared stiff, M. Poirot. Can't you understand at all?"

Her voice was lovely—deep—rich—pleading, the voice of the daughter of Linda Arden the actress.

Poirot looked gravely at her.

"If I am to believe you, Madame—and I do not say that I will *not* believe you—then you must help me."

"Help you?"

"Yes. The reason for the murder lies in the past—in that tragedy which broke up your home and saddened your young life. Take me back into the past, Mademoiselle, that I may find there the link that explains the whole thing."

"What can there be to tell you? They are all dead." She repeated mournfully: "All dead—all dead—Robert, Sonia—darling, darling Daisy. She was so sweet—so happy—she had such lovely curls. We were all just crazy about her."

"There was another victim, Madame. An indirect victim, you might say."

"Poor Susanne? Yes, I had forgotten about her. The police questioned her. They were convinced that she had something to do with it. Perhaps she had— but if so, only innocently. She had, I believe, chatted idly with someone, giving information as to the time of Daisy's outings. The poor thing got terribly wrought up—she thought she was being held responsible." She shuddered. "She threw herself out of the window. Oh! it was horrible."

She buried her face in her hands.

"What nationality was she, Madame?"

"She was French."

"What was her last name?"

"It's absurd, but I can't remember—we all called her Susanne. A pretty, laughing girl. She was devoted to Daisy."

"She was the nursery-maid, was she not?"

"Yes."

"Who was the nurse?"

"She was a trained hospital nurse. Stengelberg her name was. She too was devoted to Daisy—and to my sister."

"Now, Madame, I want you to think carefully before you answer this question. Have you, since you were on this train, seen anyone that you recognised?"

She stared at him. "I? No, no one at all."

"What about Princess Dragomiroff?"

"Oh! her. I know her, of course. I thought you meant anyone—anyone from—from that time."

"So I did, Madame. Now think carefully. Some years have passed, remember. The person might have altered his or her appearance."

Helena pondered deeply. Then she said: "No—I am sure—there is no one."

"You yourself—you were a young girl at the time—did you have no one to superintend your studies or to look after you?"

"Oh! yes, I had a dragon—a sort of governess to me and secretary to Sonia combined. She was English—or rather Scotch; a big red-haired woman."

"What was her name?"

"Miss Freebody."

"Young or old?"

"She seemed frightfully old to me. I suppose she couldn't have been more than forty. Susanne, of course, used to look after my clothes and maid me."

"And there were no other inmates of the house?"

"Only servants."

"And you are certain, quite certain, Madame, that you have recognised no one on the train?"

She replied earnestly: "No one, Monsieur. No one at all."

CHAPTER FIVE

THE CHRISTIAN NAME OF PRINCESS DRAGOMIROFF

WHEN THE Count and Countess had departed, Poirot looked across at the other two.

"You see," he said, "we make progress."

"Excellent work," said M. Bouc cordially. "On my part, I should never have dreamed of suspecting Count and Countess Andrenyi. I will admit I thought them quite *hors de combat*. I suppose there is no doubt that she committed the crime? It is rather sad. Still, they will not guillotine her. There are extenuating circumstances. A few years' imprisonment—that will be all."

"In fact you are quite certain of her guilt."

"My dear friend—surely there is no doubt of it? I thought your reassuring manner was only to smooth things over till we are dug out of the snow and the police take charge."

"You do not believe the Count's positive assertion—on his word of honour —that his wife is innocent?"

"*Mon cher*—naturally—what else *could* he say? He adores his wife. He wants to save her! He tells his lie very well—quite in the *grand seigneur* manner. But what else than a lie could it be?"

"Well, you know, I had the preposterous idea that it might be the truth."

"No, no. The handkerchief, remember. The handkerchief clinches the matter."

"Oh, I am not so sure about the handkerchief. You remember, I always told you that there were two possibilities as to the ownership of the handkerchief."

"All the same—"

M. Bouc broke off. The door at the end had opened, and Princess Dragomiroff entered the dining-car. She came straight to them and all three men rose to their feet.

She spoke to Poirot, ignoring the others.

"I believe, Monsieur," she said, "that you have a handkerchief of mine."

Poirot shot a glance of triumph at the other two.

"Is this it, Madame?"

He produced the little square of fine cambric.

"That is it. It has my initial in the corner."

"But, Madame la Princesse, that is the letter H," said M. Bouc. "Your Christian name—pardon me—is Natalia."

She gave him a cold stare.

"That is correct, Monsieur. My handkerchiefs are always initialled in the Russian characters. H is N in Russian."

M. Bouc was somewhat taken aback. There was something about this indomitable old lady which made him feel flustered and uncomfortable.

"You did not tell us that this handkerchief was yours at the inquiry this morning."

"You did not ask me," said the Princess drily.

"Pray be seated, Madame," said Poirot.

She sighed. "I may as well, I suppose." She sat down.

"You need not make a long business of this, Messieurs. Your next question will be—How did my handkerchief come to be lying by a murdered man's body? My reply to that is that I have no idea."

"You have really no idea?"

"None whatever."

"You will excuse me, Madame, but how much can we rely upon the truthfulness of your replies?"

Poirot said the words very softly.

Princess Dragomiroff answered contemptuously. "I suppose you mean because I did not tell you that Helena Andrenyi was Mrs. Armstrong's sister?"

"In fact you deliberately lied to us in the matter."

"Certainly. I would do the same again. Her mother was my friend. I believe, Messieurs, in loyalty—to one's friends and one's family and one's caste."

"You do not believe in doing your utmost to further the ends of justice?"

"In this case I consider that justice—strict justice—has been done."

Poirot leaned forward.

"You see my difficulty, Madame. In this matter of the handkerchief, even, am I to believe you? Or are you shielding your friend's daughter?"

"Oh! I see what you mean." Her face broke into a grim smile. "Well, Messieurs, this statement of mine can be easily proved. I will give you the address of the people in Paris who make my handkerchiefs. You have only to show them the one in question and they will inform you that it was made to my order over a year ago. The handkerchief is mine, Messieurs."

She rose.

"Have you anything further you wish to ask me?"

"Your maid, Madame, did she recognise this handkerchief when we showed it to her this morning?"

"She must have done so. She saw it and said nothing? Ah, well, that shows that she too can be loyal."

With a slight inclination of her head she passed out of the dining-car.

"So that was it," murmured Poirot softly. "I noticed just a trifling hesitation when I asked the maid if she knew to whom the handkerchief belonged. She was uncertain whether or not to admit that it was her mistress's. But how does that fit in with that strange central idea of mine? Yes, it might well be."

"Ah!" said M. Bouc with a characteristic gesture. "She is a terrible old lady, that!"

"Could she have murdered Ratchett?" asked Poirot of the doctor.

He shook his head.

"Those blows—the ones delivered with great force penetrating the muscle—never, never could anyone with so frail a physique inflict them."

"But the feebler ones?"

"The feebler ones, yes."

"I am thinking," said Poirot, "of the incident this morning when I said to her that the strength was in her will rather than in her arm. It was in the nature of a trap, that remark. I wanted to see if she would look down at her right or her left arm. She did neither. She looked at them both. But she made a strange reply. She said, 'No, I have no strength in these. I do not know whether to be sorry or glad.' A curious remark that. It confirms me in my belief about the crime."

"It did not settle the point about the left-handedness."

"No. By the way, did you notice that Count Andrenyi keeps his handkerchief in his right-hand breast pocket?"

M. Bouc shook his head. His mind reverted to the astonishing revelations of the last half-hour. He murmured:

"Lies—and again lies. It amazes me, the number of lies we had told to us this morning."

"There are more still to discover," said Poirot cheerfully.

"You think so?"

"I shall be very much disappointed if it is not so."

"Such duplicity is terrible," said M. Bouc. "But it seems to please you," he added reproachfully.

"It has this advantage," said Poirot. "If you confront anyone who has lied with the truth, he will usually admit it—often out of sheer surprise. It is only necessary to guess *right* to produce your effect.

"That is the only way to conduct this case. I select each passenger in turn, consider his or her evidence, and say to myself, 'If so and so is lying, on what *point* is he lying, and what is the *reason* for the lie?' And I answer, 'If he is lying—*if*, you mark—it could only be for such a reason and on such a point.' We have done that once very successfully with Countess Andrenyi. We shall now proceed to try the same method on several other persons."

"And supposing, my friend, that your guess happens to be wrong?"

"Then one person, at any rate, will be completely freed from suspicion."

"Ah!—a process of elimination."

"Exactly."

"And whom do we tackle next?"

"We are going to tackle that *pukka sahib*, Colonel Arbuthnot."

CHAPTER SIX

A SECOND INTERVIEW WITH
COLONEL ARBUTHNOT

COLONEL ARBUTHNOT was clearly annoyed at being summoned to the dining-car for a second interview. His face wore a most forbidding expression as he sat down and said:

"Well?"

"All my apologies for troubling you a second time," said Poirot. "But there is still some information that I think you might be able to give us."

"Indeed? I hardly think so."

"To begin with, you see this pipe-cleaner?"

"Yes."

"Is it one of yours?"

"Don't know. I don't put a private mark on them, you know."

"Are you aware, Colonel Arbuthnot, that you are the only man amongst the passengers in the Stamboul-Calais carriage who smokes a pipe?"

"In that case it probably is one of mine."

"Do you know where it was found?"

"Not the least idea."

"It was found by the body of the murdered man."

Colonel Arbuthnot raised his eyebrows.

"Can you tell us, Colonel Arbuthnot, how it is likely to have got there?"

"If you mean, did I drop it there myself, no, I didn't."

"Did you go into Mr. Ratchett's compartment at any time?"

"I never even spoke to the man."

"You never spoke to him and you did not murder him?"

The Colonel's eyebrows went up again sardonically.

"If I had, I should hardly be likely to acquaint you with the fact. As a matter of fact I *didn't* murder the fellow."

"Ah, well," murmured Poirot. "It is of no consequence."

"I beg your pardon?"

"I said that it was of no consequence."

"Oh!" Arbuthnot looked taken aback. He eyed Poirot uneasily.

"Because, you see," continued the little man, "the pipe-cleaner, it is of no importance. I can myself think of eleven other excellent explanations of its presence."

Arbuthnot stared at him.

"What I really wished to see you about was quite another matter," went on Poirot. "Miss Debenham may have told you, perhaps, that I overheard some words spoken to you at the station of Konya?"

Arbuthnot did not reply.

"She said, 'Not now. When it's all over. When it's behind us!' Do you know to what those words referred?"

"I am sorry, M. Poirot, but I must refuse to answer that question."

"*Pourquoi?*"

The Colonel said stiffly, "I suggest that you ask Miss Debenham herself for the meaning of those words."

"I have done so."

"And she refused to tell you?"

"Yes."

"Then I should think it would have been perfectly plain—even to you—that my lips are sealed."

"You will not give away a lady's secret?"

"You can put it that way, if you like."

"Miss Debenham told me that they referred to a private matter of her own."

"Then why not accept her word for it?"

"Because, Colonel Arbuthnot, Miss Debenham is what one might call a highly suspicious character."

"Nonsense," said the Colonel with warmth.

"It is not nonsense."

"You have nothing whatever against her."

"Not the fact that Miss Debenham was companion governess in the Armstrong household at the time of the kidnapping of little Daisy Armstrong?"

There was a minute's dead silence.

Poirot nodded his head gently.

"You see," he said. "We know more than you think. If Miss Debenham is innocent, why did she conceal that fact? Why did she tell me that she had never been in America?"

The Colonel cleared his throat. "Aren't you possibly making a mistake?"

"I am making no mistake. Why did Miss Debenham lie to me?"

Colonel Arbuthnot shrugged his shoulders. "You had better ask her. I still think that you are wrong."

Poirot raised his voice and called. One of the restaurant attendants came from the far end of the car.

"Go and ask the English lady in No. 11 if she will be good enough to come here."

"*Bien, Monsieur.*"

The man departed. The four men sat in silence. Colonel Arbuthnot's face looked as though it were carved out of wood, rigid and impassive.

The man returned.

"The lady is just coming, Monsieur."

"Thank you."

A minute or two later Mary Debenham entered the dining-car.

CHAPTER SEVEN

THE IDENTITY OF MARY DEBENHAM

SHE WORE no hat. Her head was thrown back as though in defiance. The sweep of her hair back from her face, the curve of her nostril suggested the figure-head of a ship plunging gallantly into a rough sea. In that moment she was beautiful.

Her eyes went to Arbuthnot for a minute—just a minute.

She said to Poirot, "You wished to see me?"

"I wished to ask you, Mademoiselle, why you lied to us this morning?"

"Lied to you? I don't know what you mean."

"You concealed the fact that at the time of the Armstrong tragedy you were actually living in the house. You told me that you had never been in America."

He saw her flinch for a moment and then recover herself.

"Yes," she said. "That is true."

"No, Mademoiselle, it was false."

"You misunderstood me. I mean that it is true that I lied to you."

"Ah, you admit it?"

Her lips curved into a smile. "Certainly, since you have found me out."

"You are at least frank, Mademoiselle."

"There does not seem anything else for me to be."

"Well, of course, that is true. And now, Mademoiselle, may I ask you the reason for these evasions?"

"I should have thought the reason leapt to the eye, M. Poirot?"

"It does not leap to mine, Mademoiselle."

She said in a quiet even voice with a trace of hardness in it, "I have my living to get."

"You mean—?"

She raised her eyes and looked him full in the face.

"How much do you know, M. Poirot, of the fight to get and keep decent employment? Do you think that a girl who had been detained in connection with a murder case, whose name and perhaps photograph were reproduced in the English papers—do you think that any nice ordinary middle-class Eng-lishwoman would want to engage that girl as governess to her daughters?"

"I do not see why not—if no blame attached to you."

"Oh, blame—it is not *blame*—it is the publicity! So far, M. Poirot, I have succeeded in life. I have had well-paid, pleasant posts. I was not going to risk the position I had attained when no good end could have been served."

"I will venture to suggest, Mademoiselle, that I would have been the best judge of that, not you."

She shrugged her shoulders.

"For instance, you could have helped me in the matter of identification."

"What do you mean?"

"Is it possible, Mademoiselle, that you did not recognise in the Countess Andrenyi Mrs. Armstrong's young sister whom you taught in New York?"

"Countess Andrenyi? No." She shook her head. "It may seem extraordinary to you—but I did not recognise her. She was not grown up, you see, when I knew her. That was over three years ago. It is true that the Countess reminded me of someone; it puzzled me. But she looks so foreign—I never connected her with the little American schoolgirl. I only glanced at her casually when coming into the restaurant car, and I noticed her clothes more than her face." She smiled faintly. "Women do! And then—well—I had my own preoccupations."

"You will not tell me your secret, Mademoiselle?"

Poirot's voice was very gentle and persuasive.

She said in a low voice, "I can't—I can't."

And suddenly, without warning, she broke down, dropping her face down upon her outstretched arms and crying as though her heart would break.

The Colonel sprang up and stood awkwardly beside her.

"I—look here—"

He stopped and turning round scowled fiercely at Poirot.

"I'll break every bone in your damned body, you dirty little whipper-snapper," he said.

"Monsieur," protested M. Bouc.

Arbuthnot had turned back to the girl. "Mary—for God's sake—"

She sprang up. "It's nothing. I'm all right. You don't need me any more, do you, M. Poirot? If you do, you must come and find me. Oh, what an idiot —what an idiot I'm making of myself!" She hurried out of the car.

Arbuthnot, before following her, turned once more on Poirot.

"Miss Debenham's got nothing to do with this business—nothing, do you hear? And if she's worried and interfered with, you'll have me to deal with." He strode out.

"I like to see an angry Englishman," said Poirot. "They are very amusing. The more emotional they feel, the less command they have of language."

But M. Bouc was not interested in the emotional reactions of Englishmen. He was overcome by admiration of his friend.

"*Mon cher, vous êtes épatant!*" he cried. "Another miraculous guess."

"It is incredible how you think of these things," said Dr. Constantine admiringly.

"Oh, I claim no credit this time. It was not a guess. Countess Andrenyi practically told me."

"*Comment?* Surely not?"

"You remember, I asked her about her governess or companion? I had already decided in my mind that *if* Mary Debenham were mixed up in the matter, she must have figured in the household in some such capacity."

"Yes, but the Countess Andrenyi described a totally different person."

"Exactly. A tall middle-aged woman with red hair—in fact, the exact opposite in every respect of Miss Debenham, so much so as to be quite remarkable. But then she had to invent a name quickly, and there it was that the unconscious association of ideas gave her away. She said Miss Freebody, you remember."

"Yes?"

"*Eh bien,* you may not know it, but there is a shop in London that was called until recently Debenham & Freebody. With the name Debenham running in her head, the Countess clutches at another name quickly, and the first that comes is Freebody. Naturally I understood immediately."

"That is yet another lie. Why did she do it?"

"Possibly more loyalty. It makes things a little difficult."

"*Ma foi!*" said M. Bouc with violence. "But does everybody on this train tell lies?"

"That," said Poirot, "is what we are about to find out."

CHAPTER EIGHT

FURTHER SURPRISING REVELATIONS

"NOTHING WOULD surprise me now," said M. Bouc. "Nothing! Even if everybody in the train proved to have been in the Armstrong household, I should not express surprise."

"That is a very profound remark," said Poirot. "Would you like to see what your favourite suspect, the Italian, has to say for himself?"

"You are going to make another of these famous guesses of yours?"

"Precisely."

"It is really a *most* extraordinary case," said Constantine.

"No, it is most natural."

M. Bouc flung up his arms in comic despair. "If this is what you call natural, *mon ami—*" Words failed him.

Poirot had by this time requested the dining-car attendant to fetch Antonio Foscarelli.

The big Italian had a wary look in his eye as he came in. He shot nervous glances from side to side like a trapped animal.

"What do you want?" he said. "I have nothing more to tell you—nothing, do you hear? *Per Dio—*" He struck his hand on the table.

"Yes, you have something more to tell us," said Poirot firmly. "The truth!"

"The truth?" He shot an uneasy glance at Poirot. All the assurance and geniality had gone out of his manner.

"*Mais oui.* It may be that I know it already. But it will be a point in your favour if it comes from you spontaneously."

"You talk like the American police. 'Come clean'—that is what they say—'come clean.' "

"Ah! so you have had experience of the New York police?"

"No, no, never. They could not prove a thing against me—but it was not for want of trying."

Poirot said quietly: "That was in the Armstrong case, was it not? You were the chauffeur?"

His eyes met those of the Italian. The bluster went out of the big man. He was like a pricked balloon.

"Since you know—why ask me?"

"Why did you lie this morning?"

"Business reasons. Besides, I do not trust the Jugo-Slav police. They hate the Italians. They would not have given me justice."

"Perhaps it is exactly justice that they *would* have given you!"

"No, no, I had nothing to do with this business last night. I never left my carriage. The long-faced Englishman, he can tell you so. It was not I who killed this pig—this Ratchett. You cannot prove anything against me."

Poirot was writing something on a sheet of paper. He looked up and said quietly: "Very good. You can go."

Foscarelli lingered uneasily. "You realise that it was not I? That I could have had nothing to do with it?"

"I said that you could go."

"It is a conspiracy. You are going to frame me? All for a pig of a man who should have gone to the chair! It was an infamy that he did not. If it had been me—if I had been arrested—"

"But it was not you. You had nothing to do with the kidnapping of the child."

"What is that you are saying? Why, that little one—she was the delight of the house. Tonio, she called me. And she would sit in the car and pretend to hold the wheel. All the household worshipped her! Even the police came to understand that. Ah, the beautiful little one!"

His voice had softened. The tears came into his eyes. Then he wheeled round abruptly on his heel and strode out of the dining-car.

"Pietro," called Poirot.

The dining-car attendant came at a run.

"The No. 10—the Swedish lady."

"*Bien, Monsieur.*"

"Another?" cried M. Bouc. "Ah, no—it is not possible. I tell you it is not possible."

"*Mon cher*—we have to *know*. Even if in the end everybody on the train proves to have had a motive for killing Ratchett, we have to know. Once we know, we can settle once for all where the guilt lies."

"My head is spinning," groaned M. Bouc.

Greta Ohlsson was ushered in sympathetically by the attendant. She was weeping bitterly.

She collapsed on the seat facing Poirot and wept steadily into a large handkerchief.

"Now do not distress yourself, Mademoiselle. Do not distress yourself." Poirot patted her on the shoulder. "Just a few little words of truth, that is all. You were the nurse who was in charge of little Daisy Armstrong?"

"It is true—it is true," wept the wretched woman. "Ah, she was an angel—a little sweet trustful angel. She knew nothing but kindness and love—and she was taken away by that wicked man—cruelly treated—and her poor mother—and the other little one who never lived at all. You cannot understand—you cannot know—if you had been there as I was—if you had seen the whole terrible tragedy! I ought to have told you the truth about myself this morning. But I was afraid—afraid. I did so rejoice that that evil man was dead—that he could not any more kill or torture little children. Ah! I cannot speak—I have no words. . . ."

She wept with more vehemence than ever.

Poirot continued to pat her gently on the shoulder. "There—there—I comprehend—I comprehend everything—everything, I tell you. I will ask you no more questions. It is enough that you have admitted what I know to be the truth. I understand, I tell you."

By now inarticulate with sobs, Greta Ohlsson rose and groped her way blindly towards the door. As she reached it she collided with a man coming in.

It was the valet—Masterman.

He came straight up to Poirot and spoke in his usual quiet, unemotional voice.

"I hope I'm not intruding, sir. I thought it best to come along at once, sir, and tell you the truth. I was Colonel Armstrong's batman in the War, sir, and afterwards I was his valet in New York. I'm afraid I concealed that fact this morning. It was very wrong of me, sir, and I thought I'd better come and make a clean breast of it. But I hope, sir, that you're not suspecting Tonio in any way. Old Tonio, sir, wouldn't hurt a fly. And I can swear positively that he never left the carriage all last night. So, you see, sir, he couldn't have done it. Tonio may be a foreigner, sir, but he's a very gentle creature. Not like those nasty murdering Italians one reads about."

He stopped.

Poirot looked steadily at him. "Is that all you have to say?"

"That is all, sir."

He paused; then, as Poirot did not speak, he made an apologetic little bow and after a momentary hesitation left the dining-car in the same quiet unobtrusive fashion as he had come.

"This," said Dr. Constantine, "is more wildly improbable than any *roman policier* I have ever read."

"I agree," said M. Bouc. "Of the twelve passengers in that coach, nine have been proved to have had a connection with the Armstrong case. What next, I ask you? Or should I say, who next?"

"I can almost give you the answer to your question," said Poirot. "Here comes our American sleuth, Mr. Hardman."

"Is he, too, coming to confess?"

Before Poirot could reply the American had reached their table. He cocked an alert eye at them and sitting down he drawled out: "Just exactly what's up on this train? It seems bughouse to me."

Poirot twinkled at him.

"Are you quite sure, Mr. Hardman, that you yourself were not the gardener at the Armstrong home?"

"They didn't have a garden," replied Mr. Hardman literally.

"Or the butler?"

"Haven't got the fancy manners for a place like that. No, I never had any connection with the Armstrong house—but I'm beginning to believe I'm about the only one on this train who hadn't! Can you beat it? That's what I say—can you beat it?"

"It is certainly a little surprising," said Poirot mildly.

"*C'est rigolo,*" burst from M. Bouc.

"Have you any ideas of your own about the crime, Mr. Hardman?" inquired Poirot.

"No, sir. It's got me beat. I don't know how to figure it out. They can't *all* be in it—but which one is the guilty party is beyond me. How did you get wise to all this? That's what I want to know."

"I just guessed."

"Then, believe me, you're a pretty slick guesser. Yes, I'll tell the world you're a slick guesser."

Mr. Hardman leaned back and looked at Poirot admiringly.

"You'll excuse me," he said, "but no one would believe it to look at you. I take off my hat to you. I do indeed."

"You are too kind, M. Hardman."

"Not at all. I've got to hand it to you."

"All the same," said Poirot, "the problem is not yet quite solved. Can we say with authority that we know who killed M. Ratchett?"

"Count me out," said Mr. Hardman. "I'm not saying anything at all. I'm just full of natural admiration. What about the other two you haven't had a guess at yet? The old American dame, and the lady's-maid? I suppose we can take it that they're the only innocent parties on the train?"

"Unless," said Poirot, smiling, "we can fit them into our little collection as —shall we say—housekeeper and cook in the Armstrong household?"

"Well, nothing in the world would surprise me now," said Mr. Hardman with quiet resignation. "Bughouse—that's what this business is—bughouse!"

"Ah! *mon cher,* that would be indeed stretching coincidence a little too far," said M. Bouc. "They cannot all be in it."

Poirot looked at him. "You do not understand," he said. "You do not understand at all. Tell me, do you know who killed Ratchett?"

"Do you?" countered M. Bouc.

Poirot nodded. "Oh, yes," he said. "I have known for some time. It is so clear that I wonder you have not seen it also." He looked at Hardman and asked: "And you?"

The detective shook his head. He stared at Poirot curiously. "I don't know," he said. "I don't know at all. Which of them was it?"

Poirot was silent a minute. Then he said:

"If you will be so good, M. Hardman, assemble everyone here. There are two possible solutions of this case. I want to lay them both before you all."

POIROT PROPOUNDS TWO SOLUTIONS

THE PASSENGERS came crowding into the restaurant car and took their seats round the tables. They all bore more or less the same expression, one of expectancy mingled with apprehension. The Swedish lady was still weeping, and Mrs. Hubbard was comforting her.

"Now you must just take a hold on yourself, my dear. Everything's going to be perfectly all right. You mustn't lose your grip on yourself. If one of us is a nasty murderer, we know quite well it isn't you. Why, anyone would be crazy even to think of such a thing. You sit here, and I'll stay right by you—and don't you worry any." Her voice died away as Poirot stood up.

The Wagon Lit conductor was hovering in the doorway. "You permit that I stay, Monsieur?"

"Certainly, Michel."

Poirot cleared his throat.

"*Messieurs et mesdames*, I will speak in English since I think all of you know a little of that language. We are here to investigate the death of Samuel Edward Ratchett—*alias* Cassetti. There are two possible solutions of the crime. I shall put them both before you, and I shall ask M. Bouc and Dr. Constantine here to judge which solution is the right one.

"Now you all know the facts of the case. Mr. Ratchett was found stabbed this morning. He was last known to be alive at 12.37 last night when he spoke to the Wagon Lit conductor through the door. A watch in his pyjama pocket was found to be badly dented, and it had stopped at a quarter past one. Dr. Constantine, who examined the body when found, puts the time of death as having been between midnight and two in the morning. At half an hour after midnight, as you all know, the train ran into a snowdrift. After that time *it was impossible for anyone to leave the train.*

"The evidence of Mr. Hardman, who is a member of a New York detective agency—" (Several heads turned to look at Mr. Hardman.)—"shows that no one could have passed his compartment (No. 16 at the extreme end) without being seen by him. We are therefore forced to the conclusion that the murderer is to be found among the occupants of one particular coach—the Stamboul-Calais coach.

"That, I will say, *was* our theory."

"*Comment?*" ejaculated M. Bouc, startled.

"But I will put before you an alternative theory. It is very simple. Mr. Ratchett had a certain enemy whom he feared. He gave Mr. Hardman a description of this enemy and told him that the attempt, if made at all, would most probably be made on the second night out from Stamboul.

"Now I put it to you, ladies and gentlemen, that Mr. Ratchett knew a good deal more than he told. The enemy, as Mr. Ratchett expected, joined the train *at Belgrade or else at Vincovci* by the door left open by Colonel Arbuthnot and Mr. MacQueen, who had just descended to the platform. He was provided with a suit of Wagon Lit uniform, which he wore over his ordinary clothes, and a pass-key which enabled him to gain access to Mr. Ratchett's compartment in spite of the door's being locked. Mr. Ratchett was under the influence of a sleeping draught. This man stabbed him with great ferocity and left the compartment through the communicating door leading to Mrs. Hubbard's compartment—"

"That's so," said Mrs. Hubbard, nodding her head.

"He thrust the dagger he had used into Mrs. Hubbard's sponge-bag in passing. Without knowing it, he lost a button of his uniform. Then he slipped out of the compartment and along the corridor. He hastily thrust the uniform into a suitcase in an empty compartment, and a few minutes later, dressed in ordinary clothes, he left the train just before it started off, using the same means for egress—the door near the dining-car."

Everybody gasped.

"What about that watch?" demanded Mr. Hardman.

"There you have the explanation of the whole thing. *Mr. Ratchett had omitted to put his watch back an hour as he should have done at Tzaribrod.* His watch still registered Eastern European time, which is one hour *ahead* of Central European time. It was a quarter past *twelve* when Mr. Ratchett was stabbed—not a quarter past one."

"But it is absurd, that explanation!" cried M. Bouc. "What of the voice that spoke from the compartment at twenty-three minutes to one? It was either the voice of Ratchett—or else that of his murderer."

"Not necessarily. It might have been—well—a third person. One who had gone in to speak to Ratchett and found him dead. He rang the bell to summon the conductor; then, as you express it, the wind rose in him—he was afraid of being accused of the crime, and he spoke pretending to be Ratchett."

"*C'est possible,*" admitted M. Bouc grudgingly.

Poirot looked at Mrs. Hubbard. "Yes, Madame, you were going to say—"

"Well, I don't quite know what I was going to say. Do you think I forgot to put my watch back too?"

"No, Madame. I think you heard the man pass through—but unconsciously. Later you had a nightmare of a man being in your compartment and woke up with a start and rang for the conductor."

"Well, I suppose that's possible," admitted Mrs. Hubbard.

Princess Dragomiroff was looking at Poirot with a very direct glance. "How do you explain the evidence of my maid, Monsieur?"

"Very simply, Madame. Your maid recognised the handkerchief I showed her as yours. She somewhat clumsily tried to shield you. She did encounter the man, but earlier—while the train was at Vincovci station. She pretended to have seen him at a later hour, with a confused idea of giving you a watertight alibi."

The Princess bowed her head. "You have thought of everything, Monsieur. I—I admire you."

There was a silence.

Then everyone jumped as Dr. Constantine suddenly hit the table a blow with his fist.

"But no," he said. "No, no, and again no! That is an explanation that will not hold water. It is deficient in a dozen minor points. The crime was not committed so—M. Poirot must know that perfectly well."

Poirot turned a curious glance on him. "I see," he said, "that I shall have to give you my second solution. But do not abandon this one too abruptly. You may agree with it later."

He turned back again to face the others.

"There is another possible solution of the crime. This is how I arrived at it.

"When I had heard all the evidence, I leaned back and shut my eyes, and began to *think*. Certain points presented themselves to me as worthy of attention. I enumerated these points to my two colleagues. Some I have already elucidated—such as a grease spot on a passport, and so on. I will run over the points that remain. The first and most important is a remark made to me by M. Bouc in the restaurant car at lunch on the first day after leaving Stamboul —to the effect that the company assembled was interesting because it was so varied—representing as it did all classes and nationalities.

"I agreed with him, but when this particular point came into my mind, I tried to imagine whether such an assembly was ever likely to be collected under any other conditions. And the answer I made to myself was—only in America. In America there might be a household composed of just such varied nationalities—an Italian chauffeur, an English governess, a Swedish nurse, a German lady's-maid, and so on. That led me to my scheme of 'guessing'— that is, casting each person for a certain part in the Armstrong drama much as a producer casts a play. Well, that gave me an extremely interesting and satisfactory result.

"I had also examined in my own mind each separate person's evidence, with some curious results. Take first the evidence of Mr. MacQueen. My first interview with him was entirely satisfactory. But in my second he made rather a curious remark. I had described to him the finding of a note mentioning the Armstrong case. He said, 'But surely—' and then paused and went on, 'I mean—that was rather careless of the old man.'

"Now I could feel that that was not what he had started out to say. *Supposing what he had meant to say was 'But surely that was burnt!'* In which case, *MacQueen knew of the note and of its destruction*—in other words, he was either the murderer or an accomplice of the murderer. Very good.

"Then the valet. He said his master was in the habit of taking a sleeping draught when travelling by train. That might be true, but *would Ratchett have taken one last night?* The automatic under his pillow gave the lie to that statement. Ratchett intended to be on the alert last night. Whatever narcotic was administered to him must have been given without his knowledge. By whom? Obviously by MacQueen or the valet.

"Now we come to the evidence of Mr. Hardman. I believed all that he told me about his own identity, but when it came to the actual methods he had employed to guard Mr. Ratchett, his story was neither more nor less than absurd. The only way to have protected Ratchett effectively was to pass the night actually in his compartment or in some spot where he could watch the door. The one thing that his evidence *did* show plainly was that *no one in any other part of the train could possibly have murdered Ratchett.* It drew a clear circle round the Stamboul-Calais carriage. That seemed to me a rather curious and inexplicable fact, and I put it aside to think over.

"You probably all know by now of the few words I overheard between Miss Debenham and Colonel Arbuthnot. The interesting thing to my mind was the fact that Colonel Arbuthnot called her *Mary* and was clearly on terms of intimacy with her. But the Colonel was supposed to have met her only a few days previously. And I know Englishmen of the Colonel's type—even if he had fallen in love with the young lady at first sight, he would have advanced slowly and with decorum, not rushing things. Therefore I concluded that Colonel Arbuthnot and Miss Debenham were in reality well acquainted and were for some reason pretending to be strangers. Another small point was Miss Debenham's easy familiarity with the term 'long distance' for a telephone call. Yet Miss Debenham had told me that she had never been in the States.

"To pass to another witness. Mrs. Hubbard had told us that lying in bed she had been unable to see whether the communicating door was bolted or not, and so had asked Miss Ohlsson to see for her. Now—though her statement would have been perfectly true if she had been occupying compartment No. 2, 4, 12 or any *even* number, in which the bolt is directly under the handle of the door—in the *uneven* numbers such as compartment No. 3 the bolt is well *above* the handle and could not therefore be masked by the sponge-bag in the least. I was forced to the conclusion that Mrs. Hubbard was inventing an incident that had never occurred.

"And here let me say just a word or two about *times*. To my mind the really interesting point about the dented watch is the place where it was found—in Ratchett's pyjama pocket, a singularly uncomfortable and unlikely place to keep one's watch, especially as there is a watch 'hook' provided just by the head of the bed. I felt sure, therefore, that the watch had been deliberately placed in the pocket—faked. The crime, then, was not committed at a quarter past one.

"Was it then committed earlier? To be exact, at twenty-three minutes to one? My friend M. Bouc advanced as an argument in favour of it the loud cry which awoke me from sleep. But if Ratchett had been heavily drugged, *he could not have cried out.* If he had been capable of crying out, he would have been capable of making some kind of struggle to defend himself, and there were no signs of any such struggle.

"I remembered that MacQueen had called attention, not once but twice (and the second time in a very blatant manner), to the fact that Ratchett could speak no French. I came to the conclusion that the whole business at twenty-three minutes to one was a comedy played for my benefit! Anyone might see through the watch business—it is a common enough device in detective stories. They assumed that I *should* see through it and that, pluming myself on my own cleverness, I would go on to assume that since Ratchett spoke no French, the voice I heard at twenty-three minutes to one could not have been his, and that Ratchett must have been already dead. But I am convinced that at twenty-three minutes to one Ratchett was still lying in his drugged sleep.

"But the device has succeeded! I have opened my door and looked out. I have actually heard the French phrase used. If I am so unbelievably dense as not to realise the significance of that phrase, it must be brought to my attention. If necessary, MacQueen can come right out in the open. He can say, 'Excuse me, M. Poirot, *that can't have been Mr. Ratchett speaking.* He couldn't speak French.'

"Now, what was the real time of the crime? And who killed him?

"In my opinion—and this is only an opinion—Ratchett was killed at some time very close upon two o'clock, the latest hour the doctor gives us as possible.

"As to who killed him—"

He paused, looking at his audience. He could not complain of any lack of attention. Every eye was fixed upon him. In the stillness you could have heard a pin drop.

He went on slowly:

"I was particularly struck by the extraordinary difficulty of proving a case against any one person on the train, and by the rather curious coincidence that in each case the testimony giving an alibi came from what I might describe as an 'unlikely' person. Thus, Mr. MacQueen and Colonel Arbuthnot provided alibis for each other—two persons between whom it seemed most unlikely there should have been any prior acquaintanceship. The same thing happened with the English valet and the Italian, and with the Swedish lady and the English girl. I said to myself: This is extraordinary—they cannot *all* be in it!

"And then, Messieurs, I saw light. They *were* all in it. For so many people connected with the Armstrong case to be travelling by the same train through coincidence was not only unlikely: it was *impossible.* It must be not chance, but *design.* I remembered a remark of Colonel Arbuthnot's about trial by jury. A jury is composed of twelve people—there were twelve passengers— Ratchett was stabbed twelve times. And the thing that had worried me all along—the extraordinary crowd travelling in the Stamboul-Calais coach at a slack time of year—this was explained.

"Ratchett had escaped justice in America. There was no question as to his guilt. I visualised a self-appointed jury of twelve people who had condemned him to death and who by the exigencies of the case had themselves been forced to be his executioners. And immediately, on that assumption, the whole case fell into beautiful shining order.

"I saw it as a perfect mosaic, each person playing his or her allotted part. It was so arranged that, if suspicion should fall on any one person, the evidence of one or more of the others would clear the accused person and confuse the issue. Hardman's evidence was necessary in case some outsider should be suspected of the crime and be unable to prove an alibi. The passengers in the Stamboul carriage were in no danger. Every minute detail of their evidence was worked out beforehand. The whole thing was a very cleverly planned jigsaw puzzle, so arranged that every fresh piece of knowledge that came to light made the solution of the whole more difficult. As my friend M. Bouc remarked, the case seemed fantastically impossible! That was exactly the impression intended to be conveyed.

"Did this solution explain everything? Yes, it did. The nature of the wounds—each inflicted by a different person. The artificial threatening letters —artificial since they were unreal, written only to be produced as evidence. (Doubtless there *were* real letters, warning Ratchett of his fate, which MacQueen destroyed, substituting for them these others.) Then Hardman's story of being called in by Ratchett—a lie, of course, from beginning to end. The description of the mythical 'small dark man with a womanish voice'—a convenient description since it had the merit of not incriminating any of the actual Wagon Lit conductors and would apply equally well to a man or a woman.

"The idea of stabbing is at first sight a curious one, but on reflection nothing else would fit the circumstances so well. A dagger was a weapon that could be used by everyone—strong or weak—and it made no noise. I fancy, though I may be wrong, that each person in turn entered Ratchett's darkened compartment through that of Mrs. Hubbard—and struck! They themselves would never know which blow actually killed him.

"The final letter which Ratchett had probably found on his pillow was carefully burnt. With no clue pointing to the Armstrong case there would be absolutely no reason for suspecting any of the passengers on the train. It would be put down as an outside job, and the 'small dark man with the womanish voice' would actually have been seen by one or more of the passengers leaving the train at Brod!

"I do not know exactly what happened when the conspirators discovered that this part of their plan was impossible owing to the accident to the train. There was, I imagine, a hasty consultation, and then they decided to go through with it. It was true that now one and all of the passengers were bound to come under suspicion, but that possibility had already been foreseen and provided for. The only additional thing to be done was to confuse the issue even further. Two so-called 'clues' were dropped in the dead man's compartment—one incriminating Colonel Arbuthnot (who had the strongest alibi and whose connection with the Armstrong family was probably the hardest to prove); and the second clue, the handkerchief, incriminating Princess Dragomiroff who, by virtue of her social position, her particularly frail physique and the alibi given her by her maid and the conductor, was practically in an unassailable position.

"Further to confuse the issue, a red herring was drawn across the trail— the mythical woman in the red kimono. Again I am to bear witness to this woman's existence. There is a heavy bang at my door. I get up and look out —and see the scarlet kimono disappearing in the distance. A judicious selection of people—the conductor, Miss Debenham and MacQueen—will also have seen her. It was, I think, someone with a sense of humour who thoughtfully placed the scarlet kimono on the top of my suitcase whilst I was interviewing people in the dining-car. Where the garment came from in the first place, I do not know. I suspect it is the property of Countess Andrenyi, since her luggage contained only a chiffon negligee so elaborate as to be rather a tea-gown than a dressing-gown.

"When MacQueen first learned that the letter which had been so carefully burnt had in part escaped destruction, and that the word Armstrong was exactly the word remaining, he must at once have communicated his news to the others. It was at this minute that the position of Countess Andrenyi became acute, and her husband immediately took steps to alter the passport. It was their second piece of bad luck!

"They one and all agreed to deny utterly any connection with the Armstrong family. They knew I had no immediate means of finding out the truth, and they did not believe that I should go into the matter unless my suspicions were aroused against one particular person.

"Now there was one further point to consider. Allowing that my theory of the crime was the correct one, and I believed that it *must* be the correct one, then obviously the Wagon Lit conductor himself must be privy to the plot. But if so, that gave us thirteen persons, not twelve. Instead of the usual formula 'Of so many people one is guilty,' I was faced with the problem that of thirteen persons one and one only was innocent. Which was that person?

"I came to a very odd conclusion. I came to the conclusion that the person who had taken no part in the crime was the person who would be considered the most likely to do so. I refer to Countess Andrenyi. I was impressed by the earnestness of her husband when he swore to me solemnly on his honour that his wife never left her compartment that night. I decided that Count Andrenyi took, so to speak, his wife's place.

"If so, then Pierre Michel was definitely one of the twelve. But how could one explain his complicity? He was a decent man who had been many years in the employ of the company—not the kind of man who could be bribed to assist in a crime. Then Pierre Michel must be involved in the Armstrong case. But that seemed very improbable. Then I remembered that the dead nursery-maid had been French. Supposing that that unfortunate girl had been Pierre Michel's daughter. That would explain everything—it would also explain the place chosen for the staging of the crime. Were there any others whose part in the drama was not clear? Colonel Arbuthnot I put down as a friend of the Armstrongs. They had probably been through the War together. The maid, Hildegarde Schmidt—I could guess her place in the Armstrong household. I am, perhaps, over greedy, but I sense a good cook instinctively. I laid a trap for her—she fell into it. I said I knew she was a good cook. She answered: 'Yes, indeed, all my ladies have said so.' But if you are employed as a *lady's-maid* your employers seldom have a chance of learning whether or not you are a good cook.

"Then there was Hardman. He seemed quite definitely not to belong to the Armstrong household. I could only imagine that he had been in love with the French girl. I spoke to him of the charm of foreign women—and again I obtained the reaction I was looking for. Sudden tears came into his eyes, which he pretended were dazzled by the snow.

"There remains Mrs. Hubbard. Now Mrs. Hubbard, let me say, played the most important part in the drama. By occupying the compartment communicating with that of Ratchett she was more open to suspicion than anyone else. In the nature of things she could not have an alibi to fall back upon. To play the part she played—the perfectly natural, slightly ridiculous American fond mother—an artist was needed. But there *was* an artist connected with the Armstrong family: Mrs. Armstrong's mother—Linda Arden, the actress. . . ."

He stopped.

Then in a soft rich dreamy voice, quite unlike the one she had used throughout the journey, Mrs. Hubbard said:

"I always fancied myself in comedy parts."

She went on, still dreamily:

"That slip about the sponge-bag was silly. It shows that you should always rehearse properly. We tried it on the way out—I was in an even-number compartment then, I suppose. I never thought of the bolts being in different places."

She shifted her position a little and looked straight at Poirot.

"You know all about it, M. Poirot. You're a very wonderful man. But even you can't quite imagine what it was like—that awful day in New York. I was just crazy with grief; so were the servants. And Colonel Arbuthnot was there too. He was John Armstrong's best friend."

"He saved my life in the War," said Arbuthnot.

"We decided then and there (perhaps we were mad—I don't know) that the sentence of death that Cassetti had escaped had got to be carried out. There were twelve of us—or rather eleven; Susanne's father was over in France, of course. First we thought we'd draw lots as to who should do it, but in the end we decided on this way. It was the chauffeur, Antonio, who suggested it. Mary worked out all the details later with Hector MacQueen.

He'd always adored Sonia—my daughter—and it was he who explained to us exactly how Cassetti's money had managed to get him off.

"It took a long time to perfect our plan. We had first to track Ratchett down. Hardman managed that in the end. Then we had to try and get Masterman and Hector into his employment—or at any rate one of them. Well, we managed that. Then we had a consultation with Susanne's father. Colonel Arbuthnot was very keen on having twelve of us. He seemed to think it made it more in order. He didn't like the stabbing idea much, but he agreed that it did solve most of our difficulties. Well, Susanne's father was willing. Susanne had been his only child. We knew from Hector that Ratchett would be coming back from the East sooner or later by the Orient Express. With Pierre Michel actually working on that train, the chance was too good to be missed. Besides, it would be a good way of not incriminating any outsiders.

"My daughter's husband had to know, of course, and he insisted on coming on the train with her. Hector wangled it so that Ratchett selected the right day for travelling, when Michel would be on duty. We meant to engage every carriage in the Stamboul-Calais coach, but unfortunately there was one carriage we couldn't get. It had been reserved long beforehand for a director of the company. 'Mr. Harris,' of course, was a myth. But it would have been awkward to have any stranger in Hector's compartment. And then, at the last minute, *you* came. . . ."

She stopped.

"Well," she said, "you know everything now, M. Poirot. What are you going to do about it? If it must all come out, can't you lay the blame upon me and me only? I would have stabbed that man twelve times willingly. It wasn't only that he was responsible for my daughter's death and her child's and that of the other child who might have been alive and happy now. It was more than that: there had been other children kidnapped before Daisy, and there might be others in the future. Society had condemned him—we were only carrying out the sentence. But it's unnecessary to bring all these others into it. All these good faithful souls—and poor Michel—and Mary and Colonel Arbuthnot—they love each other. . . ."

Her voice was wonderful, echoing through the crowded space—that deep, emotional, heart-stirring voice that had thrilled many a New York audience.

Poirot looked at his friend.

"You are a director of the company, M. Bouc," he said. "What do you say?"

M. Bouc cleared his throat.

"In my opinion, M. Poirot," he said, "the first theory you put forward was the correct one—decidedly so. I suggest that that is the solution we offer to the Jugo-Slavian police when they arrive. You agree, doctor?"

"Certainly I agree," said Dr. Constantine. "As regards the medical evidence, I think—er—that I made one or two fantastic suggestions."

"Then," said Poirot, "having placed my solution before you, I have the honour to retire from the case. . . ."

THE CASE OF THE CRIMSON KISS

by Erle Stanley Gardner

PREOCCUPATION WITH her own happiness prevented Fay Allison from seeing the surge of bitter hatred in Anita's eyes.

So Fay, wrapped in the warmth of romantic thoughts, went babbling on to her roommate, her tongue loosened by the double cocktail which Anita had prepared before dinner.

"*I'd* known I loved him for a long time," she said, "but honestly, Anita, it never occurred to me that Dane was the marrying kind. He'd had that one unfortunate affair, and he'd always seemed so detached and objective about things. Of course, underneath all that reserve he's romantic and tender. Anita, I'm getting a break I don't deserve."

Anita Bonsal, having pushed her dinner dishes to one side, toyed with the stem of her empty cocktail glass. Her eyes were pinpricks of black hatred which she was afraid to let Fay Allison see. "You've fixed a date?" she asked, concentrating on the rotating base of the glass.

"Just as soon as Aunt Louise can get here. I want her to be with me. I . . . and, of course, I'll want *you*, dear."

"When will Aunt Louise get here?"

"Tomorrow or next day, I think. I haven't heard from her definitely."

"You've written her?"

"Yes. She'll take the night plane. I mailed her my extra key so she can come right on in whenever she gets here, even if we aren't here."

Anita Bonsal was silent, but Fay Allison wanted to talk. "You know how Dane is. He's always been sort of impersonal. He took *you* out at first as much as he did *me*, and then he began to specialize on me. Of course, you're so popular, you don't mind. It's different with me. Anita, I was afraid to acknowledge even to myself how deeply I felt, because I thought it might lead to heartache."

"All of my congratulations, dear," Anita said.

"Don't you think it will work out, Anita? You don't seem terribly enthusiastic."

"Of course it will work out. I'm not gushing because I'm a selfish devil and it's going to make a lot of difference in my personal life—the apartment and all that. Come on, let's get the dishes done. I'm going out tonight and I presume you'll be having company."

"No, Dane's not coming over. He's going through a ceremony at his bachelors' club—one of those silly things that men belong to. He has to pay a forfeit or something, and there's a lot of horseplay. I'm so excited, I'm just walking on air."

"Well," Anita said, "I go away for a three-day week end and a lot seems to happen around here. I'll have to start looking for another roommate. This apartment is too big for me to carry by myself."

"You won't have any trouble. Just pick the person you want. How about one of the girls at the office?"

Anita shook her head, tight-lipped.

"Well, of course, I'll pay until the fifteenth and then . . ."

"Don't worry about that," Anita said lightly. "I'm something of a lone wolf at heart. I don't get along too well with most women, but I'll find someone. It'll take a little time for me to look around. Most of the girls in the office are pretty sappy."

They did the dishes, straightened up the apartment, Fay Allison talking excitedly, laughing with lighthearted merriment, Anita Bonsal moving with the swift efficiency of one who is deftly skillful with her hands, saying but little.

As soon as the dishes had been finished and put away, Anita slipped into a long black evening dress, put on her fur coat, smiled at Fay Allison and said, "You'd better take some of the sleeping pills tonight, dear. You're all wound up."

Fay said somewhat wistfully, "I am afraid I talked you to death, Anita. I wanted someone to listen while I built air castles. I . . . I'll read a book. I'll be waiting up when you get back."

"Don't," Anita said. "It'll be late."

Fay said wistfully, "You're always so mysterious about things, Anita. I really know very little about your friends. Don't you *ever* want to get married and have a home of your own?"

"Not me. I'm too fond of having my own way, and I like life as it is," Anita said, and slipped out through the door, gently pulling it shut behind her.

She walked down the corridor to the elevator, pressed the button, and when the cage came up to the sixth floor, stepped in, pressed the button for the lobby, waited until the elevator was halfway down, then pressed the stop button, then the button for the seventh floor.

The elevator rattled slowly upward, came to a stop.

Anita calmly opened her purse, took out a key, walked down the long corridor, glanced swiftly back toward the elevator, then fitted the key to apartment 702 and opened the door.

Carver L. Clements looked up from his newspaper, removed the cigar from his mouth, regarded Anita Bonsal with eyes that showed swift approval, but kept his voice detached as he said, "It took you long enough to get here."

"I had to throw a little wool in the eyes of my roommate, and listen to her prattle of happiness. She's marrying Dane Grover."

Carver Clements put down the newspaper. "The hell she is!"

"It seems he went overboard in a burst of romance, and his attentions became serious and honorable," Anita said bitterly. "Fay has written her aunt, Louise Marlow, and as soon as the aunt gets here they'll be married."

Carver Clements shifted his position slightly, as though by doing so he could look at the tall brunette from a slightly different angle. He said, "I had it figured out that you were in love with Dane Grover, yourself."

"So that's been the trouble with you lately!"

"Weren't you?"

"Heavens, no!"

"You know, my love," Clements went on, "I'd hate to lose you now."

Anger flared in her eyes. "Don't think you can own me!" she said bitterly. "You only rent me."

"Let's call it a lease," he said.

"It's a tenancy-at-will," she flared. "And kindly get up when I come into the room. After all, you might as well show some manners."

Clements arose from the chair. He was a spidery man with long arms and legs, a thick, short body, a head almost bald, but he spent a small fortune on clothes that were skillfully cut to conceal the chunkiness of his body. He smiled, and said, "My little spitfire! But I like you for it. Remember, Anita, I'm playing for keeps. As soon as I can get my divorce straightened out . . ."

"You and your divorce!" she interrupted. "You've been pulling that line . . ."

"It isn't a line. There are some very intricate property problems. I don't dare to seem too eager, and the thing can't be handled abruptly. You know that. You *should* know that."

She said, "I know that I'm tired of all this pretense. I'm tired of working. If you're playing for keeps, take me off the dole and make *me* a property settlement."

"And have my wife's lawyers suddenly drag me into court for another examination of my assets and start tracing the checks . . ."

"Make it in cash."

"And have the bank withdrawals checked? Don't be silly."

"I'm not going to be. I'm going to be practical. What if I should get dragged into your domestic mess anyway? Look at the chances I'm taking."

His eyes were somber in their steady appraisal. "I like you, Anita. I can do a lot for you. I like that fire that you have. But I want it in your heart and not in your tongue. My car's in the parking lot. You go on down, get in the car and wait. I'll be down in five minutes."

She said, "Why don't you take me out as though you weren't ashamed of me? As though . . ."

"And give my wife the opportunity she's looking for? Then you *would* have the fat in the fire. The property settlement will be completed and signed within five or six weeks. Thank heavens, I'll then be free to live my own life in my own way. Until then . . . until then, my darling, we have to be discreet in our indiscretions."

She started to say something, checked herself, turned and stalked out of the apartment.

Carver Clements' automobile was a big, luxurious sedan equipped with every possible convenience, but it was cold sitting there, waiting.

Anita waited for several minutes, then, as she felt the chill creeping through her sheer nylons, turned the ignition switch and pulled out the heater button.

It took a minute or two for warmth to generate in the heater. Then a welcome current of warm air swirled caressingly about her legs.

After ten minutes, which seemed twenty, she grew impatient. She flung open the car door, went to the entrance of the apartment house and angrily pressed the button of 702.

When there was no answer, she knew that Clements must be on his way down in the elevator, so she walked back into the shadows, to stand there, impatient, feeling a strange desire to smash something. But Clements didn't appear.

Anita used her key to enter the apartment house. The elevator was on the ground floor. She made no attempt at concealment this time, but pressed the button for the seventh floor, left the elevator, strode down the corridor, stabbed her key into the metal lock of Clements' apartment, and entered the room.

Carver L. Clements, dressed for the street, was lying sprawled on the floor.

A highball glass lay on its side, two feet from his body. It had apparently fallen from his hand, spilling contents as it rolled along the carpet. Clements' face was a peculiar hue, and there was a sharp, bitter odor which seemed intensified as she bent toward his froth-flecked lips. Since Anita had last seen him he had quite evidently had a caller. The print of half-parted lips flared in gaudy crimson from the front of his bald head.

With the expertness she had learned from a course in first aid, Anita pressed her finger against the wrist, searching for a pulse. There was none.

She opened her handbag, took out the silver cigarette case, held its smoothly polished surface close to the man's lips. There was no faintest sign of moisture which would indicate any breathing.

Quite evidently, Carver L. Clements, wealthy playboy, yachtsman, broker, gambler for high stakes, was quite dead.

In a panic, Anita Bonsal looked through the apartment.

There were all too many signs of her surreptitious and intermittent occupancy of that apartment—nightgowns, lingerie, shoes, stockings, hats, even toothbrushes and her favorite tooth paste.

Anita Bonsal turned back toward the door and quietly left the apartment. She paused in the hallway, making certain there was no one in the corridor. This time she didn't take the elevator, but walked down the fire stairs, as she had done so many times, and returned to her own apartment on the sixth floor.

Fay Allison had been listening to a musical program on the radio. She jumped up with glad surprise as Anita entered.

"Oh, Anita, I'm so glad! I thought—thought you wouldn't be in until real late. What happened? It hasn't been any time since you left."

"I developed a beastly headache," Anita said. "My escort was a trifle intoxicated, so I slapped his face and came home. I'd like to sit up and have you tell me about your plans, but I do have a headache, and you must get a good night's sleep tonight. You'll need to be looking your best tomorrow."

Fay laughed. "I don't want to waste time sleeping. While I'm unconscious I can't revel in my happiness."

"Nevertheless," Anita said firmly, "we're going to get to bed early. Let's undress, put on pajamas, have some hot chocolate, and then we'll sit in front of the electric heater and talk for just exactly twenty minutes."

"Oh, I'm so glad you came back!" Fay said.

"I'll fix the drink," Anita told her. "I'm going to make your chocolate sweet tonight. You can start worrying about your figure tomorrow. After all, you'll be a married woman before this chocolate can put any pounds on you."

She went to the kitchen, opened her purse, took out a bottle of barbiturate tablets, emptied a good half of the pills into a cup, carefully ground them up into powder, then added hot water until they were, for the most part, dissolved.

She placed chocolate on the stove, added milk and melted marshmallows, called out to Fay, "You undress, dear. I'll put on my pajamas after we've had the chocolate."

When she returned to the living room, carrying the two steaming cups frothy with melted marshmallows floating on top, Fay Allison was in her pajamas.

Anita Bonsal raised her cup. "Here's to happiness, darling."

"Lots of happiness," Fay Allison said almost dreamily.

After they had finished the first cup of chocolate, Anita talked Fay into another cup, then let Fay discuss her plans until drowsiness made the words thick, the sentences detached.

"Anita, I'm so sleepy all of a sudden. I guess it's the reaction from having been so keyed up. I . . . darling, it's all right if I . . . you don't care if I . . ."

"Not at all, dear," Anita said, and helped Fay into bed, tucked her in carefully, and then gave the situation careful consideration.

The fact that Carver Clements maintained a secret apartment in that building was known only to a few of Clements' cronies. These people knew of Carver Clements' domestic difficulties and knew why he maintained this apartment. Fortunately, however, they had never seen Anita. That was a big thing in her favor. Anita was quite certain it hadn't been a heart attack. It had been poison, some quick-acting, deadly poison. There was no use worrying herself, trying to figure out how it had been administered, or why. Carver Clements was a man who had many powerful friends and many powerful enemies.

The police would search for the woman.

It wouldn't do for Anita merely to remove her things from that apartment, and, besides, that wouldn't be artistic enough. Anita had been in love with Dane Grover. If it hadn't been for that dismal entanglement with Carver Clements . . . However, that was all past now, and Fay Allison, with her big blue eyes, her sweet, trusting disposition, had turned Dane Grover from a disillusioned wolf into an ardent suitor. Well, it was a world where the smart ones got by. Anita had washed the dishes. Fay Allison had dried them. Her fingerprints would be on glasses and on dishes. The management of the apartment house very considerately furnished dishes identical in pattern—and it only needed a little careful work on her part. She would, of course, put on gloves. The police would find Fay Allison's nightgowns in Carver Clements' secret apartment. They would find glasses that had Fay's fingerprints on them. And when they went to question Fay Allison, they would find she had taken the easy way out, an overdose of sleeping pills.

Anita would furnish the testimony that would make it all check into a composite, sordid pattern. A girl who had been the mistress of a rich playboy, then had met a younger and more attractive man who had offered her marriage. She had gone to Carver Clements and wanted to check out, but with Carver Clements one didn't simply check out. Things weren't as easy as that. So Fay had slipped the fatal poison into his drink and then had realized she was trapped when Anita returned home unexpectedly and there had been no chance for Fay to make surreptitious removal of her wearing apparel from the upstairs apartment. Anita would let the police do the figuring. Anita would be horrified, simply stunned, but, of course, co-operative.

Anita Bonsal deliberately waited three hours until things began to quiet down in the apartment house, then she took a suitcase and quietly went to work, moving with the smooth efficiency of a woman who has been accustomed to thinking out every smallest detail.

When she had finished, she carefully polished the key to apartment 702 so as to remove any possible fingerprints, and dropped it in Fay Allison's purse. She ground up all but six of the remaining sleeping tablets and mixed the powder with the chocolate which was left in the canister.

Then she donned pajamas, took the remaining six tablets, washed off the label with hot water and tossed the empty bottle out of the back window of the apartment. Then she snuggled down into her own bed and switched off the lights.

Over in the other twin bed, Fay Allison lay motionless, except for a slight chest motion as her shallow breathing raised and lowered the coverlet.

The maid was due to come at eight the next morning to clean up the apartment. She would find two still figures, one dead, one in a drugged stupor.

Two of the tablets constituted the heaviest prescribed dose. The six tablets Anita had taken began to suck at her consciousness. For a moment there was swift panic. Perhaps she had really taken too many. Could it be that . . . that . . . perhaps . . .

It was too late now. The soothing influence of the drug warmed her consciousness into acquiescence.

She wondered if she could call a drugstore and find out if . . . a moment later she was asleep.

CHAPTER TWO

LOUISE MARLOW, tired from the long airplane ride, her ears still ringing with the sound of muffled motors, paid off the taxicab in front of the apartment house.

The cab driver surveyed her solicitously. "Want me to wait until you see if your party's home?"

"I have a key," Louise Marlow said.

"How about your bags?"

"Don't worry about them. I'll get them up all right."

He helped her with her bags to the entrance door. Louise Marlow inserted the key which Fay Allison had sent her, smiled her thanks to the cab driver and picked up her bags.

Sixty-five years old, white-headed, steely-eyed, square of shoulder and broad of beam, she had experienced many and varied vicissitudes in life, and from them had extracted a salty philosophy of her own. Her love was big enough to encompass those who were dear to her with a protecting umbrella. Her hatred was bitter enough to goad her enemies into confused retreat.

With casual disregard for the fact that it was now one o'clock in the morning, she marched calmly down the corridor to the elevator, banged her suitcase and overnight bag into the corner of the cage and punched the button for the sixth floor.

The elevator moved slowly upward, then shuddered to a stop. The door slid slowly open and Aunt Louise, picking up her bags, walked down the half-darkened corridor, peering over the tops of her glasses for numbers over the doors.

At length she found the apartment she wanted, inserted her key, opened the door and groped for a light switch.

She found the light switch, clicked it on and called, "It's me, Fay!"

There was no answer.

Aunt Louise dragged her bags in, pushed the door shut, called out cheerfully, "Don't shoot," and then added by way of explanation, "I picked up a cancellation on an earlier plane, Fay."

The continued silence bothered her. She moved over to the bedroom. "Wake up, Fay. It's your Aunt Louise!"

She clicked on the bedroom light, smiled down at the two sleepers, said,

"Well, if you're going to sleep right through everything, I'll make up a bed on the davenport and say hello to you in the morning."

Then something in the color of Fay Allison's face caused the keen eyes to lose their twinkle of friendly humor and become hard with steely concentration.

"Fay!" she said.

The figures slumbered on in complete oblivion.

Aunt Louise went over and shook Fay Allison, then turned to Anita Bonsal and started shaking her.

The motion finally brought Anita back to semi-consciousness from drugged slumber.

"Who is it?" she asked thickly.

"I'm Fay Allison's Aunt Louise. I got here ahead of time. What's happened?"

Anita Bonsal knew in a drowsy manner that this was a complicating circumstance that she had not foreseen, and despite the numbing effect of the drug on her senses, managed to mouth the excuse which was to be her first waking alibi.

"Something happened," she said thickly. "The chocolate . . . we drank chocolate and it felt like . . . I can't remember . . . can't remember . . . I want to go to sleep."

She let her head swing over on a limp neck and became a dead weight in Louise Marlow's arms.

Aunt Louise put her back on the bed, snatched up a telephone directory and thumbed through the pages until she found the name, *Perry Mason, Attorney at Law.*

There was a night number—Westfield 6–59432.

Louise Marlow dialed the number.

The night operator on duty at the switchboard of the Drake Detective Agency, recognizing from the peculiar sound of the buzzing that the ringing phone was that of Mason's night number, picked up the receiver and said, "Night number of Mr. Perry Mason. Who is this talking, please?"

Louise Marlow said in a firm, steady voice, "This is Louise Marlow. I haven't met Perry Mason but I know his secretary, Della Street. I want you to get in touch with her and tell her that I'm at Keystone 97600. I'm in a mess and I want her to call me back here just as quick as she can. Yes, that's right! I know her personally. You tell her it's Louise Marlow talking and she'll get busy. I think I may need Mr. Mason before I get done; but I certainly want to talk with Della Street right now."

Louise Marlow hung up and waited.

Within less than a minute she heard the phone ring and Della Street's voice came over the line as Aunt Louise picked up the receiver and said, "Hello."

"Why, Louise Marlow, whatever are *you* doing in town?"

"I came in to attend the wedding of my niece, Fay Allison," Aunt Louise said. "Now, listen, Della. I'm at Fay's apartment. She's been drugged and

I can't wake her up. Her roommate, Anita Bonsal, has also been drugged and I managed to get her awake, but she keeps going back to sleep. Someone's tried to poison them!

"I want to get a doctor who's good, and who can keep his damn trap shut. I don't know what's back of all this, but Fay's getting married tomorrow. Someone's tried to put her under sod, and I propose to find out what's behind it. If anything should get into the newspapers about this, I'll wring someone's neck. The whole business looks fishy to me. I'm at the Mandrake Arms, apartment 604. Rush a doctor up here and then you'd better get hold of Perry Mason and . . ."

Della Street said, "I'll send a good doctor up to you right away, Mrs. Marlow. I just got in. Perry Mason, Paul Drake, the detective who handles his investigations, and I have been out nightclubbing with a client. Mr. Mason brought me home just a few minutes ago and I can catch him at his apartment. You sit tight. I'm getting busy."

CHAPTER THREE

WHEN AUNT LOUISE answered the buzzer, Della Street said, "Mrs. Marlow, this is Perry Mason. This is 'Aunt Louise,' chief. She's an old friend from my home town."

Louise Marlow gave the famous lawyer her hand and a smile. She kissed Della, said, "You haven't changed a bit, Della. Come on in. There's a mess here. I can't afford to have a word get in the newspapers. We had to get this sawbones. Now, how do we keep him from blabbing?"

"What does the doctor say?" Mason asked.

"He's working like a house afire. Anita is conscious. Fay is going to pull through all right. Another hour and it would have been too late for her."

"What happened?" Mason asked.

"Someone dumped sleeping medicine in the powdered chocolate, or else in the sugar."

"Any suspicions?" Mason asked.

She said, "Fay was marrying Dane Grover. I gather from her letters he's a wealthy but shy young man who had one bad experience with a jane years ago and had turned bitter and disillusioned, or thought he had. A cynic at twenty-six! Baloney!"

Mason smiled.

"I got here around one o'clock I guess. Fay had sent me a key. The place was closed tight as a miser's purse. I used the key. As soon as I switched on the light and looked at Fay's face, I knew that something was wrong, the color of it and the way she was breathing. I tried to wake her up and couldn't.

I finally shook some sense into Anita. She said the chocolate did it. Then I called Della. That's just about all I know about it."

"The cups they drank the chocolate from?" Mason asked. "Where are they?"

"On the kitchen sink—unwashed."

"We may need them for evidence," Mason said.

"Evidence, my eye!" Louise Marlow snorted. "I don't want the police in on this. You can imagine what'll happen if some sob sister spills a lot of printer's ink about a bride-to-be trying to kill herself on the eve of the wedding."

"Let's take a look around," Mason said.

The lawyer moved about the apartment, trying to reconstruct what had happened.

Louise Marlow followed, acting as guide, and Della Street from time to time gave the benefit of a feminine suggestion.

Mason nodded, paused as he came to street coats thrown over the back of a chair, then again as he looked at the two purses.

"Which one is Fay Allison's?" he asked.

"Heavens, I don't know. We'll have to find out," Aunt Louise said.

Mason said, "I'll let you two take the lead. Go through them carefully. See if you can find anything that would indicate whether anyone might have been in the apartment shortly before they started drinking the chocolate. Perhaps there's a letter that will give us a clue, or a card or a note."

The doctor, emerging from the bedroom, said, "I want to boil some water for another hypo."

"How are they coming?" Mason asked, as Mrs. Marlow went to the kitchen.

"The brunette is all right," the doctor said, "and I think the blonde will make it all right."

"When can I question one of them in detail?"

The doctor shook his head. "I wouldn't advise it. Not that it will hurt anything, but you might get thrown off the track. They are still groggy, and there's some evidence that the brunette is rambling and contradictory in her statements. Give her another hour and you can get some facts. Right now she's running around in circles."

The doctor boiled water for his hypo, went back to the bedroom. Della Street moved over to Mason's side, said in a low voice, "Here's something I don't understand, chief."

"What?"

"Notice the keys to the apartment house are stamped with the numbers of the apartments. Both girls have keys to this apartment in their purses. Fay Allison also has a key stamped 702. What would she be doing with the key to another apartment?"

Mason's eyes narrowed for a moment in thoughtful speculation. "What does Aunt Louise say?"

"She doesn't know. I was the one who searched Fay's purse. She went through Anita's."

"Anything else to give a clue?"

"Not the slightest thing anywhere."

Mason said, "Okay, I'm going to take a look at 702. You'd better come along, Della."

Mason made excuses to Louise Marlow. "We want to look around awhile on the outside," he said. "We'll be back in a few minutes."

He and Della took the elevator to the seventh floor, walked down to apartment 702 and Mason pushed his thumb against the bell button.

They could hear the sound of the buzzer in the apartment, but there was no faintest sound of answering motion such as would have been caused by sleepers stirring around.

Mason said, "It's a chance we shouldn't take, but I'm going to take a peek inside, just for luck."

He fitted the key to the door, clicked back the lock, gently opened the door.

The blazing lights of the living room streamed illumination out at them through the open door, showed the sprawled body on the floor, the drinking glass which had rolled from the dead fingers.

The door from an apartment across the hall jerked open. A young woman with disheveled hair, a bathrobe around her, said angrily, "After you've pressed a buzzer for five minutes at this time of the night you should have sense enough to . . ."

"We have," Mason interrupted, pulling Della Street into the apartment and kicking the door shut behind them with a quick jab of his heel.

Della Street, clinging to Mason's arm, saw the sprawled figure on the floor, the crimson lipstick on the forehead, looked at the overturned chair by the table, the glass which had rolled along the carpet, spilling part of its contents, at the other empty glass standing on the table across from the overturned chair.

Her breathing was heavy and fast, as though she had been running, but she said nothing.

"Careful, Della, we mustn't touch anything."

"Who is he?"

"Apparently he's People's Exhibit A. Do you suppose the nosy dame in the opposite apartment is out of the hall by this time? We'll have to take a chance anyway." He wrapped his hand with his handkerchief, turned the knob on the inside of the door, pulled it silently open.

The door of the apartment across the hall was closed.

Mason warned Della Street to silence with a gesture. They tiptoed out into the corridor, pulled the door closed behind them.

As the door clicked shut, the elevator came to a stop at the seventh floor. Three men and a woman came hurrying down the corridor directly toward them.

Mason's voice was low, reassuring. "Perfectly casual, Della. Just friends departing from a late card game."

They caught the curious glances of the four people, moved slightly to one side, then, after the quartet had passed, Mason took Della Street's arm, said, "Don't hurry, Della, take it easy."

"Well," Della Street said, "they'll certainly know us if they ever see us again. The way that woman looked me over . . ."

"I know," Mason said, "but we'll hope that . . . oh, oh!"

"What is it?"

"They're going to 702!"

The four paused in front of the door. One of the men pressed the buzzer button.

Almost immediately the door of the opposite apartment jerked open. The woman with the bathrobe shrilled, "I'm suffering from insomnia. I've been trying to sleep, and this . . ."

She broke off as she saw the strangers.

The man who had been pressing the button grinned and said in a booming voice which carried well down the corridor, "We're sorry, ma'am. I only just gave him one short buzz."

"Well, the other people who went in just before you made enough commotion."

"Other people *in here?*" the man asked, hesitated a moment, then went on. "Well, we won't bother him if he's got company."

Mason pulled Della Street into the elevator, pulled the door shut, pushed the button for the lobby.

"What in the world do we do now?" Della Street asked.

"Now," Mason said, his voice sharp-edged with disappointment, "we ring police headquarters and report a possible homicide. It's the only thing we *can* do. The woman only saw two people she can't identify going *in*, but that quartet will eventually identify us as going out."

There was a phone booth in the lobby. Mason dropped a nickel, dialed police headquarters and reported that he had found a corpse in apartment 702 under circumstances indicating probable homicide. He had, he said, touched nothing, but had backed right out and called the police.

While Mason was in the phone booth, the four people emerged from the elevator. There was a distinct aroma of alcohol as they pushed their way toward the door. The woman, catching sight of Della Street standing beside the phone booth, favored her with a feminine appraisal which swept from head to foot and missed no smallest detail.

Mason called Louise Marlow in apartment 604. "I think you'd better have the doctor take his patients to a sanitarium where they can have complete quiet," he said.

"He seems to think they're doing all right here."

"I distrust doctors who *seem* to think," Mason said. "I would suggest a sanitarium immediately, and *complete quiet.*"

Louise Marlow was silent for a full three seconds.

"Are you there?" Mason asked.

"I'm here," she said. "I'm just trying to get the sketch."

"I think the patients should have *complete quiet,*" Mason said.

"Damn it," Louise Marlow sputtered. "When you said it the first time I missed it. The second time I got it. You don't have to let your needle get stuck on the record! I was just trying to figure it out."

Mason heard her slam up the phone at the other end of the line.

Mason grinned, hung up the phone, took the key to 702 from his pocket, dropped it in an envelope, addressed the envelope to his office, stamped it and dropped it in the mail box by the elevator.

Outside, the four people in the car were having something of an argument. Apparently there was some sharp difference of opinion as to what action was to be taken next, but as a siren sounded they reached a sudden unanimity of decision. They were starting the car as the police car pulled in to the curb. The red beam of the police spotlight pilloried them. The siren blasted a peremptory summons.

The driver of the car looked behind him, then stepped on the throttle.

The police car shot away in angry pursuit and three minutes later, a chastened quartet swung their car back to a stop in front of the apartment house, the police car following them until the machine was safely parked at the curb. One of the radio officers walked over to the other car, took possession of the ignition keys and ushered the four people up to the door of the apartment house.

Mason hurried across the lobby to open the locked door.

The officer said, "I'm looking for a man who reported a body."

"That's right. I did. My name's Mason. The body's in 702."

"A body!" the woman screamed.

"Shut up," the radio officer said.

"But we know the . . . why he told you we'd been visiting in 702 . . . we . . ."

"Yeah, you said you'd been visiting a friend in 702, name of Carver Clements. How was he when you left him?"

There was an awkward silence, then the woman said, "We really didn't get in. We just went to the door. The woman across the way said he had company, so we left."

"Said he had company?"

"That's right. But I think the company had left. It was these two here."

"We'll go take a look," the officer said. "Come on."

CHAPTER FOUR

LIEUTENANT TRAGG, head of the Homicide Squad, finished his examination of the apartment, said wearily to Mason, "I presume by this time you've thought up a good story to explain how it all happened."

Mason said, "As a matter of fact, I don't know this man from Adam. I had never seen him alive."

"I know," Tragg said sarcastically, "wanted him as a witness to an automobile accident or something, and just happened to drop around in the wee small hours of the morning."

Mason said nothing.

"But," Tragg went on, "strange as it may seem, Mason, I'm interested to know how you got in. The woman who has the apartment across the corridor says you stood there and rang the buzzer for as much as two minutes. Then she heard the sound of a clicking bolt just as she opened her door to give you a piece of her mind, thinking you were some drunken bum trying to buzz a girl friend who had cooled off on him."

Mason nodded gravely.

Tragg said, "Either someone opened that door or the door was open. If it was ajar, I don't think you'd have buzzed for two minutes without pushing it open. If someone was in there, I want to know who it was. Now who let you in?"

"I had a key."

"A key! The hell you did!"

Mason nodded.

"Let's take a look at it."

"I'm sorry, I don't have it now."

"Well, now," Tragg said, "*isn't* that interesting! And where did you get the key, Mason?"

"Unfortunately," Mason said, "*that's* something I can't tell you."

"Don't be silly. This is a murder case."

Mason said, "The key came into my possession in a peculiar manner. I found it."

"Phooey! A client gave it to you."

"What makes you think that?"

"It's a reasonable conjecture."

Mason smiled. "Come, come, Lieutenant, if you're going to engage in pure flights of fancy, why not consider the possibility that this client might have taken a sublease on the apartment and wanted me to see that the gentleman lying there on the floor, who was unlawfully withholding possession, was ejected without trouble?"

"So you came to eject him at this time in the morning!"

"Perhaps the sublease didn't become effective until midnight."

Tragg's eyes narrowed. "It's a nice try, Mason, but you're not getting anywhere. That key you have is the dead man's key. When we searched the body we found that stuff on the table there. There's no key to this apartment on him."

Mason sparred for time, said, "And did you notice that despite the fact there's a thermos jar of ice cubes on the table, a bottle of Scotch and a siphon of soda, the fatal drink didn't have any ice in it?"

"How do you know?" Tragg asked, interested.

"Because when this glass fell from his hand and the contents spilled over the floor, it left a single small spot of moisture. If there had been ice cubes in the glass they'd have rolled out for some appreciable distance and then melted, leaving spots of moisture."

"I see," Tragg said sarcastically, "and then, having decided to commit suicide, the guy kissed himself on the forehead and . . ."

He broke off as one of the detectives, walking rapidly down the hallway, said, "We've traced that cleaning mark, Lieutenant."

Tragg glanced significantly toward Mason, said, "I'll talk with you in a minute when . . ."

The man handed Tragg a folded slip of paper.

Tragg unfolded the paper. "Well I'll be damned!" Tragg said.

Mason met Tragg's searching eyes with calm steadiness.

"And I suppose," Tragg said, "you're going to be surprised at this one. Miss Fay Allison, apartment 604, in this same building, is the person who sent the coat that was in the closet to the dry cleaner. Her mark is on it. I think, Mr. Mason, we'll have a little talk with Fay Allison, and just to see that you don't make any false moves until we get there, we'll take you right along with us. Perhaps you already know the way."

As Tragg started toward the elevator, a smartly dressed woman in the late thirties or early forties stepped out of the elevator and walked down the corridor, looking at the numbers over the doors.

Tragg stepped forward. "Looking for something?"

She started to sweep past him.

Tragg pulled back his coat, showed her his badge.

"I'm looking for apartment 702," she said.

"Who you looking for?"

"Mr. Carver Clements, if it's any of your business."

"I think it is," Tragg said. "Who are you and how do you happen to be here?"

She said, "I am Mrs. Carver L. Clements, and I'm here because I was advised over the telephone that my husband was maintaining a surreptitious apartment here."

"And that was the first you knew of it?"

"Definitely."

"And what," Tragg asked, "did you intend to do?"

"I intend to show him that he isn't getting away with anything," she said. "If you're an officer, you may as well accompany me. I feel certain that . . ."

Tragg said, "702 is down the corridor, at the corner on the right. I just came from there. You'll find a detective there in charge of things. Your husband was killed sometime between seven and nine o'clock tonight."

Dark brown eyes grew wide with surprise. "You . . . you're sure?"

Tragg said, "Dead as a mackerel. Someone slipped him a little cyanide, in his Scotch and soda. I don't suppose you'd know anything about that?"

She said slowly, "If my husband is dead . . . I can't believe it. He hated me too much to die. He was trying to force me to make a property settlement, and in order to make me properly submissive, he'd put me through a softening up process, a period during which I didn't have money enough even to dress decently. His idea was that that would make the settlement he was prepared to offer look practically irresistible to me."

"In other words," Tragg said, "you hated his guts."

She clamped her lips together. "I didn't say that!"

Tragg grinned and said, "Come along with us. We're going down to an apartment on the sixth floor. After that I'm going to take *your* fingerprints and see if they match up with those on the glass which didn't contain the poison."

CHAPTER FIVE

LOUISE MARLOW answered the buzzer.

She glanced at Tragg, then at Mrs. Clements.

Mason, raising his hat, said with grave politeness and the manner of a total stranger, "We're sorry to bother you at this hour, but . . ."

"*I'll* do the talking," Tragg said.

The formality of Mason's manner was not lost on Aunt Louise. She said, as though she had never seen him before, "Well, this is a great time . . ."

Tragg pushed his way forward. "Does Fay Allison live here?"

"That's right," Louise Marlow beamed at him. "She and another girl, Anita Bonsal, share the apartment. They aren't here now, though."

"Where are they?" Tragg asked.

She shook her head. "I'm sure I couldn't tell you."

"And who are you?"

"I'm Louise Marlow, Fay Allison's aunt."

"You're living with them?"

"Heavens, no. I just came up tonight to be here for . . . for a visit with Fay."

"How did you get in, if they weren't here?"

"I had a key, but I didn't say they weren't here then."

"You said, I believe, that they are not here now?"

"That's right."

"What time did you arrive?"

"Around one o'clock."

Tragg said, "Let's cut out the shadow boxing and get down to brass tacks, Mrs. Marlow. I want to see both of those girls."

"I'm sorry, but the girls are both sick. They're in the hospital."

"Who took them there?"

"A doctor."

"What's his name?"

Louise Marlow hesitated a moment, then said, "It's just a simple case of food poisoning. Only . . ."

"What's the doctor's name?"

"Now you listen to me," Louise Marlow said. "I tell you, these girls are too sick to be bothered, and . . ."

Lieutenant Tragg said, "Carver L. Clements, who has an apartment on the floor above here, is dead. It looks like murder. Fay Allison had evidently been living up there in the apartment with him and . . ."

"What are you talking about!" Louise Marlow exclaimed indignantly. "Why, I . . . I . . ."

"Take it easy," Tragg said. "Her clothes were up there. There's a laundry mark that has been traced to her."

"Clothes!" Louise Marlow snorted. "Why it's probably some junk she gave away somewhere, or . . ."

"I'm coming to that," Lieutenant Tragg said patiently. "I don't want to do anyone an injustice. I want to play it on the up-and-up. Now then, there are fingerprints in that apartment, the fingerprints of a woman on a drinking glass, on the handle of a toothbrush, on a tube of tooth paste. I'm not going to get tough unless I have to, but I want to get hold of Fay Allison long enough to take a set of rolled fingerprints from her hands. You try holding out on me, and see what the newspapers have to say tomorrow."

Louise Marlow reached an instant decision. "You'll find her at the Crestview Sanitarium," she said, "and if you want to make a little money, I'll give you odds of a hundred to one, in any amount you want to take, that . . ."

"I'm not a betting man," Tragg said wearily. "I've been in this game too long."

He turned to one of the detectives and said, "Keep Perry Mason and his charming secretary under surveillance and away from a telephone until I get a chance at those fingerprints. Okay, boys, let's go."

CHAPTER SIX

PAUL DRAKE, head of the Drake Detective Agency, pulled a sheaf of notes from his pocket as he settled down in the big client's chair in Mason's office.

It was ten-thirty in the morning, and the detective's face showed signs of weariness as he assumed his favorite crosswise position in the big leather chair, with his long legs hanging over one overstuffed arm, the small of his back propped against the other.

"It's a mess, Perry," he said.

"Let's have it," Mason said.

Drake said, "Fay Allison and Dane Grover were going to get married today. Last night, Fay and Anita Bonsal, who shares the apartment with her, settled down in front of the fireplace for a nice gabby little hen party. They made chocolate. Both girls had been watching their figures, but this was a celebration. Fay felt she could really let loose. She had two cups of chocolate, Anita had one. Fay evidently got about twice the dose of barbiturate that Anita did. Both girls passed out.

"Next thing Anita knew, Louise Marlow, Fay's aunt, was trying to wake her up. Fay Allison didn't recover consciousness until after she was in the sanitarium.

"The rest of the stuff you know pretty well.

"Anyhow, Tragg went out and took Fay Allison's fingerprints. They check absolutely with those on the glass. What the police call the murder glass is the one that slipped from Carver Clements' fingers and rolled around the floor. It had been carefully wiped clean of all fingerprints. Police can't even find one of Clements' prints on it. The other glass on the table had Fay's prints. It's her toothbrush. The closet was filled with her clothes. She was living there with him. It's a hell of a stink.

"Dane Grover is standing by her, but I personally don't think he can stand the gaff much longer. When a man's engaged to a girl and the newspapers scream the details of her affair with a wealthy playboy all over the front pages, you can't expect the man to appear exactly nonchalant. The aunt, Louise Marlow, tells me he's being faced with terrific pressure to repudiate the girl, publicly break the engagement and take a trip.

"The girls insist it's all part of some sinister over-all plan to frame them, that they were drugged, and all that, but how could anyone have planned it that way? For instance, how could anyone have known they were going to take the chocolate in time to . . ."

"The chocolate was drugged?" Mason asked.

Drake nodded. "They'd used up most of the chocolate, but the small amount left in the package is pretty well doped with barbiturate."

Mason began toying with a lead pencil.

"The police theory," Drake went on, "is that Fay Allison had been playing house with Carver Clements. She wanted to get married. Clements wouldn't let her go. She slipped him a little poison. She intended to return and get her things out of the apartment when it got late enough so she wouldn't meet someone in the corridor if she came walking out of 702 with her arms full of clothes. Anita, who had gone out, unexpectedly returned, and that left Fay Allison trapped. She couldn't go up and get her things out of the apartment upstairs without disturbing Anita. So she tried to drug Anita and something went wrong."

"That's a hell of a theory," Mason said.

"Try and get one that fits the case any better," Drake told him. "One thing is certain, Fay Allison was living up there in that apartment 702. As far as Dane Grover is concerned, that's the thing that will make him throw everything overboard. He's a sensitive chap, from a good family. He doesn't like having his picture in the papers. Neither does his family."

"What about Clements?"

"Successful businessman, broker, speculator, lots of dough, domestic troubles, a wife who was trying to hook him for a bigger property settlement than Clements wanted to pay. Clements has a big apartment he leases by the year, where he lives officially. This place was a playhouse. Only a few people knew he had it. His wife would have given a lot of money to have found out about it."

"What's the wife doing now?"

"Sitting pretty. They don't know yet whether Clements left a will, but she has her community property rights, and Clements' books will be open for inspection now. He'd been juggling things around pretty much, and now a lot of stuff is going to come out—safety deposit boxes and things of that sort."

"How about the four people who met us in the hall?"

"I have all the stuff on them here. The men were Richard P. Nolin, a sort of partner in some of Clements' business, Manley L. Ogden, an income tax specialist, Don B. Ralston, who acted as dummy for Clements in some business transactions, and Vera Payson, who is someone's girl friend, but I'm damned if I can find out whose. Anyhow, those people knew of the hideout apartment and would go up there occasionally for a poker game. Last night as soon as the dame across the hall said Clements had company, they knew what that meant and went away. That's the story. The newspapers are lapping it up. Dane Grover isn't going to stay put much longer. You can't blame him. Pressure's getting pretty strong. All he has is Fay Allison's tearful denial. Louise Marlow says we have to do something fast."

Mason said, "Tragg thinks I had Carver Clements' key."

"Didn't you?"

"No."

"Where *did* you get it?"

Mason shook his head.

"Well," Drake said, "Carver Clements didn't have a key."

Mason nodded. "That is the only break we have in the case, Paul. We know Clements' key is missing. No one else does, because Tragg won't believe me when I tell him Clements hadn't given me his key."

Drake said, "It won't take Tragg long to figure the answer to that one. If Clements didn't give you the key, there's only one other person who could have given it to you."

Mason said, "We won't speculate too much on that, Paul."

"I gathered we wouldn't," Drake said dryly. "Remember this, Perry, you're representing a girl who's going to be faced with a murder rap. You may be able to beat that rap. It's circumstantial evidence. But in doing it, you'll have to think out some explanation that will satisfy an embarrassed lover who's being pitied by his friends, laughed at by his enemies, and ridiculed by the public."

Mason nodded.

"Whatever explanation you're going to make has to be made fast," Drake

166 Erle Stanley Gardner

said. "My best guess is this Grover guy isn't going to stand the gaff much longer."

Mason said, "We'll push things to a quick hearing in the magistrate's court on a preliminary examination. In the meantime, Paul, find out everything you can about Carver Clements' background. Pay particular attention to Clements' wife. See if there isn't a man in her life. If she had known about that apartment . . ."

Drake shook his head dubiously. "I'll give it a once-over, Perry, but if she'd even known about that apartment, that would have been all she needed. If she could have raided that apartment with a photographer and had the deadwood on Carver Clements, she'd have boosted her property settlement another hundred grand and walked out smiling. She wouldn't have needed to use any poison."

Mason's strong, capable fingers were drumming gently on the edge of the desk. "There has to be *some* explanation, Paul."

Drake heaved himself wearily to his feet. "That's right," he said without enthusiasm, "and Tragg thinks he has it."

CHAPTER SEVEN

DELLA STREET, her eyes sparkling, entered Mason's private office from the door which led from the reception room, and said, "*He's* here, chief."

"Who's here?" Mason asked, frowning.

She laughed. "Don't be like that. As far as this office is concerned, there is only one HE."

"Dane Grover?"

"That's right."

"What sort?"

"Tall, sensitive-looking. Wavy, dark brown hair, romantic eyes, with something of the poet about him. He's terribly crushed, of course. You can see he's dying ten thousand deaths every time he meets one of his friends. Gertie, at the switchboard, can't take her eyes off of him."

Mason grinned, and said, "Let's get him in, then, before Gertie either breaks up a romance or dies of unrequited love."

Della Street went out, returned after a few moments, ushering Dane Grover into the office.

Mason shook hands, invited Grover to a seat. Grover glanced dubiously at Della Street. Mason smiled, "She's my right hand, Grover, keeps notes for me, and her thoughts to herself."

Grover said, "I suppose I'm unduly sensitive, but I can't stand it when people patronize me or snub me or pity me."

Mason nodded.

"I've had them do all three ever since the papers came out this morning."

Again, Mason's answer was merely a nod.

"But," Grover went on, "I want you to know that I'll stick."

Mason thought that over for a moment, then held Grover's eyes. "For how long?"

"All the way."

"No matter *what* the evidence shows?"

Grover said, "The *evidence* shows the woman I love was living with Carver Clements as his mistress. The evidence simply can't be right. I love her, and I'm going to stick. I want you to tell her that, and I want you to know that. What you're going to have to do is going to take money. I want it to take *lots* of money. I don't want to leave any stone unturned. I'm here to see that you have what money you need—all you want, in fact."

"That's fine," Mason said. "Primarily, what I need is a little moral support. I want to be able to tell Fay Allison that you're sticking, and I want some facts."

"What facts?"

"How long have you been going with Fay Allison?"

"A matter of three or four months. Before then I was . . . well, sort of squiring both of the girls around."

"You mean Anita Bonsal?"

"Yes. I met Anita first. I went with her for a while. Then I went with both. Then I began to gravitate toward Fay Allison. I thought I was just making dates. Actually I was falling in love."

"And Anita?"

"She's like a sister to both of us. She's been simply grand in this whole thing. She's promised me that she'll do everything she can do."

"Could Fay Allison have been living with Carver Clements?"

"She had the physical opportunity, if that's what you mean."

"You didn't see her every night?"

"No."

"What does Anita say?"

"Anita says the charge is ridiculous, absolutely absurd."

"Do you know of any place where Fay Allison could have had access to cyanide of potassium?"

"That's what I wanted to tell you about, Mr. Mason."

"Go ahead."

"Out at my place the gardener uses it. I don't know just what for, but . . . well, out there the other day, when he was showing Fay around the place . . ."

"Yes, yes," Mason said impatiently, as Grover paused, "go on."

"Well, I know the gardener was explaining to her something about it. He told her to be very careful not to touch that sack because it contained cyanide, and I remember she asked him a few questions about what he used it for, but I wasn't paying much attention. It's the basis of some sort of a spray, and then I believe it's used for the plants."

"Who else was present?"

"Just the three of us."

"Has your gardener read the papers?"

Grover nodded.

"Can you trust him?"

"With my life. He's very devoted to me. He's been with us for twenty years."

"What's his name?"

"Barney Sheff. My mother took an interest in him and . . . well, rehabilitated him."

"He'd been in trouble?"

"Yes."

"In the pen?"

"That's right."

"Then what?"

"Then he was released. He had a chance to get parole if he could get a job. Mother gave him the job. He's been terribly devoted ever since."

"You have a hothouse?"

"Yes."

"I'm wondering if you have fully explored the possibilities of orchid growing."

"We're not interested in orchid growing. We can buy them and . . ."

"I wonder," Mason said in exactly the same tone, and with the same spacing words, "if you have fully investigated the possibilities of growing orchids."

"I tell you we . . ."

"Fully investigated the possibilities of growing orchids," Mason said again.

"You mean . . . oh, you mean we should send Barney Sheff to . . ."

"Fully investigate the possibilities of growing orchids."

Dane Grover studied Mason silently for a few seconds. Then abruptly he arose from the chair, extended his hand, and said, "I brought you some money. I thought you might need it."

He carelessly tossed an envelope on the table.

"How about your mother?" Mason asked.

Grover touched his tongue to dry lips, clamped his mouth in a straight line. "Mother," he said, "is naturally embarrassed. I don't think *her* feelings need to enter into it."

And with that he marched out of the office.

Mason reached for the envelope Grover had tossed on his desk. It was well filled with hundred-dollar bills.

Della Street came over to take the money. "When I get so interested in a man," she said, "that I neglect to count the money, you know I'm becoming incurably romantic. How much, chief?"

"Plenty," Mason said.

Della Street was counting it when the unlisted telephone on her desk rang stridently.

She picked up the receiver and heard Drake's voice on the line.

"Hi, Paul," she said.

"Hi, Della. Perry there?"

"Yes."

"Okay," Drake said wearily, "I'm making a progress report. Tell him Lieutenant Tragg nabbed the Grover gardener, a chap by the name of Sheff. They're holding him as a material witness, seem to be all worked up about what they've discovered. Can't find out what it is. Think the tip-off to grab him came from Dane's mother, Caroline Manning Grover."

Della Street sat motionless at the desk, holding the receiver.

"Hello, hello," Drake said, "are you there?"

"I'm here," Della said. "I'll tell him." She hung up the phone.

CHAPTER EIGHT

IT WAS AFTER nine o'clock that night when Della Street, signing the register in the elevator, was whisked up to the floor where Perry Mason had his offices.

The offices of the Drake Detective Agency on the same floor, nearer the elevator, were kept open twenty-four hours a day. The innocent-looking entrance door showed merely a single oblong of frosted glass, the illumination back of the glass showing the offices were open, but giving no indication of the unceasing nocturnal activities of the staff which worked in a veritable rabbit warren of offices.

Della Street started to look in on Paul Drake, then changed her mind and kept on walking down the long, dark corridor, the rapid tempo of her heels echoing back at her from the night silence of the door-lined hallway.

She rounded the elbow in the corridor, and saw that lights were on in Mason's office. She fitted her latchkey to the outer door, crossed through the entrance office and opened the door of Mason's private office.

The lawyer was pacing the floor, thumbs pushed in the armholes of his vest, head shoved forward, wrapped in such concentration that he did not even notice the opening of the door.

Della Street stood for a moment watching him.

The desk was littered with photographs. There were numerous sheets of the flimsy which Paul Drake used in making reports to clients.

Della stood quietly in the doorway, watching the tall, lean-waisted man pacing back and forth. He was granite-hard of face, broad-shouldered, flat-stomached; the seething action of his restless mind demanded physical outlet in order to preserve some semblance of internal balance, and this restless pacing was but an unconscious reflex.

After almost a minute, Della Street said, "Hello, chief. Can I help?"

Mason looked up at her with a start. "What are you doing here?"

"I came up to see if you were working and if so, if there was anything I could do to help."

He smiled, said, "I'm not working. I'm like an animal running around his cage trying to find an outlet."

"Had any dinner?" she asked.

He glanced at his wrist watch, said, "Not yet."

"What time is it?" Della Street asked.

He had to look at his wrist watch again in order to tell her. "Nine-forty."

She laughed, "I knew you didn't even look the first time you went through the motions. Come on, chief, you've got to go get something to eat. The case will still be here when you get back."

"How do we know it will?" Mason said. "I've been talking with Louise Marlow on the phone. She's been in touch with Dane Grover and she knows Dane Grover's mother. Dane Grover says he'll stick. How does *he* know what he'll do? He's exploring uncharted depths in his own mind. He doesn't know what he'll find. His friends, his relatives are turning the knife in the wound with their sympathy, the silent accusation of their every glance. How the hell does he know what he's going to do? How can he tell whether he'll stick?"

"Just the same," Della Street insisted, "I think he'll do it. It's through situations such as this that character is created."

"You're just talking to keep your courage up," Mason said. "I've pulled that line with a jury once or twice, myself. Soul-seared in a crucible of adversity —the tempering fires of fate—burning away the fat of wealthy complacency as he comes to grips with the fundamentals of life—baloney!"

She smiled faintly.

"The guy's undergoing the tortures of the damned," Mason went on. "He can't help but be influenced by the evidence, by the worldly-wise, cynical skepticism of all his associates. The woman he loves on the night before the wedding having trouble trying to push herself away from the slimy embraces of the man who gave her money and a certain measure of security—until she had an opportunity to trade that security in on a newer and better model."

"Chief, you simply *have* to eat."

Mason walked over to the desk. "Look at 'em," he said, "photographs! And Drake had the devil's own time obtaining them—copies of the police photographs—the body on the floor, glass on the table, an overturned chair, a newspaper half-open by a reading chair, an ordinary, mediocre apartment as drab as the sordid affair for which it was used. And somewhere in those photographs I've got to find the clue that will establish the innocence of a woman, not only innocence of the crime of murder, but innocence of the crime of betraying the man she loved."

Mason crossed over to the desk, picked up the magnifying glass which was on his blotter, started once more examining the pictures. "And, hang it, Della," he said, "I think the thing's here somewhere. That glass on the table, a little Scotch and soda in the bottom, Fay Allison's fingerprints all over it. Then there's that brazen touch of that crimson kiss on the forehead."

"Indicating a woman was with him just before he died?"

"Not necessarily. That lipstick is a perfect imprint of a pair of lips. There was no lipstick on his lips, just there on the forehead. A shrewd man could well have smeared lipstick on his lips, pressed them against Clements' forehead after the poison had taken effect and so directed suspicion away from himself. This could well have happened if the man had known some woman was in the habit of visiting Clements there in that apartment.

"It's a clue that so obviously indicates a woman that I find myself getting suspicious of it. If there were only something to give me a starting point. If we only had a little more time."

Della Street walked over to the desk. The cool tips of her fingers slid over Mason's eyes. She said, "Stop it. Come and get something to eat. Let's talk it over . . ."

"Haven't you had dinner?"

She smiled, and shook her head. "I knew you'd be working, and that if someone didn't rescue you, you'd be pacing the floor until two or three o'clock in the morning. What's Paul Drake found out?"

She picked up the sheets of flimsy, placed them together, folded them, stacked up the photographs, put the flimsy on top of the photographs and anchored everything in place with a paper weight. "Come on, chief, I'm famished."

Mason walked over to the coat closet. Della Street had to stand on tiptoes to help him with his topcoat. The lawyer took his hat, switched out lights, and walked down the corridor with Della Street.

But he didn't really answer her question until after he had become relaxed in one of the booths in their favorite restaurant. Then he pushed back the plates containing the wreckage of a thick steak, shoestring potatoes, golden-brown toasted and buttered French bread, and a lettuce and tomato salad.

He poured more coffee, then said, "Drake hasn't found out much, just background."

"What, for instance?" Della Street asked.

Mason said wearily, "It's the same old seven and six. The wife, Marline Austin Clements, apparently was swept off her feet by Carver Clements' determination to get her, by the sheer power of the man.

"She overlooked the fact that after he had her safely listed as one of his legal chattels, with title in good order, he used that same acquisitive, aggressive tenacity of purpose to get other things he wanted. Marline was left pretty much alone. That's the price one has to pay for marrying men of that type."

"And so?" Della asked.

"And so," Mason said, "in the course of time, Carver Clements turned to other interests. Hang it, Della, we have one thing to work on, only one thing, the fact that Clements had no key on his body.

"You remember the four people who met us in the corridor. They had to get in that apartment house some way. Remember the outer door was locked.

Any of the tenants could release the latch by pressing the button of an electric release. But if the tenant of some apartment didn't press the release button, it was necessary for any visitor to have a key in order to get in.

"Now then, those four people got in. How? They must have had a key. Regardless of what they now say, one of them must have had a key."

"The missing key?" Della asked.

"That's what we have to find out."

"What story did they give the police?"

"I don't know. The police have them sewed up tight. I've got to get one of them on the stand and cross-examine him. Then we'll at least have something to go on."

"So we have to try for an immediate hearing and then go it blind?"

"That's about the size of it."

"Was that key in Fay Allison's purse Carver Clements' missing key?"

"It *could* have been. In that case either Fay was playing house, or the key was planted. In that case when was it planted, how, and by whom? I'm inclined to think Clements' key must have been on his body at the time he was murdered. It wasn't there when police arrived. That's the one really significant clue we have to work on."

Della Street shook her head. "It's too deep for me, but I guess you're going to have to wade into it. I can tell you one thing. Louise Marlow is a brick. I've known her since I was a child. If there's anything she can do to help, you can count on her."

Mason lit a cigarette. "Ordinarily I'd spar for time, but in this case I'm afraid Time is our enemy, Della. We're going to have to walk into court with all the assurance in the world and pull a very large rabbit out of a very small hat."

She smiled. "Where do we get the rabbit?"

"Back in the office," he said, "studying those photographs, looking for a clue, and . . ." Suddenly he snapped to startled attention.

"What is it, chief?"

"I was just thinking. The glass on the table in 702, there was a little whiskey and soda in the bottom of it, just a spoonful or two."

"Well?" she asked.

"What happens when you drink Scotch and soda, Della?"

"Why . . . you always have a little. It sticks to the side of the glass and then gradually settles back."

Mason shook his head. His eyes were glowing now. "You leave ice cubes in the glass," he said, "and then after a while they melt and leave an inch or so of water."

She matched his excitement. "Then there was no ice in the woman's glass?"

"And none in Carver Clements'. Yet there was a thermos jar of ice cubes on the table. Come on, Della, we're going back and *really* study those photographs!"

JUDGE RANDOLPH JORDAN ascended the bench and rapped court to order.

"People versus Fay Allison."

"Ready for the Defendant," Mason said.

"Ready for the Prosecution," Stewart Linn announced.

Linn, one of the best of the trial deputies in the district attorney's office, was a thin-faced, steely-eyed, cautious individual who had the mind of an accountant, the legal knowledge of an encyclopedia, and the cold-blooded mercilessness of a steel trap.

Linn was under no illusions as to the resourcefulness of his adversary, and he had all of the caution of a boxer approaching a heavyweight champion.

"Call Dr. Charles Keene," he said.

Dr. Keene came forward, qualified himself as a physician and surgeon who had had great experience in medical necropsies, particularly in cases of homicide.

"On the tenth of this month did you have occasion to examine a body in apartment 702 at the Mandrake Arms?"

"I did."

"What time was it?"

"It was about two o'clock in the morning."

"What did you find?"

"I found the body of a man of approximately fifty-two years of age, fairly well-fleshed, quite bald, but otherwise very well preserved for a man of his age. The body was lying on the floor, sprawled forward, head toward the door, feet toward the interior of the apartment, the left arm doubled up and lying under him, the right arm flung out, the left side of the face resting on the carpet. The man had been dead for several hours. I fix the time of death as having been during a period between seven o'clock and nine o'clock that evening. I cannot place the time of death any closer than that, but I will swear that it was within those time limits."

"And did you determine the cause of death?"

"Not at that time. I did later."

"What was the cause of death?"

"Poisoning caused by the ingestion of cyanide of potassium."

"Did you notice anything about the physical appearance of the man's body?"

"You mean with reference to lipstick?"

"Yes."

"There was a red smear on the upper part of the forehead, apparently caused by lips that had been heavily coated with lipstick and then pressed against the skin in a somewhat puckered condition."

"You mean the skin was puckered?"

"No," Dr. Linn said, smiling. "I mean the lips were puckered. It was as though some woman had administered a last kiss. The lipstick was deposited at the upper part of the forehead, where the skin across the scalp was stretched tight and smooth. It would have been above the hairline of an individual who was not bald."

"Cross-examine," Linn announced.

"No questions," Mason said.

"Call Benjamin Harlan," Linn said.

Benjamin Harlan, a huge, lumbering giant of a man, took the stand with a good-natured smile, promptly proceeded to qualify himself as a fingerprint and identification expert of some twenty years' experience.

Stewart Linn, by skillful, adroit questions, led him through an account of his activities on the date in question, the finding of the body, the dusting of various things in the apartment, the finding of no latent fingerprints on the glass which the Prosecution referred to as the "murder glass," indicating this glass had been wiped clean of prints, the finding of prints on the glass on the table which the Prosecution referred to as the "decoy glass," on the toothbrush, on the tube of tooth paste, and various other articles. These latent fingerprints had coincided with the rolled fingerprints taken from the hands of Fay Allison, the defendant in the case.

Harlan also identified a whole series of photographs taken by the police showing the position of the body when it was discovered, the furnishings in the apartment, the table, the overturned chair, the so-called murder glass which had rolled along the floor, the so-called decoy glass on the table, which bore unmistakably the fresh fingerprints of Fay Allison, the bottle of Scotch whiskey, the bottle of soda water, the thermos jar containing ice cubes.

"Cross-examine," Linn said triumphantly.

Mason said, "You have had some twenty years' experience as a fingerprint expert, Mr. Harlan?"

"That's right."

"And an identification expert?"

"Yes, sir."

"Now, you have heard Dr. Keene's testimony about the lipstick on the forehead of the dead man?"

"Yes, sir."

"And that lipstick, I believe, shows in this photograph which I now hand you?"

"Yes, sir; not only that, but I have a close-up of that lipstick stain which I myself took with one of the cameras I use for close-up photography. I have an enlargement of that negative, in case you're interested."

"I'm very much interested," Mason said. "Will you produce the enlargement, please?"

Harlan produced the photograph from his brief case, showing a section of the forehead of the dead man, with the stain of lips outlined clearly and in microscopic detail.

"What is the scale of this photograph?" Mason asked.

"Life size," Harlan said. "I have a standard of distances by which I can take photographs to a scale of exactly life size."

"Thank you," Mason said. "I'd like to have this photograph received in evidence."

"No objection," Linn said.

"And it is, is it not, a matter of fact that the little lines shown in this photograph are fully as distinctive as the ridges and whorls of a fingerprint?"

"Just what do you mean?"

"Isn't it a fact well-known to identification experts that the little wrinkles which form in a person's lips are fully as individual as the lines of a fingerprint?"

"It's not a 'well-known' fact."

"But it *is* a fact?"

"Yes, sir, it is."

"So that by measuring the distance between the little lines which are shown on this photograph, indicating the pucker lines of the skin, it would be fully as possible to identify the lips which made this lipstick print as it would be to identify a person who had left a fingerprint upon the scalp of the dead man."

"Yes, sir."

"Now, you have testified to having made rolled imprints of the defendant's fingers and compared those with the fingerprints found on the glass."

"Yes, sir."

"Have you made any attempt to take an imprint of her lips and compare that print with the print of the lipstick on the forehead of the decedent?"

"No, sir," Harlan said, shifting his position uneasily.

"Why not?"

"Well, in the first place, Mr. Mason, the fact that the pucker lines of lips are so highly individualized is not a generally known fact."

"But *you* know it."

"Yes, sir."

"And the more skilled experts in your profession know it?"

"Yes, sir."

"Why didn't you do it then?"

Harlan shifted his position again, crossed his legs, glanced somewhat helplessly at Stewart Linn, the deputy prosecutor.

"Oh, if the Court please," Linn said, promptly taking his cue from that glance, "this hardly seems to be cross-examination. The inquiry is wandering far afield. I will object to the question on the ground that it's incompetent, irrelevant and immaterial, and not proper cross-examination."

"Overruled," Judge Jordan snapped. "Answer the question!"

Harlan cleared his throat. "Well," he said, "I guess I just never thought of it."

"Think of it now," Mason said, with a gesture that was a flourish. "Go ahead and take the imprint right now and right here. Put on plenty of lipstick, Miss Allison. Let's see how your lips compare with those on the dead man's forehead."

"Oh, if the Court please," Linn said wearily, "this hardly seems to be cross-examination. If Mr. Mason wants to make Harlan his own witness and call for this test as a part of the defendant's case, that will be one thing: but this certainly isn't cross-examination."

"It may be cross-examination of Harlan's qualifications as an expert," Judge Jordan ruled.

"Oh, if the Court please! Isn't that stretching a technicality rather far?"

"Your objection was highly technical," Judge Jordan snapped. "It is overruled, and my ruling will stand. Take the impression, Mr. Harlan."

Fay Allison, with trembling hand, daubed lipstick heavily on her mouth. Then, using the makeup mirror in her purse, smoothed off the lipstick with the tip of her little finger.

"Go ahead," Mason said to Harlan, "check on her lips."

Harlan, taking a piece of white paper from his brief case, moved down to where the defendant was sitting beside Perry Mason and pressed the white paper against her lips. He removed the paper and examined the imprint.

"Go ahead," Mason said to Harlan, "make your comparison and announce the result to the Court."

Harlan said, "Of course, I have not the facilities here for making a microscopic comparison, but I can tell from even a superficial examination of the lip lines that these lips did not make that print."

"Thank you," Mason said. "That's all."

Judge Jordan was interested. "These lines appear in the lips only when the lips are puckered, as in giving a kiss?"

"No, Your Honor, they are in the lips all the time, as an examination will show, but when the lips are puckered, the lines are intensified."

"And these lip markings are different with each individual?"

"Yes, Your Honor."

"So that you are now prepared to state to the Court that despite the fingerprints of the defendant on the glass and other objects, her lips definitely could not have left the imprint on the dead man's forehead?"

"Yes, Your Honor."

"That's all," Judge Jordan said.

"Of course," Linn pointed out, "the fact that the defendant did not leave that kiss imprint on the man's forehead doesn't necessarily mean a thing, Your Honor. In fact, he may have met his death *because* the defendant found that lipstick on his forehead. The evidence of the fingerprints is quite conclusive that the defendant was in that apartment."

"The Court understands the evidence. Proceed with your case," Judge Jordan said.

"Furthermore," Linn went on angrily, "I will now show the Court that there was every possibility the print of that lipstick could have been deliberately planted by none other than the attorney for the defendant and his

charming and very efficient secretary. I will proceed to prove that by calling
Don B. Ralston to the stand."

Ralston came forward and took the stand, his manner that of a man who
wishes very much he were many miles away.

"Your name is Don B. Ralston? You reside at 2935 Creelmore Avenue
in this city?"

"Yes, sir."

"And you knew Carver L. Clements in his lifetime?"

"Yes."

"Were rather intimately associated with him?"

"Yes, sir."

"In a business way?"

"Yes, sir."

"Now, on the night, or rather, early in the morning of the 10th of this
month, did you have occasion to go to Carver L. Clements' apartment, being
apartment number 702 in the Mandrake Arms Apartments in this city?"

"I did, yes, sir."

"What time was it?"

"Around . . . well, it was between one and two in the morning . . . I
would say somewhere around one-thirty."

"Were you alone?"

"No, sir."

"Who was with you?"

"Richard P. Nolin, who is a business associate, or was a business associate
of Mr. Clements; Manley L. Ogden, who handled some of Mr. Clements'
income tax work; and a Miss Vera Payson, a friend of—well, a friend of all of
us."

"What happened when you went to that apartment? Did you enter it?"

"No, sir."

"Tell us just what happened."

"Well, we left the elevator on the seventh floor, and as we were walking
down the corridor, I noticed two people coming down the corridor toward
us."

"Now, when you say 'down the corridor,' do you mean from the direction
of apartment 702?"

"That's right, yes, sir."

"And who were these people?"

"Mr. Perry Mason and his secretary, Miss Street."

"And did you actually enter the apartment of Carver Clements?"

"I did not."

"Why not?"

"When I got to the door of apartment 702, I pushed the doorbell and
heard the sound of the buzzer on the inside of the apartment. Almost instantly the door of an apartment across the hall opened, and a woman who
seemed to be somewhat irritated complained that she had been unable to
sleep because of people ringing the buzzer of that apartment, and stated

in effect that other people were in there with Mr. Clements. So we left immediately."

"Now, then, Your Honor," Stewart Linn said, "I propose to show that the two people referred to by the person living in the apartment across the hallway were none other than Mr. Mason and Miss Street, who had actually entered that apartment and were closeted in there with the dead man and the evidence for an undetermined length of time."

"Go ahead and show it," Judge Jordan said.

"Just a moment," Mason said. "Before you do that, I want to cross-examine this witness."

"Cross-examine him, then."

"When you arrived at the Mandrake Arms, the door to the street was locked, was it not?"

"Yes, sir."

"What did you do?"

"We went up to the seventh floor and . . ."

"I understand that, but how did you get in? How did you get past the entrance door? You had a key, didn't you?"

"No, sir."

"Then how *did* you get in?"

"Why *you* let us in."

"I did?"

"Yes."

"Understand," Mason said, "I am not now referring to the time you came up from the street in the custody of the radio officer. I am now referring to the time when you first entered that apartment house on the morning of the tenth of this month—the first time you went in."

"Yes, sir. I understand. You let us in."

"What makes you say that?"

"Well, because you and your secretary were in Carver Clements' apartment, and . . ."

"You, yourself, don't *know* we were in there, do you?"

"Well, I surmise it. We met you just after you had left the apartment. You were hurrying down the hall toward the elevator."

Mason said, "I don't want your surmises. You don't even know I had been in that apartment. I want you to tell us how you got past the locked street door. No surmises now. Just how did you get in? Exactly what did you do?"

"We pressed the button of Carver Clements' apartment, and you—or at any rate someone—answered by pressing the button which released the electric door catch on the outer door. As soon as we heard the sound of buzzing, which indicated the lock was released, we pushed the door open and went in."

"Let's not have any misunderstanding about this," Mason said. "Who was it pushed the button of Carver Clements' apartment?"

"I did."

"I'm talking now about the button in front of the outer door of the apartment house."

"Yes, sir."

"And, having pressed that button, you waited until the buzzer announced the door was being opened?"

"Yes, sir."

"How long?"

"Not over a second or two."

Mason said to the witness, "One more question: did you go right up after you entered the apartment house?"

"We . . . no, sir, not *right* away. We stopped for a few moments there in the lobby to talk about the type of poker we wanted to play. Miss Payson had lost some money on one of these wild poker games where the dealer has the opportunity of calling any kind of game he wants, some of them having the one-eyed jacks wild, and others having seven cards from which five are selected, and things of that sort."

"How long were you talking?"

"Oh, a couple of minutes, perhaps."

"And you decided on the type of poker you wanted to play?"

"Yes."

"And then went right up?"

"Yes."

"Where was the elevator?"

"The elevator was . . . now, wait a minute, I don't remember exactly. It was on one of the upper floors. I remember we pressed the button and it took it a little while to come down to where we were."

"That's all," Mason said.

Della Street's fingers dug into his arm. "Aren't you going to ask him about the key?" she whispered.

"Not yet," Mason said, a light of triumph in his eyes. "I know what happened now, Della. Give us the breaks, and we've got this case in the bag. First, make him prove we were in that apartment."

Linn said, "I will now call Miss Shirley Tanner to the stand."

The young woman who advanced to the stand was very different from the disheveled, sleepless and nervous individual who had been so angry at the time Mason and Della Street had pressed the button of apartment 702.

"Your name is Shirley Tanner, and you reside in apartment 701 of the Mandrake Arms Apartments in this city?"

"Yes, sir."

"And have for how long?"

She smiled, and said, "Not very long. I put in three weeks apartment hunting and finally secured a sublease on apartment 701 on the afternoon of the 8th. I moved in on the 9th, which explains why I was tired almost to the point of having hysterics."

"You had difficulty sleeping?"

"Yes."

"And on the morning of the 10th did you have any experiences which annoyed you—that is, experiences in connection with the ringing of the buzzer in the apartment next door?"

"I most certainly did, yes, sir."

"Tell us exactly what happened."

"I had been taking sleeping medicine from time to time, but for some reason or other this night I was so nervous the sleeping medicine didn't do me any good. I had been moving and unpacking, and my nerves were all keyed up. I was physically and mentally exhausted. I tried to sleep, but I was too tired to sleep. I guess perhaps you know how it is, Your Honor," she said, turning to the judge with a winsome smile.

The judge regarded the attractive young woman, smiled in a fatherly way, nodded, and said, "We all get overtired at times. Go on with your testimony, Miss Tanner."

"Well, I was trying to sleep, and I think I had just gotten to sleep when I was awakened by a continual sounding of the buzzer over there in the apartment across the hall. It was a low, persistent noise which became exceedingly irritating to a person in my nervous state, who was trying to sleep."

"Go on," Linn said. "What did you do?"

"I finally got up and put on a robe and went to the door and flung it open. I was terribly angry at the very idea of people making so much noise at that hour of the morning. You see those apartments aren't too soundproof and there is a ventilating system over the doors of the apartments. The one over the door of 702 was apparently open and I had left mine open for nighttime ventilation. And then I was angry at myself for getting so upset over the noise. I knew my allowing myself to get so angry would prevent me from sleeping at all, which is why I lay still for what seemed an interminable time before I opened the door."

Linn smiled, "So you became angry at the people in the hallway, and then became angry at yourself for being angry?"

Her laugh was musical. "That's about the way it happened."

"And you say you *flung* open the door?"

"Yes, sir."

"What did you find?"

"Two people across the hall."

"Did you recognize them?"

"I didn't know them at the time, but I know them now."

"Who were they?"

She pointed a dramatic finger at Perry Mason.

"Mr. Perry Mason, the lawyer for the defendant, and the young woman, I believe his secretary, who is sitting there beside him—not the defendant, but the woman on the other side."

"Miss Della Street," Mason said with a bow.

"Thank you," she said.

"And," Linn went on, "what did you see those people do?"

She said, "I saw them enter the apartment."

"Did you see how they entered the apartment . . . I mean, how did they get the door open?"

"They must have used a key. Mr. Mason was just pushing the door open and I . . ."

"No surmises, please," Linn broke in. "Did you actually *see* Mr. Mason using a key?"

"Well, I heard him."

"What do you mean?"

"As I was opening my door I heard metal rasping against metal, the way a key does when it scrapes against a lock. And then when I had my door all the way open, I saw Mr. Mason pushing his way into 702."

"But you only know he must have had a key because you heard the sound of metal rubbing against metal?"

"Well, it stands to reason . . ."

"But you only heard the sound of metal against metal?"

"Yes, and the click of the lock."

"Did you say anything to Mr. Mason and Miss Street?"

"I most certainly did, and then I slammed the door and went back and tried to sleep. But I was so mad by that time I simply couldn't close my eyes and keep them closed. I couldn't understand why, if a person had a key, he would go through all that agony of ringing a doorbell and waking me up. Why didn't they simply go in there in the first place and . . ."

"Now, never mind that," Linn interrupted impatiently, holding up his hand palm outwards, and moving it back and forth as though patting the words back into her mouth. "Never mind your conclusions, never mind your reasons, just tell the Court what you *saw*."

"Yes, sir."

"What happened after that?"

"After that, when I was trying to sleep—I would say just a few seconds after that—I heard that buzzer again. And this time I was *good* and mad."

"And what did you do?"

"I swung open the door and started to give these people a piece of my mind."

"People?" Linn asked promptingly.

"There were four people standing there. The Mr. Ralston, who has just testified, two other men and a woman. They were standing there at the doorway, jabbing away at the button, and I told them this was a sweet time to be calling on someone and making a racket and that anyway the gentleman already had company, so if he didn't answer his door, it was because he didn't want to."

"Did you at that time see Mr. Mason and Miss Street walking down the corridor?"

"No. I did not. I had my door open only far enough to show me the door of apartment 702 across the way. You see, my door opens toward the end of the corridor away from the elevator. My apartment is a corner apartment and

702 is a corner apartment. So, when my door is open, I can only see just that blind end of the corridor unless I open it all the way."

"Thank you," Linn said. "Now you distinctly saw Mr. Mason and Miss Street enter that apartment?"

"Yes."

"And close the door behind them?"

"Yes."

"Cross-examine!" Linn said triumphantly.

Mason, taking a notebook from his pocket, walked up to stand beside Shirley Tanner, but his voice was good-natured. "Miss Tanner," he said, "are you certain that you heard me rub metal against the keyhole of that door?"

"Certain," she said.

"My back was towards you?"

"It was when I first opened my door, yes. I saw your face, however, just after you went in the door. You turned around and looked at me over your shoulder."

"Oh, we'll stipulate," Linn said with an exaggerated note of weariness in his voice, "that the witness couldn't see through Mr. Mason's back. Perhaps learned counsel was carrying the key in his teeth."

"Thank you," Mason said, turning toward Linn. Then suddenly stepping forward, he clapped his notebook against Shirley Tanner's face.

The witness screamed and jumped back.

Linn was on his feet. "What are you trying to do," he shouted, "intimidate the witness?"

Judge Jordan pounded with his gavel. "Mr. Mason!" he reprimanded. "That is contempt of court!"

Mason said, "Please let me explain, Your Honor. The Prosecution took the lip prints of my client. I feel that I am entitled to take the lip prints of this witness. I will cheerfully admit to being in contempt of court, in the event I am wrong, but I would like to extend this imprint of Shirley Tanner's lips to Mr. Benjamin Harlan, the identification expert, and ask him whether or not the print made by these lips is not the same as that of the lipstick kiss which was found on the dead forehead of Carver L. Clements."

There was a tense, dramatic silence in the courtroom.

Mason stepped forward and handed the notebook to Benjamin Harlan.

From the witness stand came a shrill scream of terror. Shirley Tanner tried to get to her feet, her eyes fastened on Mason, wide, round and terrified, her face the color of putty beneath the makeup which suddenly showed as dabbed-on bits of orange.

She couldn't make it. Her knees buckled. She tried to catch herself, then fell to the floor.

IT WAS WHEN order was restored in the courtroom that Perry Mason exploded his second bombshell.

"Your Honor," he said, "either Fay Allison is innocent or she is guilty. If she is innocent, someone framed the evidence which would discredit her. And if someone did frame that evidence, there is only one person who could have done it, one person who could have had access to the defendant's apartment, one person who could have transported glasses, toothbrushes, and tooth paste containing Fay Allison's fingerprints, one person who could have transported clothes bearing the unmistakable stamp of ownership of the defendant in this case.

"Your Honor, I request that Anita Bonsal be called to the stand."

There was a moment's sudden and dramatic silence.

Anita Bonsal, there in the courtroom, felt suddenly as though she had been stripped stark naked by one swift gesture.

One moment she had been sitting there completely lost in the proceedings, trying to adjust her mind to what was happening, attempting to keep pace with the swift rush of developments. The next moment everyone in the courtroom was seeking her out with staring, prying eyes.

It was as though she had been quietly bathing and the side of the building had collapsed and left her naked and exposed to the curious eyes of the gawking multitude.

In that sudden surge of panic, Anita did the worst thing she could possibly have done. She ran.

They were after her then, a throng of humanity, actuated only by the mass instinct to pursue that which ran for cover.

Elevators were too slow for Anita's frantic feet.

Behind her was the bedlam of the crowd, a babble of voices which speedily grew into a roar.

Anita dashed to the stairs, went scrambling down them, found herself in another hallway in the Hall of Justice. She dashed the length of that hallway, frantically trying to find the stairs. She could not find them.

An elevator offered her welcome haven. It was standing with the doors open, the red light on above it.

"Going down," the attendant said.

Anita fairly flung herself into the cage.

"What's the hurry?" the attendant asked.

Shreds of reason were beginning to return to Anita's fear-racked mind.

"They're calling my case," she said. "Let me off at . . ."

"I know," the man said, smiling. "Third floor. Domestic relations court."

He slid the cage to a smooth stop at the third floor. "Out to the left," he said. "Department twelve."

Anita's mind was beginning to work now, functioning smoothly, cunningly.

She smiled her thanks to the elevator attendant, walked rapidly to the left, pushed open the door of Department 12 of the Superior Court, entered the partially filled courtroom with all the assurance of a witness coming to testify in a case.

She marched down the center aisle, gave an apologetic smile to the young woman who was in the aisle seat, crossed in front of her and calmly seated herself in the middle seat in the row of benches.

She was now wrapped in anonymity. Only her breathlessness and the pounding of her pulses gave indication that she was the quarry for which the crowd was searching.

Then slowly the triumphant smile faded from her face. The realization of what was bound to be the effect of what she had done stabbed her consciousness. She had admitted her guilt. She could flee now to the farthest corners of the earth, but her guilt would always follow her. She would always be an object of scorn and contempt.

Perry Mason had shown that she had not killed Carver Clements, but he had also shown that she had done something which in the minds of all men would be even worse. She had betrayed her friendship. She had tried to besmirch Fay Allison's reputation. She had attempted the murder of her own roommate by giving an overdose of sleeping tablets.

How much would Mason have been able to prove? She had no way of knowing. The man was uncanny with his shrewdness of perception. But there was no need for him to prove now. Her flight had given Mason all the proof he needed.

She must disappear, and that would not be easy. By evening her photograph would be emblazoned upon the pages of every newspaper in the city.

CHAPTER ELEVEN

BACK IN THE COURTROOM, all but deserted now save for the county officials who were crowding around Shirley Tanner, Mason was asking questions in a low voice.

There was no more stamina left in Shirley Tanner than in a wet dishrag.

Shirley heard her own voice answering the persistent drone of Mason's searching questions.

"You knew that Clements had this apartment in 702? You deliberately made such a high offer that you were able to sublease apartment 701? You were suspicious of Clements and wanted to spy on him?"

"Yes," Shirley said, and her voice was all but inaudible to her own ears, although her eyes told her that the court reporter, standing beside her with

his hand moving unobtrusively over his notebook, was taking down all that
was said.

"You were furious when you realized that Carver Clements had *another*
mistress, that all of his talk to you about waiting until he could get his
divorce was merely another bait which you had grabbed."

Again she said, "Yes." It seemed the easiest thing to say, the only thing
that she could say. There was no strength in her any more to think up lies.

"You made the mistake of loving him," Mason said. "It wasn't his money
you were after, and you administered the poison. How did you do it, Shirley?"

She said, "I'd poisoned the drink I held in my hand. I knew it made
Carver furious when I drank because whiskey makes me lose control of myself, and he never knew what I was going to do when I was drunk.

"I rang his bell, holding that glass in my hand. I leered at him tipsily
when he opened the door, and walked on in. I said, 'Hello, Carver darling.
Meet your next-door neighbor,' and I raised the glass to my lips.

"He did just as I knew he would. He was furious. He said, 'You little
devil, what're you doing here? I've told you I'll do the drinking for both of
us.' He snatched the glass from me and drained it."

"What happened?" Mason asked.

"For a moment, nothing," she said. "He went back to the chair and sat
down. I leaned over him and pressed that kiss on his head. It was a good-by
kiss. He looked at me, frowned, suddenly jumped to his feet, tried to run to
the door, staggered and then fell face-forward."

"And what did you do?"

"I took the key to his apartment from his pocket so I could get back in to
fix things the way I wanted and get possession of the glass, but I was afraid
to be there while he was . . . retching and twisting . . . and dying."

Mason nodded. "You went back to your own apartment and then after
you had waited a few minutes and thought it was safe to go back, you
couldn't, because Anita Bonsal was at the door?"

She nodded and said, "She had a key. She went in. I supposed, of course,
she'd call the police and that they'd come at any time. I didn't dare to go
in there then. I tried to sleep and couldn't. Finally I decided the police
weren't coming after all. It was past midnight then."

"So then you went back in there? You were in there when Don Ralston
rang the bell. You . . ."

"Yes," she said. "I went back into that apartment. By that time I had put
on a bathrobe and pajamas and ruffled my hair all up. If anyone had said
anything to me, if I had been caught, I had a story all prepared to tell them,
that I had heard the door open and someone run down the corridor, that I
had opened my door and found the door of 702 ajar, and I had just that
minute looked in to see what had happened."

"All right," Mason said, "that was your story. What did you do?"

"I went across the hall. I went in and wiped all my fingerprints off that
glass on the floor. Then the buzzer sounded from the street door."

"What did you do?"

She said, "I saw someone had fixed up the evidence just the way I had been going to fix it up. A bottle of Scotch on the table, a bottle of soda, a pail of ice cubes."

"So what did you do?"

She said, "I pushed the button which released the downstairs door catch and ducked back into my own apartment. I hadn't any more than got in there than I heard the elevator stop at the seventh floor. I couldn't understand that, because I knew these people couldn't possibly have had time enough to get up to the seventh floor in the elevator. I waited, listening, and heard you two come down the corridor. I could barely hear the sound of the buzzer in the other apartment. I opened the door to chase you away and saw you were actually entering the apartment, so I had to make a quick excuse, that the sound of the buzzer had wakened me. Then I jerked the door shut. When the four people came up, I really and truly thought you were still in the apartment, and I was dying of curiosity to see what was happening."

"How long had you known him?" Mason asked.

She said sadly, "I loved him. I was the one that he wanted to marry when he left his wife. I don't know how long this other thing had been going on. I became suspicious and one time when I had an opportunity to go through his pockets, I found a key stamped 'Mandrake Arms Apartment, Number 702.' Then I thought I knew, but I wanted to be sure. I found out who had apartment 701 and made a proposition for a sublease that simply couldn't be turned down.

"I waited and watched. This brunette walked down the corridor and used *her* key to open the apartment. I slipped out into the corridor and listened at the door. I heard him give her the same old line he'd given me so many times, and my heart turned to bitter acid. I hated him. I killed him . . . and I was caught."

Mason turned to Stewart Linn and said, "There you are, young man. If you want to be the fearless prosecutor, there's your murderess, but you'll probably never be able to get a jury to think it's anything more than manslaughter."

A much chastened Linn said, "Would you mind telling me how you figured this out, Mr. Mason?"

Mason said, "Clements' key was missing. Obviously he must have had it when he entered the apartment. The murderer must have taken it from his pocket. Why? So he or she could come back. And if what Don Ralston said was true *someone* must have been in the apartment when he rang the bell from the street, someone who let him in by pressing the buzzer.

"What happened to that someone? I must have been walking down the corridor within a matter of seconds after Ralston had pressed the button on the street door. Yet I saw no one leaving the apartment. There was no one in the corridor. Obviously then, the person who pressed the buzzer must have had a place to take refuge in another near-by apartment.

"Having reasoned that far, having learned a young, attractive woman had only that very day taken a lease on the apartment opposite, the answer became so obvious it ceased to be a mystery."

Stewart Linn nodded thoughtfully. "Obvious when you have once pointed it out," he said.

Mason picked up his brief case, smiled to Della Street. "Come on, Della," he said. "Let's get Fay Allison and . . ."

He stopped as he saw Fay Allison's face. "What's happened to *your* lipstick?" he asked.

And then his eyes moved over to take in Dane Grover, who was standing by her, his face smeared diagonally across the mouth with a huge red smear of lipstick.

Fay Allison had neglected to remove the thick coating of lipstick which she had put on when Mason had asked Benjamin Harlan, the identification expert, to take an imprint of her lips. Now, the heavy mark where her mouth had been pressed against the mouth of Dane Grover gave an oddly jarring note of incongruity to the entire proceedings.

On the lower floors a mob of eagerly curious spectators were baying like hounds upon the track of Anita Bonsal. In the courtroom the long efficient arm of the law was gathering Shirley Tanner into its grasp, and there amidst the machinery of tragedy, the romance of Fay Allison and Dane Grover picked up where it had left off.

It was the gavel of Judge Randolph Jordan that brought them back to the grim realities of justice, transferred the courtroom from the scene of a dramatic confession to a crowded place, filled with chairs, tables and benches, peopled by puppets who were mechanically doing the bidding of justice.

"The Court," announced Judge Jordan, "will dismiss the case against Fay Allison. The Court will order Shirley Tanner into custody and the Court will suggest to the Prosecutor that a complaint be issued for Anita Bonsal, upon such charge as may seem expedient to the office of the District Attorney. And the Court does hereby extend its most sincere apologies to the defendant, Fay Allison. And the Court, personally, wishes to congratulate Mr. Perry Mason upon his brilliant handling of this matter."

There was a moment during which Judge Jordan's stern eyes rested upon the lipstick-smeared countenance of Dane Grover.

A faint smile twitched at the corners of His Honor's mouth.

The gavel banged once more.

"The Court," announced Judge Randolph Jordan, "is adjourned."

THE TREASURE HUNT

by Edgar Wallace

THERE IS A TRADITION in criminal circles that even the humblest of detective officers is a man of wealth and substance, and that his secret hoard was secured by thieving, bribery, and blackmail. It is the gossip of the fields, the quarries, the tailor's shop, the laundry, and the bakehouse of fifty county prisons and three convict establishments, that all highly placed detectives have by nefarious means laid up for themselves sufficient earthly treasures to make work a hobby and their official pittance the most inconsiderable portion of their incomes.

Since Mr. J. G. Reeder had for more than twenty years dealt exclusively with bank robbers and forgers, who are the aristocrats and capitalists of the underworld, legend credited him with country houses and immense secret reserves. Not that he would have a great deal of money in the bank. It was admitted that he was too clever to risk discovery by the authorities. No, it was hidden somewhere: it was the pet dream of hundreds of unlawful men that they would some day discover the hoard and live happily ever after. The one satisfactory aspect of his affluence (they all agreed) was that, being an old man—he was over 50—he couldn't take his money with him, for gold melts at a certain temperature and gilt-edged stock is seldom printed on asbestos paper.

The Director of Public Prosecutions was lunching one Saturday at his club with a judge of the King's Bench—Saturday being one of the two days in the week when a judge gets properly fed. And the conversation drifted to a certain Mr. J. G. Reeder, the chief of the Director's sleuths.

"He's capable," he confessed reluctantly, "but I hate his hat. It is the sort that So-and-so used to wear," he mentioned by name an eminent politician; "and I loathe his black frock-coat—people who see him coming into the office think he's a coroner's officer—but he's capable. His side whiskers are an abomination, and I have a feeling that, if I talked rough to him, he would burst into tears—a gentle soul. Almost too gentle for my kind of work. He apologises to the messenger every time he rings for him!"

The judge, who knew something about humanity, answered with a frosty smile.

"He sounds rather like a potential murderer to me," he said cynically.

Here, in his extravagance, he did Mr. J. G. Reeder an injustice, for Mr. Reeder was incapable of breaking the law—quite. At the same time there

Reprinted by permission of Brandt & Brandt
From *The Murder Book of J. G. Reeder*

were many people who formed an altogether wrong conception of J. G.'s harmlessness as an individual. And one of these was a certain Lew Kohl, who mixed bank-note printing with elementary burglary.

Threatened men live long, a trite saying but, like most things trite, true. In a score of cases, where Mr. J. G. Reeder had descended from the witness stand, he had met the baleful eye of the man in the dock and had listened with mild interest to divers promises as to what would happen to him in the near or the remote future. For he was a great authority on forged bank-notes and he had sent many men to penal servitude.

Mr. Reeder, that inoffensive man, had seen prisoners foaming at the mouth in their rage, he had seen them white and livid, he had heard their howling execrations and he had met these men after their release from prison and had found them amiable souls half ashamed and half amused at their nearly forgotten outbursts and horrific threats.

But when, in the early part of 1914, Lew Kohl was sentenced for ten years, he neither screamed his imprecations nor registered a vow to tear Mr. Reeder's heart, lungs, and important organs from his frail body.

Lew just smiled and his eyes caught the detective's for the space of a second—the forger's eyes were pale blue and speculative, and they held neither hate nor fury. Instead, they said in so many words:

"At the first opportunity I will kill you."

Mr. Reeder read the message and sighed heavily, for he disliked fuss of all kinds, and resented, in so far as he could resent anything, the injustice of being made personally responsible for the performance of a public duty.

Many years had passed, and considerable changes had occurred in Mr. Reeder's fortune. He had transferred from the specialised occupation of detecting the makers of forged bank-notes to the more general practice of the Public Prosecutor's bureau, but he never forgot Lew's smile.

The work in Whitehall was not heavy and it was very interesting. To Mr. Reeder came most of the anonymous letters which the Director received in shoals. In the main they were self-explanatory, and it required no particular intelligence to discover their motive. Jealousy, malice, plain mischief-making, and occasionally a sordid desire to benefit financially by the information which was conveyed, were behind the majority. But occasionally:

Sir James is going to marry his cousin, and it's not three months since his poor wife fell overboard from the Channel steamer crossing to Calais. There's something very fishy about this business. Miss Margaret doesn't like him, for she knows he's after her money. Why was I sent away to London that night? He doesn't like driving in the dark, either. It's strange that he wanted to drive that night when it was raining like blazes.

This particular letter was signed "A Friend." Justice has many such friends.

"Sir James" was Sir James Tithermite, who had been a director of some new public department during the war and had received a baronetcy for his services.

"Look it up," said the Director when he saw the letter. "I seem to remember that Lady Tithermite was drowned at sea."

"On the nineteenth of December last year," said Mr. Reeder solemnly. "She and Sir James were going to Monte Carlo, breaking their journey in Paris. Sir James, who has a house near Maidstone, drove to Dover, garaging the car at the Lord Wilson Hotel. The night was stormy and the ship had a rough crossing—they were halfway across when Sir James came to the purser and said that he had missed his wife. Her baggage was in the cabin, her passport, rail ticket, and hat, but the lady was not found, indeed was never seen again."

The Director nodded.

"I see, you've read up the case."

"I remember it." said Mr. Reeder. "The case is a favourite speculation of mine. Unfortunately, I see evil in everything and I have often thought how easy—but I fear that I take a warped view of life. It is a horrible handicap to possess a criminal mind."

The Director looked at him suspiciously. He was never quite sure whether Mr. Reeder was serious. At that moment, his sobriety was beyond challenge.

"A discharged chauffeur wrote that letter, of course," he began.

"Thomas Dayford, of 179 Barrack Street, Maidstone," concluded Mr. Reeder. "He is at present in the employ of the Kent Motor-Bus Company, and has three children, two of whom are twins and bonny little rascals."

The Chief laughed helplessly.

"I'll take it that you *know!*" he said. "See what there is behind the letter. Sir James is a big fellow in Kent, a Justice of the Peace, and he has powerful political influences. There is nothing in this letter, of course. Go warily, Reeder—if any kick comes back to this office, it goes on to you—intensified!"

Mr. Reeder's idea of walking warily was peculiarly his own. He travelled down to Maidstone the next morning, and, finding a bus that passed the lodge gates of Elfreda Manor, he journeyed comfortably and economically, his umbrella between his knees. He passed through the lodge gates, up a long and winding avenue of poplars, and presently came within sight of the grey manor house.

In a deep chair on the lawn he saw a girl sitting, a book on her knees, and evidently she saw him, for she rose as he crossed the lawn and came toward him eagerly.

"I'm Miss Margaret Letherby—are you from——?" She mentioned the name of a well-known firm of lawyers, and her face fell when Mr. Reeder regretfully disclaimed connection with those legal lights.

She was as pretty as a perfect complexion and a round, not too intellectual, face could, in combination, make her.

"I thought—do you wish to see Sir James? He is in the library. If you ring, one of the maids will take you to him."

Had Mr. Reeder been the sort of man who could be puzzled by anything, he would have been puzzled by the suggestion that any girl with money of her own should marry a man much older than herself against her own wishes. There was little mystery in the matter now. Miss Margaret would have married any strong-willed man who insisted.

"Even me," said Mr. Reeder to himself, with a certain melancholy pleasure.

There was no need to ring the bell. A tall, broad man in a golfing suit stood in the doorway. His fair hair was long and hung over his forehead in a thick flat strand; a heavy tawny moustache hid his mouth and swept down over a chin that was long and powerful.

"Well?" he asked aggressively.

"I'm from the Public Prosecutor's office," murmured Mr. Reeder. "I have had an anonymous letter."

His pale eyes did not leave the face of the other man.

"Come in," said Sir James gruffly.

As he closed the door he glanced quickly first to the girl and then to the poplar avenue.

"I'm expecting a fool of a lawyer," he said, as he flung open the door of what was evidently the library.

His voice was steady; not by a flicker of eyelash had he betrayed the slightest degree of anxiety when Reeder had told his mission.

"Well—what about this anonymous letter? You don't take much notice of that kind of trash, do you?"

Mr. Reeder deposited his umbrella and flat-crowned hat on a chair before he took a document from his pocket and handed it to the baronet, who frowned as he read. Was it Mr. Reeder's vivid imagination, or did the hard light in the eyes of Sir James soften as he read?

"This is a cock and bull story of somebody having seen my wife's jewellery on sale in Paris," he said. "There is nothing in it. I can account for every one of my poor wife's trinkets. I brought back the jewel case after that awful night. I don't recognize the handwriting: who is the lying scoundrel who wrote this?"

Mr. Reeder had never before been called a lying scoundrel, but he accepted the experience with admirable meekness.

"I thought it untrue," he said, shaking his head. "I followed the details of the case very thoroughly. You left here in the afternoon——"

"At night," said the other brusquely. He was not inclined to discuss the matter, but Mr. Reeder's appealing look was irresistible. "It is only eighty minutes' run to Dover. We got to the pier at eleven o'clock, about the same time as the boat train, and we went on board at once. I got my cabin key from the purser and put her ladyship and her baggage inside."

"Her ladyship was a good sailor?"

"Yes, a very good sailor; she was remarkably well that night. I left her in the cabin dozing, and went for a stroll on the deck——"

"Raining very heavily and a strong sea running," nodded Reeder, as though in agreement with something the other man had said.

"Yes—I'm a pretty good sailor—anyway, that story about my poor wife's jewels is utter nonsense. You can tell the Director that, with my compliments."

He opened the door for his visitor, and Mr. Reeder was some time replacing the letter and gathering his belongings.

"You have a beautiful place here, Sir James—a lovely place. An extensive estate?"

"Three thousand acres." This time he did not attempt to disguise his impatience. "Good afternoon."

Mr. Reeder went slowly down the drive, his remarkable memory at work.

He missed the bus, which he could easily have caught, and pursued an apparently aimless way along the winding road which marched with the boundaries of the baronet's property. A walk of a quarter of a mile brought him to a lane shooting off at right angles from the main road, and marking, he guessed, the southern boundary. At the corner stood an old stone lodge, on the inside of a forbidding iron gate. The lodge was in a pitiable state of neglect and disrepair. Tiles had been dislodged from the roof, the windows were grimy or broken, and the little garden was overrun with docks and thistles. Beyond the gate was a narrow, weed-covered drive that trailed out of sight into a distant plantation.

Hearing the clang of a letter-box closing, he turned to see a postman mounting his bicycle.

"What place is this?" asked Mr. Reeder, arresting the postman's departure.

"South Lodge—Sir James Tithermite's property. It's never used now. Hasn't been used for years—I don't know why; it's a short cut if they happen to be coming this way."

Mr. Reeder walked with him toward the village, and he was a skilful pumper of wells, however dry; and the postman was not dry by any means.

"Yes, poor lady! She was very frail—one of those sort of invalids that last out many a healthy man."

Mr. Reeder put a question at random and scored most unexpectedly.

"Yes, her ladyship was a bad sailor. I know because every time she went abroad she used to get a bottle of that stuff people take for seasickness. I've delivered many a bottle till Raikes, the chemist, stocked it—'Pickers' Travellers' Friend,' that's what it was called. Mr. Raikes was only saying to me the other day that he'd got half a dozen bottles on hand, and he didn't know what to do with them. Nobody in Climbury ever goes to sea."

Mr. Reeder went on to the village and idled his precious time in most unlikely places. At the chemist's, at the blacksmith shop, at the modest building yard. He caught the last bus back to Maidstone, and by great good luck the last train to London.

And, in his vague way, he answered the Director's query the next day with: "Yes, I saw Sir James: a very interesting man."

This was on the Friday. All day Saturday he was busy. The Sabbath brought him a new interest.

On this bright Sunday morning, Mr. Reeder, attired in a flowered dressing-gown, his feet encased in black velvet slippers, stood at the window of his house in Brockley Road and surveyed the deserted thoroughfare. The bell of a local church, which was accounted high, had rung for early Mass, and there was nothing living in sight except a black cat that lay asleep in a patch of sunlight on the top step of the house opposite. The hour was 7.30, and Mr. Reeder had been at his desk since six, working by artificial light, the month being October toward the close.

From the half-moon of the window bay he regarded a section of the Lewisham High Road and as much of Tanners Hill as can be seen before it dips past the railway bridge into sheer Deptford.

Returning to his table, he opened a carton of the cheapest cigarettes and, lighting one, puffed in an amateurish fashion. He smoked cigarettes rather like a woman who detests them but feels that it is the correct thing to do.

"Dear me," said Mr. Reeder feebly.

He was back at the window, and he had seen a man turn out of Lewisham High Road. He had crossed the road and was coming straight to Daffodil House—which frolicsome name appeared on the door-posts of Mr. Reeder's residence. A tall, straight man, with a sombre brown face, he came to the front gate, passed through and beyond the watcher's range of vision.

"Dear me!" said Mr. Reeder, as he heard the tinkle of a bell.

A few minutes later his housekeeper tapped on the door.

"Will you see Mr. Kohl, sir?" she asked.

Mr. J. G. Reeder nodded.

Lew Kohl walked into the room to find a middle-aged man in a flamboyant dressing-gown sitting at his desk, a pair of pince-nez set crookedly on his nose.

"Good-morning, Kohl."

Lew Kohl looked at the man who had sent him to seven and a half years of hell, and the corners of his thin lips curled.

"'Morning, Mr. Reeder." His eyes flashed across the almost bare surface of the writing-desk on which Reeder's hands were lightly clasped. "You didn't expect to see me, I guess?"

"Not so early," said Reeder in his hushed voice, "but I should have remembered that early rising is one of the good habits which are inculcated by penal servitude."

He said this in the manner of one bestowing praise for good conduct.

"I suppose you've got a pretty good idea of why I have come, eh? I'm a bad forgetter, Reeder, and a man in Dartmoor has time to think."

The older man lifted his sandy eyebrows, the steel-rimmed glasses on his nose slipped further askew.

"That phrase seems familiar," he said, and the eyebrows lowered in a frown. "Now let me think—it was in a melodrama, of course, but was it 'Souls in Harness' or 'The Marriage Vow'?"

He appeared genuinely anxious for assistance in solving this problem.

"This is going to be a different kind of play," said the long-faced Lew through his teeth. "I'm going to get you, Reeder—you can go along and tell your boss, the Public Prosecutor. But I'll get you sweet! There will be no evidence to swing me. And I'll get that nice little stocking of yours, Reeder!"

The legend of Reeder's fortune was accepted even by so intelligent a man as Kohl.

"You'll get my stocking! Dear me, I shall have to go barefooted," said Mr. Reeder, with a faint show of humour.

"You know what I mean—think that over. Some hour and day you'll go out, and all Scotland Yard won't catch me for the killing! I've thought that out——"

"One has time to think in Dartmoor," murmured Mr. J. G. Reeder encouragingly. "You're becoming one of the world's thinkers, Kohl. Do you know Rodin's masterpiece—a beautiful statue throbbing with life——"

"That's all." Lew Kohl rose, the smile still trembling at the corner of his mouth. "Maybe you'll turn this over in your mind, and in a day or two you won't be feeling so gay."

Reeder's face was pathetic in its sadness. His untidy sandy-grey hair seemed to be standing on end; the large ears, that stood out at right angles to his face, gave the illusion of quivering movement.

Lew Kohl's hand was on the door-knob.

"*Womp!*"

It was the sound of a dull weight striking a board; something winged past his cheek, before his eyes a deep hole showed in the wall, and his face was stung by flying grains of plaster. He spun round with a whine of rage.

Mr. Reeder had a long-barrelled Browning in his hand, with a barrel-shaped silencer over the muzzle, and he was staring at the weapon open-mouthed.

"Now how on earth did that happen?" he asked in wonder.

Lew Kohl stood trembling with rage and fear, his face yellow-white.

"You—you swine!" he breathed. "You tried to shoot me!"

Mr. Reeder stared at him over his glasses.

"Good gracious—you think that? Still thinking of killing me, Kohl?"

Kohl tried to speak but found no words, and, flinging open the door, he strode down the stairs and through the front entrance. His foot was on the first step when something came hurtling past him and crashed to fragments at his feet. It was a large stone vase that had decorated the window-sill of Mr. Reeder's bedroom. Leaping over the débris of stone and flower mould, he glared up into the surprised face of Mr. J. G. Reeder.

"I'll get you!" he spluttered.

"I hope you're not hurt?" asked the man at the window in a tone of concern. "These things happen. Some day and some hour——"

As Lew Kohl strode down the street, the detective was still talking.

Mr. Stan Bride was at his morning ablutions when his friend and sometime prison associate came into the little room that overlooked Fitzroy Square.

Stan Bride, who bore no resemblance to anything virginal, being a stout and stumpy man with a huge red face and many chins, stopped in the act of drying himself and gazed over the edge of the towel.

"What's the matter with you?" he asked sharply. "You look as if you'd been chased by a busy. What did you go out so early for?"

Lew told him, and the jovial countenance of his roommate grew longer and longer.

"Your poor fish!" he hissed. "To go after Reeder with that stuff! Don't you think he was waiting for you? Do you suppose he didn't know the very moment you left the Moor?"

"I've scared him, anyway," said the other, and Mr. Bride laughed.

"Good scout!" he sneered. "Scare that old person!" (He did not say "person.") "If he's as white as you, he *is* scared! But he's not. Of course he shot past you—if he'd wanted to shoot you, you'd have been stiff by now. But he didn't. Thinker, eh—he's given you somep'n' to think about."

"Where that gun came from I don't——"

There was a knock at the door and the two men exchanged glances.

"Who's there?" asked Bride, and a familiar voice answered.

"It's that busy from the Yard," whispered Bride, and opened the door. The "busy" was Sergeant Allford, C.I.D., an affable and portly man and a detective of some promise.

" 'Morning, boys—not been to church, Stan?"

Stan grinned politely.

"How's trade, Lew?"

"Not so bad." The forger was alert, suspicious.

"Come to see you about a gun—got an idea you're carrying one, Lew—Colt automatic R.7/94318. That's not right, Lew—guns don't belong to this country."

"I've got no gun," said Lew sullenly.

Bride had suddenly become an old man, for he also was a convict on licence, and the discovery might send him back to serve his unfinished sentence.

"Will you come take a little walk to the station, or will you let me go over you?"

"Go over me," said Lew, and put out his arms stiffly whilst the detective rubbed him down.

"I'll have a look round," said the detective, and his "look round" was very thorough.

"Must have been mistaken," said Sergeant Allford. And then, suddenly: "Was that what you chucked into the river as you were walking along the Embankment?"

Lew started. It was the first intimation he had received that he had been "tailed" that morning.

Bride waited till the detective was visible from the window crossing Fitzroy Square; then he turned in a fury on his companion.

"Clever, ain't you! That old hound knew you had a gun—knew the number. And if Allford had found it you'd have been 'dragged' and me too!"

"I threw it in the river," said Lew sulkily.

"Brains—not many but some!" said Bride, breathing heavily. "You cut out Reeder—he's hell and poison, and if you don't know it you're deaf! Scared him? You big stiff! He'd cut your throat and write a hymn about it."

"I didn't know they were tailing me," growled Kohl; "but I'll get him! And his money too."

"Get him from another lodging," said Bride curtly. "A crook I don't mind, being one; a murderer I don't mind, but a talking jackass makes me sick. Get his stuff if you can—I'll bet it's all invested in real estate, and you can't lift houses—but don't talk about it. I like you, Lew, up to a point; you're miles before the point and out of sight. I don't like Reeder—I don't like snakes, but I keep away from the Zoo."

So Lew Kohl went into new diggings on the top floor of an Italian's house in Dean Street, and here he had leisure and inclination to brood upon his grievances and to plan afresh the destruction of his enemy. And new plans were needed, for the schemes which had seemed so watertight in the quietude of a Devonshire cell showed daylight through many crevices.

Lew's homicidal urge had undergone considerable modification. He had been experimented upon by a very clever psychologist—though he never regarded Mr. Reeder in this light, and, indeed, had the vaguest idea as to what the word meant. But there were other ways of hurting Reeder, and his mind fell constantly back to the dream of discovering the peccant detective's hidden treasure.

It was nearly a week later that Mr. Reeder invited himself into the Director's private sanctum, and that great official listened spellbound while his subordinate offered his outrageous theory about Sir James Tithermite and his dead wife. When Mr. Reeder had finished, the Director pushed back his chair from the table.

"My dear man," he said, a little irritably, "I can't possibly give a warrant on the strength of your surmises—not even a search warrant. The story is so fantastic, so incredible, that it would be more at home in the pages of a sensational story than in a Public Prosecutor's report."

"It was a wild night, and yet Lady Tithermite was not ill," suggested the detective gently. "That is a fact to remember, sir."

The Director shook his head.

"I can't do it—not on the evidence," he said. "I should raise a storm that'd swing me into Whitehall. Can't you do anything—unofficially?"

Mr. Reeder shook his head.

"My presence in the neighbourhood has been remarked," he said primly. "I think it would be impossible to—er—cover up my traces. And yet I have located the place, and could tell you within a few inches——"

Again the Director shook his head.

"No, Reeder," he said quietly, "the whole thing is sheer deduction on your part. Oh, yes, I know you have a criminal mind—I think you have told me that before. And that is a good reason why I should not issue a warrant. You're simply crediting this unfortunate man with your ingenuity. Nothing doing!"

Mr. Reeder sighed and went back to his bureau, not entirely despondent, for there had intruded a new element into his investigations.

Mr. Reeder had been to Maidstone several times during the week, and he had not gone alone; though seemingly unconscious of the fact that he had developed a shadow, for he had seen Lew Kohl on several occasions, and had spent an uncomfortable few minutes wondering whether his experiment had failed.

On the second occasion an idea had developed in the detective's mind, and if he were a laughing man he would have chuckled aloud when he slipped out of Maidstone station one evening and, in the act of hiring a cab, had seen Lew Kohl negotiating for another.

Mr. Bride was engaged in the tedious but necessary practice of so cutting a pack of cards that the ace of diamonds remained at the bottom, when his former co-lodger burst in upon him, and there was a light of triumph in Lew's cold eye which brought Mr. Bride's heart to his boots.

"I've got him!" said Lew.

Bride put aside the cards and stood up.

"Got who?" he asked coldly. "And if it's killing, you needn't answer, but get out!"

"There's no killing."

Lew sat down squarely at the table, his hands in his pockets, a real smile on his face.

"I've been trailing Reeder for a week, and that fellow wants some trailing!"

"Well?" asked the other, when he paused dramatically.

"I've found his stocking!"

Bride scratched his chin, and was half convinced.

"You have?"

Lew nodded.

"He's been going to Maidstone a lot lately, and driving to a little village about five miles out. There I always lost him. But the other night, when he came back to the station to catch the last train, he slipped into the waiting room and I found a place where I could watch him. What do you think he did?"

Mr. Bride hazarded no suggestion.

"He opened his bag," said Lew impressively, "and took out a wad of notes as thick as that! He'd been drawing on his bank! I trailed him up to London. There's a restaurant on the station and he went in to get a cup of coffee, with me keeping well out of his sight. As he came out of the restaurant he took out his handkerchief and wiped his mouth. He didn't see the little book that dropped, but I did. I was scared sick that somebody else would see it, or that he'd wait long enough to find it himself. But he went out of the station and I got that book before you could say 'knife.' Look!"

It was a well-worn little notebook, covered with faded red morocco. Bride put out his hand to take it.

"Wait a bit," said Lew. "Are you in this with me fifty-fifty, because I want some help."

Bride hesitated.

"If it's just plain thieving, I'm with you," he said.

"Plain thieving—and sweet," said Lew exultantly, and pushed the book across the table.

For the greater part of the night they sat together talking in low tones, discussing impartially the methodical bookkeeping of Mr. J. G. Reeder and his exceeding dishonesty.

The Monday night was wet. A storm blew up from the southwest, and the air was filled with falling leaves as Lew and his companion footed the five miles which separated them from the village. Neither carried any impedimenta that was visible, yet under Lew's waterproof coat was a kit of tools of singular ingenuity, and Mr. Bride's coat pockets were weighted down with the sections of a powerful jemmy.

They met nobody in their walk, and the church bell was striking eleven when Lew gripped the bars of the South Lodge gates, pulled himself up to the top and dropped lightly on the other side. He was followed by Mr. Bride, who, in spite of his bulk, was a singularly agile man. The ruined lodge showed in the darkness, and they passed through the creaking gates to the door and Lew flashed his lantern upon the keyhole before he began manipulation with the implements which he had taken from his kit.

The door was opened in ten minutes and a few seconds later they stood in a low-roofed little room, the principal feature of which was a deep, grateless fireplace. Lew took off his mackintosh and stretched it over the window before he spread the light in his lamp, and, kneeling down, brushed the débris from the hearth, examining the joints of the big stone carefully.

"This work's been botched," he said. "Anybody could see that."

He put the claw of the jemmy into a crack and levered up the stone, and it moved slightly. Stopping only to dig a deeper crevice with a chisel and hammer he thrust the claw of the jemmy farther down. The stone came up above the edge of the floor and Bride slipped the chisel underneath.

"Now together," grunted Lew.

They got their fingers beneath the hearthstone and with one heave hinged it up. Lew picked up the lamp and, kneeling down, flashed a light into the dark cavity. And then:

"Oh, my God!" he shrieked.

A second later two terrified men rushed from the house into the drive. And a miracle had happened, for the gates were open and a dark figure stood squarely before them.

"Put up your hands, Kohl!" said a voice, and, hateful as it was to Lew Kohl, he could have fallen on the neck of Mr. Reeder.

At twelve o'clock that night Sir James Tithermite was discussing matters with his bride-to-be: the stupidity of her lawyer, who wished to safeguard her fortune, and his own cleverness and foresight in securing complete freedom of action for the girl who was to be his wife.

"These blackguards think of nothing but their fees," he began, when his footman came in unannounced, and behind him the Chief Constable of the county and a man he remembered seeing before.

"Sir James Tithermite?" said the Chief Constable unnecessarily, for he knew Sir James very well.

"Yes, Colonel, what is it?" asked the baronet, his face twitching.

"I am taking you into custody on a charge of wilfully murdering your wife, Eleanor Mary Tithermite."

*   *   *   *   *

"The whole thing turned upon the question as to whether Lady Tithermite was a good or a bad sailor," explained J. G. Reeder to his chief. "If she were a bad sailor, it was unlikely that she would be on the ship, even for five minutes, without calling for the stewardess. The stewardess did not see her ladyship, nor did anybody on board, for the simple reason that she was not on board! She was murdered within the grounds of the Manor; her body was buried beneath the hearthstone of the old lodge, and Sir James continued his journey by car to Dover, handing over his packages to a porter and telling him to take them to his cabin before he returned to put the car into the hotel garage. He had timed his arrival so that he passed on board with a crowd of passengers from the boat train, and nobody knew whether he was alone or whether he was accompanied, and, for the matter of that, nobody cared. The purser gave him his key, and he put the baggage, including his wife's hat, into the cabin, paid the porter and dismissed him. Officially, Lady Tithermite was on board, for he surrendered her ticket to the collector and received her landing voucher. And then he discovered she had disappeared. The ship was searched, but of course the unfortunate lady was not found. As I remarked before—"

"You have a criminal mind," said the Director good-humouredly. "Go on, Reeder."

"Having this queer and objectionable trait, I saw how very simple a matter it was to give the illusion that the lady was on board, and I decided that, if the murder was committed, it must have been within a few miles of the house. And then the local builder told me that he had given Sir James a little lesson in the art of mixing mortar. And the local blacksmith told me that the gate had been damaged, presumably by Sir James's car—I had seen the broken rods and all I wanted to know was when the repairs were effected. That she was beneath the hearth in the lodge I was certain. Without a search warrant it was impossible to prove or disprove my theory, and I myself could not conduct a private investigation without risking the reputation of our department—if I may say 'our'," he said apologetically.

The Director was thoughtful.

"Of course, you induced this man Kohl to dig up the hearth by pretending you had money buried there. I presume you revealed that fact in your notebook? But why on earth did he imagine that you had a hidden treasure?"

Mr. Reeder smiled sadly.

"The criminal mind is a peculiar thing," he said, with a sigh. "It harbours illusions and fairy stories. Fortunately, I understand that mind. As I have often said . . ."

MAIGRET'S CHRISTMAS

by Georges Simenon

Translated by Lawrence G. Blochman

THE ROUTINE never varied. When Maigret went to bed he must have muttered his usual, "Tomorrow morning I shall sleep late." And Mme. Maigret, who over the years should have learned to pay no attention to such casual phrases, had taken him at his word this Christmas day.

It was not quite daylight when he heard her stirring cautiously. He forced himself to breathe regularly and deeply as though he were still asleep. It was like a game. She inched toward the edge of the bed with animal stealth, pausing after each movement to make sure she had not awakened him. He waited anxiously for the inevitable finale, the moment when the bedspring, relieved of her weight, would spring back into place with a faint sigh.

She picked up her clothing from the chair and turned the knob of the bathroom door so slowly that it seemed to take an eternity. It was not until she had reached the distant fastness of the kitchen that she resumed her normal movements.

Maigret had fallen asleep again. Not deeply, nor for long. Long enough, however, for a confused and disturbing dream. Waking, he could not remember what it was, but he knew it was disturbing because he still felt vaguely uneasy.

The crack between the window drapes which never quite closed became a strip of pale, hard daylight. He waited a while longer, lying on his back with his eyes open, savoring the fragrance of fresh coffee. Then he heard the apartment door open and close, and he knew that Mme. Maigret was hurrying downstairs to buy him hot *croissants* from the bakery at the corner of the Rue Amelot.

He never ate in the morning. His breakfast consisted of black coffee. But his wife clung to her ritual: on Sundays and holidays he was supposed to lie in bed until mid-morning while she went out for *croissants*.

He got up, stepped into his slippers, put on his dressing gown, and drew the curtains. He knew he was doing wrong. His wife would be heart-broken. But while he was willing to make almost any sacrifice to please her, he simply could not stay in bed longer than he felt like it.

It was not snowing. It was nonsense, of course, for a man past 50 to be disappointed because there was no snow on Christmas morning; but then middle-aged people never have as much sense as young folks sometimes imagine.

Reprinted by permission of the author
Copyright 1953 by Mercury Publications, Inc.

A dirty, turbid sky hung low over the rooftops. The Boulevard Richard-Lenoir was completely deserted. The words *Fils et Cie.*, *Bonded Warehouses* on the sign above the porte-cochére across the street stood out as black as mourning crêpe. The *F*, for some strange reason, seemed particularly dismal.

He heard his wife moving about in the kitchen again. She came into the dining room on tiptoe, as though he were still asleep instead of looking out the window. He glanced at his watch on the night table. It was only ten past 8.

The night before the Maigrets had gone to the theatre. They would have loved dropping in for a snack at some restaurant, like everyone else on Christmas Eve, but all tables were reserved for *Réveillon* supper. So they had walked home arm in arm, getting in a few minutes before midnight. Thus they hadn't long to wait before exchanging presents.

He got a pipe, as usual. Her present was an electric coffee pot, the latest model that she had wanted so much, and, not to break with tradition, a dozen finely embroidered handkerchiefs.

Still looking out the window, Maigret absently filled his new pipe. The shutters were still closed on some of the windows across the boulevard. Not many people were up. Here and there a light burned in a window, probably left by children who had leaped out of bed at the crack of dawn to rush for their presents under the Christmas tree.

In the quiet Maigret apartment the morning promised to be a lazy one for just the two of them. Maigret would loiter in his dressing gown until quite late. He would not even shave. He would dawdle in the kitchen, talking to his wife while she put the lunch on the stove. Just the two of them.

He wasn't sad exactly, but his dream—which he couldn't remember—had left him jumpy. Or perhaps it wasn't his dream. Perhaps it was Christmas. He had to be extra-careful on Christmas Day, careful of his words, the way Mme. Maigret had been careful of her movements in getting out of bed. Her nerves, too, were especially sensitive on Christmas.

Oh, well, why think of all that? He would just be careful to say nothing untoward. He would be careful not to look out the window when the neighborhood children began to appear on the sidewalks with their Christmas toys.

All the houses in the street had children. Or almost all. The street would soon echo to the shrill blast of toy horns, the roll of toy drums, and the crack of toy pistols. The little girls were probably already cradling their new dolls.

A few years ago he had proposed more or less at random: "Why don't we take a little trip for Christmas?"

"Where?" she had replied with her infallible common sense.

Where, indeed? Whom would they visit? They had no relatives except her sister who lived too far away. And why spend Christmas in some second-rate country inn, or at a hotel in some strange town?

Oh, well, he'd feel better after he had his coffee. He was never at his best until he'd drunk his first cup of coffee and lit his first pipe.

Just as he was reaching for the knob, the door opened noiselessly and Mme. Maigret appeared carrying a tray. She looked at the empty bed, then turned her disappointed eyes upon her husband. She was on the verge of tears.

"You got up!" She looked as though she had been up for hours herself, every hair in place, a picture of neatness in her crisp clean apron. "And I was so happy about serving your breakfast in bed."

He had tried a hundred times, as subtly as he could, to make her understand that he didn't like eating breakfast in bed. It made him uncomfortable. It made him feel like an invalid or a senile old gaffer. But for Mme. Maigret breakfast in bed was the symbol of leisure and luxury, the ideal way to start Sunday or a holiday.

"Don't you want to go back to bed?"

No, he did not. Decidedly not. He hadn't the courage.

"Then come to breakfast in the kitchen. And Merry Christmas."

"Merry Christmas! . . . You're not angry?"

They were in the dining room. He surveyed the silver tray on a corner of the table, the steaming cup of coffee, the golden-brown *croissants*. He put down his pipe and ate a *croissant* to please his wife, but he remained standing, looking out the window.

"It's snowing."

It wasn't real snow. It was a fine white dust sifting down from the sky, but it reminded Maigret that when he was a small boy he used to stick out his tongue to lick up a few of the tiny flakes.

His gaze focused on the entrance to the building across the street, next door to the warehouse. Two women had just come out, both bareheaded. One of them, a blonde of about 30, had thrown a coat over her shoulders without stopping to slip her arms into the sleeves. The other, a brunette, older and thinner, was hugging a shawl.

The blonde seemed to hesitate, ready to turn back. Her slim little companion was insistent and Maigret had the impression that she was pointing up toward his window. The appearance of the concierge in the doorway behind them seemed to tip the scales in favor of the little brunette. The blonde looked back apprehensively, then crossed the street.

"What are you looking at?"

"Nothing . . . two women. . . ."

"What are they doing?"

"I think they're coming here."

The two women had stopped in the middle of the street and were looking up in the direction of the Maigret apartment.

"I hope they're not coming here to bother you on Christmas Day. My housework's not even done." Nobody would have guessed it. There wasn't a speck of dust on any of the polished furniture. "Are you sure they're coming here?"

"We'll soon find out."

To be on the safe side, he went to comb his hair, brush his teeth, and splash a little water on his face. He was still in his room, relighting his pipe, when he heard the doorbell. Mme. Maigret was evidently putting up a strong hedgehog defense, for it was some time before she came for him.

"They insist on speaking to you," she whispered. "They claim it's very important and they need advice. I know one of them."

"Which one?"

"The skinny little one, Mlle. Doncoeur. She lives across the street on the same floor as ours. She's a very nice person and she does embroidery for a firm in the Faubourg Saint-Honoré. I sometimes wonder if she isn't in love with you."

"Why?"

"Because she works near the window, and when you leave the house in the morning she sometimes gets up to watch you go down the street."

"How old is she?"

"Forty-five to fifty. Aren't you getting dressed?"

Doesn't a man have the right to lounge in his dressing gown, even if people come to bother him at 8:30 on Christmas morning? Well, he'd compromise. He'd put his trousers on underneath the robe.

The two women were standing when he walked into the dining room.

"Excuse me, mesdames . . ."

Perhaps Mme. Maigret was right. Mlle. Doncoeur did not blush; she paled, smiled, lost her smile, smiled again. She opened her mouth to speak but said nothing.

The blonde, on the other hand, was perfectly composed. She said with a touch of humor: "Coming here wasn't my idea."

"Would you sit down, please?"

Maigret noticed that the blonde was wearing a house dress under her coat and that her legs were bare. Mlle. Doncoeur was dressed as though for church.

"You perhaps wonder at our boldness in coming to you like this," Mlle. Doncoeur said finally, choosing her words carefully. "Like everyone in the neighborhood, we are honored to have such a distinguished neighbor. . . ." She paused, blushed, and stared at the tray. "We're keeping you from your breakfast."

"I've finished. I'm at your service."

"Something happened in our building last night, or rather this morning, which was so unusual that I felt it was our duty to speak to you about it immediately. Madame Martin did not want to disturb you, but I told her—"

"You also live across the street, Madame Martin?"

"Yes, Monsieur." Madame Martin was obviously unhappy at being forced to take this step. Mlle. Doncoeur, however, was now fully wound up.

"We live on the same floor, just across from your windows." She blushed again, as if she were making a confession. "Monsieur Martin is often out of town, which is natural enough since he is a traveling salesman. For the past two months their little girl has been in bed, as a result of a silly accident. . . ."

Maigret turned politely to the blonde. "You have a daughter?"

"Well, not a daughter exactly. She's our niece. Her mother died two years ago and she's been living with us ever since. The girl broke her leg on the stairs. She should have been up and about after six weeks, but there were complications."

"Your husband is on the road at present?"

"He should be in Bergerac."

"I'm listening, Mlle. Doncoeur."

Mme. Maigret had detoured through the bathroom to regain the kitchen. The clatter of pots and pans had resumed. Maigret stared through the window at the leaden sky.

"I got up early this morning as usual," said Mlle. Doncoeur, "to go to first mass."

"And you did go to church?"

"Yes. I stayed for three masses. I got home about 7:30 and prepared my breakfast. You may have seen the light in my window."

Maigret's gesture indicated he had not been watching.

"I was in a hurry to take a few goodies to Colette. It's very sad for a child to spend Christmas in bed. Colette is Madame Martin's niece."

"How old is she?"

"Seven. Isn't that right, Madame Martin?"

"She'll be seven in January."

"So at 8 o'clock I knocked at the door of their apartment—"

"I wasn't up," the blonde interrupted. "I sometimes sleep rather late."

"As I was saying, I knocked. Madame Martin kept me waiting for a moment while she slipped on her négligée. I had my arms full, and I asked if I could take my presents in to Colette."

Maigret noted that the blonde was making a mental inventory of the apartment, stopping occasionally to dart a sharp, suspicious glance in his direction.

"We opened the door to her room together. . . ."

"The child has a room of her own?"

"Yes. There are two bedrooms in the apartment, a dressing room, a kitchen, and a dining room. But I must tell you— No, I'm getting ahead of myself. We had just opened the door and since the room was dark, Madame Martin had switched on the light . . ."

"Colette was awake?"

"Yes. It was easy to see she'd been awake for some time, waiting. You know how children are on Christmas morning. If she could use her legs, she would certainly have got up long since to see what Father Christmas had brought her. Perhaps another child would have called out. But Colette is already a little lady. She's much older than her age. She thinks a lot."

Now Madame Martin was looking out the window. Maigret tried to guess which apartment was hers. It must be the last one to the right, the one with the two lighted windows.

"I wished her a Merry Christmas," Mlle. Doncoeur continued. "I said to her, and these were my exact words, 'Darling, look what Father Christmas left in my apartment for you.' "

Madame Martin was clasping and unclasping her fingers.

"And do you know what she answered me, without even looking to see what I'd brought? They were only trifles, anyhow. She said, 'I saw him.'

" 'Whom did you see?'

" 'Father Christmas.'

" 'When did you see him?' I asked. 'Where?'

" 'Right here, last night. He came to my room.'

"That's exactly what she said, isn't it, Madame Martin? With any other child, we would have smiled. But as I told you, Colette is already a little lady. She doesn't joke. I said, 'How could you see him, since it was dark?'

" 'He had a light.'

" 'You mean he turned on the electricity?'

" 'No. He had a flashlight. Look, Mama Loraine.'

"I must tell you that the little girl calls Madame Martin 'Mama,' which is natural enough, since her own mother is dead and Madame Martin has been taking her place."

The monologue had become a confused buzzing in Maigret's ears. He had not drunk his second cup of coffee and his pipe had gone out. He asked without conviction: "Did she really see someone?"

"Yes, Monsieur l'Inspecteur. And that's why I insisted that Madame Martin come to speak to you. Colette did see someone and she proved it to us. With a sly little smile she threw back the bedsheet and showed us a magnificent doll . . . a beautiful big doll she was cuddling and which I swear was not in the house yesterday."

"You didn't give your niece a doll, Madame Martin?"

"I was going to give her one, but mine was not nearly as nice. I got it yesterday afternoon at the Galeries, and I was holding it behind me this morning when we came into her room."

"In other words, someone *did* come into your apartment last night?"

"That's not all," said Mlle. Doncoeur quickly; she was not to be stopped. "Colette never tells lies. She's not a child who imagines things. And when we questioned her, she said the man was certainly Father Christmas because he wore a white beard and a bright red coat."

"At what time did she wake up?"

"She doesn't know—sometime during the night. She opened her eyes because she thought she saw a light. And there was a light, shining on the floor near the fireplace."

"I can't understand it," sighed Madame Martin. "Unless my husband has some explanation . . ."

But Mlle. Doncoeur was not to be diverted from her story. It was obvious that she was the one who had questioned the child, just as she was the one who had thought of Maigret. She resumed:

"Colette said, 'Father Christmas was squatting on the floor, and he was bending over, as though he were working at something.'"

"She wasn't frightened?"

"No. She just watched him. This morning she told us he was busy making a hole in the floor. She thought he wanted to go through the floor to visit the people downstairs—that's the Delormes who have a little boy of three—because the chimney was too narrow. The man must have sensed she was watching him, because he got up, came over to the bed, and gave Colette the big doll. Then he put his finger to his lips."

"Did she see him leave?"

"Yes."

"Through the floor?"

"No, by the door."

"Into what room does this door open?"

"Directly into the outside hall. There is another door that opens into the apartment, but the hall door is like a private entrance because the room used to be rented separately."

"Wasn't the door locked?"

"Of course," Madame Martin intervened. "I wouldn't let the child sleep in a room that wasn't locked from the outside."

"Then the door was forced?"

"Probably. I don't know. Mlle. Doncoeur immediately suggested we come to see you."

"Did you find a hole in the floor?"

Madame Martin shrugged wearily, but Mlle. Doncoeur answered for her.

"Not a hole exactly, but you could see that the floor boards had been moved."

"Tell me, Madame Martin, have you any idea what might have been hidden under the flooring?"

"No, Monsieur."

"How long have you lived in this apartment?"

"Since my marriage, five years ago."

"And this room was part of the apartment then?"

"Yes."

"You know who lived there before you?"

"My husband. He's 38. He was 33 when we were married, and he had his own furniture then. He liked to have his own home to come back to when he returned to Paris from the road."

"Do you think he might have wanted to surprise Colette?"

"He is six or seven hundred kilometers from here."

"Where did you say?"

"In Bergerac. His itinerary is planned in advance and he rarely deviates from his schedule."

"For what firm does he travel?"

"He covers the central and southwest territory for Zenith watches. It's an important line, as you probably know. He has a very good job."

"There isn't a finer man on earth!" exclaimed Mlle. Doncoeur. She blushed, then added, "Except you, Monsieur l'Inspecteur."

"As I understand it then, someone got into your apartment last night disguised as Father Christmas."

"According to the little girl."

"Didn't you hear anything? Is your room far from the little girl's?"

"There's the dining room between us."

"Don't you leave the connecting doors open at night?"

"It isn't necessary. Colette is not afraid, and as a rule she never wakes up. If she wants anything, she has a little bell on her night table."

"Did you go out last night?"

"I did not, Monsieur l'Inspecteur." Madame Martin was annoyed.

"Did you receive visitors?"

"I do not receive visitors while my husband is away."

Maigret glanced at Mlle. Doncoeur whose expression did not change. So Madame Martin was telling the truth.

"Did you go to bed late?"

"I read until midnight. As soon as the radio played *Minuit, Chrétiens,* I went to bed."

"And you heard nothing unusual?"

"Nothing."

"Have you asked the concierge if she clicked the latch to let in any strangers last night?"

"I asked her," Mlle. Doncoeur volunteered. "She says she didn't."

"And you found nothing missing from your apartment this morning, Madame Martin? Nothing disturbed in the dining room?"

"No."

"Who is with the little girl now?"

"No one. She's used to staying alone. I can't be at home all day. I have marketing to do, errands to run. . . ."

"I understand. You told me Colette is an orphan?"

"Her mother is dead."

"So her father is living. Where is he?"

"Her father's name is Paul Martin. He's my husband's brother. As to telling you where he is—" Madame Martin sketched a vague gesture.

"When did you see him last?"

"About a month ago. A little longer. It was around All Saints' Day. He was finishing a novena."

"I beg your pardon?"

"I may as well tell you everything at once," said Madame Martin with a faint smile, "since we seem to be washing our family linen." She glanced reproachfully at Mlle. Doncoeur. "My brother-in-law, especially since he lost his wife, is not quite respectable."

"What do you mean exactly?"

"He drinks. He always drank a little, but he never used to get into trouble. He had a good job with a furniture store in the Faubourg Saint-Antoine. But since the accident . . ."

"The accident to his daughter?"

"No, to his wife. He borrowed a car from a friend one Sunday about three years ago and took his wife and little girl to the country. They had lunch at a roadside inn near Mantes-la-Jolie and he drank too much white wine. He sang most of the way back to Paris—until he ran into something near the Bougival bridge. His wife was killed instantly. He cracked his own skull and it's a miracle he's still alive. Colette escaped without a scratch. Paul hasn't been a man since then. We've practically adopted the little girl. He comes to see her occasionally when he's sober. Then he starts over again. . . ."

"Do you know where he lives?"

Another vague gesture. "Everywhere. We've seen him loitering around the Bastille like a beggar. Sometimes he sells papers in the street. I can speak freely in front of Mlle. Doncoeur because unfortunately the whole house knows about him."

"Don't you think he might have dressed up as Father Christmas to call on his daughter?"

"That's what I told Mlle. Doncoeur, but she insisted on coming to see you anyhow."

"Because I see no reason for him to take up the flooring," said Mlle. Doncoeur acidly.

"Or perhaps your husband returned to Paris unexpectedly. . . ."

"It's certainly something of the sort. I'm not at all disturbed. But Mlle. Doncoeur—"

Decidedly Madame Martin had not crossed the boulevard light-heartedly. "Do you know where your husband might be staying in Bergerac?"

"Yes. At the Hotel de Bordeaux."

"You hadn't thought of telephoning him?"

"We have no phone. There's only one in the house—the people on the second floor, and they hate to be disturbed."

"Would you object to my calling the Hotel de Bordeaux?"

Madame Martin started to nod, then hesitated. "He'll think something terrible has happened."

"You can speak to him yourself."

"He's not used to my phoning him on the road."

"You'd rather he not know what's happening?"

"That's not so. I'll talk to him if you like."

Maigret picked up the phone and placed the call. Ten minutes later he was connected with the Hotel de Bordeaux in Bergerac. He passed the instrument to Madame Martin.

"Hello. . . . Monsieur Martin, please. . . . Yes, Monsieur Jean Martin. . . . No matter. Wake him up."

She put her hand over the mouthpiece. "He's still asleep. They've gone to call him."

Then she retreated into silence, evidently rehearsing the words she was to speak to her husband.

"Hello? . . . Hello, darling. . . . What? . . . Yes, Merry Christmas! . . . Yes, everything's all right. . . . Colette is fine. . . . No, that's not why I phoned. . . . No, no, no! Nothing's wrong. Please don't worry!" She repeated each word separately. "Please . . . don't . . . worry! I just want to tell you about a strange thing that happened last night. Somebody dressed up like Father Christmas and came into Colette's room. . . . No, no! He didn't hurt her. He gave her a big doll. . . . Yes, *doll!* . . . And he did queer things to the floor. He removed two boards which he put back in a hurry. . . . Mlle. Doncoeur thought I should report it to the police inspector who lives across the street. I'm there now. . . . You don't understand? Neither do I. . . . You want me to put him on?" She passed the instrument to Maigret. "He wants to speak to you."

A warm masculine voice came over the wire, the voice of an anxious, puzzled man.

"Are you sure my wife and the little girl are all right? . . . It's all so incredible! If it were just the doll, I might suspect my brother. Loraine will tell you about him. Loraine is my wife. Ask her. . . . But he wouldn't have removed the flooring. . . . Do you think I'd better come home? I can get a train for Paris at three this afternoon. . . . What? . . . Thank you so much. It's good to know you'll look out for them."

Loraine Martin took back the phone.

"See, darling? The inspector says there's no danger. It would be foolish to break your trip now. It might spoil your chances of being transferred permanently to Paris. . . ."

Mlle. Doncoeur was watching her closely and there was little tenderness in the spinster's eyes.

". . . I promise to wire you or phone you if there's anything new. . . . She's playing quietly with her new doll. . . . No, I haven't had time yet to give her your present. I'll go right home and do it now."

Madame Martin hung up and declared: "You see." Then, after a pause, "Forgive me for bothering you. It's really not my fault. I'm sure this is all the work of some practical joker . . . unless it's my brother-in-law. When he's been drinking there's no telling what he might do."

"Do you expect to see him today? Don't you think he might want to see his daughter?"

"That depends. If he's been drinking, no. He's very careful never to come around in that condition."

"May I have your permission to come over and talk with Colette a little later?"

"I see no reason why you shouldn't—if you think it worthwhile. . . ."

"Thank you, Monsieur Maigret!" exclaimed Mlle. Doncoeur. Her expression was half grateful, half conspiratorial. "She's such an interesting child! You'll see!"

She backed toward the door.

A few minutes later Maigret watched the two women cross the boulevard. Mlle. Doncoeur, close on the heels of Madame Martin, turned to look up at the windows of the Maigret apartment.

Mme. Maigret opened the kitchen door, flooding the dining room with the aroma of browning onions. She asked gently:

"Are you happy?"

He pretended not to understand. Luckily he had been too busy to think much about the middle-aged couple who had nobody to make a fuss over this Christmas morning.

It was time for him to shave and call on Colette.

He was just about to lather his face when he decided to make a phone call. He didn't bother with his dressing gown. Clad only in pajamas, he dropped into the easy chair by the window—*his* chair—and watched the smoke curling up from all the chimney pots while his call went through.

The ringing at the other end—in headquarters at the Quai des Orfèvres—had a different sound from all other rings. It evoked for him the long empty corridors, the vacant offices, the operator stuck with holiday duty at the switchboard. . . . Then he heard the operator call Lucas with the words: "The boss wants you."

He felt a little like one of his wife's friends who could imagine no greater joy—which she experienced daily—than lying in bed all morning, with her windows closed and curtains drawn, and telephoning all her friends, one after the other. By the soft glow of her night-light she managed to maintain a constant state of just having awakened. "What? Ten o'clock already? How's the weather? Is it raining? Have you been out yet? Have you done all your marketing?" And as she established telephonic connection with the hurly-burly of the workaday world, she would sink more and more voluptuously into the warm softness of her bed.

"That you, Chief?"

Maigret, too, felt a need for contact with the working world. He wanted to ask Lucas who was on duty with him, what they were doing, how the shop looked on this Christmas morning.

"Nothing new? Not too busy?"

"Nothing to speak of. Routine. . . ."

"I'd like you to get me some information. You can probably do this by phone. First of all, I want a list of all convicts released from prison the last two or three months."

"Which prison?"

"All prisons. But don't bother with any who haven't served at least five years. Then check and see if any of them has ever lived on Boulevard Richard-Lenoir. Got that?"

"I'm making notes."

Lucas was probably somewhat bewildered but he would never admit it.

"Another thing. I want you to locate a man named Paul Martin, a drunk, no fixed address, who frequently hangs out around the Place de la Bastille. I don't want him arrested. I don't want him molested. I just want to know where he spent Christmas Eve. The commissariats should help you on this one."

No use trying. Maigret simply could not reproduce the idle mood of his wife's friend. On the contrary, it embarrassed him to be lolling at home in his pajamas, unshaven, phoning from his favorite easy chair, looking out at a scene of complete peace and quiet in which there was no movement except the smoke curling up from the chimney pots, while at the other end of the wire good old Lucas had been on duty since six in the morning and was probably already unwrapping his sandwiches.

"That's not quite all, old man. I want you to call Bergerac long distance. There's a traveling salesman by the name of Jean Martin staying at the Hotel de Bordeaux there. No, Jean. It's his brother. I want to know if Jean Martin got a telegram or a phone call from Paris last night or any time yesterday. And while you're about it, find out where he spent Christmas Eve. I think that's all."

"Shall I call you back?"

"Not right away. I've got to go out for a while. I'll call you when I get home."

"Something happen in your neighborhood?"

"I don't know yet. Maybe."

Mme. Maigret came into the bathroom to talk to him while he finished dressing. He did not put on his overcoat. The smoke curling slowly upward from so many chimney pots blended with the gray of the sky and conjured up the image of just as many overheated apartments, cramped rooms in which he would not be invited to make himself at home. He refused to be uncomfortable. He would put on his hat to cross the boulevard, and that was all.

The building across the way was very much like the one he lived in—old but clean, a little dreary, particularly on a drab December morning. He avoided stopping at the concierge's lodge, but noted she watched him with some annoyance. Doors opened silently as he climbed the stairs. He heard whispering, the padding of slippered feet.

Mlle. Doncoeur, who had doubtless been watching for him, was waiting on the fourth floor landing. She was both shy and excited, as if keeping a secret tryst with a lover.

"This way, Monsieur Maigret. She went out a little while ago."

He frowned, and she noted the fact.

"I told her that you were coming and that she had better wait for you, but she said she had not done her marketing yesterday and that there was nothing in the house. She said all the stores would be closed if she waited too long. Come in."

She had opened the door into Madame Martin's dining room, a small, rather dark room which was clean and tidy.

"I'm looking after the little girl until she comes back. I told Colette that you were coming to see her, and she is delighted. I've spoken to her about you. She's only afraid you might take back her doll."

"When did Madame Martin decide to go out?"

"As soon as we came back across the street, she started dressing."

"Did she dress completely?"

"I don't understand."

"I mean, I suppose she dresses differently when she goes downtown than when she merely goes shopping in the neighborhood."

"She was quite dressed up. She put on her hat and gloves. And she carried her shopping bag."

Before going to see Colette, Maigret stepped into the kitchen and glanced at the breakfast dishes.

"Did she eat before you came to see me?"

"No. I didn't give her a chance."

"And when she came back?"

"She just made herself a cup of black coffee. I fixed breakfast for Colette while Madame Martin got dressed."

There was a larder on the ledge of the window looking out on the courtyard. Maigret carefully examined its contents: butter, eggs, vegetables, some cold meat. He found two uncut loaves of fresh bread in the kitchen cupboard. Colette had eaten *croissants* with her hot chocolate.

"How well do you know Madame Martin?"

"We're neighbors, aren't we? And I've seen more of her since Colette has been in bed. She often asks me to keep an eye on the little girl when she goes out."

"Does she go out much?"

"Not very often. Just for her marketing."

Maigret tried to analyze the curious impression he had had on entering the apartment. There was something in the atmosphere that disturbed him, something about the arrangement of the furniture, the special kind of neatness that prevailed, even the smell of the place. As he followed Mlle. Doncoeur into the dining room, he thought he knew what it was.

Madame Martin had told him that her husband had lived in this apartment before their marriage. And even though Madame Martin had lived there for five years, it had remained a bachelor's apartment. He pointed to the two enlarged photographs standing on opposite ends of the mantelpiece.

"Who are they?"

"Monsieur Martin's father and mother."

"Doesn't Madame Martin have photos of her own parents about?"

"I've never heard her speak of them. I suppose she's an orphan."

Even the bedroom was without the feminine touch. He opened a closet. Next to the neat rows of masculine clothing, the woman's clothes were hanging, mostly severely tailored suits and conservative dresses. He did not open the bureau drawers but he was sure they did not contain the usual trinkets and knickknacks that women collect.

"Mademoiselle Doncoeur!" called a calm little voice.

"Let's talk to Colette," said Maigret.

The child's room was as austere and cold as the others. The little girl lay in a bed too large for her, her face solemn, her eyes questioning but trusting.

"Are you the inspector, Monsieur?"

"I'm the inspector, my girl. Don't be afraid."

"I'm not afraid. Hasn't Mama Loraine come home yet?"

Maigret pursed his lips. The Martins had practically adopted their niece, yet the child said "Mama Loraine," not just "Mama."

"Do you believe it was Father Christmas who came to see me last night?" Colette asked Maigret.

"I'm sure it was."

"Mama Loraine doesn't believe it. She never believes me."

The girl had a dainty, attractive little face, with very bright eyes that stared at Maigret with level persistence. The plaster cast which sheathed one leg all the way to the hip made a thick bulge under the blankets.

Mlle. Doncoeur hovered in the doorway, evidently anxious to leave the inspector alone with the girl. She said: "I must run home for a moment to make sure my lunch isn't burning."

Maigret sat down beside the bed, wondering how to go about questioning the girl.

"Do you love Mama Loraine very much?" he began.

"Yes, Monsieur." She replied without hesitation and without enthusiasm.

"And your papa?"

"Which one? Because I have two papas, you know—Papa Paul and Papa Jean."

"Has it been a long time since you saw Papa Paul?"

"I don't remember. Perhaps several weeks. He promised to bring me a toy for Christmas, but he hasn't come yet. He must be sick."

"Is he often sick?"

"Yes, often. When he's sick he doesn't come to see me."

"And your Papa Jean?"

"He's away on a trip, but he'll be back for New Year's. Maybe then he'll be appointed to the Paris office and won't have to go away any more. That would make him very happy and me, too."

"Do many of your friends come to see you since you've been in bed?"

"What friends? The girls in school don't know where I live. Or maybe they know but their parents don't let them come alone."

"What about Mama Loraine's friends? Or your papa's?"

"Nobody comes, ever."

"Ever? Are you sure?"

"Only the man to read the gas meter, or for the electricity. I can hear them, because the door is almost always open. I recognize their voices. Once a man came and I didn't recognize his voice. Or twice."

"How long ago was that?"

"The first time was the day after my accident. I remember because the doctor just left."

"Who was it?"

"I didn't see him. He knocked at the other door. I heard him talking and then Mama Loraine came and closed my door. They talked for quite a while but I couldn't hear very well. Afterward Mama Loraine said it was a man who wanted to sell her some insurance. I don't know what that is."

"And he came back?"

"Five or six days ago. It was night and I'd already turned off my light. I wasn't asleep, though. I heard someone knock, and then they talked in low voices like the first time. Mademoiselle Doncoeur sometimes comes over in the evening, but I could tell it wasn't she. I thought they were quarreling and I was frightened. I called out, and Mama Loraine came in and said it was the man about the insurance again and I should go to sleep."

"Did he stay long?"

"I don't know. I think I fell asleep."

"And you didn't see him either time?"

"No, but I'd recognize his voice."

"Even though he speaks in low tones?"

"Yes, that's why. When he speaks low it sounds just like a big bumblebee. I can keep the doll, can't I? Mama Loraine bought me two boxes of candy and a little sewing kit. She bought me a doll, too, but it wasn't nearly as big as the doll Father Christmas gave me, because she's not rich. She showed it to me this morning before she left, and then she put it back in the box. I have the big one now, so I won't need the little one and Mama Loraine can take it back to the store."

The apartment was overheated, yet Maigret felt suddenly cold. The building was very much like the one across the street, yet not only did the rooms seem smaller and stuffier, but the whole world seemed smaller and meaner over here.

He bent over the floor near the fireplace. He lifted the loose floor boards, but saw nothing but an empty, dusty cavity smelling of dampness. There were scratches on the planks which indicated they had been forced up with a chisel or some similar instrument.

He examined the outside door and found indications that it had been forced. It was obviously an amateur's work, and luckily for him, the job had been an easy one.

"Father Christmas wasn't angry when he saw you watching him?"

"No, Monsieur. He was busy making a hole in the floor so he could go and see the little boy downstairs."

"Did he speak to you?"

"I think he smiled at me. I'm not sure, though, because of his whiskers. It wasn't very light. But I'm sure he put his finger to his lips so I wouldn't call anybody, because grown-ups aren't supposed to see Father Christmas. Did you ever see him?"

"A very long time ago."

"When you were little?"

Maigret heard footsteps in the hallway. The door opened and Madame Martin came in. She was wearing a gray tailored suit and a small beige hat and carried a brown shopping bag. She was visibly cold, for her skin was taut and very white, yet she must have hurried up the stairs, since there were two pink spots on her cheeks and she was out of breath. Unsmiling, she asked Maigret:

"Has she been a good girl?" Then, as she took off her jacket, "I apologize for making you wait. I had so many things to buy, and I was afraid the stores would all be closed later on."

"Did you meet anyone?"

"What do you mean?"

"Nothing. I was wondering if anyone tried to speak to you."

She had had plenty of time to go much further than the Rue Amelot or the Rue du Chemin-Vert where most of the neighborhood shops were located. She had even had time to go across Paris and back by taxi or the Metro.

Mlle. Doncoeur returned to ask if there was anything she could do. Madame Martin was about to say no when Maigret intervened: "I'd like you to stay with Colette while I step into the next room."

Mlle. Doncoeur understood that he wanted her to keep the child busy while he questioned the foster-mother. Madame Martin must have understood, too, but she gave no indication.

"Please come in. Do you mind if I take off my things?"

Madame Martin put her packages in the kitchen. She took off her hat and fluffed out her pale blonde hair. When she had closed the bedroom door, she said: "Mlle. Doncoeur is all excited. This is quite an event, isn't it, for an old maid—particularly an old maid who cuts out every newspaper article about a certain police inspector, and who finally has the inspector in her own house. . . . Do you mind?"

She had taken a cigarette from a silver case, tapped the end, and snapped a lighter. The gesture somehow prompted Maigret's next question:

"You're not working, Madame Martin?"

"It would be difficult to hold a job and take care of the house and the little girl, too, even when the child is in school. Besides, my husband won't allow me to work."

"But you did work before you met him?"

"Naturally. I had to earn a living. Won't you sit down?"

He lowered himself into a rude raffia-bottomed chair. She rested one thigh against the edge of a table.

"You were a typist?"

"I have been a typist."

"For long?"

"Quite a while."

"You were still a typist when you met Martin? You must forgive me for asking these personal questions."

"It's your job."

"You were married five years ago. Were you working then? Just a moment. May I ask your age?"

"I'm thirty-three. I was twenty-eight then, and I was working for a Monsieur Lorilleux in the Palais-Royal arcades."

"As his secretary?"

"Monsieur Lorilleux had a jewelry shop. Or more exactly, he sold souvenirs and old coins. You know those old shops in the Palais-Royal. I was salesgirl, bookkeeper, *and* secretary. I took care of the shop when he was away."

"He was married?"

"And father of three children."

"You left him to marry Martin?"

"Not exactly. Jean didn't want me to go on working, but he wasn't making very much money then and I had quite a good job. So I kept it for the first few months."

"And then?"

"Then a strange thing happened. One morning I came to work at 9 o'clock as usual, and I found the door locked. I thought Monsieur Lorilleux had overslept, so I waited. . . ."

"Where did he live?"

"Rue Mazarine with his family. At half-past 9 I began to worry."

"Was he dead?"

"No. I phoned his wife, who said he had left the house at 8 o'clock as usual."

"Where did you telephone from?"

"From the glove shop next door. I waited all morning. His wife came down and we went to the commissariat together to report him missing, but the police didn't take it very seriously. They just asked his wife if he'd ever had heart trouble, if he had a mistress—things like that. But he was never seen again, and nobody ever heard from him. Then some Polish people bought out the store and my husband made me stop working."

"How long was this after your marriage?"

"Four months."

"Your husband was already traveling in the southwest?"

"He had the same territory he has now."

"Was he in Paris when your employer disappeared?"

"No, I don't think so."

"Didn't the police examine the premises?"

"Nothing had been touched since the night before. Nothing was missing."

"Do you know what became of Madame Lorilleux?"

"She lived for a while on the money from the sale of the store. Then she bought a little dry-goods shop not far from here, in the Rue du Pas-de-la-Mule. Her children must be grown up now, probably married."

"Do you still see her?"

"I go into her shop once in a while. That's how I know she's in business in the neighborhood. The first time I saw her there I didn't recognize her."

"How long ago was that?"

"I don't know. Six months or so."

"Does she have a telephone?"

"I don't know. Why?"

"What kind of man was Lorilleux?"

"You mean physically?"

"Let's start with the physical."

"He was a big man, taller than you, and broader. He was fat, but flabby, if you know what I mean. And rather sloppy-looking."

"How old?"

"Around fifty. I can't say exactly. He had a little salt-and-pepper mustache, and his clothes were always too big for him."

"You were familiar with his habits?"

"He walked to work every morning. He got down fifteen minutes ahead of me and cleared up the mail before I arrived. He didn't talk much. He was a rather gloomy person. He spent most of the day in the little office behind the shop."

"No romantic adventures?"

"Not that I know of."

"Didn't he try to make love to you?"

"No!" The monosyllable was tartly emphatic.

"But he thought highly of you?"

"I think I was a great help to him."

"Did your husband ever meet him?"

"They never spoke. Jean sometimes came to wait for me outside the shop, but he never came in." A note of impatience, tinged with anger, crept into her voice. "Is that all you want to know?"

"May I point out, Madame Martin, that you are the one who came to get me?"

"Only because a crazy old maid practically dragged me there so she could get a close-up look at you."

"You don't like Mlle. Doncoeur?"

"I don't like people who can't mind their own business."

"People like Mlle. Doncoeur?"

"You know that we've taken in my brother-in-law's child. Believe me or not, I've done everything I can for her. I treat her the way I'd treat my own child. . . ." She paused to light a fresh cigarette, and Maigret tried unsuccessfully to picture her as a doting mother. ". . . And now that old maid is always over here, offering to help me with the child. Every time I start to go out, I find her in the hallway, smiling sweetly, and saying, 'You mustn't leave Colette all alone, Madame Martin. Let me go in and keep her company.' I sometimes wonder if she doesn't go through my drawers when I'm out."

"You put up with her, nevertheless."

"How can I help it? Colette asks for her, especially since she's been in bed. And my husband is fond of her because when he was a bachelor, she took care of him when he was sick with pleurisy."

"Have you already returned the doll you bought for Colette's Christmas?"

She frowned and glanced at the door to the child's bedroom. "I see you've been questioning the little girl. No, I haven't taken it back for the very good reason that all the big department stores are closed today. Would you like to see it?"

She spoke defiantly, expecting him to refuse, but he said nothing. He examined the cardboard box, noting the price tag. It was a very cheap doll.

"May I ask where you went this morning?"

"I did my marketing."

"Rue Amelot or Rue du Chemin-Vert?"

"Both."

"If I may be indiscreet, what did you buy?"

Furious, she stormed into the kitchen, snatched up her shopping bag, and dumped it on the dining room table. "Look for yourself!"

There were three tins of sardines, butter, potatoes, some ham, and a head of lettuce.

She fixed him with a hard, unwavering stare. She was not in the least nervous. Spiteful, rather.

"Any more questions?"

"Yes. The name of your insurance agent."

"My insurance. . . ." She was obviously puzzled.

"Insurance agent. The one who came to see you."

"I'm sorry. I was at a loss for a moment because you spoke of *my* agent as though he were really handling a policy for me. So Colette told you that, too? Actually, a man did come to see me twice, trying to sell me a policy. He was one of those door-to-door salesmen, and I thought at first he was selling vacuum cleaners, not life insurance. I had a terrible time getting rid of him."

"Did he stay long?"

"Long enough for me to convince him that I had no desire to take out a policy."

"What company did he represent?"

"He told me but I've forgotten. Something with 'Mutual' in it."

"And he came back later?"

"Yes."

"What time does Colette usually go to sleep?"

"I put out her light at 7:30, but sometimes she talks to herself in the dark until much later."

"So the second time the insurance man called, it was later than 7:30?"

"Possibly." She saw the trap. "I remember now I was washing the dishes."

"And you let him in?"

"He had his foot in the door."

"Did he call on other tenants in the building?"

"I haven't the slightest idea, but I'm sure you will inquire. Must you cross-examine me like a criminal, just because a little girl imagines she saw Santa Claus? If my husband were here—"

"By the way, does your husband carry life insurance?"

"I think so. In fact, I'm sure he does."

Maigret picked up his hat from a chair and started for the door. Madame Martin seemed surprised.

"Is that all?"

"That's all. It seems your brother-in-law promised to come and see his daughter today. If he should come, I would be grateful if you let me know. And now I'd like a few words with Mlle. Doncoeur."

There was a convent smell about Mlle. Doncoeur's apartment, but there was no dog or cat in sight, no antimacassars on the chairs, no bricabrac on the mantelpiece.

"Have you lived in this house long, Mlle. Doncoeur?"

"Twenty-five years, Monsieur l'Inspecteur. I'm one of the oldest tenants. I remember when I first moved in you were already living across the street, and you wore long mustaches."

"Who lived in the next apartment before Martin moved in?"

"A public works engineer. I don't remember his name, but I could look it up for you. He had a wife and daughter. The girl was a deaf-mute. It was very sad. They went to live somewhere in the country."

"Have you been bothered by a door-to-door insurance agent recently?"

"Not recently. There was one who came around two or three years ago."

"You don't like Madame Martin, do you?"

"Why?"

"I asked if you liked Madame Martin?"

"Well, if I had a son . . ."

"Go on."

"If I had a son I don't think I would like Madame Martin for a daughter-in-law. Especially as Monsieur Martin is such a nice man, so kind."

"You think he is unhappy with his wife?"

"I wouldn't say that. I have nothing against her, really. She can't help being the kind of woman she is."

"What kind of woman is she?"

"I couldn't say, exactly. You've seen her. You're a better judge of those things than I am. In a way, she's not like a woman at all. I'll wager she never shed a tear in her life. True, she is bringing up the child properly, decently, but she never says a kind word to her. She acts exasperated when I tell Colette a fairy tale. I'm sure she's told the girl there is no Santa Claus. Luckily Colette doesn't believe her."

"The child doesn't like her either, does she?"

"Colette is always obedient. She tries to do what's expected of her. I think she's just as happy to be left alone."

"Is she alone much?"

"Not much. I'm not reproaching Madame Martin. It's hard to explain. She wants to live her own life. She's not interested in others. She doesn't even talk much about herself."

"Have you ever met her brother-in-law—Colette's father?"

"I've seen him on the landing, but I've never spoken to him. He walks with his head down, as if he were ashamed of something. He always looks as if he slept in his clothes. No, I don't think it was he last night, Monsieur Maigret. He's not the type. Unless he was terribly drunk."

On his way out Maigret looked in at the concierge's lodge, a dark cubicle where the light burned all day.

It was noon when he started back across the boulevard. Curtains stirred at the windows of the house behind him. Curtains stirred at his own window, too. Mme. Maigret was watching for him so she would know when to put the chicken in the oven. He waved to her. He wanted very much to stick out his tongue and lick up a few of the tiny snow flakes that were drifting down. He could still remember their taste.

"I wonder if that little tike is happy over there," sighed Mme. Maigret as she got up from the table to bring the coffee from the kitchen.

She could see he wasn't listening. He had pushed back his chair and was stuffing his pipe while staring at the purring stove. For her own satisfaction she added: "I don't see how she could be happy with that woman."

He smiled vaguely, as he always did when he hadn't heard what she said, and continued to stare at the tiny flames licking evenly at the mica windows of the salamander. There were at least ten similar stoves in the house, all purring alike in ten similar dining rooms with wine and cakes on the table, a carafe of cordial waiting on the sideboard, and all the windows pale with the same hard, gray light of a sunless day.

It was perhaps this very familiarity which had been confusing his subconscious since morning. Nine times out of ten his investigations plunged him abruptly into new surroundings, set him at grips with people of a world he barely knew, people of a social level whose habits and manners he had to study from scratch. But in this case, which was not really a case since he had no official assignment, the whole approach was unfamiliar because the background was too familiar. For the first time in his career something professional was happening in his own world, in a building which might just as well be his building.

The Martins could easily have been living on his floor, instead of across the street, and it would probably have been Mme. Maigret who would look after Colette when her aunt was away. There was an elderly maiden lady living just under him who was a plumper, paler replica of Mlle. Doncoeur. The frames of the photographs of Martin's father and mother were exactly the same as those which framed Maigret's father and mother, and the enlargements had probably been made by the same studio.

Was that what was bothering him? He seemed to lack perspective. He was unable to look at people and things from a fresh, new viewpoint.

He had detailed his morning activities during dinner—a pleasant little Christmas dinner which had left him with an overstuffed feeling—and his wife had listened while looking at the windows across the street with an air of embarrassment.

"Is the concierge sure that nobody could have come in from outside?"

"She's not so sure any more. She was entertaining friends until after midnight. And after she had gone to bed, there were considerable comings and goings, which is natural for Christmas Eve."

"Do you think something more is going to happen?"

That was a question that had been plaguing Maigret all morning. First of all, he had to consider that Madame Martin had not come to see him spontaneously, but only on the insistence of Mlle. Doncoeur. If she had got up earlier, if she had been the first to see the doll and hear the story of Father Christmas, wouldn't she have kept the secret and ordered the little girl to say nothing?

And later she had taken the first opportunity to go out, even though there was plenty to eat in the house for the day. And she had been so absent-minded that she had bought butter, although there was still a pound in the cooler.

Maigret got up from the table and resettled himself in his chair by the window. He picked up the phone and called Quai des Orfèvres.

"Lucas?"

"I got what you wanted, Chief. I have a list of all prisoners released for the last four months. There aren't as many as I thought. And none of them has lived in the Boulevard Richard-Lenoir at any time."

That didn't matter any more now. At first Maigret had thought that a tenant across the street might have hidden money or stolen goods under the floor before he was arrested. His first thought on getting out of jail would be to recover his booty. With the little girl bedridden, however, the room was occupied day and night. Impersonating Father Christmas would not have been a bad idea to get into the room. Had this been the case, however, Madame Martin would not have been so reluctant to call in Maigret. Nor would she have been in so great a hurry to get out of the house afterwards on such a flimsy pretext. So Maigret had abandoned that theory.

"You want me to check each prisoner further?"

"Never mind. Any news about Paul Martin?"

"That was easy. He's known in every station house between the Bastille and the Hotel de Ville, and even on the Boulevard Saint-Michel."

"What did he do last night?"

"First he went aboard the Salvation Army barge to eat. He's a regular there one day a week and yesterday was his day. They had a special feast for Christmas Eve and he had to stand in line quite a while."

"After that?"

"About 11 o'clock he went to the Latin Quarter and opened doors for motorists in front of a night club. He must have collected enough money in tips to get himself a sinkful, because he was picked up dead drunk near the Place Maubert at 4 in the morning. He was taken to the station house to sleep it off, and was there until 11 this morning. They'd just turned him loose when I phoned, and they promised to bring him to me when they find him again. He still had a few francs in his pocket."

"What about Bergerac?"

"Jean Martin is taking the afternoon train for Paris. He was quite upset by a phone call he got this morning."

"He got only one call?"

"Only one this morning. He got a call last night while he was eating dinner."

"You know who called him?"

"The desk clerk says it was a man's voice, asking for Monsieur Jean Martin. He sent somebody into the dining room for Martin but when Martin got to the phone, the caller had hung up. Seems it spoiled his whole evening. He went out with a bunch of traveling salesmen to some local hot-spot where there were pretty girls and whatnot, but after drinking a few glasses of champagne, he couldn't talk about anything except his wife and daughter. The niece he calls his daughter, it seems. He had such a dismal evening that he went home early. Three A.M. That's all you wanted to know, Chief?"

When Maigret didn't reply, Lucas had to satisfy his curiosity. "You still phoning from home, Chief? What's happening up your way? Somebody get killed?"

"I still can't say. Right now all I know is that the principals are a seven-year-old girl, a doll, and Father Christmas."

"Ah?"

"One more thing. Try to get me the home address of the manager of Zenith Watches, Avenue de l'Opéra. You ought to be able to raise somebody there, even on Christmas Day. Call me back."

"Soon as I have something."

Mme. Maigret had just served him a glass of Alsatian plum brandy which her sister had sent them. He smacked his lips. For a moment he was tempted to forget all about the business of the doll and Father Christmas. It would be much simpler just to take his wife to the movies. . . .

"What color eyes has she?"

It took him a moment to realize that the only person in the case who interested Mme. Maigret was the little girl.

"Why, I'm not quite sure. They can't be dark. She has blonde hair."

"So they're blue."

"Maybe they're blue. Very light, in any case. And they are very serious."

"Because she doesn't look at things like a child. Does she laugh?"

"She hasn't much to laugh about."

"A child can always laugh if she feels herself surrounded by people she can trust, people who let her act her age. I don't like that woman."

"You prefer Mlle. Doncoeur?"

"She may be an old maid but I'm sure she knows more about children than that Madame Martin. I've seen *her* in the shops. Madame Martin is one of those women who watch the scales, and take their money out of their pocketbooks, coin by coin. She always looks around suspiciously, as though everybody was out to cheat her."

The telephone rang as Mme. Maigret was repeating, "I don't like that woman."

It was Lucas calling, with the address of Monsieur Arthur Godefroy, general manager in France for Zenith Watches. He lived in a sumptuous villa at Saint-Cloud, and Lucas had discovered that he was at home. He added:

"Paul Martin is here, Chief. When they brought him in, he started crying. He thought something had happened to his daughter. But he's all right now—except for an awful hangover. What do I do with him?"

"Anyone around who can come up here with him?"

"Torrence just came on duty. I think he could use a little fresh air. He looks as if he had a hard night, too. Anything more from me, Chief?"

"Yes. Call Palais-Royal station. About five years ago a man named Lorilleux disappeared without a trace. He sold jewelry and old coins in the Palais-Royal arcades. Get me all the details you can on his disappearance."

Maigret smiled as he noted that his wife was sitting opposite him with her knitting. He had never before worked on a case in such domestic surroundings.

"Do I call you back?" asked Lucas.

"I don't expect to move an inch from my chair."

A moment later Maigret was talking to Monsieur Godefroy, who had a decided Swiss accent. The Zenith manager thought that something must have happened to Jean Martin, for anyone to be making inquiries about him on Christmas Day.

"Most able . . . most devoted . . . I'm bringing him into Paris to be assistant manager next year. . . . Next week, that is . . . Why do you ask? Has anything—? Be still, you!" He paused to quiet the juvenile hubbub in the background. "You must excuse me. All my family is with me today and—"

"Tell me, Monsieur Godefroy, has anyone called your office these last few days to inquire about Monsieur Martin's current address?"

"Yesterday morning, as a matter of fact. I was very busy with the holiday rush, but he asked to speak to me personally. I forget what name he gave. He said he had an extremely important message for Jean Martin, so I told him how to get in touch with Martin in Bergerac."

"He asked you nothing else?"

"No. He hung up at once. Is anything wrong?"

"I hope not. Thank you very much, Monsieur."

The screams of children began again in the background and Maigret said goodbye.

"Were you listening?"

"I heard what you said. I didn't hear his answers."

"A man called the office yesterday morning to get Martin's address. The same man undoubtedly called Bergerac that evening to make sure Martin was still there, and therefore would not be at his Boulevard Richard-Lenoir address for Christmas Eve."

"The same man who appeared last night as Father Christmas?"

"More than likely. That seems to clear Paul Martin. He would not have to make two phone calls to find out where his brother was. Madame Martin would have told him."

"You're really getting excited about this case. You're delighted that it came up, aren't you? Confess!" And while Maigret was racking his brain for excuses, she added: "It's quite natural. I'm fascinated, too. How much longer do you think the child will have to keep her leg in a cast?"

"I didn't ask."

"I wonder what sort of complications she could have had?"

Maigret looked at her curiously. Unconsciously she had switched his mind onto a new track.

"That's not such a stupid remark you just made."

"What did I say?"

"After all, since she's been in bed for two months, she should be up and around soon, barring really serious complications."

"She'll probably have to walk on crutches at first."

"That's not the point. In a few days then, or a few weeks at most, she will no longer be confined to her room. She'll go for a walk with Madame Martin. And the coast will be clear for anyone to enter the apartment without dressing up like Father Christmas."

Mme. Maigret's lips were moving. While listening to her husband and watching his face, she was counting stitches.

"First of all, the presence of the child forced our man to use trickery. She's been in bed for two months—two months for him to wait. Without the complications the flooring could have been taken up several weeks ago. Our man must have had urgent reasons for acting at once, without further delay."

"Monsieur Martin will return to Paris in a few days?"

"Exactly."

"What do you suppose the man found underneath the floor?"

"Did he really find anything? If not, his problem is still as pressing as it was last night. So he will take further action."

"What action?"

"I don't know."

"Look, Maigret, isn't the child in danger? Do you think she's safe with that woman?"

"I could answer that if I knew where Madame Martin went this morning on the pretext of doing her shopping." He picked up the phone again and called Police Judiciaire.

"I'm pestering you again, Lucas. I want you to locate a taxi that picked up a passenger this morning between 9 and 10 somewhere near Boulevard Richard-Lenoir. The fare was a woman in her early thirties, blonde, slim but solidly built. She was wearing a gray suit and a beige hat. She carried a brown shopping bag. I want to know her destination. There couldn't have been so many cabs on the street at that hour."

"Is Paul Martin with you?"

"Not yet."

"He'll be there soon. About that other thing, the Lorilleux matter, the Palais-Royal boys are checking their files. You'll have the data in a few minutes."

Jean Martin must be taking his train in Bergerac at this moment. Little Colette was probably taking her nap. Mlle. Doncoeur was doubtless sitting behind her window curtain, wondering what Maigret was up to.

People were beginning to come out now, families with their children, the children with their new toys. There were certainly queues in front of the cinemas. . . .

A taxi stopped in front of the house. Footsteps sounded in the stairway. Mme. Maigret went to the door. The deep bass voice of Torrence rumbled: "You there, Chief?"

Torrence came in with an ageless man who hugged the walls and looked humbly at the floor. Maigret went to the sideboard and filled two glasses with plum brandy.

"To your health," he said.

The man looked at Maigret with surprised, anxious eyes. He raised a trembling, hesitant hand.

"To your health, Monsieur Martin. I'm sorry to make you come all the way up here, but you won't have far to go now to see your daughter."

"Nothing has happened to her?"

"No, no. When I saw her this morning she was playing with her new doll. You can go, Torrence. Lucas must need you."

Mme. Maigret had gone into the bedroom with her knitting. She was sitting on the edge of the bed, counting her stitches.

"Sit down, Monsieur Martin."

The man had touched his lips to the glass and set it down. He looked at it uneasily.

"You have nothing to worry about. Just tell yourself that I know all about you."

"I wanted to visit her this morning," the man sighed. "I swore I would go to bed early so I could wish her a Merry Christmas."

"I know that, too."

"It's always the same. I swear I'll take just one drink, just enough to pick me up. . . ."

"You have only one brother, Monsieur Martin?"

"Yes, Jean. He's six years younger than I am. He and my wife and my daughter were all I had to love in this world."

"You don't love your sister-in-law?"

He shivered. He seemed both startled and embarrassed.

"I have nothing against Loraine."

"You entrusted your child to her, didn't you?"

"Well, yes, that is to say, when my wife died and I began to slip. . . ."

"I understand. Is your daughter happy?"

"I think so, yes. She never complains."

"Have you ever tried to get back on your feet?"

"Every night I promise myself to turn over a new leaf, but next day I start all over again. I even went to see a doctor. I followed his advice for a few days. But when I went back, he was very busy. He said I ought to be in a special sanatorium."

He reached for his glass, then hesitated. Maigret picked up his own glass and took a swallow to encourage him.

"Did you ever meet a man in your sister-in-law's apartment?"

"No. I think she's above reproach on that score."

"Do you know where your brother first met her?"

"In a little restaurant in the Rue Beaujolais where he used to eat when he was in Paris. It was near the shop where Loraine was working."

"Did they have a long engagement?"

"I can't say. Jean was on the road for two months and when he came back he told me he was getting married."

"Were you his best man?"

"Yes. Loraine has no family in Paris. She's an orphan. So her landlady acted as her witness. Is there something wrong?"

"I don't know yet. A man entered Colette's room last night dressed as Father Christmas. He gave your girl a doll, and lifted two loose boards from the floor."

"Do you think I'm in fit condition to see her?"

"You can go over in a little while. If you feel like it you can shave here. Do you think your brother would be likely to hide anything under the floor?"

"Jean? Never!"

"Even if he wanted to hide something from his wife?"

"He doesn't hide things from his wife. You don't know him. He's one of those rare humans—a scrupulously honest man. When he comes home from the road, she knows exactly how much money he has left, to the last centime."

"Is she jealous?"

Paul Martin did not reply.

"I advise you to tell me what you know. Remember that your daughter is involved in this."

"I don't think that Loraine is especially jealous. Not of women, at least. Perhaps about money. At least that's what my poor wife always said. She didn't like Loraine."

"Why not?"

"She used to say that Loraine's lips were too thin, that she was too polite, too cold, always on the defensive. My wife always thought that Loraine set her cap for Jean because he had a good job with a future and owned his own furniture."

"Loraine had no money of her own?"

"She never speaks of her family. I understand her father died when she was very young and her mother did housework somewhere in the Glacière quarter. My poor wife used to say, 'Loraine knows what she wants.'"

"Do you think she was Lorilleux's mistress?"

Paul Martin did not reply. Maigret poured him another finger of plum brandy. Martin gave him a grateful look, but he did not touch the glass. Perhaps he was thinking that his daughter might notice his breath when he crossed the street later on.

"I'll get you a cup of coffee in a moment. . . . Your wife must have had her own ideas on the subject."

"How did you know? Please note that my wife never spoke disparagingly of people. But with Loraine it was almost pathological. Whenever we were to meet my sister-in-law, I used to beg my wife not to show her antipathy. It's funny that you should bring all that up now, at this time in my life. Do you think I did wrong in letting her take Colette? I sometimes think so. But what else could I have done?"

"You didn't answer my question about Loraine's former employer."

"Oh, yes. My wife always said it was very convenient for Loraine to have married a man who was away from home so much."

"You know where she lived before her marriage?"

"In a street just off Boulevard Sébastopol, on the right as you walk from Rue de Rivoli toward the Boulevard. I remember we picked her up there the day of the wedding."

"Rue Pernelle?"

"That's it. The fourth or fifth house on the left side of the street is a quiet rooming house, quite respectable. People who work in the neighborhood live there. I remember there were several little actresses from the Châtelet."

"Would you like to shave, Monsieur Martin?"

"I'm ashamed. Still, since my daughter is just across the street. . . ."

"Come with me."

Maigret took him through the kitchen so he wouldn't have to meet Mme. Maigret in the bedroom. He set out the necessary toilet articles, not forgetting a clothes brush.

When he returned to the dining room, Mme. Maigret poked her head through the door and whispered: "What's he doing?"

"He's shaving."

Once more Maigret reached for the telephone. He was certainly giving poor Lucas a busy Christmas Day.

"Are you indispensable at the office?"

"Not if Torrence sits in for me. I've got the information you wanted."

"In just a moment. I want you to jump over to Rue Pernelle. There's a rooming house a few doors down from the Boulevard Sébastopol. If the proprietor wasn't there five years ago, try to dig up someone who lived there then. I want everything you can find out on a certain Loraine. . . ."

"Loraine who?"

"Just a minute, I didn't think of that."

Through the bathroom door he asked Martin for the maiden name of his sister-in-law. A few seconds later he was on the phone again.

"Loraine Boitel," he told Lucas. "The landlady of this rooming house was witness at her marriage to Jean Martin. Loraine Boitel was working for Lorilleux at the time. Try to find out if she was more than a secretary to him, and if he ever came to see her. And work fast. This may be urgent. What have you got on Lorilleux?"

"He was quite a fellow. At home in the Rue Mazarine he was a good respectable family man. In his Palais-Royal shop he not only sold old coins and souvenirs of Paris, but he had a fine collection of pornographic books and obscene pictures."

"Not unusual for the Palais-Royal."

"I don't know what else went on there. There was a big divan covered with red silk rep in the back room, but the investigation was never pushed. Seems there were a lot of important names among his customers."

"What about Loraine Boitel?"

"The report barely mentions her, except that she waited all morning for Lorilleux the day he disappeared. I was on the phone about this when Langlois of the Financial Squad came into my office. The name Lorilleux rang a bell in the back of his mind and he went to check his files. Nothing definite on him, but he'd been making frequent trips to Switzerland and back, and there was a lot of gold smuggling going on at that time. Lorilleux was stopped and searched at the frontier several times, but they never found anything on him."

"Lucas, old man, hurry over to Rue Pernelle. I'm more than ever convinced that this is urgent."

Paul Martin appeared in the doorway, his pale cheeks close-shaven.

"I don't know how to thank you. I'm very much embarrassed."

"You'll visit your daughter now, won't you? I don't know how long you usually stay, but today I don't want you to leave until I come for you."

"I can't very well stay all night, can I?"

"Stay all night if necessary. Manage the best you can."

"Is the little girl in danger?"

"I don't know, but your place today is with your daughter."

Paul Martin drank his black coffee avidly, and started for the stairway. The door had just closed after him when Mme. Maigret rushed into the dining room.

"You can't let him go to see his daughter empty-handed on Christmas Day!"

"But—" Maigret was about to say that there just didn't happen to be a doll around the house, when his wife thrust a small shiny object into his hands. It was a gold thimble which had been in her sewing basket for years but which she never used.

"Give him that. Little girls always like thimbles. Hurry!"

He shouted from the landing: "Monsieur Martin! Just a minute, Monsieur Martin!"

He closed the man's fingers over the thimble. "Don't tell a soul where you got this."

Before re-entering the dining room he stood for a moment on the threshold, grumbling. Then he sighed: "I hope you've finished making me play Father Christmas."

"I'll bet she likes the thimble as well as a doll. It's something grownups use, you know."

They watched the man cross the boulevard. Before going into the house he turned to look up at Maigret's windows, as if seeking encouragement.

"Do you think he'll ever be cured?"

"I doubt it."

"If anything happens to that woman, to Madame Martin. . . ."

"Well?"

"Nothing. I was thinking of the little girl. I wonder what would become of her."

Ten minutes passed. Maigret had opened his newspaper and lighted his pipe. His wife had settled down again with her knitting. She was counting stitches when he exhaled a cloud of smoke and murmured: "You haven't even seen her."

Maigret was looking for an old envelope, on the back of which he had jotted down a few notes summing up the day's events. He found it in a drawer into which Mme. Maigret always stuffed any papers she found lying around the house.

This was the only investigation, he mused, which he had ever conducted practically in its entirety from his favorite armchair. It was also unusual in that no dramatic stroke of luck had come to his aid. True, luck had been on his side, in that he had been able to muster all his facts by the simplest and most direct means. How many times had he deployed scores of detectives on an all-night search for some minor detail. This might have happened, for instance, if Monsieur Arthur Godefroy of Zenith had gone home to Zurich for Christmas, or if he had been out of reach of a telephone. Or if Monsieur Godefroy had been unaware of the telephone inquiry regarding the whereabouts of Jean Martin.

When Lucas arrived shortly after 4 o'clock, his nose red and his face pinched with the cold, he too could report the same kind of undramatic luck.

A thick yellow fog, unusual for Paris, had settled over the city. Lights shone in all the windows, floating in the murk like ships at sea or distant beacons. Familiar details had been blotted out so completely that Maigret half-expected to hear the moan of fog horns.

For some reason, perhaps because of some boyhood memory, Maigret was pleased to see the weather thicken. He was also pleased to see Lucas walk into his apartment, take off his overcoat, sit down, and stretch out his frozen hands toward the fire.

In appearance, Lucas was a reduced-scale model of Maigret—a head shorter, half as broad in the shoulders, half as stern in expression although he tried hard. Without conscious imitation but with conscious admiration, Lucas had copied his chief's slightest gestures, postures, and changes of expression—even to the ceremony of inhaling the fragrance of the plum brandy before touching his lips to the glass.

The landlady of the rooming house in the Rue Pernelle had been killed in a subway accident two years earlier, Lucas reported. Luckily, the place had been taken over by the former night watchman, who had been in trouble with the police on morals charges.

"So it was easy enough to make him talk," said Lucas, lighting a pipe much too large for him. "I was surprised that he had the money to buy the house, but he explained that he was front man for a big investor who had money in all sorts of enterprises but didn't like to have his name used."

"What kind of dump is it?"

"Looks respectable. Clean enough. Office on the mezzanine. Rooms by the month, some by the week, and a few on the second floor by the hour."

"He remembers Loraine?"

"Very well. She lived there more than three years. I got the impression he didn't like her because she was tight-fisted."

"Did Lorilleux come to see her?"

"On my way to the Rue Pernelle I picked up a photo of Lorilleux at the Palais-Royal station. The new landlord recognized him right away."

"Lorilleux went to her room often?"

"Two or three times a month. He always had baggage with him, he always arrived around 1 o'clock in the morning, and always left before 6. I checked the timetables. There's a train from Switzerland around midnight and another at 6 in the morning. He must have told his wife he was taking the 6 o'clock train."

"Nothing else?"

"Nothing, except that Loraine was stingy with tips, and always cooked her dinner on an alcohol burner, even though the house rules said no cooking in the rooms."

"No other men?"

"No. Very respectable except for Lorilleux. The landlady was witness at her wedding."

Maigret glanced at his wife. He had insisted she remain in the room when Lucas came. She stuck to her knitting, trying to make believe she was not there.

Torrence was out in the fog, going from garage to garage, checking the trip-sheets of taxi fleets. The two men waited serenely, deep in their easy chairs, each holding a glass of plum brandy with the same pose. Maigret felt a pleasant numbness creeping over him.

His Christmas luck held out with the taxis, too. Sometimes it took days to run down a particular taxi driver, particularly when the cab in question did not belong to a fleet. Cruising drivers were the hardest to locate; they sometimes never even read the newspapers. But shortly before 5 o'clock Torrence called from Saint-Ouen.

"I found one of the taxis," he reported.

"One? Was there more than one?"

"Looks that way. This man picked up the woman at the corner of Boulevard Richard-Lenoir and Boulevard Voltaire this morning. He drove her to Rue de Maubeuge, opposite the Gare du Nord, where she paid him off."

"Did she go into the railway station?"

"No. The chauffeur says she went into a luggage shop that keeps open on Sundays and holidays. After that he doesn't know."

"Where's the driver now?"

"Right here in the garage. He just checked in."

"Send him to me, will you? Right away. I don't care how he gets here as long as it's in a hurry. Now I want you to find me the cab that brought her home."

"Sure, Chief, as soon as I get myself a coffee with a stick in it. It's damned cold out here."

Maigret glanced through the window. There was a shadow against Mlle. Doncoeur's curtains. He turned to Lucas.

"Look in the phone book for a luggage shop across from the Gare du Nord."

Lucas took only a minute to come up with a number, which Maigret dialed.

"Hello, this is the Police Judiciaire. Shortly before 10 this morning a young woman bought something in your shop, probably a valise. She was a blonde, wearing a gray suit and beige hat. She carried a brown shopping bag. Do you remember her?"

Perhaps trade was slack on Christmas Day. Or perhaps it was easier to remember customers who shopped on Christmas. In any case, the voice on the phone replied:

"Certainly, I waited on her myself. She said she had to leave suddenly for Cambrai because her sister was ill, and she didn't have time to go home for her bags. She wanted a cheap valise, and I sold her a fiber model we have on sale. She paid me and went into the bar next door. I was standing in the doorway and a little later I saw her walking toward the station, carrying the valise."

"Are you alone in your shop?"

"I have one clerk on duty."

"Can you leave him alone for half an hour? Fine! Then jump in a taxi and come to this address. I'll pay the fare, of course."

"And the return fare? Shall I have the cab wait?"

"Have him wait, yes."

According to Maigret's notes on the back of the envelope, the first taxi driver arrived at 5:50 P.M. He was somewhat surprised, since he had been summoned by the police, to find himself in a private apartment. He recognized Maigret, however, and made no effort to disguise his curious interest in how the famous inspector lived.

"I want you to climb to the fourth floor of the house just across the street. If the concierge stops you, tell her you're going to see Madame Martin."

"Madame Martin. I got it."

"Go to the door at the end of the hall and ring the bell. If a blonde opens the door and you recognize her, make some excuse— You're on the wrong floor, anything you think of. If somebody else answers, ask to speak to Madame Martin personally."

"And then?"

"Then you come back here and tell me whether or not she is the fare you drove to Rue de Maubeuge this morning."

"I'll be right back, Inspector."

As the door closed, Maigret smiled in spite of himself.

"The first call will make her worry a little. The second, if all goes well, will make her panicky. The third, if Torrence has any luck—"

Torrence, too, was having his run of Christmas luck. The phone rang and he reported:

"I think I've found him, Chief. I dug up a driver who picked up a woman answering your description at the Gare du Nord, only he didn't take her to Boulevard Richard-Lenoir. He dropped her at the corner of Boulevard Beaumarchais and the Rue du Chemin-Vert."

"Send him to me."

"He's a little squiffed."

"No matter. Where are you?"

"The Barbès garage."

"Then it won't be much out of your way to stop by the Gare du Nord. Go to the check room. Unfortunately it won't be the same man on duty, but try to find out if a small new valise was checked between 9:30 and 10 this morning. It's made of fiber and shouldn't be too heavy. Get the number of the check. They won't let you take the valise without a warrant, so try to get the name and address of the man on duty this morning."

"What next?"

"Phone me. I'll wait for your second taxi driver. If he's been drinking, better write down my address for him, so he won't get lost."

Mme. Maigret was back in the kitchen, preparing the evening meal. She hadn't dared ask whether Lucas would eat with them.

Maigret wondered if Paul Martin was still across the street with his daughter. Had Madame Martin tried to get rid of him?

The bell rang again. Two men stood at the door.

The first driver had come back from Madame Martin's and had climbed Maigret's stairs behind the luggage dealer.

"Did you recognize her?"

"Sure. She recognized me, too. She turned pale. She ran to close a door behind her, then she asked me what I wanted."

"What did you tell her?"

"That I had the wrong floor. I think maybe she wanted to buy me off, but I didn't give her a chance. But she was watching from the window when I crossed the street. She probably knows I came here."

The luggage dealer was baffled and showed it. He was a middle-aged man, completely bald and equally obsequious. When the driver had gone, Maigret explained what he wanted, and the man objected vociferously.

"One just doesn't do this sort of thing to one's customers," he repeated stubbornly. "One simply does not inform on one's customers, you know."

After a long argument he agreed to call on Madame Martin. To make sure he didn't change his mind, Maigret sent Lucas to follow him.

They returned in less than ten minutes.

"I call your attention to the fact that I have acted under your orders, that I have been compelled—"

"Did you recognize her?"

"Will I be forced to testify under oath?"

"More than likely."

"That would be very bad for my business. People who buy luggage at the last minute are very often people who dislike public mention of their comings and goings."

"You may not have to go to court. Your deposition before the examining magistrate may be sufficient."

"Very well. It was she. She's dressed differently, but I recognized her all right."

"Did she recognize you?"

"She asked immediately who had sent me."

"What did you say?"

"I . . . I don't remember. I was quite upset. I think I said I had rung the wrong bell."

"Did she offer you anything?"

"What do mean? She didn't even offer me a chair. Luckily. It would have been most unpleasant."

Maigret smiled, somewhat incredulously. He believed that the taxi driver had actually run away from a possible bribe. He wasn't so sure about this prosperous-looking shopkeeper who obviously begrudged his loss of time.

"Thank you for your cooperation."

The luggage dealer departed hastily.

"And now for Number Three, my dear Lucas."

Mme. Maigret was beginning to grow nervous. From the kitchen door she made discreet signs to her husband, beckoning him to join her. She whispered: "Are you sure the father is still across the street?"

"Why?"

"I don't know. I can't make out exactly what you're up to, but I've been thinking about the child, and I'm a little afraid. . . ."

Night had long since fallen. The families were all home again. Few windows across the street remained dark. The silhouette of Mlle. Doncoeur was still very much in evidence.

While waiting for the second taxi driver, Maigret decided to put on his collar and tie. He shouted to Lucas:

"Pour yourself another drop. Aren't you hungry?"

"I'm full of sandwiches, Chief. Only one thing I'd like when we go out: a tall beer, right from the spigot."

The second driver arrived at 6:20. At 6:35 he had returned from across the street, a gleam in his eye.

"She looks even better in her négligée than she does in her street clothes," he said thickly. "She made me come in and she asked who sent me. I didn't know what to say, so I told her I was a talent scout for the Folies Bergère. Was she furious! She's a fine hunk of woman, though, and I mean it. Did you get a look at her legs?"

He was in no hurry to leave. Maigret saw him ogling the bottle of plum brandy with envious eyes, and poured him a glass—to speed him on his way.

"What are you going to do next, Chief?" Lucas had rarely seen Maigret proceed with such caution, preparing each step with such care that he seemed to be mounting an attack on some desperate criminal. And yet the enemy was only a woman, a seemingly insignificant little housewife.

"You think she'll still fight back?"

"Fiercely. And what's more, in cold blood."

"What are you waiting for?"

"The phone call from Torrence."

As if on cue, the telephone rang. Torrence, of course.

"The valise is here all right. It feels practically empty. As you predicted, they won't give it to me without a warrant. The check-room attendant who was on duty this morning lives in the suburbs, near La Varenne-Saint-Hilaire." A snag at last? Or at least a delay? Maigret frowned. But Torrence continued. "We won't have to go out there, though. When he finishes his day's work here, he plays cornet in a *bal musette* in the Rue de Lappe."

"Go get him for me."

"Shall I bring him to your place?"

Maigret hesitated, thinking of Lucas's yearning for a glass of draft beer. "No, I'll be across the street. Madame Martin's apartment, fourth floor." He took down his heavy overcoat. He filled his pipe.

"Coming?" he said to Lucas.

Mme. Maigret ran after him to ask what time he'd be home for dinner. After a moment of hesitation, he smiled.

"The usual time," was his not very reassuring answer.

"Look out for the little girl, will you?"

At 10 o'clock that evening the investigation was still blocked. It was unlikely that anyone in the whole building had gone to sleep, except Colette. She had finally dozed off, with her father sitting in the dark by her bedside.

Torrence had arrived at 7:30 with his part-time musician and check-room attendant, who declared:

"She's the one. I remember she didn't put the check in her handbag. She slipped it into a big brown shopping bag." And when they took him into the kitchen he added, "That's the bag. Or one exactly like it."

The Martin apartment was very warm. Everyone spoke in low tones, as if they had agreed not to awaken the child. Nobody had eaten. Nobody, apparently, was even hungry. On their way over, Maigret and Lucas had each drunk two beers in a little cafe on the Boulevard Voltaire.

After the cornetist had spoken his piece, Maigret took Torrence aside and murmured fresh instructions.

Every corner of the apartment had been searched. Even the photos of Martin's parents had been taken from their frames, to make sure the baggage check had not been secreted between picture and backing. The dishes had been taken from their shelves and piled on the kitchen table. The larder had been emptied and examined closely. No baggage check.

Madame Martin was still wearing her pale blue négligée. She was chain-smoking cigarettes. What with the smoke from the two men's pipes, a thick blue haze swirled about the lamps.

"You are of course free to say nothing and answer no questions. Your husband will arrive at 11:17. Perhaps you will be more talkative in his presence."

"He doesn't know any more than I do."

"Does he know as much?"

"There's nothing to know. I've told you everything."

She had sat back and denied everything, all along the line. She had conceded only one point. She admitted that Lorilleux had dropped in to see her two or three times at night when she lived in the Rue Pernelle. But she insisted there had been nothing between them, nothing personal.

"In other words he came to talk business—at 1 o'clock in the morning?"

"He used to come to town by a late train, and he didn't like to walk the streets with large sums of money on him. I already told you he might have been smuggling gold, but I had nothing to do with it. You can't arrest me for his activities."

"Did he have large sums of money on him when he disappeared?"

"I don't know. He didn't always take me into his confidence."

"But he did come to see you in your room at night?"

Despite the evidence, she clung to her story of the morning's marketing. She denied ever having seen the two taxi drivers, the luggage dealer, or the check-room attendant.

"If I had really left a package at the Gare du Nord, you would have found the check, wouldn't you?"

She glanced nervously at the clock on the mantel, obviously thinking of her husband's return.

"Admit that the man who came last night found nothing under the floor because you changed the hiding place."

"I know of nothing that was hidden under the floor."

"When you learned of his visit, you decided to move the treasure to the check room for safekeeping."

"I haven't been near the Gare du Nord. There must be thousands of blondes in Paris who answer my description."

"I think I know where we'll find the check."

"You're so very clever."

"Sit over here at this table." Maigret produced a fountain pen and a sheet of paper. "Write your name and address."

She hesitated, then obeyed.

"Tonight every letter mailed in this neighborhood will be examined, and I'll wager we will find one addressed in your handwriting, probably to yourself."

He handed the paper to Lucas with an order to get in touch with the postal authorities. Much to his surprise, the woman reacted visibly.

"You see, it's a very old trick, Little One." For the first time he called her "Little One," the way he would have done if he were questioning her in his office, Quai des Orfèvres.

They were alone now. Maigret slowly paced the floor, while she remained seated.

"In case you're interested," Maigret said slowly, "the thing that shocks me most about you is not what you have done but the cold-blooded way you have done it. You've been dangling at the end of a slender thread since early this morning, and you still haven't blinked an eye. When your husband comes home, you'll try to play the martyr. And yet you know that sooner or later we'll discover the truth."

"But I've done nothing wrong."

"Then why do you lie?"

She did not reply. She was still far from the breaking point. Her nerves were calm, but her mind was obviously racing at top speed, seeking some avenue of escape.

"I'm not saying anything more," she declared. She sat down and pulled the hem of her négligée over her bare knees.

"Suit yourself." Maigret made himself comfortable in a chair opposite her.

"Are you going to stay here all night?" she asked.

"At least until your husband gets home."

"Are you going to tell him about Monsieur Lorilleux's visits to my room?"

"If necessary."

"You're a cad! Jean knows nothing about all this. He had no part in it."

"Unfortunately he is your husband."

When Lucas came back, they were staring at each other in silence.

"Janvier is taking care of the letter, Chief. I met Torrence downstairs. He says the man is in that little bar, two doors down from your house."

She sprang up. "What man?"

Maigret didn't move a muscle. "The man who came here last night. You must have expected him to come back, since he didn't find what he was looking for. And he might be in a different frame of mind this time."

She cast a dismayed glance at the clock. The train from Bergerac was due in twenty minutes. Her husband could be home in forty. She asked: "You know who this man is?"

"I can guess. I could go down and confirm my suspicion. I'd say it is Lorilleux and I'd say he is very eager to get back his property."

"It's not his property!"

"Let's say that, rightly or wrongly, he considers it his property. He must be in desperate straits, this man. He came to see you twice without getting what he wanted. He came back a third time disguised as Father Christmas. And he'll come back again. He'll be surprised to find you have company. I'm convinced that he'll be more talkative than you. Despite the general belief, men always speak more freely than women. Do you think he is armed?"

"I don't know."

"I think he is. He is tired of waiting. I don't know what story you've been telling him, but I'm sure he's fed up with it. The gentleman has a vicious face. There's nothing quite as cruel as a weakling with his back up."

"Shut up!"

"Would you like us to go so that you can be alone with him?"

The back of Maigret's envelope contained the following note: "10:38 P.M. —she decides to talk."

It was not a very connected story at first. It came out in bits and pieces, fragments of sentences interlarded with venomous asides, supplemented by Maigret's own guesses which she either confirmed or amended.

"What do you want to know?"

"Was it money that you left in the check room?"

"Bank notes. Almost a million."

"Did the money belong to Lorilleux?"

"No more to him than to me."

"To one of his customers?"

"Yes. A man named Julian Boissy."

"What became of him?"

"He died."

"How?"

"He was killed."

"By whom?"

"By Monsieur Lorilleux."

"Why?"

"Because I gave him to understand that if he could raise enough money—real money—I might run away with him."

"You were already married?"

"Yes."

"You're not in love with your husband?"

"I despise mediocrity. All my life I've been poor. All my life I've been surrounded by people who have had to scrimp and save, people who have had to sacrifice and count centimes. I've had to scrimp and sacrifice and count centimes myself." She turned savagely on Maigret, as if he had been responsible for all her troubles. "I just didn't want to be poor any more."

"Would you have gone away with Lorilleux?"

"I don't know. Perhaps for a while."

"Long enough to get your hands on his money?"

"I hate you!"

"How was Boissy murdered?"

"Monsieur Boissy was a regular customer of long standing."

"Pornographic literature?"

"He was a lascivious old goat, sure. So are all men. So is Lorilleux. So are you, probably. Boissy was a widower. He lived alone in a hotel room. He was very rich and very stingy. All rich people are stingy."

"That doesn't work both ways, does it? You, for instance, are not rich."

"I would have been rich."

"If Lorilleux had not come back. How did Boissy die?"

"The devaluation of the franc scared him out of his wits. Like everybody else at that time, he wanted gold. Monsieur Lorilleux used to shuttle gold in from Switzerland pretty regularly. And he always demanded payment in advance. One afternoon Monsieur Boissy came to the shop with a fortune in currency. I wasn't there. I had gone out on an errand."

"You planned it that way?"

"No."

"You had no idea what was going to happen?"

"No. Don't try to put words in my mouth. When I came back, Lorilleux was packing the body into a big box."

"And you blackmailed him?"

"No."

"Then why did he disappear after having given you the money?"

"I frightened him."

"You threatened to go to the police?"

"No. I merely told him that our neighbors in the Palais-Royal had been looking at me suspiciously and that I thought he ought to put the money in a safe place for a while. I told him about the loose floor board in my apartment. He thought it would only be for a few days. Two days later he asked me to cross the Belgian frontier with him."

"And you refused?"

"I told him I'd been stopped and questioned by a man who looked like a police inspector. He was terrified. I gave him some of the money and promised to join him in Brussels as soon as it was safe."

"What did he do with the corpse?"

"He put the box in a taxi and drove to a little country house he owned on the banks of the Marne. I suppose he either buried it there or threw it into the river. Nobody ever missed Monsieur Boissy."

"So you sent Lorilleux to Belgium without you. How did you keep him away for five years?"

"I used to write him, general delivery. I told him the police were after him, and that he probably would read nothing about it in the papers because they were setting a trap for him. I told him the police were always coming back to question me. I even sent him to South America."

"He came back two months ago?"

"About. He was at the end of his rope."

"Didn't you send him any money?"

"Not much."

"Why not?"

She did not reply. She looked at the clock.

"Are you going to arrest me? What will be the charge? I didn't kill Boissy. I wasn't there when he was killed. I had nothing to do with disposing of his body."

"Stop worrying about yourself. You kept the money because all your life you wanted money—not to spend, but to keep, to feel secure, to feel rich and free from want."

"That's my business."

"When Lorilleux came back to ask for money, or to ask you to keep your promise and run away with him, you used Colette as a pretext. You tried to scare him into leaving the country again, didn't you?"

"He stayed in Paris, hiding." Her upper lip curled slightly. "What an idiot! He could have shouted his name from the housetops and nobody would have noticed."

"The business of Father Christmas wasn't idiotic."

"No? The money wasn't under the floorboard any longer. It was right here under his nose, in my sewing basket."

"Your husband will be here in ten or fifteen minutes. Lorilleux across the street probably knows it. He's been in touch with Bergerac by phone, and

he can read a timetable. He's surely armed. Do you want to wait here for
your two men?"

"Take me away! I'll slip on a dress. . . ."

"The check-room stub?"

"General delivery, Boulevard Beaumarchais."

She did not close the bedroom door after her. Brazenly she dropped the
négligée from her shoulders and sat on the edge of the bed to pull on her
stockings. She selected a woolen dress from the closet, tossed toilet articles
and lingerie into an overnight bag.

"Let's hurry!"

"Your husband?"

"That fool? Leave him for the birds."

"Colette?"

She shrugged.

Mlle. Doncoeur's door opened a crack as they passed.

Downstairs on the sidewalk she clung fearfully to the two men, peering
into the fog.

"Take her to the Quai des Orfèvres, Lucas. I'm staying here."

She held back. There was no car in sight, and she was obviously frightened
by the prospect of walking into the night with only Lucas to protect her.
Lucas was not very big.

"Don't be afraid. Lorilleux is not in this vicinity."

"You lied to me! You—you—"

Maigret went back into the house.

The conference with Jean Martin lasted two hours.

When Maigret left the house at one-thirty, the two brothers were in serious
conversation. There was a crack of light under Mlle. Doncoeur's door, but
she did not open the door as he passed.

When he got home, his wife was asleep in a chair in the dining room. His
place at table was still set. Mme. Maigret awoke with a start.

"You're alone?" When he looked at her with amused surprise, she added,
"Didn't you bring the little girl home?"

"Not tonight. She's asleep. You can go for her tomorrow morning."

"Why, then we're going to . . ."

"No, not permanently. Jean Martin may console himself with some decent
girl. Or perhaps his brother will get back on his feet and find a new
wife. . . ."

"In other words, she won't be ours?"

"Not in fee simple, no. Only on loan. I thought that would be better than
nothing. I thought it would make you happy."

"Why, yes, of course. It will make me very happy. But . . . but . . ."

She sniffled once and fumbled for her handkerchief. When she couldn't
find it, she buried her face in her apron.

PUZZLE FOR POPPY

by Patrick Quentin

"YES, MISS CRUMP," snapped Iris into the phone. "No, Miss Crump. Oh, nuts, Miss Crump."

My wife flung down the receiver.

"Well?" I asked.

"She won't let us use the patio. It's that dog, that great fat St. Bernard. It mustn't be disturbed."

"Why?"

"It has to be alone with its beautiful thoughts. It's going to become a mother. Peter, it's revolting. There must be something in the lease."

"There isn't," I said.

When I'd rented our half of this La Jolla hacienda for my shore leave, the lease specified that all rights to the enclosed patio belonged to our eccentric co-tenant. It oughtn't to have mattered, but it did because Iris had recently skyrocketed to fame as a movie star and it was impossible for us to appear on the streets without being mobbed. For the last couple of days we had been virtually beleaguered in our apartment. We were crazy about being beleaguered together, but even Héloise and Abelard needed a little fresh air once in a while.

That's why the patio was so important.

Iris was staring through the locked French windows at the forbidden delights of the patio. Suddenly she turned.

"Peter, I'll die if I don't get things into my lungs—ozone and things. We'll just have to go to the beach."

"And be torn limb from limb by your public again?"

"I'm sorry, darling. I'm terribly sorry." Iris unzippered herself from her housecoat and scrambled into slacks and a shirt-waist. She tossed me my naval hat. "Come, Lieutenant—to the slaughter."

When we emerged on the street, we collided head on with a man carrying groceries into the house. As we disentangled ourselves from celery stalks, there was a click and a squeal of delight followed by a powerful whistle. I turned to see a small girl who had been lying in wait with a camera. She was an unsightly little girl with sandy pigtails and a brace on her teeth.

Reprinted by permission of Curtis Brown, Ltd.
Copyright 1946 by Mercury Publications, Inc.

"Geeth," she announced. "I can get two buckth for thith thnap from Barney Thtone. He'th thappy about you, Mith Duluth."

Other children, materializing in response to her whistle, were galloping toward us. The grocery man came out of the house. Passers-by stopped, stared and closed in—a woman in scarlet slacks, two sailors, a flurry of bobby-soxers, a policeman.

"This," said Iris grimly, "is the end."

She escaped from her fans and marched back to the two front doors of our hacienda. She rang the buzzer on the door that wasn't ours. She rang persistently. At length there was the clatter of a chain sliding into place and the door opened wide enough to reveal the face of Miss Crump. It was a small, faded face with a most uncordial expression.

"Yes?" asked Miss Crump.

"We're the Duluths," said Iris. "I just called you. I know about your dog, but . . ."

"Not *my* dog," corrected Miss Crump. "Mrs. Wilberframe's dog. The late Mrs. Wilberframe of Glendale who has a nephew and a niece-in-law of whom I know a great deal in Ogden Bluffs, Utah. At least, they *ought* to be in Ogden Bluffs."

This unnecessary information was flung at us like a challenge. Then Miss Crump's face flushed into sudden, dimpled pleasure.

"Duluth! Iris Duluth. You're *the* Iris Duluth of the movies?"

"Yes," said Iris.

"Oh, why didn't you tell me over the phone? My favorite actress! How exciting! Poor thing—mobbed by your fans. Of course you may use the patio. I will give you the key to open your French windows. Any time."

Miraculously the chain was off the door. It opened halfway and then stopped. Miss Crump was staring at me with a return of suspicion.

"You *are* Miss Duluth's husband?"

"Mrs. Duluth's husband," I corrected her. "Lieutenant Duluth."

She still peered. "I mean, you have proof?"

I was beyond being surprised by Miss Crump. I fumbled from my wallet a dog-eared snapshot of Iris and me in full wedding regalia outside the church. Miss Crump studied it carefully and then returned it.

"You must please excuse me. What a sweet bride! It's just that I can't be too careful—for Poppy."

"Poppy?" queried Iris. "The St. Bernard?"

Miss Crump nodded. "It is Poppy's house, you see. Poppy pays the rent."

"The dog," said Iris faintly, "pays the rent?"

"Yes, my dear. Poppy is very well-to-do. She is hardly more than a puppy, but she is one of the richest dogs, I suppose, in the whole world."

Although we entertained grave doubts as to Miss Crump's sanity, we were soon in swimming suits and stepping through our open French windows into the sunshine of the patio. Miss Crump introduced us to Poppy.

In spite of our former prejudices, Poppy disarmed us immediately. She was just a big, bouncing, natural girl unspoiled by wealth. She greeted us with great thumps of her tail. She leaped up at Iris, dabbing at her cheek with a long, pink tongue. Later, when we had settled on striped mattresses under orange trees, she curled into a big clumsy ball at my side and laid her vast muzzle on my stomach.

"Look, she likes you." Miss Crump was glowing. "Oh, I knew she would!"

Iris, luxuriating in the sunshine, asked the polite question. "Tell us about Poppy. How did she make her money?"

"Oh, she did not make it. She inherited it." Miss Crump sat down on a white iron chair. "Mrs. Wilberframe was a very wealthy woman. She was devoted to Poppy."

"And left her all her money?" I asked.

"Not quite all. There was a little nest egg for me. I was her companion, you see, for many years. But I am to look after Poppy. That is why I received the nest egg. Poppy pays me a generous salary too." She fingered nondescript beads at her throat. "Mrs. Wilberframe was anxious for Poppy to have only the best and I am sure I try to do the right thing. Poppy has the master bedroom, of course. I take the little one in front. And then, if Poppy has steak for dinner, I have hamburger." She stared intensely. "I would not have an easy moment if I felt that Poppy did not get the best."

Poppy, her head on my stomach, coughed. She banged her tail against the flagstones apologetically.

Iris reached across me to pat her. "Has she been rich for long?"

"Oh, no, Mrs. Wilberframe passed on only a few weeks ago." Miss Crump paused. "And it has been a great responsibility for me." She paused again and then blurted: "You're my friends, aren't you? Oh, I am sure you are. Please, please, won't you help me? I am all alone and I am so frightened."

"Frightened?" I looked up and, sure enough, her little bird face was peaked with fear.

"For Poppy." Miss Crump leaned forward. "Oh, Lieutenant, it is like a nightmare. Because I know. I just know they are trying to murder her!"

"They?" Iris sat up straight.

"Mrs. Wilberframe's nephew and his wife. From Ogden Bluffs, Utah."

"You mentioned them when you opened the door."

"I mention them to everyone who comes to the house. You see, I do not know what they look like and I do not want them to think I am not on my guard."

I watched her. She might have looked like a silly spinster with a bee in her bonnet. She didn't. She looked nice and quite sane, only scared.

"Oh, they are not good people. Not at all. There is nothing they would not stoop to. Back in Glendale, I found pieces of meat in the front yard. Poisoned meat, I know. And on a lonely road, they shot at Poppy. Oh, the police laughed at me. A car backfiring, they said. But I know differently. I know they won't stop till Poppy is dead." She threw her little hands up to her face. "I ran away from them in Glendale. That is why I came to La Jolla. But they have caught up with us. I know. Oh, dear, poor Poppy who is so sweet without a nasty thought in her head."

Poppy, hearing her name mentioned, smiled and panted.

"But this nephew and his wife from Ogden Bluffs, why should they want to murder her?" My wife's eyes were gleaming with a detective enthusiasm I knew of old. "Are they after her money?"

"Of course," said Miss Crump passionately. "It's the will. The nephew is Mrs. Wilberframe's only living relative, but she deliberately cut him off and I am sure I do not blame her. All the money goes to Poppy and—er—Poppy's little ones."

"Isn't the nephew contesting a screwy will like that?" I asked.

"Not yet. To contest a will takes a great deal of money—lawyers' fees and things. It would be much, much cheaper for him to kill Poppy. You see, one thing is not covered by the will. If Poppy were to die before she became a mother, the nephew would inherit the whole estate. Oh, I have done everything in my power. The moment the—er—suitable season arrived, I found a husband for Poppy. In a few weeks now, the—the little ones are expected. But these next few weeks . . ."

Miss Crump dabbed at her eyes with a small handkerchief. "Oh, the Glendale police were most unsympathetic. They even mentioned the fact that the sentence for shooting or killing a dog in this state is shockingly light—a small fine at most. I called the police here and asked for protection. They said they'd send a man around some time but they were hardly civil. So you see, there is no protection from the law and no redress. There is no one to help me."

"You've got us," said Iris in a burst of sympathy.

"Oh . . . oh . . ." The handkerchief fluttered from Miss Crump's face. "I knew you were my friends. You dear, dear things. Oh, Poppy, they are going to help us."

Poppy, busy licking my stomach, did not reply. Somewhat appalled by Iris' hasty promise but ready to stand by her, I said:

"Sure, we'll help, Miss Crump. First, what's the nephew's name?"

"Henry. Henry Blodgett. But he won't use that name. Oh, no, he will be too clever for that."

"And you don't know what he looks like?"

"Mrs. Wilberframe destroyed his photograph many years ago when he bit her as a small boy. With yellow curls, I understand. That is when the trouble between them started."

"At least you know what age he is?"

"He should be about thirty."

"And the wife?" asked Iris.

"I know nothing about her," said Miss Crump coldly, "except that she is supposed to be a red-headed person, a former actress."

"And what makes you so sure one or both of them have come to La Jolla?" Miss Crump folded her arms in her lap. "Last night. A telephone call."

"A telephone call?"

"A voice asking if I was Miss Crump, and then—silence." Miss Crump leaned toward me. "Oh, now they know I am here. They know I never let

Poppy out. They know every morning I search the patio for meat, traps. They must realize that the only possible way to reach her is to enter the house."

"Break in?"

Miss Crump shook her tight curls. "It is possible. But I believe they will rely on guile rather than violence. It is against that we must be on our guard. You are the only people who have come to the door since that telephone call. Now anyone else that comes to your apartment or mine, whatever their excuse . . ." She lowered her voice. "Anyone may be Henry Blodgett or his wife and we will have to outwit them."

A fly settled on one of Poppy's valuable ears. She did not seem to notice it. Miss Crump watched us earnestly and then gave a self-scolding cluck.

"Dear me, here I have been burdening you with Poppy's problems and you must be hungry. How about a little salad for luncheon? I always feel guilty about eating in the middle of the day when Poppy has her one meal at night. But with guests—yes, and allies—I am sure Mrs. Wilberframe would not have grudged the expense."

With a smile that was half-shy, half-conspiratorial, she fluttered away.

I looked at Iris. "Well," I said, "is she a nut or do we believe her?"

"I rather think," said my wife, "that we believe her."

"Why?"

"Just because." Iris' face wore the entranced expression which had won her so many fans in her last picture. "Oh, Peter, don't you see what fun it will be? A beautiful St. Bernard in peril. A wicked villain with golden curls who bit his aunt."

"He won't have golden curls any more," I said. "He's a big boy now."

Iris, her body warm from the sun, leaned over me and put both arms around Poppy's massive neck.

"Poor Poppy," she said. "Really, this shouldn't happen to a dog!"

The first thing happened some hours after Miss Crump's little salad luncheon while Iris and I were still sunning ourselves. Miss Crump, who had been preparing Poppy's dinner and her own in her apartment, came running to announce:

"There is a man at the door! He claims he is from the electric light company to read the meter. Oh, dear, if he is legitimate and we do not let him in, there will be trouble with the electric light company and if . . ." She wrung her hands. "Oh, what shall we do?"

I reached for a bathrobe. "You and Iris stay here. And for Mrs. Wilberframe's sake, hang on to Poppy."

I found the man outside the locked front door. He was about thirty with thinning hair and wore an army discharge button. He showed me his credentials. They seemed in perfect order. There was nothing for it but to let him in. I took him into the kitchen where Poppy's luscious steak and Miss Crump's modest hamburger were lying on the table. I hovered over the man while he located the meter. I never let him out of my sight until he had departed. In answer to Miss Crump's anxious questioning, I could only say that if the man had been Henry Blodgett he knew how much electricity she'd used in the past month—but that was all.

The next caller showed up a few minutes later. Leaving Iris, indignant at being out of things, to stand by Poppy, Miss Crump and I handled the visitor. This time it was a slim, brash girl with bright auburn hair and a navy-blue slack suit. She was, she said, the sister of the woman who owned the hacienda. She wanted a photograph for the newspapers—a photograph of her Uncle William who had just been promoted to Rear Admiral in the Pacific. The photograph was in a trunk in the attic.

Miss Crump, reacting to the unlikeliness of the request, refused entry. The red-head wasn't the type that wilted. When she started talking darkly of eviction, I overrode Miss Crump and offered to conduct her to the attic. The girl gave me one quick, experienced look and flounced into the hall.

The attic was reached by the back stairs through the kitchen. I conducted the red-head directly to her claimed destination. There were trunks. She searched through them. At length she produced a photograph of a limp young man in a raccoon coat.

"My Uncle William," she snapped, "as a youth."

"Pretty," I said.

I took her back to the front door. On the threshold she gave me another of her bold, appraising stares.

"You know something?" she said. "I was hoping you'd make a pass at me in the attic."

"Why?" I asked.

"So's I could tear your ears off."

She left. If she had been Mrs. Blodgett, she knew how to take care of herself, she knew how many trunks there were in the attic—and that was all.

Iris and I had dressed and were drinking Daiquiris under a green and white striped umbrella when Miss Crump appeared followed by a young policeman. She was very pleased about the policeman. He had come, she said, in answer to her complaint. She showed him Poppy; she babbled out her story of the Blodgetts. He obviously thought she was a harmless lunatic, but she didn't seem to realize it. After she had let him out, she settled beamingly down with us.

"I suppose," said Iris, "you asked him for his credentials?"

"I . . ." Miss Crump's face clouded. "My dear, you don't think that perhaps he wasn't a real police . . . ?"

"To me," said Iris, "everyone's a Blodgett until proved to the contrary."

"Oh, dear," said Miss Crump.

Nothing else happened. By evening Iris and I were back in our part of the house. Poppy had hated to see us go. We had hated to leave her. A mutual crush had developed between us.

But now we were alone again, the sinister Blodgetts did not seem very substantial. Iris made a creditable *Boeuf Stroganov* from yesterday's leftovers and changed into a lime green négligée which would have inflamed the whole Pacific Fleet. I was busy being a sailor on leave with his girl when the phone rang. I reached over Iris for the receiver, said "Hello," and then sat rigid listening.

It was Miss Crump's voice. But something was horribly wrong with it. It came across hoarse and gasping.

"Come," it said. "Oh, come. The French windows. Oh, please . . ."

The voice faded. I heard the clatter of a dropped receiver.

"It must be Poppy," I said to Iris. "Quick."

We ran out into the dark patio. Across it, I could see the light French windows to Miss Crump's apartment. They were half open, and as I looked Poppy squirmed through to the patio. She bounded toward us, whining.

"Poppy's all right," said Iris. "Quick!"

We ran to Miss Crump's windows. Poppy barged past us into the living room. We followed. All the lights were on. Poppy had galloped around a high-backed davenport. We went to it and looked over it.

Poppy was crouching on the carpet, her huge muzzle dropped on her paws. She was howling and staring straight at Miss Crump.

Poppy's paid companion was on the floor too. She lay motionless on her back, her legs twisted under her, her small, grey face distorted, her lips stretched in a dreadful smile.

I knelt down by Poppy. I picked up Miss Crump's thin wrist and felt for the pulse. Poppy was still howling. Iris stood, straight and white.

"Peter, tell me. Is she dead?"

"Not quite. But only just not quite. Poison. It looks like strychnine. . . ."

We called a doctor. We called the police. The doctor came, muttered a shocked diagnosis of strychnine poisoning and rushed Miss Crump to the hospital. I asked if she had a chance. He didn't answer. I knew what that meant. Soon the police came and there was so much to say and do and think that I hadn't time to brood about poor Miss Crump.

We told Inspector Green the Blodgett story. It was obvious to us that somehow Miss Crump had been poisoned by them in mistake for Poppy. Since no one had entered the house that day except the three callers, one of them, we said, must have been a Blodgett. All the Inspector had to do, we said, was to locate those three people and find out which was a Blodgett.

Inspector Green watched us poker-faced and made no comment. After he'd left, we took the companionless Poppy back to our part of the house. She climbed on the bed and stretched out between us, her tail thumping, her head flopped on the pillows. We didn't have the heart to evict her. It was not one of our better nights.

Early next morning, a policeman took us to Miss Crump's apartment. Inspector Green was waiting in the living room. I didn't like his stare.

"We've analyzed the hamburger she was eating last night," he said. "There was enough strychnine in it to kill an elephant."

"Hamburger!" exclaimed Iris. "Then that proves she was poisoned by the Blodgetts!"

"Why?" asked Inspector Green.

"They didn't know how conscientious Miss Crump was. They didn't know she always bought steak for Poppy and hamburger for herself. They saw the steak and the hamburger and they naturally assumed the hamburger was for Poppy, so they poisoned that."

"That's right," I cut in. "The steak and the hamburger were lying right on the kitchen table when all three of those people came in yesterday."

"I see," said the Inspector.

He nodded to a policeman who left the room and returned with three people—the balding young man from the electric light company, the red-headed vixen, and the young policeman. None of them looked happy.

"You're willing to swear," the Inspector asked us, "that these were the only three people who entered this house yesterday."

"Yes," said Iris.

"And you think one of them is either Blodgett or his wife?"

"They've got to be."

Inspector Green smiled faintly. "Mr. Burns here has been with the electric light company for five years except for a year when he was in the army. The electric light company is willing to vouch for that. Miss Curtis has been identified as the sister of the lady who owns this house and the niece of Rear Admiral Moss. She has no connection with any Blodgetts and has never been in Utah." He paused. "As for Officer Patterson, he has been a member of the police force here for eight years. I personally sent him around yesterday to follow up Miss Crump's complaint."

The Inspector produced an envelope from his pocket and tossed it to me. "I've had these photographs of Mr. and Mrs. Henry Blodgett flown from the files of the Ogden Bluffs *Tribune*."

I pulled the photographs out of the envelope. We stared at them. Neither Mr. or Mrs. Blodgett looked at all the sort of person you would like to know. But neither of them bore the slightest resemblance to any of the three suspects in front of us.

"It might also interest you," said the Inspector quietly, "that I've checked with the Ogden Bluffs police. Mr. Blodgett has been sick in bed for over a week and his wife has been nursing him. There is a doctor's certificate to that effect."

Inspector Green gazed down at his hands. They were competent hands. "It looks to me that the whole Blodgett story was built up in Miss Crump's mind—or yours." His grey eyes stared right through us. "If we have to eliminate the Blodgetts and these three people from suspicion, that leaves only two others who had the slightest chance of poisoning the hamburger."

Iris blinked. "Us?"

"You," said Inspector Green almost sadly.

They didn't arrest us, of course. We had no conceivable motive. But Inspector Green questioned us minutely and when he left there was a policeman lounging outside our door.

We spent a harried afternoon racking our brains and getting nowhere. Iris was the one who had the inspiration. Suddenly, just after she had fed Poppy the remains of the *Stroganov*, she exclaimed:

"Good heavens above, of course!"

"Of course, what?"

She spun to me, her eyes shining. "Barney Thtone," she lisped. "Why didn't we realize? Come on!"

She ran out of the house into the street. She grabbed the lounging policeman by the arm.

"You live here," she said. "Who's Barney Stone?"

"Barney Stone?" The policeman stared. "He's the son of the druggist on the corner."

Iris raced me to the drugstore. She was attracting quite a crowd. The policeman followed, too.

In the drugstore, a thin young man with spectacles stood behind the prescription counter.

"Mr. Stone?" asked Iris.

His mouth dropped open. "Gee, Miss Duluth. I never dreamed . . . Gee, Miss Duluth, what can I do for you? Cigarettes? An alarm clock?"

"A little girl," said Iris. "A little girl with sandy pigtails and a brace on her teeth. What's her name? Where does she live?"

Barney Stone said promptly: "You mean Daisy Kornfeld. Kind of homely. Just down the block. 712. Miss Duluth, I certainly . . ."

"Thanks," cut in Iris and we were off again with our ever growing escort.

Daisy was sitting in the Kornfeld parlor, glumly thumping the piano. Ushered in by an excited, cooing Mrs. Kornfeld, Iris interrupted Daisy's rendition of *The Jolly Farmer*.

"Daisy, that picture you took of me yesterday to sell to Mr. Stone, is it developed yet?"

"Geeth no, Mith Duluth. I ain't got the developing money yet. Theventy-five thenth. Ma don't give me but a nickel an hour for practithing thith gothdarn piano."

"Here." Iris thrust a ten-dollar bill into her hand. "I'll buy the whole roll. Run get the camera. We'll have it developed right away."

"Geeth." The mercenary Daisy stared with blank incredulity at the ten-dollar bill.

I stared just as blankly myself. I wasn't being bright at all.

I wasn't much brighter an hour later. We were back in our apartment, waiting for Inspector Green. Poppy, all for love, was trying to climb into my lap. Iris, who had charmed Barney Stone into developing Daisy's films, clutched the yellow envelope of snaps in her hand. She had sent our policeman away on a secret mission, but an infuriating passion for the dramatic had kept her from telling or showing me anything. I had to wait for Inspector Green.

Eventually Iris' policeman returned and whispered with her in the hall.

Then Inspector Green came. He looked cold and hostile. Poppy didn't like him. She growled. Sometimes Poppy was smart.

Inspector Green said: "You've been running all over town. I told you to stay here."

"I know." Iris' voice was meek. "It's just that I wanted to solve poor Miss Crump's poisoning."

"Solve it?" Inspector Green's query was skeptical.

"Yes. It's awfully simple really. I can't imagine why we didn't think of it from the start."

"You mean you know who poisoned her?"

"Of course." Iris smiled, a maddening smile. "Henry Blodgett."

"But . . ."

"Check with the airlines. I think you'll find that Blodgett flew in from Ogden Bluffs a few days ago and flew back today. As for his being sick in bed under his wife's care, I guess that'll make Mrs. Blodgett an accessory before the fact, won't it?"

Inspector Green was pop-eyed.

"Oh, it's my fault really," continued Iris. "I said no one came to the house yesterday except those three people. There was someone else, but he was so ordinary, so run-of-the-mill, that I forgot him completely."

I was beginning to see then. Inspector Green snapped: "And this run-of-the-mill character?"

"The man," said Iris sweetly, "who had the best chance of all to poison the hamburger, *the man who delivered it*—the man from the Supermarket."

"We don't have to guess. We have proof." Iris fumbled in the yellow envelope. "Yesterday morning as we were going out, we bumped into the man delivering Miss Crump's groceries. Just at that moment, a sweet little girl took a snap of us. This snap."

She selected a print and handed it to Inspector Green. I moved to look at it over his shoulder.

"I'm afraid Daisy is an impressionistic photographer," murmured Iris. "That hip on the right is me. The buttocks are my husband. But the figure in the middle—quite a masterly likeness of Henry Blodgett, isn't it? Of course, there's the grocery apron, the unshaven chin . . ."

She was right. Daisy had only winged Iris and me but with the grocery man she had scored a direct hit. And the grocery man was unquestionably Henry Blodgett.

Iris nodded to her policeman. "Sergeant Blair took a copy of the snap around the neighborhood groceries. They recognized Blodgett at the Supermarket. They hired him day before yesterday. He made a few deliveries this morning, including Miss Crump's, and took a powder without his pay."

"Well . . ." stammered Inspector Green. "Well . . ."

"Just how many charges can you get him on?" asked my wife hopefully. "Attempted homicide, conspiracy to defraud, illegal possession of poisonous drugs. . . . The rat, I hope you give him the works when you get him."

"We'll get him all right," said Inspector Green.

Iris leaned over and patted Poppy's head affectionately.

"Don't worry, darling. I'm sure Miss Crump will get well and we'll throw a lovely christening party for your little strangers. . . ."

Iris was right about the Blodgetts. Henry got the works. And his wife was held as an accessory. Iris was right about Miss Crump too. She is still in the hospital but improving steadily and will almost certainly be well enough to attend the christening party.

Meanwhile, at her request, Poppy is staying with us, awaiting maternity with rollicking unconcern.

It's nice having a dog who pays the rent.

THE SECRET

by Mary Roberts Rinehart

CHAPTER ONE

HILDA ADAMS was indignant. She snapped her bag shut and got up.

"So that's that," she said. "I'm not young enough or strong enough to go abroad, but I can work my head off here. Maybe if I'd had a new permanent and a facial I'd have got by."

The man behind the desk smiled at her.

"I'm sorry," he said. "It looks as though this war is about over. Anyhow your heart—"

"What's the matter with my heart?"

"It skips a beat now and then. Nothing serious. You'll probably live to a ripe old age. But—"

"It skipped a beat because I was making up my mind to commit a murder," she said coldly.

She put a hand on the desk. It was alarmingly near an ink well, and the medical man looked slightly uneasy.

"Now look, Miss Adams," he said. "I didn't make these rules. We need nurses over there, all we can get. But suppose you had to fly at twenty thousand feet?"

"I'd like it." However she had moved her hand, and he was relieved. "All right," she said. "Maybe I did want to be useful, Dr. Forbes. And maybe I wanted some excitement too. At my age there isn't a great deal. Well, I know when I'm licked."

She did not say good-bye. She walked out, and Forbes looked after her thoughtfully. She was a small neat woman, with short graying hair and child-like blue eyes. Her black suit and white blouse showed a sturdy body, and he scowled as he pressed a button on his desk.

"Get me Inspector Fuller," he said to the girl who came in. "Here's his number."

He shoved a piece of paper across the desk and sat back. Damn it all, they could have used the Adams woman abroad. She was capable. No nerves, he thought, and she was a motherly sort of woman, too old to upset the boys and not too old to take care of them. But the Board had ruled against her.

When the telephone rang he took it up sharply.

"Fuller here," said a voice. "How about it, doctor?"

"I wish you fellows would keep out of my hair," he said, disregarding the fact that he had little or none. "We had to turn her down, if that's what you want to know."

"Why? What reason?"

"She's no chicken," the doctor said sourly. "She has a heart too."

Fuller's voice was startled.

"Good God! What's wrong with her heart?"

"Nothing that will kill her. Skips a beat now and then. She says it was because she was feeling like murdering some one. Maybe we can review the case. I'd be damned glad to use her over here anyhow."

There was more than a hint of alarm in Fuller's voice.

"Now look," he said, "lay off that for a week or so, won't you? I may need her."

"She says there isn't much excitement in life at her age," the doctor said drily. "I had an idea that wasn't exactly true. However . . ."

Fuller was apparently stunned into silence. He grunted.

"Besides, as I've said, whether the war's over or not we still need nurses, Inspector."

"Crime's never over," Fuller said, recovering somewhat. "And she's one of my best operatives." His voice was almost pleading. "Don't let that face of hers fool you, Forbes. She sees more with those blue eyes of hers than you'd believe. I plant her in a house, and what comes up would make your hair curl. This idea of hers has had me running in circles."

Dr. Forbes was unmoved.

"I wouldn't count too much on her," he said. "She looked pretty sore when she left here. Said there wasn't much excitement in life at her age."

Fuller laughed.

"I wonder what she calls excitement," he said. "The last case she was on she warned the guilty woman to kill herself or she would go to the chair."

"And did she?"

"Did she what? Oh, the woman! Yes, of course. Put a bullet in her brain. Well, thanks a lot, Forbes. I don't mind her nursing soldiers, but I didn't want her to be where we couldn't get her when we need her."

"Better send her a box of flowers," Forbes suggested. "She's not feeling very happy just now. Nor am I," he added and slapped down the receiver.

Hilda went back to her tidy apartment that afternoon, to her small sitting room with its bright chintzes, where above a Boston fern a canary hopped about in its cage and piped a welcome. And to her austere bedroom where in a locked suitcase she kept the small bone-handled automatic which was as much a part of her nursing equipment as her hypodermic, forceps, bandage, scissors, thermometer, and so on.

She took off her neat black hat and ran her hand over her short hair. Then, which was unusual for her, she lit a cigarette and stood by the sitting room window, staring out. All she saw was a series of flat roofs and chimneys, but she was not really looking at them. Her mind was back in the office she had just left. They should have taken her. She knew all about her heart, which had taken a lot of beating and could still take a lot more. Even if she wasn't young she was strong. She could work circles around most of the younger women she knew.

The canary beside her chirped again, and absently she got some lettuce from her small icebox and gave it to him. It wasn't good for him, she thought, but after all why not get some enjoyment out of life? It was dull enough as it was. She had lost a month trying to get to the war. Any part of the war. Now with things as they were she would have to register for a case again. She was needed. They were all needed.

She was too disgusted to go out for dinner. She fried an egg on the two-burner electric stove in her kitchenette and made coffee in a percolator. Then, having put up a card table and covered it with a white cloth, she sat down to her supper.

She was still there playing with the food when the flowers came. The landlady brought them up, avid with curiosity.

"Somebody sure thinks a lot of you," she said. "That box is as big as a coffin."

But Hilda was staring at it suspiciously.

"Thanks," she said. "I guess I know who they're from. And if I had a chance I'd throw them in his face."

"Well, really!" The landlady looked shocked. "I must say, if some one sent me a box like that I'd be pleased, to say the least."

"That depends on why they're sent," Hilda said coldly, and closed the door with firmness. She didn't look at the flowers. She merely took the lid off, glanced at the card—which said "To Miss Pinkerton, with admiration and regards"—and, ignoring the remainder of her meal, went to the telephone and dialed a number.

"Give me Inspector Fuller," she said, and waited, her face a frozen mask.

When she heard his voice she was so shaken with fury that her hands trembled. Her voice was steady, however, steady and very very cold.

"Why the flowers?" she inquired briefly.

"Now listen, Hilda—"

"Why the flowers? How did you know I'd been turned down?"

"Well, you see, I happened to know Forbes. So when he told me what had happened today—"

"Don't lie to me. It was a put-up job and you know it. I'm to stay at home and do your dirty work. That's it, isn't it?"

"Look, Hilda, don't you suppose I want to be in this thing, too. I've pulled all the wires I can and here I am. The country's got to go on, you know. Anyhow, what with your heart and the fact that we're neither of us as young as—"

He realized then that she had hung up, and sat gazing rather forlornly at the receiver.

Hilda did not finish her supper. It was her custom when off duty to take a brief walk in the evening, and in many ways she was a creature of habit. In the winter she walked a certain number of blocks. When the weather was warm enough she walked to the park and sat there on a bench with her knitting. Now, taking the box of flowers under one arm and her knitting bag on the other, she stalked downstairs. She left the flowers outside the landlady's sitting room, and with a grim face started for the park.

She did not even look up when a man sat down on the bench beside her. She knitted bleakly and determinedly until she heard him laugh.

"What a face!" he said. "And I'll bet you're skipping stitches, Hilda."

She said nothing, and Fuller realized it was serious. But then it was always serious. Hilda did not like working for the police.

"Heard a curious story today," he said. "I call it the mystery of the black dot."

She looked up then. "Do I have to listen?" she inquired coldly. "I like it here, but I can go home."

"It's nothing to do with you, or me," he said. "Just a nice little spy story. A black dot on a letter to certain prisoners of war in Germany. The letters weren't meant to reach the prisoners, and didn't. They were picked up and the dot magnified from the size of a pinhead to a complete message. Neat, wasn't it?"

He watched her. At least she had stopped knitting, but she made no comment. Not for the first time he thought that, except for her hair and her small mature body, she looked almost girlish. It was her skin, he considered, and the clear blue of her eyes. But her face had not relaxed.

"I might as well tell you now," she said. "I'm not working for you any more. I'm too old, and I have a bad heart. I'm going to the country and raise chickens. I've always wanted to."

"Oh, my God. Is that what they've done to you?" he said unhappily. "Now listen, Hilda. I put no pressure on that situation. I said if they wanted you they'd have to take you. But I said I could use you if they couldn't. And I can. Right now."

"I want no more murder," she said flatly.

"Would it interest you to try to stop one? After all, life is life, here or at the front, Hilda. There's a situation building up that's got me worried. At least let me talk about it. Sometimes it helps me."

"I can't stop your talking," she said briefly, and picked up her knitting again.

He lit a cigarette and stared out over the park. The October sun had set. The nurses had long ago taken their small charges home to early supper and bed, and now the children playing about had come from the tenement districts. For this little hour the park was theirs. His eyes softened as he looked at them.

"Life's a damned queer thing," he said. "Look at those kids. They haven't

much, but they like what they have. There are other children who have
everything and don't like anything." He cleared his throat. "I'm thinking
about a girl. She's perfectly rational, so far as I know. She's nice to look at,
she has money and clothes, she has a young officer who wants to marry her.
And I think she intends to kill her mother."

Hilda looked startled.

"What has the mother done?"

"That's the devil of it. Nobody knows. There's an aunt, and she's about
frantic. She thinks it's a fixed idea, abnormal. I'm not so sure."

In spite of her anger Hilda was interested.

"There are such things as psychiatrists."

"She's smart. We've tried it. No soap. She wouldn't talk."

"How do you know she has this idea?"

"She's tried it already. Twice."

He stopped at that. Hilda turned exasperated eyes on him.

"Is this like the sailor who promised to tell the little boy how he'd lost
his leg, if he wouldn't ask any more questions?"

"Well, how did he lose it?"

"He said it was bit off," Hilda said calmly, and Fuller laughed.

"All right," he said. "The first time she shot at her. The idea is that she
was walking in her sleep. Went to the door of her mother's room and let go
twice. Only she missed. That was about two months ago."

"People do walk in their sleep."

"They don't fire a gun twice. The first shot would waken them. And they
don't run cars into trees in their sleep. She did that too, with her mother
in the car. This time it was to be an accident."

"The psychiatrists claim there are no accidents, don't they?"

"I wouldn't know," Fuller said, restraining a feeling of triumph. "What
I get out of it is that she's tried twice and weakened each time. I've seen
where the car hit. Ten feet further on it would have gone into a ravine. The
tree saved them."

She was silent for some time. Darkness was falling, and the children were
wandering back to whatever dingy spots they called home. Overhead the
lights of a plane flashed on and off. Its muffled beat mingled with the sounds
of traffic, of buses and cars and trucks, to make the subdued roar of the city
at night.

"I don't like it," Hilda said, after a pause. "I don't know anything about
abnormal psychology, and I loathe neurotic girls."

"She isn't neurotic," Fuller said positively. "She's in trouble of some sort."

"And murder's the way out?"

"There's one motive the crime writers never touch on, Hilda. That's desperation."

"What has driven the girl to that?"

"I wish to God I knew," he said heavily. "Anyhow the aunt fell downstairs
today and cracked some ribs. Apparently it's okay. She wasn't pushed. But
they need a nurse there. You might think about it."

"I've told you I'm taking no more cases for you."

He had to leave it at that. They walked slowly back to her small apartment, but Fuller did not go in. He said a few rather awkward words about her disappointment, to which she replied with frozen silence. But as he was leaving she spoke abruptly.

"That girl," she said. "Does *she* say these things are accidents?"

"She doesn't say anything. I gather it's the mother who does the explaining, sleepwalking and faulty steering gear."

"Anybody hurt in the car?"

"The girl hurt her arm. That's all. The aunt's been to see me. Says they took an X-ray at the hospital. No break. She behaved nicely, apparently. Thanked everybody but wasn't talking much. I've seen the surgeon who examined it. He says she didn't look crazy. She looked—well, defeated was his word. Otherwise she seemed like a nice child."

"She doesn't sound like it," Hilda said drily. But she made no further comment, and he left her at her door and went on. All things considered, he thought, he had done rather well. Hilda would think it over, and after that either she would call him or something would happen and he would call her. She might not like crime work, but her bump of curiosity was very large.

CHAPTER TWO

HE WENT BACK to his comfortable bachelor apartment and telephoned his office. There was no message however, and he mixed himself a mild drink and sat down in an ancient leather chair to think.

It was the aunt, Alice Rowland, who had consulted him. As he had told Hilda, he had known her slightly, a frail middle-aged woman, and she had told him the story, first with an attempt to conceal the identity of the girl involved and finally laying all her cards on the table.

She was, as he knew, unmarried and until the war she had lived alone in the large Rowland house on Center Avenue. Her brother Charles was a colonel in the Army. He had been stationed in Honolulu, and his wife and daughter had been with him there. He had got them out after the Japanese attacked, but had remained himself. Now he was somewhere in the Pacific, and his family was living with the aunt.

The first two or three years had been all right, she said. At the beginning Nina—the sister-in-law—had been suffering from shock, and the daughter had been overanxious. She was only sixteen then, but she might have been the mother rather than the child.

"It worried me at the time," Miss Rowland said. "I laid it to what had happened, but she wouldn't talk about the attack, or even about the islands.

Nina did. She loved Honolulu. But Tony, the daughter, would get up and leave the room if it was even mentioned."

"She gave no reason, I suppose?"

"No, and she got over it in time. She became entirely normal. She went to boarding school and made friends there. She was very popular, I believe. When she graduated she came back, and a year ago I had an informal tea and gave her as much of a debut as I could in wartime. She's been home ever since. Nina's rather delicate, but we all got along splendidly. Or did. Then about two months ago Tony—her name is really Antoinette, after my mother—Tony began to change."

"Just how? What did you notice?"

Alice Rowland looked distressed.

"It's hard to put into words," she said. "She was sick for a day or two, but she got over that. I thought it was because something had happened and she broke her engagement. Maybe that was part of it, but it was the other change in her."

"What sort of change?"

"Well, she began to watch her mother. Nina's always been in bed a good bit—she likes being coddled—and Tony's room is across the hall. Then she practically stopped going out, and she kept her door open all the time. Whenever I went in to see her mother she went in too. I got the idea she didn't want me to see her. Not alone anyhow. And she never let her go out of the house if she could help it. I began to wonder . . ."

She hesitated, coloring faintly.

"You see," she explained, "my sister-in-law is a really beautiful woman. She's always had a great deal of admiration. And Tony worships her father. I—well, I thought there might be some one in love with her and Tony knew it. But nobody calls her up, so far as I know, and I don't see her mail. As a matter of fact"—she looked embarrassed—"I don't even know if she sees all of it. Tony watches for the postman and gets it first."

She came to a full stop. Her hands were moist with nervousness, and she got a handkerchief from her bag and wiped them.

"I hate doing this," she said. "It—this part of it really isn't a police matter. I just need advice. But one of my friends wrote asking Nina to lunch and bridge. She got a telephoned regret from Tony. Later I spoke to Nina about it. I thought she looked very queer, as if she hadn't known about it."

"But she accepts all this—attention?"

"She's used to being looked after. My brother spoiled her. If she and Tony disagree I wouldn't know about it. Since the accident with the car Nina's been in bed a good bit. Dr. Wynant says it's merely shock, but she has some neuritis too. In her arms."

"When did this shooting take place?"

"Two months ago. I really do think Tony was walking in her sleep then. She was very unhappy. She'd broken her engagement, just when everything was ready for the wedding. That was probably the reason." She wiped her hands again. "Such a nice boy, too. Johnny Hayes. He's a lieutenant in the Army. I suppose he's gone now, or on his way."

"Did Mrs. Rowland object to the marriage?"

"No. She was delighted. We all were."

"Did Tony ever say why she broke her engagement?"

"No. She simply said it was all off. She was quite definite about it. She sent back the presents and took her trousseau up to a closet on the third floor. It's still there, her wedding dress and everything."

"About this shooting. Did she say she'd been walking in her sleep?"

"She didn't say anything. She never has, since. But the gun was under some clothes in a drawer in Nina's room. Charles had given it to them after the attack. It was loaded, and none of us knew how to unload it."

"Can you remember that night, Miss Rowland? You heard the shots, I suppose. What then?"

"I ran in, in my nightdress. Nina's room is behind mine, and Tony's is across the hall. I found Tony on the floor just inside her mother's door, with the gun beside her. She had fainted, and Nina was trying to get out of bed. She didn't seem to know what had happened."

"She wasn't hurt? Your sister-in-law, I mean."

"No, but she was badly shocked. It was late at night, and with the house being detached only the servants heard the shots. They ran down and helped put Tony to bed. Nina wasn't any use. She never is in an emergency. But she said Tony had often walked in her sleep as a child, especially if she was worried."

"And Tony? How did she react?"

"She seemed dazed. When we put her to bed she just lay there. I tried to find her pulse, but she had hardly any. I called Dr. Wynant, and he gave her a hypodermic of some sort. I told him a little. I didn't say she'd fired at her mother, but she had, Inspector. I found one bullet in the head of the bed. The other must have gone out the window. It was open."

"This was two months ago?"

"Yes. She was in bed for a week or so. But I'm very anxious. You see, she fired twice. That's the part I don't understand. You'd think, if she were really asleep, one shot would have wakened her."

About the car accident she was more vague. She had not been there, and Nina had said something had gone wrong with the steering gear. After all the car was old, and few mechanics were available. What she couldn't understand was where it had happened.

"We have very little gas," she said. "I can't imagine Tony going out to the country at all with things as they are, or Nina going with her. Yet she did, and it happened on a remote road. Only Tony was the one who was injured. She hurt her arm, and it's still stiff. Nina isn't much good in an emergency, but Tony walked a mile or two, holding her arm and not making any fuss about it. Nina says she was very pale but quite calm."

"Then all this has been in the last two months? Things were normal before that."

"Yes."

"Was there anything else to worry her, outside of breaking her engagement?"

"I don't know. I don't know why she broke it. And Nina doesn't either."

"Didn't she explain it all?"

"I don't know what she told Johnny. She merely told her mother the bare fact, as she did me. But she's very unhappy. She doesn't sleep or eat. She's dreadfully thin."

"Have you talked to young Hayes?"

"Once. He's bewildered like the rest of us. He doesn't know what it's all about. He had to go back to camp of course. We haven't seen him since. He'll be going to the Pacific anytime now."

Fuller was thoughtful.

"Of course I'm no psychiatrist," he said, "but certainly there's an emotional upset there. Some sort of mental conflict, I imagine. If we knew why she broke off with young Hayes . . . You're sure there was nothing else?"

"I can't think of anything to worry her. In fact, there was good news. My brother wrote that he was probably coming back on some military business."

"Was this before or after she broke her engagement?"

"After. Why would that affect her anyhow, Inspector? She worships her father. But even that's strange. She . . ."

She hesitated, as if unwilling to go on.

"Yes?" he prompted her.

"Well, ordinarily I'd have expected her to be pleased, or at least excited. She hasn't seen him for more than three years. She wasn't. She acted—well, as though she didn't want him to come. It worried Nina. She couldn't understand it either."

She got up then and laid a package on the table.

"I brought the gun," she explained. "None of us knows anything about guns, and it seemed better to have it out of the house. You know how Honolulu was after the attack, with so many Japanese around. Charles gave it to them—Nina and Tony—and told them how to take the safety catch off. But we were afraid to unload it."

He opened the parcel. The automatic was lying in a bed of cotton in what looked like a shoe box, and he took it out and examined it. It was a heavy Colt automatic, which had been fired and not cleaned.

"There were two shots fired?"

"Yes."

"Close together?"

"I think so. Yes."

"How far from her mother's door was she when she fired? How many feet?"

"I don't know. The bed is at the side of the room. Perhaps ten or twelve feet. Maybe more. Our rooms are large."

"That's pretty close. How could she miss?"

But Alice Rowland did not know. She stood there, nervously clutching her bag, not relaxing until he had emptied the magazine and put the gun down. Then she opened the bag.

"I brought one of the bullets," she said. "I dug it out of the bed. I don't know whether you want it or not."

She produced it, wrapped neatly in tissue paper, and laid it in front of him.

"I do hope you understand." Her voice was unsteady. "I don't want Tony to suffer. I don't want the police around. What I need is advice. What am I to do, Inspector? I can't talk to Nina about it. She is convinced Tony was walking in her sleep."

"And you are not?"

"I don't know what to think," she said evasively.

She was preparing to go, but Fuller pushed a pad and pencil across the desk to her.

"Suppose you draw a rough sketch of Mrs. Rowland's room," he suggested. "Make it of the second floor, showing the general layout. I'll get you a chair."

He had done so, and Alice had drawn a shaky outline. It showed four main bedrooms, with a center hall; her own room at the front, her sister-in-law's behind it, a guest room—also at the front of the house—across from hers, and a wing extending beyond Nina Rowland's room, containing a room she called the sewing room, a servants' staircase, and some storage closets. Nina's bed was to the right of the door from the hall, and there was no window beside it. The two windows shown were opposite the door.

Fuller examined it carefully.

"If the second shot went out the open window she was pretty far off the mark," he observed. "You're sure it's not in the room?"

Alice was positive. She had examined every part of the room carefully. The screens had been taken out, and the window was wide open. There had been two shots and only one bullet. Therefore . . .

It was after this that Fuller had suggested the psychiatrist, and the family doctor, Wynant, had agreed. It had not been easy. Tony had at first refused entirely. She hadn't walked in her sleep for years. If they were afraid of her they could lock her in her room at night. In the end however she had gone, only to remain stubbornly non-co-operative.

"I never even chipped the surface," the psychiatrist had reported to Fuller. "It was like working on a china nestegg. She was polite enough, but she simply wouldn't talk. However she's got something in her mind, Fuller, and I'd say it isn't healthy. She's—well, she's unnatural for a girl of twenty. Too quiet, for one thing. I had an idea she was hating me like the devil all the time."

"Maybe she was afraid of you."

"She's afraid of something. That's certain."

But he had noticed one reaction. Her hands began to shake when he mentioned Honolulu.

"I don't like guessing," he said, "but I'd say something happened to her there. They got out after the attack, didn't they?"

"Yes," Fuller said. "And why wait almost four years for it to send her off?"

The psychiatrist shrugged.

"The mind's a curious thing. The more I work with it the less I seem to know! But I'd say she's heading for trouble."

Alice Rowland's story had stuck in the Inspector's mind. One day he went around to the garage where the car had been taken after Tony wrecked it. It was still there, waiting the delivery of some new parts. He looked it over carefully.

"Got quite a bump," the garage man said. "Smashed the radiator, for one thing. It's a wonder the girl and her mother didn't go out through the windshield."

"How did it happen?"

"Well, you know how some women drive. Turn their heads to talk to the person with them and socko, they're off the road."

"Then it wasn't the steering gear?"

The garage man stared at him.

"Is that the girl's story?" he inquired. "Well, take it from me she's lying. The insurance people were here almost as soon as the car was. They know what happened."

That was as much as Fuller knew. He had had one other talk with Alice Rowland. She had been frightened, both for and about Tony, but any suggestion to her mother that a rest in one of the institutions for nervous cases would help had only met with furious resentment. However, nothing had happened, and Fuller had stopped wondering about the case and devoted himself to a crime wave near one of the Army camps. Then, the morning of the day he saw Hilda Adams, Dr. Wynant had called him up.

"I have a message for you, Inspector," he said. "Alice Rowland fell down the stairs today and cracked some ribs. It's all right, according to her. Purely accidental. There was no one near her at the time. But she asked me to tell you."

"Tony's not involved?"

"So Alice thinks, but I wondered if that nurse you use sometimes is available. What is it you call her?"

"Miss Pinkerton. Her name's Adams, of course."

"Well, nurses are scarce, and I think Alice is uneasy. She's going to be flat in bed for a few days. Pretty helpless too."

"You mean she's afraid of the girl?"

"I don't know. But her sister-in-law isn't much good in a sickroom. As a matter of fact she's laid up herself. Don't ask me what's wrong. She won't see me. Seems I offended her after the automobile accident. I asked her if she thought it was deliberate and she blew up. I suppose it's a combination of her old neuritis, plus shock and resentment. Tony's looking after both of them now."

"It's all right, I suppose. Safe, I mean?"

"Tony's never shown any animus against Alice, but that's as far as I go."

Which was the state of affairs when Fuller mixed himself another drink that night after his appeal to Hilda and went to bed. He slept rather badly however, and was awake at six when his telephone rang. He was not surprised to find Hilda on the wire.

"I've been thinking about that girl," she said. "What's all this about desperation? Can't she be manic-depressive or dementia praecox or something simple like that?"

"Could be."

"Well, what do you think?" she asked impatiently.

He yawned.

"I'm not at my best at this hour," he said. "I think she's in trouble. I don't think she wants her mother to know, and that it's bad enough for murder and suicide—in her own mind anyhow."

"You think she meant to kill herself too?"

"Why try to wreck a car and hope to escape yourself? I thought you were going to raise chickens. The market's good these days."

She ignored that.

"Where's the house, and who's the doctor?"

"Wynant. You know him."

"All right. I'll call him," she said and rang off, leaving Fuller smiling to himself.

CHAPTER THREE

IT WAS HALF AFTER SEVEN that morning when Hilda got into her taxi and perched her small suitcase on the seat beside her. She looked washed and ironed, as Fuller always said, but also she looked slightly starched. Her child-like face was rather set. Jim, the local taxi driver who usually drove her on her cases, took a quick glance at her in his rearview mirror.

"Thought you were going to the war," he said. "My wife said she'd be glad to take your canary if you did."

Hilda's face stiffened still more.

"I'm too old, and I've got a bad heart," she said sourly. "I can work my legs off here at home, but I can't do the same thing overseas."

"Bad heart! You sure look well enough."

"I *am* well. If I'd dyed my hair I dare say I could have made it."

He helped her out with the suitcase when they reached the address she had given. The Rowland house stood by itself, a large four-square brick structure with handsomely curtained windows and an air of complete dignity and self-respect. It was a civilized house, Hilda thought, eying it as she went up the cement walk to the porch across its front; the sort of building which implied wealth and security rather than—what was Fuller's word? Desperation. That what had been a handsome lawn around the building showed neglect meant nothing. Men were scarce, as indeed was all sorts of help.

This was borne out when an elderly maid admitted her. She looked as though she had dressed hastily and she was still tying a white apron around her heavy waist. Hilda stepped into the hall and put down her bag.

"I'm Miss Adams," she said. "Dr. Wynant sent me. If you'll show me where to put on my uniform . . ."

"I'm surely glad you've come," the woman said. "My name is Aggie, miss. I'll take your bag up. Would you like some breakfast?"

"I've had mine, thanks."

"We're short of help," Aggie said, picking up the bag. "The chambermaid's gone, and the butler left for a war job two years ago. Of course Miss Tony helps all she can."

Hilda said nothing. She was surveying the long hall, with its heavy carpet, its mirrors and consoles, and the big square rooms opening off it. The effect was handsome but gloomy. The stillness too was startling, as though nothing lived or moved in the house save the heavy figure of Aggie noiselessly mounting the stairs. The stairs, she thought, down which Alice Rowland had either fallen or been thrown the day before. She had a feeling of surprise too. A Tony who helped with the housework was hard to reconcile with a neurotic or possibly insane girl who had twice tried to kill her mother.

Her surprise was augmented when she met Tony in the upper hall, a slender girl in a skirt and a pull-over sweater, with shining dark hair loose over her shoulders, and looking about sixteen. What was even more important, a friendly girl, with a charming sensitive face and a sweet but unsmiling mouth.

What was all this about, Hilda thought resentfully. She's a child, and a nice child. Before she knew it she was shaking hands and Tony was saying: "I'm so glad you could come. I can do housework, but I'm not much good with sick people. Would you like to see your room? It's old-fashioned, but comfortable."

It was both, the large guest room Alice had shown on her diagram, and facing the street. The furniture was obviously of the nineties or earlier, but some hasty attempt had been made to prepare it for her, a bunch of flowers on the bureau, a magazine on the table. It had its own bathroom, too, and Hilda heaved a sigh of relief.

The whole layout looked better than she had expected, and the hard core of anxiety which had brought her there began to relax. Then she got her first real look at Tony herself. The hall had been dark. Now in the bright morning light of the bedroom she had to revise her first impression of the girl. She was certainly young and attractive. But the friendliness had been forced, and the lines around her mouth were too tight. Also she looked tired, tired to the point of exhaustion, as though she had not slept for many nights, and there was a silk sling around her neck, although she was not using it.

Aggie had brought in the bag and gone out, and rather unexpectedly Tony closed the door behind her.

"I hope you don't mind," she said, her eyes anxiously searching Hilda's face. "My mother isn't very well. She's nervous, and she likes me to look after her. Anyhow, I expect Aunt Alice will take all your time."

Hilda took off her neat black hat and placed it on the closet shelf. Casually as it had been done, she had been warned off Mrs. Rowland, and she knew it. Her face was bland as she turned.

"I suppose your aunt's accident has been a shock, too," she said. "Just how did it happen?"

"We don't know. She doesn't know herself. It might have been the cat. She lies on the stairs sometimes, and she's dark like the carpet. She's hard to see."

"Does Miss Rowland think that?"

She was aware that the girl was watching her, as if she were suddenly suspicious.

"It doesn't really matter, does it?" she said coolly. "She fell. That's bad enough. If you'll come in when you're ready—it's the room across—I'll give you the doctor's orders."

She went out, her slim body held rather stiffly, and Hilda felt she had made a bad start. Yet after seeing Tony Rowland the whole story lost credibility. She thought again of Fuller and his statement about desperation as a motive for crime. There was something unusual about the girl, of course; that statement that she would herself look after her mother, for one thing. But she did not look like a psychopathic case, and on the other hand the house, Aggie, even Tony herself in her short skirt and pull-over sweater and with her hair sweeping over her shoulders, seemed the very antithesis of tragedy. Only the girl's eyes . . .

She got into her uniform, pinning her cap securely to the top of her head. One of the first things she observed to Fuller when she took her first case for him was about her cap. "I don't wear it like a barrel about to go over Niagara Falls," she said. "I wear it where it belongs." It was where it belonged as she crossed the hall to her patient's room.

Alice Rowland lay in the big double bed where she had almost certainly been born. She was only a name and some cracked ribs to Hilda at this point, and she surveyed her without emotion. She saw a thin middle-aged woman with a long nose and a fretful mouth, now forcing a smile.

"Good morning," Hilda said briskly. "Have you had your breakfast?"

"Yes, thanks. I wasn't hungry. So stupid of me to fall downstairs, wasn't it? I've gone down those stairs all my life. To be helpless just now . . ."

She didn't complete the sentence, and Hilda wondered if she suspected her identity. Apparently she did not, for she lay back looking more relaxed.

"I don't remember having had a nurse for years," she said. "But two of us were really too much for the servants."

"Two of you?"

"My sister-in-law is not very well. Nerves, largely. She's in bed a good bit of the time. They were all in Honolulu during the raid, and she hasn't got over it yet. Then of course she worries about her husband, my brother Charles. He's a colonel in the regular Army. He's in the Pacific somewhere."

So that was to be the story, Hilda reflected as she got out her old-fashioned watch and took her patient's pulse. Everything was to be laid to the war. Mrs. Rowland was worried about her husband and still suffering from Pearl Harbor, after almost four years. Her daughter had shot at her twice and tried to kill her in a car, but the trouble was still to be the Japs.

"Tony looks after her," Alice said, as Hilda put her watch—it had been her mother's, an old-fashioned open-case one with a large second hand—back in her bag on the bureau. "He left Nina in her care." She looked sharply at Hilda. "I suppose she warned you off, didn't she? She's a jealous child, you know. She was frightfully upset when I told her you were coming."

"That doesn't make sense," Hilda said brusquely. "Why should she mind?"

"I wish I knew," Alice said, and submitted to having a bedbath and to having her linen changed. She did not revert to Tony, and Hilda, moving her skillfully, saw that her adhesive-strapped body was thin and angular. She was a spinsterish fifty, certainly unattractive and as certainly worried. But she was evidently not going to discuss her niece.

"How did you happen to fall?" she inquired, as she drew the last sheet in place.

"I caught my heel near the top and stumbled. It was awkward of me, wasn't it?"

"Were you alone when it happened?"

"Quite alone," Alice said rather sharply. "Why? I'd have fallen just the same."

"I asked because I noticed your niece had hurt her arm. I thought perhaps—"

"That was some time ago. She bruised it."

As this was evidently all Alice intended to say Hilda went on with her work. She finished the bed, brushed her patient's thin hair, and then carried out the soiled linen. The hall was empty, the door into Nina Rowland's room closed and no one in sight. On her way back she went to the staircase and starting at the top examined it carefully. There was always the possibility that some trap had been laid, a string stretched across to catch a heel perhaps. She found no sign of anything of the sort however, and she was still stooping over, her back to the lower hall, when she heard Tony's voice behind her.

"What on earth are you doing?" she asked.

Hilda was startled out of her usual composure.

"I dropped my class pin," she said, rather too hastily. "It's all right. I've got it."

Tony stood watching her as she went back to Alice's room, but Hilda felt a wave of almost palpable suspicion and distrust. And she had made a mistake. Since she had been on the stairs she should have gone on down, to see the cook about the patient's diet, to use the telephone, almost anything but her ignominious retreat.

The case was already getting on her nerves, she realized. Of the two women she had seen, Alice Rowland seemed far more the neurotic type than the girl. She began to question whatever story Fuller had heard. After all people did walk in their sleep. There were automobile accidents too without any implication of murder and suicide. Yet the girl's face haunted her.

She saw her only at a distance after that until lunchtime. Once, glancing out, she saw her meet the postman on the front walk and take the mail from him. The other time she was dressed for the street, returning later with what looked like the morning marketing. She looked older for she had rolled her hair back and had used lipstick and rouge. But she walked slowly, as though she dreaded coming back to the house again.

At noon Hilda went downstairs to the kitchen to discuss Alice's lunch. The cook was there alone, a thin little woman who said her name was Stella, and who seemed to carry a perpetual grouch.

"I've got a chop for Miss Alice," she said, unsmilingly. "You'll have to eat fish, like the rest of us."

Hilda was accustomed to dealing with obstreperous cooks. She did so now.

"I don't care for fish. You can boil me an egg. Four minutes, please."

Stella stared at her and Hilda stared back. But Stella had met her match. Her eyes dropped first.

"All right, miss," she said. "Four minutes."

This being settled Hilda went to the kitchen door. There was a brick walk outside, leading a hundred feet or so to a garage and an alley. The next houses stood some distance away, the grounds separated by low privet hedges. Behind her she could hear Stella banging pans about. She turned and looked at her, and the noise ceased.

"Been here long?" she inquired pleasantly.

"Thirty years."

"Always have a cat?"

Stella glanced at her.

"What's the cat got to do with it?"

"Miss Rowland thinks her aunt tripped over it."

"That cat was right here when she fell. I've told Miss Tony that. Miss Alice don't like cats. She says they carry germs. She's fussy about things like that. Anyhow it's my cat. It stays with me."

And as if to answer a black cat emerged stretching from behind the range. Hilda stooped and stroked it, and Stella's face softened.

"That fall was an accident," she said. "Don't you go thinking anything else."

"Why should I?" Hilda asked, simulating surprise. "Of course it was an accident."

Stella however had tightened her mouth and said nothing more.

Alice was dozing when she went back to her, so she ate her lunch alone with Tony in the big square dining room, with its sideboard crowded with old-fashioned silver. The girl had evidently abandoned her suspicions. She even made an effort to talk, the difficulty of buying food with two invalids to care for. Her mother was not sick, of course, but she was very nervous. She didn't like to see people, and she slept badly.

She ate very little, Hilda noticed. She smoked through the meal, taking only a puff or two of a cigarette and then crushing it out on an ash tray, while Aggie agitatedly hung over her.

"Just a bite of this, Miss Tony. It's caramel custard. You always liked it."

And Tony taking a little and pushing it around on her plate but only tasting it.

It was toward the end of the meal that she put down her third cigarette and asked Hilda a question, her eyes curiously intent.

"How long have you been nursing?"

"Twenty-odd years."

"You must have had all sorts of cases in that time."

"I have indeed. Everything from delirium tremens to smallpox and nervous breakdowns."

Tony's eyes were still fixed on her, but if she meant to say more Aggie's entrance stopped her. Was she about to ask about somnambulism, she wondered?

She was puzzled as she carried Alice's lunch tray up to her. It had been Fuller's custom when she took a case for him more or less to lay the situation before her, with all its various angles. The night before however she had cut him off before he could really discuss it with her, and her own decision to come had been sudden. So now she wondered what Tony had not said, and at the look of anxiety in her eyes.

She was twenty or so, Hilda thought. Then she must have been not more than seventeen, probably less, when she left the islands. Too young for a love affair, very likely, certainly for one to last so long. And what would that have had to do with two attempts to kill her mother? If indeed she had made such attempts at all.

She was to be increasingly bewildered as she passed Mrs. Rowland's door. A plaintive voice beyond it was speaking.

"Tony," it called. "Is that you, Tony?"

Hilda stopped.

"It's Miss Rowland's nurse," she said. "Can I get you something?"

She shifted the tray to one hand and put the other on the doorknob. To her astonishment the door did not open. It was locked. She stared at it.

"I'm afraid it's locked," she called.

There was a short silence. Then the woman inside laughed lightly.

"Good gracious," she said. "The catch must have slipped. Don't bother. I only wanted to tell Tony I'd have tea instead of coffee."

Hilda became aware then that Tony had come up the stairs with her mother's tray. She had stopped abruptly when she saw Hilda, and this time there was no mistake about it. She was frightened. She whirled and set the tray on a hall table.

"I forgot something," she gasped, and ran down the stairs again.

Hilda was baffled. Why did Mrs. Rowland lock herself in her room? Was she afraid of something in the house? Whoever it was, certainly it was not Tony. Then who, or what? When she went back to her patient she found her watching the door.

"I thought I heard Nina calling," she said. "Is—is everything all right?"

"Tony forgot something for her mother's tray," Hilda said placidly. "I could have carried it up for her if I'd known. With her arm. . . ."

"There are still two servants in the house," Alice said shortly. "It's perfectly silly for her to do it."

CHAPTER FOUR

IF HILDA had hoped that Alice Rowland would talk to her that day she was mistaken. Beyond saying that her sister-in-law was what she called delicate she did not refer to the family again. But there was certainly tension in the house. That evening, when Hilda prepared for her usual walk before settling down for the night, it became obvious that Alice did not intend to be left alone and helpless in her bed.

"I have some things to talk over with Aggie," she said. "She's been here for years. In a way she's more of a housekeeper than anything else. Do you mind asking her to come up?"

So Aggie was there when Hilda left, and she was still there, with the door into the hall closed, when she came back.

She came back, as a matter of fact, rather shaken.

She was in the corner drugstore when it happened. She had been in the booth trying to locate Inspector Fuller, and coming out she saw a good-looking young man in uniform with a first lieutenant's insignia staring at her over the Coke he held in his hand. She had thrown her cape over her white nurse's uniform, and at first she thought this was what had interested him. As she started out however she saw him paying hastily for his drink. He was on her heels when she reached the street, and he spoke to her before she had gone a dozen feet.

"I'm sorry to bother you," he said, "but I saw you coming out of the Rowland house. Is anything wrong there?"

There was a sort of sick anxiety in his voice. Hilda halted and looked up at him. He was a tall young man, and just then with the pleading eyes of a whipped dog.

"Who are you?" she asked.

"I'm John Hayes. I'm—I used to be a friend of Tony Rowland's. She's not ill, is she?"

"She's perfectly all right. Her aunt fell downstairs and hurt herself yesterday. That's why I'm here. It's not serious."

It was not like Hilda to explain, but she felt confident she knew who the boy was. Also she liked what she could see of him. He was not too handsome, for one thing. She had a vague suspicion of all handsome men. And his uniform entitled him to consideration.

He did not leave her. He walked along beside her, trying to fit his long steps to her short ones and then abandoning the idea. At first he did not speak, nor did she. When at last he did it was to surprise her.

"Why have they kicked me out?" he inquired. "Do you know? Have they said anything?"

"I only got there this morning. No one mentioned you—unless you are the man Tony Rowland was to marry."

"That's right," he said morosely.

"I'm afraid I don't know anything about it, except that the wedding was postponed."

"Postponed!" His voice was incredulous. "So that's what they say. Postponed! Tony gave me the complete brush-off two months ago, without any warning. I'd got leave, the plans were all made, I'd . . ." His voice broke. "She sent back her engagement ring. We'd even got the license. And then—good-bye and be a good boy and take it nicely. Hell," he said thickly. "I don't know why I'm still hanging around."

"Well, why are you?" Hilda asked.

He took this literally. He seemed to be a literal young man.

"I got the measles," he said. "Missed my outfit when it sailed. I'll be going soon, of course."

This seeming slightly anticlimactic, Hilda smiled in the darkness.

"What explanation did she give?" she asked.

"Said she'd changed her mind. Said it was all over. Said she didn't care for me as she'd thought she did, which was a damned dirty lie." He stopped and shakily lit a cigarette, offering Hilda one which she refused. "It's her mother," he said sullenly. "Her mother or that aunt of hers. I've got a mother too. She thinks I'm good enough. Plenty. What's the matter with them?"

"What about Tony herself?" Hilda said. "Young girls do queer things sometimes. They are neurotic, or they get odd ideas."

He laughed without mirth.

"Tony's twenty," he said. "She's no neurotic kid, Miss . . ."

"Adams is my name."

"Well, if she's neurotic she got it pretty suddenly, Miss Adams. She was as normal as any girl I ever saw. She visited my sister Nancy, and the whole family fell for her. They still can't understand it. They think I must have done something."

"When was all this?"

"A year ago last summer. That's when I met her. I had thirty days' leave. We have a summer place in Massachusetts, and if she was having any queer ideas she darned well hid them. She swam and sailed and danced—" He stopped abruptly and stood still. "I suppose I'm making a fool of myself," he said. "Thanks a lot, Miss Adams. Good night."

He gave her a stiff-armed salute, wheeled and left her standing in the darkness, rather open-mouthed with astonishment.

She did not see Fuller until the next night. Nothing had happened in the interval, and on the surface everything was normal in the Rowland household. Alice, still strapped with adhesive, was fretful but comfortable. Dr. Wynant paid a hasty visit, said she would be up in a few days and hurried away. Tony seemed to have accepted Hilda, with reservations. The house ran smoothly, with Tony doing the marketing and helping with the housework.

Then, on that second day, Nina Rowland asked to see her. Tony brought the message, looking resentful as she did so.

"She's worried about Aunt Alice," she said. "It's silly. I've told her she's all right." And she added: "She's very excitable. Please don't stay long. All sorts of things upset her."

"Is it only nerves?"

"She has a touch of neuritis in one arm," Tony said unwillingly.

"What does the doctor say?"

Tony moved abruptly.

"She's fed up with doctors," she said. "All she needs is rest, and to be let alone. Is three o'clock all right?"

She might, Hilda thought wryly, have been making a call on royalty. Nevertheless at three o'clock precisely by her old-fashioned watch she knocked at Nina Rowland's door. Tony admitted her and she stood blinking in a blaze of autumn sunlight. Her first impression was one of brilliant color, of flowers everywhere and bright hangings and chintzes.

Then she saw the woman in the bed. Hilda was startled. What she had expected she did not know, but what she saw was a very beautiful woman, not looking her forty-odd years, and with a breath-taking loveliness that even Hilda—no admirer of feminine good looks—found startling. She was dark, like Tony, but there the resemblance ended. She knew Tony was watching her, but so great was her surprise that it was Nina who spoke first.

"It seemed rather unneighborly not to see you, Miss Adams," she said. "My little girl takes almost too good care of me. I'm much better today."

Tony said nothing, and Hilda did not sit down. She stood rather stiffly near the foot of the bed.

"I'm glad you're better," she said. "If there is anything I can do. . . ." She felt awkward.

Tony was still watching her, and now she spoke.

"We won't take you from Aunt Alice," she said quickly. "She needs you. We don't."

Nina Rowland smiled pleasantly, showing beautiful teeth.

"No, of course not. How is poor Alice? Of all things, to fall down the stairs. It's so—undignified."

"She's more comfortable today. The doctor says she will be quite all right."

But now she was aware that Nina too was watching her. She was still smiling, but her eyes were sharp and wary.

"What does she think happened?" she asked.

So that was it. Hilda had been brought in because the woman in the bed was uneasy. But she had no chance to answer. It was Tony who spoke.

"I've told you all that, mother. She stumbled. I was in the kitchen when I heard her fall."

"She's lived here all her life. I don't understand it."

She did not look at Tony, but obviously the remark was made for her. For an instant Hilda wondered if there was some buried resentment there; if the girl and the woman were on less friendly terms than Alice had indicated. It passed quickly however. Nina Rowland put her arms up and fixed a pillow under her head, and Tony moved quickly to help her. She was too late, however. The sleeve of Nina's bed jacket had fallen back, and showed a heavy bandage on the arm nearest the door.

Hilda glanced away hastily.

"What lovely flowers," she said. "May I look at them?"

When she turned back the bandage was hidden again, but Tony was very pale. She stayed only a minute or two after that, but she left with a firm conviction that one of the two shots Tony had fired at her mother had struck her arm, and it had not yet been healed.

She told Fuller that night when she found him outside the house as she left for her evening walk, and he seemed impressed.

"Although I don't know why the secrecy," he said. "Dr. Wynant knows she shot at her mother, and if the bullet's still there it may cause trouble."

"I don't understand it." Hilda was thoughtful. "Miss Rowland isn't the sort to keep quiet about a thing like that. I imagine she's been spoiled and petted all her life."

"Well, mother love, my girl!" he said drily. "If Tony actually shot her she may be keeping her mouth shut to save the girl."

"I don't think she's as fond of her as all that."

He eyed her.

"What would you expect? She's tried to kill her twice."

"But she doesn't know that, does she?"

He stopped abruptly.

"Now look," he said. "What's on your mind? Did Tony push her aunt down the stairs?"

She shook her head.

"I think not. She was in the kitchen when it happened. Alice seems pretty positive she stumbled. It's just—it almost looks as though Nina is suspicious of the girl. Why should she be?"

That was when he told her in detail the story as she knew it from Alice Rowland, the flight from Honolulu, the quiet years, the broken engagement, the shooting, the automobile accident, the psychiatrist's failure, as well as his statement that Tony had something on her mind and might be heading for trouble. She listened attentively.

"So that's the layout," he finished. "Now you've seen them all. What do you make of it?"

"None of it makes sense," she said testily. "The girl's certainly devoted to her mother. Maybe she's protecting somebody else."

"Who?"

"I don't know. Alice Rowland perhaps. If Alice wanted to throw dust in your eyes she might have done what she did, gone to you saying Tony's crazy. She's no crazier than I am."

"You don't like Alice, do you?"

"I take care of my patients. I don't have to love them."

He laughed a little as they walked on. Hilda's sharp tongue and warm heart always amused him.

"What motive would she have had? Alice, I mean."

"Well, look at it," Hilda said more reasonably. "She's lived alone all her adult life. She's had servants and money. Her house was her own, and her time. Then what happens? She finds her brother's family parked on her, some of the servants leave, her whole scheme of living is changed, and she's —well, she's at a time of life when women are not always responsible. On the other hand. . . ."

She stopped. Fuller eyed her curiously.

"On the other hand what?" he inquired.

"Tony locks her mother in her room when she has to leave her."

Fuller stopped and stared down at her.

"That's fantastic," he said. "Are you sure of it?"

"I don't usually make statements I'm not sure about," Hilda said stiffly. "I found it out yesterday. Last night I put the light out in my room and watched her go down to dinner. She looked around to be sure I wasn't in sight, took a key from the neck of her dress and locked the door from the hall."

"Then the mother knows?"

"I'm not sure. She's in bed most of the time. Tony's been doing it only since I came."

"Hell's bells, Hilda!" he said, exasperated. "Why don't you tell me what you know, without my having to get it bit by bit? How do you know she's afraid of you? Not that I blame her," he added. "That baby face of yours never fools me. You're as dangerous as a rattlesnake, and even *it* rattles before it strikes."

Very properly Hilda ignored that.

"Aggie's bunions," she said succinctly.

He stopped.

"Aggie's what?"

"Aggie's the housemaid. She has bunions. I told her what to do for them, so she talks. Are we walking or standing still? I need exercise."

He went on and she explained. When Hilda had gone out the night before Tony had gone out too, and when Aggie tried to take fresh towels to Nina's room the door was locked, and no key inside it.

"She said it scared the daylights out of her," Hilda said reflectively.

"Now just why," Fuller inquired, "did that scare the daylights out of her?"

"Because it hadn't happened before. Because she doesn't think Tony fired those shots at all. Because she thinks Nina Rowland tried to kill herself and Tony got the gun from her and took the blame."

"Could be," Fuller said. "So now she locks her mother up. What sort of woman is she anyhow? The mother."

"I've told you. Beautiful, spoiled, and self-indulgent. Scared too about something. Maybe about Tony. Maybe about her sister-in-law."

"So now it's Nina who's crazy!"

Hilda was silent for a moment.

"I don't think any one of them is crazy," she said finally. "Something has happened, either to them all, or to one or two of them. Personally, I think it happened to Tony."

"But it's bad enough to set them all on edge? To put it mildly," he added smiling.

Hilda did not smile.

"We have only Tony's word that she was driving the car when the accident happened," she said. "Maybe the mother did that too. But I'd say she's pretty fond of her pretty self. She likes lying in bed, with flowers all around her and Tony waiting on her hand and foot."

"Not the suicidal type, eh?"

"Definitely not."

They had almost reached the Rowland house. Hilda stopped, and Fuller put a hand on her shoulder.

"Look," he said. "I want you to take care of yourself in that house. I'm beginning to wish you hadn't gone. This isn't a question of crime. No real crime's been committed, according to the way I see it. But one may be. There's tension there, and it may snap. Keep out of the way, Hilda. Watch yourself."

He left her then, and Hilda walked on. She was quite sure she saw a masculine figure lurking in the shrubbery across the street and wondered if it was Johnny. He did not approach her, however, and looking back from the porch she realized that whoever it was was not in uniform.

CHAPTER FIVE

THAT NIGHT Alice Rowland asked Hilda to sleep in the room with her. Hilda had given her an alcohol rub and the tablet the doctor had ordered to make her sleep, and Alice held the pill in her hand and looked at it.

"I suppose it's all right, isn't it?" she said, with a bleak smile. "I mean—one or two odd things have happened, and—I suppose I'm being childish, but will you look at it?"

Hilda examined the pill.

"It's all right. That's the way they're always marked. What do you mean by odd things, Miss Rowland?"

Alice did not answer directly. She took the pill with a swallow of water and put her head back on her pillow.

"You've been here a day or two," she said. "I wonder what you think of us."

"I haven't seen much of the others," Hilda said calmly. "Miss Rowland seems very fond of her mother. I've only had a glimpse of Mrs. Rowland."

"I'm thinking of Tony. You've seen her quite a bit. Do you think she's worried about anything?"

"She seems rather serious, for a girl of that age," Hilda said evasively.

"That's all? You think she's perfectly normal? Please be honest, Miss Adams. I'm anxious about her. She broke her engagement a couple of months ago, and she hasn't been the same since."

"It may have upset her more than you realize. Unless she didn't care for the man."

"Care for him! She was quite shamelessly in love with him."

Hilda raised the window for the night before she made any comment. The man across the street had apparently gone. She was more and more sure it had not been Johnny, but her face was bland as she went back to the bed and pulled up an extra blanket.

"I may have seen him last night," she said. "A young officer saw my uniform and spoke to me. He was afraid Tony was sick."

"I don't see why he would care." Alice said, her voice sharp. "She treated him outrageously. Everything was ready. His people were coming to stay here, and the presents were lovely. Then all at once it was over. I felt like a fool. It was too late to do anything but announce the postponement in the newspapers, and people kept calling up. All I could say was that he had been moved unexpectedly. I didn't say he'd gone overseas, but I let them think so."

"I see," Hilda said. "Was that when she started walking in her sleep?" Alice looked startled.

"Who told you that?"

"Aggie said something about it."

"What else did she tell you?"

"Just that Tony was inclined to sleepwalking, and not to waken her suddenly."

Alice's suspicions were lulled. She settled back on her pillows.

"It was about that time," she said. "Things were pretty confused here, what with calling off the wedding and everything. Her mother went to bed in a sort of collapse, and Tony looked like a ghost. Then she walked in her sleep one night and—I suppose you'll hear it sooner or later—she found a loaded gun and almost shot her mother."

Hilda registered the proper surprise and horror.

"Perhaps she was remembering the Japs," she said. "Where did she find the gun?"

"Nina had it in her room. Tony knew where it was, of course. You see, don't you, why I'm worried about the child? And now I'm afraid she's sleep-walking again. I thought, if you didn't mind the couch here tonight—you'll find it quite comfortable."

"What makes you think she's walking in her sleep," Hilda persisted.

"She came in here last night after you had gone to bed. It must have been about two o'clock. I wakened to find her standing beside the bed looking down at me, with the oddest look on her face. She—I spoke to her, and she gave a start and shot out without saying a word."

"You're sure it was Tony?"

"She'd left the door open into the hall, and the light was on there. I saw her plainly."

"Maybe she merely wanted to talk to you, and then decided against it?"

"Why should she go like that? I was awake, and she knew it."

"Then you don't think she was walking in her sleep?"

Alice looked annoyed.

"I don't know," she said fretfully. "I don't know anything about girls. I certainly don't know anything about Tony these days. She's changed. She's not herself at all. I'm half afraid of her."

Hilda slept on the couch in Alice's room that night. Or rather she lay there, keeping an eye on the door and trying to think things out. That Fuller was right, and that the tension in the house was building toward a crisis of some sort she felt confident, but what such a crisis might be she did not know. The vulnerable person was Alice, comparatively helpless in her bed. Yet she could see no rational reason for any danger unless she was involved in the shooting episode. Someone had fired the shots. According to Fuller's story Tony had been found in a faint just inside her mother's door, with a gun beside her and Nina trying to get out of bed. If Nina had been wounded she had managed to conceal it in the general excitement. Would that be possible, she wondered? Still, as Fuller said, if she was protecting her own child . . .

It would have required considerable stoicism, she thought, but it could have been done, the bloody sheets rinsed out in the bathroom, a self-applied tourniquet to stop the bleeding, and perhaps the assistance of one of the servants. Not the garrulous Aggie. Stella, possibly. She determined to talk to Stella the next morning.

Alice had had her tablet and slept soundly. Because the night was warm Hilda had left the door open, and at two o'clock she heard a faint noise in the hall. It sounded like a door being stealthily opened and closed again, and unconsciously she braced herself. Nobody came into the room, however, and she got up quickly and looked out.

Some one was moving quickly and quietly down the staircase. She could not see who it was. The lower hall was dark, but whoever it was below was moving toward the back of the house, with the ease of long familiarity.

Hilda caught up her kimono and put it on as she went. For a woman of her build she could move rapidly and quietly, and she did so now. She was at the foot of the stairs almost before the door into the service wing at the rear had closed. After that however she went more cautiously. The back hall was dark and empty, but someone was in the kitchen beyond. She heard the lifting of a stove lid and the striking of a match. There was a brief interval after that, practically noiseless. Then, so rapidly that Hilda had barely time to get out of the way, the unknown was opening the door in the darkness and on the way upstairs again.

Hilda had to make a split-second decision, whether to follow and identify the figure or to see what had been put in the stove. She chose the latter and went quickly to the kitchen.

It was quite dark, save for a small gleam of something on fire in the range. She made her way to it, striking her shins on a chair and making considerable noise as she did so. There was no indication that she had been heard, however, and she limped to the stove and managed to pry up the lid. The fire beneath was low, and whatever was burning had not been entirely consumed.

She found a box of matches by fumbling over the top of the plate heater where she knew Stella kept them, and lit one. The mass slowly charring was a surgical dressing of cotton and gauze bandage. Only an end of the bandage remained. The cotton was practically gone, but she had no doubt whatever as to what it was. Some one had burned a dressing from Nina Rowland's arm.

She felt a little cold as she went back to her room. Any one in the house except Alice could have crept downstairs, but why the secrecy? There seemed to be no question that Tony had fired the shots at her mother. But if she had really injured her why run the risk of infection now? Could there have been another gun in the case, and Tony's shooting a cover-up, perhaps for Nina, perhaps for Alice Rowland? Had the story as Alice had told it to Fuller been a clever device to protect some one, possibly herself?

Yet, if it had been Tony the night before in the kitchen, she seemed entirely natural the next morning at the breakfast table. She was wearing again the sweater and short skirt, with her hair loose about her face, making her look about sixteen again. And she ate a normal breakfast, to Hilda's relief. In fact she looked as though she had had a reprieve of some sort, which was the more surprising because of what she said.

"We've had a letter from my father," she observed. "He's not coming home after all. Things in the Pacific have changed. Everything is moving fast now."

"That must be rather a blow," Hilda said drily, and saw Tony flush.

"It *has* rather upset mother," she said. "She was counting on seeing him soon. But he's a soldier. He wouldn't want to miss anything even if he could."

Hilda made her way upstairs. To her surprise Nina's door was open and her room empty. And as she reached the upper hall she heard voices in Alices room. Evidently Nina was there, and equally evidently the sisters-in-law were quarreling. Nina's voice was raised and shrill.

"You're having her watched," she said stormily. "That's why the nurse is here, isn't it? First a psychiatrist, now a nurse. What are you trying to do? Prove she's crazy?"

Alice's voice was hard.

"I think you're hysterical," she said. "You can't blame me because Charles isn't coming home. As for Tony, if you think it's normal for a girl to shoot at her own mother . . ."

"She never shot at me, and you know it. She had the gun and it went off in her hand. She'd never fired one in her life before."

"She did pretty well, in that case," Alice said drily.

"Just remember, *you* found her. She doesn't remember anything about it. It's your story, not hers. And I'm no fool, Alice." Nina's voice was still high. "I know you don't want us here. I begged Charles to make other arrangements, but he said you would be hurt if he did. If he'd only come home . . ."

Hilda heard Tony coming up with Nina's breakfast tray and had only time to duck into her own room. When some time later she went back to her patient she found her indignant and highly nervous. She looked up at Hilda resentfully.

"Nina's been here," she said. "She thinks I'm trying to have Tony put away."

"And are you?" Hilda asked bluntly.

Alice looked shocked.

"Certainly not. But I am worried. She may do something dangerous, to herself or some one else."

"I suppose," Hilda said, "there's no chance Mrs. Rowland had the gun that night and Tony tried to take it from her?"

Alice laughed.

"To shoot herself?" she said bitterly. "With looks like that? And a husband who adores her? I assure you she likes to live, Miss Adams. She likes clothes and money. She's fond of herself, too. She's had a wonderful life. While I . . ."

She did not finish, and Hilda, going methodically about her work that morning, realized that there were undercurrents in the house which were being carefully concealed from her. Nevertheless in spite of the quarrel between the two women the day was better than the preceding one. After she had settled her patient with a book that afternoon she wandered down to the kitchen.

Tony was out, and Stella was pouring milk out of a bottle for the cat. She gave Hilda a curt good afternoon. Hilda merely nodded and sat down.

"I want to ask you about the night of the shooting," she said without preamble. "What do you know about it?"

"Me? Nothing. I heard the shots and came down. So did Aggie."

"Is that all?"

"I don't know what you mean, miss."

"Who attended to Mrs. Rowland's arm that night?"

"Her arm? I never heard anything about her arm. What was wrong with it?"

Hilda watched her, but Stella's thin face was impassive. She tried again.

"How often do you find that something's been burned in your stove when you come down in the morning, Stella?"

This time Stella gave her a sharp look, and turned away.

"My stove's the way I leave it, miss. If you don't mind my asking, what business is it of yours?"

Hilda knew defeat when she faced it.

"All right," she said resignedly. "Who put Mrs. Rowland to bed the night this shooting took place?"

Stella looked relieved. "She never really got out of it. She was faint, as well she might be. Miss Alice helped get her settled after the doctor came for Miss Tony. Or maybe it was Aggie. That's all I know."

It was possible, Hilda thought as she got up. Alice might have tried to avoid scandal by dressing Nina's arm herself. The story that one bullet had gone out the open window had been hers. She could have washed the sheets too, and ironed them in the sewing room where an electric iron was kept ready for use. But when she followed Dr. Wynant down the stairs later and put the question to him in the library he merely laughed at her.

"Nina shot!" he said. "You don't know her. If she banged her finger she'd rouse the neighborhood."

"Her arm is bandaged."

"My dear girl," he added pontifically. "Don't ask me why she wears a bandage. Don't ask me why she lies up there in bed either. She's a perfectly strong healthy woman who likes to be coddled, that's all. And that," he added, "is one of the reasons why she doesn't have me any more. I told her so."

Hilda eyed him coldly.

"So that's all?" she said, her blue eyes icy. "It's easy, isn't it? Tony has tried twice to kill her mother, but her mother likes to be coddled, so it's all right with you."

"My dear Miss Adams . . ."

"Don't dear Miss Adams me," she said tartly. "They don't have you any more. You think none of this is your business. Well, I'm sorry, but it is mine."

"I suggested that you come here. You might remember that," he said, highly affronted.

"Then I have a right to know certain things." She watched him put down his bag and look at her resignedly. "How were they—Tony and her mother— when they first came here from Hawaii? You saw them then, didn't you?"

"Certainly. Nina was complaining, but all right. Tony didn't adjust very well. In the sense that a neurotic cannot adapt himself to a change of environment. I suppose you can say she was neurotic. She avoided me, for one thing. I thought she was rather afraid of me. We became good friends later, of course."

"And Mrs. Rowland? What did she complain about?"

"Oh, just small things. The cold weather, a personal maid she'd been fond of had to be left behind, Alice's rather rigid housekeeping. Nothing serious."

"And Miss Rowland herself?"

"She did her best. It was rather hard on her. She and Nina are not very congenial, but as Nina spends most of her time in her room it hasn't mattered much. It has helped since Tony came back from school, of course. She's a friendly child, even if she does walk in her sleep."

He picked up his bag. He was not young, and he looked very tired. Hilda felt rather sorry for him, although she stiffened at his parting words.

"Don't let your imagination carry you away, Miss Adams," he said. "There's nothing wrong with Nina Rowland except a chronic case of inertia and an occasional neuritis in the arm. You'll find that's the trouble now, and Tony has merely tied her up as usual."

CHAPTER SIX

HILDA FOUND Alice asleep when she went upstairs, and an Aggie with the face of a conspirator waiting for her in the hall.

"Miss Tony's gone," she whispered. "The car's back and she's trying it out. Would you like to see the wedding dress and her other things? I'm going to pack them away tomorrow, so if you care to look."

Hilda agreed. Nina's door was closed, and she had nothing to do for the moment. She found that the trousseau had been relegated to the third floor, a floor she had not seen, and she surveyed it with interest. In general it followed the pattern of the second, with the servants' quarters in the rear. The wedding clothes were in closets in the room over her own, and Hilda cautiously opened the door and going across raised a window shade.

"The dresses are in the closet," she said. "Such lovely things! And the wedding dress is a dream—wait until you see it."

But it became evident after a moment that Hilda was to wait some time to see it, if ever. Aggie moved the sheet which had covered it and turned a bewildered face to her.

"It's gone!" she whispered. "Look, here's where it was. Whoever could have taken it?"

"Maybe she took it herself."

"Why? Where is it? It's not in her room." She poked around among the things hanging there. "Her cocktail dress is gone too. Do you think—maybe she's changed her mind. Maybe she's going to marry him anyhow. Everything was here yesterday. I showed them to Stella's sister."

"Did you see her going out today?" Hilda asked practically.

"No. I didn't. Maybe Stella did."

But Stella had not seen Tony leave the house. She had been upstairs changing her uniform after lunch, and after cautioning both women to silence Hilda went back upstairs.

Tony's room was still empty when she went along the hall, and after ascertaining that Alice was still asleep Hilda went back to it and stepped inside. It was the usual girl's room, feminine with its pale blue carpet, its white curtains, and its rose-colored bedspread and silk quilt neatly folded at the foot of the *chaise longue*. There was a tennis racket in a frame, and on the toilet table the photograph of a man in uniform, evidently of her father. Hilda inspected it carefully. He was a fine-looking man with a strong nose and jutting jaw, but with Tony's sensitive mouth. It was inscribed "To Tony, my own girl, from Dad."

But the wedding dress was not in the closet, and the small desk by a window yielded nothing. The only incongruous thing, in fact, was the doorstop. It was Volume XIII of the *Encyclopedia Britannica*, and she was stooping over it when she heard Aggie behind her.

"Is it here?"

"Is what here?"

"The dress. I'm scared, Miss Adams. I was responsible for it. Only yesterday Miss Alice asked me about it and I said it was all right."

"They won't blame you," Hilda said soothingly. "I imagine she took it herself. She may be giving it to someone."

"Giving it away!" Aggie screeched. "It cost a fortune. Her father sent her the money for it. She'd never do that."

There was no use asking Aggie about the *Encyclopedia*. She was running around like a wild woman, looking under the bed, frantically opening bureau drawers and moaning to herself. Her search was only interrupted by the ringing of the front doorbell. She tried to smooth her hair as she went down the stairs, and Hilda watched her as she opened the front door.

Standing on the porch outside was a woman in the early fifties, gray-haired and handsomely dressed.

Aggie stood as if stunned, staring at her, and the woman smiled faintly.

"I want to see Miss Tony, Aggie," she said. "I know she's at home. I just saw her driving back to the garage."

Aggie found her tongue.

"I'm sorry, Mrs. Hayes. Maybe she's in, but I don't think . . ."

Mrs. Hayes however showed grim determination. She walked into the hall and stood there, planted with dignity and firmness.

"Either she sees me now or I'll wait until she does," she said flatly. Then she saw Hilda in her uniform at the head of the stairs. "Is someone sick? I didn't know . . ."

Aggie explained, her voice bleak, and when she had finished Mrs. Hayes walked with deliberation into the living room, leaving Aggie staring at her.

Behind her Hilda heard Tony's voice.

"Who is it?"

She turned. Tony was standing near her door, her hand holding to the frame of it as if for support. Her face had lost all its color.

"I think it's a Mrs. Hayes."

Tony said nothing. She seemed to be bracing herself. Then with her head held high and a strange look of determination in her face she passed Hilda and went down the stairs. The living-room door closed behind her, and an agitated Aggie came up and sat down abruptly on a hall chair.

"I couldn't help it, Miss Adams," she said wretchedly. "You saw how she walked in. Right over me, so to speak. It's his mother."

"So I gathered," Hilda said. "Don't worry. You couldn't stop her. Aggie, how long has that book been holding back Miss Tony's door?"

"What book? I didn't notice. She does her own room these days."

"Will you do something for me? Get another volume from the encyclopedia set in the library, and put that one in my room. Hide it in a drawer. I'd like to look at it."

She went back to her patient's room, and a few minutes later she saw from the front window Mrs. Hayes going down the walk to her waiting taxicab. She walked slowly and almost unsteadily, and before she got into the cab she looked back at the house with her pleasant face bleak and incredulous. It was some time before Tony came up again. She did not go into her mother's room. She went into her own and closed and locked the door.

There was no sign of her that night at dinner. To Hilda's surprise Nina was there, in a flowing housecoat with long sleeves, and with a troubled look on her face.

"Tony won't be down," she said. "She's not well. She said she didn't want a tray. I wish she would eat more," she added as Hilda sat down. "She's so very thin lately. Perhaps I don't understand girls any more. It's a long time since I was one myself."

"Why not have Dr. Wynant go over her?"

"She won't let him. She's been very odd the last few weeks. She used to be so gay, Miss Adams. I don't understand it at all."

Hilda saw that she was using both arms, but the left one rather stiffly. And she did not mention Tony again. She chattered amiably through the meal. It was nice to be out of her room again. And wasn't it sad that her husband was not to get back after all. She missed him dreadfully. And she missed the personal maid she had had so long in Honolulu. In fact of the two, Hilda considered as she ate stolidly, the husband's absence was a grievance, but the maid's was a grief.

"She gave such wonderful massage," Nina said, and sighed. "And she was so good with hair. I have never looked the same since."

Not receiving the expected comment on this she went on. The maid's name was Delia, and she was to have sailed with them to the mainland. Only at the last minute she didn't show up. Her brother came instead, with some story about Delia's being suspected of working with the Japs. Of course it was all nonsense. Colonel Rowland never kept any papers in the house.

There was more, of course; her resentment at losing Delia, the inability to get the beauty treatments she was used to, and Alice's niggardly house-keeping "with only two servants." Hilda ended her meal with the feeling that Nina was a completely self-centered self-indulgent woman, and a little puzzled too about Delia, the paragon, who was suspected of working with the Japanese.

"This maid of yours," she said as she got up. "What does she say about this accusation?"

"I don't know." Nina's voice was resentful. "She's never even written to me. As good as I'd been to her, too."

"But you think she is innocent?"

"Maybe she had her price. Most of us have, haven't we? Only I don't see how she could know anything important, when we didn't even know it ourselves."

Neither one of them had mentioned Mrs. Hayes's visit, and after dinner Nina went upstairs again. Hilda heard her rapping at Tony's door, but there seemed to be no answer.

At Alice's request Hilda again left Aggie in her patient's room that night when she went out for her evening walk. Alice was nervous, either because of the scene that morning with Nina or because she had learned of Mrs. Hayes's visit. Evidently she had, for she was querying Aggie as Hilda in the room across got her cape and her bag.

"What did Tony tell her?"

"I don't know, Miss Alice. I don't listen at doors."

"You do when it suits you." Alice said petulantly. "Now, when I need to know you go virtuous. How did Mrs. Hayes act when you let her out?"

"I didn't let her out. She just went."

They were still bickering when Hilda left the house. And after what had happened she was not surprised to find young Hayes waiting for her across the street. He angled over and caught up with her, and under a street lamp she saw that his young face looked set and stern.

"I've been waiting for you," he said without preamble. "What goes on in that house? What sort of song-and-dance did Tony give mother this afternoon?"

"I haven't an idea," said Hilda mildly.

"You're sure you don't know?"

"I don't usually listen at doors," Hilda recalled Aggie and smiled faintly. "Why? What happened?"

"All I know is that mother is in bed at her hotel, the Majestic. She won't talk, but she's in poor shape, crying and carrying on, and I've been across the street here for hours. What's wrong anyhow? It must be pretty bad. Mother's got plenty of guts usually. All she says now is that I mustn't try to see Tony again, or bother her."

Hilda was silent. Had Tony told Mrs. Hayes about shooting her mother? Was that it? Or was there something else, something which went deeper, of which the shooting was a result? Whatever it was she was confident it was not over. But she could not say that to the boy beside her.

"I'll tell you this," she said at last. "Tony didn't do whatever she did easily, Lieutenant. She's still shut in her room."

He drew a long breath.

"I've been over everything," he said. "There may be insanity in the family. Mother would be terrified of that. It must be something," he added naively. "She did care for me, you know. We were frightfully in love. She wrote me every day in camp, I have her letters and I keep rereading them. They're wonderful."

"You never did anything to make her change her mind? Or cause this change in her?"

"Never. There's nothing in my past, either. I've been around a bit. Who hasn't? But nothing that matters. Certainly not since I knew her."

He left her soon after, a sadly perplexed and dejected young man, and Hilda turned back to the house. She was as bewildered as he was, and she was still debating the situation when she approached the house. In her rubber heels she walked lightly, and the street lamps left a small oasis of darkness at the foot of the walk. She roused suddenly to see two people there, a man and a girl, and to realize the girl was Tony. She was confident they had not noticed her, and she turned sharply and crossed the street, stopping in the shadows to watch.

She could not hear much that they were saying. The street was wide and their voices low. That there was an argument of some sort going on was evident, however for once Tony tried to break away and the man caught her by the arm and raised his voice.

"Maybe you'd like me to report it," he said. "It would make a nice story, wouldn't it?"

"You wouldn't. You don't dare to." Tony's voice was raised too.

"Oh, wouldn't I? Wait and see."

Hilda heard no more. A moment later Tony had rushed back to the house. Hilda thought she was crying. But her own eyes had turned to the window of Alice's room upstairs. Some one, probably Aggie, had been standing there.

CHAPTER SEVEN

THE SCENE had roused Hilda's quick curiosity, and as the man started down the street she trailed him at a safe distance. At the end of two or three blocks he stopped, evidently waiting for a bus. The street however was dark. He was only a vague rather sinister figure as he stood there, and as the bus rumbled along she decided to follow him. He paid no attention to her. He got on first, throwing away a cigarette as he did so and swinging on easily. Even then she could only get a general impression of him, a man of probably forty, in a shabby blue suit and a well-worn brown hat.

If he had noticed her he gave no indication of it. He seemed to be absorbed in thought, and Hilda decided to find out his destination. But he stayed on the bus almost to the end of the line, and she began to worry about her patient. Then abruptly he got up. Two or three other passengers alighted also, and Hilda was the last to leave. He was some distance ahead of her when, drawing her blue cape around her, she set out to follow him.

He stopped once to light a cigarette, and so far as she could tell he was still unaware of her. She was in a part of town she did not know, but he seemed at home in it. The streets were empty, the buildings dark and forbidding, and his own figure not too distinct. She began to feel uncomfortable. Then she lost him altogether, in front of one of a row of small dilapidated houses. So far as she could tell they had no numbers, and she began counting from the end of the block. She had lost him at either six or seven, and she went on past, making a mental note of the location.

Which was the last mental note she made of anything for some time.

When she came to she found herself lying on the pavement of a narrow dirty alley between two houses, with her purse gone and her head aching wildly. It was a number of minutes before she could get to her feet, and then it was to find herself retching violently and her legs almost unable to hold her.

There was no sign of her assailant. The street was empty and quiet when she staggered to it, and she sat down on a doorstep and tried to reconsider her situation. She was miles from the Rowland house or from her own apartment, she had no money, and what was even worse she had fallen for what was the cheapest and most obvious of tricks.

It was some time before she could think coherently. Evidently he had known who she was all along. Probably Tony had seen her and told him when he tried to hold her.

"My aunt's nurse is watching you across the street. Let me go or I'll call her."

It had been easy enough after that, she thought sourly. Her uniform, her hatless head, and the long wait for the bus. When she had followed him . . .

She felt better after a few minutes. Her head still ached but her legs would at least obey her. She managed with several stops to reach a drugstore, and the man behind the counter looked startled when she more or less stumbled through the door.

"I'm sorry," she gasped. "I've been knocked down and robbed. May I use the telephone? I have no money."

"Sure," he said. "Don't bother with the booth. Use this."

He put the instrument out on the counter and she sat down gratefully. It was a moment or two before she felt able to use it, however, and she looked up to see him putting a glass in front of her.

"Aromatic ammonia," he said. "It may help."

She drank it and before long was able to call Fuller at his apartment. "It's Hilda," she said. "I'm at . . ." The man supplied the address and she gave it. "I've had a little trouble. Been knocked out and robbed. Can you send for me?"

"I'll come myself. What the hell are you doing out there?"

"It's a long story," she said, and hung up abruptly.

When at last he arrived she had lost the aromatic ammonia and divers other things in the gutter outside, and the man from the drugstore was standing on the pavement beside her, offering paper tissues in lieu of handkerchiefs. He looked surprised when he saw the police car with its uniformed driver.

"Lady's in poor shape," he said when he saw the Inspector. "Guess you'd better take her to a hospital."

"I'm all right," Hilda said disgustedly. "Just a plain damned fool, that's all. Do I get in the car or do I stand here all night?"

Fuller smiled. Hilda was herself again, he realized. She might look like the wrath of God, as indeed she did, but she was practically normal. He made no fuss over her as she got into the back of the car. He simply followed her, rolled up the glass to cut off the men in front, and lit a cigarette.

"Talk when you're ready," he said cheerfully. "That bump may ache but it won't kill you."

"I wish you had it. You wouldn't be so happy."

"All right. When one of my best operatives lets herself be lured to this part of town and is knocked out, either she isn't smart or she had a good reason. Which is it?"

"He fooled me. He didn't pay any attention to me. I ought to know better, at my age."

Fuller eyed her.

"Very clear. Very lucid," he said. "Maybe we'd better go to a hospital after all."

"I'm going back to my case," she said firmly. "It all started there. He was talking to Tony Rowland on the street. That's why I followed him."

She told her story as briefly as she could, describing the man and the method by which he had disposed of her. Especially however she related Tony's crying, her attempt to escape, the man's threat to report something or other, and the likelihood that he had then been told who and where she was, and that she might overhear.

"He put on a good act," she said. "But then everybody's doing it in the house. Tony or some one else burns a surgical dressing at night in the kitchen stove. Today her wedding dress is missing. It cost a fortune, and it's gone. She uses the *Encyclopedia Britannica* for a doorstop, and this afternoon she saw Johnny Hayes's mother and sent her back to her hotel in hysterics."

"Good God," Fuller said. "Are you sure you're all right? It sounds like delirium."

"It's all true," Hilda said, trying to lean her head back against the car cushion and deciding against it.

"And after all that you still think the girl is normal?"

"I'm not sure I'm normal myself."

She was determined to go back to her case, and it was useless to argue with her. Fuller tried it, only to meet with stubborn silence. Finally he turned on the top light and surveyed her. Some of her color had come back, although her face was dirty, her short gray hair standing in every direction and her white uniform smeared. But her eyes were cold and hard and very Hilda-ish at her most obstinate.

"All right," he said resignedly. "If you can take it I can. It's your head and your headache."

Before he left her however he got a description of her assailant and was thoughtful for some time, trying to assort the various items. The surgical dressing he did not bother about. "If she shot her mother and doesn't want it known that's their affair." But the wedding dress puzzled him.

"Would she burn it?" he suggested. "After all it couldn't have been a pleasant thing to have around."

"The furnace isn't going. She may have sold it."

"I see. You think this man was after money?"

"He was after mine," she said drily. "He got my mother's watch too. That's all I care about."

He got a description of the watch, in case it was sold or pawned. Then he sat back and looked at her again.

"Now see here," he said. "What we want to know is why the girl shot at her mother, if she did. Why they had the car accident, and if there may be another one. That's why you're there. You must have some idea by this time."

"Ideas!" she said bitterly. "I'm filled with them. One thing I'd like to know is why Tony is consulting Volume Thirteen of the *Encyclopedia Britannica*."

He eyed her with annoyance.

"See here," he said, almost violently, "if you've got any theory on this case I want to hear it. It's no time to hold out on me."

But Hilda merely shook her head, a gesture which proved disastrous, and remained silent.

CHAPTER EIGHT

IT WAS ONE in the morning before they reached the house, and some time later before Aggie in a dressing gown opened the front door an inch or two and gazed with terrified eyes at the two of them. Hilda was urbanely calm.

"Sorry to bother you," she said. "I was knocked down and my bag taken. This gentleman found me and kindly brought me home. Is everything all right?"

Aggie had found her tongue.

"I've been scared to death about you," she said. "Yes, they're all asleep. Maybe I'd better stay with Miss Alice tonight."

"I'm perfectly all right," said Hilda, staggering slightly. "Go to bed, Aggie, and don't worry." She turned to Fuller formally. "And thank you very much. You've been most kind."

The Inspector took the hint, mumbled something and departed, while Hilda sat down on a chair in the hall and watched the walls rotate and finally settle back to where they belonged. Aggie was still looking startled.

"Who did it?" she asked. "I declare, the amount of crime since this war makes a body wonder. Did you see him?"

"I caught a glimpse of him," Hilda said cautiously. "A man about forty, not very well dressed. He had a dark skin. That's all I saw."

Aggie stared at her.

"Him?" she said. "Why should he be knocking you down?"

"You know who he is?"

But Aggie pursed her lips.

"No, miss," she said stolidly. "I thought for a minute it was somebody I'd seen around. But it couldn't be."

If she knew more she was not talking, and with her help a dirty and exasperated Hilda climbed the stairs. Alice had taken her sleeping tablet and was quiet, and Aggie followed Hilda into her room.

"I put the book in your bureau," she said, with the air of a conspirator. "She never noticed the change. She was out for a while and when she came in she looked queer. I feel kind of worried about her."

Hilda sat down dizzily on the edge of the bed.

"I haven't told Miss Alice about the dresses," Aggie said, still cautiously. "I've been everywhere. They're not in this house. I'll take my Bible oath on it."

Hilda got up and began to take off her filthy uniform. She was not listening to Aggie's account of the wedding dress. She was back in the car, talking to Fuller and he was saying it sounded like delirium. So it did, but it had a definite beginning, if not yet an end.

"Try to think back, Aggie," she said. "How were things here before Miss Tony broke her engagement?"

"Just the way they'd always been, miss. Except for the excitement, packages coming and clothes and all that. The florist in to see about the flowers for the reception, and the caterer about what they were to eat."

"How about Miss Tony?"

"She was singing all over the place. Very happy she was, miss, and that crazy about the Lieutenant it would make you want to cry."

"When did that stop?"

Aggie thought.

"Well, about ten days before the wedding. I remember Stella saying her breakfast tray hadn't been touched. The next day I saw her coming downstairs, looking sort of sicklike. She went into the library and stayed there a couple of hours. I guess she'd used the telephone, for when she came up she went to her Aunt Alice's door and said there wouldn't be any wedding at all."

"How did they take it? Her mother and Miss Alice?"

"They acted like they thought she was out of her mind. But she wouldn't budge an inch. Her mother about had a fit. She hasn't really been the same since."

"What reason did she give?"

"I don't know as she gave any, miss."

"And how long after that did Tony walk in her sleep?"

"On her wedding night," Hilda said impressively. "Can you blame the poor child, miss? She'd been queer all day. She did her room and her mother's. Then she locked herself in and I never saw her until that night, when I heard the shots."

"Just what did you see then?"

"Stella and I both heard the noise. We didn't wait to put anything on. We ran to the stairs, and down below Miss Alice was bending over Tony on the floor, just inside her mother's door. Mrs. Rowland was screaming in her bed. When I got there she was trying to get out of it."

"What happened to her afterwards?"

"Mrs. Rowland? Well, she looked kind of faint and I made her get back. She was shaking all over."

"You didn't think a bullet had struck her?"

Aggie started.

"You mean she was shot!" she said incredulously. "And said nothing about it? Not her, Miss Adams. She'd have raised the roof."

"There was no blood about?"

"Not that I saw. I wasn't there but a minute."

"Then why does she wear a bandage on one arm?"

Aggie looked relieved.

"Oh, that," she said. "She has neuritis. It's been worse the last few weeks. That's why she's in bed so much."

"How about the lights that night, Aggie? You say you saw Tony on the floor. Was the hall light on?"

"It always is. Miss Alice is the nervous sort."

"And Mrs. Rowland's room? Was that light on too?"

Aggie hesitated.

"Well, now I come to think of it it wasn't. I could see well enough though, with the door open. I didn't turn it on until later, after we'd got Miss Tony to bed and kind of settled."

She went up to bed after that, and Hilda washed and took another look at her patient. Alice however was still comfortably asleep. Hilda went back to her room and took the heavy volume Aggie had left from her bureau drawer. It was Volume XIII, Jere to Libe, and she put it on her bed and examined it. If there were any markers in it she could not see them, and no part of it appeared to have been used more than any other. Finally she picked it up and shook it. A small piece of blank paper fell out, and she was annoyed at her carelessness. She should have gone through it page by page, she reflected, and in a very bad humor and with a worse headache put herself to bed on Alice's couch.

She had not yet gone to sleep when Tony came carefully into the room. She stood in the doorway as if she was uncertain for a minute or so. Then she came directly to Hilda and stood looking down at her. She had been so quiet that had Hilda not been awake she could not have heard her. She was not walking in her sleep, however, and she seemed relieved when she saw Hilda was awake.

"I wonder if I may have a sleeping tablet," she whispered. "Mother's are all gone, and I've been awake for hours."

In the half light from the hall she looked young and rather pathetic. Evidently she did not know what had happened. She was shaking however and Hilda reached out and caught her wrist. Her pulse was fast and irregular. On impulse she drew her out into the hall and closed the door.

"What's wrong, Tony?" she said. "There is something, isn't there? I'm a nurse. I'm used to all sorts of things. Maybe I can help you."

Tony gave her a thin smile.

"That's kind of you," she said. "There isn't anything really." Then, as if she had just thought of it, "When I'm nervous I sometimes walk in my sleep. I don't want to tonight. That's all."

"If you're worried about your mother . . ."

"What about my mother?" Her voice had changed, was sharp and challenging.

"I saw the bandage on her arm, you know. I don't want to worry you, but if she's had an injury—"

"What on earth are you talking about?" Tony asked coldly.

Hilda lost patience at last.

"Don't be a little idiot," she said sharply. "I'm saying that if your mother has been shot in the arm it ought to be properly cared for."

Tony gasped.

"Who told you that? About the shooting?" she demanded.

"My dear child, it's not a secret, is it?" Hilda said practically. "People do queer things in their sleep. I had a patient once who almost choked her own baby to death. She thought she was choking a burglar."

Some of the suspicion died in Tony's face, but she looked ready to collapse.

"I see," she said. "The doctor and the servants. Especially Aggie. And Aunt Alice, of course. But I didn't shoot my mother, Miss Adams. You can ask her yourself."

Hilda was certain Nina would deny it with her last breath, no matter what the fact. She said nothing, however. She brought the tablet and Tony swallowed it with a sip of water and handed back the glass.

"That man I was talking to tonight," she said. "He's the brother of a maid we had in Honolulu. He's out of work, he says. But there are plenty of jobs. I don't want mother to be bothered about him."

Hilda nodded. She was not to mention this man, evidently. And she had been right. Tony had seen her across the street, had probably used her as a threat too. But she could have no idea of what had happened since, or that the police were after him; that Fuller had inaugurated a citywide search for him.

Hilda felt better the next morning. Her neck was stiff, and she had bruised a knee and torn a stocking in falling. Otherwise she was all right. She was uneasy, however. The case would not last much longer. Alice was much improved. She was to sit up in a chair that day, and she was no nearer the solution of the problem than when she came. Rather less, in fact. It had looked at the start like a neurotic or unbalanced young woman, desperately determined to kill her mother, even if she finished herself in doing so.

But she was convinced now that Tony Rowland was not psychopathic. She was a desperately frightened and unhappy girl, with a trouble she was refusing to share with anyone. Her thoughts were busy as later on she got Alice up in a chair by the window and turned her mattress. What was this secret? And as if she had read her mind Alice spoke.

"You've seen Tony now for two or three days," she said. "How does she impress you?"

"She seems worried," Hilda observed.

"Worried!" Alice smiled her thin smile. "That's a polite word for it. She's not herself at all. She really ought to be in a sanitarium, but what can I do?"

"You have no idea what the trouble is?"

"None, unless it's in her own mind. We did send her to a psychiatrist, but she wouldn't talk to him. He was furious. You see, she may have been asleep the night she fired those shots. She certainly wasn't asleep in broad daylight when she wrecked my car."

"I don't think you've told me about that," Hilda said.

"Well, perhaps I shouldn't now. Only I keep thinking about it. That accident when Tony hurt her arm. At least they say it was an accident. Something about the steering gear. But the steering gear was all right, Miss Adams. The garage says so, and Tony won't even talk about it."

"That would look as though she meant them both to—to have the accident," Hilda said thoughtfully. "It doesn't sound like her, does it? She's a devoted daughter. If she wanted to kill herself why kill them both?" Alice shrugged her thin shoulders.

"She loves her father too. Then why was she relieved when she found he wasn't coming to America? She was, you know."

Hilda smoothed the spread over the bed, and eyed it. The effect was sufficiently geometrical to satisfy her.

"I've been wondering," she said, giving a pillow a final pat. "The attack on Honolulu must have been quite a shock. Did she lose anyone in it? Anyone she cared about?"

"I don't know. After all she was only sixteen. If you mean a man . . . There is one strange thing. Nina likes to talk about the Islands. She hopes to go back there when the war's over. She's done her room here much as it was there, and Tony keeps it full of flowers. But Tony hates the place. In the almost four years she's been here she's hardly ever mentioned it. She seems to hate the thought of it."

Hilda considered this. She was no moving picture fan, but she had seen the films of Pearl Harbor. Even when the attack was over they could not have felt safe there. Colonel Rowland had given his wife a gun, had sent them to the mainland as soon as possible. And with the lights out everywhere . . .

"Something must have happened to her there," she suggested. "Something Mrs. Rowland doesn't know. Something nobody but Tony knows. There are such things as psychic scars. If she had been attacked—"

"I'm sure it was nothing of the sort," Alice said, flushing. "And she got over it, Miss Adams. She was perfectly normal after the first month or two."

"Does she get any letters from the Islands?"

"I never see her mail. She gets it first."

While Hilda straightened the bathroom Alice had evidently been thinking, for when she emerged she threw her first words like a bomb.

"What was Herbert Johnson saying to Tony last night, Miss Adams? Aggie says you were across the street."

Hilda managed to keep her voice smooth.

"She was talking to a man. I didn't know who it was."

"You didn't hear anything?"

"I was pretty far away."

Alice looked disappointed.

"I think he's been bothering her off and on for the last four years," she said fretfully. "His sister Delia was Nina's personal maid in Hawaii, and he comes from there too. He's no good and I've told them so, but they were fond of Delia." She eyed Hilda. "Would you think Tony gave him any money last night?"

"I don't know, Miss Rowland, I didn't see it if she did."

Alice was obviously disappointed. She was silent for some time. Then what she said was apparently a *non sequitur*.

"My sister-in-law is a very attractive woman," she observed drily. "I imagine a good many men have envied my brother. It's just possible that Nina—"

But she didn't finish and Hilda made no comment.

CHAPTER NINE

THAT MORNING Fuller saw Commissioner Bayard. They were old friends. The Commissioner offered him a cigar and Fuller sat down. Bayard had a cold, and was using a paper towel as a handkerchief. He crumpled it up and threw it in the wastebasket.

"Dab the thigs," he said. "Bight as well use a dutbeg grater. Why dod't they bake theb out of cottod? South's full of it. What's wrog with you? You look as though you hadd't beed in bed."

"Hilda Adams had a narrow escape last night."

"Od a case for you?"

Fuller nodded.

"Knocked out and her bag taken. Luckily it had an old-fashioned watch in it. If the fellow tries to sell or pawn it we've got him. But I'm not very easy. I'd like to have a man or two to keep an eye on the house where she's working. There's some sort of trouble there."

The Commissioner sneezed.

"Good God," he exploded. "Dod't you know we're dowd to less thad two-thirds of the force? What's the matter? The Adabs wobad cad take care of herself. She always has."

"She's never had a case like this," Fuller said, and proceeded to tell what he knew. The Commissioner listened grimly.

"So we watch a girl who's god batty!" he said with disgust. "What good is a cop across the street? To call the Bedical Exabiner after it's all over?"

"It's going to be done, if I have to do it myself."

"Dod't be a fool. You've got a job to do."

In the end however Fuller got what he wanted, or a part of it. A plain-clothes man would watch the Rowland house at night, and follow Hilda if she persisted in her evening walks. But Hilda did not go out that night.

She chose the afternoon instead.

"I'd like to get some fresh uniforms," she told Alice after lunch. "If you'll be all right I won't be long."

Alice yawned.

"I'll take a nap," she said. "Go right ahead. Just tell Aggie to look in now and then."

So Hilda went downstairs, in her neat black suit and hat and in her comfortable flat-heeled shoes. As usual she walked quietly, and in the lower hall she saw Tony in the library at the telephone. She hung up hastily when she saw Hilda, and the expression on her pale face was one of shocked alarm. Hilda saw it and ignored it.

"I'm going out for an hour or two," she said. "Miss Rowland will try to sleep."

Tony did not answer at once. She stood staring at Hilda, and when she spoke her lips seemed stiff.

"Aggie says you met with an accident last night."

"I was knocked down and robbed," Hilda said cheerfully. "I'm all right today. It takes a lot to kill me."

She thought Tony went even whiter, and she was puzzled as she went out to the street. Did Tony suspect what had really happened to her, she wondered? And what was the truth about the man last night? What hold had this Herbert Johnson had on her? A hold of some sort he certainly had. He had shown it when he caught her arm and jerked her back. And what was it he had threatened to report? To report to whom?

She was still thoughtful as she took a bus downtown. For contrary to her statement to Alice she did not go at once to her apartment. She went instead to the Majestic Hotel and inquired for Mrs. Hayes. Mrs. Hayes, it appeared, was not well and seeing nobody. However on the mention of Tony Rowland's name over the telephone she was told to go up.

The door was open into the sitting room, and when she knocked a voice called her to come in. She found Johnny's mother in bed, still pulling on a bed jacket and looking exhausted and pale.

"You're Alice Rowland's nurse, aren't you?" she said. "I saw you in the hall yesterday."

Hilda agreed and sat down. She had no bag, so she folded her hands in her lap and eyed Mrs. Hayes serenely.

"I came because your son told me you were worried about Tony Rowland," she said. "I don't mind saying I am too, Mrs. Hayes. I thought if we could get together . . ."

Mrs. Hayes' mouth tightened.

"I'm afraid I can't discuss her, Miss Adams. I am seeing you to ask you to talk to Johnny. He might listen to you. He won't—to me. I don't want him ever to see Tony again, or to try to."

Hilda raised her eyebrows.

"That's rather drastic, isn't it?" she said politely. "Unless you have a very good reason."

"I can't discuss the reason." Mrs. Hayes' voice was frozen. "It's not my secret. I've sworn not to talk about it. But any marriage, any engagement, is out of the question. Tony knows that herself. If she sent you . . ."

"No. She doesn't know I'm here. I wondered—did she tell you there was insanity in the family? Because if I'm any judge she's as sane as I am."

Mrs. Hayes remained stiffly silent, and Hilda went on. "There *is* something wrong, Mrs. Hayes. I know that. Tony Rowland is pretty close to desperate. I'm only afraid . . . She may try to take her own life, you see."

"I'm sorry, Miss Adams. I'm fond of her, or I was. But I assure you there is nothing I can do."

Hilda eyed her, her handsome flushed face, reminiscent of Johnny's masculine one, the platinum wedding ring and large square-cut diamond on her hand. The sort of woman, she thought, who would be a good homemaker, a good wife and mother. But also a woman without imagination.

She got up.

"It's just possible," she said, "that by keeping this secret to yourself you may actually cause trouble. How can I help Tony if I don't know anything?"

"I'm afraid I'm more interested in my son. There must be no marriage, Miss Adams, if I had to sacrifice everything I care for to prevent it. And Tony knows it."

On that note Hilda took her departure, feeling frustrated and more anxious than she had since she had taken the case. Her apartment when she reached it looked orderly and peaceful, and she sat down for a minute or two to try to assort her ideas. Mrs. Hayes had had an air of finality in everything she said. That she had been profoundly shocked by her talk with Tony was certain. Then what had Tony told her?

She was rummaging for a bag to replace her stolen one when her landlady puffed up the stairs to give her a message relayed from the Rowland house. It was to call Fuller, and she was tempted not to do it, to sit down for an hour or so in her comfortable easy chair and rest her head, still sore from the attack. Instead she took two aspirins and picked up the telephone.

Fuller was in a bad humor. He snapped a hello at her, stated that she ought to be in bed, and then said he wanted to know what sort of monkey business was going on in the Rowland house.

"I don't know what you mean. If it's because I saw Mrs. Hayes—"

"Oh, you thought of that, did you? No. It's about your watch. It was sold this morning to a pawnbroker downtown who is known to traffic in stolen jewelry, and bought this afternoon. I'll give you three guesses who bought it."

"How would I know?"

"Tony Rowland," he said. "Your nice gentle little friend. The girl who tried to kill her mother. Remember? She walked in there as bold as brass an hour or so ago, asked to look at watches and selected yours. Did you tell her you'd lost it?"

"No."

"Then you see where that leaves it. She knew the fellow had it. He got word to her, describing it. He was probably scared we'd trace it. So she protects him by getting it first."

Hilda was very still. It looked as though, instead of using her the night before to protect herself, Tony had warned him against her. She found her hands shaking.

"That's your angel child," Fuller said. "Now maybe you'll change some of your ideas. Find out if she got a note or a telephone message some time today. It may help if we can trace it. We've got a good description of the fellow. It's your man all right."

"She did get a telephone message. I know that."

"When?"

"About half past two. I was on my way out."

"That's it, then. She hot-footed it down to the shop, getting there at three. What do you bet you'll find it in your room when you get back?"

"I think it's the last place I'll find it," Hilda said curtly. "She's no fool. She'll send it here or hide it, if she hasn't dropped it in the river. The man's name is Herbert Johnson, if he's using it. He came from Honolulu after Pearl Harbor, and his sister was Nina Rowland's personal maid. I think he's blackmailing her."

"That's my girl!" He was pleased with her. He always was when she came out coldly with important bits of information. "Fellow a Hawaiian?"

"No, and they'd cut me off the wire if I told you what I think he is."

She hung up and, after looking in at the landlady's quarters to see her canary, made her way stolidly back to the Rowland house. There was no Tony in sight, and she met the postman on the pavement and took the mail from him. There was a letter for Alice from Honolulu, and Alice looked triumphant when she took it.

"Maybe I'll know something about Herbert now," she said as she ripped it open. "I wrote to a friend of mine out there." She glanced up at Hilda. "Did Tony see you get it?"

"No. I met the postman on the pavement."

She was reading the letter when Hilda went back to her room to change into uniform again. As she had expected the watch was not there. The room was as she had left it, except for one thing. Volume XIII of the *Encyclopedia* in her bureau drawer had been changed to XIV, Libi to Mary, and a heavy china elephant with large pink roses painted on it was now propped against Tony's open door.

When she went back to her patient there was no sign of the letter, and Alice had got out of bed and was standing in her nightgown in front of a chest of drawers, with a key in her hand. But something had happened to her. She had lost all her color, and she staggered as she turned to look at Hilda.

"I'm sorry," she said. "I'm not as strong as I thought I was."

Hilda had to help her back to her bed, and she lay there for some time, not speaking and with her eyes closed. It was some time before she spoke, and then it was not to explain anything.

"I'm all right now," she said. "Just some bad news from Honolulu."

A little later however, as her color came back, she said: "So it was Herbert Johnson who knocked you down and robbed you last night! I know you followed him. It's the sort of thing he would do. Why didn't you tell me?"

"I don't bother my patients with my personal troubles," Hilda said stiffly. "Why is he blackmailing Tony, Miss Rowland? If that's what he's doing?"

But Alice did not answer, and Hilda went down to dinner confused and in a bad humor. Except that Tony was present the meal that night was more or less a repetition of the night before. Nina for some reason chose to talk about Hawaii, and her hope to go back there eventually. Tony ate almost nothing, said even less, and smoked one cigarette after another. But there was something wrong with Aggie. She was clumsy and nervous and Hilda suspected that the *Encyclopedia* was involved.

She had a sudden desire to break the polite veneer of the meal, to destroy the illusion of well-dressed civilized people eating a highly civilized meal, to see the mask of Nina's beautiful face change, if it ever did. She even made an attempt at it.

"I saw a rather dark-skinned man loitering on the pavement last night," she said. "He looked as though he might be waiting for some one."

If looks could have killed Tony's would have slain her. Nina however was only politely interested.

"Was that Herbert again?" she inquired. "I thought you'd got rid of him, Tony." She turned to Hilda. "He's the brother of the maid I told you about in Honolulu," she explained. "He's no good, Tony. I wish you wouldn't see him."

Tony got up, her face set.

"I'm sorry," she said. "I have some things to do," and left without further explanation.

So Herbert was not to be discussed, Hilda reflected. He had taken her bag, suspected the police were after him and it, and got Tony to salvage the watch. But he was not to be suspected. What was the hold he had over the girl? Did it involve her alone, or was she protecting her mother. After all, four years . . .

With Tony gone, Nina looked at Hilda.

"I didn't like to ask before Tony," she said. "She's very nervous these days. Aggie says you had some trouble last night. I hope it wasn't serious."

Hilda glanced at her. If she suspected Herbert it did not show in her face.

"I did a silly thing," she admitted. "I took a bus ride, and got out in a low part of town. Some one knocked me down and robbed me."

"How dreadful! Are you sure you ought to be up and around?"

"I'm quite all right, thanks."

"Did you lose much? If that's too personal, forget it. I just thought . . ."

"I never carry much money. I lost my mother's watch. I valued that, of course."

"What a pity! Have you notified the police?"

Hilda looked at her, but she was eating her chocolate souffle calmly and with enjoyment.

"I believe they're trying to trace the watch," she said warily. "They seem to have located it, but some one bought it today. I'm afraid it's gone."

But Nina had dismissed the watch. She waited until Aggie brought in the fingerbowls. Then she showed the first real emotion Hilda had seen since her arrival. She leaned forward and lowered her voice.

"I'm worried about Tony, Miss Adams. She's not herself at all. And she does such strange things. I'm quite sure she reads my mail before I get it, for one thing. She steams the letters open in the sewing room, and once or twice since you came I know she has locked my door. I hate telling you this, but Alice thinks she's not—well, that she has some mental condition. The way she broke her engagement, for one thing, with everything ready."

It was Hilda's chance.

"You have no idea why she did that?"

"Not the slightest."

"Of course Pearl Harbor was a shock. Sometimes those things are late in developing, Mrs. Rowland."

But Nina shook her head.

"She got over that very soon. Only a couple of months. It was terrible, of course."

Hilda was silent. Whatever had happened Nina obviously had no idea of it.

"Sometimes these nervous upsets come from something held over from childhood," she said after the pause. "Can you recall anything of the sort?"

Nina reached over and took a cigarette from Tony's package on the table. She was thinking back, her handsome face troubled.

"She was a very happy child," she said. "She had a nurse she adored, a Hawaiian woman. Then when she was ten we had to let her go. The nurse, I mean. It was dreadful. Tony fretted for a long time. But it was necessary to send her away. You see she—"

The sentence was not finished. Tony came back. If she had heard what Nina had said she made no comment. She was very pale, although her voice was gentle.

"You've been up a good while," she said to Nina, avoiding Hilda's eyes. "How about bed and a game of gin rummy?"

In her room that night after Alice was settled for the night Hilda went over the situation. Since the conversation with Nina she was confident that the secret Tony was guarding was hers alone. And that whatever it was, up to a short time before Tony had been a happy normal girl, falling in love, getting her trousseau together, writing daily letters to her *fiancé*, and opening and exclaiming over the wedding gifts as they arrived. Then something had happened and it was all over.

Hilda was no prude. She knew the temptations of beautiful women, and Nina was all of that. Had there been a lover, and had Herbert knowledge of it? But Tony was a modern girl. She might resent such knowledge bitterly, but she would not try to kill her mother for such a lapse.

She considered the maid, Delia Johnson. What was it Nina had said about every one having his price? Had she, Nina, had her price? And had Delia known it?

But that was absurd. Selfish she might be, and self-indulgent she certainly was. But to attempt to connect her with the Japanese was preposterous. All in all Hilda knew that night that she had failed, and that her case was almost over.

But how nearly over she had no idea.

CHAPTER TEN

LATER HILDA was to try to bring the events of that night into some sort of order, and to find it difficult.

She remembered the walk with Tony, of course. She had found the girl in the lower hall, looking lonely and lost, and for once the woman in her triumphed over the detective.

"Why not come out and get some air?" she asked. "I'd like company anyhow, after last night."

The girl's face was pitiful as she looked at her.

"I'm afraid I haven't been very nice to you, Miss Adams," she said unexpectedly. "You see, I've been in sort of a jam. And I had no idea . . ."

She hesitated, and Hilda thought she might bring up the matter of the watch. She did not, however.

"I'll get a coat," she said, and ran quickly up the stairs.

They had not had their walk after all, of course. They started companionably enough, after Tony had shot a quick glance up and down the street. But neither Johnny Hayes nor Herbert was in sight. Only a man in plain dark clothes who began suddenly to whistle for an invisible dog, and they had reached the corner of the block before a tall uniformed figure detached itself from the shadows and confronted them.

Tony stopped and caught her breath.

"Just what," said Johnny Hayes sternly, "did you mean by upsetting mother the way you did yesterday?"

Hilda thought she was about to turn and run. So evidently did Johnny, for he caught her by the shoulder and forced her to face him.

"No, you don't," he said. "You're staying right where you are. We're having this out, here and now."

"Let go of me," Tony gasped.

"Not yet," he said. "Not ever, if I can help it. You crazy little fool, what notion have you got in your head anyhow? I'm not going to the Pacific with some fantastic bit of nonsense between us. What if you did walk in your sleep? Hell, yes, I know about that. Aggie's a friend of mine. D'you think I care?"

He dropped his hand, but Tony did not move. She was trembling. She put out a hand and reached blindly for Hilda, as though to steady herself. The man across the street was walking toward them. Hilda recognized him. He was a plainclothes man named Rogers from headquarters, and she wished furiously that he would mind his own business.

"Anyhow, you gave me the brush-off before that," Johnny was saying. "What was it? What did I do?"

"It has nothing to do with you, Johnny," Tony said, her voice shaking. "Only if you ever cared for me you'll let me alone now. I couldn't go on with it. That's all. I can't go on with it. Ever."

"Why? That's all I want to know. Why? You did love me. I think you still do. What crazy idea have you got in your head?" Then, still ignoring Hilda, he put his arms around Tony and held her. "Tell Johnny, darling. Let me help. You know I'll do anything, everything. Tell Johnny, won't you?"

Tony shook her head, but her iron composure suddenly broke. Against his uniform she began to cry, great heavy sobs which shook her whole body, and he was wisely silent. He let her cry it out, while Hilda saw that Rogers had turned back and was the plainclothes man once more whistling for his imaginary dog.

When it was over Tony released herself.

"Give me a little time, Johnny," she said brokenly. "Maybe things will be better soon. I'm sorry about your mother. I just tried—I do care, Johnny. Always remember that, won't you?"

"What do you mean, remember?"

"When you're overseas I'll write. I promise I'll write," she said, her voice feverish. "There's nobody else. Just you. You can be sure of that."

She turned and started back toward the house, and young Hayes stared gloomily after her.

"Now what the hell do you make of that?" he asked.

Hilda was cautious.

"I don't know," she said. "She's in some sort of trouble. I may learn about it before long. Why not give her time? That's what she asked for."

"Time's the one thing I haven't got," he said, and turning on his heel left her abruptly.

Hilda found Rogers waiting for her on her way back, a middle-aged man with shrewd intelligent eyes.

"Nice little scene," he observed. "Only what did it mean? Boy's been waiting for a couple of hours. Not the fellow who got you last night, I gather?"

"No," Hilda said absently. "He used to be engaged to her. He's sailing soon, and she's worried."

He let that go. "I'll be around," he told her. "Just watch your step," and went back to his lonely vigil in the shadows.

That matters were approaching a crisis of some sort Hilda felt in her very bones that night as she put on her dressing gown over her long-sleeved night-dress and placed her slippers under Alice's couch. But tired as she was she did not go to bed at once. She carried up Volume XIII of the *Encyclopedia Britannica* and went through it page by page in her room. At one place it had apparently been laid face down on something which had smeared it slightly, and she stopped at one rather brief article. Was it possible, she thought? But she dismissed the idea and put the book away, yawning. She had had little real rest the night before, and because she was still bruised she had taken a couple of aspirins. After an hour or so she went to bed and dozed off.

She wakened some time after two in the morning, to find her neck stiff and to try to rearrange her pillows. There was some light in the room from the hall, and after her custom she glanced at her patient's bed. The first intimation she had that anything was wrong was that the bed was empty.

She looked at the bathroom, but the door was open and there was no one in it. Still she was not apprehensive. Alice had not been able to sleep and was wandering around somewhere in her new freedom. Nevertheless she put on her slippers and went out into the hall. Everything was quiet. Nina's door was closed and locked. Tony's door was closed too. And of Alice there was no sign whatever.

When she looked downstairs the front hall was dark and empty, and for the first time she began to feel anxious. She tried to reassure herself. Alice had been hungry and had managed to get down to the kitchen, and because it was nearer she made her way to the back stairs. She stopped sharply as she reached them.

Below her some one was coming up, or trying to. All she could see was a dark huddling figure near the foot of the staircase, a figure which seemed to be on its hands and knees, and which was making small painful noises as it scrabbled at the steps.

"Miss Rowland!" she said sharply. "Wait there. I'll come for you."

She could not find the light switch, and so it was not until she had reached the figure and stooped over it that she realized it was Tony; a Tony who gave a small gasp as she touched her and then fainted dead away. Hilda reached down and felt her pulse. It was slow and feeble, and she hardly knew what to do. In the end she decided to get her down rather than up, and getting below Tony's body she half carried, half dragged it to the floor below. There she laid her out flat and felt for the light switch. The glare almost blinded her as she went back to the girl. She had not moved. Her face had no color whatever, and there was blood on her hands and on the front of her white blouse.

Even in the shock of this discovery Hilda realized that Tony was fully dressed. She had changed from what she had worn at dinner to her usual skirt and blouse, but she had discarded the sweater. The blood was coming from a deep cut on the palm of one hand. Otherwise she seemed uninjured.

There was no sign of Alice as she straightened and looked about her. The door from the small back hall to the kitchen was closed, and when she opened it she thought at first that the kitchen itself was empty. On the table, however, there had been set what was the making of a light meal; a loaf of bread with a knife beside it, a small pat of butter and some sliced cold meat and mustard. At the edge of the table was a bloody print as though some one had laid a hand flat on it.

Tony had not moved when she glanced back at her, and she moved into the room. Only then did she see Alice Rowland, face down on the floor beyond the table, with the back of her head crushed and the fragments of a milk bottle on the floor beside her.

She was dead, beyond a hope.

Hilda stood over the body, with a sense of helpless rage which fairly shook her. She had come on this case to prevent further trouble, and she had not only failed, she had slept while a murder was being committed. Worse than that, it was her patient who had died. Only once in her long experience had such a thing happened, and the picture was too plain to be ignored. Whatever she thought—if she was thinking at all—she knew the police would be sure Tony had done this thing; the Tony who was now lying with blank open eyes on the floor in the hall, staring at the ceiling but seeing nothing at all.

That was when she saw the envelope. It was lying a few feet from the body. She picked it up almost automatically. It was addressed to Alice Rowland, and it was quite obviously the one she had taken from the postman that day. She thrust it hastily inside her uniform and leaving Tony where she was ran upstairs to Nina Rowland's room. It was still locked, and she pounded on it furiously. If Nina had been awake she gave an excellent imitation of shocked arousing.

"What is it?" she called, her voice frightened. "Who's there?"

"Open the door," Hilda shouted. "It's locked. And hurry. Please hurry."

Nina unlocked her door. She was in her nightdress, her feet bare and her hair in curlers with a net over them. In her short-sleeved gown the bandage on her arm showed plainly. She was very pale.

"What's wrong?" she managed. "I was asleep. What's happened?"

Hilda surveyed both Nina and the room. It looked like any normal bedroom where a sleeper had been disturbed, the windows open, the bed clothing thrown back and a jar of skin cream with some tissues on the toilet table. The memory of the quarrel between Alice and the woman in front of her was strong in her mind, but she had no time to investigate.

"Tony's all right," she said. "She's cut her hand. I . . . Maybe you'd better get your clothes on, Mrs. Rowland. There's been some trouble, and Tony's fainted."

She did not wait. She ran down the front stairs, stopping only to turn on a light. Across the street Rogers was sitting on a low stone wall smoking a cigarette. When she called to him he came over on the run.

"We've had a murder here," Hilda said breathlessly. "Come in and call the Inspector. I'll be in the back hall downstairs."

She showed him the telephone in the library and went back to Tony, still lying where she had left her, and with her eyes still open. They were less blank, however. They moved slowly from Hilda to the stairs and then to the green-painted walls.

"How did I get here?" she asked slowly.

"Don't you know?"

"No. I . . ." She began to remember then, for she lifted her injured hand and stared at it. "Aunt Alice?" she said, with an effort. "Is she . . . ?"

"Can you sit up?" Hilda put an arm around her and raised her, but it seemed to make her dizzy. She let her down again. She could hear Rogers in the front hall, coming back, and went quickly to meet him. He began to speak, but she silenced him with a gesture.

"Tony Rowland has fainted back here," she said hastily. "Don't talk about what's happened before her. I want to get her out of the way. The other's in the kitchen."

"Tony the little girl with the officer?"

"Yes. You'll have to carry her."

He picked Tony up easily, to be confronted by Nina at the head of the back stairs, a Nina who had thrown on a dressing gown but had not removed her curlers, and who only stared when she saw what he held.

"What's the matter?" she said shakily. "She isn't hurt, is she?"

But Tony did not move or speak. She lay back in Rogers' arms with her eyes closed, and she did not open them even when she had been put in her bed and Nina bent over her. She saw the blood and gave Hilda a horrified look.

"She's hurt, Miss Adams. Badly hurt."

Hilda on her way out stopped in the doorway.

"I told you. Her hand's cut. That's all. Call the maids, won't you?"

But Nina was calling no maids that night. She sank into a chair, evidently on the verge of collapse, and turned a desperate face to Hilda.

"Who found her?"

"I did," Hilda said quietly. "I might as well tell you, Mrs. Rowland. Miss Alice has had an accident. I'm afraid it was fatal."

That was when Nina Rowland fainted, and Hilda had two patients on her hands. Not until the two maids had come and they got Nina to her bed across the hall did Hilda get downstairs again. She found Rogers in the kitchen, staring down at the body and looking rather shaken.

"Who did it? The girl?" he asked.

"I don't know," she said shortly. "You got Inspector Fuller, I suppose. I'll get the doctor."

"Little late for that, isn't it?"

"The family doctor. The girl's cut her hand."

"On the bottle? Or on this knife?"

She saw the knife then. She had hardly noticed it before. It was on the table, and there was blood on the long blade. He gave her a forced grin.

"What was it anyhow?" he asked. "A duel? The one with a knife and the other a milk bottle! Where were you while all this was going on?"

"Asleep," she said bitterly and went forward as the doorbell rang.

Two police officers stood outside, their squad car parked at the curb. She sent them back to the kitchen and ran up the stairs, to meet both maids in the upper hall. She felt incapable of coping with them just then. She brushed past them and into Tony's room. The girl had not moved since Rogers had carried her up, except that now her eyes were closed.

"You're not asleep, Tony, and you're not fainting," she said firmly. "You can hear what I say perfectly well."

There was no movement, but Tony opened her eyes. There was such misery in them that Hilda felt like an executioner. She bent over the bed.

"Listen, my dear," she said, her voice one Inspector Fuller had never heard. "You must tell what you know. The police are here. You can't help anybody now by hiding things."

"Is she . . . ?"

"Yes, Tony."

The eyes closed again. "I'm tired," she said. "Please let me alone. I want to sleep."

Aggie had followed Hilda into the room. Now she spoke.

"Why don't you let her alone?" she said sharply. "She's sick. What happened to her anyhow? What are those policemen doing downstairs?"

Hilda straightened.

"Miss Alice is dead, Aggie," she said. "Somebody killed her, down in the kitchen. And Tony here either saw it done or found her there."

Aggie gasped.

"Dead!" she said. "But why? Who would do a thing like that?"

"Ask Tony," Hilda said briefly. "I think she knows."

But there was no time to ask Tony anything. Dr. Wynant came into the room, and downstairs Fuller had arrived and was asking for Hilda. She went down, to find him in the front hall. He surveyed her dourly.

"Well, what do you make of this? Still holding out for the girl?"

He did not wait for a reply. He stalked back to the kitchen and she followed him. The two men from the cruise car and Rogers were standing near the kitchen door. They stood back to let him survey the body, but he did nothing more than that.

"The Half-Truck will be here soon," he said. "Just hold everything until it comes."

The Half-Truck was the humorous name given by the force to the Police Mobile Laboratory. It carried everything from pulmotors to a sound-amplifying device for bombs, and its crew consisted of print experts, several technicians, a photographer, a chemist and a variety of tools. Fuller was proud of it, but now he wanted Hilda's story. She told it to him in the library.

She gave him only the bare facts as she knew them, and he listened attentively.

"All right," he said when she finished. "You don't claim the girl was sleepwalking this time, do you?"

"I don't claim anything."

"You saw the kitchen table. One of them came down to get something to eat, and the other followed. They quarreled, and perhaps the aunt got scared. She picked up a knife, so the girl took it from her and then got the milk bottle. That's the way it looks from here, anyhow."

"What would take Alice Rowland downstairs? She was barely able to walk."

"Yet she did go down. She's still down. Don't forget that, Miss Pinkerton."

Angry color rose in Hilda's cheeks.

"So Tony killed her!" she said. "What about the other people in this house? What about that open kitchen door, and the man who attacked me last night?"

He was not obliged to answer. The Half-Truck arrived just then with its crew, and Fuller followed it back. But Hilda did not go with him. She knew the ritual too well, and there was nothing she could do anyhow. When some time later he came forward again he found her sitting on the stairs, her head buried in her hands and her whole small body dejected and hopeless. She looked up at him as though she did not see him.

"What took Tony downstairs?" she said, her voice unsteady. "And why did Alice follow her? If I knew that . . ."

"It might have been the other way."

She shook her head.

"Alice was still far from well. She'd never have gone down alone anyhow, with me there. She followed Tony. I'm sure of that. If she thought she was sleepwalking—"

"Cutting bread and butter in her sleep! And I suppose she's still asleep when she picks up a milk bottle and brains her aunt."

Hilda got up slowly. She felt drained of all vitality.

"It's just possible she'll say exactly that," she said drearily.

Fuller's look at her was fond but exasperated.

"Why?" he said. "Don't act the sphinx with me. You're no good at it. Why would she say that?"

"She probably thinks she has to," she said.

CHAPTER ELEVEN

SHE FOLLOWED him stiffly up the stairs to the girl's room. The doctor was in the bathroom preparing a hypodermic, while Aggie hovered over the bed. Tony's hand had been neatly dressed by that time. There was no sign of Nina, but both servants were in the room. Fuller cleared it of every one except Wynant.

Tony lay with her eyes closed, and he went to the bed and stood looking down at her.

"I want you to tell me what happened downstairs tonight," he said sternly. "Everything. Why you were there. How you cut your hand. And what happened to your aunt."

"I don't know," she said weakly, not opening her eyes. "I went down to get something to eat and she followed me. I went into the pantry for something. I was still there when I heard—when I heard her fall," she shuddered. "I found her—like that."

"How did you cut your hand?"

She raised her hand and looked at the bandage, as though she had not seen it before.

"I don't know," she whispered. "Maybe the knife slipped."

"Did your aunt have the knife? And did you try to take it from her?"

"No," she said, and began to cry, slow tears which rolled unnoticed down her white cheeks. "She never touched it. I was fond of her. We didn't quarrel, if that's what you mean. She was good to me."

"Were you in the habit of going down for a night supper?"

She shook her head, without replying.

"You saw nothing? Or nobody?"

But here the doctor intervened. Tony was badly shocked. The questions could wait. Just now she needed rest and quiet. And Fuller too realized that the girl had said all she intended to. After Dr. Wynant had given the hypodermic both men left, and Hilda alone with her at last, went quietly to the bed. Tony lay very still with her eyes closed, but Hilda knew she was conscious. There was no softness in her voice now.

"Was Herbert in the kitchen tonight?" she asked. "You'd better talk, Tony. I'm warning you."

"Herbert!" Tony gasped, trying to sit up. "What do you know about him?

He hasn't anything to do with all this. He wasn't even here. He . . ." She gulped and stopped. Hilda's face was stony.

"I think he was here tonight," she said gravely. "I think he came here tonight to hide from the police, and that you were getting food for him. That's when your Aunt Alice discovered him, wasn't it?" And when Tony said nothing: "He's been blackmailing you, hasn't he? And today your aunt got a letter from Honolulu. She had it in her hand when she followed you to the kitchen."

"Oh God!" Tony lay back in her bed, shivering. "Please don't tell any one about it. It—it hasn't anything to do with what happened."

"What became of it, Tony?" Hilda said, her voice still hard. "I want it. Where have you hidden it?"

"I haven't got it. I never did have it."

"But you know what was in it, don't you?"

Tony however only shook her head and closed her eyes. She refused to speak again, and Hilda stood looking down at her, divided between anger and pity. Any psychiatrist would say she was a mental case, she thought. But she did not believe it.

It was imperative, she realized, to see Nina. But the Nina she found in the bed across the hall was a wild-eyed, hysterical creature, entirely beyond reason, who dared her to think Tony had done anything wrong and tried to order her out of the house. She was not prepared however for Nina's rage when she told her she had been working for the police, and still was.

"So that's it!" she said furiously. "You've been here snooping all the time, and my poor Tony . . ."

Hilda listened as long as she could. When Nina stopped she spoke quietly.

"I would like to see that arm of yours, Mrs. Rowland," she said. "I assure you it's necessary. If you have been wounded and infection has set in, it needs attention."

Whatever she had expected it was not what followed. For Nina almost immediately went into a fit of screaming hysteria, laughing and crying wildly. It was necessary for Dr. Wynant to give her a hypodermic before she quieted, and after it had taken effect he followed Hilda out of the room.

"I don't know whether you are staying here or not, Miss Adams," he said. "I do advise you to keep away from her. Let the maids look after her. She's pretty badly shocked. What set her off this time?"

"I asked to see her arm."

"Still harping on that?" he said indulgently. "Well, keep away from her anyhow. It's *her* arm."

Tony lay in a drugged stupor the rest of the night, while the usual reporters crowded the grounds and used various devices to get into the house; while late as it was a crowd gathered on the pavement and in the alley back of the house, to be held in bounds by the police; while flash-bulbs burst, meas-urements were taken, the bottle fragments carefully gathered up and while at last Alice Rowland left her home for the last time.

Hilda, not needed elsewhere, spent the time in a search for the letter which she was confident Alice had carried downstairs with her. It was not in Tony's room, and if it had been burned the kitchen stove showed no sign of it. The kitchen was quiet again, and by daylight only the smear on the floor remained to remind her of the tragedy. The police and the crowds had gone, the Half-Truck had departed, the grounds had been examined, and only a policeman outside, a guard in the lower hall and Fuller drinking coffee in the dining room with Dr. Wynant remained.

They paid no attention to her when she joined them. The doctor put down his cup. He looked tired and unhappy.

"I can't believe it," he said. "I like the girl. Always have. It was a fine family—until lately, at least."

"When did you notice a change?"

"Only recently. Mind you, I'm not saying Tony's abnormal even now. She's not been herself since she broke her engagement, of course. But a thing like this . . . !"

Fuller lit a cigarette and surveyed the doctor over it.

"How do you get around the other facts? She did try to shoot her mother, didn't she? And there was the automobile accident later. Why all that? Does she hate her?"

The doctor looked shocked.

"Hate her!" he said. "Hate Nina! She is and has been devoted to her. Perhaps like most girls at her age she cared most for her father, but as for hate—that's absurd."

"Then you do think she was walking in her sleep when she fired the gun?" Fuller persisted.

"Something of the sort."

"It wasn't possible Alice did it, I suppose? And that last night was the result of Tony's knowing it?"

"I'd consider it highly unlikely," the doctor said gravely. "Alice Rowland had her faults. But she took in her brother's family and looked after them. Not too amiably, perhaps. As I say, she was pretty difficult at times. But she did it as well as she could, I imagine."

Fuller looked thoughtful.

"The boys think they have a case against Tony," he said. "That story of hers won't wash. They got her prints on the knife and the table, both bloody. If they find any on the pieces of the milk bottle and they turn out to be hers we'll have to take her in for questioning. Hilda's going to fight that, I suppose."

He looked at Hilda and smiled.

"Why?" The doctor was puzzled. He too stared at Hilda, who said nothing. She had poured herself a cup of coffee and was slowly sipping it.

"Don't ask me. Ask her. One of her hunches probably. Something she's got in her head about Honolulu. But four years is a long time." He got up and, picking up his hat, set it carefully on his head. "I have a great deal of respect for her hunches," he said, and went out.

The doctor looked at Hilda.

"What's all this about Honolulu?" he said gruffly. "I don't believe in hunches, but if you know anything . . ."

Hilda did not reply directly. She put down her coffee cup and looked at him stonily.

"When you see Nina Rowland again will you examine her arm?" she inquired.

"What the hell has her arm got to do with Alice's murder?"

"That's what I want to find out."

He was irritated. He got up and gazed down at her with extreme distaste.

"I'll examine her arm when and if she asks me to," he said. "Not before."

"You may be sorry," she told him. But he picked up his bag and flung out of the room without replying.

She did not see Fuller again that morning. Now that it was daylight he wandered around the lawns surrounding the house. But he found nothing and at last he got into his car and drove to his office. He found a message there from the Commissioner, and discovered that gentleman surrounded by morning papers and a distinct aura of unpleasantness. His cold was better, however, so he was articulate. Very completely articulate.

"What sort of mess is this?" he demanded. "I give you one of my best men to watch the house, you put the Pinkerton woman in it, and under both their noses we have murder." He eyed Fuller coldly. "At least you saved Hilda Adams. That probably pleases you."

"It does," Fuller said. "I'm very fond of Hilda."

"Well, dammit, she was there. How did she let this happen?"

"She was asleep," Fuller said serenely. "She'd been knocked on the head the night before, and she was about all in."

"And who the hell did that?" said the Commissioner. "Not that I haven't felt like doing it myself every now and then. And to some other people I could name," he added darkly, as Fuller grinned.

When he got back to his office, having left his chief in a state bordering on apoplexy, he found a young officer waiting for him, a tall boy with a white face and a pair of desperately clenched hands holding his cap.

"Lieutenant Hayes, sir," he said. "I've just come from the Rowland house."

"I see," Fuller said politely. "Sit down, son, and relax. No use getting into a dither about it, you know. Easy does it."

The lieutenant did not sit down. He stood stiffly, staring at Fuller.

"Are you going to arrest Tony Rowland?" he asked. "Because if you are—"

"We don't arrest people as easy as you seem to think, Lieutenant. This isn't the Army."

If he had hoped his last words would distract Johnny Hayes he failed. That single-tracked young man ignored them.

"Then why did you take her prints?" he demanded. "Aggie—one of the maids—says you did."

"We print everybody in a case like this."

Hayes however refused to relax.

"I got the story from Aggie," he said. "You're going to pin this on her,

aren't you? Because she got hold of a gun once in her sleep and it went off
. . . What sort of evidence is that? She never killed anybody, or tried to.
I know her."

"She hasn't been accused yet, Lieutenant." He pushed a box of cigarettes
across the desk. "Have one and get hold of yourself. I'd like to ask you a
question or two. Just why did she break her engagement to you?"

Hayes sat down. He did not take the proffered cigarette, however. He got
a leather case from his pocket and lit one of his own. His hands were not
steady.

"That's a private matter, sir," he said.

"Rather sudden, wasn't it?" And when there was no reply to this: "I understand all the plans were made. Then out of a blue sky—"

"Oh, for God's sake. If she changed her mind that's her business."

Fuller studied him. He looked like a nice boy, the clean-cut type the
Army either produces or discovers.

"Is that all? Did she merely change her mind, or did something happen
between you?"

"Nothing happened."

"There was no quarrel?"

"No, sir."

"You realize, of course, that she isn't in a very happy position, Lieutenant.
I'm not referring to the shooting a couple of months ago. I'm speaking of
last night. On the surface it looks as though she and her aunt had quarreled,
that Alice Rowland picked up a knife, that Tony took it from her—her prints
are on it—and then struck her aunt with a milk bottle which was on the
table. On the surface, I say. If her prints are on any of the glass from the
broken bottle it won't look very good."

"But you haven't got them?"

"The bottle broke, and the milk hasn't helped any. They're working on
them now."

The telephone rang at his elbow. He picked it up, aware of the boy's eyes
on him. He listened for a minute or so, then said thanks and put down the
receiver. Hayes was standing by that time.

"A good many blurred prints on the glass," he said. "Some that seem to be
hers. They're still working on it. I'm sorry, Lieutenant. It isn't decisive. Not
yet."

Hayes however was not listening. He jerked his cap on his head, gave a
halfhearted automatic salute and departed. Fuller sat for some time, after
he had gone. He had liked the boy's looks, and damn it all, with what was
ahead of him . . . He picked up the telephone again.

"Work on those other prints," he said. "If we haven't got them try Washington. Maybe they are the milkman's, but maybe they're not. That's what
I want to know."

AT THE HOUSE Hilda had had a trying day. The uniformed officer still patrolled outside the house, and another one remained in the lower hall, looking bored and now and then slipping into the library for a surreptitious cigarette. Nina's door was locked and Tony was still only semiconscious. Hilda ate her lunch alone, feeling useless and inadequate. Before she went upstairs she went back to the kitchen.

Stella was alone there. She had mopped the milk from the floor and cleaned up generally. Now she was at the table drinking strong black tea to settle her nerves. She was not cordial, but she seemed glad to see anybody.

"You've been here a long time, Stella," Hilda said. "Was it usual for Miss Tony to get a night lunch for herself or her mother?"

"No, miss. I said that to Aggie today. I've known her to get a piece of cheese or something like that. But that's all, and only once in a while. As for that milk bottle, she never touched milk." Stella's face crumpled. Unexpectedly she began to cry. "The poor child!" she said. "So nice and kind and then breaking her engagement and now this. When I think of her carrying out her wedding dress yesterday—"

"Are you sure of that?" Hilda asked sharply.

"Well, Aggie says it's missing. Another dress too. And she had the car out. I saw her come back."

Hilda was puzzled.

"Why on earth would she do a thing like that, Stella?"

"I suppose she just wanted to get rid of it. Couldn't bear to have it around, poor dear. And so crazy she was about it when it came!"

Hilda digested this in silence. When Stella had wiped her eyes and regained some of her composure Hilda opened the door to the basement staircase.

"I suppose the police were down there?" she asked.

"They were all over. The dirt in this place you'd hardly believe. They even went into the butler's room! It's empty, of course; has been since we got rid of that Herbert Johnson."

In spite of herself Hilda started.

"Herbert Johnson?" she said. "When was he here?"

"Miss Tony found him somewhere. They knew him in the islands. He wasn't rightly a butler. More of a houseman really. And he wasn't any good. Always sort of snooping around. Miss Alice fired him, and not too soon if you ask me."

"When was this?"

"Oh, two—three months ago. We really got him because of the wedding. His sister Delia used to be Mrs. Rowland's maid. If she wasn't any better than he was . . ."

"Where is the butler's room?"

"Off the back hall, so he could answer the doorbell. It's closed now. Nothing there."

Hilda left the kitchen, but she did not go upstairs. She found the door to the room, slipped inside and closed it carefully behind her. The window was closed and the shade drawn, but a glance told her that some one had been in it briefly and recently. Possibly the police too. But certainly the police had not put a blanket on the dismantled bed, or a fresh cake of soap and a towel on the stationary washstand in the corner. Both soap and towel had been used, and the under side of the soap was still moist.

Some one had made hasty preparations to sleep there the night before. To get a supper of sorts and then to sleep, and she had no doubt whatever as to who it had been. When she went back to the kitchen Stella was pouring milk into a saucer for her cat and looking rather sulky.

"I guess I talk too much," she said. "But if that Herbert was here last night he'd be the one who did it. Him and his goings-on, scaring Miss Tony half to death and getting her little bit of money from her."

"How do you mean he scared her?"

"I wouldn't know. Something about that sister of his—as if anybody cared! And Tony slipping him into her mother's room when she thought nobody was around! I didn't draw a full breath until Miss Alice fired him."

Hilda went back upstairs. She had not told Fuller about the envelope from the kitchen floor, and she had no real doubt as to why it had been where she found it. To make certain however she went into Alice's room and to the chest where she had locked the letter the day before.

The chest was not locked now. The keys were hanging in the upper drawer and Hilda opened it. It contained nothing, however, but neatly arranged piles of stockings and gloves, and the other drawers were equally innocent. If she had had any doubt that Alice had had the letter in her hand when she went downstairs that night the doubt was gone.

Just to be certain she searched the rest of the room. The letter had definitely disappeared, however, and the picture of the murder grew clearer in her mind; of Alice, letter in hand, following Tony to the kitchen, of her telling or reading its contents, and of a Herbert, hiding from the police and seeking sanctuary in his old room, overhearing her. Coming up behind her maybe and picking up the milk bottle.

Still, in the light of what she already knew, why had he killed her? Either he had only meant to knock her down and escape, or she had some knowledge which made it necessary for her to die.

Somewhat grimly, Hilda picked up the telephone on the bedside table and called Fuller.

"Can you talk to Honolulu by wire?" she inquired.

"I can. I'll be monitored, of course. Why Honolulu?"

"Herbert Johnson came from there."

"Herbert Johnson?"

"The man who knocked me down and robbed me. You may recall that," she said drily. "He was butler or something of the sort here two or three months ago. Tony got him, but Alice Rowland fired him."

He whistled.

"I think he was here last night," she went on. "Tony seems to have hidden him here, or some one did. He comes from Hawaii. He may have a record there. You'd better find out all you can about him. About his sister too. You might see what you can find out about the Rowlands at the same time."

Fuller was duly impressed.

"You think this Herbert's the killer, don't you?" he inquired. "Anybody but Tony Rowland, eh?"

"I'm only saying he's been hiding out, and Tony was probably getting him something to eat last night. If Alice came in and recognized him . . . She may have known him. Or she may have written to some one in Hawaii about him. She got a letter from there yesterday, and I can't find it."

"If he was there why didn't Tony say so?"

"She probably has a reason," Hilda said drily and put down the receiver.

He sat back and considered this after he had put in his Honolulu call. He had in fact some hours to consider it, due to wartime delay. He went back to the beginning of the case and Alice's story to him when she brought the gun. Getting out the rough sketch she had drawn of Nina's room he studied it again, the doorway, the bed, the location of the open window. Suppose this Herbert had been the one who shot at Nina and missed her? Hilda was laying emphasis on him. Was he in the house as butler at that time?

He looked over his notes. No. Only the family and the two women servants, he saw. Of course some one might have admitted him, Tony by choice. In that case why had she protected him? As she was still doing, he thought irritably; getting Hilda's watch before the police found it, and hiding him the night before. Unless it was blackmail, and of a serious sort. Not of Tony probably. Very possibly of her mother. What he had seen of her had shown him a beautiful and not too intelligent woman, the sort who expected admiration from men and undoubtedly received it. What did Herbert have? Letters and photographs were the usual stock of the blackmailer. Outside of those . . .

At five o'clock he called Hilda on the phone.

"We've picked up a dozen or so fellows who more or less answer your Herbert's description," he said. "Can you come down?"

She did not answer at once, and when she did she was doubtful.

"I can," she said. "I'd rather not, of course. Tony's beginning to rouse. I don't like to leave her."

"Put Aggie there. How's the mother?"

"Still shut away. Perhaps I ought to tell you she's sent one word. I'm fired."

"You seem to be still there!"

"What do *you* think?" she inquired.

She agreed to come however, leaving Aggie with Tony, and before six she was viewing a sorry-looking line of men in the glare of the line-up. None of them was Herbert and Hilda, looking them over much as she would a row of Christmas turkeys, rejected them in much the same businesslike manner and prepared to go. He followed her to the door.

"If Tony's coming out of the hypo I'd better talk to her," he said. "It's time she spoke up."

Hilda stopped and turned chilly blue eyes up to his.

"You're not going to question her until I get the bandage off her mother's arm," she said coldly, and walked out.

So Hilda still thought Tony had shot her mother, he reflected. Well, what if she had? And once more his mind turned to a possible lover, to blackmail, and the girl's probable resentment at both. But it was Alice who had been murdered, not an attractive but certainly an inoffensive onlooker. Or was she?

He went back to his office to wait for his call and—he thought grimly—for Hilda to get the bandage off Nina Rowland's lovely white arm. How had they managed it, he wondered. After all a bullet wound was a serious matter, even if it only plowed through the flesh. There would have been blood to hide, and pain to conceal. Not for the first time he wondered if Hilda had not got off on the wrong foot. But long experience had taught him to respect her methods.

He decided to give her a few hours more, which turned out to be a mistake. And an almost fatal one at that.

CHAPTER THIRTEEN

WHEN HILDA got back to the Rowland house she found the young police officer in the hall below staring up the stairs.

"Say," he said. "I thought the girl was sick."

"So she is. What's wrong?"

He scratched an ear reflectively.

"I don't know as it's anything," he said. "I just saw somebody up there out of the tail of my eye. Looked like a young lady. Maybe I'm wrong."

Hilda scuttled up the stairs, but everything was quiet. Tony was in bed, awake but not moving. Aggie, however had disappeared, and Hilda was immediately suspicious. Nothing seemed to be wrong, but she was confident Tony had been in the hall for some purpose of her own.

"How long have you been alone?" she demanded.

"Only a minute or two." Tony's voice was flat. "She went to get me some soup."

Hilda glanced around the room. Nothing was apparently changed. Colonel Rowland's picture still stood on the toilet table. The few drops of blood on the blue carpet from Tony's cut hand had been washed up, her slippers and dressing gown were in the closet as before. But Tony was watching her with the eyes of a sick child. She walked over to the bed.

"What have you been doing?" she asked bluntly. "You've been up to something, haven't you? That policeman downstairs saw you."

"Can't I even see my own mother?"

"Not at the head of the stairs. Where were you? What were you doing?"

Tony however refused to answer, and Hilda felt vaguely uneasy. She looked down at the girl.

"Now you're awake," she said, still bluntly. "I'd like my watch again. It belonged to my mother, and I know you have it."

"It's in the toe of a shoe in the closet," Tony said indifferently. "When are they going to arrest me?"

"Why do you think they *are* going to arrest you?"

"Because I did it," she said, with that strange new indifference. "They needn't look any further. You can tell that man downstairs. Or maybe I'd better tell him myself."

"You killed your aunt? With a milk bottle?" Hilda inquired blandly, "and that stiff arm of yours?"

"I did it. That's enough, isn't it?"

Hilda's patience gave way.

"Now listen to me," she said crossly. "You're behaving like a child. You're too old to go on dramatizing yourself. Who are you protecting? Herbert Johnson? Did he kill your Aunt Alice?"

"I told you I did it."

Hilda wanted to shake her.

"Has it occurred to you," she said, "that you've done more than your share of damage? That if you'd acted like a sane person your Aunt Alice might be alive now?" And when Tony only shuddered and closed her eyes—"And that you haven't helped anybody or anything? Suppose I tell you that the police are looking up Herbert Johnson's record in Honolulu right now."

To her horror and dismay she realized that the girl had fainted again. She was still not conscious when Aggie came in with the soup, and to turn a blistering tongue on her.

She went back to her room after Tony was better. But she was uneasy. What had the girl been doing in the upper hall? And why had she fainted when she had learned about Herbert's record in Honolulu? She felt defeated and deflated as she changed from her street clothes into her uniform again. Nina's door was still obstinately closed and probably locked. There had been no sound from it. And there was still no word from Fuller.

She went downstairs to her supper in an unhappy frame of mind. Even the theory she had been slowly evolving seemed farfetched and unlikely. After all why kill Alice? If anyone had to be killed it should have been Herbert Johnson. Unless . . .

She ate very little. She was still too uneasy to be hungry. Outside in the hall she saw Aggie carrying a supper tray to the library for the police officer, and saw him eating it as she went up the stairs again. Nothing suspicious had happened, however. Tony was not asleep, but she refused to talk, and there was no sound from Nina's room. She located her watch where Tony said she would find it, and wound and set it automatically by the bedside clock.

It was eight o'clock, she was to remember later.

For two hours she sat in the dim light in the bedroom, aware that Tony was watching her. But she made no effort to speak or to get out of bed, and at last Hilda got stiffly to her feet and prepared to go to her room and get ready for the night.

Tony asked for a glass of water then, the first time she had spoken. Hilda placed it beside the bed and stood watching her. But she did not drink it. She lay there looking up with tired sunken young eyes.

"Don't worry," she said. "I won't get up. And I'm sorry I've given you so much trouble, Miss Adams." She smiled faintly.

"That's a promise, is it?" Hilda looked down at her.

"Absolutely. I'm going to sleep." She yawned, and turned on her side.

That was at ten o'clock. As she went out Hilda heard Aggie and Stella going up to their rooms on the third floor, and she looked down into the front hall for the officer there. Rather to her surprise he was not in sight, and she suspected him of being in the kitchen searching for food or in the library smoking.

One of her profoundest beliefs being that men were all right in their place but seldom in it, she made her usual systematic preparations for the night. She took a short bath, brushed her teeth and her hair, began to wind her watch and remembered she had already done so, put on her nightgown and a warm dressing gown over it, and then having switched out her light went to her door. To her astonishment it did not open. She pulled at it vigorously, but nothing happened. And when she found the switch and turned on the lights again she saw the key was not in it.

For the first time she felt terrified. She stood staring at it incredulously. This could not be happening, not to her, Hilda Adams. It happened to people like Nina, but not to her. She shook it violently and called.

"Officer!" she said. "Officer, some one has locked me in."

There was no reply however, and she looked around her helplessly. She could open the window and shout, she thought. But she hesitated to do it. Anyhow the house was a detached one, and the patrolman was not in sight on the pavement outside. What had happened to the guard in the hall? Was he dead? Had some one knocked him out?"

It was wrong. All wrong. Something was going on in the house, and she was helpless. The nearest telephone was across the hall in Alice Rowland's room, and it chose that moment to ring violently. It kept on ringing for some time, while she looked around for a method of escape. She glanced up at the closed transom over the door. She had no illusions that she could get through it, but at least she could look out, maybe call so some one would hear her. It took some time to move the table under it, and to mount by means of a chair. The transom too had apparently not been opened for years. She managed it at last, to realize that the light in both upper and lower halls had been extinguished, and that if the guard was there he was either unconscious or dead.

She called without result, and as she was getting down from her perch the chair slipped and fell. She sat on the floor for a minute or two, a small and ignominious figure of defeat. A frightened one, too. For almost the first time in her life she felt helpless and desperate.

To add to her confusion the telephone across the hall was ringing again, and she realized that something would have to be done, and done soon.

She limped to the window and looked out. The policeman was still missing, but a man was walking along the pavement. He had a dog on a leash, and he stopped sharply and looked up when she called.

"Do you mind ringing the doorbell?" she asked.

"Doing what?"

"Ringing the doorbell. I'm locked in my room and can't get out."

He let the dog go and came up the walk. He was middle-aged and carrying his hat. He seemed to be quite bald.

"There's nothing wrong, is there?" he asked. "I mean—this is the Rowland house, isn't it?"

"Yes. I don't know what's happened. Do try the bell. I think it rings on the third floor too. The servants will hear it."

He climbed the steps and put a thumb on the push button. The dog had followed him, looking interested. Through the open transom Hilda could hear the bell far away, and after an interval Aggie's heavy steps coming down the stairs from the third floor. She exclaimed when she saw the dark hall, and evidently turned on a light, for it was reflected in Hilda's room. Hilda called to her.

"You needn't go down," she said. "I'm locked in here. It's Miss Adams. See if you can find the key and let me out."

"Whoever did that?" said Aggie. "Maybe the door's stuck. There's no key here."

Hilda went back to the window and leaned out.

"It's all right," she said to the man below. "Thanks a lot. One of the maids is here now."

He went away looking vaguely disappointed, as though he had expected something more dramatic. But Hilda wasted no time on him. She was back at the door.

"Try Miss Alice's key," she said urgently, "and see if that policeman is around. I don't know what's happened to him."

It took some time to find a key which fitted. Aggie moved slowly, and her hands fumbled as she tried one after another. Hilda was on the verge of shrieking hysteria when at last the door opened and she shot out into the hall.

Somewhere not far away the engine of a car had started to roar, then settled down to a purr. The telephone had stopped ringing, and save for the guard missing from the lower hall everything seemed quiet. But she saw that

Tony's door, which she had left open, was now closed. She felt her throat tighten as she ran back to it.

It was not locked, however. She threw it open and stepped inside, to find the bed empty and no sign of Tony in the room.

Alarmed as she was, even then Hilda had no idea of the extent of the calamity. With Aggie at her heels she crossed to Nina's door and banged on it. It took a long time to rouse her, but at last she came to the door and Hilda asked rather wildly if Tony was there.

"Tony?" Nina said thickly. "Why no. What's wrong? Where is she?"

Hilda did not wait. She scurried forward to Alice's room, and from there down the front stairs. In the library the young police officer was heavily asleep on the leather couch. He was breathing noisily, and a cigarette had fallen from his hand and burned a small hole in the carpet.

There was no sign of Tony anywhere. In the back of the house the lights were out, but the kitchen door was standing wide open, and she ran frantically outside. Back along the alley the garage was closed and locked, and by the light of a nearby street lamp she could see that the car was still there. But there was no sound of the motor running, and she drew a long breath of relief. If Tony had only run away, and not . . .

She was dripping with perspiration, although the night was cool. Her one fear had been that the girl had found herself facing an insoluble problem and had killed herself. It was still possible, of course. She could have made her way to the river, or there were a dozen other sickening possibilities. But in that case she would have had to dress. Had there been time enough for that, she wondered. How long had she been locked in her room?

She never even heard the doorbell as she ran back to the house, and she only realized Aggie had admitted Fuller when he caught her by the arm and held her.

"Why the hell don't you answer your telephone?" he demanded angrily.

She looked at him, her face blank.

"Tony's disappeared," she said.

"Disappeared?" he said incredulously. "Where's she gone?"

"How would I know? I've been locked in my room, and the policeman on the street probably went to the drugstore for cigarettes. All she had to do was to walk out."

He followed her up the stairs. The servants had roused Nina and she was standing in the door of her room. Dulled as she was by the opiate she had been given, there could be no doubt of her bewilderment.

"Where could she go?" she was saying, her eyes staring in her white face. "She wasn't even dressed, was she?" She caught Fuller by the arm. "You've got to find her, for God's sake. Before it's too late. Before she does something dreadful."

Hilda did not wait. She caught Aggie's eye and went into Tony's room.

"You know her clothes," she said. "Look and see if anything is missing."

But nothing was missing. Aggie inspected the closet and the bed.

"Her clothes are all here," she said, her voice flat. "But there's a blanket gone from her bed. And her slippers aren't here."

Hilda reported that to Fuller as he came in, followed by a terrified Nina. He ignored the matter of the clothing, however. He looked from Aggie to Nina, his face dark with anger.

"The officer downstairs has been drugged," he said sternly. "What do you women know about it? Did you drug him so your daughter could escape, Mrs. Rowland?"

She stared at him blankly.

"Me?" she said. "Why would I do a thing like that?"

"Somebody did," he said, his voice gruff. "Some one in this house. And some one has taken your daughter away. What do you know about that?"

"I don't know anything," she said. "And I wouldn't tell you if I did. At least you can't arrest her now."

"We had no idea of arresting her," he said, his voice grim. "We've got Herbert Johnson, Mrs. Rowland, if that means anything to you."

She looked even more pale, if that was possible. But there was no doubt of her surprise.

"Herbert?" she said unbelievingly. "But what has Herbert got to do with this?"

He was compelled to believe her. Whatever had been going on, at least she did not connect Herbert Johnson with it. He sent her back to her bed, to comfort a Hilda who for once had lost her composure. She was coming from Alice's room, a small empty bottle in her hand, and she held it out to him, her face a frozen mask.

"Sleeping tablets," she said. "I'm afraid she's taken all of them."

Fuller stiffened as he took the bottle and examined it.

"How long do you think it is since she took them?"

"It can't be more than an hour and a half. She was awake when I left her. But I was locked in for a good while, and before that I was getting ready for the night."

"How many tablets were there?"

"Plenty. If we don't find her soon it will be too late."

Neither of them had noticed Aggie, standing by. The first warning they had was a heavy crash behind them as she fainted and fell to the floor.

CHAPTER FOURTEEN

NO ONE PAID any attention to her. At some period she must have revived and got up, have gone upstairs to her room and packed her clothing, sobbing bitterly as she did so. At some time later too she must have crept down the back stairs and left the house by the kitchen door. But by that time Fuller had been to the garage and seen the car still there.

For once in his life he was thoroughly at a loss. Obviously Tony had not gone of her own volition. She had been carried away, wrapped in a blanket, and she might easily die before she was located. He had an idea what had happened, but that was all, and the likelihood that they could locate her before it was too late was small indeed.

When later on he decided to talk to Aggie she was gone, bag and baggage. That Tony had been taken away in a car was evident, but the policeman who belonged in front of the house had seen none. He appeared as Fuller went down the stairs.

"I saw the lights on," he said. "Is anything wrong, sir?"

"Only a kidnaping," Fuller said shortly. "A girl's been stolen out of this house, the nurse was locked in her room and you weren't around. Where the hell were you?"

He looked astounded. He had heard a window break somewhere near, he said, and saw a man running down the street. He had followed him for two or three blocks, but he was pretty fast. He had lost him near the bus stop.

"Funny thing, sir," he said. "He could have dodged into any of the places around here and got away. He didn't. He—just kept going."

He had no description of him, except that from the way he ran, he was young. And that he was without a hat. Kind of a light-colored suit, he thought. As to the broken window, he'd located it across the street and notified the family.

Fuller went into the library. The young guard was sitting rather dazedly on the couch in the library.

"I don't know what happened to me," he said, his voice shaken. "I got sleepy all at once. I couldn't even stand up. I came in here and—well, that's all I remember. I just passed out."

Fuller's face was grim as he turned to see a stiff-faced Hilda pushing Stella down the stairs.

Stella looked frightened. Her thin body was trembling.

"It's about Aggie," she said. "She didn't take a bath."

"What the hell's that got to do with it?"

"She said she was. I heard the water running. But she wasn't. She was downstairs."

"What Stella means," Hilda interposed, "is that Aggie locked me in my room and turned out the lights. In that case she probably doped Price's supper tray. You see what that means, of course."

"Are you saying that Aggie took the girl away?"

With a magnificent gesture Hilda deplored the stupidity of all men, pushed into the library and picked up the telephone book. After that, with Fuller's baffled eyes still on her, she dialed a number.

"Hotel Majestic?" she said politely. "Give me Mrs. Hayes. Mrs. Arthur Hayes. It's urgent."

She waited. The room behind her was filled with faces: Fuller's, Nina's,

Stella's, the two police officers. So far as she was concerned they were not
there.

"Mrs. Hayes?" she said. "I'm sorry to disturb you, but it's important. Have
you a car in town?"

Mrs. Hayes's voice, surprised and not too pleasant, could be heard by everyone.

"In town? No. What on earth . . . Is it Johnny? Has he had an accident?"

"I imagine he's quite well," Hilda said, rapidly but still politely. "What
sort of car is it, Mrs. Hayes?"

"A black limousine. But I don't really see—"

"Do you mind giving me the number of the license? And your home telephone too. We want to call up and see if it's there. And hurry, please. It's a
matter of life and death."

But Mrs. Hayes was firm. She was giving no information until she knew
what the trouble was, and Fuller—finally seeing the light—took the phone himself, using his best authoritative manner.

"This is Inspector Fuller of the Police Department," he said. "Please give
me the license number of the car at once. I think it's been used to kidnap
Tony Rowland. If it goes over the State line it's a capital offense."

"Johnny?" she gasped. "You mean Johnny has done that?"

"It looks like it."

Her reaction surprised him. She was indignant and terrified.

"You can't mean he is going to marry her? It's impossible. It's dreadful.
You must find him, Inspector."

"I've got to find him, and soon. Or the charge may be murder."

She gasped for breath, but she gave both numbers, and at Hilda's suggestion the location of the summer place in Massachusetts. "But he can't go
there," she protested. "It's closed. There's nobody there."

"There might be an excellent reason," he said drily, and put down the receiver. After that he spent a busy quarter of an hour over the phone. He
augmented his earlier orders with the license number of the car, and after a
long wait Mr. Hayes in Connecticut reported the limousine gone.

"The chauffeur says a sergeant—a young fellow—came here late this afternoon with a note from my son John. He wanted to borrow the car for overnight. As I use a coupe myself he let it go. What's wrong? John in trouble
about it?"

"Very definitely," said Fuller, and put down the receiver.

Aggie was gone by the time they looked for her, sitting red-eyed and terrified in a jolting bus. She had nowhere to go, after thirty years in the Rowland
house. When the bus reached the end of the line she was still there. The
driver looked back at her.

"What's the idea?" he said. "Just taking a ride?"

She said nothing. At the end of the trip she was back where she had
started, and she picked up her bag automatically and got out. She walked
doggedly back to the house and up the stairs, to confront a Hilda remarkable

in her dressing gown and magnificent in her fury. Aggie did not give her a chance to speak.

"It was to be only for a minute, Miss Adams. Just long enough to get her out," she sobbed, her heavy shoulders shaking. "How could I know?" she protested, tears rolling down her cheeks. "He called me on the telephone this afternoon. He didn't want her to be arrested. He knew she didn't do it. All he wanted was to get her away until they found out who killed Miss Alice."

"So you locked my door. You doped that guard downstairs, too. Where were you when he carried her out?"

"Up in my room. I was to wait and when the car drove off in the alley I was to unlock your door again. I didn't mean any harm. I was trying to help."

"Help her to die, you mean," Hilda said bitterly. "If they don't find her in time that's what will happen, Aggie. Think that over. Then go up to your room and pray. She needs it."

It was some time before she went downstairs again. Fuller was once more hanging up the receiver, after issuing orders, statewide and including near-by states as well, to pick up any car answering the vague description he had, and containing a girl, probably asleep and wrapped in a dark blanket. It was pretty hopeless, he knew. Tony might be on the floor in the back of the car, or the car might already be garaged and hidden somewhere. But it was a fight against time. Something had to be done.

When he turned from the telephone he surveyed Hilda with his usual mixture of pride and irritation. He did not notice that she looked on the verge of collapse.

"The Honolulu message is in," he said. "Johnson's wanted for murder out there. Nothing on the sister yet. Your hunch was good, Hilda."

She still said nothing. There was, as a matter of fact, no time for her to say anything. A car drove up to the curb, and two young men got out. One of them carried a figure wrapped in a dark blanket. The other ran ahead and rang the bell. Both men were in uniform, one of them a sergeant, and it was Johnny Hayes who brought Tony into the house, a Johnny pale to the lips and visibly shaking.

"Look, for God's sake!" he said hoarsely. "We can't wake her up. There's something wrong."

He attempted to carry her up the stairs, but Fuller blocked the way.

"Get her back into the car, you young fool!" he shouted. "She's had a poisonous dose of sleeping tablets. The hospital's not far. You two damned idiots may have killed her."

They did not resent it. They were scared and pitiful. They did not even notice Hilda—still in dressing gown and slippers—as she got in with them. It is doubtful if they realized that Fuller was grimly telling them they were under arrest for abduction, or that kidnaping was a capital crime. The other boy drove while Johnny sat in the rear holding Tony, his face filled with despair. He spoke only twice. Once he said: "I couldn't let her be arrested. I only meant to hide her for a while." And again: "Who gave her the poison?"

"She took it herself," Fuller said grimly.

HOURS LATER, with a cold October sun shining into the hospital windows, Fuller roused himself from sleep in the straight chair outside Tony's room. He felt stiff and hungry, and the sight of Hilda, in a borrowed uniform and a cap set uncompromisingly on top of her head made him also feel guilty.

"See here," he said roughly, "how about home and bed? She's all right, isn't she?"

She looked worriedly at him.

"She'll live. I don't think she wants to."

"She's young, Hilda. She'll get over it. And we have Herbert. Don't forget that."

She looked up at him. He seemed relieved and self-confident. She made a move toward the pocket of her dressing gown, then abandoned the idea. In an endeavor to cheer her Fuller laughed.

"I don't want a night like that again," he said cheerfully. "Quite a plan those youngsters had, wasn't it? The sergeant to break a window and call off the man in front, and Johnny to grab the girl. Then when it was all over to see the sergeant topple over in a faint! I hope to God the Army doesn't hear it."

Hilda however refused to be cheered. She sat staring ahead of her, her eyes blank, and his gaze grew more intent.

"What's wrong with you, Hilda?"

She stirred then, but she still did not look at him.

"Nothing," she said, and got up heavily. "I meant to tell you. I got the bandage off Nina Rowland's arm last night."

"And Tony had shot her?"

"No. Nobody had shot her." She reached up and took off her cap. "I'd better go home. I'm not needed now."

He felt confused as he took her down to a waiting police car, still in the ridiculous borrowed uniform, with her bathrobe over her arm. She had refused to say anything more, and he thought she walked as though she felt slightly dizzy. He was still puzzled as he went back to his vigil outside Tony's door.

To his disgust Johnny Hayes was there again, prowling the hall, with a face which needed a shave and could have stood a washing.

Fuller groaned when he saw him.

"Why don't you go somewhere else?" he said irritably. "Get a bath and go to bed, for instance."

Johnny looked astounded.

"Bed, sir?" he said. "I thought I was under arrest."

"Oh, for God's sake!" Fuller said sourly. "Get out of my sight. Go and get some breakfast. Get that sergeant of yours and beat it. Let the Army take care of you. You're its baby. Not mine."

Johnny made a gesture which threw the Army at least temporarily overboard. He stood in front of Fuller, rocking slightly on a pair of excellent shoes, and with his unshaven jaw set.

"I'm entitled to some information, sir," he said, not without dignity. "Why did she take that stuff? If she did take it."

"I imagine she blamed herself for her aunt's death."

"But that's ridiculous!"

"Not entirely," said Fuller gravely. "She was sheltering a fugitive from justice, a man named Herbert Johnson. Alice Rowland must have found him there and threatened to call the police."

"It doesn't sound like Tony, Inspector."

"I expect she had her reasons," Fuller said, his voice dry. "Let her tell you herself when she's able to. Now go and get some breakfast and a shave. And take that window-breaking sergeant of yours with you. I have other things to do."

Which proved to be more true than he had anticipated. For one thing when he was finally admitted to Tony's room at first she would not talk to him. She looked small and young in the high hospital bed, with her shining hair spread over the flat pillow. But she only shuddered when she saw him and turned her head away.

He sat down beside the bed and took her hand.

"I'm glad you're better, my dear," he said. "It's all over now. And you needn't be afraid of Herbert any more. He's under arrest. It's all right."

He felt her hand give a convulsive jerk. Then she said the only thing she said while he was there.

"Why didn't you let me alone last night?"

"Let you die?" he said lightly. "My dear child, with a long happy life ahead of you, and a young man ready to break down that door at any minute! Don't be foolish."

But although he tried questioning her as to the events leading to Alice Rowland's death she said nothing more. When the nurse came in she was apparently asleep, her sensitive mouth set and her eyes closed. He went out feeling frustrated and slightly bewildered, to go back to his office, put his feet on his desk, and sleep peacefully for several hours.

It was afternoon when the telephone wakened him. . . .

Hilda was alone in her apartment that night when he arrived. She had been sitting in the dark, her hands folded in her lap and her eyes gazing out at the roof and chimneys beyond the window. She was still sitting there when, receiving no answer to his knock, he opened the door and walked in. He did not see her at first. Then he made out her smallish huddled body and put his hat down on the table.

"I've been thinking things over," he said coldly. "Perhaps you'd better raise chickens. You won't mind cutting their heads off, will you?"

"What's the difference between using an ax and breaking their necks?"

"That's no excuse for what you have done. And you know it."

"There were only two alternatives."

But this was not the old Hilda. There was defense in her voice, not resentment. He lit a cigarette and pulled up a chair. He was still furiously resentful.

"How long did you know this thing?" he demanded.

"What thing?"

"The secret Tony Rowland was trying to keep. The hold Johnson had over her."

"I didn't know it. I only suspected it. I kept trying to have somebody look at Nina's arm. Nobody would do it." She was still indignant. "Last night I made her show it to me. It wasn't what they were afraid of, and I told her so."

"I see. And that's the reason she—"

"I had nothing to do with that," she said hastily.

"But you suspected something wrong from the start?" he persisted.

She moved in her chair.

"If I had I'd have saved Alice. All I was sure of was that Tony Rowland was not a psychopathic case. I didn't think she'd shot her mother in her sleep, either."

"But you thought she had shot her?"

"What was I to think? At first, anyhow," she said defensively. "I hadn't been in the house five minutes before she told me to keep away from her mother's room. And she locked the door at first, too, until she saw I was minding my own business."

Fuller smiled rather wryly. The idea of Hilda on a case minding her own business amused him.

"All right," he said. "You were attending strictly to your job. Then something set you off. What was it?"

It was some time before she answered. The room was still dark. Over her head the canary chirped sleepily. That and the cries of children playing in the street below were all that broke the silence. When she did speak her voice was tired and dispirited.

"I don't know much about girls," she said. "But it isn't usual for them to lock their mothers in their rooms, is it? And there was Herbert, of course. He had to fit in somewhere."

"Don't tell me you suspected him because he knocked you down and robbed you!"

Some of the resentment was gone from his voice.

"I wasn't within a mile of the truth at that time," she confessed. "Tony had a secret of some sort. I knew that. And the Johnson man was involved in it. But it seemed queer for her to be using the *Encyclopedia Britannica* for a doorstop."

He looked astonished.

"The *Encyclopedia!* What on earth did that have to do with it?"

She sighed. "Did you ever go through a whole volume of it, page by page?

It's horribly tiring. But one page had a smear on it, as if it had been put face down on something."

"I see. Of course that explained everything!"

She ignored the irony in his voice. Probably she never noticed it, engrossed as she was in what she knew.

"It simply suggested something. Why for instance Tony burned the bandages from her mother's arm at night. And I never was really certain, even then. It was just a possibility—until the end."

"Why for God's sake didn't you take me into your confidence?" he demanded. "You could at least have told me what you suspected."

"Why should I? Nobody had been killed then. If Tony had a secret like that it was hers, not mine. But if she had, Herbert knew it too. There had to be some reason why she bought my watch. Apparently she didn't want him arrested. Then she'd sold a couple of dresses, so she evidently needed money, probably for him. But I began to suspect something very serious after I talked to Stella, the cook. She said he had been in the house as a butler just before Tony broke her engagement and tried to kill both her mother and herself. You gave me the clue to that yourself before I even took the case."

He stared at her.

"I gave you the clue! What sort of clue?"

"In the park that night. You said there was one motive for crime usually forgotten. That was desperation. Tony Rowland was desperate. Any idiot could have seen that."

Angry as he was Fuller grinned in the darkness. This was Hilda again, not the cowering creature he had found on his arrival. And a Hilda ready to talk, to justify the thing she had done.

"I suppose I began by wondering why Tony locked her mother's door. She relaxed later, but it was a queer thing for a girl to do. Then there was her broken engagement. No one knew why, even Nina herself. After Herbert appeared I decided it was a case of blackmail, but blackmail didn't explain everything. The queer thing was that her mother didn't seem to know anything about it. She was perfectly willing to talk about Herbert and his sister Delia, who had been her maid. She even talked about the change in Tony.

"I thought of everything from Japs to a lover for Nina Rowland. I even wondered if Alice had tried to shoot her sister-in-law, and Tony was taking the blame. Then I saw Mrs. Hayes. She worried me. She wouldn't talk, except that her son was to keep away from the girl. She looked shocked and half sick. It was more than his marrying her. She didn't even want him near her. I thought Tony had told her the truth, or what she thought was the truth, so—"

"So you went to the *Encyclopedia?*" He looked at her with a sort of awe. "Don't tell me, on the basis of what you had, you went through twenty-four volumes, including the Atlas!"

"Only one. She had been using it as a doorstop."

"Of course. Why not?" he said, his mouth twitching. "I always thought there must be some practical use for the damned things."

She remained unsmiling, however.

"Later she changed it for a china elephant, but I found it in the library. I didn't have a chance to go through it until just before Alice Rowland was killed. I should have acted at once, of course. I blame myself. After all Alice had had the letter and hidden it, and it came from Hawaii. Up to that time Tony had watched the mail, but that day she happened to be out. I took it to Alice myself."

Fuller looked baffled.

"What letter? What on earth are you talking about?"

"The letter about Herbert's sister Delia, the reason she didn't sail with them from Honolulu. Alice got the letter, and everything broke wide open."

"Where is this letter now?" he inquired impatiently.

"I have it," she said. "I found it last night. But maybe I'd better tell you how I think things happened when Alice Rowland was killed."

And this is the story of the murder, as she told it, and as it actually happened.

CHAPTER SIXTEEN

TONY HAD NOT been asleep that night. She was waiting for the household to settle down before she burned the dressings from her mother's arm. But also the meeting with Johnny Hayes had upset her. When she finally slipped into her mother's room Nina had been awake and irritable.

"You've been crying again," Nina said, eyeing her. "I don't understand you, Tony. It isn't enough that you spoil everyone's plans, including my own. You go around looking like a ghost yourself."

"I'm sorry, mother. I'm all right, really."

"And why all this secrecy?" Nina demanded. "Why not tell Alice and be through with it? She can't do anything about it, can she?"

"You know how she is, mother. She'd raise a row. She'd get Dr. Wynant in, for one thing."

Nina subsided. She loathed Wynant. Then too she was never certain of Tony these days. The night of the shooting, for instance. Had she been walking in her sleep? Or was Alice right after all and there was something wrong in Tony's mind?

Tony was dressing her arm by that time. It looked better, but she said nothing, and Nina lapsed into sulky silence. She lay back against her pillows and submitted glumly. Seen thus, even with her hair in curlers and a thin gleam of cold cream on her face she still looked attractive. She waited until Tony had washed her hands in the bathroom and came back.

"What happened to your wedding dress?" she said abruptly. "I happen to know it's missing."

Tony did not answer. She was wrapping the dressings in a towel, and Nina went on petulantly.

"Don't you think you've acted the fool long enough?" she demanded. "What happened between you and Johnny Hayes? I've a good notion to send for his mother and see what she knows. She's in town. I saw it in the paper."

Tony stiffened, and her young face set in hard lines.

"If you do I'll never forgive you, mother."

"Am I supposed to sit back and see my only child eating her heart out? No wonder Alice thinks you've lost your mind. I'm not sure she isn't right."

"I'm doing what I think is best. If that's crazy I can't help it."

She left the room, closing the door carefully behind her, and went down the stairs. The house was very quiet, and following her usual custom she deposited the dressings in the stove and set fire to them. The kitchen was dark until she lit the match, but she was startled as she replaced the stove lid to hear some one rapping on the window outside.

She stood still, afraid to move. There was no light from the stove now and the darkness was thick. But beyond the window a distant street light showed her a figure which she all too surely recognized.

"It's Herbert," said the voice. "Let me in, quick. The police are after me."

She stood uncertain for a moment. Then she went to the door and unlocked it, and Herbert burst into the room. He sounded as though he had been running, and he was in an ugly mood.

"Who put them onto me?" he demanded. "If it was you, you know what that means."

"I didn't. How do you know they're after you?"

"I've got ways of finding out," he said cryptically. "It's that damned watch. Look, pull down the shade and let's have a light. I need food and a bed. How about my old room?"

She was shaking, but she steadied her voice.

"Did you have to come here? It isn't safe, for either of us. Even if you do stay you'll have to be out of there before Stella comes down in the morning. Suppose she finds you there?"

"What if she does?" he said, impatiently. "Look, I'm hungry. How about something to eat?"

She was trapped. She was afraid of him. She always had been afraid of him. Even in Honolulu. Even when he came to the ship and, taking her aside, had told her about Delia.

She had never told any one about that.

Now she tried to steady herself. She got soap and towels and a blanket and put them in the bedroom off the back hall. When she went back to the kitchen Herbert was comfortably settled in a chair, smoking a cigarette and with Stella's cat on his lap. The sight made her flush with anger.

"You know your way around here," she said coldly. "Why don't you get your own supper?"

His terror had apparently gone. He grinned at her.

"You know your way too," he said insolently. "What did you do with that watch?"

"That's none of your business."

"Well, you better bury it. It won't be nice if you're found with it."

She had gone to the refrigerator and was getting out some food. Now with the milk bottle in her hand she turned and looked at him.

"I wonder why I haven't killed you before this," she told him. "I've wanted to long enough. I lie awake at night and think about how to do it."

He threw back his head and laughed.

"Killing takes a lot of nerve, Tony. You ought to know that. You've tried it twice, haven't you? Only not me."

He looked wary however as she took a long bread knife from a drawer. She did not approach him, however. She went out into the pantry, and was there at the bread box when to her horror she heard the door into the rear hall open again, and Alice's voice, high and shrill with fury.

"What are you doing in this house?"

Herbert was startled. He leaped to his feet, dropping the cat. His cock-sureness had dropped away, and he was trying to smile.

"Now look, Miss Rowland," he said. "There's no harm in my bumming a little supper, is there? Miss Tony's known me for years, and when I saw her in here . . ."

Tony was in the doorway by that time, the bread knife in her hand. Herbert saw her, but Alice did not. She was holding a letter in her hand, and her face was hard.

"You're getting out of here," she said. "Right now, before I put in a call for the police. You're doing no more blackmailing. I know now what I should have known all along. Leave the house and don't try to come back, or I'll set the police on you."

He moved toward the door, picking up his hat as he went. But some of his cocky manner had come back.

"You'll set the police on me!" he said. "Ask your niece there about that. She won't like it."

He left then, closing the door behind him. Tony was still near the pantry, the knife in her hand. Neither she nor Alice had seen the knob turn to the back hall, or that there was a motionless figure behind the door there.

Alice sat down by the table. She looked collapsed, but the face she turned to Tony was stone cold.

"How long have you known?" she asked.

"Known what?"

"Don't try to act the innocent with me. I have this letter in my hand. Shall I read it to you? It came from the Islands today." She drew it out of the envelope. "But of course you know what it says. You've known all along, haven't you? That's why you broke your engagement, isn't it? Listen, I'm going to read this to you."

And read it she did, Alice by the table and Tony with the knife still in her hand and unconscious of it. Neither of them saw Nina open the door and stand listening, her face livid with amazement and horror. Neither of them knew she was in the room until she struggled to take the knife from Tony. And the letter was still in Alice's hand when Nina picked up the milk bottle and struck with all her strength at Alice's head.

CHAPTER SEVENTEEN

THAT WAS THE STORY as Fuller heard it that night from Hilda, and as he learned it in detail later. At the time he merely listened carefully, putting in a question now and then. When she had finished she reached over to the table and turned on a lamp.

"The letter's here," she said, picking it up. "Shall I read it? Or will you?"

"Carry on," he said. "It's your case, apparently. Not mine."

She made no comment on that. She put on the shell-rimmed glasses which made her look like a baby-faced owl, and under the light he saw her hands shaking. Her voice, however, was steady enough.

"My dear Alice:" she read. "I was terribly shocked when your letter came. It does look like it, doesn't it? Why else the secret dressings at night and Tony burning them? And the refusal to see Dr. Wynant, or any doctor.

"After all Tony would know. She has seen it here in the Islands. I remember years ago they had to dismiss her nurse for letting her see an advanced case. And you *must* have medical advice at once. I say that because I find that Delia, for whom you inquired, has it and is at present in a leprosarium. I happen to know that she had it before they left and was not allowed to sail for that reason. The family did not know it, of course.

"It sounds brutal, Alice, but you must get Nina out of the house at once. They have institutions for lepers in the States, I believe, and that is where she will have to go. I believe . . ."

Hilda stopped reading. She put the letter down.

"There's more," she said, her voice flat. "It doesn't matter."

Fuller had found his voice.

"Good God!" he said hoarsely. "No wonder Nina picked up the milk bottle!"

"No. She was hardly sane. She was a beautiful woman, and she thought she was facing exile and horror."

"And Tony thought so too?"

"Yes. She knew what it meant. Her father had told her to look after her mother, and when Herbert for his own reasons lied and told her it was what she was afraid of, she was desperate. You see, she had seen it as a child. It must have left a terrific scar on her."

"Nina never suspected?"

"No. Alice Rowland had a morbid fear of infection of any sort. She would never touch Stella's cat, for instance. When Nina's trouble developed that was how Tony kept her quiet about it. But Tony had learned about Delia before they sailed, and she'd been on the watch for four years."

When Fuller said nothing she went on rather drearily.

"You can see how it was for Tony. It was the end of the world for her. It had been ever since Herbert had lied to her about it. She must have let him see the arm somehow. And remember this, she'd been watching for trouble. And what she thought had happened to her mother was horrible beyond words."

"So she tried to kill her. Better death than what was happening, I suppose."

"She meant to kill herself too. Remember that," Hilda said defensively.

"All right," he agreed. "Now let's get to last night. Just what did you do to Nina Rowland last night to make her do what she did?"

There was a longish silence. When Hilda broke it her voice was unsteady.

"I did nothing," she said finally. "I made her let me see her arm, and I told her it was a harmless skin trouble. Psoriasis, I imagine. Nasty but not what Tony had thought it was."

"I see," Fuller said, not ungently. "Only where did that leave her? It was all for nothing. She had committed a murder and Tony had tried to kill herself. All for nothing." His voice sharpened. "What could she do? What's the difference between using an ax or breaking a neck? That's it, isn't it? Don't tell me you didn't know what would happen, Hilda."

She made no effort to defend herself.

"She made her own choice. What could she expect? Disgrace and life imprisonment, or maybe the chair. If her choice was to drive the car into the river I couldn't stop her. I was at the hospital."

Fuller said nothing for some time. Then he got out his cigarette case and in the dim light held it out.

"For God's sake take a cigarette and remind me that you're merely human," he said. "And even a damned fine woman—at times."

He leaned over and lit it for her. In the lamplight he saw that she was close to breaking down. He made an effort to rally her.

"You know," he observed, "there are a good many times when you absolutely terrify me. Here you had a locked door to start with, a bandage on Nina Rowland's arm, a volume of the *Encyclopedia* as a doorstop, a bump on your head, a stolen watch returned, a lady named Hayes who registered horror, and a letter from Honolulu. That's all you had for quite a while, isn't it? Until Alice was killed. And you make a case out of it!"

She looked rather relaxed, as he had hoped. She even took a puff of the cigarette, coughed, and then put it down.

"I had Tony," she said, almost apologetically. "I liked her, you know. And what about her mother was so dreadful that she didn't want her father to come home? Or that she didn't want either the doctor or me to know about it? I—I stuck to my bullet in Nina's arm for quite a while." She smiled faintly. "I feel rather stupid about the whole thing, really. I should have known the night she burned the bandages. And there was that article in the *Encyclopedia*. Only in this country we don't think about such things."

He looked over at her, his expression one of genuine fondness tempered by exasperation.

"I wish to God you'd work *with* me on my cases," he said. "Not against me. But I don't mind telling you you've done a damn fine job. Or advising you to go to bed for a week. Why not?" he added as she shook her head. "Tony will get over this. She's faced worse than death for her mother. And she's got Johnny Hayes. We've had to put a guard around her, to keep him out of her room. He ought to be a Commando, that boy."

"You haven't arrested him?"

He smiled sheepishly.

"I can sympathize with young lovers too," he said. "I'm not so damned old myself. Anyhow both those boys are on their way to a war. Who am I to stop them? Only by heck they're going to pay for that window they broke." He grinned. "Quite a neat little plot they hatched with Aggie, wasn't it?" he went on. "The kitchen door unlocked, and the sergeant breaking the window across the street and running like blazes while our man followed him. And you shut in your room! I'd like to have seen your face then. It must have been something to see."

"It's never been anything to see," she observed drily.

"Still and all I rather like it."

He went over and stood looking down at her.

"You don't mean this chicken stuff, do you?" he inquired. "After all, Hilda, I need you. Maybe in more ways than you know."

If Hilda flushed he did not see it.

"Oh, for heaven's sake don't go sentimental on me," she said brusquely. "I'm tired and I need a bath. So do you probably. Go home and get a night's sleep. That's what I mean to do."

And it was not until he was outside in the cool October night that he felt a faint sense of relief. He had his job and his comfortable bachelor quarters. And a policeman had no business with a wife.

He grinned as he realized that Hilda had once more saved him from a grave mistake.

THE INCAUTIOUS BURGLAR
(formerly A GUEST IN THE HOUSE)
by John Dickson Carr

TWO GUESTS, who were not staying the night at Cranleigh Court, left at shortly past eleven o'clock. Marcus Hunt saw them to the front door. Then he returned to the dining-room, where the poker-chips were now stacked into neat piles of white, red, and blue.

"Another game?" suggested Rolfe.

"No good," said Derek Henderson. His tone, as usual, was weary. "Not with just the three of us."

Their host stood by the sideboard and watched them. The long, low house, overlooking the Weald of Kent, was so quiet that their voices rose with startling loudness. The dining-room, large and panelled, was softly lighted by electric wall-candles which brought out the sombre colours of the paintings. It is not often that anybody sees, in one room of an otherwise commonplace country house, two Rembrandts and a Van Dyck. There was a kind of defiance about those paintings.

To Arthur Rolfe—the art dealer—they represented enough money to make him shiver. To Derek Henderson—the art critic—they represented a problem. What they represented to Marcus Hunt was not apparent.

Hunt stood by the sideboard, his fists on his hips, smiling. He was a middle-sized, stocky man, with a full face and a high complexion. Equip him with a tuft of chin-whisker, and he would have looked like a Dutch burgher for a Dutch brush. His shirt-front bulged out untidily. He watched with ironical amusement while Henderson picked up a pack of cards in long fingers, cut them into two piles, and shuffled with a sharp flick of each thumb which made the cards melt together like a conjuring trick.

Henderson yawned.

"My boy," said Hunt, "you surprise me."

"That's what I try to do," answered Henderson, still wearily. He looked up. "But why do you say so, particularly?"

Henderson was young, he was long, he was lean, he was immaculate; and he wore a beard. It was a reddish beard, which moved some people to hilarity. But he wore it with an air of complete naturalness.

Reprinted by permission of Harper & Brothers
and Pearn, Pollinger & Higham, Ltd.
Copyright 1947 by Mercury Publications, Inc.

"I'm surprised," said Hunt, "that you enjoy anything so bourgeois—so plebeian—as poker."

"I enjoy reading people's characters," said Henderson. "Poker's the best way to do it, you know."

Hunt's eyes narrowed. "Oh? Can you read my character, for instance?"

"With pleasure," said Henderson. Absently he dealt himself a poker-hand, face up. It contained a pair of fives, and the last card was the ace of spades. Henderson remained staring at it for a few seconds before he glanced up again.

"And I can tell you," he went on, "that *you* surprise *me*. Do you mind if I'm frank? I had always thought of you as the Colossus of Business; the smasher; the plunger; the fellow who took the long chances. Now, you're not like that at all."

Marcus Hunt laughed. But Henderson was undisturbed.

"You're tricky, but you're cautious. I doubt if you ever took a long chance in your life. Another surprise"—he dealt himself a new hand—"is Mr. Rolfe here. He's the man who, given the proper circumstances, would take the long chances."

Arthur Rolfe considered this. He looked startled, but rather flattered. Though in height and build not unlike Hunt, there was nothing untidy about him. He had a square, dark face, with thin shells of eyeglasses, and a worried forehead.

"I doubt that," he declared, very serious about this. Then he smiled. "A person who took long chances in my business would find himself in the soup." He glanced round the room. "Anyhow, I'd be too cautious to have three pictures, with an aggregate value of thirty thousand pounds, hanging in an unprotected downstairs room with French windows giving on a terrace." An almost frenzied note came into his voice. "Great Scot! Suppose a burglar——"

"Damn!" said Henderson unexpectedly.

Even Hunt jumped.

Ever since the poker-party, an uneasy atmosphere had been growing. Hunt had picked up an apple from a silver fruit-bowl on the sideboard. He was beginning to pare it with a fruit-knife, a sharp wafer-thin blade which glittered in the light of the wall-lamps.

"You nearly made me slice my thumb off," he said, putting down the knife. "What's the matter with you?"

"It's the ace of spades," said Henderson, still languidly. "That's the second time it's turned up in five minutes."

Arthur Rolfe chose to be dense. "Well? What about it?"

"I think our young friend is being psychic," said Hunt, good-humoured again. "Are you reading characters, or only telling fortunes?"

Henderson hesitated. His eyes moved to Hunt, and then to the wall over the sideboard where Rembrandt's "Old Woman with Cap" stared back with the immobility and skin-colouring of a red Indian. Then Henderson looked towards the French windows opening on the terrace.

"None of my affair," shrugged Henderson. "It's your house and your collection and your responsibility. But this fellow Butler: what do you know about him?"

Marcus Hunt looked boisterously amused.

"Butler? He's a friend of my niece's. Harriet picked him up in London, and asked me to invite him down here. Nonsense! Butler's all right. What are you thinking, exactly?"

"Listen!" said Rolfe, holding up his hand.

The noise they heard, from the direction of the terrace, was not repeated. It was not repeated because the person who had made it, a very bewildered and uneasy young lady, had run lightly and swiftly to the far end, where she leaned against the balustrade.

Lewis Butler hesitated before going after her. The moonlight was so clear that one could see the mortar between the tiles which paved the terrace, and trace the design of the stone urns along the balustrade. Harriet Davis wore a white gown with long and filmy skirts, which she lifted clear of the ground as she ran.

Then she beckoned to him.

She was half sitting, half leaning against the rail. Her white arms were spread out, fingers gripping the stone. Dark hair and dark eyes became even more vivid by moonlight. He could see the rapid rise and fall of her breast; he could even trace the shadow of her eyelashes.

"That was a lie, anyhow," she said.

"What was?"

"What my Uncle Marcus said. You heard him." Harriet Davis's fingers tightened still more on the balustrade. But she nodded her head vehemently, with fierce accusation. "About my knowing you. And inviting you here. I never saw you before this week-end. Either Uncle Marcus is going out of his mind, or . . . will you answer me just one question?"

"If I can."

"Very well. Are you by any chance a crook?"

She spoke with as much simplicity and directness as though she had asked him whether he might be a doctor or a lawyer. Lewis Butler was not unwise enough to laugh. She was in that mood where, to any woman, laughter is salt to a raw wound; she would probably have slapped his face.

"To be quite frank about it," he said, "I'm not. Will you tell me why you asked?"

"This house," said Harriet, looking at the moon, "used to be guarded with burglar alarms. If you as much as touched a window, the whole place started clanging like a fire-station. He had all the burglar alarms removed last week. Last week." She took her hands off the balustrade, and pressed them together hard. "The pictures used to be upstairs, in a locked room next to his bedroom. He had them moved downstairs—last week. It's almost as though my uncle *wanted* the house to be burgled."

Butler knew that he must use great care here.

"Perhaps he does." (Here she looked at Butler quickly, but did not comment.) "For instance," he went on idly, "suppose one of his famous Rembrandts turned out to be a fake? It might be a relief not to have to show it to his expert friends."

The girl shook her head.

"No." She said. "They're all genuine. You see, I thought of that too."

Now was the time to hit, and hit hard. To Lewis Butler, in his innocence, there seemed to be no particular problem. He took out his cigarette-case, and turned it over without opening it.

"Look here, Miss Davis, you're not going to like this. But I can tell you of cases in which poeple were rather anxious to have their property 'stolen.' If a picture is insured for more than its value, and then it is mysteriously 'stolen' one night——?"

"That might be all very well too," answered Harriet, still calmly. "Except that not one of those pictures has been insured."

The cigarette-case, which was of polished metal, slipped through Butler's fingers and fell with a clatter on the tiles. It spilled cigarettes, just as it spilled and confused his theories. As he bent over to pick it up, he could hear a church clock across the Weald strike the half-hour after eleven.

"You're sure of that?"

"I'm perfectly sure. He hasn't insured any of his pictures for as much as a penny. He says it's a waste of money."

"But——"

"Oh, I know! And I don't know why I'm talking to you like this. You're a stranger, aren't you?" She folded her arms, drawing her shoulders up as though she were cold. Uncertainty, fear, and plain nerves flicked at her eyelids. "But then Uncle Marcus is a stranger too. Do you know what I think? *I* think he's going mad."

"Hardly as bad as that, is it?"

"Yes, go on," the girl suddenly stormed at him. "*Say* it: go on and say it. That's easy enough. But you don't see him when his eyes seem to get smaller, and all that genial-country-squire look goes out of his face. He's not a fake: he hates fakes, and goes out of his way to expose them. But, if he hasn't gone clear out of his mind, what's he up to? What can he be up to?"

In something over three hours, they found out.

The burglar did not attack until half-past two in the morning. First he smoked several cigarettes in the shrubbery below the rear terrace. When he heard the church clock strike, he waited a few minutes more, and then slipped up the steps to the French windows of the dining-room.

A chilly wind stirred at the turn of the night, in the hour of suicides and bad dreams. It smoothed grass and trees with a faint rustling. When the man glanced over his shoulder, the last of the moonlight distorted his face: it showed less a face than the blob of a black cloth mask, under a greasy cap pulled down over his ears.

He went to work on the middle window, with the contents of a folding tool-kit not so large as a motorist's. He fastened two short strips of adhesive tape to the glass just beside the catch. Then his glass-cutter sliced out a small semi-circle inside the tape.

It was done not without noise: it crunched like a dentist's drill in a tooth, and the man stopped to listen.

There was no answering noise. No dog barked.

With the adhesive tape holding the glass so that it did not fall and smash, he slid his gloved hand through the opening and twisted the catch. The weight of his body deadened the creaking of the window when he pushed inside.

He knew exactly what he wanted. He put the tool-kit into his pocket, and drew out an electric torch. Its beam moved across to the sideboard; it touched gleaming silver, a bowl of fruit, and a wicked little knife thrust into an apple as though into someone's body; finally, it moved up the hag-face of the "Old Woman with Cap."

This was not a large picture, and the burglar lifted it down easily. He pried out glass and frame. Though he tried to roll up the canvas with great care, the brittle paint cracked across in small stars which wounded the hag's face. The burglar was so intent on this that he never noticed the presence of another person in the room.

He was an incautious burglar: he had no sixth sense which smelt murder.

Up on the second floor of the house, Lewis Butler was awakened by a muffled crash like that of metal objects falling.

He had not fallen into more than a half doze all night. He knew with certainty what must be happening, though he had no idea of why, or how, or to whom.

Butler was out of bed, and into his slippers, as soon as he heard the first faint clatter from downstairs. His dressing-gown would, as usual, twist itself up like a rolled umbrella and defy all attempts to find the arm-holes whenever he wanted to hurry. But the little flashlight was ready in the pocket.

That noise seemed to have roused nobody else. With certain possibilities in his mind, he had never in his life moved so fast once he managed to get out of his bedroom. Not using his light, he was down two flights of deep-carpeted stairs without noise. In the lower hall he could feel a draught, which meant that a window or door had been opened somewhere. He made straight for the dining-room.

But he was too late.

Once the pencil-beam of Butler's flashlight had swept round, he switched on a whole blaze of lights. The burglar was still here, right enough. But the burglar was lying very still in front of the sideboard; and, to judge by the amount of blood on his sweater and trousers, he would never move again.

"That's done it," Butler said aloud.

A silver service, including a tea-urn, had been toppled off the sideboard. Where the fruit-bowl had fallen, the dead man lay on his back among a litter of oranges, apples, and a squashed bunch of grapes. The mask still covered the burglar's face; his greasy cap was flattened still further on his ears; his gloved hands were thrown wide.

Fragments of smashed picture-glass lay round him, together with the empty frame, and the "Old Woman with Cap" had been half crumpled up under his body. From the position of the most conspicuous bloodstains, one judged that he had been stabbed through the chest with the stained fruit-knife beside him.

"*What is it?*" said a voice almost at Butler's ear.

He could not have been more startled if the fruit-knife had pricked his ribs. He had seen nobody turning on lights in the hall, nor had he heard Harriet Davis approach. She was standing just behind him, wrapped in a Japanese kimono, with her dark hair round her shoulders. But, when he explained what had happened, she would not look into the dining-room; she backed away, shaking her head violently, like an urchin ready for flight.

"You had better wake up your uncle," Butler said briskly, with a confidence he did not feel. "And the servants. I must use your telephone." Then he looked her in the eyes. "Yes, you're quite right. I think you've guessed it already. I'm a police-officer."

She nodded.

"Yes. I guessed. Who are you? And is your name really Butler?"

"I'm a sergeant of the Criminal Investigation Department. And my name really is Butler. Your uncle brought me here."

"Why?"

"I don't know. He hasn't got round to telling me."

This girl's intelligence, even when over-shadowed by fear, was direct and disconcerting. "But, if he wouldn't say why he wanted a police-officer, how did they come to send you? He'd have to tell them, wouldn't he?"

Butler ignored it. "I must see your uncle. Will you go upstairs and wake him, please?"

"I can't," said Harriet. "Uncle Marcus isn't in his room."

"Isn't——?"

"No. I knocked at the door on my way down. He's gone."

Butler took the stairs two treads at a time. Harriet had turned on all the lights on her way down, but nothing stirred in the bleak, over-decorated passages.

Marcus Hunt's bedroom was empty. His dinner-jacket had been hung up neatly on the back of a chair, shirt laid across the seat with collar and tie on top of it. Hunt's watch ticked loudly on the dressing-table. His money and keys were there too. But he had not gone to bed, for the bedspread was undisturbed.

The suspicion which came to Lewis Butler, listening to the thin insistent ticking of that watch in the drugged hour before dawn, was so fantastic that he could not credit it.

He started downstairs again, and on the way he met Arthur Rolfe blundering out of another bedroom down the hall. The art dealer's stocky body was wrapped in a flannel dressing-gown. He was not wearing his eyeglasses, which gave his face a bleary and rather caved-in expression. He planted himself in front of Butler, and refused to budge.

"Yes," said Butler. "You don't have to ask. It's a burglar."

"I knew it," said Rolfe calmly. "Did he get anything?"

"No. He was murdered."

For a moment Rolfe said nothing, but his hand crept into the breast of his dressing-gown as though he felt pain there.

"Murdered? You don't mean the *burglar* was murdered?"

"Yes."

"But why? By an accomplice, you mean? Who is the burglar?"

"That," snarled Lewis Butler, "is what I intend to find out."

In the lower hall he found Harriet Davis, who was now standing in the doorway of the dining-room and looking steadily at the body by the sideboard. Though her face hardly moved a muscle, her eyes brimmed over.

"You're going to take off the mask, aren't you?" she asked, without turning round.

Stepping with care to avoid squashed fruit and broken glass, Butler leaned over the dead man. He pushed back the peak of the greasy cap; he lifted the black cloth mask, which was clumsily held by an elastic band; and he found what he expected to find.

The burglar was Marcus Hunt—stabbed through the heart while attempting to rob his own house.

"You see, sir," Butler explained to Dr. Gideon Fell on the following afternoon, "that's the trouble. However you look at it, the case makes no sense."

Again he went over the facts.

"Why should the man burgle his own house and steal his own property? Every one of those paintings is valuable, and not a single one is insured! Consequently, why? Was the man a simple lunatic? What did he think he was doing?"

The village of Sutton Valence, straggling like a grey-white Italian town along the very peak of the Weald, was full of hot sunshine. In the apple orchard behind the white inn of the *Tabard*, Dr. Gideon Fell sat at a garden table among wasps, with a pint tankard at his elbow. Dr. Fell's vast bulk was clad in a white linen suit. His pink face smoked in the heat, and his wary lookout for wasps gave him a regrettably wall-eyed appearance as he pondered.

He said:

"Superintendent Hadley suggested that I might—harrumph—look in here. The local police are in charge, aren't they?"

"Yes. I'm merely standing by."

"Hadley's exact words to me were, 'It's so crazy that nobody but you will understand it.' The man's flattery becomes more nauseating every day." Dr. Fell scowled. "I say. Does anything else strike you as queer about this business?"

"Well, why should a man burgle his own house?"

"No, no, no!" growled Dr. Fell. "Don't be obsessed with that point. Don't become hypnotized by it. For instance"—a wasp hovered near his tankard, and he distended his cheeks and blew it away with one vast puff like Father Neptune—"for instance, the young lady seems to have raised an interesting question. If Marcus Hunt wouldn't say why he wanted a detective in the house, why did the C.I.D. consent to send you?"

Butler shrugged his shoulders.

"Because," he said, "Chief Inspector Ames thought Hunt was up to funny business, and meant to stop it."

"What sort of funny business?"

"A faked burglary to steal his own pictures for the insurance. It looked like the old, old game of appealing to the police to divert suspicion. In other words, sir, exactly what this appeared to be: until I learned (and to-day proved) that not one of those damned pictures has ever been insured for a penny."

Butler hesitated.

"It can't have been a practical joke," he went on. "Look at the elaborateness of it! Hunt put on old clothes from which all tailors' tabs and laundry marks were removed. He put on gloves and a mask. He got hold of a torch and an up-to-date kit of burglar's tools. He went out of the house by the back door; we found it open later. He smoked a few cigarettes in the shrubbery below the terrace; we found his footprints in the soft earth. He cut a pane of glass . . . but I've told you all that."

"And then," mused Dr. Fell, "somebody killed him."

"Yes. The last and worst 'why.' Why should anybody have killed him?"

"H'm. Clues?"

"Negative." Butler took out his notebook. "According to the police surgeon, he died of a direct heart-wound from a blade (presumably that fruit-knife) so thin that the wound was difficult to find. There were a number of his finger-prints, but nobody else's. We did find one odd thing, though. A number of pieces in the silver service off the sideboard were scratched in a queer way. It looked almost as though, instead of being swept off the sideboard in a struggle, they had been piled up on top of each other like a tower; and then pushed——"

Butler paused, for Dr. Fell was shaking his big head back and forth with an expression of Gargantuan distress.

"Well, well, well," he was saying; "well, well, well. And you call that negative evidence?"

"Isn't it? It doesn't explain why a man burgles his own house."

"Look here," said the doctor mildly. "I should like to ask you just one question. What is the most important point in this affair? One moment! I did not say the most interesting; I said the most important. Surely it is the fact that a man has been murdered?"

"Yes, sir. Naturally."

"I mention the fact"—the doctor was apologetic—"because it seems in danger of being overlooked. It hardly interests you. You are concerned only with Hunt's senseless masquerade. You don't mind a throat being cut; but you can't stand a leg being pulled. Why not try working at it from the other side, and asking who killed Hunt?"

Butler was silent for a long time.

"The servants are out of it," he said at length. "They sleep in another wing on the top floor; and for some reason," he hesitated, "somebody locked them in last night." His doubts, even his dreads, were beginning to take form. "There was a fine blow-up over that when the house was roused. Of course, the murderer could have been an outsider."

"You know it wasn't," said Dr. Fell. "Would you mind taking me to Cranleigh Court?"

They came out on the terrace in the hottest part of the afternoon.

Dr. Fell sat down on a wicker settee, with a dispirited Harriet beside him. Derek Henderson, in flannels, perched his long figure on the balustrade. Arthur Rolfe alone wore a dark suit and seemed out of place. For the pale green and brown of the Kentish lands, which rarely acquired harsh colour, now blazed. No air stirred, no leaf moved, in that brilliant thickness of heat; and down in the garden, towards their left, the water of the swimming-pool sparkled with hot, hard light. Butler felt it like a weight on his eyelids.

Derek Henderson's beard was at once languid and yet aggressive.

"It's no good," he said. "Don't keep on asking me why Hunt should have burgled his own house. But I'll give you a tip."

"Which is?" inquired Dr. Fell.

"Whatever the reason was," returned Henderson, sticking out his neck, "it was a good reason. Hunt was much too canny and cautious ever to do anything without a good reason. I told him so last night."

Dr. Fell spoke sharply. "Cautious? Why do you say that?"

"Well, for instance. I take three cards on the draw. Hunt takes one. I bet; he sees me and raises. I cover that, and raise again. Hunt drops out. In other words, it's fairly certain he's filled his hand, but not so certain I'm holding much more than a pair. Yet Hunt drops out. So with my three sevens I bluff him out of his straight. He played a dozen hands last night just like that."

Henderson began to chuckle. Seeing the expression on Harriet's face, he checked himself and became preternaturally solemn.

"But then, of course," Henderson added, "he had a lot on his mind last night."

Nobody could fail to notice the change of tone.

"So? And what did he have on his mind?"

"Exposing somebody he had always trusted," replied Henderson coolly. "That's why I didn't like it when the ace of spades turned up so often."

"You'd better explain that," said Harriet, after a pause. "I don't know what you're hinting at, but you'd better explain that. He told you he intended to expose somebody he had always trusted?"

"No. Like myself, he hinted at it."

It was the stolid Rolfe who stormed into the conversation then. Rolfe had the air of a man determined to hold hard to reason, but finding it difficult.

"Listen to me," snapped Rolfe. "I have heard a great deal, at one time or another, about Mr. Hunt's liking for exposing people. Very well!" He slid one hand into the breast of his coat, in a characteristic gesture. "But where in the name of sanity does that leave us? He wants to expose someone. And, to do that, he puts on outlandish clothes and masquerades as a burglar. Is that sensible? I tell you, the man was mad! There's no other explanation."

"There are five other explanations," said Dr. Fell.

Derek Henderson slowly got up from his seat on the balustrade, but he sat down again at a savage gesture from Rolfe.

Nobody spoke.

"I will not, however," pursued Dr. Fell, "waste your time with four of them. We are concerned with only one explanation: the real one."

"And you know the real one?" asked Henderson sharply.

"I rather think so."

"Since when?"

"Since I had the opportunity of looking at all of you," answered Dr. Fell.

He settled back massively in the wicker settee, so that its frame creaked and cracked like a ship's bulkhead in a heavy sea. His vast chin was out-thrust, and he nodded absently as though to emphasize some point that was quite clear in his own mind.

"I've already had a word with the local inspector," he went on suddenly. "He will be here in a few minutes. And, at my suggestion, he will have a request for all of you. I sincerely hope nobody will refuse."

"Request?" said Henderson. "What request?"

"It's a very hot day," said Dr. Fell, blinking towards the swimming-pool. "He's going to suggest that you all go in for a swim."

Harriet uttered a kind of despairing mutter, and turned as though appealing to Lewis Butler.

"That," continued Dr. Fell, "will be the politest way of drawing attention to the murderer. In the meantime, let me call your attention to one point in the evidence which seems to have been generally overlooked. Mr. Henderson, do you know anything about direct heart-wounds, made by a steel blade as thin as a wafer?"

"Like Hunt's wound? No. What about them?"

"There is practically no exterior bleeding," answered Dr. Fell.

"But——!" Harriet was beginning, when Butler stopped her.

"The police surgeon, in fact, called attention to that wound which was so 'difficult to find.' The victim dies almost at once; and the edges of the wound compress. But in that case," argued Dr. Fell, "how did the late Mr. Hunt come to have so much blood on his sweater, and even splashed on his trousers?"

"Well?"

"He didn't," answered Dr. Fell simply. "Mr. Hunt's blood never got on his clothes at all."

"I can't stand this," said Harriet, jumping to her feet. "I—I'm sorry, but have you gone mad yourself? Are you telling us we didn't see him lying by that sideboard, with blood on him?"

"Oh, yes. You saw that."

"Let him go on," said Henderson, who was rather white round the nostrils. "Let him rave."

"It is, I admit, a fine point," said Dr. Fell. "But it answers your question, repeated to the point of nausea, as to why the eminently sensible Mr. Hunt chose to dress up in burglar's clothes and play burglar. The answer is short and simple. He didn't."

"It must be plain to everybody," Dr. Fell went on, opening his eyes wide, "that Mr. Hunt was deliberately setting a trap for someone—the real burglar.

"He believed that a certain person might try to steal one or several of his pictures. He probably knew that this person had tried similar games before, in other country houses: that is, an inside job which was carefully planned to look like an outside job. So he made things easy for this thief, in order to trap him, with a police-officer in the house.

"The burglar, a sad fool, fell for it. This thief, a guest in the house, waited until well past two o'clock in the morning. He then put on his old clothes, mask, gloves, and the rest of it. He let himself out by the back door. He went through all the motions we have erroneously been attributing to Marcus Hunt. Then the trap snapped. Just as he was rolling up the Rembrandt, he heard a noise. He swung his light round. And he saw Marcus Hunt, in pyjamas and dressing-gown, looking at him.

"Yes, there was a fight. Hunt flew at him. The thief snatched up a fruit-knife and fought back. In that struggle, Marcus Hunt forced his opponent's hand back. The fruit-knife gashed the thief's chest, inflicting a superficial but badly bleeding gash. It sent the thief over the edge of insanity. He wrenched Marcus Hunt's wrist half off, caught up the knife, and stabbed Hunt to the heart.

"Then, in a quiet house, with a little beam of light streaming out from the torch on the sideboard, the murderer sees something that will hang him. He sees the blood from his own superficial wound seeping down his clothes.

"How is he to get rid of those clothes? He cannot destroy them, or get them away from the house. Inevitably the house will be searched, and they will be found. Without the blood-stains, they would seem ordinary clothes in his wardrobe. But with the blood-stains——

"There is only one thing he can do."

Harriet Davis was standing behind the wicker settee, shading her eyes against the glare of the sun. Her hand did not tremble when she said:

"He changed clothes with my uncle."

"That's it," growled Dr. Fell. "That's the whole sad story. The murderer dressed the body in his own clothes, making a puncture with the knife in sweater, shirt, and undervest. He then slipped on Mr. Hunt's pyjamas and dressing-gown, which at a pinch he could always claim as his own. Hunt's wound had bled hardly at all. His dressing-gown, I think, had come open in the fight; so that all the thief had to trouble him was a tiny puncture in the jacket of the pyjamas.

"But, once he had done this, he had to hypnotize you all into the belief that there would have been no time for a change of clothes. He had to make it seem that the fight occurred just *then*. He had to rouse the house. So he brought down echoing thunders by pushing over a pile of silver, and slipped upstairs."

Dr. Fell paused.

"The burglar could never have been Marcus Hunt, you know," he added. "We learn that Hunt's fingerprints were all over the place. Yet the murdered man was wearing gloves."

There was a swishing of feet in the grass below the terrace, and a tread of heavy boots coming up the terrace steps. The local Inspector of police, buttoned up and steaming in his uniform, was followed by two constables.

Dr. Fell turned round a face of satisfaction.

"Ah!" he said, breathing deeply. "They've come to see about that swimming-party, I imagine. It is easy to patch up a flesh-wound with lint and cotton, or even a handkerchief. But such a wound will become infernally conspicuous in anyone who is forced to climb into bathing-trunks."

"But it couldn't have been——" cried Harriet. Her eyes moved round. Her fingers tightened on Lewis Butler's arm, an instinctive gesture which he was to remember long afterwards, when he knew her even better.

"Exactly," agreed the doctor, wheezing with pleasure. "It could not have been a long, thin, gangling fellow like Mr. Henderson. It assuredly could not have been a small and slender girl like yourself.

"There is only one person who, as we know, is just about Marcus Hunt's height and build; who could have put his own clothes on Hunt without any suspicion. That is the same person who, though he managed to staunch the wound in his chest, has been constantly running his hand inside the breast of his coat to make certain the bandage is secure. Just as Mr. Rolfe is doing now."

Arthur Rolfe sat very quiet, with his right hand still in the breast of his jacket. His face had grown smeary in the hot sunlight, but the eyes behind those thin shells of glasses remained inscrutable. He spoke only once, through dry lips, after they had cautioned him.

"I should have taken the young pup's warning," he said. "After all, he told me I would take long chances."

THE LAMP OF GOD

by Ellery Queen

IF A STORY BEGAN: "Once upon a time in a house cowering in wilderness there lived an old and eremitical creature named Mayhew, a crazy man who had buried two wives and lived a life of death; and this house was known as *The Black House*"—if a story began in this fashion, it would strike no one as especially remarkable. There are people like that who live in houses like that, and very often mysteries materialize like ectoplasm about their wild-eyed heads.

Now however disorderly Mr. Ellery Queen may be by habit, mentally he is an orderly person. His neckties and shoes might be strewn about his bedroom helter-skelter, but inside his skull hums a perfectly oiled machine, functioning as neatly and inexorably as the planetary system. So if there was a mystery about one Sylvester Mayhew, deceased, and his buried wives and gloomy dwelling, you may be sure the Queen brain would seize upon it and worry it and pick it apart and get it all laid out in neat and shiny rows. Rationality, that was it. No esoteric mumbo-jumbo could fool *that* fellow. Lord, no! His two feet were planted solidly on God's good earth, and one and one made two—always—and that's all there was to that.

Of course, Macbeth had said that stones have been known to move and trees to speak; but, pshaw! for these literary fancies. In this day and age, with its *Cominterns*, its wars of peace, its *fasces* and its rocketry experiments? Nonsense! The truth is, Mr. Queen would have said, there is something about the harsh, cruel world we live in that's very rough on miracles. Miracles just don't happen any more, unless they are miracles of stupidity or miracles of national avarice. Everyone with a grain of intelligence knows that.

"Oh, yes," Mr. Queen would have said; "there are yogis, voodoos, fakirs, shamans, and other tricksters from the effete East and primitive Africa, but nobody pays any attention to such pitiful monkeyshines—I mean, nobody with sense. This is a reasonable world and everything that happens in it must have a reasonable explanation."

You couldn't expect a sane person to believe, for example, that a three-dimensional, flesh-and-blood, veritable human being could suddenly stoop,

grab his shoelaces, and fly away. Or that a water-buffalo could change into
a golden-haired little boy before your eyes. Or that a man dead one hundred
and thirty-seven years could push aside his tombstone, step out of his grave,
yawn, and then sing three verses of *Mademoiselle from Armentières*. Or even,
for that matter, that a stone could move or a tree speak—yea, though it were
in the language of Atlantis or Mu.

Or . . . *could you?*

The tale of Sylvester Mayhew's house is a strange tale. When what happened happened, proper minds tottered on their foundations and porcelain
beliefs threatened to shiver into shards. Before the whole fantastic and incomprehensible business was done, God Himself came into it. Yes, God came
into the story of Sylvester Mayhew's house, and that is what makes it quite
the most remarkable adventure in which Mr. Ellery Queen, that lean and in-
defatigable agnostic, has ever become involved.

The early mysteries in the Mayhew case were trivial—mysteries merely because certain pertinent facts were lacking; pleasantly provocative mysteries,
but scarcely savorous of the supernatural.

Ellery was sprawled on the hearthrug before the hissing fire that raw January morning, debating with himself whether it was more desirable to brave
the slippery streets and biting wind on a trip to Centre Street in quest of
amusement, or to remain where he was in idleness but comfort, when the
telephone rang.

It was Thorne on the wire. Ellery, who never thought of Thorne without
perforce visualizing a human monolith—a long-limbed, gray-thatched male
figure with marbled cheeks and agate eyes, the whole man coated with a
veneer of ebony, was rather startled. Thorne was excited; every crack and blur
in his voice spoke eloquently of emotion. It was the first time, to Ellery's
recollection, that Thorne had betrayed the least evidence of human feeling.

"What's the matter?" Ellery demanded. "Nothing's wrong with Ann, I
hope?" Ann was Thorne's wife.

"No, no." Thorne spoke hoarsely and rapidly, as if he had been running.

"Where the deuce have you been? I saw Ann only yesterday and she said
she hadn't heard from you for almost a week. Of course, your wife's used to
your preoccupation with those interminable legal affairs, but an absence of
six days——"

"Listen to me, Queen, and don't hold me up. I must have your help. Can
you meet me at Pier 54 in half an hour? That's North River."

"Of course."

Thorne mumbled something that sounded absurdly like: "Thank God!"
and hurried on: "Pack a bag. For a couple of days. And a revolver. Especially
a revolver, Queen."

"I see," said Ellery, not seeing at all.

"I'm meeting the Cunarder *Coronia*. Docking this morning. I'm with a
man by the name of Reinach, Dr. Reinach. You're my colleague; get that?

Act stern and omnipotent. Don't be friendly. Don't ask him—or me—questions. And don't allow yourself to be pumped. Understood?"

"Understood," said Ellery, "but not exactly clear. Anything else?"

"Call Ann for me. Give her my love and tell her I shan't be home for days yet, but that you're with me and that I'm all right. And ask her to telephone my office and explain matters to Crawford."

"Do you mean to say that not even your partner knows what you've been doing?"

But Thorne had hung up.

Ellery replaced the receiver, frowning. It was stranger than strange. Thorne had always been a solid citizen, a successful attorney who led an impeccable private life and whose legal practice was dry and unexciting. To find old Thorne entangled in a web of mystery. . . .

Ellery drew a happy breath, telephoned Mrs. Thorne, tried to sound reassuring, yelled for Djuna, hurled some clothes into a bag, loaded his .38 police revolver with a grimace, scribbled a note for Inspector Queen, dashed downstairs and jumped into the cab Djuna had summoned, and landed on Pier 54 with thirty seconds to spare.

There was something terribly wrong with Thorne, Ellery saw at once, even before he turned his attention to the vast fat man by the lawyer's side. Thorne was shrunken within his Scotch-plaid greatcoat like a pupa which has died prematurely in its cocoon. He had aged years in the few weeks since Ellery had last seen him. His ordinarily sleek cobalt cheeks were covered with a straggly stubble. Even his clothing looked tired and uncared-for. And there was a glitter of furtive relief in his bloodshot eyes as he pressed Ellery's hand that was, to one who knew Thorne's self-sufficiency and aplomb, almost pathetic.

But he merely remarked: "Oh, hello, there, Queen. We've a longer wait than we anticipated, I'm afraid. Want you to shake hands with Dr. Herbert Reinach. Doctor, this is Ellery Queen."

"'D'you do," said Ellery curtly, touching the man's immense gloved hand. If he was to be omnipotent, he thought, he might as well be rude, too.

"Surprise, Mr. Thorne?" said Dr. Reinach in the deepest voice Ellery had ever heard; it rumbled up from the caverns of his chest like the echo of thunder. His little purplish eyes were very, very cold.

"A pleasant one, I hope," said Thorne.

Ellery snatched a glance at his friend's face as he cupped his hands about a cigaret, and he read approval there. If he had struck the right tone, he knew how to act thenceforth. He flipped the match away and turned abruptly to Thorne. Dr. Reinach was studying him in a half-puzzled, half-amused way.

"Where's the *Coronia?*"

"Held up in quarantine," said Thorne. "Somebody's seriously ill aboard with some disease or other and there's been difficulty in clearing her passengers. It will take hours, I understand. Suppose we settle down in the waiting-room for a bit."

They found places in the crowded room, and Ellery set his bag between his feet and disposed himself so that he was in a position to catch every expression on his companions' faces. There was something in Thorne's repressed excitement, an even more piquing aura enveloping the fat doctor, that violently whipped his curiosity.

"Alice," said Thorne in a casual tone, as if Ellery knew who Alice was, "is probably becoming impatient. But that's a family trait with the Mayhews, from the little I saw of old Sylvester. Eh, Doctor? It's trying, though, to come all the way from England only to be held up on the threshold."

So they were to meet an Alice Mayhew, thought Ellery, arriving from England on the *Coronia*. Good old Thorne! He almost chuckled aloud. "Sylvester" was obviously a senior Mayhew, some relative of Alice's.

Dr. Reinach fixed his little eyes on Ellery's bag and rumbled politely: "Are you going away somewhere, Mr. Queen?"

Then Reinach did not know Ellery was to accompany them—wherever they were bound for.

Thorne stirred in the depths of his greatcoat, rustling like a sack of desiccated bones. "Queen's coming back with me, Dr. Reinach." There was something brittle and hostile in his voice.

The fat man blinked, his eyes buried beneath half-moons of damp flesh. "Really?" he said, and by contrast his bass voice was tender.

"Perhaps I should have explained," said Thorne abruptly. "Queen is a colleague of mine, Doctor. This case has interested him."

"Case?" said the fat man.

"Legally speaking. I really hadn't the heart to deny him the pleasure of helping me—ah—protect Alice Mayhew's interests. I trust you won't mind?"

This was a deadly game, Ellery became certain. Something important was at stake, and Thorne in his stubborn way was determined to defend it by force or guile.

Reinach's puffy lids dropped over his eyes as he folded his paws on his stomach. "Naturally, naturally not," he said in a hearty tone. "Only too happy to have you, Mr. Queen. A little unexpected, perhaps, but delightful surprises are as essential to life as to poetry. Eh?" And he chuckled.

Samuel Johnson, thought Ellery, recognizing the source of the doctor's remark. The physical analogy struck him. There was iron beneath those layers of fat and a good brain under that dolichocephalic skull. The man sat there on the waiting-room bench like an octopus, lazy and inert and peculiarly indifferent to his surroundings. Indifference—that was it, thought Ellery; the man was a colossal remoteness, as vague and darkling as a storm cloud on an empty horizon.

Thorne said in a weary voice: "Suppose we have lunch. I'm famished."

By three in the afternoon Ellery felt old and worn. Several hours of nervous, cautious silence, threading his way smiling among treacherous shoals, had told him just enough to put him on guard. He often felt knotted-up and tight inside when a crisis loomed or danger threatened from an unknown quarter. Something extraordinary was going on.

As they stood on the pier watching the *Coronia's* bulk being nudged alongside, he chewed on the scraps he had managed to glean during the long, heavy, pregnant hours. He knew definitely now that the man called Sylvester Mayhew was dead, that he had been a pronounced paranoic, that his house was buried in an almost inaccessible wilderness on Long Island. Alice Mayhew, somewhere on the decks of the *Coronia*, doubtless straining her eyes pierward, was the dead man's daughter, parted from her father since childhood.

And he had placed the remarkable figure of Dr. Reinach in the puzzle. The fat man was Sylvester Mayhew's half-brother. He had also acted as Mayhew's physician during the old man's last illness. This illness and death seemed to have been very recent, for there had been some talk of "the funeral" in terms of fresh if detached sorrow. There was also a Mrs. Reinach glimmering unsubstantially in the background, and a queer old lady who was the dead man's sister. But what the mystery was, or why Thorne was so perturbed, Ellery could not figure out.

The liner tied up to the pier at last. Officials scampered about, whistles blew, gangplanks appeared, passengers disembarked in droves to the accompaniment of the usual howls and embraces.

Interest crept into Dr. Reinach's little eyes, and Thorne was shaking.

"There she is!" croaked the lawyer. "I'd know her anywhere from her photographs. That slender girl in the brown turban!"

As Thorne hurried away Ellery studied the girl eagerly. She was anxiously scanning the crowd, a tall charming creature with an elasticity of movement more esthetic than athletic and a harmony of delicate features that approached beauty. She was dressed so simply and inexpensively that he narrowed his eyes.

Thorne came back with her, patting her gloved hand and speaking quietly to her. Her face was alight and alive, and there was a natural gayety in it which convinced Ellery that whatever mystery or tragedy lay before her, it was still unknown to her. At the same time there were certain signs about her eyes and mouth—fatigue, strain, worry, he could not put his finger on the exact cause—which puzzled him.

"I'm so glad," she murmured in a cultured voice, strongly British in accent. Then her face grew grave and she looked from Ellery to Dr. Reinach.

"This is your uncle, Miss Mayhew," said Thorne. "Dr. Reinach. This other gentleman is not, I regret to say, a relative. Mr. Ellery Queen, a colleague of mine."

"Oh," said the girl; and she turned to the fat man and said tremulously: "Uncle Herbert. How terribly odd. I mean—I've felt so all alone. You've been just a legend to me, Uncle Herbert, you and Aunt Sarah and the rest, and now . . ." She choked a little as she put her arms about the fat man and kissed his pendulous cheek.

"My dear," said Dr. Reinach solemnly; and Ellery could have struck him for the Judas quality of his solemnity.

"But you must tell me everything! Father—how is father? It seems so strange to be . . . to be saying that."

"Don't you think, Miss Mayhew," said the lawyer quickly, "that we had better see you through the Customs? It's growing late and we have a long trip before us. Long Island, you know."

"Island?" Her candid eyes widened. "That sounds so exciting!"

"Well, it's not what you might think——"

"Forgive me. I'm acting the perfect gawk." She smiled. "I'm entirely in your hands, Mr. Thorne. Your letter was more than kind."

As they made their way toward the Customs, Ellery dropped a little behind and devoted himself to watching Dr. Reinach. But that vast lunar countenance was as inscrutable as a gargoyle.

Dr. Reinach drove. It was not Thorne's car; Thorne had a regal new Lincoln limousine and this was a battered if serviceable old Buick sedan.

The girl's luggage was strapped to the back and sides; Ellery was puzzled by the scantness of it—three small suitcases and a tiny steamer-trunk. Did these four pitiful containers hold all of her worldly possessions?

Sitting beside the fat man, Ellery strained his ears. He paid little attention to the road Reinach was taking.

The two behind were silent for a long time. Then Thorne cleared his throat with an oddly ominous finality. Ellery saw what was coming; he had often heard that throat-clearing sound emanate from the mouths of judges pronouncing sentence of doom.

"We have something sad to tell you, Miss Mayhew. You may as well learn it now."

"Sad?" murmured the girl after a moment. "Sad? Oh, it's not——"

"Your father," said Thorne inaudibly. "He's dead."

She cried: "Oh!" in a small helpless voice; and then she grew quiet.

"I'm dreadfully sorry to have to greet you with such news," said Thorne in the silence. "We'd anticipated . . . And I realize how awkward it must be for you. After all, it's quite as if you had never known him at all. Love for a parent, I'm afraid, lies in direct ratio to the degree of childhood association. Without any association at all . . ."

"It's a shock, of course," Alice said in a muffled voice. "And yet, as you say, he was a stranger to me, a mere name. As I wrote you, I was only a toddler when mother got her divorce and took me off to England. I don't remember father at all. And I've not seen him since, or heard from him."

"Yes," muttered the attorney.

"I might have learned more about father if mother hadn't died when I was six; but she did, and my people—her people—in England. . . . Uncle John died last fall. He was the last one. And then I was left all alone. When your letter came I was—I was so glad, Mr. Thorne. I didn't feel lonely any more. I was really happy for the first time in years. And now—" She broke off to stare out the window.

Dr. Reinach swiveled his massive head and smiled benignly. "But you're not alone, my dear. There's my unworthy self, and your Aunt Sarah, and Milly—Milly's my wife, Alice; naturally you wouldn't know anything about her —and there's even a husky young fellow named Keith who works about the place—bright lad who's come down in the world." He chuckled. "So you see there won't be a dearth of companionship for you."

"Thank you, Uncle Herbert," she murmured. "I'm sure you're all terribly kind. Mr. Thorne, how did father . . . When you replied to my letter you wrote me he was ill, but——"

"He fell into a coma unexpectedly nine days ago. You hadn't left England yet and I cabled you at your antique-shop address. But somehow it missed you."

"I'd sold the shop by that time and was flying about, patching up things. When did he . . . die?"

"A week ago Thursday. The funeral . . . Well, we couldn't wait, you see. I might have caught you by cable or telephone on the *Coronia*, but I didn't have the heart to spoil your voyage."

"I don't know how to thank you for all the trouble you've taken." Without looking at her Ellery knew there were tears in her eyes. "It's good to know that someone——"

"It's been hard for all of us," rumbled Dr. Reinach.

"Of course, Uncle Herbert. I'm sorry." She fell silent. When she spoke again, it was as if there were a compulsion expelling the words. "When Uncle John died, I didn't know where to reach father. The only American address I had was yours, Mr. Thorne, which some patron or other had given me. It was the only thing I could think of. I was sure a solicitor could find father for me. That's why I wrote to you in such detail, with photographs and all."

"Naturally we did what we could." Thorne seemed to be having difficulty with his voice. "When I found your father and went out to see him the first time and showed him your letter and photographs, he . . . I'm sure this will please you, Miss Mayhew. He wanted you badly. He'd apparently been having a hard time of late years—ah, mentally, emotionally. And so I wrote you at his request. On my second visit, the last time I saw him alive, when the question of the estate came up——"

Ellery thought that Dr. Reinach's paws tightened on the wheel. But the fat man's face bore the same bland, remote smile.

"Please," said Alice wearily. "Do you greatly mind, Mr. Thorne? I—I don't feel up to discussing such matters now."

The car was fleeing along the deserted road as if it were trying to run away from the weather. The sky was gray lead; a frowning, gloomy sky under which the countryside lay cowering. It was growing colder, too, in the dark and draughty tonneau; the cold seeped in through the cracks and their over-clothes.

Ellery stamped his feet a little and twisted about to glance at Alice Mayhew. Her oval face was a glimmer in the murk; she was sitting stiffly, her hands clenched into tight little fists in her lap. Thorne was slumped miserably by her side, staring out the window.

"By George, it's going to snow," announced Dr. Reinach with a cheerful puff of his cheeks.

No one answered.

The drive was interminable. There was a dreary sameness about the landscape that matched the weather's mood. They had long since left the main highway to turn into a frightful byroad, along which they jolted in an unsteady eastward curve between ranks of leafless woods. The road was pitted and frozen hard; the woods were tangles of dead trees and underbrush densely packed but looking as if they had been repeatedly seared by fire. The whole effect was one of wide-spread and oppressive desolation.

"Looks like No Man's Land," said Ellery at last from his bouncing seat beside Dr. Reinach. "And feels like it, too."

Dr. Reinach's cetaceous back heaved in a silent mirth. "Matter of fact, that's exactly what it's called by the natives. Land-God-forgot, eh? But then Sylvester always swore by the Greek unities."

The man seemed to live in a dark and silent cavern, out of which he maliciously emerged at intervals to poison the atmosphere.

"It isn't very inviting-looking, is it?" remarked Alice in a low voice. It was clear she was brooding over the strange old man who had lived in this wasteland, and of her mother who had fled from it so many years before.

"It wasn't always this way," said Dr. Reinach, swelling his cheeks like a bullfrog. "Once it was pleasant enough; I remember it as a boy. Then it seemed as if it might become the nucleus of a populous community. But progress has passed it by, and a couple of uncontrollable forest fires did the rest."

"It's horrible," murmured Alice, "simply horrible."

"My dear Alice, it's your innocence that speaks there. All life is a frantic struggle to paint a rosy veneer over the ugly realities. Why not be honest with yourself? Everything in this world is stinking rotten; worse than that, a bore. Hardly worth living, in any impartial analysis. But if you have to live, you may as well live in surroundings consistent with the rottenness of everything."

The old attorney stirred beside Alice, where he was buried in his greatcoat. "You're quite a philosopher, Doctor," he snarled.

"I'm an honest man."

"Do you know, Doctor," murmured Ellery, despite himself, "you're beginning to annoy me."

The fat man glanced at him. Then he said: "And do you agree with this mysterious friend of yours, Thorne?"

"I believe," snapped Thorne, "that there is a platitude extant which says that actions speak with considerably more volume than words. I haven't shaved for six days, and today has been the first time I left Sylvester Mayhew's house since his funeral."

"Mr. Thorne!" cried Alice, turning to him. "Why?"

The lawyer muttered: "I'm sorry, Miss Mayhew. All in good time, in good time."

"You wrong us all," smiled Dr. Reinach, deftly skirting a deep rut in the road. "And I'm afraid you're giving my niece quite the most erroneous impression of her family. We're odd, no doubt, and our blood is presumably turning sour after so many generations of cold storage; but then don't the finest vintages come from the deepest cellars? You've only to glance at Alice to see my point. Such vital loveliness could only have been produced by an old family."

"My mother," said Alice, with a faint loathing in her glance, "had something to do with that, Uncle Herbert."

"Your mother, my dear," replied the fat man, "was merely a contributory factor. You have the typical Mayhew features."

Alice did not reply. Her uncle, whom until today she had not seen, was an obscene enigma; the others, waiting for them at their destination, she had never seen at all, and she had no great hope that they would prove better. A livid streak ran through her father's family; he had been a paranoic with delusions of persecution. The Aunt Sarah in the dark distance, her father's surviving sister, was apparently something of a character. As for Aunt Milly, Dr. Reinach's wife, whatever she might have been in the past, one had only to glance at Dr. Reinach to see what she undoubtedly was in the present.

Ellery felt prickles at the nape of his neck. The farther they penetrated this wilderness the less he liked the whole adventure. It smacked vaguely of a foreordained theatricalism, as if some hand of monstrous power were setting the stage for the first act of a colossal tragedy. . . . He shrugged this sophomoric foolishness off, settling deeper into his coat. It was queer enough, though. Even the lifelines of the most indigent community were missing; there were no telephone poles and, so far as he could detect, no electric cables. That meant candles. He detested candles.

The sun was behind them, leaving them. It was a feeble sun, shivering in the pallid cold. Feeble as it was, Ellery wished it would stay.

They crashed on and on, endlessly, shaken like dolls. The road kept lurching toward the east in a stubborn curve. The sky grew more and more leaden. The cold seeped deeper and deeper into their bones.

When Dr. Reinach finally rumbled: "Here we are," and steered the jolting car leftward off the road into a narrow, wretchedly gravelled driveway, Ellery came to with a start of surprise and relief. So their journey was really over, he thought. Behind him he heard Thorne and Alice stirring; they must be thinking the same thing.

He roused himself, stamping his icy feet, looking about. The same desolate tangle of woods to either side of the byroad. He recalled now that they had not once left the main road nor crossed another road since turning off the highway. No chance, he thought grimly, to stray off this path to perdition.

Dr. Reinach twisted his fat neck and said: "Welcome home, Alice."

Alice murmured something incomprehensible; her face was buried to the eyes in the moth-eaten laprobe Reinach had flung over her. Ellery glanced sharply at the fat man; there had been a note of mockery, of derision, in that heavy rasping voice. But the face was smooth and damp and bland, as before.

Dr. Reinach ran the car up the driveway and brought it to rest a little before, and between, two houses. These structures flanked the drive, standing side by side, separated by only the width of the drive, which led straight ahead to a ramshackle garage. Ellery caught a glimpse of Thorne's glittering Lincoln within it's crumbling walls.

The three buildings huddled in a ragged clearing, surrounded by the tangle of woods, like three desert islands in an empty sea.

"That," said Dr. Reinach heartily, "is the ancestral mansion, Alice. To the left."

The house to the left was of stone; once gray, but now so tarnished by the elements and perhaps the ravages of fire that it was almost black. Its face was blotched and streaky, as if it had succumbed to an insensate leprosy. Rising three stories, elaborately ornamented with stone flora and gargoyles, it was unmistakably Victorian in its architecture. The façade had a neglected, granular look that only the art of great age could have etched. The whole structure appeared to have thrust its roots immovably into the forsaken landscape.

Ellery saw Alice Mayhew staring at it with a sort of speechless horror; it had nothing of the pleasant hoariness of old English mansions. It was simply old, old with the dreadful age of this seared and blasted countryside. He cursed Thorne beneath his breath for subjecting the girl to such a shocking experience.

"Sylvester called it The Black House," said Dr. Reinach cheerfully as he turned off the ignition. "Not pretty, I admit, but as solid as the day it was built, seventy-five years ago."

"Black House," grunted Thorne. "Rubbish."

"Do you mean to say," whispered Alice, "that father . . . mother lived here?"

"Yes, my dear. Quaint name, eh, Thorne? Another illustration of Sylvester's preoccupation with the morbidly colorful. Built by your grandfather, Alice. The old gentleman built this one, too, later; I believe you'll find it considerably more habitable. Where the devil is everyone?"

He descended heavily and held the rear door open for his niece. Mr. Ellery Queen slipped down to the driveway on the other side and glanced about with the sharp, uneasy sniff of a wild animal. The old mansion's companion-house was a much smaller and less pretentious dwelling, two stories high and built of an originally white stone which had turned gray. The front door was shut and the curtains at the lower windows were drawn. But there was a fire burning somewhere inside; he caught the tremulous glimmers. In the next moment they were blotted out by the head of an old woman, who pressed her face to one of the panes for a single instant and then vanished. But the door remained shut.

"You'll stop with us, of course," he heard the doctor say genially; and Ellery circled the car. His three companions were standing in the driveway, Alice pressed close to old Thorne as if for protection. "You won't want to sleep in the Black House, Alice. No one's there, it's in rather a mess; and a house of death, y'know. . . ."

"Stop it," growled Thorne. "Can't you see the poor child is half-dead from fright as it is? Are you trying to scare her away?"

"Scare me away?" repeated Alice, dazedly.

"Tut, tut," smiled the fat man. "Melodrama doesn't become you at all, Thorne. I'm a blunt old codger, Alice, but I mean well. It will really be more comfortable in the White House." He chuckled suddenly again. "White House. That's what *I* named it to preserve a sort of atmospheric balance."

"There's something frightfully wrong here," said Alice in a tight voice. "Mr. Thorne, what is it? There's been nothing but innuendo and concealed hostility since we met at the pier. And just why *did* you spend six days in father's house after the funeral? I think I've a right to know."

Thorne licked his lips. "I shouldn't——"

"Come, come, my dear," said the fat man. "Are we to freeze here all day?"

Alice drew her thin coat more closely about her. "You're all being beastly. Would you mind, Uncle Herbert? I should like to see the inside—where father and mother . . ."

"I don't think so, Miss Mayhew," said Thorne hastily.

"Why not?" said Dr. Reinach tenderly, and he glanced once over his shoulder at the building he had called the White House. "She may as well do it now and get it over with. There's still light enough to see by. Then we'll go over, wash up, have a hot dinner, and you'll feel worlds better." He seized the girl's arm and marched her toward the dark building, across the dead, twig-strewn ground. "I believe," continued the doctor blandly, as they mounted the steps of the stone porch, "that Mr. Thorne has the keys."

The girl stood quietly waiting, her dark eyes studying the faces of the three men. The attorney was pale, but his lips were set in a stubborn line. He did not reply. Taking a bunch of large rusty keys out of a pocket, he fitted one into the lock of the front door. It turned over with a creak.

Then Thorne pushed open the door and they stepped into the house.

It was a tomb. It smelled of must and damp. The furniture, ponderous pieces which once no doubt had been regal, was uniformly dilapidated and dusty. The walls were peeling, showing broken, discolored laths beneath. There was dirt and débris everywhere. It was inconceivable that a human being could once have inhabited this grubby den.

The girl stumbled about, her eyes a blank horror, Dr. Reinach steering her calmly. How long the tour of inspection lasted Ellery did not know; even to him, a stranger, the effect was so oppressive as to be almost unendurable. They wandered about, silent, stepping over trash from room to room, impelled by something stronger than themselves.

Once Alice said in a strangled voice: "Uncle Herbert, didn't anyone . . . take care of father? Didn't anyone ever clean up this horrible place?"

The fat man shrugged. "Your father had notions in his old age, my dear.

There wasn't much anyone could do with him. Perhaps we had better not go into that."

The sour stench filled their nostrils. They blundered on, Thorne in the rear, watchful as an old cobra. His eyes never left Dr. Reinach's face.

On the middle floor they came upon a bedroom in which, according to the fat man, Sylvester Mayhew had died. The bed was unmade; indeed, the impress of the dead man's body on the mattress and tumbled sheets could still be discerned.

It was a bare and mean room, not as filthy as the others, but infinitely more depressing. Alice began to cough.

She coughed and coughed, hopelessly, standing still in the center of the room and staring at the dirty bed in which she had been born.

Then suddenly she stopped coughing and ran over to a lopsided bureau with one foot missing. A large, faded chromo was propped on its top against the yellowed wall. She looked at it for a long time without touching it. Then she took it down.

"It's mother," she said slowly. "It's really mother. I'm glad now I came. He did love her, after all. He's kept it all these years."

"Yes, Miss Mayhew," muttered Thorne. "I thought you'd like to have it."

"I've only one portrait of mother, and that's a poor one. This—why, she was beautiful, wasn't she?"

She held the chromo up proudly, almost laughing in her hysteria. The time-dulled colors revealed a stately young woman with hair worn high. The features were piquant and regular. There was little resemblance between Alice and the woman in the picture.

"Your father," said Dr. Reinach with a sigh, "often spoke of your mother toward the last, and of her beauty."

"If he had left me nothing but this, it would have been worth the trip from England." Alice trembled a little. Then she hurried back to them, the chromo pressed to her breast. "Let's get out of here," she said in a shriller voice. "I—I don't like it here. It's ghastly. I'm . . . afraid."

They left the house with half-running steps, as if someone were after them. The old lawyer turned the key in the lock of the front door with great care, glaring at Dr. Reinach's back as he did so. But the fat man had seized his niece's arm and was leading her across the driveway to the White House, whose windows were now flickeringly bright with light and whose front door stood wide open.

As they crunched along behind, Ellery said sharply to Thorne: "Thorne. Give me a clue. A hint. Anything. I'm completely in the dark."

Thorne's unshaven face was haggard in the setting sun. "Can't talk now," he muttered. "Suspect everything, everybody. I'll see you tonight, in your room. Or wherever they put you, if you're alone . . . Queen, for God's sake, be careful!"

"Careful?" frowned Ellery.

"As if your life depended on it." Thorne's lips made a thin, grim line. "For all I know, it does."

Then they were crossing the threshold of the White House.

Ellery's impressions were curiously vague. Perhaps it was the effect of the sudden smothering heat after the hours of cramping cold outdoors; perhaps he thawed out too suddenly, and the heat went to his brain.

He stood about for a while in a state almost of semi-consciousness, basking in the waves of warmth that eddied from a roaring fire in a fireplace black with age. He was only dimly aware of the two people who greeted them, and of the interior of the house. The room was old, like everything else he had seen, and its furniture might have come from an antique shop. They were standing in a large living-room, comfortable enough; strange to his senses only because it was so old-fashioned in its appointments. There were actually antimacassars on the overstuffed chairs! A wide staircase with worn brass treads wound from one corner to the sleeping quarters above.

One of the two persons awaiting them was Mrs. Reinach, the doctor's wife. The moment Ellery saw her, even as she embraced Alice, he knew that this was inevitably the sort of woman the fat man would choose for a mate. She was a pale and weazened midge, almost fragile in her delicacy of bone and skin; and she was plainly in a silent convulsion of fear. She wore a hunted look on her dry and bluish face; and over Alice's shoulder she glanced timidly, with the fascinated obedience of a whipped bitch, at her husband.

"So you're Aunt Milly," sighed Alice, pushing away. "You'll forgive me if I . . . It's all so very new to me."

"You must be exhausted, poor darling," said Mrs. Reinach in the chirping twitter of a bird; and Alice smiled wanly and looked grateful. "And I quite understand. After all, we're no more than strangers to you. Oh!" she said, and stopped. Her faded eyes were fixed on the chromo in the girl's hands. "Oh," she said again. "I see you've been over to the other house *already*."

"Of course she has," said the fat man; and his wife grew even paler at the sound of his bass voice. "Now, Alice, why don't you let Milly take you upstairs and get you comfortable?"

"I am rather done in," confessed Alice; and then she looked at her mother's picture and smiled again. "I suppose you think I'm very silly, dashing in this way with just—" She did not finish; instead, she went to the fireplace. There was a broad flame-darkened mantel above it, crowded with gewgaws of a vanished era. She set the chromo of the handsome Victorian-garbed woman among them. "There! Now I feel ever so much better."

"Gentlemen, gentlemen," said Dr. Reinach. "Please don't stand on ceremony. Nick! Make yourself useful. Miss Mayhew's bags are strapped to the car."

A gigantic young man, who had been leaning against the wall, nodded in a surly way. He was studying Alice Mayhew's face with a dark absorption. He went out.

"Who," murmured Alice, flushing, "is that?"

"Nick Keith." The fat man slipped off his coat and went to the fire to warm his flabby hands. "My morose protégé. You'll find him pleasant company, my dear, if you can pierce that thick defensive armor he wears. Does odd jobs about the place, as I believe I mentioned, but don't let that hold you back. This is a democratic country."

"I'm sure he's very nice. Would you excuse me? Aunt Milly, if you'd be kind enough to . . ."

The young man reappeared under a load of baggage, clumped across the living-room, and plodded up the stairs. And suddenly, as if at a signal, Mrs. Reinach broke out into a noisy twittering and took Alice's arm and led her to the staircase. They disappeared after Keith.

"As a medical man," chuckled the fat man, taking their wraps and depositing them in a hall-closet, "I prescribe a large dose of . . . this, gentlemen." He went to a sideboard and brought out a decanter of brandy. "Very good for chilled bellies." He tossed off his own glass with an amazing facility, and in the light of the fire the finely etched capillaries in his bulbous nose stood out clearly. "Ah-h! One of life's major compensations. Warming, eh? And now I suppose you feel the need of a little sprucing up yourselves. Come along, and I'll show you to your rooms."

Ellery shook his head in a dogged way, trying to clear it. "There's something about your house, Doctor, that's unusually soporific. Thank you, I think both Thorne and I would appreciate a brisk wash."

"You'll find it brisk enough," said the fat man, shaking with silent laughter. "This is the forest primeval, you know. Not only haven't we any electric light or gas or telephone, but we've no running water, either. Well behind the house keeps us supplied. The simple life, eh? Better for you than the pampering influences of modern civilization. Our ancestors may have died more easily of bacterial infections, but I'll wager they had a greater body immunity to coryza! . . . Well, well, enough of this prattle. Up you go."

The chilly corridor upstairs made them shiver, but the very shiver revived them; Ellery felt better at once. Dr. Reinach, carrying candles and matches, showed Thorne into a room overlooking the front of the house, and Ellery into one on the side. A fire burned crisply in the large fireplace in one corner, and the basin on the old-fashioned washstand was filled with icy-looking water.

"Hope you find it comfortable," drawled the fat man, lounging in the doorway. "We were expecting only Thorne and my niece, but one more can always be accommodated. Ah—colleague of Thorne's, I believe he said?"

"Twice," replied Ellery. "If you don't mind—"

"Not at all." Reinach lingered, eying Ellery with a smile. Ellery shrugged, stripped off his coat, and made his ablutions. The water *was* cold; it nipped his fingers like the mouths of little fishes. He scrubbed his face vigorously.

"That's better," he said, drying himself. "Much. I wonder why I felt so peaked downstairs."

"Sudden contrast of heat after cold, no doubt." Dr. Reinach made no move to go.

Ellery shrugged again. He opened his bag with pointed nonchalance. There, plainly revealed on his haberdashery, lay the .38 police revolver. He tossed it aside.

"Do you always carry a gun, Mr. Queen?" murmured Dr. Reinach.

"Always." Ellery picked up the revolver and slipped it into his hip pocket.

"Charming!" The fat man stroked his triple chin. "Charming. Well, Mr. Queen, if you'll excuse me I'll see how Thorne is getting on. Stubborn fellow, Thorne. He could have taken pot luck with us this past week, but he insisted on isolating himself in that filthy den next door."

"I wonder," murmured Ellery, "why."

Dr. Reinach eyed him. Then he said: "Come downstairs when you're ready. Mrs. Reinach has an excellent dinner prepared and if you're as hungry as I am, you'll appreciate it." Still smiling, the fat man vanished.

Ellery stood still for a moment, listening. He heard the fat man pause at the end of the corridor; a moment later the heavy tread was audible again, this time descending the stairs.

Ellery went swiftly to the door on tiptoe. He had noticed that the instant he had come into the room.

There was no lock. Where a lock had been there was a splintery hole, and the splinters had a newish look about them. Frowning, he placed a rickety chair against the door-knob and began to prowl.

He raised the mattress from the heavy wooden bedstead and poked beneath it, searching for he knew not what. He opened closets and drawers; he felt the worn carpet for wires.

But after ten minutes, angry with himself, he gave up and went to the window. The prospect was so dismal that he scowled in sheer misery. Just brown stripped woods and the leaden sky; the old mansion picturesquely known as The Black House was on the other side, invisible from this window.

A veiled sun was setting; a bank of storm clouds slipped aside for an instant and the brilliant rim of the sun shone directly into his eyes, making him see colored, dancing balls. Then other clouds, fat with snow, moved up and the sun slipped below the horizon. The room darkened rapidly.

Lock taken out, eh? Someone had worked fast. They could not have known he was coming, of course. Then someone must have seen him through the window as the car stopped in the drive. The old woman who had peered out for a moment? Ellery wondered where she was. At any rate, a few minutes' work by a skilled hand at the door . . . He wondered, too, if Thorne's door had been similarly mutilated. And Alice Mayhew's.

Thorne and Dr. Reinach were already seated before the fire when Ellery came down, and the fat man was rumbling: "Just as well. Give the poor girl a chance to return to normal. With the shock she's had today, it might be the finisher. I've told Mrs. Reinach to break it to Sarah gently . . . Ah, Queen. Come over here and join us. We'll have dinner as soon as Alice comes down."

"Dr. Reinach was just apologizing," said Thorne casually, "for this Aunt

Sarah of Miss Mayhew's—Mrs. Fell, Sylvester Mayhew's sister. The excitement of anticipating her niece's arrival seems to have been a bit too much for her."

"Indeed," said Ellery, sitting down and planting his feet on the nearest firedog.

"Fact is," said the fat man, "my poor half-sister is cracked. The family paranoia. She's off-balance; not violent, you know, but it's wise to humor her. She isn't normal, and for Alice to see her——"

"Paranoia," said Ellery. "An unfortunate family, it seems. Your half-brother Sylvester's weakness seems to have expressed itself in rubbish and solitude. What's Mrs. Fell's delusion?"

"Common enough—she thinks her daughter is still alive. As a matter of fact, poor Olivia was killed in an automobile accident three years ago. It shocked Sarah's maternal instinct out of plumb. Sarah's been looking forward to seeing Alice, her brother's daughter, and it may prove awkward. Never can tell how a diseased mind will react to an unusual situation."

"For that matter," drawled Ellery, "I should have said the same remark might be made about any mind, diseased or not."

Dr. Reinach laughed silently. Thorne, hunched by the fire, said: "This Keith boy."

The fat man set his glass down slowly. "Drink, Queen?"

"No, thank you."

"This Keith boy," said Thorne again.

"Eh? Oh, Nick. Yes, Thorne? What about him?"

The lawyer shrugged. Dr. Reinach picked up his glass again. "Am I imagining things, or is there the vaguest hint of hostility in the circumambient ether?"

"Reinach—" began Thorne harshly.

"Don't worry about Keith, Thorne. We let him pretty much alone. He's sour on the world, which demonstrates his good sense; but I'm afraid he's unlike me in that he hasn't the emotional buoyancy to rise above his wisdom. You'll probably find him anti-social. . . . Ah, there you are, my dear! Lovely, lovely."

Alice was wearing a different gown, a simple unfrilled frock, and she had freshened up. There was color in her cheeks and her eyes were sparkling with a light and tinge they had not had before. Seeing her for the first time without her hat and coat, Ellery thought she looked different, as all women contrive to look different divested of their outer clothing and refurbished by the mysterious activities which go on behind the closed doors of feminine dressing-rooms. Apparently the ministrations of another woman, too, had cheered her; there were still rings under her eyes, but her smile was more cheerful.

"Thank you, Uncle Herbert." Her voice was slightly husky. "But I do think I've caught a nasty cold."

"Whisky and hot lemonade," said the fat man promptly. "Eat lightly and go to bed early."

"To tell the truth, I'm famished."

"Then eat as much as you like. I'm one hell of a physician, as no doubt you've already detected. Shall we go in to dinner?"

"Yes," said Mrs. Reinach in a frightened voice. "We shan't wait for Sarah, or Nicholas."

Alice's eyes dulled a little. Then she sighed and took the fat man's arm and they all trooped into the dining-room.

Dinner was a failure. Dr. Reinach divided his energies between Gargantuan inroads on the viands and copious drinking. Mrs. Reinach donned an apron and served, scarcely touching her own food in her haste to prepare the next course and clear the plates; apparently the household employed no domestic. Alice gradually lost her color, the old strained look reappearing on her face; occasionally she cleared her throat. The oil lamp on the table flickered badly, and every mouthful Ellery swallowed was flavored with the taste of oil. Besides, the *pièce de résistance* was curried lamb: if there was one dish he detested, it was lamb; and if there was one culinary style that sickened him, it was curry. Thorne ate stolidly, not raising his eyes from his plate.

As they returned to the living-room the old lawyer managed to drop behind. He whispered to Alice: "Is everything all right? Are you?"

"I'm a little scarish, I think," she said quietly. "Mr. Thorne, please don't think me a child, but there's something so strange about—everything. . . . I wish now I hadn't come."

"I know," muttered Thorne. "And yet it was necessary, quite necessary. If there was any way to spare you this, I should have taken it. But you obviously couldn't stay in that horrible hole next door——"

"Oh, no," she shuddered.

"And there isn't a hotel for miles and miles. Miss Mayhew, has any of these people——"

"No, no. It's just that they're so strange to me. I suppose it's my imagination and this cold. Would you greatly mind if I went to bed? Tomorrow will be time enough to talk."

Thorne patted her hand. She smiled gratefully, murmured an apology, kissed Dr. Reinach's cheek, and went upstairs with Mrs. Reinach again.

They had just settled themselves before the fire again and were lighting cigarets when feet stamped somewhere at the rear of the house.

"Must be Nick," wheezed the doctor. "Now where's *he* been?"

The gigantic young man appeared in the living-room archway, glowering. His boots were soggy with wet. He growled: "Hello," in his surly manner and went to the fire to toast his big reddened hands. He paid no attention whatever to Thorne, although he glanced once, swiftly, at Ellery in passing.

"Where've you been, Nick? Go in and have your dinner."

"I ate before you came."

"What's been keeping you?"

"I've been hauling in firewood. Something you didn't think of doing." Keith's tone was truculent, but Ellery noticed that his hands were shaking.

Damnably odd! His manner was noticeably not that of a servant, and yet he was apparently employed in a menial capacity. "It's snowing."

"Snowing?"

They crowded to the front windows. The night was moonless and palpable, and big fat snowflakes were sliding down the panes.

"Ah, snow," sighed Dr. Reinach; and for all the sigh there was something in his tone that made the nape of Ellery's neck prickle. "'The whited air hides hills and woods, the river, and the heaven, and veils the farmhouse at the garden's end.'"

"You're quite the countryman, Doctor," said Ellery.

"I like Nature in her more turbulent moods. Spring is for milksops. Winter brings out the fundamental iron." The doctor slipped his arm about Keith's broad shoulders. "Smile, Nick. Isn't God in His heaven?"

Keith flung the arm off without replying.

"Oh, you haven't met Mr. Queen. Queen, this is Nick Keith. You know Mr. Thorne already." Keith nodded shortly. "Come, come, my boy, buck up. You're too emotional, that's the trouble with you. Let's all have a drink. The disease of nervousness is infectious."

Nerves! thought Ellery grimly. His nostrils were pinched, sniffing the little mysteries in the air. They tantalized him. Thorne was tied up in knots, as if he had cramps; the veins at his temples were pale blue swollen cords and there was sweat on his forehead. Above their heads the house was soundless.

Dr. Reinach went to the sideboard and began hauling out bottles—gin, bitters, rye, vermouth. He busied himself mixing drinks, talking incessantly. There was a purr in his hoarse undertones, a vibration of pure excitement. What in Satan's name, thought Ellery in a sort of agony, was going on here?

Keith passed the cocktails around, and Ellery's eyes warned Thorne. Thorne nodded slightly; they had two drinks apiece and refused more. Keith drank doggedly, as if he were anxious to forget something.

"Now that's better," said Dr. Reinach, settling his bulk into an easy-chair. "With the women out of the way and a fire and liquor, life becomes almost endurable."

"I'm afraid," said Thorne, "that I shall prove an unpleasant influence, Doctor. I'm going to make it unendurable."

Dr. Reinach blinked. "Well, now," he said. "Well, now." He pushed the brandy decanter carefully out of the way of his elbow and folded his pudgy paws on his stomach. His purple little eyes shone.

Thorne went to the fire and stood looking down at the flames, his back to them. "I'm here in Miss Mayhew's interests, Dr. Reinach," he said, without turning. "In her interests alone. Sylvester Mayhew died last week very suddenly. Died while waiting to see the daughter whom he hadn't seen since his divorce from her mother almost twenty years ago."

"Factually exact," rumbled the doctor, without stirring.

Thorne spun about. "Dr. Reinach, you acted as Mayhew's physician for over a year before his death. What was the matter with him?"

"A variety of things. Nothing extraordinary. He died of cerebral hemorrhage."

"So your certificate claimed." The lawyer leaned forward. "I'm not entirely convinced," he said slowly, "that your certificate told the truth."

The doctor stared at him for an instant, then he slapped his bulging thigh. "Splendid!" he roared. "Splendid! A man after my own heart. Thorne, for all your desiccated exterior you have juicy potentialities." He turned on Ellery, beaming. "You heard that, Mr. Queen? Your friend openly accuses me of murder. This is becoming quite exhilarating. So! Old Reinach's a fratricide. What do you think of that, Nick? Your patron accused of coldblooded murder. Dear, dear."

"That's ridiculous, Mr. Thorne," growled Nick Keith. "You don't believe it yourself."

The lawyer's gaunt cheeks sucked in. "Whether I believe it or not is immaterial. The possibility exists. But I'm more concerned with Alice Mayhew's interests at the moment than with a possible homicide. Sylvester Mayhew is dead, no matter by what agency—divine or human; but Alice Mayhew is very much alive."

"And so?" asked Reinach softly.

"And so I say," muttered Thorne, "it's damnably queer her father should have died when he did. Damnably."

For a long moment there was silence. Keith put his elbows on his knees and stared into the flames, his shaggy boyish hair over his eyes. Dr. Reinach sipped a glass of brandy with enjoyment.

Then he set his glass down and said with a sigh: "Life is too short, gentlemen, to waste in cautious skirmishings. Let us proceed without feinting movements to the major engagement. Nick Keith is in my confidence and we may speak freely before him." The young man did not move. "Mr. Queen, you're very much in the dark, aren't you?" went on the fat man with a bland smile.

Ellery did not move, either. "And how," he murmured, "did you know that?"

Reinach kept smiling. "Pshaw. Thorne hadn't left The Black House since Sylvester's funeral. Nor did he receive or send any mail during his self-imposed vigil last week. This morning he left me on the pier to telephone someone. You showed up shortly after. Since he was gone only a minute or two, it was obvious that he hadn't had time to tell you much, if anything. Allow me to felicitate you, Mr. Queen, upon your conduct today. It's been exemplary. An air of omniscience covering a profound and desperate ignorance."

Ellery removed his *pince-nez* and began to polish their lenses. "You're a psychologist as well as a physician, I see."

Thorne said abruptly: "This is all beside the point."

"No, no, it's all very much *to* the point," replied the fat man in a sad bass. "Now the canker annoying your friend, Mr. Queen—since it seems a shame to keep you on tenterhooks any longer—is roughly this: My half-brother

Sylvester, God rest his troubled soul, was a miser. If he'd been able to take his gold with him to the grave—with any assurance that it would remain there —I'm sure he would have done so."

"Gold?" asked Ellery, raising his brows.

"You may well titter, Mr. Queen. There was something mediaeval about Sylvester; you almost expected him to go about in a long black velvet gown muttering incantations in Latin. At any rate, unable to take his gold with him to the grave, he did the next best thing. He hid it."

"Oh, lord," said Ellery. "You'll be pulling clanking ghosts out of your hat next."

"Hid," beamed Dr. Reinach, "the filthy lucre in The Black House."

"And Miss Alice Mayhew?"

"Poor child, a victim of circumstances. Sylvester never thought of her until recently, when she wrote from London that her last maternal relative had died. Wrote to friend Thorne, he of the lean and hungry eye, who had been recommended by some friend as a trustworthy lawyer. As he is, as he is! You see, Alice didn't even know if her father was alive, let alone where he was. Thorne, good Samaritan, located us, gave Alice's exhaustive letters and photographs to Sylvester, and has acted as *liaison* officer ever since. And a downright circumspect one, too, by thunder!"

"This explanation is wholly unnecessary," said the lawyer stiffly. "Mr. Queen knows——"

"Nothing," smiled the fat man, "to judge by the attentiveness with which he's been following my little tale. Let's be intelligent about this, Thorne." He turned to Ellery again, nodding very amiably. "Now, Mr. Queen, Sylvester clutched at the thought of his new-found daughter with the pertinacity of a drowning man clutching a life-preserver. I betray no secret when I say that my half-brother, in his paranoic dotage, suspected his own family— imagine!—of having evil designs on his fortune."

"A monstrous slander, of course."

"Neatly put, neatly put! Well, Sylvester told Thorne in my presence that he had long since converted his fortune into specie, that he'd hidden this gold somewhere in the house next door, and that he wouldn't reveal the hiding-place to anyone but Alice, his daughter, who was to be his sole heir. You see?"

"I see," said Ellery.

"He died before Alice's arrival, unfortunately. Is it any wonder, Mr. Queen, that Thorne thinks dire things of us?"

"This is fantastic," snapped Thorne, coloring. "Naturally, in the interests of my client, I couldn't leave the premises unguarded with that mass of gold lying about loose somewhere——"

"Naturally not," nodded the doctor.

"If I may intrude my still, small voice," murmured Ellery, "isn't this a battle of giants over a mouse? The possession of gold is a clear violation of the law in this country, and has been for several years. Even if you found it, wouldn't the government confiscate it?"

"There's a complicated legal situation, Queen," said Thorne; "but one which cannot come into existence before the gold is found. Therefore my efforts to——"

"And successful efforts, too," grinned Dr. Reinach. "Do you know, Mr. Queen, your friend has slept behind locked, barred doors, with an old cutlass in his hand—one of Sylvester's prized mementoes of a grandfather who was in the Navy? It's terribly amusing."

"I don't find it so," said Thorne shortly. "If you insist on playing the buffoon——"

"And yet—to go back to this matter of your little suspicions, Thorne—have you analyzed the facts? Whom do you suspect, my dear fellow? Your humble servant? I assure you that I am spiritually an ascetic——"

"An almighty fat one!" snarled Thorne.

"—and that money, *per se*, means nothing to me," went on the doctor imperturbably. "My half-sister Sarah? An anile wreck living in a world of illusion, quite as antediluvian as Sylvester—they were twins, you know—who isn't very long for this world. Then that leaves my estimable Milly and our saturnine young friend Nick. Milly? Absurd; she hasn't had an idea, good or bad, for two decades. Nick? Ah, an outsider—we may have struck something there. Is it Nick you suspect, Thorne?" chuckled Dr. Reinach.

Keith got to his feet and glared down into the bland damp lunar countenance of the fat man. He seemed quite drunk. "You damned porker," he said thickly.

Dr. Reinach kept smiling, but his little porcine eyes were wary. "Now, now, Nick," he said in a soothing rumble.

It all happened very quickly. Keith lurched forward, snatched the heavy cut-glass brandy decanter, and swung it at the doctor's head. Thorne cried out and took an instinctive forward step; but he might have spared himself the exertion. Dr. Reinach jerked his head back like a fat snake and the blow missed. The violent effort pivoted Keith's body completely about; the decanter slipped from his fingers and flew into the fireplace, crashing to pieces. The fragments splattered all over the fireplace, strewing the hearth, too; the little brandy that remained in the bottle hissed into the fire, blazing with a blue flame.

"That decanter," said Dr. Reinach angrily, "was almost a hundred and fifty years old!"

Keith stood still, his broad back to them. They could see his shoulders heaving.

Ellery sighed with the queerest feeling. The room was shimmering as in a dream, and the whole incident seemed unreal, like a scene in a play on a stage. Were they acting? Had the scene been carefully planned? But, if so, why? What earthly purpose could they have hoped to achieve by pretending to quarrel and come to blows? The sole result had been the wanton destruction of a lovely old decanter. It didn't make sense.

"I think," said Ellery, struggling to his feet, "that I shall go to bed before the Evil One comes down the chimney. Thank you for an altogether extraordinary evening, gentlemen. Coming, Thorne?"

He stumbled up the stairs, followed by the lawyer, who seemed as weary as he. They separated in the cold corridor without a word to stumble to their respective bedrooms. From below came a heavy silence.

It was only as he was throwing his trousers over the footrail of his bed that Ellery recalled hazily Thorne's whispered intention hours before to visit him that night and explain the whole fantastic business. He struggled into his dressing-gown and slippers and shuffled down the hall to Thorne's room. But the lawyer was already in bed, snoring stertorously.

Ellery dragged himself back to his room and finished undressing. He knew he would have a head the next morning; he was a notoriously poor drinker. His brain spinning, he crawled between the blankets and fell asleep almost stertorously.

He opened his eyes after a tossing, tiring sleep with the uneasy conviction that something was wrong. For a moment he was aware only of the ache in his head and the fuzzy feel of his tongue; he did not remember where he was. Then, as his glance took in the faded wall-paper, the pallid patches of sunlight on the worn blue carpet, his trousers tumbled over the footrail where he had left them the night before, memory returned; and, shivering, he consulted his wrist-watch, which he had forgotten to take off on going to bed. It was five minutes to seven. He raised his head from the pillow in the frosty air of the bedroom; his nose was half-frozen. But he could detect nothing wrong; the sun looked brave if weak in his eyes; the room was quiet and exactly as he had seen it on retiring; the door was closed. He snuggled between the blankets again.

Then he heard it. It was Thorne's voice. It was Thorne's voice raised in a thin faint cry, almost a wail, coming from somewhere outside the house.

He was out of bed and at the window in his bare feet in one leap. But Thorne was not visible at this side of the house, upon which the dead woods encroached directly; so he scrambled back to slip shoes on his feet and his gown over his pajamas, darted toward the footrail and snatched his revolver out of the hip pocket of his trousers, and ran out into the corridor, heading for the stairs, the revolver in his hand.

"What's the matter?" grumbled someone, and he turned to see Dr. Reinach's vast skull protruding nakedly from the room next to his.

"Don't know. I heard Thorne cry out," and Ellery pounded down the stairs and flung open the front door.

He stopped within the doorway, gaping.

Thorne, fully dressed, was standing ten yards in front of the house, facing Ellery obliquely, staring at something outside the range of Ellery's vision with the most acute expression of terror on his gaunt face Ellery had ever seen on a human countenance. Beside him crouched Nicholas Keith, only half-dressed; the young man's jaws gaped foolishly and his eyes were enormous glaring discs.

Dr. Reinach shoved Ellery roughly aside and growled: "What's the matter? What's wrong?" The fat man's feet were encased in carpet slippers and he had pulled a raccoon coat over his night-shirt, so that he looked like a particularly obese bear.

Thorne's Adam's-apple bobbed nervously. The ground, the trees, the world were blanketed with snow of a peculiarly unreal texture; and the air was saturated with warm woolen flakes, falling softly. Deep drifts curved upwards to clamp the boles of trees.

"Don't move," croaked Thorne as Ellery and the fat man stirred. "Don't move, for the love of God. Stay where you are." Ellery's grip tightened on the revolver and he tried perversely to get past the doctor; but he might have been trying to budge a stone wall. Thorne stumbled through the snow to the porch, paler than his background, leaving two deep ruts behind him. "Look at me," he shouted. "*Look at me*. Do I seem all right? Have I gone mad?"

"Pull yourself together, Thorne," said Ellery sharply. "What's the matter with you? I don't see anything wrong."

"Nick!" bellowed Dr. Reinach. "Have you gone crazy, too?"

The young man covered his sunburnt face suddenly with his hands; then he dropped his hands and looked again.

He said in a strangled voice: "Maybe we all have. This is the most—Take a look yourself."

Reinach moved then, and Ellery squirmed by him to land in the soft snow beside Thorne, who was trembling violently. Dr. Reinach came lurching after. They ploughed through the snow toward Keith, squinting, straining to see.

They need not have strained. What was to be seen was plain for any seeing eye to see. Ellery felt his scalp crawl as he looked; and at the same instant he was aware of the sharp conviction that this was inevitable, this was the only possible climax to the insane events of the previous day. The world had turned topsy-turvy. Nothing in it meant anything reasonable or sane.

Dr. Reinach gasped once; and then he stood blinking like a huge owl. A window rattled on the second floor of the White House. None of them looked up. It was Alice Mayhew in a wrapper, staring from the window of her bedroom, which was on the side of the house facing the driveway. She screamed once; and then she, too, fell silent.

There was the house from which they had just emerged, the house Dr. Reinach had dubbed the White House, with its front door quietly swinging open and Alice Mayhew at an upper side window. Substantial, solid, an edifice of stone and wood and plaster and glass and the patina of age. It was everything a house should be. That much was real, a thing to be grasped.

But beyond it, beyond the driveway and the garage, where The Black House had stood, the house in which Ellery himself had set foot only the afternoon before, the house of the filth and the stench, the house of the equally stone walls, wooden facings, glass windows, chimneys, gargoyles, porch; the house of the blackened look; the old Victorian house built during the Civil War where Sylvester Mayhew had died, where Thorne had barricaded himself with a cutlass for a week; the house which they had all seen, touched, smelled . . . there, *there stood nothing.*

No walls. No chimney. No roof. No ruins. No débris. No house. Nothing. Nothing but empty space covered smoothly and warmly with snow.

The house had vanished during the night.

CHAPTER TWO

"THERE'S EVEN," thought Mr. Ellery Queen dully, "a character named Alice."

He looked again. The only reason he did not rub his eyes was that it would have made him feel ridiculous; besides, his sight, all his senses, had never been keener.

He simply stood there in the snow and looked and looked and looked at the empty space where a three-story stone house seventy-five years old had stood the night before.

"Why, it isn't there," said Alice feebly from the upper window. "It . . . isn't . . . there."

"Then I'm not insane." Thorne stumbled toward them. Ellery watched the old man's feet sloughing through the snow, leaving long tracks. A man's weight still counted for something in the universe, then. Yes, and there was his own shadow; so material objects still cast shadows. Absurdly, the discovery brought a certain faint relief.

"It *is* gone!" said Thorne in a cracked voice.

"Apparently." Ellery found his own voice thick and slow; he watched the words curl out on the air and become nothing. "Apparently, Thorne." It was all he could find to say.

Dr. Reinach arched his fat neck, his wattles quivering like a gobbler's. "Incredible. Incredible!"

"Incredible," said Thorne in a whisper.

"Unscientific. It can't be. I'm a man of sense. Of senses. My mind is clear. Things like this—damn it, they just don't happen!"

"As the man said who saw a giraffe for the first time," sighed Ellery. "And yet . . . there it was."

Thorne began wandering helplessly about in a circle. Alice stared, bewitched into stone, from the upper window. And Keith cursed and began to run across the snow-covered driveway toward the invisible house, his hands outstretched before him like a blind man's.

"Hold on," said Ellery. "Stop where you are."

The giant halted, scowling. "What d'ye want?"

Ellery slipped his revolver back into his pocket and sloshed through the snow to pause beside the young man in the driveway. "I don't know precisely. Something's wrong. Something's out of kilter either with us or with the world. It isn't the world as we know it. It's almost . . . almost a matter of transposed dimensions. Do you suppose the solar system has slipped out of its niche in the universe and gone stark crazy in the uncharted depths of spacetime? I suppose I'm talking nonsense."

"You know best," shouted Keith. "I'm not going to let this screwy business stampede *me*. There was a solid house on that plot last night, by God, and nobody can convince me it still isn't there. Not even my own eyes. We've —we've been hypnotized! The hippo could do it here—he could do anything. Hypnotized. You hypnotized us, Reinach!"

The doctor mumbled: "What?" and kept glaring at the empty lot.

"I tell you it's there!" cried Keith angrily.

Ellery sighed and dropped to his knees in the snow; he began to brush aside the white, soft blanket with chilled palms. When he had laid the ground bare, he saw wet gravel and a rut.

"This *is* the driveway, isn't it?" he asked without looking up.

"The driveway," snarled Keith, "or the road to hell. You're as mixed up as we are. Sure it's the driveway! Can't you see the garage? Why shouldn't it be the driveway?"

"I don't know." Ellery got to his feet, frowning. "I don't know anything. I'm beginning to learn all over again. Maybe—maybe it's a matter of gravitation. Maybe we'll all fly into space any minute now."

Thorne groaned: "My God."

"All I can be sure of is that something very strange happened last night."

"I tell you," growled Keith, "it's an optical illusion!"

"Something strange." The fat man stirred. "Yes, decidedly. What an inadequate word! A house has disappeared. Something strange." He began to chuckle in a choking, mirthless way.

"Oh that," said Ellery impatiently. "Certainly. Certainly, Doctor. That's a *fact*. As for you, Keith, you don't really believe this mass-hypnosis bilge. The house is gone, right enough. . . . It's not the fact of its being gone that bothers me. It's the agency, the *means*. It smacks of—of—" He shook his head. "I've never believed in . . . this sort of thing, damn it all!"

Dr. Reinach threw back his vast shoulders and glared, red-eyed, at the empty snow-covered space. "It's a trick," he bellowed. "A rotten trick, that's what it is. That house is right there in front of our noses. Or— Or— They can't fool *me!*"

Ellery looked at him. "Perhaps," he said, "Keith has it in his pocket?"

Alice clattered out on the porch in high-heeled shoes over bare feet, her hair streaming, a cloth coat flung over her night-clothes. Behind her crept little Mrs. Reinach. The women's eyes were wild.

"Talk to them," muttered Ellery to Thorne. "Anything; but keep their minds occupied. We'll all go balmy if we don't preserve at least an air of sanity. Keith, get me a broom."

He shuffled up the driveway, skirting the invisible house very carefully and not once taking his eyes off the empty space. The fat man hesitated; then he lumbered along in Ellery's tracks. Thorne stumbled back to the porch and Keith strode off, disappearing behind the White House.

There was no sun now. A pale and eerie light filtered down through the cold clouds. The snow continued its soft, thick fall.

They looked like dots, small and helpless, on a sheet of blank paper.

Ellery pulled open the folding doors of the garage and peered. A healthy odor of raw gasoline and rubber assailed his nostrils. Thorne's car stood within, exactly as Ellery had seen it the afternoon before, a black monster with glittering chrome-work. Beside it, apparently parked by Keith after their arrival, stood the battered Buick in which Dr. Reinach had driven them from the city. Both cars were perfectly dry.

He shut the doors and turned back to the driveway. Aside from the catenated links of their footprints in the snow, made a moment before, the white covering on the driveway was virgin.

"Here's your broom," said the giant. "What are you going to do—ride it?"

"Hold your tongue, Nick," growled Dr. Reinach.

Ellery laughed. "Let him alone, Doctor. His angry sanity is infectious. Come along, you two. This may be the Judgment Day, but we may as well go through the motions."

"What do you want with a broom, Queen?"

"It's hard to decide whether the snow was an accident or part of the plan," murmured Ellery. "Anything may be true today. Literally anything."

"Rubbish," snorted the fat man. "Abracadabra. *Om mani padme hum.* How could a man have planned a snowfall? You're talking gibberish."

"I didn't say a human plan, Doctor."

"Rubbish, rubbish, rubbish!"

"You may as well save your breath. You're a badly scared little boy whistling in the dark—for all your bulk, Doctor."

Ellery gripped the broom tightly and stamped out across the driveway. He felt his own foot shrinking as he tried to make it step upon the white rectangle. His muscles were gathered in, as if in truth he expected to encounter the adamantine bulk of a house which was still there but unaccountably impalpable. When he felt nothing but cold air, he laughed a little self-consciously and began to wield the broom on the snow in a peculiar manner. He used the most delicate of sweeping motions, barely brushing the surface crystals away; so that layer by layer he reduced the depth of the snow. He scanned each layer with anxiety as it was uncovered. And he continued to do this until the ground itself lay revealed; and at no depth did he come across the minutest trace of a human imprint.

"Elves," he complained. "Nothing less than elves. I confess it's beyond me."

"Even the foundation—" began Dr. Reinach heavily.

Ellery poked the tip of the broom at the earth. It was hard as corundum.

The front door slammed as Thorne and the two women crept into the White House. The three men outside stood still, doing nothing.

"Well," said Ellery at last, "this is either a bad dream or the end of the world." He made off diagonally across the plot, dragging the broom behind him like a tired charwoman, until he reached the snow-covered drive; and then he trudged down the drive towards the invisible road, disappearing around a bend under the stripped white-dripping trees.

It was a short walk to the road. Ellery remembered it well. It had curved steadily in a long arc all the way from the turn-off at the main highway. There had been no crossroad in all the jolting journey.

He went out into the middle of the road, snow-covered now but plainly distinguishable between the powdered tangles of woods as a gleaming, empty strip. There was the long curve exactly as he remembered it. Mechanically he used the broom again, sweeping a small area clear. And there were the pits and ruts of the old Buick's journeys.

"What are you looking for," said Nick Keith quietly, "gold?"

Ellery straightened up by degrees, turning about slowly until he was face to face with the giant. "So you thought it was necessary to follow me? Or—no, I beg your pardon. Undoubtedly it was Dr. Reinach's idea."

The sun-charred features did not change expression. "You're crazy as a bat. Follow you? I've got all I can do to follow myself."

"Of course," said Ellery. "But did I understand you to ask me if I was looking for gold, my dear young Prometheus?"

"You're a queer one," said Keith as they made their way back toward the house.

"Gold," repeated Ellery. "Hmm. There was gold in that house, and now the house is gone. In the shock of the discovery that houses fly away like birds, I'd quite forgotten that little item. Thank you, Mr. Keith," said Ellery grimly, "for reminding me."

"Mr. Queen," said Alice. She was crouched in a chair by the fire, white to the lips. "What's happened to us? What are we to do? Have we . . . Was yesterday a dream? Didn't we walk into that house, go through it, touch things? . . . I'm frightened."

"If yesterday *was* a dream," smiled Ellery, "then we may expect that tomorrow will bring a vision; for that's what holy Sanskrit says, and we may as well believe in parables as in miracles." He sat down, rubbing his hands briskly. "How about a fire, Keith? It's arctic in here."

"Sorry," said Keith with surprising amiability, and he went away.

"We could use a vision," shivered Thorne. "My brain is—sick. It just isn't possible. It's horrible." His hand slapped his side and something jangled in his pocket.

"Keys," said Ellery, "and no house. It *is* staggering."

Keith came back under a mountain of firewood. He grimaced at the litter in the fireplace, dropped the wood, and began sweeping together the fragments of glass, the remains of the brandy decanter he had smashed against the brick wall the night before. Alice glanced from his broad back to the chromo of her mother on the mantel. As for Mrs. Reinach, she was as silent as a scared bird; she stood in a corner like a weazened little gnome, her wrapper drawn about her, her stringy sparrow-colored hair hanging down her back, and her glassy eyes fixed on the face of her husband.

"Milly," said the fat man.

"Yes, Herbert, I'm going," said Mrs. Reinach instantly, and she crept up the stairs and out of sight.

"Well, Mr. Queen, what's the answer? Or is this riddle too esoteric for your taste?"

"No riddle is esoteric," muttered Ellery, "unless it's the riddle of God; and that's no riddle—it's a vast blackness. Doctor, is there any way of reaching assistance?"

"Not unless you can fly."

"No phone," said Keith without turning, "and you saw the condition of the road for yourself. You'd never get a car through those drifts."

"If you had a car," chuckled Dr. Reinach. Then he seemed to remember the disappearing house, and his chuckle died.

"What do you mean?" demanded Ellery. "In the garage are—"

"Two useless products of the machine age. Both cars are out of fuel."

"And mine," said old Thorne suddenly, with a resurrection of grim personal interest, "mine has something wrong with it besides. I left my chauffeur in the city, you know, Queen, when I drove down last time. Now I can't get the engine running on the little gasoline that's left in the tank."

Ellery's fingers drummed on the arm of his chair. "Bother! Now we can't even call on other eyes to test whether we've been bewitched or not. By the way, Doctor, how far is the nearest community? I'm afraid I didn't pay attention on the drive down."

"Over fifteen miles by road. If you're thinking of footing it, Mr. Queen, you're welcome to the thought."

"You'd never get through the drifts," muttered Keith. The drifts appeared to trouble him.

"And so we find ourselves snowbound," said Ellery, "in the middle of the fourth dimension—or perhaps it's the fifth. A pretty kettle! Ah there, Keith, that feels considerably better."

"You don't seem bowled over by what's happened," said Dr. Reinach, eying him curiously. "I'll confess it's given even me a shock."

Ellery was silent for a moment. Then he said lightly: "There wouldn't be any point to losing our heads, would there?"

"I fully expect dragons to come flying over the house," groaned Thorne. He eyed Ellery a bit bashfully. "Queen . . . perhaps we had better . . . try to get out of here."

"You heard Keith, Thorne."

Thorne bit his lip. "I'm frozen," said Alice, drawing nearer the fire. "That was well done, Mr. Keith. It—it—a fire like this makes me think of home, somehow." The young man got to his feet and turned around. Their eyes met for an instant.

"It's nothing," he said shortly. "Nothing at all."

"You seem to be the only one who—*Oh!*"

An enormous old woman with a black shawl over her shoulders was coming downstairs. She might have been years dead, she was so yellow and emaciated and mummified. And yet she gave the impression of being very much alive, with a sort of ancient, ageless life; her black eyes were young and bright and cunning, and her face was extraordinarily mobile. She was sidling down stiffly, feeling her way with one foot and clutching the banister with two dried claws, while her lively eyes remained fixed on Alice's face. There was a curious hunger in her expression, the flaring of a long-dead hope suddenly, against all reason.

"Who— Who—" began Alice, shrinking back.

"Don't be alarmed," said Dr. Reinach quickly. "It's unfortunate that she got away from Milly. . . . Sarah!" In a twinkling he was at the foot of the staircase, barring the old woman's way. "What are you doing up at this hour? You should take better care of yourself, Sarah."

She ignored him, continuing her snail's pace down the stairs until she reached his pachyderm bulk. "Olivia," she mumbled, with a vital eagerness. "It's Olivia come back to me. Oh, my sweet, sweet darling. . . ."

"Now, Sarah," said the fat man, taking her hand gently. "Don't excite yourself. This isn't Olivia, Sarah. It's Alice—Alice Mayhew, Sylvester's girl, come from England. You remember Alice, little Alice? Not Olivia, Sarah."

"Not Olivia?" The old woman peered across the banister, her wrinkled lips moving. "Not Olivia?"

The girl jumped up. "I'm Alice, Aunt Sarah. Alice—"

Sarah Fell darted suddenly past the fat man and scurried across the room to seize the girl's hand and glare into her face. As she studied those shrinking features her expression changed to one of despair. "Not Olivia. Olivia's beautiful black hair. . . . Not Olivia's voice. Alice? Alice?" She dropped into Alice's vacated chair, her skinny broad shoulders sagging, and began to weep. They could see the yellow skin of her scalp through the sparse gray hair.

Dr. Reinach roared: "Milly!" in an enraged voice. Mrs. Reinach popped into sight like Jack-in-the-box. "Why did you let her leave her room?"

"B-but I thought she was—" began Mrs. Reinach, stammering.

"Take her upstairs at once!"

"Yes, Herbert," whispered the sparrow, and Mrs. Reinach hurried downstairs in her wrapper and took the old woman's hand and, unopposed, led her away. Mrs. Fell kept repeating, between sobs: "Why doesn't Olivia come back? Why did they take her away from her mother?" until she was out of sight.

"Sorry," panted the fat man, mopping himself. "One of her spells. I knew it was coming on from the curiosity she exhibited the moment she heard you were coming, Alice. There *is* a resemblance; you can scarcely blame her."

"She's—she's horrible," said Alice faintly. "Mr. Queen—Mr. Thorne, must we stay here? I'd feel so much easier in the city. And then my cold, these frigid rooms——"

"By heaven," burst out Thorne, "I feel like chancing it on foot!"

"And leave Sylvester's gold to our tender mercies?" smiled Dr. Reinach. Then he scowled.

"I don't want father's legacy," said Alice desperately. "At this moment I don't want anything but to get away. I—I can manage to get along all right. I'll find work to do—I can do so many things. I want to go away. Mr. Keith, couldn't you possibly——"

"*I'm* not a magician," said Keith rudely; and he buttoned his mackinaw and strode out of the house. They could see his tall figure stalking off behind a veil of snowflakes.

Alice flushed, turning back to the fire.

"Nor are any of us," said Ellery. "Miss Mayhew, you'll simply have to be a brave girl and stick it out until we can find a means of getting out of here."

"Yes," murmured Alice, shivering; and stared into the flames.

"Meanwhile, Thorne, tell me everything you know about this case, especially as it concerns Sylvester Mayhew's house. There may be a clue in your father's history, Miss Mayhew. If the house has vanished, so has the gold *in* the house; and whether you want it or not, it belongs to you. Consequently we must make an effort to find it."

"I suggest," muttered Dr. Reinach, "that you find the house first. House!" he exploded, waving his furred arms. And he made for the sideboard.

Alice nodded listlessly. Thorne mumbled: "Perhaps, Queen, you and I had better talk privately."

"We made a frank beginning last night; I see no reason why we shouldn't continue in the same candid vein. You needn't be reluctant to speak before Dr. Reinach. Our host is obviously a man of parts—unorthodox parts."

Dr. Reinach did not reply. His globular face was dark as he tossed off a water-goblet full of gin.

Through air metallic with defiance, Thorne talked in a hardening voice; not once did he take his eyes from Dr. Reinach.

His first suspicion that something was wrong had been germinated by Sylvester Mayhew himself.

Hearing by post from Alice, Thorne had investigated and located Mayhew. He had explained to the old invalid his daughter's desire to find her father, if he still lived. Old Mayhew, with a strange excitement, had acquiesced; he was eager to be reunited with his daughter; and he seemed to be living, explained Thorne defiantly, in mortal fear of his relatives in the neighboring house.

"Fear, Thorne?" The fat man sat down, raising his brows. "You know he was afraid, not of us, but of poverty. He was a miser."

Thorne ignored him. Mayhew had instructed Thorne to write Alice and bid her come to America at once; he meant to leave her his entire estate and wanted her to have it before he died. The repository of the gold he had cunningly refused to divulge, even to Thorne; it was "in the house," he had said, but he would not reveal its hiding-place to anyone but Alice herself. The "others," he had snarled, had been looking for it ever since their "arrival."

"By the way," drawled Ellery, "how long have you good people been living in this house, Dr. Reinach?"

"A year or so. You certainly don't put any credence in the paranoic ravings of a dying man? There's no mystery about our living here. I looked Sylvester up over a year ago after a long separation and found him still in the old homestead, and this house boarded up and empty. The White House, this house, incidentally, was built by my stepfather—Sylvester's father—on Sylvester's marriage to Alice's mother; Sylvester lived in it until my stepfather died, and then moved back to The Black House. I found Sylvester, a degenerated hulk of what he'd once been, living on crusts, absolutely alone and badly in need of medical attention."

"Alone—here, in this wilderness?" said Ellery incredulously.

"Yes. As a matter of fact, the only way I could get his permission to move back to this house, which belonged to him, was by dangling the bait of free medical treatment before his eyes. I'm sorry, Alice; he was quite unbalanced. . . . And so Milly and Sarah and I—Sarah had been living with us ever since Olivia's death—moved in here."

"Decent of you," remarked Ellery. "I suppose you had to give up your medical practice to do it, Doctor?"

Dr. Reinach grimaced. "I didn't have much of a practice to give up, Mr. Queen."

"But it was an almost pure brotherly impulse, eh?"

"Oh, I don't deny that the possibility of falling heir to some of Sylvester's fortune had crossed our minds. It was rightfully ours, we believed, not knowing anything about Alice. As it's turned out—" he shrugged his fat shoulders. "I'm a philosopher."

"And don't deny, either," shouted Thorne, "that when I came back here at the time Mayhew sank into that fatal coma you people watched me like a —like a band of spies! I was in your way!"

"Mr. Thorne," whispered Alice, paling.

"I'm sorry, Miss Mayhew, but you may as well know the truth. Oh, you didn't fool me, Reinach! You wanted that gold, Alice or no Alice. I shut myself up in that house just to keep you from getting your hands on it!"

Dr. Reinach shrugged again; his rubbery lips compressed.

"You want candor; here it is!" rasped Thorne. "I was in that house, Queen, for six days after Mayhew's funeral and before Miss Mayhew's arrival, *looking for the gold*. I turned that house upside down. And I didn't find the slightest trace of it. I tell you it isn't there." He glared at the fat man. "I tell you it was stolen before Mayhew died!"

"Now, now," sighed Ellery. "That makes less sense than the other. Why then has somebody intoned an incantation over the house and caused it to disappear?"

"I don't know," said the old lawyer fiercely. "I know only that the most dastardly thing's happened here, that everything is unnatural, veiled in that—that false creature's smile! Miss Mayhew, I'm sorry I must speak this way about your own family. But I feel it my duty to warn you that you've fallen among human wolves. Wolves!"

"I'm afraid," said Reinach sourly, "that I shouldn't come to you, my dear Thorne, for a reference."

"I wish," said Alice in a very low tone, "I truly wish I were dead."

But the lawyer was past control. "That man Keith," he cried. "Who is he? What's he doing here? He looks like a gangster. I suspect him, Queen——"

"Apparently," smiled Ellery, "you suspect everybody."

"Mr. Keith?" murmured Alice. "Oh, I'm sure not. I—I don't think he's that sort at all, Mr. Thorne. He looks as if he's had a hard life. As if he's suffered terribly from something."

Thorne threw up his hands, turning to the fire.

"Let us," said Ellery amiably, "confine ourselves to the problem at hand. We were, I believe, considering the problem of a disappearing house. Do any architect's plans of the so-called Black House exist?"

"Lord, no," said Dr. Reinach.

"Who has lived in it since your stepfather's death besides Sylvester Mayhew and his wife?"

"Wives," corrected the doctor, pouring himself another glassful of gin. "Sylvester married twice; I suppose you didn't know that, my dear." Alice shivered by the fire. "I dislike raking over old ashes, but since we're at confessional . . . Sylvester treated Alice's mother abominably."

"I—guessed that," whispered Alice.

"She was a woman of spirit and she rebelled; but when she'd got her final decree and returned to England, the reaction set in and she died very shortly afterward, I understand. Her death was recorded in the New York papers."

"When I was a baby," whispered Alice.

"Sylvester, already unbalanced, although not so anchoretic in those days as he became later, then wooed and won a wealthy widow and brought her out here to live. She had a son, a child by her first husband, with her. Father'd died by this time, and Sylvester and his second wife lived in The Black House. It was soon evident that Sylvester had married the widow for her money; he persuaded her to sign it over to him—a considerable fortune for those days—and promptly proceeded to devil the life out of her. Result: the woman vanished one day, taking her child with her."

"Perhaps," said Ellery, seeing Alice's face, "we'd better abandon the subject, Doctor."

"We never did find out what actually happened—whether Sylvester drove her out or whether, unable to stand his brutal treatment any longer, she left voluntarily. At any rate, I discovered by accident, a few years later, through an obituary notice, that she died in the worst sort of poverty."

Alice was staring at him with a wrinkled-nosed nausea. "Father . . . did that?"

"Oh, stop it," growled Thorne. "You'll have the poor child gibbering in another moment. What has all this to do with the house?"

"Mr. Queen asked," said the fat man mildly. Ellery was studying the flames as if they fascinated him.

"The real point," snapped the lawyer, "is that you've watched me from the instant I set foot here, Reinach. Afraid to leave me alone for a moment. Why, you even had Keith meet me in your car on both my visits—to 'escort' me here! And I didn't have five minutes alone with the old gentleman—you saw to that. And then he lapsed into the coma and was unable to speak again before he died. Why? Why all this surveillance? God knows I'm a forbearing man; but you've given me every ground for suspecting your motives."

"Apparently," chuckled Dr. Reinach, "you don't agree with Caesar."

"I beg your pardon?"

" 'Would,' " quoted the fat man, " 'he were fatter.' Well, good people, the end of the world may come, but that's no reason why we shouldn't have breakfast. Milly!" he bellowed.

Thorne awoke sluggishly, like a drowsing old hound dimly aware of danger. His bedroom was cold; a pale morning light was struggling in through the window. He groped under his pillow.

"Stop where you are!" he said harshly.

"So you have a revolver, too?" murmured Ellery. He was dressed and looked as if he had slept badly. "It's only I, Thorne, stealing in for a conference. It's not so hard to steal in here, by the way."

"What do you mean?" grumbled Thorne, sitting up and putting his old-fashioned revolver away.

"I see your lock has gone the way of mine, Alice's, The Black House, and Sylvester Mayhew's elusive gold."

Thorne drew the patchwork comforter about him, his old lips blue. "Well, Queen?"

Ellery lit a cigaret and for a moment stared out Thorne's window at the streamers of crêpy snow still dropping from the sky. The snow had fallen without a moment's let-up the entire previous day. "This is a curious business all round, Thorne. The queerest medley of spirit and matter. I've just reconnoitered. You'll be interested to learn that our young friend the Colossus is gone."

"Keith gone?"

"His bed hasn't been slept in at all. I looked."

"And he was away most of yesterday, too!"

"Precisely. Our surly Crichton, who seems afflicted by a particularly acute case of *Weltschmerz*, periodically vanishes. Where does he go? I'd give a good deal to know the answer to that question."

"He won't get far in those nasty drifts," mumbled the lawyer.

"It gives one, as the French say, to think. Comrade Reinach is gone, too." Thorne stiffened. "Oh, yes; his bed's been slept in, but briefly, I judge. Have they eloped together? Separately? Thorne," said Ellery thoughtfully, "this becomes an increasingly subtle devilment."

"It's beyond me," said Thorne with another shiver. "I'm just about ready to give up. I don't see that we're accomplishing a thing here. And then there's always that annoying, incredible fact . . . the house—vanished."

Ellery sighed and looked at his wristwatch. It was a minute past seven.

Thorne threw back the comforter and groped under the bed for his slippers. "Let's go downstairs," he snapped.

"Excellent bacon, Mrs. Reinach," said Ellery. "I suppose it must be a trial carting supplies up here."

"We've the blood of pioneers," said Dr. Reinach cheerfully, before his wife could reply. He was engulfing mounds of scrambled eggs and bacon. "Luckily, we've enough in the larder to last out a considerable siege. The winters are severe out here—we learned that last year."

Kieth was not at the breakfast table. Old Mrs. Fell was. She ate voraciously, with the unconcealed greed of the very old, to whom nothing is left of the sensual satisfactions of life but the filling of the belly. Nevertheless, although she did not speak, she contrived as she ate to keep her eyes on Alice, who wore a haunted look.

"I didn't sleep very well," said Alice, toying with her coffee-cup. Her voice was huskier. "This abominable snow! Can't we manage somehow to get away today?"

"Not so long as the snow keeps up, I'm afraid," said Ellery gently. "And you, Doctor? Did you sleep badly, too? Or hasn't the whisking away of a whole house from under your nose affected your nerves at all?"

The fat man's eyes were red-rimmed and his lids sagged. Nevertheless, he chuckled and said: "I? I always sleep well. Nothing on my conscience. Why?"

"Oh, no special reason. Where's friend Keith this morning? He's a seclusive sort of chap, isn't he?"

Mrs. Reinach swallowed a muffin whole. Her husband glanced at her and she rose and fled to the kitchen. "Lord knows," said the fat man. "He's as unpredictable as the ghost of Banquo. Don't bother yourself about the boy; he's harmless."

Ellery sighed and pushed back from the table. "The passage of twenty-four hours hasn't softened the wonder of the event. May I be excused? I'm going to have another peep at the house that isn't there any more." Thorne started to rise. "No, no, Thorne; I'd rather go alone."

He put on his warmest clothes and went outdoors. The drifts reached the lower windows now; and the trees had almost disappeared under the snow. A crude path had been hacked by someone from the front door for a few feet; already it was half-refilled with snow.

Ellery stood still in the path, breathing deeply of the raw air and staring off to the right at the empty rectangle where The Black House had once stood. Leading across that expanse to the edge of the woods beyond were barely discernible tracks. He turned up his coat-collar against the cutting wind and plunged into the snow waist-deep.

It was difficult going, but not unpleasant. After a while he began to feel quite warm. The world was white and silent—a new, strange world.

When he had left the open area and struggled into the woods, it was with a sensation that he was leaving even that new world behind. Everything was so still and white and beautiful, with a pure beauty not of the earth; the snow draping the trees gave them a fresh look, making queer patterns out of old forms.

Occasionally a clump of snow fell from a low branch, pelting him.

Here, where there was a roof between ground and sky, the snow had not filtered into the mysterious tracks so quickly. They were purposeful tracks, unwandering, striking straight as a dotted line for some distant goal. Ellery pushed on more rapidly, excited by a presentiment of discovery.

Then the world went black.

It was a curious thing. The snow grew gray, and grayer, and finally very dark gray, becoming jet black at the last instant, as if flooded from underneath by ink. And with some surprise he felt the cold wet kiss of the drift on his cheek.

He opened his eyes to find himself flat on his back in the snow and Thorne in the great-coat stooped over him, nose jutting from blued face like a winter thorn.

"Queen!" cried the old man, shaking him. "Are you all right?"

Ellery sat up, licking his lips. "As well as might be expected," he groaned. "What hit me? It felt like one of God's angrier thunderbolts." He caressed the back of his head, and staggered to his feet. "Well, Thorne, we seem to have reached the border of the enchanted land."

"You're not delirious?" asked the lawyer anxiously.

Ellery looked about for the tracks which should have been there. But except for the double line at the head of which Thorne stood, there were none. Apparently he had lain unconscious in the snow for a long time.

"Farther than this," he said with a grimace, "we may not go. Hands off. Nose out. Mind your own business. Beyond this invisible boundary-line lie Sheol and Domdaniel and Abaddon. *Lasciate ogni speranza voi ch'entrate.* . . . Forgive me, Thorne. Did you save my life?"

Thorne jerked about, searching the silent woods. "I don't know. I think not. At least I found you lying here, alone. Gave me quite a start—thought you were dead."

"As well," said Ellery with a shiver, "I might have been."

"When you left the house Alice went upstairs, Reinach said something about a cat-nap, and I wandered out of the house. I waded through the drifts on the road for a spell, and then I thought of you and made my way back. Your tracks were almost obliterated; but they were visible enough to take me across the clearing to the edge of the woods, and I finally blundered upon you. By now the tracks are gone."

"I don't like this at all," said Ellery, "and yet in another sense I like it very much."

"What do you mean?"

"I can't imagine," said Ellery, "a divine agency stooping to such a mean assault."

"Yes, it's open war now," muttered Thorne. "Whoever it is—he'll stop at nothing."

"A benevolent war, at any rate. I was quite at his mercy, and he might have killed me as easily as——"

He stopped. A sharp report, like a pine-knot snapping in a fire or an ice-stiffened twig breaking in two, but greatly magnified, had come to his ears. Then the echo came to them, softer but unmistakable.

It was the report of a gun.

"From the house!" yelled Ellery. "Come on!"

Thorne was pale as they scrambled through the drifts. "Gun . . . I forgot. I left my revolver under the pillow in my bedroom. Do you think——?"

Ellery scrabbled at his own pocket. "Mine's still here. . . . No, by George, I've been scotched!" His cold fingers fumbled with the cylinder. "Bullets taken out. And I've no spare ammunition." He fell silent, his mouth hardening.

They found the women and Reinach running about like startled animals, searching for they knew not what.

"Did you hear it, too?" cried the fat man as they burst into the house. He seemed extraordinarily excited. "Someone fired a shot!"

"Where?" asked Ellery, his eyes on the rove. "Keith?"

"Don't know where he is. Milly says it might have come from behind the house. I was napping and couldn't tell. Revolvers! At least he's come out in the open."

"Who has?" asked Ellery.

The fat man shrugged. Ellery went through to the kitchen and opened the back door. The snow outside was smooth, untrodden. When he returned to the living-room Alice was adjusting a scarf about her neck with fingers that shook.

"I don't know how long you people intend to stay in this ghastly place," she said in a passionate voice. "But I've had *quite* enough, thank you. Mr. Thorne, I insist you take me away at once. At once! I shan't stay another instant."

"Now, now, Miss Mayhew," said Thorne in a distressed way, taking her hands. "I should like nothing better. But can't you see——"

Ellery, on his way upstairs three steps at a time, heard no more. He made for Thorne's room and kicked the door open, sniffing. Then, with rather a grim smile, he went to the tumbled bed and pulled the pillow away. A long-barreled, old-fashioned revolver lay there. He examined the cylinder; it was empty. Then he put the muzzle to his nose.

"Well?" said Thorne from the doorway. The English girl was clinging to him.

"Well," said Ellery, tossing the gun aside, "we're facing fact now, not fancy. It's war, Thorne, as you said. The shot was fired from your revolver. Barrel's still warm, muzzle still reeks, and you can smell the burnt gunpowder if you sniff this cold air hard enough. *And* the bullets are gone."

"But what does it mean?" moaned Alice.

"It means that somebody's being terribly cute. It was a harmless trick to get Thorne and me back to the house. Probably the shot was a warning as well as a decoy."

Alice sank onto Thorne's bed. "You mean we——"

"Yes," said Ellery, "from now on we're prisoners, Miss Mayhew. Prisoners who may not stray beyond the confines of the jail. I wonder," he added with a frown, "precisely why."

The day passed in a timeless haze. The world of outdoors became more and more choked in the folds of the snow. The air was a solid white sheet. It seemed as if the very heavens had opened to admit all the snow that ever was, or ever would be.

Young Keith appeared suddenly at noon, taciturn and leaden-eyed, gulped down some hot food, and without explanation retired to his bedroom. Dr. Reinach shambled about quietly for some time; then he disappeared, only to show up, wet, grimy, and silent, before dinner. As the day wore on, less and less was said. Thorne in desperation took to a bottle of whisky. Keith came down at eight o'clock, made himself some coffee, drank three cups, and went upstairs again. Dr. Reinach appeared to have lost his good nature; he was morose, almost sullen, opening his mouth only to snarl at his wife.

And the snow continued to fall.

They all retired early, without conversation.

At midnight the strain was more than even Ellery's iron nerves could bear. He had prowled about his bedroom for hours, poking at the brisk fire in the grate, his mind leaping from improbability to fantasy until his head throbbed with one great ache. Sleep was impossible.

Moved by an impulse which he did not attempt to analyze, he slipped into his coat and went out into the frosty corridor.

Thorne's door was closed; Ellery heard the old man's bed creaking and groaning. It was pitch-dark in the hall as he groped his way about. Suddenly Ellery's toe caught in a rent in the carpet and he staggered to regain his balance, coming up against the wall with a thud, his heels clattering on the bare planking at the bottom of the baseboard.

He had no sooner straightened up than he heard the stifled exclamation of a woman. It came from across the corridor; if he guessed right, from Alice Mayhew's bedroom. It was such a weak, terrified exclamation that he sprang across the hall, fumbling in his pockets for a match as he did so. He found match and door in the same instant; he struck one and opened the door and stood still, the tiny light flaring up before him.

Alice was sitting up in bed, quilt drawn about her shoulders, her eyes gleaming in the quarter-light. Before an open drawer of a tallboy across the room, one hand arrested in the act of scattering its contents about, loomed Dr. Reinach, fully dressed. His shoes were wet; his expression was blank; and his eyes were slits.

"Please stand still, Doctor," said Ellery softly as the match sputtered out. "My revolver is useless as a percussion weapon, but it still can inflict damage as a blunt instrument." He moved to a nearby table, where he had seen an oil-lamp before the match went out, struck another match, lighted the lamp, and stepped back again to stand against the door.

"Thank you," whispered Alice.

"What happened, Miss Mayhew?"

"I . . . don't know. I slept badly. I came awake a moment ago when I heard the floor creak. And then you dashed in." She cried suddenly: "Bless you!"

"You cried out."

"Did I?" She sighed like a tired child. "I . . . Uncle Herbert!" she said suddenly, fiercely. "What's the meaning of this? What are you doing in my room?"

The fat man's eyes came open, innocent and beaming; his hand withdrew from the drawer and closed it; and he shifted his elephantine bulk until he was standing erect. "Doing, my dear?" he rumbled. "Why, I came in to see if you were all right." His eyes were fixed on a patch of her white shoulders visible above the quilt. "You were so overwrought today. Purely an avuncular impulse, my child. Forgive me if I startled you."

"I think," sighed Ellery, "that I've misjudged you, Doctor. That's not clever of you at all. Downright clumsy, in fact; I can only attribute it to a certain understandable confusion of the moment. Miss Mayhew isn't normally to be found in the top drawer of a tallboy, no matter how capacious it may be."

He said sharply to Alice: "Did this fellow touch you?"

"Touch me?" Her shoulders twitched with repugnance. "No. If he had, in the dark, I—I think I should have died."

"What a charming compliment," said Dr. Reinach ruefully.

"Then what," demanded Ellery, "*were* you looking for, Dr. Reinach?"

The fat man turned until his right side was toward the door. "I'm notoriously hard of hearing," he chuckled, "in my right ear. Good night, Alice; pleasant dreams. May I pass, Sir Launcelot?"

Ellery kept his gaze on the fat man's bland face until the door closed. For some time after the last echo of Dr. Reinach's chuckle died away they were silent.

Then Alice slid down in the bed and clutched the edge of the quilt. "Mr. Queen, please! Take me away tomorrow. I mean it. I truly do. I—can't tell you how frightened I am of . . . all this. Every time I think of that—that . . . How can such things be? We're not in a place of sanity, Mr. Queen. We'll all go mad if we remain here much longer. Won't you take me away?"

Ellery sat down on the edge of her bed. "Are you really so upset, Miss Mayhew?" he asked gently.

"I'm simply terrified," she whispered.

"Then Thorne and I will do what we can tomorrow." He patted her arm through the quilt. "I'll have a look at his car and see if something can't be done with it. He said there's some gas left in the tank. We'll go as far as it will take us and walk the rest of the way."

"But with so little petrol . . . Oh, I don't care!" She stared up at him wide-eyed. "Do you think . . . he'll let us?"

"He?"

"Whoever it is that . . ."

Ellery rose with a smile. "We'll cross that bridge when it gets to us. Meanwhile, get some sleep; you'll have a strenuous day tomorrow."

"Do you think I'm—he'll——"

"Leave the lamp burning and set a chair under the doorknob when I leave." He took a quick look about. "By the way, Miss Mayhew, is there anything in your possession which Dr. Reinach might want to appropriate?"

"That's puzzled me, too. I can't imagine what I've got he could possibly want. I'm so poor, Mr. Queen—quite the Cinderella. There's nothing; just my clothes, the things I came with."

"No old letters, records, mementoes?"

"Just one very old photograph of mother."

"Hmm, Dr. Reinach doesn't strike me as *that* sentimental. Well, good night. Don't forget the chair. You'll be quite safe, I assure you."

He waited in the frigid darkness of the corridor until he heard her creep out of bed and set a chair against the door. Then he went into his own room.

And there was Thorne in a shabby dressing-gown, looking like an ancient and dishevelled spectre of gloom.

"What ho! The ghost walks. Can't you sleep, either?"

"Sleep!" The old man shuddered. "How can an honest man sleep in this God-forsaken place? I notice you seem rather cheerful."

"Not cheerful. Alive." Ellery sat down and lit a cigaret. "I heard you tossing about your bed a few minutes ago. Anything happen to pull you out into this cold?"

"No. Just nerves." Thorne jumped up and began to pace the floor. "Where have you been?"

Ellery told him. "Remarkable chap, Reinach," he concluded. "But we mustn't allow our admiration to overpower us. We'll really have to give this thing up, Thorne, at least temporarily. I *had* been hoping . . . But there! I've promised the poor girl. We're leaving tomorrow as best we can."

"And be found frozen stiff next March by a rescue party," said Thorne miserably. "Pleasant prospect! And yet even death by freezing is preferable to this abominable place." He looked curiously at Ellery. "I must say I'm a trifle disappointed in you, Queen. From what I'd heard about your professional cunning . . ."

"I never claimed," shrugged Ellery, "to be a magician. Or even a theologian. What's happened here is either the blackest magic or palpable proof that miracles can happen."

"It would seem so," muttered Thorne. "And yet, when you put your mind to it . . . It goes against reason, by thunder!"

"I see," said Ellery dryly, "the man of law is recovering from the initial shock. Well, it's a shame to have to leave here now, in a way. I detest the thought of giving up—especially at the present time."

"At the present time? What do you mean?"

"I dare say, Thorne, you haven't emerged far enough from your condition of shock to have properly analyzed this little problem. I gave it a lot of thought today. The goal eludes me—but I'm near it," he said softly, "very near it."

"You mean," gasped the lawyer, "you mean you actually——"

"Remarkable case," said Ellery. "Oh, extraordinary—there isn't a word in the English language or any other, for that matter, that properly describes it. If I were religiously inclined . . ." He puffed away thoughtfully. "It gets down to very simple elements, as all truly great problems do. A fortune in gold exists. It is hidden in a house. The house disappears. To find the gold, then, you must first find the house. I believe . . ."

"Aside from that mumbo-jumbo with Keith's broom the other day," cried Thorne, "I can't recall that you've made a single effort in that direction. Find the house!—why, you've done nothing but sit around and wait."

"Exactly," murmured Ellery.

"What?"

"Wait. That's the prescription, my lean and angry friend. That's the sigil that will exorcise the spirit of The Black House."

"Sigil?" Thorne stared. "Spirit?"

"Wait. Precisely. Lord, how I'm waiting!"

Thorne looked puzzled and suspicious, as if he suspected Ellery of a contrary midnight humor. But Ellery sat soberly smoking. "Wait! For what, man? You're more exasperating than that fat monstrosity! What are you waiting for?"

Ellery looked at him. Then he rose and flung his butt into the dying fire and placed his hand on the old man's arm. "Go to bed, Thorne. You wouldn't believe me if I told you."

"Queen, you *must*. I'll go mad if I don't see daylight on this thing soon!"

Ellery looked shocked, for no reason that Thorne could see. And then, just as inexplicably, he slapped Thorne's shoulder and began to chuckle.

"Go to bed," he said, still chuckling.

"But you must tell me!"

Ellery sighed, losing his smile. "I can't. You'd laugh."

"I'm not in a laughing mood!"

"Nor is it a laughing matter. Thorne, I began to say a moment ago that if I, poor sinner that I am, possessed religious susceptibilities, I should have become permanently devout in the past three days. I suppose I'm a hopeless case. But even I see a power not of earth in this."

"Play-actor," growled the old lawyer. "Professing to see the hand of God in . . . Don't be sacrilegious, man. We're not all heathen."

Ellery looked out his window at the moonless night and the glimmering grayness of the snow-swathed world.

"Hand of God?" he murmured. "No, not hand, Thorne. If this case is ever solved, it will be by . . . a lamp."

"Lamp?" said Thorne faintly. "Lamp?"

"In a manner of speaking. *The lamp of God.*"

CHAPTER THREE

THE NEXT DAY dawned sullenly, as ashen and hopeless a morning as ever was. Incredibly, it still snowed in the same thick fashion, as if the whole sky were crumbling bit by bit.

Ellery spent the better part of the day in the garage, tinkering at the big black car's vitals. He left the doors wide open, so that anyone who wished might see what he was about. He knew little enough of automotive mechanics, and he felt from the start that he was engaged in a futile business.

But in the late afternoon, after hours of vain experimentation, he suddenly came upon a tiny wire which seemed to him to be out of joint with its environment. It simply hung, a useless thing. Logic demanded a connection. He experimented. He found one.

As he stepped on the starter and heard the cold motor sputter into life, a shape darkened the entrance of the garage. He turned off the ignition quickly and looked up.

It was Keith, a black mass against the background of snow, standing with widespread legs, a large can hanging from each big hand.

"Hello, there," murmured Ellery. "You've assumed human shape again, I see. Back on one of your infrequent jaunts to the world of men, Keith?"

Keith said quietly: "Going somewhere, Mr. Queen?"

"Certainly. Why—do you intend to stop me?"

"Depends on where you're going."

"Ah, a threat. Well, suppose I tell *you* where to go?"

"Tell all you want. You don't get off these grounds until I know where you're bound for."

Ellery grinned. "There's a naive directness about you, Keith, that draws me in spite of myself. Well, I'll relieve your mind. Thorne and I are taking Miss Mayhew back to the city."

"In that case it's all right." Ellery studied his face; it was worn deep with ruts of fatigue and worry. Keith dropped the cans to the cement floor of the garage. "You can use these, then. Gas."

"Gas! Where on earth did you get it?"

"Let's say," said Keith grimly, "I dug it up out of an old Indian tomb." "Very well."

"You've fixed Thorne's car, I see. Needn't have. I could have done it." "Then why didn't you?"

"Because nobody asked me to." The giant swung on his heel and vanished.

Ellery sat still, frowning. Then he got out of the car, picked up the cans, and poured their contents into the tank. He reached into the car again, got the engine running, and leaving it to purr away like a great cat he went back to the house.

He found Alice in her room, a coat over her shoulders, staring out her window. She sprang up at his knock.

"Mr. Queen, you've got Mr. Thorne's car going!"

"Success at last," smiled Ellery. "Are you ready?"

"Oh, yes! I feel so much better, now that we're actually to leave. Do you think we'll have a hard time? I saw Mr. Keith bring those cans in. Petrol, weren't they? Nice of him. I never did believe such a nice young man—" She flushed. There were hectic spots in her cheeks and her eyes were brighter than they had been for days. Her voice seemed less husky, too.

"It may be hard going through the drifts, but the car is equipped with chains. With luck we should make it. It's a powerful——"

Ellery stopped very suddenly indeed, his eyes fixed on the worn carpet at his feet, stony yet startled.

"Whatever is the matter, Mr. Queen?"

"Matter?" Ellery raised his eyes and drew a deep, deep breath. "Nothing at all. God's in His heaven and all's right with the world."

She looked down at the carpet. "Oh . . . the sun!" With a little squeal of delight she turned to the window. "Why, Mr. Queen, it's stopped snowing. There's the sun setting—at last!"

"And high time, too," said Ellery briskly. "Will you please get your things on? We leave at once." He picked up her bags and left her, walking with a springy vigor that shook the old boards. He crossed the corridor to his room opposite hers and began, whistling, to pack his bag.

The living-room was noisy with a babble of adieux. One would have said that this was a normal household, with normal people in a normal human situation. Alice was positively gay, quite as if she were not leaving a fortune in gold for what might turn out to be all time.

She set her purse down on the mantel next to her mother's chromo, fixed her hat, flung her arms about Mrs. Reinach, pecked gingerly at Mrs. Fell's withered cheek, and even smiled forgivingly at Dr. Reinach. Then she dashed back to the mantel, snatched up her purse, threw one long enigmatic glance at Keith's drawn face, and hurried outdoors as if the devil himself were after her.

Thorne was already in the car, his old face alight with incredible happiness, as if he had been reprieved at the very moment he was to set his foot beyond the little green door. He beamed at the dying sun.

Ellery followed Alice more slowly. The bags were in Thorne's car; there was nothing more to do. He climbed in, raced the motor, and then released the brake.

The fat man filled the doorway, shouting: "You know the road, now, don't you? Turn to the right at the end of this drive. Then keep going in a straight line. You can't miss. You'll hit the main highway in about . . ."

His last words were drowned in the roar of the engine. Ellery waved his hand. Alice, in the tonneau beside Thorne, twisted about and laughed a little hysterically. Thorne sat beaming at the back of Ellery's head.

The car, under Ellery's guidance, trundled unsteadily out of the drive and made a right turn into the road.

It grew dark rapidly. They made slow progress. The big machine inched its way through the drifts, slipping and lurching despite its chains. As night fell, Ellery turned the powerful headlights on.

He drove with unswerving concentration.

None of them spoke.

It seemed hours before they reached the main highway. But when they did the car leaped to life on the road, which had been partly cleared by snowplows, and it was not long before they were entering the nearby town.

At the sight of the friendly electric lights, the paved streets, the solid blocks of houses, Alice gave a cry of sheer delight. Ellery stopped at a gasoline station and had the tank filled.

"It's not far from here, Miss Mayhew," said Thorne reassuringly. "We'll be in the city in no time. The Triborough Bridge . . ."

"Oh, it's wonderful to be alive!"

"Of course you'll stay at my house. My wife will be delighted to have you. After that . . ."

"You're so kind, Mr. Thorne. I don't know how I shall ever be able to thank you enough." She paused, startled. "Why, what's the matter, Mr. Queen?"

For Ellery had done a strange thing. He had stopped the car at a traffic intersection and asked the officer on duty something in a low tone. The officer stared at him and replied with gestures. Ellery swung the car off into another street. He drove slowly.

"What's the matter?" asked Alice again, leaning forward.

Thorne said, frowning: "You can't have lost your way. There's a sign which distinctly says . . ."

"No, it's not that," said Ellery in a preoccupied way. "I've just thought of something."

The girl and the old man looked at each other, puzzled. Ellery stopped the car at a large stone building with green lights outside and went in, remaining there for fifteen minutes. He came out whistling.

"Queen!" said Thorne abruptly, eyes on the green lights. "What's up?"

"Something that must be brought down." Ellery swung the car about and headed it for the traffic intersection. When he reached it he turned left.

"Why, you've taken the wrong turn," said Alice nervously. "This is the direction from which we've just come. I'm sure of that."

"And you're quite right, Miss Mayhew. It is." She sank back, pale, as if the very thought of returning terrified her. "We're going back, you see," said Ellery.

"Back!" exploded Thorne, sitting up straight.

"Oh, can't we just forget all those horrible people?" moaned Alice.

"I've a viciously stubborn memory. Besides, we have reinforcements. If you'll look back you'll see a car following us. It's a police car, and in it are the local Chief of Police and a squad of picked men."

"But why, Mr. Queen?" cried Alice. Thorne said nothing; his happiness had quite vanished, and he sat gloomily staring at the back of Ellery's neck.

"Because," said Ellery grimly, "I have my own professional pride. Because I've been on the receiving end of a damnably cute magician's trick."

"Trick?" she repeated dazedly.

"Now I shall turn magician myself. You saw a house disappear." He laughed softly. "I shall make it appear again!"

They could only stare at him, too bewildered to speak.

"And then," said Ellery, his voice hardening, "even if we chose to overlook such trivia as dematerialized houses, in all conscience we can't overlook . . . *murder*."

CHAPTER FOUR

AND THERE WAS The Black House again. Not a wraith. A solid house, a strong dirty time-encrusted house, looking as if it would never dream of taking wing and flying off into space.

It stood on the other side of the driveway, where it had always stood.

They saw it even as they turned into the drive from the drift-covered road, its bulk looming black against the brilliant moon, as substantial a house as could be found in the world of sane things.

Thorne and the girl were incapable of speech; they could only gape, dumb witnesses of a miracle even greater than the disappearance of the house in the first place.

As for Ellery, he stopped the car, sprang to the ground, signalled to the car snuffling up behind, and darted across the snowy clearing to the White House, whose windows were bright with lamp- and fire-light. Out of the police car swarmed men, and they ran after Ellery like hounds. Thorne and Alice followed in a daze.

Ellery kicked open the White House door. There was a revolver in his hand and there was no doubt, from the way he gripped it, that its cylinder had been replenished.

"Hello again," he said, stalking into the living-room. "Not a ghost; Inspector Queen's little boy in the too, too solid flesh. Nemesis, perhaps. I bid you good evening. What—no welcoming smile, Dr. Reinach?"

The fat man had paused in the act of lifting a glass of Scotch to his lips. It was wonderful how the color seeped out of his pouchy cheeks, leaving them gray. Mrs. Reinach whimpered in a corner, and Mrs. Fell stared stupidly. Only Nick Keith showed no great astonishment. He was standing by a window, muffled to the ears; and on his face there was bitterness and admiration and, strangely, a sort of relief.

"Shut the door." The detectives behind Ellery spread out silently. Alice stumbled to a chair, her eyes wild, studying Dr. Reinach with a fierce intensity. . . . There was a sighing little sound and one of the detectives lunged toward the window at which Keith had been standing. But Keith was no longer there. He was bounding through the snow toward the woods like a huge deer.

"Don't let him get away!" cried Ellery. Three men dived through the window after the giant, their guns out. Shots began to sputter. The night outside was streaked with orange lightning.

Ellery went to the fire and warmed his hands. Dr. Reinach slowly, very slowly, sat down in the armchair. Thorne sank into a chair, too, putting his hands to his head.

Ellery turned around and said: "I've told you, Captain, enough of what's happened since our arrival to allow you an intelligent understanding of what I'm about to say." A stocky man in uniform nodded curtly.

"Thorne, last night for the first time in my career," continued Ellery whimsically, "I acknowledged the assistance of . . . Well, I tell you, who are implicated in this extraordinary crime, that had it not been for the good God above you would have succeeded in your plot against Alice Mayhew's inheritance."

"I'm disappointed in you," said the fat man from the depths of the chair.

"A loss I keenly feel." Ellery looked at him, smiling. "Let me show you, skeptic. When Mr. Thorne, Miss Mayhew and I arrived the other day, it was late afternoon. Upstairs, in the room you so thoughtfully provided, I looked out the window and saw the sun setting. This was nothing and meant nothing, surely: sunset. Mere sunset. A trivial thing, interesting only to poets, meteorologists, and astronomers. But this was one time when the sun was vital to a man seeking truth . . . a veritable lamp of God shining in the darkness.

"For, see. Miss Mayhew's bedroom that first day was on the opposite side of the house from mine. If the sun *set* in my window, then I faced west and she faced east. So far, so good. We talked, we retired. The next morning I awoke at seven—shortly after sunrise in this winter month—and what did I see? *I saw the sun streaming into my window.*"

A knot hissed in the fire behind him. The stocky man in the blue uniform stirred uneasily.

"Don't you understand?" cried Ellery. "The sun had *set* in my window, and now it was *rising* in my window!"

Dr. Reinach was regarding him with a mild ruefulness. The color had come back to his fat cheeks. He raised the glass he was holding in a gesture curiously like a salute. Then he drank, deeply.

And Ellery said: "The significance of this unearthly reminder did not strike me at once. But much later it came back to me; and I dimly saw that chance, cosmos, God, whatever you may choose to call it, had given me the instrument for understanding the colossal, the mind-staggering phenomenon of a house which vanished overnight from the face of the earth."

"Good lord," muttered Thorne.

"But I was not sure; I did not trust my memory. I needed another demonstration from heaven, a bulwark to bolster my own suspicions. And so, as it snowed and snowed and snowed, the snow drawing a blanket across the face of the sun through which it could not shine, I waited. I waited for the snow to stop, and for the sun to shine again."

He sighed. "When it shone again, there could no longer be any doubt. It appeared first to me in Miss Mayhew's room, which had faced east the afternoon of our arrival. But what was it I saw in Miss Mayhew's room late this afternoon? I saw the sun *set*."

"Good lord," said Thorne again; he seemed incapable of saying anything else.

"Then her room faced west today. How could her room face west today when it had faced east the day of our arrival? How could my room face west the day of our arrival and face east today? Had the sun stood still? Had the world gone mad? Or was there another explanation—one so extraordinarily simple that it staggered the imagination?"

Thorne muttered: "Queen, this is the most——"

"Please," said Ellery, "let me finish. The only logical conclusion, the only conclusion that did not fly in the face of natural law, of science itself, was that while the house we were in today, the rooms we occupied, *seemed* to be identical with the house and the rooms we had occupied on the day of our arrival, *they were not*. Unless this solid structure had been turned about on its foundation like a toy on a stick, which was palpably absurd, then *it was not the same house*. It looked the same inside and out, it had identical furniture, identical carpeting, identical decorations . . . but it was not the same house. It was another house. It was another house exactly like the first in every detail except one: and that was its terrestrial position in relation to the sun."

A detective outside shouted a message of failure, a shout carried away by the wind under the bright cold moon.

"See," said Ellery, softly, "how everything fell into place. If this White House we were in was not the same White House in which we had slept that first night, but was a twin house in a different position in relation to the sun, then The Black House, which apparently had vanished, had not vanished at all. It was where it had always been. It was not The Black House which had vanished, but we who had vanished. It was not The Black House which had moved away, but we who had moved away. We had been transferred during that first night to a new location, where the surrounding woods looked similar, where there was a similar driveway with a similar garage at its terminus, where the road outside was similarly old and pitted, where everything was similar except that there was no Black House, only an empty clearing.

"So we must have been moved, body and baggage, to this twin White House during the time we retired the first night and the time we awoke the next morning. We, Miss Mayhew's chromo on the mantel, the holes in our doors where locks had been, even the fragments of a brandy decanter which had been shattered the night before in a cleverly staged scene against the brick wall of the fireplace at the original house . . . all, all transferred to the twin house to further the illusion that we were still in the original house the next morning."

"Drivel," said Dr. Reinach, smiling. "Such pure drivel that it smacks of fantasmagoria."

"It was beautiful," said Ellery. "A beautiful plan. It had symmetry, the polish of great art. And it made a beautiful chain of reasoning, too, once I was set properly at the right link. For what followed? Since we had been transferred without our knowledge during the night, it must have been while we were unconscious. I recalled the two drinks Thorne and I had had, and the fuzzy tongue and head that resulted the next morning. Mildly drugged, then; and the drinks had been mixed the night before by Dr. Reinach's own hand. Doctor—drugs; very simple." The fat man shrugged with amusement, glancing sidewise at the stocky man in blue. But the stocky man in blue wore a hard, unchanging mask.

"But Dr. Reinach alone?" murmured Ellery. "Oh, no, impossible. One man could never have accomplished all that was necessary in the scant few hours available . . . fix Thorne's car, carry us and our clothes and bags from the one White House to its duplicate—by machine—put Thorne's car out of commission again, put us to bed again, arrange our clothing identically, transfer the chromo, the fragments of the cut-glass decanter in the fireplace, perhaps even a few knickknacks and ornaments not duplicated in the second White House, and so on. A prodigious job, even if most of the preparatory work had been done before our arrival. Obviously the work of a whole group. Of accomplices. Who but everyone in the house? With the possible exception of Mrs. Fell, who in her condition could be swayed easily enough, with no clear perception of what was occurring."

Ellery's eyes gleamed. "And so I accuse you all—including young Mr. Keith, who has wisely taken himself off—of having aided in the plot whereby you would prevent the rightful heiress of Sylvester Mayhew's fortune from taking possession of the house in which it was hidden."

Dr. Reinach coughed politely, flapping his paws together like a great seal. "Terribly interesting, Queen, terribly. I don't know when I've been more captivated by sheer fiction. On the other hand, there are certain personal allusions in your story which, much as I admire their ingenuity, cannot fail to provoke me." He turned to the stocky man in blue. "Certainly, Captain," he chuckled, "you don't credit this incredible story? I believe Mr. Queen has gone a little mad from sheer shock."

"Unworthy of you, Doctor," sighed Ellery. "The proof of what I say lies in the very fact that we are here, at this moment."

"You'll have to explain that," said the police chief, who seemed out of his depth.

"I mean that we are now in the original White House. I led you back here, didn't I? And I can lead you back to the twin White House, for now I know the basis of the illusion. After our departure this evening, incidentally, all these people returned to this house. The other White House had served its purpose and they no longer needed it.

"As for the geographical trick involved, it struck me that this side-road we're on makes a steady curve for miles. Both driveways lead off this same road, one some six miles farther up the road; although, because of the curve, which is like a number 9, the road makes a wide sweep and virtually doubles back on itself, so that as the crow flies the two settlements are only a mile or so apart, although by the curving road they are six miles apart.

"When Dr. Reinach drove Thorne and Miss Mayhew and me out here the day the *Coronia* docked, he deliberately passed the almost imperceptible drive leading to the substitute house and went on until he reached this one, the original. We didn't notice the first driveway.

"Thorne's car was put out of commission deliberately to prevent his driving. The driver of a car will observe landmarks when his passengers notice little or nothing. Keith even met Thorne on both Thorne's previous visits to May- hew—ostensibly 'to lead the way,' actually to prevent Thorne from familiariz- ing himself with the road. And it was Dr. Reinach who drove the three of us here that first day. They permitted me to drive away tonight for what they hoped was a one-way trip because we started from the substitute house —of the two, the one on the road nearer to town. We couldn't possibly, then, pass the tell-tale second drive and become suspicious. And they knew the relatively shorter drive would not impress our consciousness."

"But even granting all that, Mr. Queen," said the policeman, "I don't see what these people expected to accomplish. They couldn't hope to keep you folks fooled forever."

"True," cried Ellery, "but don't forget that by the time we caught on to the various tricks involved they hoped to have laid hands on Mayhew's fortune and disappeared with it. Don't you see that the whole illusion was planned *to give them time?* Time to dismantle The Black House without interference, raze it to the ground if necessary, to find that hidden hoard of gold? I don't doubt that if you examine the house next door you'll find it a shambles and a hollow shell. That's why Reinach and Keith kept disappearing. They were taking turns at The Black House, picking it apart, stone by stone, in a frantic search for the cache, while we were occupied in the duplicate White House with an apparently supernatural phenomenon. That's why someone—prob- ably the worthy doctor here—slipped out of the house behind your back, Thorne, and struck me over the head when I rashly attempted to follow Keith's tracks in the snow. I could not be permitted to reach the original settlement, for if I did the whole preposterous illusion would be revealed."

"How about that gold?" growled Thorne.

"For all I know," said Ellery with a shrug, "they've found it and salted it away again."

"Oh, but we didn't," whimpered Mrs. Reinach, squirming in her chair. "Herbert, I *told* you not to——"

"Idiot," said the fat man. "Stupid swine." She jerked as if he had struck her.

"If you hadn't found the loot," said the police chief to Dr. Reinach brusquely, "why did you let these people go tonight?"

Dr. Reinach compressed his blubbery lips; he raised his glass and drank quickly.

"I think I can answer that," said Ellery in a gloomy tone. "In many ways it's the most remarkable element of the whole puzzle. Certainly it's the grimmest and least excusable. The other illusion was child's play compared to it. For it involves two apparently irreconcilable elements—Alice Mayhew and a murder."

"A murder!" exclaimed the policeman, stiffening.

"Me?" said Alice in bewilderment.

Ellery lit a cigaret and flourished it at the policeman. "When Alice Mayhew came here that first afternoon, she went into The Black House with us. In her father's bedroom she ran across an old chromo—I see it's not here, so it's still in the other White House—portraying her long-dead mother as a girl. Alice Mayhew fell on the chromo like a Chinese refugee on a bowl of rice. She had only one picture of her mother, she explained, and that a poor one. She treasured this unexpected discovery so much that she took it with her, then and there, to the White House—this house. And she placed it on the mantel over the fireplace here in a prominent position."

The stocky man frowned; Alice sat very still; Thorne looked puzzled. And Ellery put the cigaret back to his lips and said: "Yet when Alice Mayhew fled from the White House in our company tonight for what seemed to be the last time, *she completely ignored her mother's chromo,* that treasured memento over which she had gone into such raptures the first day! She could not have failed to overlook it in, let us say, the excitement of the moment. She had placed her purse on the mantel, a moment before, next to the chromo. She returned to the mantel for her purse. And yet she passed the chromo up without a glance. Since its sentimental value to her was overwhelming, by her own admission, it's the one thing in all this property she would not have left. *If she had taken it in the beginning, she would have taken it on leaving.*"

Thorne cried: "What in the name of heaven are you saying, Queen?" His eyes glared at the girl, who sat glued to her chair, scarcely breathing.

"I am saying," said Ellery curtly, "that we were blind. I am saying that not only was a house impersonated, but a woman as well. *I am saying that this woman is not Alice Mayhew.*"

The girl raised her eyes after an infinite interval in which no one, not even the policemen present, so much as stirred a foot.

"I thought of everything," she said with the queerest sigh, and quite without the husky tone, "but that. And it was going off so beautifully."

"Oh, you fooled me very neatly," drawled Ellery. "That pretty little bedroom scene last night. . . . I know now what happened. This precious Dr. Reinach of yours had stolen into your room at midnight to report to you on the progress of the search at The Black House, perhaps to urge you to persuade Thorne and me to leave today—at any cost. I happened to pass along the hall outside your room, stumbled, and fell against the wall with a clatter; not knowing who it might be or what the intruder's purpose, you both fell instantly into that cunning deception. . . . Actors! Both of you missed a career on the stage."

The fat man closed his eyes; he seemed asleep. And the girl murmured, with a sort of tired defiance: "Not missed, Mr. Queen. I spent several years in the theatre."

"You were devils, you two. Psychologically this plot has been the conception of evil genius. You knew that Alice Mayhew was unknown to anyone in this country except by her photographs. Moreover, there was a startling resemblance between the two of you, as Miss Mayhew's photographs showed. And you knew Miss Mayhew would be in the company of Thorne and me for only a few hours, and then chiefly in the murky light of a sedan."

"Good lord," groaned Thorne, staring at the girl in horror.

"Alice Mayhew," said Ellery grimly, "walked into this house and was whisked upstairs by Mrs. Reinach. *And Alice Mayhew, the English girl, never appeared before us again.* It was you, who came downstairs; you, who had been secreted from Thorne's eyes during the past six days deliberately, so that he would not even suspect your existence; you, who probably conceived the entire plot when Thorne brought the photographs of Alice Mayhew here, and her gossipy, informative letters; you, who looked enough like the real Alice Mayhew to get by with an impersonation in the eyes of two men to whom Alice Mayhew was a total stranger. I did think you looked different, somehow, when you appeared for dinner that first night; but I put it down to the fact that I was seeing you for the first time refreshed, brushed up, and without your hat and coat. Naturally, after that, the more I saw of you the less I remembered the details of the real Alice Mayhew's appearance and so became more and more convinced, unconsciously, that you were Alice Mayhew. As for the husky voice and the excuse of having caught cold on the long automobile ride from the pier, that was a clever ruse to disguise the inevitable difference between your voices. The only danger that existed lay in Mrs. Fell, who gave us the answer to the whole riddle the first time we met her. She thought you were her own daughter Olivia. Of course. *Because that's who you are!*"

Dr. Reinach was sipping brandy now with a steady indifference to his surroundings. His little eyes were fixed on a point miles away. Old Mrs. Fell sat gaping stupidly at the girl.

"You even covered that danger by getting Dr. Reinach to tell us beforehand that trumped-up story of Mrs. Fell's 'delusion' and Olivia Fell's 'death' in an automobile accident several years ago. Oh, admirable! Yet even this poor creature, in the frailty of her anile faculties, was fooled by a difference in voice and hair—two of the most easily distinguishable features. I suppose you fixed up your hair at the time Mrs. Reinach brought the real Alice Mayhew upstairs and you had a living model to go by. . . . I could find myself moved to admiration if it were not for one thing."

"You're so clever," said Olivia Fell coolly. "Really a fascinating monster. What do you mean?"

Ellery went to her and put his hand on her shoulder. "Alice Mayhew vanished and you took her place. Why did you take her place? For two possible reasons. One—to get Thorne and me away from the danger zone as quickly as possible, and to keep us away by 'abandoning' the fortune or dismissing us, which as Alice Mayhew would be your privilege: in proof, your vociferous insistence that we take you away. Two—of infinitely greater importance to the scheme: if your confederates did not find the gold at once, you were still Alice Mayhew in our eyes. You could then dispose of the house when and as you saw fit. Whenever the gold was found, it would be yours and your accomplices'.

"But the real Alice Mayhew vanished. For you, her impersonator, to be in a position to go through the long process of taking over Alice Mayhew's inheritance, it was necessary that Alice Mayhew remain *permanently invisible*. For you to get possession of her rightful inheritance and live to enjoy its fruits, it was necessary that Alice Mayhew die. And that, Thorne," snapped Ellery, gripping the girl's shoulder hard, "is why I said that there was something besides a disappearing house to cope with tonight. Alice Mayhew was murdered."

There were three shouts from outside which rang with tones of great excitement. And then they ceased, abruptly.

"Murdered," went on Ellery, "by the only occupant of the house who was not *in* the house when this impostor came downstairs that first evening—Nicholas Keith. A hired killer. Although these people are all accessories to that murder."

A voice said from the window: "Not a hired *killer*."

They wheeled sharply, and fell silent. The three detectives who had sprung out of the window were there in the background, quietly watchful. Before them were two people.

"Not a killer," said one of them, a woman. "That's what he was supposed to be. Instead, and without their knowledge, he saved my life . . . dear Nick."

And now the pall of grayness settled over the faces of Mrs. Fell, and of Olivia Fell, and of Mrs. Reinach, and of the burly doctor. For by Keith's side stood Alice Mayhew. She was the same woman who sat near the fire only in general similitude of feature. Now that both women could be compared in proximity, there were obvious points of difference. She looked worn and grim, but happy withal; and she was holding to the arm of bitter-mouthed Nick Keith with a grip that was quite possessive.

AFTERWARDS, when it was possible to look back on the whole amazing fabric of plot and event, Mr. Ellery Queen said: "The scheme would have been utterly impossible except for two things: the character of Olivia Fell and the—in itself—fantastic existence of that duplicate house in the woods."

He might have added that both of these would in turn have been impossible except for the aberrant strain in the Mayhew blood. The father of Sylvester Mayhew—Dr. Reinach's stepfather—had always been erratic, and he had communicated his unbalance to his children. Sylvester and Sarah, who became Mrs. Fell, were twins, and they had always been insanely jealous of each other's prerogatives. When they married in the same month, their father avoided trouble by presenting each of them with a specially-built house, the houses being identical in every detail. One he had erected next to his own house and presented to Mrs. Fell as a wedding gift; the other he built on a piece of property he owned some miles away and gave to Sylvester.

Mrs. Fell's husband died early in her married life; and she moved away to live with her half-brother Herbert. When old Mayhew died, Sylvester boarded up his own house and moved into the ancestral mansion. And there the twin houses stood for many years, separated by only a few miles by road, completely and identically furnished inside—fantastic monuments to the Mayhew eccentricity.

The duplicate White House lay boarded up, waiting, idle, requiring only the evil genius of an Olivia Fell to be put to use. Olivia was beautiful, intelligent, accomplished, and as unscrupulous as Lady Macbeth. It was she who had influenced the others to move back to the abandoned house next to The Black House for the sole purpose of coercing or robbing Sylvester Mayhew. When Thorne appeared with the news of Sylvester's long-lost daughter, she recognized the peril to their scheme and, grasping her own resemblance to her English cousin from the photographs Thorne brought, conceived the whole extraordinary plot.

Then obviously the first step was to put Sylvester out of the way. With perfect logic, she bent Dr. Reinach to her will and caused him to murder his patient before the arrival of Sylvester's daughter. (A later exhumation and autopsy revealed traces of poison in the corpse.) Meanwhile, Olivia perfected the plans of the impersonation and illusion.

The house illusion was planned for the benefit of Thorne, to keep him sequestered and bewildered while The Black House was being torn down in the search for the gold. The illusion would perhaps not have been necessary had Olivia felt certain that her impersonation would succeed perfectly.

The illusion was simpler, of course, than appeared on the surface. The house was there, completely furnished, ready for use. All that was necessary was to take the boards down, air the place out, clean up, put fresh linen in. There was plenty of time before Alice's arrival for this preparatory work.

The one weakness of Olivia Fell's plot was objective, not personal. That woman would have succeeded in anything. But she made the mistake of selecting Nick Keith for the job of murdering Alice Mayhew. Keith had originally insinuated himself into the circle of plotters, posing as a desperado prepared to do anything for sufficient pay. Actually, he was the son of Sylvester Mayhew's second wife, who had been so brutally treated by Mayhew and driven off to die in poverty.

Before his mother expired she instilled in Keith's mind a hatred for Mayhew that waxed, rather than waned, with the ensuing years. Keith's sole motive in joining the conspirators was to find his stepfather's fortune and take that part of it which Mayhew had stolen from his mother. He had never intended to murder Alice—his ostensible rôle. When he carried her from the house that first evening under the noses of Ellery and Thorne, it was not to strangle and bury her, as Olivia had directed, but to secrete her in an ancient shack in the nearby woods known only to himself.

He had managed to smuggle provisions to her while he was ransacking The Black House. At first he had held her frankly prisoner, intending to keep her so until he found the money, took his share, and escaped. But as he came to know her he came to love her, and he soon confessed the whole story to her in the privacy of the shack. Her sympathy gave him new courage; concerned now with her safety above everything else, he prevailed upon her to remain in hiding until he could find the money and outwit his fellow-conspirators. Then they both intended to unmask Olivia.

The ironical part of the whole affair, as Mr. Ellery Queen was to point out, was that the goal of all this plotting and counterplotting—Sylvester Mayhew's gold—remained as invisible as The Black House apparently had been. Despite the most thorough search of the building and grounds no trace of it had been found.

"I've asked you to visit my poor diggings," smiled Ellery a few weeks later, "because something occurred to me that simply cried out for investigation."

Keith and Alice glanced at each other blankly; and Thorne, looking clean, rested, and complacent for the first time in weeks, sat up straighter in Ellery's most comfortable chair.

"I'm glad something occurred to somebody," said Nick Keith with a grin. "I'm a pauper; and Alice is only one jump ahead of me."

"You haven't the philosophic attitude towards wealth," said Ellery dryly, "that's so charming a part of Dr. Reinach's personality. Poor Colossus! I wonder how he likes our jails. . . ." He poked a log into the fire. "By this time, Miss Mayhew, our common friend Thorne has had your father's house virtually annihilated. No gold. Eh, Thorne?"

"Nothing but dirt," said the lawyer sadly. "Why, we've taken that house apart stone by stone."

"Exactly. Now there are two possibilities, since I am incorrigibly categorical:

either your father's fortune exists, Miss Mayhew, or it does not. If it does not and he was lying, there's an end to the business, of course, and you and your precious Keith will have to put your heads together and agree to live either in noble, ruggedly individualistic poverty or by the grace of the Relief Administration. But suppose there was a fortune, as your father claimed, and suppose he did secrete it somewhere in that house. What then?"

"Then," sighed Alice, "it's flown away."

Ellery laughed. "Not quite; I've had enough of vanishments for the present, anyway. Let's tackle the problem differently. Is there anything which was in Sylvester Mayhew's house before he died which is not there now?"

Thorne stared. "If you mean the—er—the body . . ."

"Don't be gruesome, Literal Lyman. Besides, there's been an exhumation. No, guess again."

Alice looked slowly down at the package in her lap. "So that's why you asked me to fetch this with me today!"

"You mean," cried Keith, "the old fellow was deliberately putting everyone off the track when he said his fortune was gold?"

Ellery chuckled and took the package from the girl. He unwrapped it and for a moment gazed appreciatively at the large old chromo of Alice's mother.

And then, with the self-assurance of the complete logician, he stripped away the back of the frame.

Gold-and-green documents cascaded into his lap.

"Converted into bonds," grinned Ellery. "Who said your father was cracked, Miss Mayhew? A very clever gentleman! Come, come, Thorne, stop rubber-necking and let's leave these children of fortune alone!"

THE CASE OF THE WHITE ELEPHANT

by Margery Allingham

MR CAMPION, piloting his companion through the crowded courtyard at Burlington House, became aware of the old lady in the Daimler partly because her chauffeur almost ran over him and partly because she gave him a stare of such vigorous and personal disapproval that he felt she must either know him very well indeed or have mistaken him for someone else entirely.

Juliet Fysher-Sprigge, who was leaning on his arm with all the weariness of a two-hour trek round the academy's Summer Exhibition, enlightened him.

"We were *not* amused, were we?" she said. "Old-fashioned people have minds that are just too prurient, my dear. After all, I have known you for years, haven't I, and I'm not even married to Philip. Besides, the academy is so respectable. It isn't as though she'd seen me sneaking out of the National Gallery."

Mr Campion handed her into a taxicab.

"Who was she?" he enquired, hoisting his lank form in after her.

Juliet laughed. Her laughter was one of her most charming attributes, for it wiped the sophistication from her débutante's face and left her the schoolgirl he had known three years before.

"My dear, didn't you recognize her? That would have been the last straw for the poor darling! That's Florence, Dowager Countess of Marle. Philip's Auntie Flo."

Mr Campion's pale blue eyes grew momentarily more intelligent behind his horn-rimmed spectacles.

"Ah, hence the disgust," he said. "You'll have to explain me away. The police are always doing it."

Juliet turned to him with the wide-eyed ingenuousness of one who perceives a long-awaited opening.

"You still dabble in police and detection and things, then?" she said breathlessly and not very tactfully, since his reputation as a criminologist was considerable. "Do tell me, what is the low-down on these terribly exciting burglaries? Are the police really beaten or are they being bribed? No one talks of anything else these days. I just had to see you and find out."

Her companion leant back in the leathery depths of the cab and sighed regretfully.

"When you phoned me and demanded to be taken to this execrable exhibition I was vain enough to think it was my companionship you were after," he said. "Now it turns out to be merely a vulgar pursuit of the material for gossip. Well, my girl, you're going to be disappointed. The clever gentleman doesn't know a thing and, what's more, he doesn't care. Have you lost anything yourself?"

"Me?" Juliet's gratification at the implied compliment all but outweighed her disappointment. "Of course I haven't. It's only the really worth-while collections that have gone. That's why it's so interesting. The De Breuil diamonds went first. Then the Denver woman lost her emeralds and the glorious Napoleon necklace. Josephine Pharoah had her house burgled and just lost her tiara, which was the one really good thing she had, and now poor old Mrs Dacre has had her diamonds and rubies pinched, including the famous dog collar. Forty-two diamonds, my dear!—each one quite as big as a pea. They say it's a cat burglar and the police know him quite well but they can't find him—at least, that's one story. The other one is that it's all being done for the insurance and the police are in it. What do you think?"

Mr Campion glanced at her affectionately and noted that the gold hair under her small black hat curled as naturally as ever.

"Both stories are equally good," he announced placidly. "Come and have some tea, or has Philip's Auntie Flo got spies everywhere?"

Miss Fysher-Sprigge blushed. "I don't care if she has," she said. "I've quarrelled with Philip, anyway."

It took Mr Campion several minutes, until they were seated at a table on the edge of the Hotel Monde's smaller dance floor, in fact, before he fully digested this piece of information. Juliet was leaning back in her chair, her eyes roving over the gathering in a frank search for old acquaintances, when he spoke again.

"Seriously?" he enquired.

Juliet met his eyes and again he saw her sophistication vanish.

"I hope not," she said soberly. "I've been rather an ass. Can I tell you about it?"

Mr Campion smiled ruefully. It was a sign of the end of the thirties, he supposed, when one submitted cheerfully to the indignity of taking a young woman out only to hear about her hopes and fears concerning a younger man. Juliet went on blissfully, lowering her voice so that the heart searchings of the balalaika orchestra across the floor concealed it from adjoining tables.

"Philip is a dear, but he has to be so filthily careful about the stupidest things," she said, accepting a rhumbaba. "The F.O. casts a sort of white light over people, have you noticed? His relations are like it, too, only worse. You can't talk of anything without getting warned off. The aunt we saw today bit my head off the other evening for merely mentioning these cat burglaries, which, after all, are terribly exciting. 'My child,' she said, 'we can't afford to know about such things,' and went on talking about her old White Elephant until I nearly wept."

"White Elephant?" Mr Campion looked blank. "The charity?"

Juliet nodded. " 'Send your white elephant to Florence, Countess of Marle, and she will find it a home where it will be the pet of the family,' " she quoted. "It's quite an important affair, patronised by royalty and blessed by every archbishop in the world. I pointed out it was only a glorified jumble sale and she nearly had a fit. She works herself to death for it. I go and help pack up parcels sometimes—or I did before this row with Philip. I've been rather silly. I've done something infuriating. Philip's livid with me now and I don't know what's going to happen when he finds out everything. I must tell somebody. Can I tell you?"

A faint smile passed over Mr Campion's thin face.

"You're quite a nice girl," he said, "but you won't stay twenty-one for ever. Stop treating me as though I was a maiden uncle."

"You must be thirty-six at least," said Miss Fysher-Sprigge brutally, "and I'm rather glad, because presumably you're sensible. Look here, if a man has a criminal record it doesn't mean he's always going to be stealing things, does it? Not if he promises to go straight?"

Her companion frowned. "I don't quite follow," he said. "Age is stopping the brain from functioning. I thought we were talking about Philip Graysby, Auntie Flo's nephew?"

"So we are," said Juliet. "He hasn't got the record, of course, but Henry Swan has. Henry Swan is—or, rather, was—Philip's man. He'd been with Philip for eighteen months and been perfectly good, and then this came out about him. Philip said he was awfully sorry but he'd have to go. Philip couldn't help it, I suppose—I do see that now—but at the time I was furious. It seemed so unfair, and we had a quarrel. I said some beastly things and so did he, but he wouldn't give in and Swan went."

She paused and eyed her companion dubiously. Mr Campion shrugged his shoulders.

"It doesn't seem very serious," he said.

Juliet accepted the cigarette he offered her and seemed engrossed in the tip of it.

"No," she agreed. "That part isn't. But you see, I'm a very impulsive person and I was stupidly cross at the time and so when I had a wonderful idea for getting my own back I acted on it. I got Swan a job with the most respectable person I knew and, in order to do it, I gave him a reference. To make it a good reference I didn't say anything about the record. How's that?"

"Not so good," he admitted. "Who's the most respectable person harbouring this human bomb?"

Juliet avoided his eyes. "Philip's Auntie Flo," she said. "She's the stiffest, thorniest, most conventional of them all. Philip doesn't go there often so he hasn't seen Swan yet, but when he does and makes enquiries and hears about me—well, it's going to be awkward. D'you think he'll ever forgive me? He stands to get a fortune from Auntie Flo if he doesn't annoy her. It was a silly thing of me to do, wasn't it?"

"Not bright," agreed Mr Campion. "Are you in love with Philip?"

"Horribly," said Juliet Fysher-Sprigge and looked away across the dance floor.

Mr Campion had spent some time expounding a wise course of action, in which a clean breast to all concerned figured largely, when he became aware that he was not being heard. Juliet was still staring across the room, her eyes puzzled.

"I say," she said unexpectedly, "this place is wildly expensive, isn't it?"

"I hope not," said Mr Campion mildly.

Juliet did not smile. Her cheeks were faintly flushed and her eyes questioning.

"Don't be a fool. You know what I mean. This is probably the most expensive place in London, isn't it? How queer! It looks as though Auntie Flo really has got her spies everywhere. That's her manicurist over there, having tea alone."

He glanced casually across the room.

"The woman sitting directly under the orchestra?" he enquired. "The one who looks like a little bull in a navy hat? She's an interesting type, isn't she? Not very nice."

Juliet's eyes were still thoughtful.

"That's her. Miss Matisse. A visiting manicurist," she said. "She goes to dozens of people I know. I believe she's very good. How funny for her to come to tea alone, here of all places . . ."

Mr Campion's casual interest in the small square figure who managed somehow to look flamboyant in spite of her sober clothes showed signs of waning.

"She may be waiting for someone," he suggested.

"But she's ordered her tea and started it."

"Oh well, perhaps she just felt like eating."

"Rubbish!" said Juliet. "You pay ten and sixpence just to sit in this room because you can dance if you want to."

Her host laughed. "Auntie Flo has a pretty turn of speed if she tracked us down here and then whipped round and set her manicuring bloodhound on us, all in half an hour," he said.

Juliet ignored him. Her attention had wandered once again.

"I say," she murmured, "can you see through that mirror over there? See that man eating alone? I thought at first he was watching Miss Matisse, but I believe it's you he's most interested in."

Her companion turned his head and his eyes widened.

"Apologies," he said. "I underestimated you. That's Detective Sergeant Blower, one of the best men in the public-school and night-club tradition. I wonder who he's tailing. Don't watch him—it's unkind."

Juliet laughed. "You're a most exciting person to have tea with," she said. "I do believe . . ."

The remainder of her remark was lost as, in common with all but one visitor in the room, she was silenced by what was, for the Hotel Monde, a rather extraordinary incident.

The balalaika orchestra had ceased to play for a moment or so and the dance floor was practically deserted when, as though taking advantage of the lull, the woman in the navy hat rose from her chair and shouted down the whole length of the long room, in an effort, apparently, to attract the attention of a second woman who had just entered.

"Mrs Gregory!" Her voice was powerful and well articulated. "Mrs Gregory! Mrs Gregory!"

The newcomer halted as all eyes were turned upon her, and her escort expostulated angrily to the excited maître d'hotel who hurried forward.

Miss Matisse sat down, and in the silence Mr Campion heard her explaining in a curiously flat voice to the waiter who came up to her.

"I am sorry. I thought I recognised a friend. I was mistaken. Bring me my bill, please."

Juliet stared across the table, her young face shocked.

"What a very extraordinary thing to do," she said.

Mr Campion did not reply. From his place of vantage he could see in the mirror that Detective Sergeant Blower had also called for his bill and was preparing to leave.

Some little time later, when Mr Campion deposited Juliet on her Mount Street doorstep, she was in a more cheerful mood.

"Then you think if I go to Philip and tell him the worst and say that I'm sorry he'll forgive me?" she said as they parted.

"If he's human he'll forgive you anything," Mr Campion assured her gallantly.

Juliet sighed. "Age does improve the manners," she said unnecessarily. "I'll forgive you for disappointing me about the burglaries. I really had hoped to get all the dirt. Good-bye."

"Damn the burglaries!" said Mr Campion and took a taxi home.

Three days later he said the same thing again but for a different reason. This reason arrived by post. It came in a fragrant green box designed to contain a large flask of familiar perfume and it lay upon his breakfast table winking at him with evil amusement. It was Mrs Dacre's ruby-and-diamond dog collar and it was not alone. In a nest of cotton wool beneath it were five diamond rings of considerable value, a pair of exquisite ruby ear clips, and a small hooped bracelet set with large alternate stones.

Mr Campion, who was familiar with the "stolen" list which the police send round to their local stations and circularise to the jewellers and pawnbrokers of the kingdom, had no difficulty in recognising the collection as the haul of the last cat burglary.

The sender of so dubious a gift might have been harder to identify had it not been for the familiarity of the perfume and the presence of a small card on which was printed in shaky, ill-disguised characters a simple request and a specious promise:

Get these back where they belong and I'll love you for ever, darling.

Mr Campion had a considerable respect for the law but he spent some time that morning in acquiring a box of similar design but different and more powerful perfume, and it was not until the jewelry was freshly housed and the card burned that he carried his responsibility to Scotland Yard and laid it with a sigh of relief on the desk of Chief Detective Inspector Stanislaus Oates, his friend and partner in many adventures.

The original wrapping he decided to retain. Its ill-written address might have been scrawled by anyone and the fact that it was grossly overfranked showed that it had been dropped into a public box and not passed over a post-office counter.

He let the chief, who was a tall, disconsolate personage with a grey face and dyspepsia, recover from his first transports of mingled relief and suspicion before regretting his inability to help him further. Oates regarded him.

"It's my duty to warn you that you're under suspicion," he said with the portentous solemnity which passed with him for wit.

Campion laughed. "My cat-burglary days are over," he said. "Or am I the fence?"

"That's more like it." The chief passed his cigarette case. "I can't tell you how glad I am to see this lot. But it doesn't help us very much unless we know where it came from. These cat jobs are done by The Sparrow. We knew that as soon as we saw the first one. You remember him, Campion?—a sleek, handsome chap with an insufferable manner. These jobs have his trademarks all over them. Pane cut out with a diamond and the glass removed with a sucker—no fingerprints, no noise, no mistakes." He paused and caressed his ear sadly. "It's getting on my nerves," he said. "The commissioner is sarcastic and the papers are just libellous. It's hard on us. We know who and where the fellow is but we can't get him. We've held him as long as we dared, three separate times this summer, but we haven't got a thing we can fix on him. I've been trusting the stuff would turn up somewhere so that we could work back on him from that angle, but frankly this is the first scrap of it I've seen. Where's all the early swag? This was only pinched five days ago."

Mr Campion remained unhelpful. "I got it this morning," he said. "It just came out of the air. Ask the postman."

"Oh, I know . . ." The chief waved the suggestion aside. "You'll help us just as much as you can, which means as much as you care to. Some society bit is mixed up in this somewhere, I'm sure of it. Look here, I'll tell you what I'll do. I'll put my cards on the table. This isn't official; this is the truth. Edward Borringer, alias The Sparrow, is living with his wife in digs in Kilburn. They're very respectable at the moment, just a quiet hard-working couple. He takes classes in the local gym and she does visiting manicure work."

"Under the name of Matisse?"

"Exactly!" The inspector was jubilant. "Now you've given yourself away, my lad. What do you know about Margot Matisse?"

"Not much," his visitor confessed affably. "She was pointed out to me as a manicurist at a thé dansant at the Hotel Monde on Tuesday. Looking round, I saw Blower on her trail, so naturally when you mentioned manicurists I put two and two together."

"Who pointed her out to you?"

"A lady who had seen her at work in a relation's house."

"All right." The policeman became depressed again. "Well, there you are. It's quite obvious how they're working it. She goes round to the big houses and spots the stuff and the lie of the land, and then he calls one night and does the job. It's the old game worked very neatly. Too neatly, if you ask me. What we can't fathom is how they're disposing of the stuff. They certainly haven't got it about them, and their acquaintance just now is so respectable, not to say aristocratic, that we can barely approach it. Besides, to make this big stuff worth the risk they must be using an expert. Most of these stones are so well known that they must go to a first-class fellow to be recut."

Mr Campion hesitated. "I seem to remember that Edward Borringer was once associated with our old friend Bertrand Meyer and his ménage," he ventured. "Are they still functioning?"

"Not in England." The chief was emphatic. "And if these two are getting their stuff out of the country I'll eat my hat. The customs are co-operating with us. We thought a maid in one of the houses which the Matisse woman visits might be in it and so if you've heard a squawk from your society pals about severity at the ports, that's our work. I don't mind telling you it's all very difficult. You can see for yourself. These are the Matisse clients."

Mr Campion scanned the typewritten page and his sympathy for his friend deepened.

"Oh yes, Caesar's wives," he agreed. "Every one of 'em. Servants been in the families for years, I suppose?"

"Unto the third and fourth generations," said the chief bitterly.

His visitor considered the situation.

"I suppose they've got alibis fixed up for the nights of the crimes?" he enquired.

"Fixed up?" The chief's tone was eloquent. "The alibis are so good that we ought to be able to arrest 'em on suspicion alone. An alibi these days doesn't mean anything except that the fellow knows his job. Borringer does, too, and so does his wife. We've had them both on the carpet for hours without getting a glimmer from them. No, it's no use, Campion; we've got to spot the middleman and then the fence, and pin it on to them that way. Personally, I think the woman actually passes the stuff, but we've had Blower on her for weeks and he swears she doesn't speak to a soul except these superior clients of hers. Also, of course, neither of them post anything. We thought we'd got something once and got the postal authorities to help us, but all we got for our trouble was a p.c. to a viscountess about an appointment for chiropody."

Mr Campion was silent for some time.

"It was funny, her shouting out like that in the Hotel Monde," he said at last.

The chief grunted. "Mrs Gregory," he said. "Yes, I heard about that. A little show for Blower's benefit, if you ask me. Thought she'd give him something to think about. The Borringers are like that, cocky as hell."

Once again there was thoughtful silence in the light airy office and this time it was Stanislaus Oates who spoke first.

"Look here, Campion," he said, "you and I know one another. Let this be a word of friendly warning. If you suspect anyone you know of getting mixed up in this—for a bit of fun, perhaps—see that she's careful. If The Sparrow and his wife are still tied up with the Meyer lot, and they very well may be, the Meyer crowd aren't a pretty bunch. In fact, you know as well as I do, they're dirty and they're dangerous."

His visitor picked up the list again. Philip Graysby's aunt's name headed the second column. He made up his mind.

"I don't know anything," he said. "I'm speaking entirely from guesswork and I rely on you to go into this in stockinged feet and with your discretion wrapping you like a blanket. But if I were you I should have a little chat with one Henry Swan, employed by Florence, Dowager Countess of Marle."

"Ah," said the chief with relief, "that's where the wind blows, does it? I thought you'd come across."

"I don't promise anything," Campion protested.

"Who does?" said Stanislaus Oates and pulled a pad towards him. . . .

Mr Campion kept late hours. He was sitting up by the open window of his flat in Bottle Street, the cul-de-sac off Piccadilly, when the chief detective inspector called upon him just after midnight on the evening of his visit to Scotland Yard. The policeman was unusually fidgety. He accepted a drink and sat down before mentioning the purpose of his visit, which was, in fact, to gossip.

Campion, who knew him, let him take his time.

"We pulled that chap Swan in this afternoon," he volunteered at last. "He's a poor weedy little beggar who did a stretch for larceny in twenty-three and seems to have gone straight since. We had quite a time with him. He wouldn't open his mouth at first. Fainted when he thought we were going to jug him. Finally, of course, out it came, and a very funny story it was. Know anything about the White Elephant Society, Campion?"

His host blinked. "Nothing against it," he admitted. "Ordinary charity stunt. Very decently run, I believe. The dowager does it herself."

"I know." There was a note of mystification in the chief's voice. "See this?"

From his wallet he took a small green stick-on label. It was an ornate product embellished with a design of angels in the worst artistic taste. Across the top was a printed heading:

This is a gift from the White Elephant Society (Secy, Florence, Countess of Marle) and contains— A blank space had been filled up with the legend *Two Pairs of Fancy Woollen Gloves* in ink. The address, which was also in ink, was that of a well-known orphanage and the addressee was the matron.

"That's how they send the white elephants out," Oates explained. "There's a word or two inside in the countess's own handwriting. This is a specimen label. See what it means? It's as good as a diplomatic pass with that old woman's name on it."

"Who to?" demanded Mr Campion dubiously.

"Anyone," declared the chief triumphantly. "Especially the poor chap in the customs office who's tired of opening parcels. Even if he does open 'em he's not going to examine 'em. Now here's Swan's story. He admits he found the jewelry, which he passed on to a friend whose name he will not divulge. That friend must have sent it to you. It sounds like a woman to me but I'm not interested in her at the moment."

"Thank God for that," murmured his host devoutly. "Go on. Where did he find the stuff?"

"In a woollen duck inside one of these White Elephant parcels," said the chief unexpectedly. "We've got the duck; homemade toy with little chamois pockets under its wings. The odd thing is that Swan swears the old lady gave the parcel to him herself, told him to post it, and made such a fuss about it that he became suspicious and opened it up."

"Do you believe that?" Mr Campion was grinning and Oates frowned.

"I do," he said slowly. "Curiously enough I do, in the main. In the first place, this chap honestly wants to go straight. One dose of clink has put him in terror of it for life. Secondly, if he was in on the theft why give the whole game away? Why produce the duck? What I do think is that he recognised the address. He says he can't remember anything about it except that it was somewhere abroad, but that's just what he would say if he recognised it and thought it was dangerous and was keeping quiet for fear of reprisals. Anyway, I believed him sufficiently to go down and interview the old lady."

"Did you, by Jove!" murmured Mr Campion with respect.

Stanislaus Oates smiled wryly and ran his finger round the inside of his collar.

"Not a homely woman," he observed. "Ever met someone who made you feel you wanted a haircut, Campion? I was very careful, of course. Kid gloves all the way. Had to. I tell you one funny thing, though: she was rattled."

Mr Campion sat up. He knew his friend to be one of the soberest judges of humanity in the police force, where humanity is deeply studied.

"Sure?" he demanded incredulously.

"Take my dying oath on it," said the chief. "Scared blue, if you ask me."

The young man in the horn-rimmed spectacles made polite but depreciating noises. The chief shook his head.

"It's the truth. I gave her the facts—well, most of them. I didn't explain how we came to open the parcel, since that part of the business wasn't strictly orthodox. But I gave her the rest of the story just as I've given it to you, and instead of being helpful she tried to send me about my business with a flea in my ear. She insisted that she had directed each outgoing parcel during the last four weeks herself and swore that the Matisse woman could never have had access to any of them. Also, which is significant, she would not give me a definite reply about the duck. She was not sure if she'd ever seen it before. I ask you!—a badly made yellow duck in a blue pullover. Anyone'd know it again."

Mr Campion grinned. "What was the upshot of this embarrassing interview?" he enquired.

The chief coughed. "When she started talking about her son in the Upper House I came away," he said briefly. "I thought I'd let her rest for a day or two. Meanwhile, we shall keep a wary eye on Swan and the Borringers, although if those three are working together I'll resign."

He was silent for a moment.

"She certainly was rattled," he repeated at last. "I'd swear it. Under that magnificent manner of hers she was scared. She had that set look about the eyes. You can't mistake it. What d'you make of that, my lad?"

"I don't," said Campion discreetly. "It's absurd."

Oates sighed. "Of course it is," he agreed. "And so what?"

"Sleep on it," his host suggested and the chief took the hint. . . .

It was unfortunate for everyone concerned that Mr Campion should have gone into the country early the following morning on a purely personal matter concerning a horse which he was thinking of buying and should not have returned to his flat until the evening. When he did get back he found Juliet and the dark, good-looking Philip Graysby, with whom she had presumably made up her differences, waiting for him. To Mr Campion they both seemed very young and very distressed. Juliet appeared to have been crying and it was she who broke the news.

"It's Auntie Flo," she said in a small tragic voice. "She's bunked, Albert."

It took Mr Campion some seconds to assimilate this interesting development, and by that time young Graysby had launched into hurried explanations.

"That's putting it very crudely," he said. "My aunt caught the Paris plane this morning. Certainly she travelled alone, which was unusual, but that may not mean anything. Unfortunately, she did not leave an address, and although we've got into touch with the Crillon she doesn't seem to have arrived there."

He hesitated and his dark face became suddenly ingenuous.

"It's so ridiculously awkward, her going off like this without telling anyone just after Detective Inspector Oates called on her last night. I don't know what the interview was about, of course—nobody does—but there's an absurd feeling in the household that it wasn't very pleasant. Anyway, the inspector was very interested to hear that she had gone away when he called round this afternoon. It was embarrassing not being able to give him any real information about her return, and precious little about her departure. You see, we shouldn't have known she'd taken the plane if the chauffeur hadn't driven her to Croydon. She simply walked out of the house this morning and ordered the car. She didn't even take a suitcase, which looks as though she meant to come back tonight, and, of course, there's every possibility that she will."

Mr Campion perched himself on the table and his eyes were grave.

"Tell me," he said quietly, "had Lady Florence an appointment with her manicurist today?"

"Miss Matisse?" Juliet looked up. "Why, yes, she had, as a matter of fact. I went round there quite early this morning. Swan phoned me and told me Aunt had left rather hurriedly so I—er—I went to see him."

She shot an appealing glance at Philip, who grimaced at her, and she hurried on.

"While I was there Miss Matisse arrived and Bennett, Aunt's maid, told her all the gossip before I could stop her. Oh my dear, you don't think . . . ?"

Instead of replying Mr Campion reached for the telephone and dialled a famous Whitehall number. Chief Detective Inspector Oates was glad to hear his voice. He said so. He was also interested to know if Mr Campion had heard of the recent developments in The Sparrow case.

"No," he said in reply to Mr Campion's sharp question. "The two Borringers are behaving just as usual. Blower's had the girl under his eye all day. . . . No, she hasn't communicated with anyone. . . . What? . . . Wait a minute. I've got notes on Blower's telephoned report here. Here we are. 'On leaving the Dowager Countess of Marle's house Miss Matisse went to the Venetian Cinema in Regent Street for the luncheon programme.' Nothing happened there except that she pulled Blower's leg again."

"Did she shout to someone?" Mr Campion's tone was urgent.

"Yes. Called to a woman named Mattie, who she said she thought was in the circle. Same silly stunt as last time. What's the matter?"

Campion checked his exasperation. He was desperately in earnest and his face as he bent over the instrument was frighteningly grave.

"Oates," he said quietly, "I'm going to ring you again in ten minutes and then you've got to get busy. Remember our little talk about the Meyers? This may be life or death."

"Good . . ." began the chief and was cut off.

Mr Campion hustled his visitors out of the flat.

"We're going down to see Swan," he said, "and the quicker we get there the better."

Henry Swan proved to be a small frightened man who was inclined to be more than diffident until he had had matters explained to him very thoroughly. Then he was almost pathetically anxious to help.

"The address on the duck parcel, sir?" he said, echoing Mr Campion's question nervously. "I daren't tell the police that. It might have been more than my life was worth. But if you think her ladyship——"

"Let's have it," cut in Graysby irritably.

"Please," murmured Juliet.

Mr Swan came across. "Nineteen A, Rue Robespierre, Lyons, France," he blurted out. "I've burned the label but I remember the address. In fact, to tell you the truth, it was because of the address I opened the box in the first place. I never had such a fright in all me life, sir, really."

"I see. Who was the parcel sent to?" Mr Campion's manner was comfortingly reassuring.

Henry Swan hesitated. "Maurice Bonnet," he said at last, "and I once met a man who called himself that."

Mr Campion's eyes flickered. "On those occasions when he wasn't calling himself Meyer, I suppose?" he remarked.

The small man turned a shade or so paler and dropped his eyes.

"I shouldn't like to say, sir," he murmured.

"Very wise," Campion agreed. "But you've got nothing to worry about now. We've got the address and that's all that matters. You run along. Graysby, you and I have got to hurry. I'll just have a word with Oates on the phone and then we'll nip down to Croydon and charter a plane."

Juliet caught his arm. "You don't mean Philip's aunt might be in *danger?*" she said.

Mr Campion smiled down at her. "Some people do resent interference so, my dear," he said, "especially when they have quite a considerable amount to lose. . . ."

The Rue Robespierre is not in the most affluent quarter of Lyons and just before midnight on a warm spring evening it is not seen at its best. There silent figures loll in the dark doorways of houses which have come down in the world, and the night life has nothing to do with gaiety.

From Scotland Yard the wires had been busy and Campion and Graysby were not alone as they hurried down the centre of the wide street. A military little capitaine and four gendarmes accompanied them, but even so they were not overstaffed.

As their small company came to a stop before the crumbling façade of number nineteen A an upper window was thrown open and a shot spat down upon them. The capitaine drew his own gun and fired back, while the others put their shoulders to the door.

As they pitched into the dark musty hall a rain of fire met them from the staircase. A bullet took Mr Campion's hat from his head, and one of the gendarmes stepped back swearing, his left hand clasping a shattered right elbow.

The raiding party defended itself. For three minutes the darkness was streaked with fire, while the air became heavy with the smell of cordite.

The end came suddenly. There was a scream from the landing and a figure pitched over the balustrade onto the flags below, dragging another with it in its flight, while pattering footsteps flying up to the top story testified to the presence of a fugitive.

Mr Campion plunged forward, the others at his heels. They found Florence, Dowager Countess of Marle, at last in a locked bedroom on the third floor. She had defended herself and had suffered for it. Her black silk was torn and dusty and her coiffure dishevelled. But her spirit was unbroken and the French police listened to her tirade with a respect all the more remarkable since they could not understand one word of it.

Graysby took his aunt back to her hotel in a police car and Mr Campion remained to assist in the cleaning up.

Bertrand Meyer himself actually succeeded in getting out onto the roof, but he was brought back finally and the little capitaine had the satisfaction of putting the handcuffs on him.

One of the gang had been killed outright when his head had met the flagstones of the hall, and the remaining member was hurried off to a prison hospital with a broken thigh.

Mr Campion looked at Meyer with interest. He was an oldish man, square and powerful, with strong sensitive hands and the hot angry eyes of a fanatic. His workroom revealed many treasures. A jeweller's bench, exquisitely fitted with all the latest appliances, contained also a drawer which revealed the dismembered fragments of the proceeds of the first three London burglaries, together with some French stones in particular request by the Sûreté.

Campion looked round him. "Ah," he said with satisfaction, "and there's the wireless set. I wondered when some of you fellows were going to make use of the outside broadcasting programmes. How did you work it? Had someone listening to the first part of the first programme to be broadcast from a London public place each day, I suppose? It really is amazing how clearly those asides come, her voice quite fearless and yet so natural that it wasn't until some time afterwards that I realised she had been standing just below the orchestra's live microphone."

Meyer did not answer. His face was sullen and his eyes were fixed on the stones which the Frenchmen were turning out of little chamois leather bags onto the baize surface of the bench. . . .

It was some days later, back in the flat in Bottle Street, when Chief Detective Inspector Oates sipped a whisky and soda and beamed upon his friend.

"I take off my hat to the old girl," he said disrespectfully. "She's got courage and a great sense of justice. She says she'll go into the witness box if we need her and she apologised handsomely to me for taking the law into her own hands."

"Good," said Mr Campion. "You've got the Borringers, of course?"

The chief grinned. "We've got 'em as safe as a couple of ferrets in a box," he declared. "The man's an expert, but the woman's a genius. The story she told the old lady, for instance. That was more than brains. After she'd got her ladyship interested in her she broke down one day and told a pretty little yarn about her cruel husband in France who had framed a divorce and got the custody of the kid. She told a harrowing story about the little presents she had made for it herself and had had sent back to her pronto. It didn't take her long to get the old woman to offer to send them as though they'd come from the White Elephant Society. Every woman has a streak of sentimentality in her somewhere. So all the Borringer—alias Matisse—girl had to do was to bring along the toys in her manicure case from time to time and have 'em despatched free, gratis, with a label which almost guaranteed 'em a free pass. Very nice, eh?"

"Very," Campion agreed. "Almost simple."

The chief nodded. "She did it well," he said; "so well that even after I'd given the old lady the facts she didn't trust me. She believed so strongly in this fictitious kid that she went roaring over to Lyons to find out the truth for herself before she gave the girl away. Unfortunately, the Borringers had that means of wireless communication with Meyer and so when she arrived the gang was ready for her. It's a good thing you got there, Campion. They're a hot lot. I wonder what they'd have done with her."

"Neat," muttered Mr Campion. "That wireless stunt, I mean."

"It was." Oates was still impressed. "The use of the names made it sound so natural. What was the code exactly? Do you know?"

His host pulled a dictionary from a shelf at his side and turned over the leaves until he came to a small section at the end.

"It's childish," he said. "Funny how these people never do any inventing if they can help it. Look it all up."

The chief took the book and read the heading aloud.

"The More Common British Christian Names and Their Meanings."

He ran his eyes down the columns.

"Gregory," he read. *"A watcher.* Good Lord, that was to tell 'em Blower was on their track, I suppose. And Mattie . . . what's Mattie?"

He paused. *"Diminutive of Matilda,"* he said at last. *"Mighty Battle Maid.* I don't get that."

"Dangerous, indignant and female," translated Mr Campion. "It rather sums up Philip Graysby's Auntie Flo, don't you think?"

It was after the chief had gone and he was alone that Juliet phoned. She was jubilant and her clear voice bubbled over the wire.

"I can't thank you," she said. "I don't know what to say. Aunt Florence is perfectly marvellous about everything. And I say, Albert . . ."

"Yes?"

"Philip says we can keep Swan if we have him at the country house. We're going to be married quite soon, you know. Our reconciliation rather hurried things along. . . . Oh, what did you say?"

Mr Campion smiled. "I said I'll have to send you a wedding present then," he lied.

There was a fraction of silence at the other end of the wire.

"Well, darling . . . it would be just too terribly sweet if you really *wanted* to," said Miss Fysher-Sprigge.

REAR WINDOW

by William Irish (Cornell Woolrich)

I DIDN'T KNOW their names. I'd never heard their voices. I didn't even know them by sight, strictly speaking, for their faces were too small to fill in with identifiable features at that distance. Yet I could have constructed a time-table of their comings and goings, their daily habits and activities. They were the rear-window dwellers around me.

Sure, I suppose it *was* a little bit like prying, could even have been mistaken for the fevered concentration of a Peeping Tom. That wasn't my fault, that wasn't the idea. The idea was, my movements were strictly limited just around this time. I could get from the window to the bed, and from the bed to the window, and that was all. The bay window was about the best feature my rear bedroom had in the warm weather. It was unscreened, so I had to sit with the light out or I would have had every insect in the vicinity in on me. I couldn't sleep, because I was used to getting plenty of exercise. I'd never acquired the habit of reading books to ward off boredom, so I hadn't that to turn to. Well, what should I do, sit there with my eyes tightly shuttered?

Just to pick a few at random: Straight over, and the windows square, there was a young jitter-couple, kids in their teens, only just married. It would have killed them to stay home one night. They were always in such a hurry to go, wherever it was they went, they never remembered to turn out the lights. I don't think it missed once in all the time I was watching. But they never for-got altogether, either. I was to learn to call this delayed action, as you will see. He'd always come skittering madly back in about five minutes, probably from all the way down in the street, and rush around killing the switches. Then fall over something in the dark on his way out. They gave me an inward chuckle, those two.

The next house down, the windows already narrowed a little with perspec-tive. There was a certain light in that one that always went out each night too. Something about it, it used to make me a little sad. There was a woman living there with her child, a young widow I suppose. I'd see her put the child to bed, and then bend over and kiss her in a wistful sort of way. She'd shade the light off her and sit there painting her eyes and mouth. Then she'd go out. She'd never come back till the night was nearly spent. Once I was still up, and I looked and she was sitting there motionless with her head buried in her arms. Something about it, it used to make me a little sad.

The third one down no longer offered any insight, the windows were just slits like in a medieval battlement, due to foreshortening. That brings us around to the one on the end. In that one, frontal vision came back full-depth again, since it stood at right angles to the rest, my own included, sealing up the inner hollow all these houses backed on. I could see into it, from the rounded projection of my bay window, as freely as into a doll house with its rear wall sliced away. And scaled down to about the same size.

It was a flat building. Unlike all the rest it had been constructed originally as such, not just cut up into furnished rooms. It topped them by two stories and had rear fire escapes, to show for this distinction. But it was old, evidently hadn't shown a profit. It was in the process of being modernized. Instead of clearing the entire building while the work was going on, they were doing it a flat at a time, in order to lose as little rental income as possible. Of the six rearward flats it offered to view, the topmost one had already been completed, but not yet rented. They were working on the fifth-floor one now, disturbing the peace of everyone all up and down the "inside" of the block with their hammering and sawing.

I felt sorry for the couple in the flat below. I used to wonder how they stood it with that bedlam going on above their heads. To make it worse the wife was in chronic poor health, too; I could tell that even at a distance by the listless way she moved about over there, and remained in her bathrobe without dressing. Sometimes I'd see her sitting by the window, holding her head. I used to wonder why he didn't have a doctor in to look her over, but maybe they couldn't afford it. He seemed to be out of work. Often their bedroom light was on late at night behind the drawn shade, as though she were unwell and he was sitting up with her. And one night in particular he must have had to sit up with her all night, it remained on until nearly daybreak. Not that I sat watching all that time. But the light was still burning at three in the morning, when I finally transferred from chair to bed to see if I could get a little sleep myself. And when I failed to, and hopscotched back again around dawn, it was still peering wanly out behind the tan shade.

Moments later, with the first brightening of day, it suddenly dimmed around the edges of the shade, and then shortly afterward, not that one, but a shade in one of the other rooms—for all of them alike had been down—went up, and I saw him standing there looking out.

He was holding a cigarette in his hand. I couldn't see it, but I could tell it was that by the quick, nervous little jerks with which he kept putting his hand to his mouth, and the haze I saw rising around his head. Worried about her, I guess. I didn't blame him for that. Any husband would have been. She must have only just dropped off to sleep, after night-long suffering. And then in another hour or so, at the most, that sawing of wood and clattering of buckets was going to start in over them again. Well, it wasn't any of my business, I said to myself, but he really ought to get her out of there. If I had an ill wife on my hands. . . .

He was leaning slightly out, maybe an inch past the window frame, carefully scanning the back faces of all the houses abutting on the hollow square that lay before him. You can tell, even at a distance, when a person is looking fixedly. There's something about the way the head is held. And yet his scrutiny wasn't held fixedly to any one point, it was a slow, sweeping one, moving along the houses on the opposite side from me first. When it got to the end of them, I knew it would cross over to my side and come back along there. Before it did, I withdrew several yards inside my room, to let it go safely by. I didn't want him to think I was sitting there prying into his affairs. There was still enough blue night-shade in my room to keep my slight withdrawal from catching his eye.

When I returned to my original position a moment or two later, he was gone. He had raised two more of the shades. The bedroom one was still down. I wondered vaguely why he had given that peculiar, comprehensive, semicircular stare at all the rear windows around him. There wasn't anyone at any of them, at such an hour. It wasn't important, of course. It was just a little oddity, it failed to blend in with his being worried or disturbed about his wife. When you're worried or disturbed, that's an internal preoccupation, you stare vacantly at nothing at all. When you stare around you in a great sweeping arc at windows, that betrays external preoccupation, outward interest. One doesn't quite jibe with the other. To call such a discrepancy trifling is to add to its importance. Only someone like me, stewing in a vacuum of total idleness, would have noticed it at all.

The flat remained lifeless after that, as far as could be judged by its windows. He must have either gone out or gone to bed himself. Three of the shades remained at normal height, the one masking the bedroom remained down. Sam, my day houseman, came in not long after with my eggs and morning paper, and I had that to kill time with for awhile. I stopped thinking about other people's windows and staring at them.

The sun slanted down on one side of the hollow oblong all morning long, then it shifted over to the other side for the afternoon. Then it started to slip off both alike, and it was evening again—another day gone.

The lights started to come on around the quadrangle. Here and there a wall played back, like a sounding board, a snatch of radio program that was coming in too loud. If you listened carefully you could hear an occasional clink of dishes mixed in, faint, far off. The chain of little habits that were their lives unreeled themselves. They were all bound in them tighter than the tightest straitjacket any jailer ever devised, though they all thought themselves free. The jitterbugs made their nightly dash for the great open spaces, forgot their lights, he came careening back, thumbed them out, and their place was dark until the early morning hours. The woman put her child to bed, leaned mournfully over its cot, then sat down with heavy despair to redden her mouth.

In the fourth-floor flat at right angles to the long, interior "street" the three shades had remained up, and the fourth shade had remained at full length, all day long. I hadn't been conscious of that because I hadn't particularly been looking at it, or thinking of it, until now. My eyes may have rested on those windows at times, during the day, but my thoughts had been elsewhere. It was only when a light suddenly went up in the end room behind one of the raised shades, which was their kitchen, that I realized that the shades had been untouched like that all day. That also brought something else to my mind that hadn't been in it until now: I hadn't seen the woman all day. I hadn't seen any sign of life within those windows until now.

He'd come in from outside. The entrance was at the opposite side of their kitchen, away from the window. He'd left his hat on, so I knew he'd just come in from the outside.

He didn't remove his hat. As though there was no one there to remove it for any more. Instead, he pushed it farther to the back of his head by pronging a hand to the roots of his hair. That gesture didn't denote removal of perspiration, I knew. To do that a person makes a sidewise sweep—this was up over his forehead. It indicated some sort of harassment or uncertainty. Besides, if he'd been suffering from excess warmth, the first thing he would have done would be to take off his hat altogether.

She didn't come out to greet him. The first link, of the so-strong chain of habit, of custom, that binds us all, had snapped wide open.

She must be so ill she had remained in bed, in the room behind the lowered shade, all day. I watched. He remained where he was, two rooms away from there. Expectancy became surprise, surprise incomprehension. Funny, I thought, that he doesn't go in to her. Or at least go as far as the doorway, look in to see how she is.

Maybe she was asleep, and he didn't want to disturb her. Then immediately: but how can he know for sure that she's asleep, without at least looking in at her? He just came in himself.

He came forward and stood there by the window, as he had at dawn. Sam had carried out my tray quite some time before, and my lights were out. I held my ground, I knew he couldn't see me within the darkness of the bay window. He stood there motionless for several minutes. And now his attitude was the proper one for inner preoccupation. He stood there looking downward at nothing, lost in thought.

He's worried about her, I said to myself, as any man would be. It's the most natural thing in the world. Funny, though, he should leave her in the dark like that, without going near her. If he's worried, then why didn't he at least look in on her on returning? Here was another of those trivial discrepancies, between inward motivation and outward indication. And just as I was thinking that, the original one, that I had noted at daybreak, repeated itself. His head went up with renewed alertness, and I could see it start to give that slow circular sweep of interrogation around the panorama of rearward windows again. True, the light was behind him this time, but there was enough of it falling on him to show me the microscopic but continuous shift of direction his head made in the process. I remained carefully immobile until the distant glance had passed me safely by. Motion attracts.

Why is he so interested in other people's windows, I wondered detachedly. And of course an effective brake to dwelling on that thought too lingeringly clamped down almost at once: Look who's talking. What about you yourself?

An important difference escaped me. I wasn't worried about anything. He, presumably, was.

Down came the shades again. The lights stayed on behind their beige opaqueness. But behind the one that had remained down all along, the room remained dark.

Time went by. Hard to say how much—a quarter of an hour, twenty minutes. A cricket chirped in one of the back yards. Sam came in to see if I wanted anything before he went home for the night. I told him no, I didn't— it was all right, run along. He stood there for a minute, head down. Then I saw him shake it slightly, as if at something he didn't like. "What's the matter?" I asked.

"You know what that means? My old mammy told it to me, and she never told me a lie in her life. I never once seen it to miss, either."

"What, the cricket?"

"Any time you hear one of them things, that's a sign of death—someplace close around."

I swept the back of my hand at him. "Well, it isn't in here, so don't let it worry you."

He went out, muttering stubbornly: "It's somewhere close by, though. Somewhere not very far off. Got to be."

The door closed after him, and I stayed there alone in the dark.

It was a stifling night, much closer than the one before. I could hardly get a breath of air even by the open window at which I sat. I wondered how he— that unknown over there—could stand it behind those drawn shades.

Then suddenly, just as idle speculation about this whole matter was about to alight on some fixed point in my mind, crystallize into something like suspicion, up came the shades again, and off it flitted, as formless as ever and without having had a chance to come to rest on anything.

He was in the middle windows, the living room. He'd taken off his coat and shirt, was bare-armed in his undershirt. He hadn't been able to stand it himself, I guess—the sultriness.

I couldn't make out what he was doing at first. He seemed to be busy in a perpendicular, up-and-down way rather than lengthwise. He remained in one place, but he kept dipping down out of sight and then straightening up into view again, at irregular intervals. It was almost like some sort of calisthenic exercise, except that the dips and rises weren't evenly timed enough for that. Sometimes he'd stay down a long time, sometimes he'd bob right up again, sometimes he'd go down two or three times in rapid succession. There was some sort of a widespread black V railing him off from the window. Whatever it was, there was just a sliver of it showing above the upward inclination to which the window sill deflected my line of vision. All it did was strike off the bottom of his undershirt, to the extent of a sixteenth of an inch maybe. But I hadn't seen it there at other times, and I couldn't tell what it was.

Suddenly he left it for the first time since the shades had gone up, came out around it to the outside, stooped down into another part of the room, and straightened again with an armful of what looked like varicolored pennants at the distance at which I was. He went back behind the V and allowed them to fall across the top of it for a moment, and stay that way. He made one of his dips down out of sight and stayed that way a good while.

The "pennants" slung across the V kept changing color right in front of my eyes. I have very good sight. One moment they were white, the next red, the next blue.

Then I got it. They were a woman's dresses, and he was pulling them down to him one by one, taking the topmost one each time. Suddenly they were all gone, the V was black and bare again, and his torso had reappeared. I knew what it was now, and what he was doing. The dresses had told me. He confirmed it for me. He spread his arms to the ends of the V, I could see him heave and hitch, as if exerting pressure, and suddenly the V had folded up, become a cubed wedge. Then he made rolling motions with his whole upper body, and the wedge disappeared off to one side.

He'd been packing a trunk, packing his wife's things into a large upright trunk.

He reappeared at the kitchen window presently, stood still for a moment. I saw him draw his arm across his forehead, not once but several times, and then whip the end of it off into space. Sure, it was hot work for such a night. Then he reached up along the wall and took something down. Since it was the kitchen he was in, my imagination had to supply a cabinet and a bottle.

I could see the two or three quick passes his hand made to his mouth after that. I said to myself tolerantly: That's what nine men out of ten would do after packing a trunk—take a good stiff drink. And if the tenth didn't, it would only be because he didn't have any liquor at hand.

Then he came closer to the window again, and standing edgewise to the side of it, so that only a thin paring of his head and shoulder showed, peered watchfully out into the dark quadrilateral, along the line of windows, most of them unlighted by now, once more. He always started on the left-hand side, the side opposite mine, and made his circuit of inspection from there on around.

That was the second time in one evening I'd seen him do that. And once at daybreak, made three times altogether. I smiled mentally. You'd almost think he felt guilty about something. It was probably nothing, just an odd little habit, a quirk, that he didn't know he had himself. I had them myself, everyone does.

He withdrew into the room again, and it blacked out. His figure passed into the one that was still lighted next to it, the living room. That blacked next. It didn't surprise me that the third room, the bedroom with the drawn shade, didn't light up on his entering there. He wouldn't want to disturb her, of course—particularly if she was going away tomorrow for her health, as his packing of her trunk showed. She needed all the rest she could get, before making the trip. Simple enough for him to slip into bed in the dark.

It did surprise me, though, when a match-flare winked some time later, to have it still come from the darkened living room. He must be lying down in there, trying to sleep on a sofa or something for the night. He hadn't gone near the bedroom at all, was staying out of it altogether. That puzzled me, frankly. That was carrying solicitude almost too far.

Ten minutes or so later, there was another match-wink, still from that same living room window. He couldn't sleep.

The night brooded down on both of us alike, the curiosity-monger in the bay window, the chain-smoker in the fourth-floor flat, without giving any answer. The only sound was that interminable cricket.

I was back at the window again with the first sun of morning. Not because of him. My mattress was like a bed of hot coals. Sam found me there when he came in to get things ready for me. "You're going to be a wreck, Mr. Jeff," was all he said.

First, for awhile, there was no sign of life over there. Then suddenly I saw his head bob up from somewhere down out of sight in the living room, so I knew I'd been right; he'd spent the night on a sofa or easy chair in there. Now, of course, he'd look in at her, to see how she was, find out if she felt any better. That was only common ordinary humanity. He hadn't been near her, so far as I could make out, since two nights before.

He didn't. He dressed, and he went in the opposite direction, into the kitchen, and wolfed something in there, standing up and using both hands. Then he suddenly turned and moved off side, in the direction in which I knew the flat-entrance to be, as if he had just heard some summons, like the doorbell.

Sure enough, in a moment he came back, and there were two men with him in leather aprons. Expressmen. I saw him standing by while they laboriously maneuvered that cubed black wedge out between them, in the direction they'd just come from. He did more than just stand by. He practically hovered over them, kept shifting from side to side, he was so anxious to see that it was done right.

Then he came back alone, and I saw him swipe his arm across his head, as though it was he, not they, who was all heated up from the effort.

So he was forwarding her trunk, to wherever it was she was going. That was all.

He reached up along the wall again and took something down. He was taking another drink. Two. Three. I said to myself, a little at a loss: Yes, but he hasn't just packed a trunk this time. That trunk has been standing packed and ready since last night. Where does the hard work come in? The sweat and the need for a bracer?

Now, at last, after all those hours, he finally did go in to her. I saw his form pass through the living room and go beyond, into the bedroom. Up went the shade, that had been down all this time. Then he turned his head and looked around behind him. In a certain way, a way that was unmistakable, even from where I was. Not in one certain direction, as one looks at a person. But from side to side, and up and down, and all around, as one looks at—*an empty room*.

He stepped back, bent a little, gave a fling of his arms, and an unoccupied mattress and bedding upended over the foot of a bed, stayed that way, emptily curved. A second one followed a moment later.

She wasn't in there.

They use the expression "delayed action." I found out then what it meant. For two days a sort of formless uneasiness, a disembodied suspicion, I don't know what to call it, had been flitting and volplaning around in my mind, like an insect looking for a landing place. More than once, just as it had been ready to settle, some slight thing, some slight reassuring thing, such as the raising of the shades after they had been down unnaturally long, had been enough to keep it winging aimlessly, prevent it from staying still long enough for me to recognize it. The point of contact had been there all along, waiting to receive it. Now, for some reason, within a split second after he tossed over the empty mattresses, it landed—*zoom!* And the point of contact expanded—or exploded, whatever you care to call it—into a certainty of murder.

In other words, the rational part of my mind was far behind the instinctive, subconscious part. Delayed action. Now the one had caught up to the other. The thought-message that sparked from the synchronization was: He's done something to her!

I looked down and my hand was bunching the goods over my kneecap, it was knotted so tight. I forced it to open. I said to myself, steadyingly: Now wait a minute, be careful, go slow. You've seen nothing. You know nothing. You only have the negative proof that you don't see her any more.

Sam was standing there looking over at me from the pantry way. He said accusingly: "You ain't touched a thing. And your face looks like a sheet."

It felt like one. It had that needling feeling, when the blood has left it involuntarily. It was more to get him out of the way and give myself some elbow room for undisturbed thinking, than anything else, that I said: "Sam, what's the street address of that building down there? Don't stick your head too far out and gape at it."

"Somep'n or other Benedict Avenue." He scratched his neck helpfully.

"I know that. Chase around the corner a minute and get me the exact number on it, will you?"

"Why you want to know that for?" he asked as he turned to go.

"None of your business," I said with the good-natured firmness that was all that was necessary to take care of that once and for all. I called after him just as he was closing the door: "And while you're about it, step into the entrance and see if you can tell from the mailboxes who has the fourth-floor rear. Don't get me the wrong one now. And try not to let anyone catch you at it."

He went out mumbling something that sounded like, "When a man ain't got nothing to do but just sit all day, he sure can think up the blamest things——" The door closed and I settled down to some good constructive thinking.

I said to myself: What are you really building up this monstrous supposition on? Let's see what you've got. Only that there were several little things wrong with the mechanism, the chain-belt, of their recurrent daily habits over there. 1. The lights were on all night the first night. 2. He came in later than usual the second night. 3. He left his hat on. 4. She didn't come out to greet him— she hasn't appeared since the evening before the lights were on all night.

5. He took a drink after he finished packing her trunk. But he took three stiff drinks the next morning, immediately after her trunk went out. 6. He was inwardly disturbed and worried, yet superimposed upon this was an unnatural external concern about the surrounding rear windows that was off-key. 7. He slept in the living room, didn't go near the bedroom, during the night before the departure of the trunk.

Very well. If she had been ill that first night, and he had sent her away for her health, that automatically canceled out points 1, 2, 3, 4. It left points 5 and 6 totally unimportant and unincriminating. But when it came up against 7, it hit a stumbling block.

If she went away immediately after being ill that first night, why didn't he want to sleep in their bedroom *last night*? Sentiment? Hardly. Two perfectly good beds in one room, only a sofa or uncomfortable easy chair in the other. Why should he stay out of there if she was already gone? Just because he missed her, was lonely? A grown man doesn't act that way. All right, then she was still in there.

Sam came back parenthetically at this point and said: "That house is Number 525 Benedict Avenue. The fourth-floor rear, it got the name of Mr. and Mrs. Lars Thorwald up."

"Sh-h," I silenced, and motioned him backhand out of my ken.

"First he want it, then he don't," he grumbled philosophically, and retired to his duties.

I went ahead digging at it. But if she was still in there, in that bedroom last night, then she couldn't have gone away to the country, because I never saw her leave today. She could have left without my seeing her in the early hours of yesterday morning. I'd missed a few hours, been asleep. But this morning I had been up before he was himself, I only saw his head rear up from that sofa after I'd been at the window for some time.

To go at all she would have had to go yesterday morning. Then why had he left the bedroom shade down, left the mattresses undisturbed, until today? Above all, why had he stayed out of that room last night? That was evidence that she hadn't gone, was still in there. Then today, immediately after the trunk had been dispatched, he went in, pulled up the shade, tossed over the mattresses, and showed that she hadn't been in there. The thing was like a crazy spiral.

No, it wasn't either. *Immediately after the trunk had been dispatched—* The trunk.

That did it.

I looked around to make sure the door was safely closed between Sam and me. My hand hovered uncertainly over the telephone dial a minute. Boyne, he'd be the one to tell about it. He was on Homicide. He had been, anyway, when I'd last seen him. I didn't want to get a flock of strange dicks and cops into my hair. I didn't want to be involved any more than I had to. Or at all, if possible.

They switched my call to the right place after a couple of wrong tries, and I got him finally.

"Look, Boyne? This is Hal Jeffries——"

"Well, where've you been the last sixty-two years?" he started to enthuse.

"We can take that up later. What I want you to do now is take down a name and address. Ready? Lars Thorwald. Five twenty-five Benedict Avenue. Fourth-floor rear. Got it?"

"Fourth-floor rear. Got it. What's it for?"

"Investigation. I've got a firm belief you'll uncover a murder there if you start digging at it. Don't call on me for anything more than that—just a conviction. There's been a man and wife living there until now. Now there's just the man. Her trunk went out early this morning. If you can find someone who saw *her* leave herself——"

Marshaled aloud like that and conveyed to somebody else, a lieutenant of detectives above all, it did sound flimsy, even to me. He said hesitantly, "Well, but——" Then he accepted it as was. Because I was the source. I even left my window out of it completely. I could do that with him and get away with it because he'd known me years, he didn't question my reliability. I didn't want my room all cluttered up with dicks and cops taking turns nosing out of the window in this hot weather. Let them tackle it from the front.

"Well, we'll see what we see," he said. "I'll keep you posted."

I hung up and sat back to watch and wait events. I had a grandstand seat. Or rather a grandstand seat in reverse. I could only see from behind the scenes, but not from the front. I couldn't watch Boyne go to work. I could only see the results, when and if there were any.

Nothing happened for the next few hours. The police work that I knew must be going on was as invisible as police work should be. The figure in the fourth-floor windows over there remained in sight, alone and undisturbed. He didn't go out. He was restless, roamed from room to room without staying in one place very long, but he stayed in. Once I saw him eating again—sitting down this time—and once he shaved, and once he even tried to read the paper, but he didn't stay with it long.

Little unseen wheels were in motion around him. Small and harmless as yet, preliminaries. If he knew, I wondered to myself, would he remain there quiescent like that, or would he try to bolt out and flee? That mightn't depend so much upon his guilt as upon his sense of immunity, his feeling that he could outwit them. Of his guilt I myself was already convinced, or I wouldn't have taken the step I had.

At three my phone rang. Boyne calling back. "Jeffries? Well, I don't know. Can't you give me a little more than just a bald statement like that?"

"Why?" I fenced. "Why do I have to?"

"I've had a man over there making inquiries. I've just had his report. The building superintendent and several of the neighbors all agree she left for the country, to try and regain her health, early yesterday morning."

"Wait a minute. Did any of them *see* her leave, according to your man?"

"No."

"Then all you've gotten is a second-hand version of an unsupported statement by him. Not an eyewitness account."

"He was met returning from the depot, after he'd bought her ticket and seen her off on the train."

"That's still an unsupported statement, once removed."

"I've sent a man down there to the station to try and check with the ticket agent if possible. After all, he should have been fairly conspicuous at that early hour. And we're keeping him under observation, of course, in the meantime, watching all his movements. The first chance we get we're going to jump in and search the place."

I had a feeling that they wouldn't find anything, even if they did.

"Don't expect anything more from me. I've dropped it in your lap. I've given you all I have to give. A name, an address, and an opinion."

"Yes, and I've always valued your opinion highly before now, Jeff——"

"But now you, don't, that it?"

"Not at all. The thing is, we haven't turned up anything that seems to bear out your impression so far."

"You haven't gotten very far along, so far."

He went back to his previous cliché. "Well, we'll see what we see. Let you know later."

Another hour or so went by, and sunset came on. I saw him start to get ready to go out, over there. He put on his hat, put his hand in his pocket and stood still looking at it for a minute. Counting change, I guess. It gave me a peculiar sense of suppressed excitement, knowing they were going to come in the minute he left. I thought grimly, as I saw him take a last look around: If you've got anything to hide, brother, now's the time to hide it.

He left. A breath-holding interval of misleading emptiness descended on the flat. A three-alarm fire couldn't have pulled my eyes off those windows. Suddenly the door by which he had just left parted slightly and two men insinuated themselves, one behind the other. There they were now. They closed it behind them, separated at once, and got busy. One took the bedroom, one the kitchen, and they started to work their way toward one another again from those extremes of the flat. They were thorough. I could see them going over everything from top to bottom. They took the living room together. One cased one side, the other man the other.

They'd already finished before the warning caught them. I could tell that by the way they straightened up and stood facing one another frustratedly for a minute. Then both their heads turned sharply, as at a tip-off by doorbell that he was coming back. They got out fast.

I wasn't unduly disheartened, I'd expected that. My own feeling all along had been that they wouldn't find anything incriminating around. The trunk had gone.

He came in with a mountainous brown-paper bag sitting in the curve of one arm. I watched him closely to see if he'd discover that someone had been there in his absence. Apparently he didn't. They'd been adroit about it.

He stayed in the rest of the night. Sat tight, safe and sound. He did some desultory drinking, I could see him sitting there by the window and his hand would hoist every once in awhile, but not to excess. Apparently everything was under control, the tension had eased, now that—the trunk was out.

Watching him across the night, I speculated: Why doesn't he get out? If I'm right about him, and I am, why does he stick around—after it? That brought its own answer: Because he doesn't know anyone's on to him yet. He doesn't think there's any hurry. To go too soon, right after she has, would be more dangerous than to stay awhile.

The night wore on. I sat there waiting for Boyne's call. It came later than I thought it would. I picked the phone up in the dark. He was getting ready to go to bed, over there, now. He'd risen from where he'd been sitting drinking in the kitchen, and put the light out. He went into the living room, that. He started to pull his shirt-tail up out of his belt. Boyne's voice was in my ear as my eyes were on him, over there. Three-cornered arrangement.

"Hello, Jeff? Listen, absolutely nothing. We searched the place while he was out——"

I nearly said, "I know you did, I saw it," but checked myself in time.

"—and didn't turn up a thing. But——" He stopped as though this was going to be important. I waited impatiently for him to go ahead.

"Downstairs in his letter box we found a post card waiting for him. We fished it up out of the slot with bent pins——"

"And?"

"And it was from his wife, written only yesterday from some farm up-country. Here's the message we copied: 'Arrived O. K. Already feeling a little better. Love, Anna.'"

I said, faintly but stubbornly: "You say, written only yesterday. Have you proof of that? What was the postmark-date on it?"

He made a disgusted sound down in his tonsils. At me, not it. "The postmark was blurred. A corner of it got wet, and the ink smudged."

"All of it blurred?"

"The year-date," he admitted. "The hour and the month came out O. K. August. And seven thirty P.M., it was mailed at."

This time I made the disgusted sound, in my larynx. "August, seven thirty P.M.—1937 or 1939 or 1942. You have no proof how it got into that mail box, whether it came from a letter carrier's pouch or from the back of some bureau drawer!"

"Give up, Jeff," he said. "There's such a thing as going too far."

I don't know what I would have said. That is, if I hadn't happened to have my eyes on the Thorwald flat living room windows just then. Probably very little. The post card *had* shaken me, whether I admitted it or not. But I was looking over there. The light had gone out as soon as he'd taken his shirt off. But the bedroom didn't light up. A match-flare winked from the living room, low down, as from an easy chair or sofa. With two unused beds in the bedroom, he was *still staying out of there*.

"Boyne," I said in a glassy voice, "I don't care what post cards from the other world you've turned up, I say that man has done away with his wife!

Trace that trunk he shipped out. Open it up when you've located it—and I think you'll find her!"

And I hung up without waiting to hear what he was going to do about it. He didn't ring back, so I suspected he was going to give my suggestion a spin after all, in spite of his loudly proclaimed skepticism.

I stayed there by the window all night, keeping a sort of deathwatch. There were two more match-flares after the first, at about half-hour intervals. Nothing more after that. So possibly he was asleep over there. Possibly not. I had to sleep some time myself, and I finally succumbed in the flaming light of the early sun. Anything that he was going to do, he would have done under cover of darkness and not waited for broad daylight. There wouldn't be anything much to watch, for a while now. And what was there that he needed to do any more, anyway? Nothing, just sit tight and let a little disarming time slip by.

It seemed like five minutes later that Sam came over and touched me, but it was already high noon. I said irritably: "Didn't you lamp that note I pinned up, for you to let me sleep?"

He said: "Yeah, but it's your old friend Inspector Boyne. I figured you'd sure want to——"

It was a personal visit this time. Boyne came into the room behind him without waiting, and without much cordiality.

I said to get rid of Sam: "Go inside and smack a couple of eggs together."

Boyne began in a galvanized-iron voice: "Jeff, what do you mean by doing anything like this to me? I've made a fool out of myself, thanks to you. Sending my men out right and left on wild-goose chases. Thank God, I didn't put my foot in it any worse than I did, and have this guy picked up and brought in for questioning."

"Oh, then you don't think that's necessary?" I suggested, drily.

The look he gave me took care of that. "I'm not alone in the department, you know. There are men over me I'm accountable to for my actions. That looks great, don't it, sending one of my fellows one-half-a-day's train ride up into the sticks to some God-forsaken whistle-stop or other at departmental expense——"

"Then you located the trunk?"

"We traced it through the express agency," he said flintily.

"And you opened it?"

"We did better than that. We got in touch with the various farmhouses in the immediate locality, and Mrs. Thorwald came down to the junction in a produce-truck from one of them and opened it for him herself, with her own keys!"

Very few men have ever gotten a look from an old friend such as I got from him. At the door he said, stiff as a rifle barrel: "Just let's forget all about it, shall we? That's about the kindest thing either one of us can do for the other. You're not yourself, and I'm out a little of my own pocket money, time and temper. Let's let it go at that. If you want to telephone me in future I'll be glad to give you my home number."

The door went *whopp!* behind him.

For about ten minutes after he stormed out my numbed mind was in a sort of straitjacket. Then it started to wriggle its way free. The hell with the police. I can't prove it to them, maybe, but I can prove it to myself, one way or the other, once and for all. Either I'm wrong or I'm right. He's got his armor on against them. But his back is naked and unprotected against me.

I called Sam in. "Whatever became of that spyglass we used to have, when we were bumming around on that cabin-cruiser that season?"

He found it some place downstairs and came in with it, blowing on it and rubbing it along his sleeve. I let it lie idle in my lap first. I took a piece of paper and a pencil and wrote six words on it: *What have you done with her?*

I sealed it in an envelope and left the envelope blank. I said to Sam: "Now here's what I want you to do, and I want you to be slick about it. You take this, go in that building 525, climb the stairs to the fourth-floor rear, and ease it under the door. You're fast, at least you used to be. Let's see if you're fast enough to keep from being caught at it. Then when you get safely down again, give the outside doorbell a little poke, to attract attention."

His mouth started to open.

"And don't ask me any questions, you understand? I'm not fooling."

He went, and I got the spyglass ready.

I got him in the right focus after a minute or two. A face leaped up, and I was really seeing him for the first time. Dark-haired, but unmistakable Scandinavian ancestry. Looked like a sinewy customer, although he didn't run to much bulk.

About five minutes went by. His head turned sharply, profilewards. That was the bell-poke, right there. The note must be in already.

He gave me the back of his head as he went back toward the flat-door. The lens could follow him all the way to the rear, where my unaided eyes hadn't been able to before.

He opened the door first, missed seeing it, looked out on a level. He closed it. Then he dipped, straightened up. He had it. I could see him turning it this way and that.

He shifted in, away from the door, nearer the window. He thought danger lay near the door, safety away from it. He didn't know it was the other way around, the deeper into his own rooms he retreated the greater the danger.

He'd torn it open, he was reading it. God, how I watched his expression. My eyes clung to it like leeches. There was a sudden widening, a pulling—the whole skin of his face seemed to stretch back behind the ears, narrowing his eyes to Mongoloids. Shock. Panic. His hand pushed out and found the wall, and he braced himself with it. Then he went back toward the door again slowly. I could see him creeping up on it, stalking it as though it were something alive. He opened it so slenderly you couldn't see it at all, peered fearfully through the crack. Then he closed it, and he came back, zigzag, off balance from sheer reflex dismay. He toppled into a chair and snatched up a drink. Out of the bottle neck itself this time. And even while he was holding it to his lips, his head was turned looking over his shoulder at the door that had suddenly thrown his secret in his face.

I put the glass down.

Guilty! Guilty as all hell, and the police be damned!

My hand started toward the phone, came back again. What was the use? They wouldn't listen now any more than they had before. "You should have seen his face, etc." And I could hear Boyne's answer: "Anyone gets a jolt from an anonymous letter, true or false. You would yourself." They had a real live Mrs. Thorwald to show me—or thought they had. I'd have to show them the dead one, to prove that they both weren't one and the same. I, from my window, had to show them a body.

Well, he'd have to show me first.

It took hours before I got it. I kept pegging away at it, pegging away at it, while the afternoon wore away. Meanwhile he was pacing back and forth there like a caged panther. Two minds with but one thought, turned inside-out in my case. How to keep it hidden, how to see that it wasn't kept hidden.

I was afraid he might try to light out, but if he intended doing that he was going to wait until after dark, apparently, so I had a little time yet. Possibly he didn't want to himself, unless he was driven to it—still felt that it was more dangerous than to stay.

The customary sights and sounds around me went on unnoticed, while the main stream of my thoughts pounded like a torrent against that one obstacle stubbornly damming them up: how to get him to give the location away to me, so that I could give it away in turn to the police.

I was dimly conscious, I remember, of the landlord or somebody bringing in a prospective tenant to look at the sixth-floor apartment, the one that had already been finished. This was two over Thorwald's; they were still at work on the in-between one. At one point an odd little bit of synchronization, completely accidental of course, cropped up. Landlord and tenant both happened to be near the living room windows on the sixth at the same moment that Thorwald was near those on the fourth. Both parties moved onward simultaneously into the kitchen from there, and, passing the blind spot of the wall, appeared next at the kitchen windows. It was uncanny, they were almost like precision-strollers or puppets manipulated on one and the same string. It probably wouldn't have happened again just like that in another fifty years. Immediately afterwards they digressed, never to repeat themselves like that again.

The thing was, something about it had disturbed me. There had been some slight flaw or hitch to mar its smoothness. I tried for a moment or two to figure out what it had been, and couldn't. The landlord and tenant had gone now, and only Thorwald was in sight. My unaided memory wasn't enough to recapture it for me. My eyesight might have if it had been repeated, but it wasn't.

It sank into my subconscious, to ferment there like yeast, while I went back to the main problem at hand.

I got it finally. It was well after dark, but I finally hit on a way. It mightn't work, it was cumbersome and roundabout, but it was the only way I could think of. An alarmed turn of the head, a quick precautionary step in one certain direction, was all I needed. And to get this brief, flickering, transitory give-away, I needed two phone calls and an absence of about half an hour on his part between them.

I leafed a directory by matchlight until I'd found what I wanted: *Thorwald, Lars. 525 Bndct. . . . SWansea 5-2114.*

I blew out the match, picked up the phone in the dark. It was like television. I could see to the other end of my call, only not along the wire but by a direct channel of vision from window to window.

He said "Hullo?" gruffly.

I thought: How strange this is. I've been accusing him of murder for three days straight, and only now I'm hearing his voice for the first time.

I didn't try to disguise my own voice. After all, he'd never see me and I'd never see him. I said: "You got my note?"

He said guardedly: "Who is this?"

"Just somebody who happens to know."

He said craftily: "Know what?"

"Know what you know. You and I, we're the only ones."

He controlled himself well. I didn't hear a sound. But he didn't know he was open another way too. I had the glass balanced there at proper height on two large books on the sill. Through the window I saw him pull open the collar of his shirt as though its stricture was intolerable. Then he backed his hand over his eyes like you do when there's a light blinding you.

His voice came back firmly. "I don't know what you're talking about."

"Business, that's what I'm talking about. It should be worth something to me, shouldn't it? To keep it from going any further." I wanted to keep him from catching on that it was the windows. I still needed them, I needed them now more than ever. "You weren't very careful about your door the other night. Or maybe the draft swung it open a little."

That hit him where he lived. Even the stomach-heave reached me over the wire. "You didn't see anything. There wasn't anything to see."

"That's up to you. Why should I go to the police?" I coughed a little. "If it would pay me not to."

"Oh," he said. And there was relief of a sort in it. "D'you want to—see me? Is that it?"

"That would be the best way, wouldn't it? How much can you bring with you for now?"

"I've only got about seventy dollars around here."

"All right, then we can arrange the rest for later. Do you know where Lakeside Park is? I'm near there now. Suppose we make it there." That was about thirty minutes away. Fifteen there and fifteen back. "There's a little pavilion as you go in."

"How many of you are there?" he asked cautiously.

"Just me. It pays to keep things to yourself. That way you don't have to divvy up."

He seemed to like that too. "I'll take a run out," he said, "just to see what it's all about."

I watched him more closely than ever, after he'd hung up. He flitted straight through to the end room, the bedroom, that he didn't go near any more. He disappeared into a clothes-closet in there, stayed a minute, came out again. He must have taken something out of a hidden cranny or niche in there that even the dicks had missed. I could tell by the piston-like motion of his hand, just before it disappeared inside his coat, what it was. A gun.

It's a good thing, I thought, I'm not out there in Lakeside Park waiting for my seventy dollars.

The place blacked and he was on his way.

I called Sam in. "I want you to do something for me that's a little risky. In fact, damn risky. You might break a leg, or you might get shot, or you might even get pinched. We've been together ten years, and I wouldn't ask you anything like that if I could do it myself. But I can't, and it's got to be done." Then I told him. "Go out the back way, cross the back yard fences, and see if you can get into that fourth-floor flat up the fire escape. He's left one of the windows down a little from the top."

"What do you want me to look for?"

"Nothing." The police had been there already, so what was the good of that? "There are three rooms over there. I want you to disturb everything just a little bit, in all three, to show someone's been in there. Turn up the edge of each rug a little, shift every chair and table around a little, leave the closet doors standing out. Don't pass up a thing. Here, keep your eyes on this." I took off my own wrist watch, strapped it on him. "You've got twenty-five minutes, starting from now. If you stay within those twenty-five minutes, nothing will happen to you. When you see they're up, don't wait any longer, get out and get out fast."

"Climb back down?"

"No." He wouldn't remember, in his excitement, if he'd left the windows up or not. And I didn't want him to connect danger with the back of his place, but with the front. I wanted to keep my own window out of it. "Latch the window down tight, let yourself out the door, and beat it out of the building the front way, for your life!"

"I'm just an easy mark for you," he said ruefully, but he went.

He came out through our own basement door below me, and scrambled over the fences. If anyone had challenged him from one of the surrounding windows, I was going to backstop for him, explain I'd sent him down to look for something. But no one did. He made it pretty good for anyone his age. He isn't so young any more. Even the fire escape backing the flat, which was drawn up short, he managed to contact by standing up on something. He got in, lit the light, looked over at me. I motioned him to go ahead, not weaken.

I watched him at it. There wasn't any way I could protect him, now that he was in there. Even Thorwald would be within his rights in shooting him down—this was break and entry. I had to stay in back behind the scenes, like I had been all along. I couldn't get out in front of him as a lookout and shield him. Even the dicks had had a lookout posted.

He must have been tense, doing it. I was twice as tense, watching him do it. The twenty-five minutes took fifty to go by. Finally he came over to the window, latched it fast. The lights went, and he was out. He'd made it. I blew out a bellyful of breath that was twenty-five minutes old.

I heard him keying the street door, and when he came up I said warningly: "Leave the light out in here. Go and build yourself a great big two-story whisky punch; you're as close to white as you'll ever be."

Thorwald came back twenty-nine minutes after he'd left for Lakeside Park. A pretty slim margin to hang a man's life on. So now for the finale of the long-winded business, and here was hoping. I got my second phone call in before he had time to notice anything amiss. It was tricky timing but I'd been sitting there with the receiver ready in my hand, dialing the number over and over, then killing it each time. He came in on the 2 of 5–2114, and I saved that much time. The ring started before his hand came away from the light switch.

This was the one that was going to tell the story.

"You were supposed to bring money, not a gun; that's why I didn't show up." I saw the jolt that threw into him. The window still had to stay out of it. "I saw you tap the inside of your coat, where you had it, as you came out on the street." Maybe he hadn't, but he wouldn't remember by now whether he had or not. You usually do when you're packing a gun and aren't an habitual carrier.

"Too bad you had your trip out and back for nothing. I didn't waste my time while you were gone, though. I know more now than I knew before." This was the important part. I had the glass up and I was practically fluoroscoping him. "I've found out where—it is. You know what I mean. I know now where you've got—it. I was there while you were out."

Not a word. Just quick breathing.

"Don't you believe me? Look around. Put the receiver down and take a look for yourself. I found it."

He put it down, moved as far as the living room entrance, and touched off the lights. He just looked around him once, in a sweeping, all-embracing stare, that didn't come to a head on any one fixed point, didn't center at all.

He was smiling grimly when he came back to the phone. All he said, softly and with malignant satisfaction, was: "You're a liar."

Then I saw him lay the receiver down and take his hand off it. I hung up at my end.

The test had failed. And yet it hadn't. He hadn't given the location away as I'd hoped he would. And yet that "You're a liar" was a tacit admission that it was there to be found, somewhere around him, somewhere on those premises. In such a good place that he didn't have to worry about it, didn't even have to look to make sure.

So there was a kind of sterile victory in my defeat. But it wasn't worth a damn to me.

He was standing there with his back to me, and I couldn't see what he was doing. I knew the phone was somewhere in front of him, but I thought he was just standing there pensive behind it. His head was slightly lowered, that was all. I'd hung up at my end. I didn't even see his elbow move. And if his index finger did, I couldn't see it.

He stood like that a moment or two, then finally he moved aside. The lights went out over there; I lost him. He was careful not even to strike matches, like he sometimes did in the dark.

My mind no longer distracted by having him to look at, I turned to trying to recapture something else—that troublesome little hitch in synchronization that had occurred this afternoon, when the renting agent and he both moved simultaneously from one window to the next. The closest I could get was this: it was like when you're looking at someone through a pane of imperfect glass, and a flaw in the glass distorts the symmetry of the reflected image for a second, until it has gone on past that point. Yet that wouldn't do, that was not it. The windows had been open and there had been no glass between. And I hadn't been using the lens at the time.

My phone rang. Boyne, I supposed. It wouldn't be anyone else at this hour. Maybe, after reflecting on the way he'd jumped all over me— I said "Hello" unguardedly, in my own normal voice.

There wasn't any answer.

I said: "Hello? Hello? Hello?" I kept giving away samples of my voice. There wasn't a sound from first to last.

I hung up finally. It was still dark over there, I noticed.

Sam looked in to check out. He was a bit thick-tongued from his restorative drink. He said something about "Awri' if I go now?" I half heard him. I was trying to figure out another way of trapping *him* over there into giving away the right spot. I motioned my consent absently.

He went a little unsteadily down the stairs to the ground floor and after a delaying moment or two I heard the street door close after him. Poor Sam, he wasn't much used to liquor.

I was left alone in the house, one chair the limit of my freedom of movement.

Suddenly a light went on over there again, just momentarily, to go right out again afterwards. He must have needed it for something, to locate something that he had already been looking for and found he wasn't able to put his hands on readily without it. He found it, whatever it was, almost immediately, and moved back at once to put the lights out again. As he turned to do so, I saw him give a glance out the window. He didn't come to the window to do it, he just shot it out in passing.

Something about it struck me as different from any of the others I'd seen him give in all the time I'd been watching him. If you can qualify such an elusive thing as a glance, I would have termed it a glance with a purpose. It was certainly anything but vacant or random, it had a bright spark of fixity in it. It wasn't one of those precautionary sweeps I'd seen him give, either. It hadn't started over on the other side and worked its way around to my side, the right. It had hit dead-center at my bay window, for just a split second while it lasted, and then was gone again. And the lights were gone, and he was gone.

Sometimes your senses take things in without your mind translating them into their proper meaning. My eyes saw that look. My mind refused to smelter it properly. "It was meaningless," I thought. "An unintentional bull's-eye, that just happened to hit square over here, as he went toward the lights on his way out."

Delayed action. A wordless ring of the phone. To test a voice? A period of bated darkness following that, in which two could have played at the same game—stalking one another's window-squares, unseen. A last-moment flicker of the lights, that was bad strategy but unavoidable. A parting glance, radio-active with malignant intention. All these things sank in without fusing. My eyes did their job, it was my mind that didn't—or at least took its time about it.

Seconds went by in packages of sixty. It was very still around the familiar quadrangle formed by the back of the houses. Sort of a breathless stillness. And then a sound came into it, starting up from nowhere, nothing. The un-mistakable, spaced clicking a cricket makes in the silence of the night. I thought of Sam's superstition about them, that he claimed had never failed to fulfill itself yet. If that was the case, it looked bad for somebody in one of these slumbering houses around here——

Sam had been gone only about ten minutes. And now he was back again, he must have forgotten something. That drink was responsible. Maybe his hat, or maybe even the key to his own quarters uptown. He knew I couldn't come down and let him in, and he was trying to be quiet about it, thinking perhaps I'd dozed off. All I could hear was this faint jiggling down at the lock of the front door. It was one of those old-fashioned stoop houses, with an outer pair of storm doors that were allowed to swing free all night, and then a small vestibule, and then the inner door, worked by a simple iron key. The liquor had made his hand a little unreliable, although he'd had this dif-ficulty once or twice before, even without it. A match would have helped him find the keyhole quicker, but then, Sam doesn't smoke. I knew he wasn't likely to have one on him.

The sound had stopped now. He must have given up, gone away again, decided to let whatever it was go until tomorrow. He hadn't gotten in, because I knew his noisy way of letting doors coast shut by themselves too well, and there hadn't been any sound of that sort, that loose slap he always made.

Then suddenly it exploded. Why at this particular moment, I don't know. That was some mystery of the inner workings of my own mind. It flashed like waiting gunpowder which a spark has finally reached along a slow train. Drove all thoughts of Sam, and the front door, and this and that completely out of my head. It had been waiting there since midafternoon today, and only now—— More of that delayed action. Damn that delayed action.

The renting agent and Thorwald had both started even from the living room window. An intervening gap of blind wall, and both had reappeared at the kitchen window, still one above the other. But some sort of a hitch or flaw or jump had taken place, right there, that bothered me. The eye is a reliable surveyor. There wasn't anything the matter with their timing, it was with their parallel-ness, or whatever the word is. The hitch had been vertical, not horizontal. There had been an upward "jump."

Now I had it, now I knew. And it couldn't wait. It was too good. They wanted a body? Now I had one for them.

Sore or not, Boyne would *have* to listen to me now. I didn't waste any time, I dialed his precinct-house then and there in the dark, working the slots in my lap by memory alone. They didn't make much noise going around, just a light click. Not even as distinct as that cricket out there——

"He went home long ago," the desk sergeant said.

This couldn't wait. "All right, give me his home phone number."

He took a minute, came back again. "Trafalgar," he said. Then nothing more.

"Well? Trafalgar what?" Not a sound.

"Hello? Hello?" I tapped it. "Operator, I've been cut off. Give me that party again." I couldn't get her either.

I hadn't been cut off. My wire had been cut. That had been too sudden, right in the middle of—— And to be cut like that it would have to be done somewhere right here inside the house with me. Outside it went underground.

Delayed action. This time final, fatal, altogether too late. A voiceless ring of the phone. A direction-finder of a look from over there. "Sam" seemingly trying to get back in a while ago.

Surely, death was somewhere inside the house here with me. And I couldn't move, I couldn't get up out of this chair. Even if I had gotten through to Boyne just now, that would have been too late. There wasn't time enough now for one of those camera-finishes in this. I could have shouted out the window to that gallery of sleeping rear-window neighbors around me, I supposed. It would have brought them to the windows. It couldn't have brought them over here in time. By the time they had even figured which particular house it was coming from, it would stop again, be over with. I didn't open my mouth. Not because I was brave, but because it was so obviously useless.

He'd be up in a minute. He must be on the stairs now, although I couldn't hear him. Not even a creak. A creak would have been a relief, would have placed him. This was like being shut up in the dark with the silence of a gliding, coiling cobra somewhere around you.

There wasn't a weapon in the place with me. There were books there on the wall, in the dark, within reach. Me, who never read. The former owner's books. There was a bust of Rousseau or Montesquieu, I'd never been able to decide which, one of those gents with flowing manes, topping them. It was a monstrosity, bisque clay, but it too dated from before my occupancy.

I arched my middle upward from the chair seat and clawed desperately up at it. Twice my fingertips slipped off it, then at the third raking I got it to teeter, and the fourth brought it down into my lap, pushing me down into the chair. There was a steamer rug under me. I didn't need it around me in this weather, I'd been using it to soften the seat of the chair. I tugged it out from under and mantled it around me like an Indian brave's blanket. Then I squirmed far down in the chair, let my head and one shoulder dangle out over the arm, on the side next to the wall. I hoisted the bust to my other, upward shoulder, balanced it there precariously for a second head, blanket tucked around its ears. From the back, in the dark, it would look—I hoped——

I proceeded to breathe adenoidally, like someone in heavy upright sleep. It wasn't hard. My own breath was coming nearly that labored anyway, from tension.

He was good with knobs and hinges and things. I never heard the door open, and this one, unlike the one downstairs, was right behind me. A little eddy of air puffed through the dark at me. I could feel it because my scalp, the real one, was all wet at the roots of the hair right then.

If it was going to be a knife or head-blow, the dodge might give me a second chance, that was the most I could hope for, I knew. My arms and shoulders are hefty. I'd bring him down on me in a bear-hug after the first slash or drive, and break his neck or collarbone against me. If it was going to be a gun, he'd get me anyway in the end. A difference of a few seconds. He had a gun, I knew, that he was going to use on me in the open, over at Lakeside Park. I was hoping that here, indoors, in order to make his own escape more practicable——

Time was up.

The flash of the shot lit up the room for a second, it was so dark. Or at least the corners of it, like flickering, weak lightning. The bust bounced on my shoulder and disintegrated into chunks.

I thought he was jumping up and down on the floor for a minute with frustrated rage. Then when I saw him dart by me and lean over the window sill to look for a way out, the sound transferred itself rearwards and downwards, became a pummeling with hoof and hip at the street door. The camera-finish after all. But he still could have killed me five times.

I flung my body down into the narrow crevice between chair arm and wall, but my legs were still up, and so was my head and that one shoulder.

He whirled, fired at me so close that it was like looking a sunrise in the face. I didn't feel it, so—it hadn't hit.

"You——" I heard him grunt to himself. I think it was the last thing he said. The rest of his life was all action, not verbal.

He flung over the sill on one arm and dropped into the yard. Two-story drop. He made it because he missed the cement, landed on the sod-strip in the middle. I jacked myself up over the chair arm and flung myself bodily forward at the window, nearly hitting it chin first.

He went all right. When life depends on it, you go. He took the first fence, rolled over that bellywards. He went over the second like a cat, hands and feet pointed together in a spring. Then he was back in the rear yard of his own building. He got up on something, just about like Sam had—— The rest was all footwork, with quick little corkscrew twists at each landing stage.

Sam had latched his windows down when he was over there, but he'd re-opened one of them for ventilation on his return. His whole life depended now on that casual, unthinking little act——

Second, third. He was up to his own windows. He'd made it. Something went wrong. He veered out away from them in another pretzel-twist, flashed up toward the fifth, the one above. Something sparked in the darkness of one of his own windows where he'd been just now, and a shot thudded heavily out around the quadrangle-enclosure like a big bass drum.

He passed the fifth, the sixth, got up to the roof. He'd made it a second time. Gee, he loved life! The guys in his own windows couldn't get him, he was over them in a straight line and there was too much fire escape interlacing in the way.

I was too busy watching him to watch what was going on around me. Suddenly Boyne was next to me, sighting. I heard him mutter: "I almost hate to do this, he's got to fall so far."

He was balanced on the roof parapet up there, with a star right over his head. An unlucky star. He stayed a minute too long, trying to kill before he was killed. Or maybe he was killed, and knew it.

A shot cracked, high up against the sky, the window pane flew apart all over the two of us, and one of the books snapped right behind me.

Boyne didn't say anything more about hating to do it. My face was pressing outward against his arm. The recoil of his elbow jarred my teeth. I blew a clearing through the smoke to watch him go.

It was pretty horrible. He took a minute to show anything, standing up there on the parapet. Then he let his gun go, as if to say: "I won't need this any more." Then he went after it. He missed the fire escape entirely, came all the way down on the outside. He landed so far out he hit one of the projecting planks, down there out of sight. It bounced his body up, like a springboard. Then it landed again—for good. And that was all.

I said to Boyne: "I got it. I got it finally. The fifth-floor flat, the one over his, that they're still working on. The cement kitchen floor, raised above the level of the other rooms. They wanted to comply with the fire laws and also obtain a dropped living room effect, as cheaply as possible. Dig it up——"

He went right over then and there, down through the basement and over the fences, to save time. The electricity wasn't turned on yet in that one, they had to use their torches. It didn't take them long at that, once they'd got started. In about half an hour he came to the window and wigwagged over for my benefit. It meant yes.

He didn't come over until nearly eight in the morning; after they'd tidied up and taken them away. Both away, the hot dead and the cold dead. He said: "Jeff, I take it all back. That damn fool that I sent up there about the trunk—well, it wasn't his fault, in a way. I'm to blame. He didn't have orders to check on the woman's description, only on the contents of the trunk. He came back and touched on it in a general way. I go home and I'm in bed already, and suddenly pop! into my brain—one of the tenants I questioned two whole days ago had given us a few details and they didn't tally with his on several important points. Talk about being slow to catch on!"

"I've had that all the way through this damn thing," I admitted ruefully. "I call it delayed action. It nearly killed me."

"I'm a police officer and you're not."

"That how you happened to shine at the right time?"

"Sure. We came over to pick him up for questioning. I left them planted there when we saw he wasn't in, and came on over here by myself to square it up with you while we were waiting. How did you happen to hit on that cement floor?"

I told him about the freak synchronization. "The renting agent showed up taller at the kitchen window in proportion to Thorwald, than he had been a moment before when both were at the living room windows together. It was no secret that they were putting in cement floors, topped by a cork composition, and raising them considerable. But it took on new meaning. Since the top floor one has been finished for some time, it had to be the fifth. Here's the way I have it lined up, just in theory. She's been in ill health for years, and he's been out of work, and he got sick of that and of her both. Met this other——"

"She'll be here later today, they're bringing her down under arrest."

"He probably insured her for all he could get, and then started to poison her slowly, trying not to leave any trace. I imagine—and remember, this is pure conjecture—she caught him at it that night the light was on all night. Caught on in some way, or caught him in the act. He lost his head, and did the very thing he had wanted all along to avoid doing. Killed her by violence —strangulation or a blow. The rest had to be hastily improvised. He got a better break than he deserved at that. He thought of the apartment upstairs, went up and looked around. They'd just finished laying the floor, the cement hadn't hardened yet, and the materials were still around. He gouged a trough out of it just wide enough to take her body, put her in it, mixed fresh cement and recemented over her, possibly raising the general level of the flooring an inch or two so that she'd be safely covered. A permanent, odorless coffin. Next day the workmen came back, laid down the cork surfacing on top of it without noticing anything, I suppose he'd used one of their own trowels to smooth it. Then he sent his accessory upstate fast, near where his wife had been several summers before, but to a different farmhouse where she wouldn't be recognized, along with the trunk keys. Sent the trunk up after her, and dropped himself an already used post card into his mailbox, with the year-date blurred. In a week or two she would have probably committed 'suicide' up there as Mrs. Anna Thorwald. Despondency due to ill health. Written him a farewell note and left her clothes beside some body of deep water. It was risky, but they might have succeeded in collecting the insurance at that."

By nine Boyne and the rest had gone. I was still sitting there in the chair, too keyed up to sleep. Sam came in and said: "Here's Doc Preston."

He showed up rubbing his hands, in that way he has. "Guess we can take that cast off your leg now. You must be tired of sitting there all day doing nothing."

JOURNEY INTO FEAR

by Eric Ambler

THE STEAMER, *Sestri Levante*, stood high above the dock side, and the watery sleet, carried on the wind blustering down from the Black Sea, had drenched even the small shelter deck. In the after well the Turkish stevedores, with sacking tied round their shoulders, were still loading cargo.

Graham saw the steward carry his suit-case through a door marked PASSEGGIERI, and turned aside to see if the two men who had shaken hands with him at the foot of the gangway were still there. They had not come aboard lest the uniform of one of them should draw attention to him. Now they were walking away across the crane lines towards the warehouses and the dock gates beyond. As they reached the shelter of the first shed they looked back. He raised his left arm and saw an answering wave. They walked on out of sight.

For a moment he stood there shivering and staring out of the mist that shrouded the domes and spires of Stambul. Behind the rumble and clatter of the winches, the Turkish foreman was shouting plaintively in bad Italian to one of the ship's officers. Graham remembered that he had been told to go to his cabin and stay there until the ship sailed. He followed the steward through the door.

The man was waiting for him at the head of a short flight of stairs. There was no sign of any of the nine other passengers.

"*Cinque, signore?*"

"Yes."

"*Da queste parte.*"

Graham followed him below.

Number five was a small cabin with a single bunk, a combined wardrobe and washing cabinet, and only just enough floor space left over to take him and his suit-case. The porthole fittings were caked with verdigris, and there was a strong smell of paint. The steward manhandled the suit-case under the bunk, and squeezed out into the alley-way.

"*Favorisca di darmi il suo biglietto ed il suo passaporto, signore. Li portero al Commissario.*"

Graham gave him the ticket and passport, and, pointing to the porthole, made the motions of unscrewing and opening it.

The steward said, "*Subito, signore,*" and went away.

Graham sat down wearily on the bunk. It was the first time for nearly twenty-four hours that he had been left alone to think. He took his right hand carefully out of his overcoat pocket, and looked at the bandages swathed round it. It throbbed and ached abominably. If that was what a bullet graze felt like, he thanked his stars that the bullet had not really hit him.

He looked round the cabin, accepting his presence in it as he had accepted so many other absurdities since he had returned to his hotel in Pera the night before. The acceptance was unquestioning. He felt only as if he had lost something valuable. In fact, he had lost nothing of any value but a sliver of skin and cartilage from the back of his right hand. All that had happened to him was that he had discovered the fear of death.

By the husbands of his wife's friends, Graham was considered lucky. He had a highly paid job with a big armaments manufacturing concern, a pleasant house in the country an hour's drive from his office, and a wife whom everyone liked. Not that he didn't deserve it all. He was, though you would never think it to look at him, a brilliant engineer; quite an important one if some of the things you heard were true; something to do with guns. He went abroad a good deal on business. He was a quiet, likeable sort of chap, and generous with his whisky. You couldn't, of course, imagine yourself getting to know him very well (it was hard to say which was worse—his golf or his bridge), but he was always friendly. Nothing effusive; just friendly; a bit like an expensive dentist trying to take your mind off things. He looked rather like an expensive dentist, too, when you came to think of it: thin and slightly stooping, with well-cut clothes, a good smile, and hair going a bit grey. But if it was difficult to imagine a woman like Stephanie marrying him for anything except his salary, you had to admit that they got on extraordinarily well together. It only went to show . . .

Graham himself also thought that he was lucky. From his father, a diabetic school-master, he had inherited, at the age of seventeen, an easy-going disposition, five hundred pounds in cash from a life insurance policy, and a good mathematical brain. The first legacy had enabled him to endure without resentment the ministrations of a reluctant and cantankerous guardian; the second had made it possible for him to use the scholarship he had won to a university; the third resulted in his securing in his middle twenties a science doctorate. The subject of his thesis had been a problem in ballistics, and an abridged version of it had appeared in a technical journal. By the time he was thirty he was in charge of one of his employers' experimental departments, and a little surprised that he should be paid so much money for doing something that he liked doing. That same year he had married Stephanie.

It never occurred to him to doubt that his attitude towards his wife was that of any other man towards a wife to whom he has been married for ten years. He had married her because he had been tired of living in furnished rooms, and had assumed (correctly) that she had married him to get away from her father—a disagreeable and impecunious doctor. He was pleased by her good looks, her good humour, and her capacity for keeping servants and making friends, and if he sometimes found the friends tiresome, was inclined to blame himself rather than them. She, on her part, accepted the fact that he was more interested in his work than in anyone or anything else as a matter of course and without resentment. She liked her life exactly as it was. They lived in an atmosphere of good-natured affection and mutual tolerance, and thought their marriage as successful as one could reasonably expect a marriage to be.

The outbreak of war in September nineteen thirty-nine had little effect on the Graham household. Having spent the previous two years with the certain knowledge that such an outbreak was as inevitable as the going down of the sun, Graham was neither astonished nor dismayed when it occurred. He had calculated to a nicety its probable effects on his private life, and by October he was able to conclude that his calculations had been correct. For him, the war meant more work; but that was all. It touched neither his economic nor his personal security. He could not, under any circumstances, become liable for combatant military service. The chances of a German bomber unloading its cargo anywhere near either his house or his office were remote enough to be disregarded. When he learned, just three weeks after the signing of the Anglo-Turkish treaty of alliance, that he was to go to Turkey on company business, he was troubled only by the dismal prospect of spending Christmas away from home.

He had been thirty-two when he had made his first business trip abroad. It had been a success. His employers had discovered that, in addition to his technical ability, he had the faculty, unusual in a man with his particular qualifications, of making himself amiable to—and liked by—foreign government officials. In the years that followed, occasional trips abroad had become part of his working life. He enjoyed them. He liked the actual business of getting to a strange city almost as much as he liked discovering its strangeness. He liked meeting men of other nationalities, learning smatterings of their languages, and being appalled at his lack of understanding of both. He had acquired a wholesome dislike of the word "typical."

Towards the middle of November, he reached Istanbul, by train from Paris, and left it almost immediately for Izmir and, later, Gallipoli. By the end of December he had finished his work in those two places, and on the first of January took a train back to Istanbul, the starting point of his journey home.

He had had a trying six weeks. His job had been a difficult one made more difficult by his having to discuss highly technical subjects through interpreters. The horror of the Anatolian earthquake disaster had upset him nearly as much as it had upset his hosts. Finally, the train service from Gallipoli to Istanbul had been disorganized by floods. By the time he arrived back in Istanbul he was feeling tired and depressed.

He was met at the station by Kopeikin, the company's representative in Turkey.

Kopeikin had arrived in Istanbul with sixty-five thousand other Russian refugees in nineteen twenty-four, and had been, by turns, card-sharper, part owner of a brothel, and army clothing contractor before he had secured— the Managing Director alone knew how—the lucrative agency he now held. Graham liked him. He was a plump, exuberant man with large projecting ears, irrepressible high spirits, and a vast fund of low cunning.

He wrung Graham's hand enthusiastically. "Have you had a bad trip? I am so sorry. It is good to see you back again. How did you get on with Fethi?"

"Very well, I think. I imagined something much worse from your description of him."

"My dear fellow, you underrate your charm of manner. He is known to be difficult. But he is important. Now everything will go smoothly. But we will talk business over a drink. I have engaged a room for you—a room with a bath, at the Adler-Palace, as before. For to-night I have arranged a farewell dinner. The expense is mine."

"It's very good of you."

"A great pleasure, my dear fellow. Afterwards we will amuse ourselves a little. There is a box that is very popular at the moment—Le Jockey Cabaret. You will like it, I think. It is very nicely arranged, and the people who go there are quite nice. No riff-raff. Is this your luggage?"

Graham's heart sank. He had expected to have dinner with Kopeikin, but he had been promising himself that about ten o'clock he would have a hot bath and go to bed with a Tauchnitz detective story. The last thing he wanted to do was to "amuse" himself at Le Jockey Cabaret, or any other night place. He said, as they followed the porter out to Kopeikin's car: "I think that perhaps I ought to get to bed early to-night, Kopeikin. I've got four nights in a train in front of me."

"My dear fellow, it will do you good to be late. Besides, your train does not go until eleven to-morrow morning, and I have reserved a sleeper for you. You can sleep all the way to Paris if you feel tired."

Over dinner at the Pera Palace Hotel, Kopeikin gave war news. For him, the Soviets were still "the July assassins" of Nicholas the Second, and Graham heard much of Finnish victories and Russian defeats. The Germans had sunk more British ships and lost more submarines. The Dutch, the Danes, the Swedes and the Norwegians were looking to their defences. The world awaited a bloody spring. They went on to talk about the earthquake. It was half-past ten when Kopeikin announced that it was time for them to leave for Le Jockey Cabaret.

It was in the Beyoglu quarter; just off the Grande Rue de Pera, and in a street of buildings obviously designed by a French architect of the middle nineteen twenties. Kopeikin took his arm affectionately as they went in.

"It is a very nice place, this," he said. "Serge, the proprietor, is a friend of mine, so they will not cheat us. I will introduce you to him."

For the man he was, Graham's knowledge of the night life of cities was surprisingly extensive. For some reason, the nature of which he could never discover, his foreign hosts always seemed to consider that the only form of entertainment acceptable to an English engineer was that to be found in the rather less reputable *Nachtlokalen*. He had been in such places in Buenos Aires and in Madrid, in Valparaiso and in Bucharest, in Rome and in Mexico; and he could not remember one that was very much different from any of the others. He could remember the business acquaintances with whom he had sat far into the early morning hours drinking outrageously expensive drinks; but the places themselves had merged in his mind's eye into one prototypical picture of a smoke-filled basement room with a platform for the band at one end, a small space for dancing surrounded by tables, and a bar with stools, where the drinks were alleged to be cheaper, to one side.

He did not expect Le Jockey Cabaret to be any different. It was not.

The mural decorations seemed to have caught the spirit of the street outside. They consisted of a series of immense vorticisms involving sky-scrapers at camera angles, coloured saxophone players, green all-seeing eyes, telephones, Easter Island masks, and ash-blond hermaphrodites with long cigarette holders. The place was crowded and very noisy. Serge was a sharp-featured Russian with bristly grey hair and the air of one whose feelings were constantly on the point of getting the better of his judgment. To Graham, looking at his eyes, it seemed unlikely that they ever did: but he greeted them graciously enough, and showed them to a table beside the dance floor. Kopeikin ordered a bottle of brandy.

The band brought an American dance tune, which they had been playing with painful zeal, to an abrupt end and began, with more success, to play a rumba.

"It is very gay here," said Kopeikin. "Would you like to dance? There are plenty of girls. Say which you fancy and I will speak to Serge."

"Oh, don't bother. I really don't think I ought to stay long."

"You must stop thinking about your journey. Drink some more brandy and you will feel better." He got to his feet. "I shall dance now and find a nice girl for you."

Graham felt guilty. He should, he knew, be displaying more enthusiasm. Kopeikin was, after all, being extraordinarily kind. It could be no pleasure for him to try to entertain a train-weary Englishman who would have preferred to be in bed. He drank some more brandy determinedly. More people were arriving. He saw Serge greet them warmly and then, when their backs were turned, issue a furtive instruction to the waiter who was to serve them: a drab little reminder that Le Jockey Cabaret was in business neither for his own pleasure nor for theirs. He turned his head to watch Kopeikin dancing.

The girl was thin and dark and had large teeth. Her red satin evening dress drooped on her as if it had been made for a bigger woman. She smiled a great deal. Kopeikin held her slightly away from him and talked all the time they were dancing. To Graham, he seemed, despite the grossness of his body, to be the only man on the floor who was completely self-possessed.

He was the ex-brothel-proprietor dealing with something he understood perfectly. When the music stopped he brought the girl over to their table.

"This is Maria," he said. "She is an Arab. You would not think it to look at her, would you?"

"No, you wouldn't."

"She speaks a little French."

"*Enchanté, Mademoiselle.*"

"*Monsieur.*" Her voice was unexpectedly harsh, but her smile was pleasant. She was obviously good natured.

"Poor child!" Kopeikin's tone was that of a governess who hoped that her charge would not disgrace her before visitors. "She has only just recovered from a sore throat. But she is a very nice girl and has good manners. *Assieds-toi,* Maria."

She sat down beside Graham. "*Je prends du champagne,*" she said.

"*Oui, oui, mon enfant. Plus tard,*" said Kopeikin vaguely. "She gets extra commission if we order champagne," he remarked to Graham, and poured out some brandy for her.

She took it without comment, raised it to her lips, and said, "*Skål!*"

"She thinks you are a Swede," said Kopeikin.

"Why?"

"She likes Swedes, so I said you were a Swede." He chuckled. "You cannot say that the Turkish agent does nothing for the company."

She had been listening to them with an uncomprehending smile. Now, the music began again and, turning to Graham, she asked him if he would like to dance.

She danced well; well enough for him to feel that he, too, was dancing well. He felt less depressed and asked her to dance again. The second time she pressed her thin body hard against him. He saw a grubby shoulder strap begin to work its way out from under the red satin and smelt the heat of her body behind the scent she used. He found that he was getting tired of her.

She began to talk. Did he know Istanbul well? Had he been there before? Did he know Paris? And London? He was lucky. She had never been to those places. She hoped to go to them. And to Stockholm, too. Had he many friends in Istanbul? She asked because there was a gentleman who had come in just after him and his friend who seemed to know him. This gentleman kept looking at him.

Graham had been wondering how soon he could get away. He realised suddenly that she was waiting for him to say something. His mind had caught her last remark.

"Who keeps looking at me?"

"We cannot see him now. The gentleman is sitting at the bar."

"No doubt he's looking at you." There seemed nothing else to say.

But she was evidently serious. "It is in you that he is interested, Monsieur. It is the one with the handkerchief in his hand."

They had reached a point on the floor from which he could see the bar.

The man was sitting on a stool with a glass of vermouth in front of him.

He was a short, thin man with a stupid face: very bony with large nostrils, prominent cheekbones, and full lips pressed together as if he had sore gums or were trying to keep his temper. He was intensely pale and his small, deep-set eyes and thinning, curly hair seemed in consequence darker than they were. The hair was plastered in streaks across his skull. He wore a crumpled brown suit with lumpy padded shoulders, a soft shirt with an almost invisible collar, and a new grey tie. As Graham watched him he wiped his upper lip with the handkerchief as if the heat of the place were making him sweat.

"He doesn't seem to be looking at me now," Graham said. "Anyway, I don't know him, I'm afraid."

"I did not think so, Monsieur." She pressed his arm to her side with her elbow. "But I wished to be sure. I do not know him either, but I know the type. You are a stranger here, Monsieur, and you perhaps have money in your pocket. Istanbul is not like Stockholm. When such types look at you more than once, it is advisable to be careful. You are strong, but a knife in the back is the same for a strong man as for a small one."

Her solemnity was ludicrous. He laughed; but he looked again at the man by the bar. He was sipping at his vermouth; an inoffensive creature. The girl was probably trying, rather clumsily, to demonstrate that her own intentions were good.

He said: "I don't think that I need worry."

She relaxed the pressure on his arm. "Perhaps not, Monsieur." She seemed suddenly to lose interest in the subject. The band stopped and they returned to the table.

"She dances very nicely, doesn't she?" said Kopeikin.

"Very."

She smiled at them, sat down and finished her drink as if she were thirsty. Then she sat back. "We are three," she said and counted round with one finger to make sure they understood; "would you like me to bring a friend of mine to have a drink with us? She is very sympathetic. She is my greatest friend."

"Later, perhaps," said Kopeikin. He poured her out another drink.

At that moment, the band played a resounding "chord-on" and most of the lights went out. A spotlight quivered on the floor in front of the platform.

"The attractions," said Maria. "It is very good."

Serge stepped into the spotlight and pattered off a long announcement in Turkish which ended in a flourish of the hand towards a door beside the platform. Two dark young men in pale blue dinner jackets promptly dashed out on to the floor and proceeded to do an energetic tap dance. They were soon breathless and their hair became dishevelled, but the applause, when they had finished, was lukewarm. Then they put on false beards and, pretending to be old men, did some tumbling. The audience was only slightly more enthusiastic. They retired, rather angrily Graham thought, dripping with perspiration. They were followed by a handsome coloured woman with long thin legs who proved to be a contortionist. Her contortions were ingeniously obscene and evoked gusts of laughter. In response to shouts, she followed her contortions with a snake dance. This was not so successful, as the snake, produced from a gilt wicker crate as cautiously as if it had been a fully grown anaconda, proved to be a small and rather senile python with a tendency to fall asleep in its mistress's hands. It was finally bundled back into its crate while she did some more contortions. When she had gone, the proprietor stepped once more into the spotlight and made an announcement that was greeted with clapping.

The girl put her lips to Graham's ear. "It is Josette and her partner, José. They are dancers from Paris. This is their last night here. They have had a great success."

The spotlight became pink and swept to the entrance door. There was a roll of drums. Then, as the band struck up the Blue Danube waltz, the dancers glided on to the floor.

For the weary Graham, their dance was as much a part of the cellar convention as the bar and the platform for the band: it was something to justify the prices of the drinks: a demonstration of the fact that, by applying the laws of classical mechanics, one small, unhealthy looking man with a broad sash round his waist could handle an eight stone woman as if she were a child. Josette and her partner were remarkable only in that, although they carried out the standard "specialty" routine rather less efficiently than usual, they managed to do so with considerably more effect.

She was a slim woman with beautiful arms and shoulders and a mass of gleaming fair hair. Her heavily lidded eyes, almost closed as she danced, and the rather full lips, fixed in a theatrical half-smile, contradicted in a curious way the swift neatness of her movements. Graham saw that she was not a dancer but a woman who had been trained to dance and who did so with a sort of indolent sensuality, conscious of her young-looking body, her long legs, and the muscles below the smooth surfaces of her thighs and stomach. If her performance did not succeed as a dance, as an *attraction* at Le Jockey Cabaret it succeeded perfectly and in spite of her partner.

He was a dark, preoccupied man with tight, disagreeable lips, a smooth sallow face, and an irritating way of sticking his tongue hard in his cheek as he prepared to exert himself. He moved badly and was clumsy, his fingers shifting uncertainly as he grasped her for the lifts as if he were uncertain of the point of balance. He was constantly steadying himself.

But the audience was not looking at him, and when they had finished called loudly for an encore. It was given. The band played another "chord-on." Mademoiselle Josette took a bow and was presented with a bouquet of flowers by Serge. She returned several times and bowed and kissed her hand.

"She is quite charming, isn't she?" Kopeikin said in English as the lights went up. "I promised you that this place was amusing."

"She's quite good. But it's a pity about the moth-eaten Valentino."

"José? He does well for himself. Would you like to have her to the table for a drink?"

"Very much. But won't it be rather expensive?"

"Gracious no! She does not get commission."

"Will she come?"

"Of course. The *patron* introduced me. I know her well. You might take to her, I think. This Arab is a little stupid. No doubt Josette is stupid, too; but she is very attractive in her way. If I had not learned too much when I was too young, I should like her myself."

Maria stared after him as he went across the floor, and remained silent for a moment. Then she said: "He is very good, that friend of yours."

Graham was not quite sure whether it was a statement, a question, or a feeble attempt to make conversation. He nodded. "Very good."

She smiled. "He knows the proprietor well. If you desire it, he will ask Serge to let me go when you wish instead of when the place closes."

He smiled as regretfully as he could. "I'm afraid, Maria, that I have to pack my luggage and catch a train in the morning."

She smiled again. "It does not matter. But I specially like the Swedes. May I have some more brandy, Monsieur?"

"Of course." He refilled her glass.

She drank half of it. "Do you like Mademoiselle Josette?"

"She dances very well."

"She is very sympathetic. That is because she has a success. When people have a success they are sympathetic. José, nobody likes. He is a Spaniard from Morocco, and very jealous. They are all the same. I do not know how she stands him."

"I thought you said they were Parisians."

"They have danced in Paris. She is from Hungary. She speaks languages —German, Spanish, English—but not Swedish, I think. She has had many rich lovers." She paused. "Are you a business man, Monsieur?"

"No, an engineer." He realised, with some amusement, that Maria was less stupid than she seemed, and that she knew exactly why Kopeikin had left them. He was being warned, indirectly but unmistakably, that Mademoiselle Josette was very expensive, that communication with her would be difficult, and that he would have a jealous Spaniard to deal with.

She drained her glass again, and stared vaguely in the direction of the bar. "My friend is looking very lonely," she said. She turned her head and looked directly at him. "Will you give me a hundred piastres, Monsieur?"

"What for?"

"A tip, Monsieur." She smiled, but in not quite so friendly a fashion as before.

He gave her a hundred piastre note. She folded it up, put it in her bag, and stood up. "Will you excuse me, please? I wish to speak to my friend. I will come back if you wish." She smiled.

He saw her red satin dress disappear in the crowd gathered round the bar. Kopeikin returned almost immediately.

"Where is the Arab?"

"She's gone to speak to her best friend. I gave her a hundred piastres."

"A hundred! Fifty would have been plenty. But perhaps it is as well. Josette asks us to have a drink with her in her dressing-room. She is leaving Istanbul to-morrow, and does not wish to come out here. She will have to speak to so many people, and she has packing to do."

"Shan't we be rather a nuisance?"

"My dear fellow, she is anxious to meet you. She saw you while she was dancing. When I told her that you were an Englishman, she was delighted. We can leave these drinks here."

Mademoiselle Josette's dressing-room was a space about eight feet square, partitioned off from the other half of what appeared to be the proprietor's office by a brown curtain. The three solid walls were covered with faded pink wall-paper with stripes of blue: there were greasy patches here and there where people had leaned against them. The room contained two bent-wood chairs and two rickety dressing tables littered with cream jars and dirty make-up towels. There was a mixed smell of stale cigarette smoke, face powder, and damp upholstery.

As they went in in response to a grunt of "*Entrez*" from the partner, José, he got up from his dressing table. Still wiping the grease paint from his face, he walked out without a glance at them. For some reason, Kopeikin winked at Graham. Josette was leaning forward in her chair dabbing intently at one of her eyebrows with a swab of damp cotton-wool. She had discarded her costume, and put on a rose velvet house-coat. Her hair hung down loosely about her head as if she had shaken it out and brushed it. It was really, Graham thought, very beautiful hair. She began to speak in slow, careful English, punctuating the words with dabs.

"Please excuse me. It is this filthy paint. It . . . *Merde!*"

She threw the swab down impatiently, stood up suddenly, and turned to face them.

In the hard light of the unshaded bulb above her head she looked smaller than she had looked on the dance floor; and a trifle haggard. Graham, thinking of his Stephanie's rather buxom good looks, reflected that the woman before him would probably be quite plain in ten years' time. He was in the habit of comparing other women with his wife. As a method of disguising from himself the fact that other women still interested him, it was usually effective. But Josette was unusual. What she might look like in ten years' time was altogether beside the point. At that moment she was a very attractive, self-possessed woman with a soft, smiling mouth, slightly protuberant blue eyes, and a sleepy vitality that seemed to fill the room.

"This, my dear Josette," said Kopeikin, "is Mr. Graham."

"I enjoyed your dancing very much, Mademoiselle," he said.

"So Kopeikin told me." She shrugged. "It could be better, I think, but it is very good of you to say that you like it. It is nonsense to say that Englishmen are not polite." She flourished her hand round the room. "I do not like to ask you to sit down in this filth, but please try to make yourself comfortable.

There is José's chair for Kopeikin, and if you could push José's things away, the corner of his table will be for you. It is too bad that we cannot sit together in comfort outside, but there are so many of these men who make some *chichi* if one does not stop and drink some of their champagne. The champagne here is filthy. I do not wish to leave Istanbul with a headache. How long do you stay here, Mr. Graham?"

"I, too, leave to-morrow." She amused him. Her posturing was absurd. Within the space of a minute she had been a great actress receiving wealthy suitors, a friendly woman of the world, and a disillusioned genius of the dance. Every movement, every piece of affectation was calculated: it was as if she were still dancing.

Now she became a serious student of affairs. "It is terrible, this travelling. And you go back to your war. I am sorry. These filthy Nazis. It is such a pity that there must be wars. And if it is not wars, it is earthquakes. Always death. It is so bad for business. I am not interested in death. Kopeikin is, I think. Perhaps it is because he is a Russian."

"I think nothing of death," said Kopeikin. "I am concerned only that the waiter shall bring the drinks I ordered. Will you have a cigarette?"

"Please, yes. The waiters here are filthy. There must be much better places than this in London, Mr. Graham."

"The waiters there are very bad, too. Waiters are, I think, mostly very bad. But I should have thought you had been to London. Your English . . ."

Her smile tolerated his indiscretion, the depths of which he could not know. As well to have asked the Pompadour who paid her bills. "I learned it from an American and in Italy. I have a great sympathy for Americans. They are so clever in business, and yet so generous and sincere. I think it is most important to be sincere. Was it amusing dancing with that little Maria, Mr. Graham?"

"She dances very well. She seems to admire you very much. She says that you have a great success. You do, of course."

"A great success! Here?" The disillusioned genius raised her eyebrows. "I hope you gave her a good tip, Mr. Graham."

"He gave her twice as much as was necessary," said Kopeikin. "Ah, here are the drinks!"

They talked for a time about people whom Graham did not know, and about the war. He saw that behind her posturing she was quick and shrewd, and wondered if the American in Italy had ever regretted his "sincerity." After a while Kopeikin raised his glass.

"I drink," he said pompously, "to your two journeys." He lowered his glass suddenly without drinking. "No, it is absurd," he said, irritably. "My heart is not in the toast. I cannot help thinking that it is a pity that there should be two journeys. You are both going to Paris. You are both friends of mine, and so you have"—he patted his stomach—"much in common."

Graham smiled, trying not to look startled. She was certainly very attractive, and it was pleasant to sit facing her as he was; but the idea that the acquaintance might be extended had simply not occurred to him. He was confused by it. He saw that she was watching him with amusement in her eyes, and had an uncomfortable feeling that she knew exactly what was passing through his mind.

He put the best face on the situation that he could. "I was hoping to suggest the same thing. I think you should have left me to suggest it, Kopeikin. Mademoiselle will wonder if I am as sincere as an American." He smiled at her. "I am leaving by the eleven o'clock train."

"And in the first class, Mr. Graham?"

"Yes."

She put out her cigarette. "Then there are two obvious reasons why we cannot travel together. I am not leaving by that train and, in any case, I travel in the second class. It is perhaps just as well. José would wish to play cards with you all the way, and you would lose your money."

There was no doubt that she expected them to finish their drinks and go. Graham felt oddly disappointed. He would have liked to stay. He knew, besides, that he had behaved awkwardly.

"Perhaps," he said, "we could meet in Paris."

"Perhaps." She stood up and smiled kindly at him. "I shall stay at the Hotel des Belges near Trinité, if it is still open. I shall hope to meet you again. Kopeikin tells me that as an engineer you are very well known."

"Kopeikin exaggerates—just as he exaggerated when he said that we should not hinder you and your partner in your packing. I hope you have a pleasant journey."

"It has been so good to meet you. It was so kind of you, Kopeikin, to bring Mr. Graham to see me."

"It was his idea," said Kopeikin. "Good-bye, my dear Josette, and *bon voyage*. We should like to stay, but it is late, and I insisted on Mr. Graham's getting some sleep. He would stay talking until he missed the train if I permitted it."

She laughed. "You are very nice, Kopeikin. When I come next to Istanbul, I shall tell you first. *Au 'voir*, Mr. Graham, and *bon voyage*." She held out her hand.

"The Hotel des Belges near Trinité," he said: "I shall remember." He spoke very little less than the truth. During the ten minutes that his taxi would take to get from the Gare de l'Est to the Gare St. Lazare, he probably would remember.

She pressed his fingers gently. "I'm sure you will," she said. "*Au 'voir*, Kopeikin. You know the way?"

"I think," said Kopeikin, as they waited for their bill, "I think that I am a little disappointed in you, my dear fellow. You made an excellent impression. She was yours for the asking. You had only to ask her the time of her train."

"I am quite sure that I made no impression at all. Frankly, she embarrassed me. I don't understand women of that sort."

"That sort of woman, as you put it, likes a man who is embarrassed by her. Your diffidence was charming."

"Heavens! Anyway, I said that I would see her in Paris."

"My dear fellow, she knows perfectly well that you have not the smallest intention of seeing her in Paris. It is a pity. She is, I know, quite particular. You were lucky, and you chose to ignore the fact."

"Good gracious, man, you seem to forget that I'm a married man!"

Kopeikin threw up his hands. "The English point of view! One cannot reason; one can only stand amazed." He sighed profoundly. "Here comes the bill."

On their way out they passed Maria sitting at the bar with her best friend, a mournful-looking Turkish girl. They received a smile. Graham noticed that the man in the crumpled brown suit had gone.

It was cold in the street. A wind was beginning to moan through the telephone wires bracketed on the wall. At three o'clock in the morning the city of Sulyman the Magnificent was like a railway station after the last train had gone.

"We shall be having snow," said Kopeikin. "Your hotel is quite near. We will walk if you like. It is to be hoped," he went on as they began to walk, "that you will miss the snow on your journey. Last year there was a Simplon Orient express delayed for three days near Salonika."

"I shall take a bottle of brandy with me."

Kopeikin grunted. "Still, I do not envy you the journey. I think perhaps I am getting old. Besides, travelling at this time . . ."

"Oh, I'm a good traveller. I don't get bored easily."

"I was not thinking of boredom. So many unpleasant things can happen in war time."

"I suppose so."

Kopeikin buttoned up his overcoat collar. "To give you only one example . . .

"During the last war an Austrian friend of mine was returning to Berlin from Zürich, where he had been doing some business. He sat in the train with a man who said that he was a Swiss from Lugano. They talked a lot on the journey. This Swiss told my friend about his wife and his children, his business, and his home. He seemed a very nice man. But soon after they had crossed the frontier, the train stopped at a small station and soldiers came on with police. They arrested the Swiss. My friend had also to leave the train as he was with the Swiss. He was not alarmed. His papers were in order. He was a good Austrian. But the man from Lugano was terrified. He turned very pale and cried like a child. They told my friend afterwards that the man was not a Swiss but an Italian spy and that he would be shot. My friend was upset. You see, one can always tell when a man is speaking about something he loves, and there was no doubt that all that this man had said about his wife and children was true: all except one thing—they were in Italy instead of Switzerland. War," he added solemnly, "is unpleasant."

"Quite so." They had stopped outside the Adler-Palace Hotel. "Will you come in for a drink?"

Kopeikin shook his head. "It is kind of you to suggest it, but you must get some sleep. I feel guilty now at having kept you out so late, but I have enjoyed our evening together."

"So have I. I'm very grateful to you."

"A great pleasure. No farewells now. I shall take you to the station in the morning. Can you be ready by ten?"

"Easily."

"Then good night, my dear fellow."

"Good night, Kopeikin."

Graham went inside, stopped at the hall porter's desk for his key and to tell the night porter to call him at eight. Then, as the power for the lift was switched off at night, he climbed wearily up the stairs to his room on the second floor.

It was at the end of the corridor. He put the key in the lock, turned it, pushed the door open and, with his right hand, felt along the wall for the light switch.

The next moment there was a splinter of flame in the darkness and an ear-splitting detonation. A piece of plaster from the wall beside him stung his cheek. Before he could move or even think, the flame and the noise came again and it seemed as if a bar of white-hot metal had been suddenly pressed against the back of his hand. He cried out with pain and stumbled forward out of the light from the corridor into the darkness of the room. Another shot scattered plaster behind him.

There was silence. He was half leaning, half crouching against the wall by the bed, his ears singing from the din of the explosions. He was dimly aware that the window was open and that someone was moving by it. His hand seemed to be numb, but he could feel blood beginning to trickle between his fingers.

He remained motionless, his heart hammering at his head. The air reeked of cordite fumes. Then, as his eyes became used to the darkness, he saw that whoever had been at the window had left by it.

There would, he knew, be another light switch beside the bed. With his left hand he fumbled along the wall towards it. Then his hand touched the telephone. Hardly knowing what he was doing, he picked it up.

He heard a click as the night porter plugged in at the switchboard.

"Room thirty-six," he said and was surprised to find that he was shouting. "Something has happened. I need help."

He put the telephone down, blundered towards the bathroom and switched on the light there. The blood was pouring from a great gash across the back of his hand. Through the waves of nausea flowing from his stomach to his head, he could hear doors being flung open and excited voices in the corridor. Someone started hammering at the door.

THE STEVEDORES had finished loading and were battening down. One winch was still working but it was hoisting the steel bearers into place. The bulk-head against which Graham was leaning vibrated as they thudded into their sockets. Another passenger had come aboard and the steward had shown him to a cabin farther along the alley-way. The newcomer had a low, grumbling voice and had addressed the steward in hesitant Italian.

Graham stood up and with his unbandaged hand fumbled in his pocket for a cigarette. He was beginning to find the cabin oppressive. He looked at his watch. The ship would not be sailing for another hour. He wished he had asked Kopeikin to come aboard with him. He tried to think of his wife in England, to picture her sitting with her friends having tea; but it was as if someone behind him were holding a stereoscope to his mind's eyes; someone who was steadily sliding picture after picture between him and the rest of his life to cut him off from it; pictures of Kopeikin and Le Jockey Cabaret, of Maria and the man in the crumpled suit, of Josette and her partner, of stabbing flames in a sea of darkness and of pale, frightened faces in the hotel corridor. He had not known then what he knew now, what he learnt in the cold, beastly dawn that had followed. The whole thing had seemed different then: unpleasant, decidedly unpleasant, but reasonable, accountable. Now he felt as if a doctor had told him that he was suffering from some horrible and deadly disease; as if he had become part of a different world, a world of which he knew nothing but that it was detestable.

The hand holding the match to his cigarette was trembling. "What I need," he thought, "is sleep."

As the waves of nausea subsided and he stood there in the bathroom, shivering, sounds began once more to penetrate the blanket of cotton wool that seemed to have enveloped his brain. There was a sort of irregular thudding coming from a long distance. He realised that someone was still knocking at the bedroom door.

He wrapped a face towel round his hand, went back into the bedroom and switched on the light. As he did so, the knocking ceased and there was a clinking of metal. Someone had got a pass key. The door burst open.

It was the night porter who came in first, blinking round uncertainly. Behind him in the corridor were the people from the neighbouring rooms, drawing back now for fear of seeing what they hoped to see. A small, dark man in a red dressing gown over blue striped pyjamas pushed past the night porter. Graham recognised the man who had shown him to his room.

"There were shots," he began in French. Then he saw Graham's hand and went white. "I . . . You are wounded. You are . . ."

Graham sat down on the bed. "Not seriously. If you will send for a doctor to bandage my hand properly, I will tell you what has happened. But first: the man who fired the shots left through the window. You might try and catch him. What is below the window?"

"But . . ." began the man shrilly. He stopped, visibly pulling himself together. Then he turned to the night porter and said something in Turkish. The porter went out, shutting the door behind him. There was a burst of excited chatter from outside.

"The next thing," said Graham, "is to send for the manager."

"Pardon, Monsieur, he has been sent for. I am the Assistant Manager." He wrung his hands. "What has happened? Your hand, Monsieur. . . . But the doctor will be here immediately."

"Good. You'd better know what happened. I have been out this evening with a friend. I returned a few minutes ago. As I opened the door here, someone standing there just inside the window fired three shots at me. The second one hit my hand. The other two hit the wall. I heard him moving but I did not see his face. I imagine that he was a thief and that my unexpected return disturbed him."

"It is an outrage!" said the Assistant Manager hotly. His face changed. "A thief! Has anything been stolen, Monsieur?"

"I haven't looked. My suit-case is over there. It was locked."

The Assistant Manager hurried across the room and went down on his knees beside the suit-case. "It is still locked," he reported with a sigh of relief.

Graham fumbled in his pocket. "Here are the keys. You'd better open it."

The man obeyed. Graham glanced at the contents of the case. "It has not been touched."

"A blessing!" He hesitated. He was obviously thinking fast. "You say that your hand is not seriously hurt, Monsieur?"

"I don't think it is."

"It is a great relief. When the shots were heard, Monsieur, we feared an unbelievable horror. You may imagine. . . . But this is bad enough." He went to the window and looked out. "The pig! He must have escaped through the gardens immediately. Useless to search for him." He shrugged despairingly. "He is gone now, and there is nothing to be done. I need not tell you, Monsieur, how profoundly we regret that this thing should happen to you in the Adler-Palace. Never before has such a thing happened here." He hesitated again and then went on quickly: "Naturally, Monsieur, we shall do everything in our power to alleviate the distress which has been caused to you. I have told the porter to bring some whisky for you when he has telephoned for the doctor. English whisky! We have a special supply. Happily, nothing has been stolen. We could not, of course, have foreseen that an accident of such a kind should happen; but we shall ourselves see that the best medical attention is given. And there will, of course, be no question of any charge for your stay here. But . . ."

"But you don't want to call in the police and involve the hotel. Is that it?"

The Assistant Manager smiled nervously. "No good can be done, Monsieur. The police would merely ask questions and make inconveniences for all." Inspiration came to him. "For *all*, Monsieur," he repeated emphatically. "You are a business man. You wish to leave Istanbul this morning. But if the police are brought in, it might be difficult. There would be, inevitably, delays. And for what purpose?"

"They might catch the man who shot me."

"But how, Monsieur? You did not see his face. You cannot identify him. There is nothing stolen by which he could be traced."

Graham hesitated. "But what about this doctor you are getting? Supposing he reports to the police the fact that there is someone here with a bullet wound."

"The doctor's services, Monsieur, will be paid for liberally by the management."

There was a knock at the door and the porter came in with whisky, soda-water, and glasses which he set down on the table. He said something to the Assistant Manager who nodded and then motioned him out.

"The doctor is on his way, Monsieur."

"Very well. No, I don't want any whisky. But drink some yourself. You look as though you need it. I should like to make a telephone call. Will you tell the porter to telephone the Crystal Apartments in the rue d'Italie? The number is forty-four, nine hundred and seven, I think. I want to speak to Monsieur Kopeikin."

"Certainly, Monsieur. Anything you wish." He went to the door and called after the porter. There was another incomprehensible exchange. The Assistant Manager came back and helped himself generously to the whisky.

"I think," he said, returning to the charge, "that you are wise not to invoke the police, Monsieur. Nothing has been stolen. Your injury is not serious. There will be no trouble. It is thus and thus with the police here, you understand."

"I haven't yet decided what to do," snapped Graham. His head was aching violently and his hand was beginning to throb. He was getting tired of the Assistant Manager.

The telephone bell rang. He moved along the bed and picked up the telephone.

"Is that you, Kopeikin?"

He heard a mystified grunt. "Graham? What is it? I have only just this moment come in. Where are you?"

"Sitting on my bed. Listen! Something stupid has happened. There was a burglar in my room when I got up here. He took pot shots at me with a gun before escaping via the window. One of them hit me in the hand."

"Merciful God! Are you badly hurt?"

"No. It just took a slice of the back of my right hand. I don't feel too good, though. It gave me a nasty shock."

"My dear fellow! Please tell me exactly what has happened."

Graham told him. "My suit-case was locked," he went on, "and nothing is missing. I must have got back just a minute or so too soon. But there are complications. The noise seems to have roused half the hotel, including the Assistant Manager who is now standing about drinking whisky. They've sent for a doctor to bandage me up, but that's all. They made no attempt to get out after the man. Not, I suppose, that it would have done any good if they had, but at least they might have seen him. I didn't. They say he must have got away by the gardens. The point is that they won't call in the police unless I turn nasty and insist. Naturally, they don't want police tramping about the place, giving the hotel a bad name. They put it to me that the police would prevent my travelling on the eleven o'clock train if I lodged a complaint. I expect they would. But I don't know the laws of this place; and I don't want to put myself in a false position by failing to lodge a complaint. They propose, I gather, to square the doctor. But that's their look-out. What do *I* do?"

There was a short silence. Then: "I think," said Kopeikin, slowly, "that you should do nothing at the moment. Leave the matter to me. I will speak to a friend of mine about it. He is connected with the police, and has great influence. As soon as I have spoken to him, I will come to your hotel."

"But there's no need for you to do that, Kopeikin. I . . ."

"Excuse me, my dear fellow, there is every need. Let the doctor attend to your wound and then stay in your room until I arrive."

"I wasn't going out," said Graham, acidly; but Kopeikin had rung off.

As he hung up the telephone, the doctor arrived. He was thin and quiet, with a sallow face, and wore an overcoat with a black lamb's wool collar over his pyjamas. Behind him came the Manager, a heavy, disagreeable-looking man who obviously suspected that the whole thing was a hoax concocted expressly to annoy him.

He gave Graham a hostile stare, but before he could open his mouth his assistant was pouring out an account of what had occurred. There was a lot of gesturing and rolling of eyes. The Manager exclaimed as he listened, and looked at Graham with less hostility and more apprehension. At last the assistant paused, and then broke meaningly into French.

"Monsieur leaves Istanbul by the eleven o'clock train, and so does not wish to have the trouble and inconvenience of taking this matter to the police. I think you will agree, Monsieur le Directeur, that his attitude is wise."

"Very wise," agreed the Manager pontifically, "and most discreet." He squared his shoulders. "Monsieur, we infinitely regret that you should have been put to such pain, discomfort and indignity. But not even the most luxurious hotel can fortify itself against thieves who climb through windows. Nevertheless," he went on, "the Hotel Adler-Palace recognises its responsibilities towards its guests. We shall do everything humanly possible to arrange the affair."

"If it would be humanly possible to instruct the doctor then to attend to my hand, I should be grateful."

"Ah yes. The doctor. A thousand pardons."

The doctor, who had been standing gloomily in the background, now came forward and began snapping out instructions in Turkish. The windows were promptly shut, the heating turned up, and the Assistant Manager dispatched on an errand. He returned, almost immediately, with an enamel bowl which was then filled with hot water from the bathroom. The doctor removed the towel from Graham's hand, sponged the blood away, and inspected the wound. Then he looked up and said something to the Manager.

"He says, Monsieur," reported the Manager, complacently, "that it is not serious—no more than a little scratch."

"I already knew that. If you wish to go back to bed, please do so. But I should like some hot coffee. I am cold."

"Immediately, Monsieur." He snapped his fingers to the Assistant Manager, who scuttled out. "And if there is anything else, Monsieur?"

"No, thank you. Nothing. Good night."

"At your service, Monsieur. It is all most regrettable. Good night."

He went. The doctor cleaned the wound carefully, and began to dress it. Graham wished that he had not telephoned Kopeikin. The fuss was over. It was now nearly four o'clock. But for the fact that Kopeikin had promised to call in to see him, he might have had a few hours' sleep. He was yawning repeatedly. The doctor finished the dressing, patted it reassuringly, and looked up. His lips worked.

"*Maintenant,*" he said laboriously, "*il faut dormir.*"

Graham nodded. The doctor got to his feet and repacked his bag with the air of a man who has done everything possible for a difficult patient. Then he looked at his watch and sighed. "*Très tard,*" he said. "*Gitéceğ-im. Adiyo, efendi.*"

Graham mustered his Turkish. "*Adiyo, hekim efendi. Cok teşekkür ederim.*"

"*Birsey değil. Adiyo.*" He bowed and went.

A moment later, the Assistant Manager bustled in with the coffee, set it down with a businesslike flourish clearly intended to indicate that he, too, was about to return to his bed, and collected the bottle of whisky.

"You may leave that," said Graham; "a friend is on his way to see me. You might tell the porter . . ."

But as he spoke, the telephone rang, and the night porter announced that Kopeikin had arrived. The Assistant Manager retired.

Kopeikin came into the room looking preternaturally grave.

"My dear fellow!" was his greeting. He looked round. "Where is the doctor?"

"He's just left. Just a graze. Nothing serious. I feel a bit jumpy but, apart from that, I'm all right. It's really very good of you to turn out like this. The grateful management has presented me with a bottle of whisky. Sit down and help yourself. I'm having coffee."

Kopeikin sank into the arm-chair. "Tell me exactly how it happened."

Graham told him. Kopeikin heaved himself out of the arm-chair and walked over to the window. Suddenly he stooped and picked something up. He held it up: a small brass cartridge case.

"A nine millimetre calibre self-loading pistol," he remarked. "An unpleasant thing!" He dropped it on the floor again, opened the window and looked out.

Graham sighed. "I really don't think it's any good playing detectives, Kopeikin. The man was in the room; I disturbed him, and he shot at me. Come in, shut that window, and drink some whisky."

"Gladly, my dear fellow, gladly. You must excuse my curiosity."

Graham realised that he was being a little ungracious. "It's extremely kind of you, Kopeikin, to take so much trouble. I seem to have made a lot of fuss about nothing."

"It is good that you have." He frowned. "Unfortunately a lot more fuss must be made."

"You think we ought to call in the police? I don't see that it can do any good. Besides, my train goes at eleven. I don't want to miss it."

Kopeikin drank some whisky and put his glass down with a bang. "I am afraid, my dear fellow, that you cannot under any circumstances leave on the eleven o'clock train."

"What on earth do you mean? Of course I can. I'm perfectly all right."

Kopeikin looked at him curiously. "Fortunately you are. But that does not alter facts."

"Facts?"

"Did you notice that both your windows and the shutters outside have been forced open?"

"I didn't. I didn't look. But what of it?"

"If you will look out of the window you will see that there is a terrace below which gives on the garden. Above the terrace there is a steel framework which reaches almost to the second floor balconies. In the summer it is covered with straw matting so that people can eat and drink on the terrace, out of the sun. This man obviously climbed up by the framework. It would be easy. I could almost do it myself. He could reach the balconies of all the rooms on this floor of the hotel that way. But can you tell me why he chooses to break into one of the few rooms with both shutters and windows locked?"

"Of course I can't. I've always heard that criminals were fools."

"You say nothing was stolen. Your suit-case was not even opened. A coincidence that you should return just in time to prevent him."

"A lucky coincidence. For goodness' sake, Kopeikin, let's talk about something else. The man's escaped. That's the end of it."

Kopeikin shook his head. "I'm afraid not, my dear fellow. Does he not seem to you to have been a very curious thief? He behaves like no other hotel thief ever behaved. He breaks in, and through a locked window as well. If you had been in bed, he would certainly have awakened you. He must, therefore, have known beforehand that you were not there. He must also have discovered your room number. Have you anything so obviously valuable that a thief finds it worth his while to make such preparations? No. A curious thief! He carries, too, a pistol weighing at least a kilogramme with which he fires three shots at you."

"Well?"

Kopeikin bounced angrily out of his chair. "My dear fellow, does it not occur to you that this man was shooting to kill you, and that he came here for no other purpose?"

Graham laughed. "Then all I can say is that he was a pretty bad shot. Now you listen to me carefully, Kopeikin. Have you ever heard the legend about Americans and Englishmen? It persists in every country in the world where English isn't spoken. The story is that all Americans and Englishmen are millionaires, and that they always leave vast amounts of loose cash about the place. And now, if you don't mind, I'm going to try to snatch a few hours' sleep. It was very good of you to come round, Kopeikin, and I'm very grateful, but now . . ."

"Have you ever," demanded Kopeikin, "tried firing a heavy pistol in a dark room at a man who's just come through the door? There's no direct light from the corridor outside. Merely a glow of light. Have you ever tried? No. You might be able to see the man, but it's quite another thing to hit him. Under these circumstances even a good shot might miss first time as this man missed. That miss would unnerve him. He does not perhaps know that Englishmen do not usually carry firearms. You may fire back. He fires again, quickly, and clips your hand. You probably cry out with the pain. He probably thinks that he has wounded you seriously. He fires another shot for luck, and goes."

"Nonsense, Kopeikin! You must be out of your senses. What conceivable reason could anyone have for wanting to kill me? I'm the most harmless man alive."

Kopeikin glared at him stonily. "Are you?"

"Now what does *that* mean?"

But Kopeikin ignored the question. He finished his whisky. "I told you that I was going to telephone a friend of mine. I did so." He buttoned up his coat deliberately. "I am sorry to tell you, my dear fellow, that you must come with me to see him immediately. I have been trying to break the news to you gently, but now I must be frank. A man tried to murder you to-night. Something must be done about it at once."

Graham got to his feet. "Are you mad?"

"No, my dear fellow, I am not. You ask me why anyone should want to murder you. There is an excellent reason. Unfortunately, I cannot be more explicit. I have my official instructions."

Graham sat down. "Kopeikin, I shall go crazy in a minute. Will you kindly tell me what you are babbling about? Friend? Murder? Official instructions? What is all this nonsense?"

Kopeikin was looking acutely embarrassed. "I am sorry, my dear fellow. I can understand your feelings. Let me tell you this much. This friend of mine is not, strictly speaking, a friend at all. In fact, I dislike him. But his name is Colonel Haki, and he is the head of the Turkish secret police. His office is in Galata, and he is expecting us to meet him there now to discuss this affair. I may also tell you that I anticipated that you might not wish to go, and told him so. He said, forgive me, that if you did not go you would be fetched. My dear fellow, it is no use your being angry. The circumstances are exceptional. If I had not known that it was necessary both in your interests and in mine to telephone him, I would not have done so. Now then, my dear fellow, I have a taxi outside. We ought to be going."

Graham got slowly to his feet again. "Very well. I must say, Kopeikin, that you have surprised me. Friendly concern, I could understand and appreciate. But this . . . Hysteria is the last thing I should have expected from you. To get the head of the secret police out of bed at this hour seems to me a fantastic thing to do. I can only hope that he doesn't object to being made a fool of."

Kopeikin flushed. "I am neither hysterical nor fantastic, my friend. I have something unpleasant to do, and I am doing it. If you will forgive my saying so, I think . . ."

"I can forgive almost anything except stupidity," snapped Graham. "However, this is your affair. Do you mind helping me on with my overcoat?"

They drove to Galata in grim silence. Kopeikin was sulking. Graham sat hunched up in his corner staring out miserably at the cold, dark streets, and wishing that he had not telephoned Kopeikin. It was, he kept telling himself, absurd enough to be shot at by a hotel sneak thief: to be bundled out in the early hours of the morning to tell the head of the secret police about it was worse than absurd; it was ludicrous. He felt, too, concerned on Kopeikin's account. The man might be behaving like an idiot; but it was not very pleasant to think of him making an ass of himself before a man who might well be able to do him harm in his business. Besides, he, Graham, had been rude.

He turned his head. "What's this Colonel Haki like?"

Kopeikin grunted. "Very *chic* and polished—a ladies' man. There is also a legend that he can drink two bottles of whisky without getting drunk. It may be true. He was one of Ataturk's men, a deputy in the provisional government of nineteen-nineteen. There is also another legend—that he killed prisoners by tying them together in pairs and throwing them into the river to save both food and ammunition. I do not believe everything I hear, nor am I a prig, but, as I told you, I do not like him. He is, however, very clever. But you will be able to judge for yourself. You can speak French to him."

"I still don't see . . ."

"You will."

They pulled up soon afterwards behind a big American car which almost blocked the narrow street into which they had turned. They got out. Graham found himself standing in front of a pair of double doors which might have been the entrance to a cheap hotel. Kopeikin pressed a bell push.

One of the doors was opened almost immediately by a sleepy-looking caretaker who had obviously only just been roused from his bed.

"*Haki efendi evde midir,*" said Kopeikin.

"*Efendi var-dir. Yokari.*" The man pointed to the stairs.

They went up.

Colonel Haki's office was a large room at the end of a corridor on the top floor of the building. The Colonel himself walked down the corridor to meet them.

He was a tall man with lean, muscular cheeks, a small mouth and grey hair cropped Prussian fashion. A narrow frontal bone, a long beak of a nose and a slight stoop gave him a somewhat vultural air. He wore a very well-cut officer's tunic with full riding breeches and very tight, shiny cavalry boots; he walked with the slight swagger of a man who is used to riding. But for the intense pallor of his face and the fact that it was unshaven, there was nothing about him to show that he had recently been asleep. His eyes were grey and very wide-awake. They surveyed Graham with interest.

"Ah! *Nasil-siniz. Fransizca konus-abilir misin.* Yes? Delighted, Mr. Graham. Your wound, of course." Graham found his unbandaged hand being gripped with considerable force by long rubbery fingers. "I hope that it is not too painful. Something must be done about this rascal who tries to kill you."

"I'm afraid," said Graham, "that we have disturbed your rest unnecessarily, Colonel. The man stole nothing."

Colonel Haki looked quickly at Kopeikin.

"I have told him nothing," said Kopeikin placidly. "At your suggestion, Colonel, you may remember. I regret to say that he thinks that I am either mad or hysterical."

Colonel Haki chuckled. "It is the lot of you Russians to be misunderstood. Let us go into my office where we can talk."

They followed him: Graham with the growing conviction that he was involved in a nightmare and that he would presently wake up to find himself at his dentist's. The corridor was, indeed, as bare and featureless as the corridors of a dream. It smelt strongly, however, of stale cigarette smoke.

The Colonel's office was large and chilly. They sat down facing him across his desk. He pushed a box of cigarettes towards them, lounged back in his chair and crossed his legs.

"You must realise, Mr. Graham," he said suddenly, "that an attempt was made to kill you to-night."

"Why?" demanded Graham irritably. "I'm sorry, but I don't see it. I returned to my room to find that a man had got in through the window. Obviously he was some sort of thief. I disturbed him. He fired at me and then escaped. That is all."

"You have not, I understand, reported the matter to the police."

"I did not consider that reporting it could do any good. I did not see the man's face. Besides, I am leaving for England this morning on the eleven o'clock train. I did not wish to delay myself. If I have broken the law in any way I am sorry."

"*Zarar yok!* It does not matter." The Colonel lit a cigarette and blew smoke at the ceiling. "I have a duty to do, Mr. Graham," he said. "That duty is to protect you. I am afraid that you cannot leave on the eleven o'clock train."

"But protect me from *what?*"

"I will ask you questions, Mr. Graham. It will be simpler. You are in the employ of Messrs. Cator and Bliss, Ltd., the English armament manufacturers?"

"Yes. Kopeikin here is the company's Turkish agent."

"Quite so. You are, I believe, Mr. Graham, a naval ordnance expert."

Graham hesitated. He had the engineer's dislike of the word "expert." His managing director sometimes applied it to him when writing to foreign naval authorities; but he could, on those occasions, console himself with the reflection that his managing director would describe him as a full-blooded Zulu to impress a customer. At other times he found the word unreasonably irritating.

"Well, Mr. Graham?"

"I'm an engineer. Naval ordnance happens to be my subject."

"As you please. The point is that Messrs. Cator and Bliss, Ltd., have contracted to do some work for my Government. Good. Now, Mr. Graham, I do not know exactly what that work is"—he waved his cigarette airily—"that is the affair of the Ministry of Marine. But I have been told some things. I know that certain of our naval vessels are to be rearmed with new guns and torpedo tubes and that you were sent to discuss the matter with our dockyard experts. I also know that our authorities stipulated that the new equipment should be delivered by the spring. Your company agreed to that stipulation. Are you aware of it?"

"I have been aware of nothing else for the past two months."

"*Iyi dir!* Now I may tell you, Mr. Graham, that the reason for that stipulation as to time was not mere caprice on the part of our Ministry of Marine. The international situation demands that we have that new equipment in our dockyards by the time in question."

"I know that, too."

"Excellent. Then you will understand what I am about to say. The naval authorities of Germany and Italy and Russia are perfectly well aware of the fact that these vessels are being rearmed and I have no doubt that the moment the work is done, or even before, their agents will discover the details known at the moment only to a few men, yourself among them. That is unimportant. No navy can keep that sort of secret: no navy expects to do so. We might even consider it advisable, for various reasons, to publish the details ourselves. But"—he raised a long, well-manicured finger—"at the moment you are in a curious position, Mr. Graham."

"That, at least, I can believe."

The Colonel's small grey eyes rested on him coldly. "I am not here to make jokes, Mr. Graham."

"I beg your pardon."

"Not at all. Please take another cigarette. I was saying that at the moment your position is curious. Tell me! Have you ever regarded yourself as indispensable in your business, Mr. Graham?"

Graham laughed. "Certainly not. I could tell you the names of dozens of other men with my particular qualifications."

"Then," said Colonel Haki, "allow me to inform you, Mr. Graham, that for once in your life you *are* indispensable. Let us suppose for the moment that your thief's shooting had been a little more accurate and that at this moment you were, instead of sitting talking with me, lying in hospital on an operating table with a bullet in your lungs. What would be the effect on this business you are engaged in now?"

"Naturally, the company would send another man out immediately."

Colonel Haki affected a look of theatrical astonishment. "So? That would be splendid. So typically British! Sporting! One man falls—immediately another, undaunted, takes his place. But wait!" The Colonel held up a forbidding arm. "Is it necessary? Surely, Mr. Kopeikin here could arrange to have your papers taken to England. No doubt your colleagues there could find out from your notes, your sketches, your drawings, exactly what they wanted to know even though your company did not build the ships in question, eh?"

Graham flushed. "I gather from your tone that you know perfectly well that the matter could not be dealt with so simply. I was forbidden, in any case, to put certain things on paper."

Colonel Haki tilted his chair. "Yes, Mr. Graham,"—he smiled cheerfully— "I do know that. Another expert would have to be sent out to do some of your work over again." His chair came forward with a crash. "And meanwhile," he said through his teeth, "the spring would be here and those ships would still be lying in the dockyards of Izmir and Gallipoli, waiting for their new guns and torpedo tubes. Listen to me, Mr. Graham! Turkey and Great Britain are allies. It is in the interests of your country's enemies that, when the snow melts and the rain ceases, Turkish naval strength should be exactly what it is now. *Exactly what it is now!* They will do anything to see that it is so. *Anything*, Mr. Graham! Do you understand?"

Graham felt something tightening in his chest. He had to force himself to smile. "A little melodramatic, aren't you? We have no proof that what you say is true. And, after all, this is real life, not . . ." He hesitated.

"Not what, Mr. Graham?" The Colonel was watching him like a cat about to streak after a mouse.

". . . the cinema, I was going to say, only it sounded a little impolite."

Colonel Haki stood up quickly. "Melodrama! Proof! Real life! The cinema! Impolite!" His lips curled round the words as if they were obscene. "Do you think I care what you say, Mr. Graham? It's your carcass I am interested in. Alive, it's worth something to the Turkish Republic. I'm going to see that it stays alive as long as I've any control over it. There is a war on in Europe. Do you understand *that?*"

Graham said nothing.

The Colonel stared at him for a moment and then went on quietly. "A little more than a week ago, while you were still in Gallipoli, we discovered —that is, my agents discovered—a plot to murder you there. The whole thing was very clumsy and amateurish. You were to be kidnapped and knifed. Fortunately, we are not fools. We do not dismiss as melodramatic anything that does not please us. We were able to persuade the arrested men to tell us that they had been paid by a German agent in Sofia—a man named Moeller about whom we have known for some time. He used to call himself an American until the American Legation objected. His name was Fielding then. I imagine that he claims any name and nationality that happens to suit him. However, I called Mr. Kopeikin in to see me and told him about it but suggested that nothing should be said about it to you. The less these things are talked about the better and, besides, there was nothing to be gained by upsetting you while you were so hard at work. I think I made a mistake. I had reason to believe that this Moeller's further efforts would be directed elsewhere. When Mr. Kopeikin, very wisely, telephoned me immediately he knew of this fresh attempt, I realised that I had underestimated the determination of this gentleman in Sofia. He tried again. I have no doubt that he will try a third time if we give him a chance." He leaned back in his chair. "Do you understand now, Mr. Graham? Has your excellent brain grasped what I have been trying to say? It is perfectly simple! Someone is trying to kill you."

CHAPTER THREE

ON THE RARE OCCASIONS—when matters concerned with insurance policies had been under consideration—on which Graham had thought about his own death, it had been to reaffirm the conviction that he would die of natural causes and in bed. Accidents did happen, of course; but he was a careful driver, an imaginative pedestrian and a strong swimmer; he neither rode horses nor climbed mountains; he was not subject to attacks of dizziness; he did not hunt big game and he had never had even the smallest desire to jump in front of an approaching train. He had felt, on the whole, that the conviction was not unreasonable. The idea that anyone else in the world might so much as hope for his death had never occurred to him. If it had done so he would probably have hastened to consult a nerve specialist. Confronted by the proposition that someone was, in fact, not merely hoping for his death but deliberately trying to murder him, he was as profoundly shocked as if he had been presented with incontrovertible proofs that a^2 no longer equalled $b^2 + c^2$ or that his wife had a lover.

He was a man who had always been inclined to think well of his fellow creatures; and the first involuntary thought that came into his head was that he must have done something particularly reprehensible for anyone to want to murder him. The mere fact that he was doing his job could not be sufficient reason. He was not dangerous. Besides, he had a wife dependent on him. It was impossible that anyone should wish to kill him. There must be some horrible mistake.

He heard himself saying: "Yes. I understand."

He didn't understand, of course. It was absurd. He saw Colonel Haki looking at him with a frosty little smile on his small mouth.

"A shock, Mr. Graham? You do not like it, eh? It is not pleasant. War is war. But it is one thing to be a soldier in the trenches: the enemy is not trying to kill you in particular because you are Mr. Graham: the man next to you will do as well: it is all impersonal. When you are a marked man it is not so easy to keep your courage. I understand, believe me. But you have advantages over the soldier. You have only to defend yourself. You do not have to go into the open and attack. And you have no trench or fort to hold. You may run away without being a coward. You must reach London safely. But it is a long way from Istanbul to London. You must, like the soldier, take precautions against surprise. You must know your enemy. You follow me?"

"Yes. I follow you."

His brain was icily calm now, but it seemed to have lost control of his body. He knew that he must try to look as if he were taking it all very philosophically, but his mouth kept filling with saliva, so that he was swallowing repeatedly, and his hands and legs were trembling. He told himself that he was behaving like a schoolboy. A man had fired three shots at him. What difference did it make whether the man had been a thief or an intending murderer? He had fired three shots, and that was that. But all the same, it did somehow make a difference . . .

"Then," Colonel Haki was saying, "let us begin with what has just happened." He was obviously enjoying himself. "According to Mr. Kopeikin, you did not see the man who shot at you."

"No, I didn't. The room was in darkness."

Kopeikin chipped in. "He left cartridge cases behind him. Nine millimetre calibre ejected from a self-loading pistol."

"That does not help a great deal. You noticed nothing about him, Mr. Graham?"

"Nothing, I'm afraid. It was all over so quickly. He had gone before I realised it."

"But he had probably been in the room for some time waiting for you. You didn't notice any perfume in the room?"

"All I could smell was cordite."

"What time did you arrive in Istanbul?"

"At about six p.m."

"And you did not return to your hotel until three o'clock this morning. Please tell me where you were during that time."

"Certainly. I spent the time with Kopeikin. He met me at the station, and we drove in a taxi to the Adler-Palace, where I left my suitcase and had a wash. We then had some drinks and dined. Where did we have the drinks, Kopeikin?"

"At the Rumca Bar."

"Yes, that was it. We went on to the Pera Palace to dine. Just before eleven we left there, and went on to Le Jockey Cabaret."

"Le Jockey Cabaret! You surprise me! What did you do there?"

"We danced with an Arab girl named Maria, and saw the cabaret."

"We? Was there, then, only one girl between you?"

"I was rather tired, and did not want to dance much. Later we had a drink with one of the cabaret dancers, Josette, in her dressing-room." To Graham it all sounded rather like the evidence of detectives in a divorce case.

"A nice girl, this Josette?"

"Very attractive."

The Colonel laughed: the doctor keeping the patient's spirits up. "Blonde or brunette?"

"Blonde."

"Ah! I must visit Le Jockey. I have missed something. And what happened then?"

"Kopeikin and I left the place. We walked back to the Adler-Palace together where Kopeikin left me to go on to his apartment."

The Colonel looked humorously astonished. "You left this dancing blonde?"—he snapped his fingers—"just like that? There were no—little games?"

"No. No little games."

"Ah, but you have told me that you were tired." He swung round suddenly in his chair to face Kopeikin. "These women—this Arab and this Josette —what do you know of them?"

Kopeikin stroked his chin. "I know Serge, the proprietor of Le Jockey Cabaret. He introduced me to Josette some time ago. She is a Hungarian, I believe. I know nothing against her. The Arab girl is from a house in Alexandria."

"Very well. We will see about them later." He turned again to Graham. "Now, Mr. Graham, we shall see what we can find out from you about the enemy. You were tired, you say?"

"Yes."

"But you kept your eyes open, eh?"

"I suppose so."

"Let us hope so. You realise that you must have been followed from the moment you left Gallipoli?"

"I hadn't realised that."

"It must be so. They knew your hotel and your room in it. They were waiting for you to return. They must have known of every movement you made since you arrived."

He got up suddenly and, going to a filing cabinet in the corner, extracted from it a yellow manila folder. He brought it back and dropped it on the desk in front of Graham. "Inside that folder, Mr. Graham, you will find photographs of fifteen men. Some of the photographs are clear; most are very blurred and indistinct. You will have to do the best you can. I want you to cast your mind back to the time you boarded the train at Gallipoli yesterday, and remember every face you saw, even casually, between that time and three o'clock this morning. Then I want you to look at those photographs and see if you recognise any of the faces there. Afterwards Mr. Kopeikin can look at them, but I wish you to see them first."

Graham opened the folder. There was a series of thin white cards in it. Each was about the size of the folder, and had a photograph gummed to the top half of it. The prints were all the same size, but they had obviously been copied from original photographs of varying sizes. One was an enlargement of part of a photograph of a group of men standing in front of some trees. Underneath each print was a paragraph or two of typewritten matter in Turkish: presumably the description of the man in question.

Most of the photographs were, as the Colonel had said, blurred. One or two of the faces were, indeed, no more than blobs of grey with dark patches marking the eyes and mouths. Those that were clear looked like prison photographs. The men in them stared sullenly at their tormentors. There was one of a negro wearing a tarboosh with his mouth wide open as if he were shouting at someone to the right of the camera. Graham turned the cards over, slowly and hopelessly. If he had ever seen any of these men in his life, he could not recognise them now.

The next moment his heart jolted violently. He was looking at a photograph taken in very strong sunshine of a man in a hard straw hat standing in front of what might have been a shop, and looking over his shoulder at the camera. His right arm and his body below the waist were out of the picture, and what was in was rather out of focus; in addition the photograph looked as if it had been taken at least ten years previously; but there was no mistaking the doughy, characterless features, the long-suffering mouth, the small deep-set eyes. It was the man in the crumpled suit.

"Well, Mr. Graham!"

"This man. He was at Le Jockey Cabaret. It was the Arab girl who drew my attention to him while we were dancing. She said that he came in just after Kopeikin and me, and that he kept looking at me. She warned me against him. She seemed to think that he might stick a knife in my back and take my wallet."

"Did she know him?"

"No. She said that she recognised the type."

Colonel Haki took the card and leaned back. "That was very intelligent of her. Did you see this man, Mr. Kopeikin?"

Kopeikin looked, and then shook his head.

"Very well." Colonel Haki dropped the card on the desk in front of him. "You need not trouble to look at any more of the photographs, gentlemen. I know now what I wanted to know. This is the only one of the fifteen that interests us. The rest I put with it merely to make sure that you identified this one of your own accord."

"Who is he?"

"He is a Roumanian by birth. His name is supposed to be Petre Banat; but as Banat is the name of a Roumanian province, I think it very probable that he never had a family name. We know, indeed, very little about him. But what we do know is enough. He is a professional gunman. Ten years ago he was convicted, in Jassy, of helping to kick a man to death, and was sent to prison for two years. Soon after he came out of prison he joined Codreanu's Iron Guard. In nineteen thirty-three he was charged with the assassination of a police official at Bucova. It appears that he walked into the official's house one Sunday afternoon, shot the man dead, wounded his wife, and then calmly walked out again. He is a careful man, but he knew that he was safe. The trial was a farce. The court-room was filled with Iron Guards with pistols, who threatened to shoot the judge and everyone connected with the trial if Banat were convicted. He was acquitted. There were many such trials in Roumania at that time. Banat was afterwards responsible for at least four other murders in Roumania. When the Iron Guard was proscribed, however, he escaped from the country, and has not returned there. He spent some time in France until the French police deported him. Then he went to Belgrade. But he got into trouble there, too, and has since moved about Eastern Europe.

"There are men who are natural killers. Banat is one of them. He is very fond of gambling, and is always short of money. At one time it was said that his price for killing a man was as little as five thousand French francs and expenses.

"But all that is of no interest to you, Mr. Graham. The point is that Banat is here in Istanbul. I may tell you that we receive regular reports on the activities of this man Moeller in Sofia. About a week ago it was reported that he had been in touch with Banat, and that Banat had afterwards left Sofia. I will admit to you, Mr. Graham, that I did not attach any importance to the fact. To be frank, it was another aspect of this agent's activities which was interesting me at the time. It was not until Mr. Kopeikin telephoned me that I remembered Banat and wondered if, by any chance, he had come to Istanbul. We know now that he is here. We know also that Moeller saw him just after those other arrangements for killing you had been upset. There can be no doubt, I think, that it was Banat who was waiting for you in your room at the Adler-Palace."

Graham strove to seem unimpressed. "He looked harmless enough."

"That," said Colonel Haki, sagely, "is because you are not experienced, Mr. Graham. The real killer is not a mere brute. He may be quite sensitive. Have you studied abnormal psychology?"

"I'm afraid not."

"It is very interesting. Apart from detective stories, Krafft-Ebing and Stekel are my favourite reading. I have my own theory about men such as Banat. I believe that they are perverts with an *idée fixe* about the father whom they identify not with a virile god"—he held up a cautionary finger—"but with their own impotence. When they kill, they are thus killing their own weakness. There is no doubt of it, I think."

"Very interesting, I feel sure. But can't you arrest this man?"

Colonel Haki cocked one gleaming boot over the arm of his chair, and pursed his lips. "That raises an awkward problem, Mr. Graham. In the first place, we have to find him. He will certainly be travelling with a false passport and under a false name. I can and, of course, will circulate his description to the frontier posts so that we shall know if he leaves the country, but as for arresting him . . . You see, Mr. Graham, the so-called democratic forms of government have serious drawbacks for a man in my position. It is impossible to arrest and detain people without absurd legal formalities." He threw up his hands—a patriot bemoaning his country's decadence. "On what charge can we arrest him? We have no evidence against him. We could, no doubt, invent a charge and then apologise, but what good will it do? No! I regret it, but we can do nothing about Banat. I do not think it matters a great deal. What we must think of now is the future. We must consider how to get you home safely."

"I have, as I have already told you, a sleeping berth on the eleven o'clock train. I fail to see why I shouldn't use it. It seems to me that the sooner I leave here the better."

Colonel Haki frowned. "Let me tell you, Mr. Graham, that if you were to take that or any other train, you would be dead before you reached Belgrade. Don't imagine for one moment that the presence of other travellers would deter them. You must not underrate the enemy, Mr. Graham. It is a fatal mistake. In a train you would be caught like a rat in a trap. Picture it for yourself! There are innumerable stops between the Turkish and French frontiers. Your assassin might get on the train at any of them. Imagine yourself sitting there for hour after hour after hour trying to stay awake lest you should be knifed while you slept; not daring to leave the compartment for fear of being shot down in the corridor; living in terror of everyone—from the man sitting opposite to you in the restaurant car to the Customs officials. Picture it, Mr. Graham, and then reflect that a transcontinental train is the safest place in the world in which to kill a man. Consider the position! These people do not wish you to reach England. So they decide, very wisely and logically, to kill you. They have tried twice and failed. They will wait now to see what you will do. They will not try again in this country. They will know that you will now be too well protected. They will wait until you come out in the open. No! I am afraid that you cannot travel by train."

"Then I don't see. . . ."

"If," continued the Colonel, "the air line services had not been suspended we could send you by aeroplane to Brindisi. But they *are* suspended—the earthquake, you understand. Everything is disorganized. The planes are being used for relief work. But we can do without them. It will be best if you go by sea."

"But surely . . ."

"There is an Italian shipping line which runs a weekly service of small cargo boats between here and Genoa. Sometimes, when there is a cargo, they go up as far as Constanza, but usually they run only as far as here, calling at the Piræus on the way. They carry a few passengers, fifteen at the most, and we can make sure that every one of them is harmless before the boat is given its clearance papers. When you get to Genoa, you will have only the short train journey between Genoa and the French frontier to put you out of reach of German agents."

"But as you yourself pointed out, time is an important factor. To-day is the second. I am due back on the eighth. If I have to wait for boats I shall be days late. Besides, the journey itself will take at least a week."

"There will be no delay, Mr. Graham," sighed the Colonel. "I am not stupid. I telephoned the port police before you arrived. There is a boat leaving in two days' time for Marseilles. It would have been better if you could have travelled on that even though it does not ordinarily take passengers. But the Italian boat leaves to-day at four-thirty in the afternoon. You will be able to stretch your legs in Athens to-morrow afternoon. You will dock in Genoa early Saturday morning. You can, if you wish and if your visas are in order, be in London by Monday morning. As I have told you, a marked man has advantages over his enemies: he can run away—disappear. In the middle of the Mediterranean, you will be as safe as you are in this office."

Graham hesitated. He glanced at Kopeikin; but the Russian was staring at his finger nails.

"Well, I don't know, Colonel. This is all very good of you, but I can't help thinking that, in view of the circumstances which you have explained to me, I ought to get in touch with the British Consul here, or with the British Embassy, before deciding anything."

Colonel Haki lit a cigarette. "And what do you expect the Consul or the Ambassador to do? Send you home in a cruiser?" He laughed unpleasantly. "My dear Mr. Graham, I am not asking you to decide anything. I am telling you what you must do. You are, I must again remind you, of great value to my country in your present state of health. You must allow me to protect my country's interests in my own way. I think that you are probably tired now and a little upset. I do not wish to harass you, but I must explain that, if you do not agree to follow my instructions, I shall have no alternative but to arrest you, have an order issued for your deportation and put you on board the *Sestri Levante* under guard. I hope that I make myself clear."

Graham felt himself reddening. "Quite clear. Would you like to handcuff me now? It will save a lot of trouble. You need . . ."

"I think," put in Kopeikin hastily, "that I should do as the Colonel suggests, my dear fellow. It is the best thing."

"I prefer to be my own judge of that, Kopeikin." He looked from one to the other of them angrily. He felt confused and wretched. Things had been moving too quickly for him. Colonel Haki he disliked intensely. Kopeikin seemed to be no longer capable of thinking for himself. He felt that they were making decisions with the glib irresponsibility of schoolboys planning a game of Red Indians. And yet the devil of it was that those conclusions were inescapably logical. His life was threatened. All they were asking him to do was to go home by another and safer route. It was a reasonable request but. . . . Then he shrugged his shoulders. "All right. I seem to have no choice."

"Exactly, Mr. Graham." The Colonel smoothed out his tunic with the air of one who has reasoned wisely with a child. "Now we can make our arrangements. As soon as the shipping company's offices are open Mr. Kopeikin can arrange for your passage and obtain a refund for your railway ticket. I will see that the names and particulars of the other passengers are submitted to me for approval before the ship sails. You need have no fears, Mr. Graham, of your fellow travellers. But I am afraid that you will not find them very *chic* or the boat very comfortable. This line is actually the cheapest route to and from Istanbul if you live in the west. But you will not, I am sure, mind a little discomfort if you have peace of mind to compensate for it."

"As long as I get back to England by the eighth, I don't care how I travel."

"That is the right spirit. And now I suggest that you remain in this building until it is time for you to leave. We will make you as comfortable as possible. Mr. Kopeikin can collect your suit-case from the hotel. I will see that a doctor looks at your hand later on to see that it is still all right." He looked at his watch. "The concierge can make us some coffee now. Later, he can get some food for you from the restaurant round the corner." He stood up. "I will go and see about it now. We cannot save you from bullets to let you die of starvation, eh?"

"It's very kind of you," said Graham; and then, as the Colonel disappeared down the corridor: "I owe you an apology Kopeikin. I behaved badly."

Kopeikin looked distressed. "My dear fellow! You cannot be blamed. I am glad everything has been settled so quickly."

"Quickly, yes." He hesitated. "Is this man Haki to be trusted?"

"You do not like him either, eh?" Kopeikin chuckled. "I would not trust him with a woman; but with you—yes."

"You approve of my going on this boat?"

"I do. By the way, my dear fellow," he went on mildly, "have you a gun in your luggage?"

"Good heavens, no!"

"Then you had better take this." He pulled a small revolver out of his overcoat pocket. "I put it in my pocket when I came out after you telephoned. It is fully loaded."

"But I shan't need it."

"No, but it will make you feel better to have it."

"I doubt that. Still. . . ." He took the revolver and stared at it distastefully. "I've never fired one of these things, you know."

"It is easy. You release the safety catch, point it, pull the trigger and hope for the best."

"All the same . . ."

"Put it in your pocket. You can give it to the French Customs officials at Modano."

Colonel Haki returned. "The coffee is being prepared. Now, Mr. Graham, we will decide how you are to amuse yourself until it is time for you to go." He caught sight of the revolver in Graham's hand. "Ah-ha! You are arming yourself!" He grinned. "A little melodrama is sometimes unavoidable, eh, Mr. Graham?"

The decks were silent now and Graham could hear the sounds within the ship: people talking, doors slamming, quick businesslike footsteps in the alleyways. There was not long to wait now. Outside it was getting dark. He looked back upon a day which had seemed interminable, surprised that he could remember so little of it.

Most of it he had spent in Colonel Haki's office, his brain hovering uncertainly on the brink of sleep. He had smoked innumerable cigarettes and read some fortnight old French newspapers. There had been an article in one of them, he remembered, about the French mandate in the Cameroons. A doctor had been, reported favourably on the state of his wound, dressed it and gone. Kopeikin had brought him his suit-case and he had made a bloody attempt to shave with his left hand. In the absence of Colonel Haki they had shared a cool and soggy meal from the restaurant. The Colonel had returned at two to inform him that there were nine other passengers travelling on the boat, four of them women, that none of them had booked for the journey less than three days previously, and that they were all harmless.

The gangway was down now and the last of the nine, a couple who sounded middle-aged and spoke French, had come aboard and were in the cabin next to his. Their voices penetrated the thin wooden bulkhead with dismaying ease. He could hear almost every sound they made. They had argued incessantly, in whispers at first as if they had been in church; but the novelty of their surroundings soon wore off and they spoke in ordinary tones.

"The sheets are damp."

"No, it is simply that they are cold. In any case it does not matter."

"You think not? You think not?" She made a noise in her throat. "You may sleep as you wish, but do not complain to me about your kidneys."

"Cold sheets do not harm the kidneys, *chérie*."

"We have paid for our tickets. We are entitled to comfort."

"If you never sleep in a worse place you will be lucky. This is not the *Normandie*."

"That is evident." The washing cabinet clicked open. "Ah! Look at this. Look! Do you expect me to wash in it?"

"It is only necessary to run the water. A little dust."

"Dust! It is *dirty*. Filthy! It is for the steward to clean it. I will not touch it. Go and fetch him while I unpack the luggage. My dresses will be crushed. Where is the W.C.?"

"At the end of the corridor."

"Then find the steward. There is no room for two while I unpack. We should have gone by train."

"Naturally. But it is I who must pay. It is I who must give the steward a tip."

"It is you who make too much noise. Quickly. Do you want to disturb everyone?"

The man went out and the woman sighed loudly. Graham wondered whether they would talk all night. And one or both of them might snore. He would have to cough loudly once or twice so that they would realise how thin the partition was. But it was strangely comforting to hear people talking about damp sheets and dirty wash basins and W.C.'s as if—the phrase was in his mind before he realised it—as if they were matters of life and death.

Life and death! He got to his feet and found himself staring at the framed instructions for lifeboat drill.

"CINTURE DI SALVATAGGIO, CEINTURES DE SAUVETAGE, RETRUNGSGÜRTEL. LIFEBELTS. . . . *In case of danger, the signal will be given by six short blasts on the whistle followed by one long blast and the ringing of alarm bells. Passengers should then put on their lifebelts and assemble at boat station number 4.*"

He had seen the same sort of thing dozens of times before but now he read it carefully. The paper it was printed on was yellow with age. The life-belt on top of the washing cabinet looked as if it had not been moved for years. It was all ludicrously reassuring. *"In case of danger. . . ."* In case! But you couldn't get away from danger! It was all about you, all the time. You could live in ignorance of it for years: you might go to the end of your days believing that some things couldn't possibly happen to *you*, that death could only come to you with the sweet reason of disease or an "act of God": but it was there just the same, waiting to make nonsense of all your comfortable ideas about your relations with time and chance, ready to remind you—in case you had forgotten—that civilisation was a word and that you still lived in the jungle.

The ship swayed gently. There was a faint clanging from the engine room telegraph. The floor began to vibrate. Through the smeared glass of the port-hole he saw a light begin to move. The vibration ceased for a moment or two; then the engines went astern and the water glass rattled in its bracket on the wall. Another pause and then the engines went ahead again, slowly and steadily. They were free of the land. With a sigh of relief he opened the cabin door and went up on deck.

It was cold but the ship had turned and was taking the wind on her port side. She seemed stationary on the oily water of the harbour but the dock lights were sliding past them and receding. He drew the cold air into his lungs. It was good to be out of the cabin. His thoughts no longer seemed to worry him. Istanbul, Le Jockey Cabaret, the man in the crumpled suit, the Adler-Palace and its manager, Colonel Haki—they were all behind him. He could forget about them.

He began to pace slowly along the deck. He would, he told himself, be able to laugh at the whole business soon. It was already half-forgotten; there was already an air of the fantastic about it. He might almost have dreamed it. He was back in the ordinary world: he was on his way home.

He passed one of his fellow passengers, the first he had seen, an elderly man leaning on the rail staring at the lights of Istanbul coming into view as they cleared the mole. Now, as he reached the end of the deck and turned about, he saw that a woman in a fur coat had just come out of the saloon door and was walking towards him.

The light on the deck was dim and she was within a few yards of him before
he recognised her.

It was Josette.

FOR A MOMENT they stared blankly at one another. Then she laughed. "Merciful God! It is the Englishman. Excuse me, but this is extraordinary."

"Yes, isn't it."

"And what happened to your first-class compartment on the Orient Express?"

He smiled. "Kopeikin thought that a little sea air would do me good."

"And you needed doing good?" The straw-coloured hair was covered with
a woollen scarf tied under the chin, but she held her head back to look at
him as if she were wearing a hat that shaded her eyes.

"Evidently." On the whole, he decided, she looked a good deal less attractive than she had looked in her dressing-room. The fur coat was shapeless, and
the scarf did not suit her. "Since we are talking about trains," he added, "what
happened to your second-class compartment?"

She frowned with a smile at the corners of her mouth. "This way is so much
less expensive. Did I say that I was travelling by train?"

Graham flushed. "No, of course not." He realised that he was being rather
rude. "In any case, I am delighted to see you again so soon. I have been wondering what I should do if I found that the Hotel des Belges was closed."

She looked at him archly. "Ah! You were really going to telephone me,
then?"

"Of course. It was understood, wasn't it?"

She discarded the arch look and replaced it with a pout. "I do not think
that you are sincere after all. Tell me truthfully why you are on this boat."

She began to walk along the deck. He could do nothing but fall in step beside her.

"You don't believe me?"

She lifted her shoulders elaborately. "You need not tell me if you do not
wish to. I am not inquisitive."

He thought he saw her difficulty. From her point of view there could be
only two explanations of his presence on the boat: either his claim to be travelling first class on the Orient Express had been a pretentious lie intended to
impress her—in which case he would have very little money—or he had somehow discovered that she was travelling on the boat, and had abandoned the
luxury of the Orient Express in order to pursue her—in which case he would
probably have plenty of money. He had a sudden absurd desire to startle her
with the truth.

"Very well," he said. "I am travelling this way to avoid someone who is trying to shoot me."

She stopped dead. "I think it is too cold out here," she said calmly. "I shall go in."

He was so surprised that he laughed.

She turned on him quickly. "You should not make such stupid jokes."

There was no doubt about it; she was genuinely angry. He held up his bandaged hand. "A bullet grazed it."

She frowned. "You are very bad. If you have hurt your hand I am sorry, but you should not make jokes about it. It is very dangerous."

"Dangerous!"

"You will have bad luck, and so shall I. It is very bad luck to joke in that way."

"Oh, I see." He grinned. "I am not superstitious."

"That is because you do not know. I would sooner see a raven flying than joke about killing. If you wish me to like you, you must not say such things."

"I apologise," said Graham, mildly. "Actually I cut my hand with a razor."

"Ah, they are dangerous things! In Algiers José saw a man with his throat cut from ear to ear with a razor."

"Suicide?"

"No, no! It was his *petite amie* who did it. There was a lot of blood. José will tell you about it if you ask him. It was very sad."

"Yes, I can imagine. José is travelling with you, then?"

"Naturally." And then, with a sidelong look: "He is my husband."

Her husband! That explained why she "put up with" José. It also explained why Colonel Haki had omitted to tell him that the "dancing blonde" was travelling on the boat. Graham remembered the promptitude with which José had retired from the dressing-room. That, no doubt, had been a matter of business. *Attractions* at a place like Le Jockey Cabaret were not quite so attractive if they were known to have husbands in the vicinity. He said: "Kopeikin didn't tell me that you were married."

"Kopeikin is very nice, but he does not know everything. But I will tell you confidentially that with José and me it is an arrangement. We are partners, nothing more. He is jealous about me only when I neglect business for pleasure."

She said it indifferently, as if she were discussing a clause in her contract. "Are you going to dance in Paris now?"

"I do not know. I hope so; but so much is closed on account of the war."

"What will you do if you can't get an engagement?"

"What do you think? I shall starve. I have done it before." She smiled bravely. "It is good for the figure." She pressed her hands on her hips and looked at him, inviting his considered opinion. "Do you not think it would be good for my figure to starve a little? One grows fat in Istanbul." She posed. "You see?"

Graham nearly laughed. The picture being presented for his approval had all the simple allure of a full-page drawing in *La Vie Parisienne*. Here was the "business man's" dream come true: the beautiful blonde dancer, married but unloved, in need of protection: something expensive going cheap.

"A dancer's must be a very hard life," he said drily.

"Ah, yes! Many people think that it is so gay. If they knew!"

"Yes, of course. It is getting a little cold, isn't it? Shall we go inside and have a drink?"

"That would be nice." She added with a tremendous air of candour: "I am so glad we are travelling together. I was afraid that I was going to be bored. Now, I shall enjoy myself."

He felt that his answering smile was probably rather sickly. He was beginning to have an uncomfortable suspicion that he was making a fool of himself. "We go this way, I think," he said.

The *salone* was a narrow room about thirty feet long, with entrances from the shelter deck and from the landing at the head of the stairs to the cabins. There were grey upholstered *banquettes* round the walls and, at one end, three round dining tables bolted down. Evidently there was no separate dining-room. Some chairs, a card table, a shaky writing desk, a radio, a piano and a threadbare carpet completed the furnishings. Opening off the room at the far end was a cubby hole with half doors. The lower door had a strip of wood screwed to the top of it to make a counter. This was the bar. Inside it, the steward was opening cartons of cigarettes. Except for him, the place was deserted. They sat down.

"What would you like to drink, Mrs. . . . ," began Graham tentatively.

She laughed. "José's name is Gallindo, but I detest it. You must call me Josette. I would like some English whisky and a cigarette, please."

"Two whiskies," said Graham.

The steward put his head out and frowned at them. "Viski? *E molto caro*," he said warningly; "*très cher. Cinque lire*. Five lire each. Vair dear."

"Yes, it is, but we will have them just the same."

The steward retired into the bar, and made a lot of noise with the bottles.

"He is very angry," said Josette. "He is not used to people who order whisky." She had obviously derived a good deal of satisfaction from the ordering of the whisky, and the discomfiture of the steward. In the light of the saloon her fur coat looked cheap and old; but she had unbuttoned it and arranged it round her shoulders as if it had been a thousand guinea mink. He began, against his better judgment, to feel sorry for her.

"How long have you been dancing?"

"Since I was ten. That is twenty years ago. You see," she remarked, complacently, "I do not lie to you about my age. I was born in Serbia, but I say that I am Hungarian because it sounds better. My mother and father were very poor."

"But honest, no doubt."

She looked faintly puzzled. "Oh no, my father was not at all honest. He was a dancer, and he stole some money from someone in the troupe. They put him in prison. Then the war came, and my mother took me to Paris. A very rich man took care of us for a time, and we had a very nice apartment." She gave a nostalgic sigh: an impoverished *grande dame* lamenting past glories. "But he lost his money, and so my mother had to dance again. My mother died when we were in Madrid, and I was sent back to Paris, to a convent. It was terrible there. I do not know what happened to my father. I think perhaps he was killed in the war."

"And what about José?"

"I met him in Berlin when I was dancing there. He did not like his partner. She was," she added simply, "a terrible bitch."

"Was this long ago?"

"Oh, yes. Three years. We have been to a great many places." She examined him with affectionate concern. "But you are tired. You look tired. You have cut your face, too."

"I tried to shave with one hand."

"Have you got a very nice house in England?"

"My wife likes it."

"*Oh là-là!* And do you like your wife?"

"Very much."

"I do not think," she said reflectively, "that I would like to go to England. So much rain and fog. I like Paris. There is nothing better to live in than an apartment in Paris. It is not expensive."

"No?"

"For twelve hundred francs a month one can have a very nice apartment. In Rome it is not so cheap. I had an apartment in Rome that was very nice, but it cost fifteen hundred lire. My fiancé was very rich. He sold automobiles."

"That was before you married José?"

"Of course. We were going to be married but there was some trouble about his divorce from his wife in America. He always said that he would fix it, but in the end it was impossible. I was very sorry. I had that apartment for a year."

"And that was how you learned English?"

"Yes, but I had learned a little in that terrible convent." She frowned. "But I tell you everything about myself. About you I know nothing except that you have a nice house and a wife, and that you are an engineer. You ask questions, but you tell me nothing. I still do not know why you are here. It is very bad of you."

But he did not have to reply to this. Another passenger had entered the saloon, and was advancing towards them, clearly with the intention of making their acquaintance.

He was short, broad-shouldered and unkempt, with a heavy jowl and a fringe of scurfy grey hair round a bald pate. He had a smile, fixed like that of a ventriloquist's doll: a standing apology for the iniquity of his existence.

The boat had begun to roll slightly; but from the way he clutched for support at the backs of chairs as he crossed the room, it might have been riding out a full gale.

"There is lot of movement, eh?" he said in English, and subsided into a chair. "Ah! That is better, eh?" He looked at Josette with obvious interest, but turned to Graham before he spoke again. "I hear English spoken so I am interested at once," he said. "You are English, sir?"

"Yes. And you?"

"Turkish. I also go to London. Trade is very good. I go to sell tobacco. My name is Mr. Kuvetli, sir."

"My name is Graham. This is Señora Gallindo."

"So good," said Mr. Kuvetli. Without getting up from his chair, he bowed from the waist. "I don't speak English very well," he added, unnecessarily.

"It is a very difficult language," said Josette, coldly. She was obviously displeased by the intrusion.

"My wife," continued Mr. Kuvetli, "does not speak English any. So I do not bring her with me. She has not been to England."

"But you have?"

"Yes, sir. Three times, and to sell tobacco. I do not sell much before, but now I sell lot. It is war. United States ships do not come to England any more. English ships bring guns and aeroplanes from U.S. and have no room for tobacco, so England now buys lot of tobacco from Turkey. It is good business for my boss. Firm of Pazar and Co."

"It must be."

"He would come to England himself, but cannot speak English any. Or he cannot write. He is very ignorant. I reply to all favours from England and elsewhere abroad. But he knows lot about tobacco. We produce best." He plunged his hand into his pocket and produced a leather cigarette case. "Please try cigarette made from tobacco by Pazar and Co." He extended the case to Josette.

She shook her head. *"Tesekkür ederim."*

The Turkish phrase irritated Graham. It seemed to belittle the man's polite efforts to speak a language foreign to him.

"Ah!" said Mr. Kuvetli, "you speak my language. That is very good. You have been long in Turkey?"

"Dört ay." She turned to Graham. "I would like one of *your* cigarettes, please."

It was a deliberate insult but Mr. Kuvetli only smiled a little more. Graham took one of the cigarettes.

"Thank you very much. It's very good of you. Will you have a drink, Mr. Kuvetli?"

"Ah, no, thank you. I must go to arrange my cabin before it is dinner."

"Then later, perhaps."

"Yes, please." With a broadened smile and a bow to each of them he got to his feet and made his way to the door.

Graham lit his cigarette. "Was it absolutely necessary to be so rude? Why drive the man away?"

She frowned. "Turks! I do not like them. They are"—she ransacked the automobile salesman's vocabulary for an epithet—"they are goddamned dagoes. See how thick his skin is! He does not get angry. He only smiles."

"Yes, he behaved very well."

"I do not understand it," she burst out angrily. "In the last war you fought with France against the Turks. In the convent they told me much about it. They are heathen animals, these Turks. There were the Armenian atrocities and the Syrian atrocities and the Smyrna atrocities. Turks killed babies with their bayonets. But now it is all different. You like the Turks. They are your allies and you buy tobacco from them. It is the English hypocrisy. I am a Serb. I have a longer memory."

"Does your memory go back to nineteen twelve? I was thinking of the Serbian atrocities in Turkish villages. Most armies commit what are called atrocities at some time or other. They usually call them reprisals."

"Including the British army, perhaps?"

"You would have to ask an Indian or an Afrikaner about that. But every country has its madmen. Some countries have more than others. And when you give such men a license to kill they are not always particular about the way they kill. But I am afraid that the rest of their fellow countrymen remain human beings. Personally, I like the Turks."

She was clearly angry with him. He suspected that her rudeness to Mr. Kuvetli had been calculated to earn his approval and that she was annoyed because he had not responded in the way she had expected. "It is stuffy in here," she said, "and there is a smell of cooking. I should like to walk outside again. You may come with me if you wish."

Graham seized the opportunity. He said, as they walked towards the door: "I think that I should unpack my suit-case. I shall hope to see you at dinner."

Her expression changed quickly. She became an international beauty humouring, with a tolerant smile, the extravagances of a love-sick boy. "As you wish. José will be with me later. I shall introduce you to him. He will want to play cards."

"Yes, I remember you told me that he would. I shall have to try to remember a game that I can play well."

She shrugged. "He will win in any case. But I have warned you."

"I shall remember that when I lose."

He returned to his cabin and stayed there until the steward came round beating a gong to announce dinner. When he went upstairs he was feeling better. He had changed his clothes. He had managed to complete the shave which he had begun in the morning. He had an appetite. He was prepared to take an interest in his fellow passengers.

Most of them were already in their places when he entered the saloon.

The ship's officers evidently ate in their own quarters. Only two of the dining tables were laid. At one of them sat Mr. Kuvetli, a man and woman who looked as if they might be the French couple from the cabin next to his, Josette, and with her a very sleek José. Graham smiled courteously at the assembly and received in return a loud "good evening" from Mr. Kuvetli, a lift of the eyebrows from Josette, a cool nod from José, and a blank stare from the French couple. There was about them an air of tension which seemed to him to be more than the ordinary restraint of passengers on a boat sitting down together for the first time. The steward showed him to the other table.

One of the places was already filled by the elderly man whom he had passed on his walk round the deck. He was a thick, round-shouldered man with a pale heavy face, white hair and a long upper lip. As Graham sat down next to him he looked up. Graham met a pair of prominent pale blue eyes.

"Mr. Graham?"

"Yes. Good evening."

"My name is Haller. Doctor Fritz Haller. I should explain that I am a German, a good German, and that I am on my way back to my country." He spoke very good, deliberate English in a deep voice.

Graham realised that the occupants of the other table were staring at them in breathless silence. He understood now their air of tension.

He said calmly: "I am an Englishman. But I gather you knew that."

"Yes, I knew it." Haller turned to the food in front of him. "The Allies seem to be here in force and unhappily the steward is an imbecile. The two French people at the next table were placed here. They objected to eating with the enemy, insulted me and moved. If you wish to do the same I suggest that you do so now. Everyone is expecting the scene."

"So I see." Graham cursed the steward silently.

"On the other hand," Haller continued, breaking his bread, "you may find the situation humorous. I do myself. Perhaps I am not as patriotic as I should be. No doubt I should insult you before you insult me; but, quite apart from the unfair differences in our ages, I can think of no effective way of insulting you. One must understand a person thoroughly before one can insult him effectively. The French lady, for example, called me a filthy Bosche. I am unmoved. I bathed this morning and I have no unpleasant habits."

"I see your point. But . . ."

"But there is a matter of etiquette involved. Quite so. Fortunately, I must leave that to you. Move or not, as you choose. Your presence here would not embarrass me. If it were understood that we were to exclude international politics from our conversation we might even pass the next half-hour in a civilised manner. However, as the newcomer on the scene, it is for you to decide."

Graham picked up the menu. "I believe it is the custom for belligerents on neutral ground to ignore each other if possible and in any case to avoid embarrassing the neutrals in question. Thanks to the steward, we cannot ignore each other. There seems to be no reason why we should make a difficult situation unpleasant. No doubt we can rearrange the seating before the next meal."

Haller nodded approval. "Very sensible. I must admit that I am glad of your company to-night. My wife suffers from the sea and will stay in her cabin this evening. I think that Italian cooking is very monotonous without conversation."

"I am inclined to agree with you." Graham smiled intentionally and heard a rustle from the next table. He also heard an exclamation of disgust from the Frenchwoman. He was annoyed to find that the sound made him feel guilty.

"You seem," said Haller, "to have earned some disapproval. It is partly my fault. I am sorry. Perhaps it is that I am old, but I find it extremely difficult to identify men with their ideas. I can dislike, even hate an idea, but the man who has it seems to be still a man."

"Have you been long in Turkey?"

"A few weeks. I came there from Persia."

"Oil?"

"No, Mr. Graham, archeology. I was investigating the early pre-Islamic cultures. The little I have been able to discover seems to suggest that some of the tribes who moved westward to the plains of Iran about four thousand years ago assimilated the Sumerian culture and preserved it almost intact until long after the fall of Babylon. The form of perpetuation of the Adonis myth alone was instructive. The weeping for Tammuz was always a focal point of the pre-historic religions—the cult of the dying and risen god. Tammuz, Osiris and Adonis are the same Sumerian deity personified by three different races. But the Sumerians called this god Dumuzida. So did some of the pre-Islamic tribes of Iran! And they had a most interesting variation of the Sumerian epic of Gilgamish and Enkidu which I had not heard about before. But forgive me, I am boring you already."

"Not at all," said Graham politely. "Were you in Persia for long?"

"Two years only. I would have stayed another year but for the war."

"Did it make so much difference?"

Haller pursed his lips. "There was a financial question. But even without that I think that I might not have stayed. We can learn only in the expectation of life. Europe is too preoccupied with its destruction to concern itself with such things: a condemned man is interested only in himself, the passage of hours and such intimations of immortality as he can conjure from the recesses of his mind."

"I should have thought that a preoccupation with the past. . . ."

"Ah yes, I know. The scholar in his study can ignore the noise in the market place. Perhaps—if he is a theologian or a biologist or an antiquarian. I am none of those things. I helped in the search for a logic of history. We should have made of the past a mirror with which to see round the corner that separates us from the future. Unfortunately, it no longer matters what we could have seen. We are returning the way we came. Human understanding is re-entering the monastery."

"Forgive me but I thought you said that you were a *good* German."

He chuckled. "I am old. I can afford the luxury of despair."

"Still, in your place, I think that I should have stayed in Persia and luxuriated at a distance."

"The climate, unfortunately, is not suitable for any sort of luxuriating. It is either very hot or very cold. My wife found it particularly trying. Are you a soldier, Mr. Graham?"

"No, an engineer."

"That is much the same thing. I have a son in the army. He has always been a soldier. I have never understood why he should be my son. As a lad of fourteen he disapproved of me because I had no duelling scars. He disapproved of the English, too, I am afraid. We lived for some time in Oxford while I was doing some work there. A beautiful city! Do you live in London?"

"No, in the North."

"I have visited Manchester and Leeds. I preferred Oxford. I live in Berlin myself. I don't think it is any uglier than London." He glanced at Graham's hand. "You seem to have had an accident."

"Yes. Fortunately it's just as easy to eat ravioli with the left hand."

"There is that to be said for it, I suppose. Will you have some of this wine?"

"I don't think so, thank you."

"Yes, you're wise. The best Italian wines never leave Italy." He dropped his voice. "Ah! Here are the other two passengers."

They looked like mother and son. The woman was about fifty and unmistakably Italian. Her face was very hollow and pale and she carried herself as if she had been seriously ill. Her son, a handsome lad of eighteen or so, was very attentive to her and glared defensively at Graham, who had risen to draw back her chair for her. They both wore black.

Haller greeted them in Italian to which the boy replied briefly. The woman inclined her head to them but did not speak. It was obvious that they wished to be left to themselves. They conferred in whispers over the menu. Graham could hear José talking at the next table.

"War!" he was saying in thick, glutinous French; "it makes it very difficult for all to earn money. Let Germany have all the territory she desires. Let her choke herself with territory. Then let us go to Berlin and enjoy ourselves. It is ridiculous to fight. It is not businesslike."

"Ha!" said the Frenchman. "You, a Spaniard, say that! Ha! That is very good. Magnificent!"

"In the civil war," said José, "I took no sides. I had my work to do, my living to earn. It was madness. I did not go to Spain."

"War is terrible," said Mr. Kuvetli.

"But if the Reds had won . . ." began the Frenchman.

"Ah yes!" exclaimed his wife. "If the Reds had won. . . . They were antiChrist. They burnt churches and broke sacred images and relics. They violated nuns and murdered priests."

"It was all very bad for business," repeated José obstinately. "I know a man in Bilbao who had a big business. It was all finished by the war. War is very stupid."

"The voice of the fool," murmured Haller, "with the tongue of the wise. I think that I will go and see how my wife is. Will you excuse me, please?"

Graham finished his meal virtually alone. Haller did not return. The mother and son opposite to him ate with their heads bent over their plates. They seemed to be in communion over some private sorrow. He felt as if he were intruding. As soon as he had finished he left the saloon, put on his overcoat and went out on deck to get some air before going to bed.

The lights on the land were distant now, and the ship was rustling through the sea before the wind. He found the companionway up to the boat deck and stood for a time in the lee of a ventilator idly watching a man with a lamp on the well deck below tapping the wedges which secured the hatch tarpaulins. Soon the man finished his task, and Graham was left to wonder how he was going to pass the time on the boat. He made up his mind to get some books in Athens the following day. According to Kopeikin, they would dock at the Piræus at about two o'clock in the afternoon, and sail again at five. He would have plenty of time to take the tram into Athens, buy some English cigarettes and books, send a telegram to Stephanie and get back to the dock.

He lit a cigarette, telling himself that he would smoke it and then go to bed; but, even as he threw the match away, he saw that Josette and José had come on to the deck, and that the girl had seen him. It was too late to retreat. They were coming over to him.

"So you are here," she said accusingly. "This is José."

José, who was wearing a very tight black overcoat and a grey soft hat with a curly brim, nodded reluctantly, and said: "*Enchanté, Monsieur*," with the air of a busy man whose time is being wasted.

"José does not speak English," she explained.

"There is no reason why he should. It is a pleasure to meet you, Señor Gallindo," he went on in Spanish. "I very much enjoyed the dancing of you and your wife."

José laughed rudely. "It is nothing. The place was impossible."

"José was angry all the time because Coco—the negress with the snake, you remember?—had more money from Serge than we did, although we were the principal attraction."

José said something unprintable, in Spanish.

"She was," said Josette, "Serge's lover. You smile, but it is true. Is it not true, José?"

José made a loud noise with his lips.

"José is very vulgar," commented Josette. "But it is true about Serge and Coco. It is a very *drôle* story. There was a great joke about Fifi, the snake. Coco was very fond of Fifi, and always used to take it to bed with her. But Serge did not know that until he became her lover. Coco says that when he found Fifi in the bed, he fainted. She made him increase her wages to double before she would consent to Fifi's sleeping alone in its basket. Serge is no fool: even José says that Serge is no fool; but Coco treats him like dirt. It is because she has a very great temper that she is able to do it."

"He needs to hit her with his fist," said José.

"Ah! *Salop!*" She turned to Graham. "And you! Do you agree with José?"

"I have no experience of snake dancers."

"Ah! You do not answer. You are brutes, you men!"

She was obviously amusing herself at his expense. He said to José: "Have you made this trip before?"

José stared suspiciously. "No. Why? Have you?"

"Oh no."

José lit a cigarette. "I am already very tired of this ship," he announced. "It is dull and dirty, and it vibrates excessively. Also the cabins are too near the lavabos. Do you play poker?"

"I *have* played. But I don't play very well."

"I told you!" cried Josette.

"She thinks," said José sourly, "that because I win I cheat. I do not care a damn what she thinks. People are not compelled by law to play cards with me. Why should they squeal like stuck pigs when they lose?"

"It is," Graham admitted, tactfully, "illogical."

"We will play now if you like," said José, as if someone had accused him of refusing a challenge.

"If you don't mind, I'd sooner leave it until to-morrow. I'm rather tired to-night. In fact, I think that if you will excuse me I shall get to bed now."

"So soon!" Josette pouted, and broke into English. "There is only one interesting person on the boat, and he goes to bed. It is too bad. Ah yes, you are being very bad. Why did you sit next to that German at dinner?"

"He did not object to my sitting beside him. Why should *I* object? He is a very pleasant and intelligent old fellow."

"He is a German. For you no German should be pleasant or intelligent. It is as the French people were saying. The English are not serious about these things."

José turned suddenly on his heel. "It is very boring to listen to English," he said, "and I am cold. I shall go and drink some brandy."

Graham was beginning to apologise when the girl cut him short. "He is very unpleasant to-day. It is because he is disappointed. He thought there were going to be some pretty little girls for him to roll his eyes at. He always has a great success with pretty little girls—and old women."

She had spoken loudly, and in French. José, who had reached the top of the companionway, turned and belched deliberately before descending.

"He is gone," said Josette. "I am glad. He has very bad manners." She drew in her breath, and looked up at the clouds. "It is a lovely night. I do not see why you wish to go to bed. It is early."

"I'm very tired."

"You cannot be too tired to walk across the deck with me."

"Of course not."

There was a corner of the deck below the bridge where it was very dark. She stopped there, turned abruptly and leaned with her back to the rail so that he was facing her.

"I think you are angry with me?"

"Good gracious, no! Why should I be?"

"Because I was rude to your little Turk."

"He's not *my* little Turk."

"But you are angry?"

"Of course not."

She sighed. "You are very mysterious. You have still not told me why you are travelling on this boat. I am very interested to know. It cannot be because it is cheap. Your clothes are expensive!"

He could not see her face, only a vague outline of her; but he could smell the scent she was using, and the mustiness of the fur coat. He said: "I can't think why you should be interested."

"But you know perfectly well that I am."

She had come an inch or two nearer to him. He knew that, if he wanted to do so, he could kiss her and that she would return the kiss. He knew also that it would be no idle peck, but a declaration that their relationship was to be the subject of discussion. He was surprised to find that he did not reject the idea instantaneously, that the immediate prospect of feeling her full smooth lips against his was more than attractive. He was cold and tired: she was near, and he could sense the warmth of her body. It could do no one any harm if . . . He said: "Are you travelling to Paris via Modane?"

"Yes. But why ask? It is the way to Paris."

"When we get to Modane I will tell you exactly why I travelled this way, if you are still interested."

She turned and they walked on. "Perhaps it is not so important," she said. "You must not think I am inquisitive." They reached the companionway. Her attitude towards him had changed perceptibly. She looked at him with friendly concern. "Yes, my dear sir, you are tired. I should not have asked you to stay up here. I shall finish my walk alone. Good night."

"Good night, Señora."

She smiled. "Señora! You must not be so unkind. Good night."

He went below amused and irritated by his thoughts. Outside the door of the saloon he came face to face with Mr. Kuvetli.

Mr. Kuvetli broadened his smile. "First officer says we shall have good weather, sir."

"Splendid." He remembered with a sinking heart that he had invited the man to have a drink. "Will you join me in a drink?"

"Oh no, thank you. Not now." Mr. Kuvetli placed one hand on his chest. "Matter of fact, I have pain because of wine at table. Very strong acid stuff!"

"So I should imagine. Until to-morrow, then."

"Yes, Mr. Graham. You will be glad to arrive back at your home, eh?" He seemed to want to talk.

"Oh yes, very glad."

"You go to Athens when we stop to-morrow?"

"I was thinking of doing so."

"Do you know Athens well, I suppose?"

"I've been there before."

Mr. Kuvetli hesitated. His smile became oily. "You are in a position to do me service, Mr. Graham."

"Oh yes?"

"I do not know Athens. I have never been. Would you allow me to go with you?"

"Yes, of course. I should be glad of company. But I was only going to buy some English books and cigarettes."

"I am most grateful."

"Not at all. We get in just after lunch, don't we?"

"Yes, yes. That is quite right. But I will find out exact time. You leave that to me."

"Then that's settled. I think I shall go to bed now. Good night, Mr. Kuvetli."

"Good night, sir. And I thank you for your favour."

"Not at all. Good night."

He went to his cabin, rang for the steward and said that he wanted his breakfast coffee in his cabin at nine-thirty. Then he undressed and got into his bunk.

For a few minutes he lay on his back enjoying the gradual relaxing of his muscles. Now, at last, he could forget Haki, Kopeikin, Banat, and the rest of it. He was back in his own life, and could sleep. The phrase "asleep almost as soon as his head touched the pillow" passed through his mind. That was how it would be with him. God knew he was tired enough. He turned on his side. But sleep did not come so easily. His brain would not stop working. It was as if the needle were trapped in one groove on the record. He'd made a fool of himself with that wretched woman Josette. He'd made a fool . . . He jerked his thoughts forward. Ah yes! He was committed to three unalloyed hours of Mr. Kuvetli's company. But that was to-morrow. And now, sleep. But his hand was throbbing again, and there seemed to be a lot of noise going on. That boor José was right. The vibration *was* excessive. The cabins *were* too near the lavatories. There were footsteps overhead, too: people walking round the shelter deck. Round and round. Why, for Heaven's sake, must people always be walking?

He had been lying awake for half an hour when the French couple entered their cabin.

They were quiet for a minute or two, and he could only hear the sounds they made as they moved about the cabin, and an occasional grunted comment. Then the woman began.

"Well, that is the first evening over! Three more! It is too much to think of."

"It will pass." A yawn. "What is the matter with the Italian woman and her son?"

"You did not hear? Her husband was killed in the earthquake at Erzurum. The first officer told me. He is very nice, but I had hoped that there would be at least one French person to talk to."

"There are people who speak French. The little Turk speaks it very well. And there are the others."

"They are not French. That girl and that man—the Spaniard. They say that they are dancers, but I ask you."

"She is pretty."

"Certainly. I do not dispute it. But you need not think little thoughts. She is interested in the Englishman. I do not like him. He does not look like an Englishman."

"You think the English are all *milords* with sporting clothes and monocles. Ha! I saw the Tommies in nineteen fifteen. They are all small and ugly with very loud voices. They talk very quickly. This type is more like the officers who are thin and slow, and look as if things do not smell very nice."

"This type is not an English officer. He likes the Germans."

"You exaggerate. An old man like that! I would have sat with him myself."

"Ah! So you say. I will not believe it."

"No? When you are a soldier you do not call the Bosche 'the filthy Bosche.' That is for the women, the civilians."

"You are mad. They are filthy. They are beasts like those in Spain who violated nuns and murdered priests."

"But, my little one, you forget that there were many of Hitler's Bosches who fought *against* the Reds in Spain. You forget. You are not logical."

"They are not the same as those who attack France. They were Catholic Germans."

"You are ridiculous! Was I not hit in the guts by a bullet fired by a Bavarian Catholic in 'seventeen? You make me tired. You are ridiculous. Be silent."

"No, it is you who . . ."

They went on. Graham heard little more. Before he could make up his mind to cough loudly, he was asleep.

He awoke only once in the night. The vibration had ceased. He looked at his watch, saw that the time was half-past two, and guessed that they had stopped at Chanaq to drop the pilot. A few minutes later, as the engines started again, he went to sleep again.

It was not until the steward brought his coffee seven hours later that he learned that the pilot cutter from Chanaq had brought a telegram for him. It was addressed: "GRAHAM, VAPUR SESTRI LEVANTE, CANAKKALE." He read:

"H. REQUESTS ME INFORM YOU B. LEFT FOR SOFIA HOUR AGO. ALL WELL. BEST WISHES. KOPEIKIN."

It had been handed in at Beyoglu at seven o'clock the previous evening.

CHAPTER FIVE

IT WAS AN Ægean day: intensely coloured in the sun and with small pink clouds drifting in a bleached indigo sky. A stiff breeze was blowing and the amethyst of the sea was broken with white. The *Sestri Levante* was burying her stem in it and lifting clouds of spray which the breeze whipped across the well-deck like hail. The steward had told him that they were within sight of the island of Makronisi and as he went out on deck he saw it: a thin golden line shimmering in the sun and stretched out ahead of them like a sand bar at the entrance to a lagoon.

There were two other persons on that side of the deck. There was Haller and with him, on his arm, a small desiccated woman with thin grey hair, who was evidently his wife. They were steadying themselves at the rail and he was holding his head up to the wind as if to draw strength from it. He had his hat off and the white hair quivered with the air streaming through it.

Evidently they had not seen him. He made his way up to the boat deck. The breeze there was stronger. Mr. Kuvetli and the French couple stood by the rail clutching at their hats and watching the gulls following the ship. Mr. Kuvetli saw him immediately and waved. He went over to them.

"Good morning. *Madame. Monsieur.*"

They greeted him guardedly but Mr. Kuvetli was enthusiastic.

"It *is* good morning, eh? You sleep well? I look forward to our excursion this afternoon. Permit me to present Monsieur and Madame Mathis. Monsieur Graham."

There was handshaking. Mathis was a sharp-featured man of fifty or so with lean jaws and a permanent frown. But his smile, when it came, was good and his eyes were alive. The frown was the badge of his ascendancy over his wife. She had bony hips and wore an expression which said that she was determined to keep her temper however sorely it were tried. She was like her voice.

"Monsieur Mathis," said Mr. Kuvetli, whose French was a good deal more certain than his English, "is from Eskeshehir, where he has been working with the French railway company."

"It is a bad climate for the lungs," said Mathis. "Do you know Eskeshehir, Monsieur Graham?"

"I was there for a few minutes only."

"That would have been quite enough for me," said Madame Mathis. "We have been there three years. It was never any better than the day we arrived."

"The Turks are a great people," said her husband. "They are hard and they endure. But we shall be glad to return to France. Do you come from London, Monsieur?"

"No, the North of England. I have been in Turkey for a few weeks on business."

"To us, war will be strange after so many years. They say that the towns in France are darker than the last time."

"The towns are damnably dark both in France and in England. If you do not have to go out at night it is better to stay in."

"It is war," said Mathis sententiously.

"It is the filthy Bosche," said his wife.

"War," put in Mr. Kuvetli, stroking an unshaven chin, "is a terrible thing. There is no doubt of it. But the Allies must win."

"The Bosche is strong," said Mathis. "It is easy to say that the Allies must win, but they yet have the fighting to do. And do we yet know whom we are going to fight or where? There is a front in the East as well as in the West. We do not yet know the truth. When that is known the war will be over."

"It is not for us to ask questions," said his wife.

His lips twisted and in his brown eyes was the bitterness of years. "You are right. It is not for us to ask questions. And why? Because the only people who can give us the answers are the bankers and the politicians at the top, the boys with the shares in the big factories which make war materials. They will not give us answers. Why? Because they know that if the soldiers of France and England knew those answers they would not fight."

His wife reddened. "You are mad! Naturally the men of France would fight to defend us from the filthy Bosche." She glanced at Graham. "It is bad to say that France would not fight. We are not cowards."

"No, but neither are we fools." He turned quickly to Graham. "Have you heard of Briey, Monsieur? From the mines of the Briey district comes ninety per cent. of France's iron ore. In nineteen fourteen those mines were captured by the Germans, who worked them for the iron they needed. They worked them hard. They have admitted since that without the iron they mined at Briey they would have been finished in nineteen seventeen. Yes, they worked Briey hard. I, who was at Verdun, can tell you that. Night after night we watched the glare in the sky from the blast furnaces of Briey a few kilometres away; the blast furnaces that were feeding the German guns. Our artillery and our bombing aeroplanes could have blown those furnaces to pieces in a week. But our artillery remained silent; an airman who dropped one bomb on the Briey area was court-martialled. Why?" His voice rose. "I will tell you why, Monsieur. Because there were orders that Briey was not to be touched. Whose orders? Nobody knew. The orders came from someone at the top. The Ministry of War said that it was the generals. The generals said that it was the Ministry of War. We did not find out the facts until after the war. The orders had been issued by Monsieur de Wendel of the Comité des Forges who owned the Briey mines and blast furnaces. We were fighting for our lives, but our lives were less important than that the property of Monsieur de Wendel should be preserved to make fat profits. No, it is not good for those who fight to know too much. Speeches, yes! The truth, no!"

His wife sniggered. "It is always the same. Let someone mention the war and he begins to talk about Briey—something that happened twenty-four years ago."

"And why not?" he demanded. "Things have not changed so much. Because we do not know about such things until after they have happened it does not mean that things like it are not happening now. When I think of war I think also of Briey and the glare of the blast furnaces in the sky to remind myself that I am an ordinary man who must not believe all that he is told. I see the newspapers from France with the blanks in them to show where the censor has been at work. They tell me certain things, these newspapers. France, they say, is fighting with England against Hitler and the Nazis for democracy and liberty."

"And you don't believe that?" Graham asked.

"I believe that *the peoples* of France and England are so fighting, but is that the same thing? I think of Briey and wonder. Those same newspapers once told me that the Germans were not taking ore from the Briey mines and that all was well. I am an invalid of the last war. I do not have to fight in this one. But I can think."

His wife laughed again. "Ha! It will be different when he gets to France again. He talks like a fool but you should take no notice, Messieurs. He is a good Frenchman. He won the Croix de Guerre."

He winked. "A little piece of silver outside the chest to serenade the little piece of steel inside, eh? It is the women, I think, who should fight these wars. They are more ferocious as patriots than the men."

"And what do you think, Mr. Kuvetli?" said Graham.

"Me? Ah, please!" Mr. Kuvetli looked apologetic. "I am neutral, you understand. I know nothing. I have no opinion." He spread out his hands. "I sell tobacco. Export business. That is enough."

The Frenchman's eyebrows went up. "Tobacco? So? I arranged a great deal of transport for the tobacco companies. What company is that?"

"Pazar of Istanbul."

"Pazar?" Mathis looked slightly puzzled. "I don't think . . ."

But Mr. Kuvetli interrupted him. "Ah! See! There is Greece!"

They looked. There, sure enough, was Greece. It looked like a low bank of cloud on the horizon beyond the end of the golden line of Makronisi, a line that was contracting slowly as the ship ploughed on its way through the Zea channel.

"Beautiful day!" enthused Mr. Kuvetli. "Magnificent!" He drew a deep breath and exhaled loudly. "I anticipate very much to see Athens. We get to Piræus at two o'clock."

"Are you and Madame going ashore?" said Graham to Mathis.

"No, I think not. It is too short a time." He turned his coat collar up and shivered. "I agree that it is a beautiful day, but it is cold."

"If you did not stand talking so much," said his wife, "you would keep warm. And you have no scarf."

"Very well, very well!" he said irritably. "We will go below. Excuse us, please."

"I think that I, too, will go," said Mr. Kuvetli. "Are you coming down, Mr. Graham?"

"I'll stay a little." He would have enough of Mr. Kuvetli later.

"Then at two o'clock."

"Yes."

When they had gone he looked at his watch, saw that it was eleven-thirty, and made up his mind to walk round the boat deck ten times before he went down for a drink. He was, he decided as he began to walk, a good deal better for his night's rest. For one thing, his hand had ceased throbbing and he could bend the fingers a little, without pain. More important, however, was the fact that the feeling of moving in a nightmare which he had had the previous day had now gone. He felt whole again and cheerful. Yesterday was years away. There was, of course, his bandaged hand to remind him of it but the wound no longer seemed significant. Yesterday it had been a part of something horrible. To-day it was a cut on the back of his hand, a cut which would take a few days to heal. Meanwhile he was on his way home, back to his work. As for Mademoiselle Josette, he had had, fortunately, enough sense left not to behave really stupidly. That he should actually have wanted, even momentarily, to kiss her was fantastic enough. However, there were extenuating circumstances. He had been tired and confused; and, while she was a woman whose needs and methods of fulfilling them were only too apparent, she was undeniably attractive in a blowzy way.

He had completed his fourth circuit when the subject of these reflections appeared on the deck. She had on a camel hair coat instead of the fur, a green cotton scarf round her head in place of the woollen one, and wore sports shoes with cork "platform" soles. She waited for him to come over to her.

He smiled and nodded. "Good morning."

She raised her eyebrows. "Good morning! Is that all you have to say?"

He was startled. "What should I say?"

"You have disappointed me. I thought that all Englishmen got out of bed early to eat a great English breakfast. I get out of bed at ten but you are nowhere to be found. The steward says that you are still in your cabin."

"Unfortunately they don't serve English breakfasts on this boat. I made do with coffee and drank it in bed."

She frowned. "Now, you do not ask why I wished to see you. Is it so natural that I should wish to see you as soon as I left my bed?"

The mock severity was appalling. Graham said: "I'm afraid I didn't take you seriously. Why *should* you want to find me?"

"Ah, that is better. It is not good but it is better. Are you going into Athens this afternoon?"

"Yes."

"I wished to ask you if you would let me come with you."

"I see. I should be . . ."

"But now it is too late."

"I'm so sorry," said Graham happily. "I should have been delighted to take you."

She shrugged. "It is too late. Mr. Kuvetli, the little Turk, has asked me and, *faut de mieux*, I accepted. I do not like him but he knows Athens very well. It will be interesting."

"Yes, I should think it would be."

"He is a very interesting man."

"Evidently."

"Of course, I might be able to persuade him . . ."

"Unfortunately, there is a difficulty. Last night Mr. Kuvetli asked me if I minded his going with me as he had never been in Athens before."

It gave him a great deal of pleasure to say it; but she was disconcerted only momentarily. She burst out laughing.

"You are not at all polite. Not at all. You let me say what you know to be untrue. You do not stop me. You are unkind." She laughed again. "But it is a good joke."

"I'm really very sorry."

"You are too kind. I wished only to be friendly to you. I do not care whether I go to Athens or not."

"I'm sure Mr. Kuvetli would be delighted if you came with us. So should I, of course. You probably know a great deal more about Athens than I do."

Her eyes narrowed suddenly. "What, please, do you mean by that?"

He had not meant anything at all beyond the plain statement. He said, with a smile that he intended to be reassuring: "I mean that you have probably danced there."

She stared at him sullenly for a moment. He felt the smile, still clinging fatuously to his lips, fading. She said slowly: "I do not think I like you as much as I thought. I do not think that you understand me at all."

"It's possible. I've known you for such a short time."

"Because a woman is an artiste," she said angrily, "you think that she must be of the *milieu*."

"Not at all. The idea hadn't occurred to me. Would you like to walk round the deck?"

She did not move. "I am beginning to think that I do not like you at all."

"I'm sorry. I was looking forward to your company on the journey."

"But you have Mr. Kuvetli," she said viciously.

"Yes, that's true. Unfortunately, he's not as attractive as you are."

She laughed sarcastically. "Oh, you have seen that I am attractive? That is very good. I am so pleased. I am honoured."

"I seem to have offended you," he said. "I apologise."

She waved one hand airily. "Do not trouble. I think that it is perhaps because you are stupid. You wish to walk. Very well, we will walk."

"Splendid."

They had taken three steps when she stopped again and faced him. "Why do you have to take this little Turk to Athens?" she demanded. "Tell him that you cannot go. If you were polite you would do that."

"And take you? Is that the idea?"

"If you asked me, I would go with you. I am bored with this ship and I like to speak English."

"I'm afraid that Mr. Kuvetli might not think it so polite."

"If you liked me it would not matter to you about Mr. Kuvetli." She shrugged. "But I understand. It does not matter. I think that you are very unkind, but it does not matter. I am bored."

"I'm sorry."

"Yes, you are sorry. That is all right. But I am still bored. Let us walk." And then, as they began to walk: "José thinks that you are indiscreet."

"Does he? Why?"

"That old German you talked to. How do you know that he is not a spy?"

He laughed outright. "A spy! What an extraordinary idea!"

She glanced at him coldly. "And why is it extraordinary?"

"If you had talked to him you would know quite well that he couldn't possibly be anything of the sort."

"Perhaps not. José is always very suspicious of people. He always believes that they are lying about themselves."

"Frankly, I should be inclined to accept José's disapproval of a person as a recommendation."

"Oh, he does not disapprove. He is just interested. He likes to find things out about people. He thinks that we are all animals. He is never shocked by anything people do."

"He sounds very stupid."

"You do not understand José. He does not think of good things and evil things as they do in the convent, but only of things. He says that a thing that is good for one person may be evil for another, so that it is stupid to talk of good and evil."

"But people sometimes do good things simply because those things *are* good."

"Only because they feel nice when they do them—that is what José says."

"What about the people who stop themselves from doing evil because it *is* evil?"

"José says that if a person *really* needs to do something he will not trouble about what others may think of him. If he is really hungry, he will steal. If he is in real danger, he will kill. If he is really afraid, he will be cruel. He says that it was people who were safe and well fed who invented good and evil so that they would not have to worry about the people who were hungry and unsafe. What a man does depends on what he needs. It is simple. You are not a murderer. You say that murder is evil. José would say that you are as much a murderer as Landru or Weidmann and that it is just that fortune has not made it necessary for you to murder anyone. Someone once told him that there was a German proverb which said that a man is an ape in velvet. He always likes to repeat it."

"And do you agree with José? I don't mean about my being a potential murderer. I mean about why people are what they are."

"I do not agree or disagree. I do not care. For me, some people are nice, some people are sometimes nice and others are not at all nice." She looked at him out of the corners of her eyes. "You are sometimes nice."

"What do you think about yourself?"

She smiled. "Me? Oh, I am sometimes nice, too. When people are nice to me, I am a little angel." She added: "José thinks that he is as clever as God."

"Yes, I can see that he would."

"You do not like him. I am not surprised. It is only the old women who like José."

"Do *you* like him?"

"He is my partner. With us it is business."

"Yes, you told me that before. But do you *like* him?"

"He makes me laugh sometimes. He says amusing things about people. You remember Serge? José said that Serge would steal straw from his mother's kennel. It made me laugh very much."

"It must have done. Would you like a drink now?"

She looked at a small silver watch on her wrist and said that she would.

They went down. One of the ship's officers was leaning by the bar with a beer in his hand, talking to the steward. As Graham ordered the drinks, the officer turned his attention to Josette. He obviously counted on being successful with women: his dark eyes did not leave hers while he was talking to her. Graham, listening to the Italian with bored incomprehension, was ignored. He was content to be ignored. He got on with his drink. It was not until the gong sounded for lunch and Haller came in that he remembered that he had done nothing about changing his place at table.

The German nodded in a friendly way as Graham sat down beside him. "I did not expect to have your company to-day."

"I completely forgot to speak to the steward. If you . . ."

"No, please. I take it as a compliment."

"How is your wife?"

"Better, though she is not yet prepared to face a meal. But she took a walk this morning. I showed her the sea. This is the way Xerxes' great ships sailed to their defeat at Salamis. For those Persians that grey mass on the horizon was the country of Themistocles and the Attic Greeks of Marathon. You will think that it is my German sentimentality but I must say that the fact that for me that grey mass is the country of Venizelos and Metaxas is as regrettable as it could be. I was at the German Institute in Athens for several years when I was young."

"Shall you go ashore this afternoon?"

"I do not think so. Athens can only remind me of what I know already—that I am old. Do you know the city?"

"A little. I know Salamis better."

"That is now their big naval base, isn't it?"

Graham said yes rather too carelessly. Haller glanced sideways and smiled slightly. "I beg your pardon. I see that I am on the point of being indiscreet."

"I shall go ashore to get some books and cigarettes. Can I get anything for you?"

"It is very kind of you, but there is nothing. Are you going alone?"

"Mr. Kuvetli, the Turkish gentleman at the next table, has asked me to show him round. He has never been to Athens."

Haller raised his eyebrows. "Kuvetli? So that is his name. I talked with him this morning. He speaks German quite well and knows Berlin a little."

"He speaks English, too, and very good French. He seems to have travelled a lot."

Haller grunted. "I should have thought that a Turk who had travelled a lot would have been to Athens."

"He sells tobacco. Greece grows its own tobacco."

"Yes, of course. I had not thought of that. I am apt to forget that most people who travel do so not to see but to sell. I talked with him for twenty minutes. He has a way of talking without saying anything. His conversation consists of agreements or indisputable statements."

"I suppose it's something to do with his being a salesman. 'The world is my customer and the customer is always right.'"

"He interests me. In my opinion he is too simple to be true. The smile is a little too stupid, the conversation a little too evasive. He tells you some things about himself within the first minutes of your meeting him and then tells you no more. That is curious. A man who begins by telling you about himself usually goes on doing so. Besides, who ever heard of a simple Turkish business man? No, he makes me think of a man who has set out to create a definite impression of himself in people's minds. He is a man who wishes to be underrated."

"But why? He's not selling us tobacco."

"Perhaps, as you suggest, he regards the world as his customer. But you will have an opportunity of probing a little this afternoon." He smiled. "You see, I assume, quite unwarrantably, that you are interested. I must ask your pardon. I am a bad traveller who has had to do a great deal of travelling. To pass the time I have learned to play a game. I compare my own first impressions of my fellow travellers with what I can find out about them."

"If you are right you score a point? If you are wrong you lose one?"

"Precisely. Actually I enjoy losing more than winning. It is an old man's game, you see."

"And what is your impression of Señor Gallindo?"

Haller frowned. "I am afraid that I am only too right about that gentleman. He is not really very interesting."

"He has a theory that all men are potential murderers and is fond of quoting a German proverb to the effect that a man is an ape in velvet."

"It does not surprise me," was the acid reply. "Every man must justify himself somehow."

"Aren't you a little severe?"

"Perhaps. I regret to say that I find Señor Gallindo a very ill-mannered person."

Graham's reply was interrupted by the entrance of the man himself, looking as if he had just got out of bed. He was followed by the Italian mother and son. The conversation became desultory and over-polite.

The *Sestri Levante* was tied up alongside the new wharf on the north side of the harbour of the Piræus soon after two o'clock. As, with Mr. Kuvetli, Graham stood on the deck waiting for the passenger gangway to be hoisted into position, he saw that Josette and José had left the saloon and were standing behind him. José nodded to them suspiciously as if he were afraid that they were thinking of borrowing money from him. The girl smiled. It was the tolerant smile that sees a friend disregarding good advice.

Mr. Kuvetli spoke up eagerly. "Are you going ashore, Monsieur-dame?"

"Why should we?" demanded José. "It is a waste of time to go."

But Mr. Kuvetli was not sensitive. "Ah! Then you know Athens, you and your wife?"

"Too well. It is a dirty town."

"I have not seen it. I was thinking that if you and Madame were going, we might all go together." He beamed round expectantly.

José set his teeth and rolled his eyes as if he were being tortured. "I have already said that we are *not* going."

"But it is very kind of you to suggest it," Josette put in graciously.

The Mathises came out of the saloon. "Ah!" he greeted them. "The adventurers! Do not forget that we leave at five. We shall not wait for you."

The gangway thudded into position and Mr. Kuvetli clambered down it nervously. Graham followed. He was beginning to wish that he had decided to stay on board. At the foot of the gangway he turned and looked up—the inevitable movement of a passenger leaving a ship. Mathis waved his hand.

"He is very amiable, Monsieur Mathis," said Mr. Kuvetli.

"Very."

Beyond the Customs shed there was a fly-blown old Fiat landaulet with a notice on it in French, Italian, English and Greek, saying that an hour's tour of the sights and antiquities of Athens for four persons cost five hundred drachmes.

Graham stopped. He thought of the electric trains and trams he would have to clamber on to, of the hill up to the Acropolis, of the walking he would have to do, of the exhausting boredom of sightseeing on foot. Any way of avoiding the worst of it was, he decided, worth thirty shillingsworth of drachmes.

"I think," he said, "that we will take this car."

Mr. Kuvetli looked worried. "There is no other way? It is very expensive."

"That's all right. I'll pay."

"But it is you who do favour to me. I must pay."

"Oh, I should have taken a car in any case. Five hundred drachmes is not really expensive."

Mr. Kuvetli's eyes opened very wide. "Five hundred? But that is for four persons. We are two."

Graham laughed. "I doubt if the driver will look at it that way. I don't suppose it costs him any less to take two instead of four."

Mr. Kuvetli looked apologetic. "I have little Greek. You will permit me to ask him?"

"Of course. Go ahead."

The driver, a predatory looking man wearing a suit several sizes too small for him and highly polished tan shoes without socks, had leapt out at their approach and was holding the door open. Now he began to shout. "*Allez! Allez! Allez!*" he exhorted them; "*très bon marché. Cinque-cento, solamente.*"

Mr. Kuvetli strode forward, a stout, grubby little David going out to do battle with a lean Goliath in stained blue serge. He began to speak.

He spoke Greek fluently; there was no doubt of it. Graham saw the surprised look on the driver's face replaced by one of fury as a torrent of words poured from Mr. Kuvetli's lips. He was disparaging the car. He began to point. He pointed to every defect in the thing from a patch of rust on the luggage grid to a small tear in the upholstery, from a crack in the windshield to a worn patch on the running board. He paused for breath and the angry driver seized the opportunity of replying. He shouted and thumped the door panels with his fist to emphasise his remarks and made long streamlining gestures. Mr. Kuvetli smiled sceptically and returned to the attack. The driver spat on the ground and counterattacked. Mr. Kuvetli replied with a short, sharp burst of fire. The driver flung up his hands, disgusted but defeated.

Mr. Kuvetli turned to Graham. "Price," he reported simply, "is now three hundred drachmes. It is too much, I think, but it will take time to reduce more. But if you think . . ."

"It seems a very fair price," said Graham hurriedly.

Mr. Kuvetli shrugged. "Perhaps. It could be reduced more, but . . ." He turned and nodded to the driver, who suddenly grinned broadly. They got into the cab.

"Did you say," said Graham, as they drove off, "that you had never been in Greece before?"

Mr. Kuvetli's smile was bland. "I know little Greek," he said. "I was born in Izmir."

The tour began. The Greek drove fast and with dash, twitching the wheel playfully in the direction of slow moving pedestrians, so that they had to run for their lives, and flinging a running commentary over his right shoulder as he went. They stopped for a moment on the road by the Theseion and again on the Acropolis where they got out and walked round. Here, Mr. Kuvetli's curiosity seemed inexhaustible. He insisted on a century by century history of the Parthenon and prowled round the museum as if he would have liked to spend the rest of the day there; but at last they got back into the car and were whisked round to the theatre of Dionysos, the arch of Hadrian, the Olympieion, and the Royal Palace. It was, by now, four o'clock and Mr. Kuvetli had been asking questions and saying "very nice" and "*formidable*" for well over the allotted hour. At Graham's suggestion they stopped in the Syntagma, changed some money and paid off the driver, adding that if he liked to wait in the square he could earn another fifty drachmes by driving them back to the wharf later. The driver agreed. Graham bought his cigarettes and books and sent his telegram. There was a band playing on the terrace of one of the cafés when they got back to the square and at Mr. Kuvetli's suggestion they sat down at a table to drink coffee before returning to the port.

Mr. Kuvetli surveyed the square regretfully. "It is very nice," he said with a sigh. "One would like to stay longer. So many magnificent ruins we have seen!"

Graham remembered what Haller had said at lunch about Mr. Kuvetli's evasions. "Which is your favourite city, Mr. Kuvetli?"

"Ah, that is difficult to say. All cities have their magnificences. I like all cities." He breathed the air. "It is most kind of you to bring me here to-day, Mr. Graham."

Graham stuck to the point. "A great pleasure. But surely you have some preference."

Mr. Kuvetli looked anxious. "It is so difficult. I like London very much."

"Personally I like Paris better."

"Ah, yes. Paris is also magnificent."

Feeling rather baffled, Graham sipped his coffee. Then he had another idea. "What do you think of Señor Gallindo, Mr. Kuvetli?"

"Señor Gallindo? It is so difficult. I do not know him. His manner is strange."

"His manner," said Graham, "is damnably offensive. Don't you agree?"

"I do not like Señor Gallindo very much," conceded Mr. Kuvetli. "But he is Spanish."

"What can that have to do with it? The Spanish are an exceedingly polite race."

"Ah, I have not been to Spain." He looked at his watch. "It is quarter-past four now. Perhaps we should go, eh? It has been very nice this afternoon."

Graham nodded wearily. If Haller wanted Mr. Kuvetli "probed" he could do the probing himself. His, Graham's, personal opinion was that Mr. Kuvetli was an ordinary bore whose conversation, such as it was, sounded a little unreal because he used languages with which he was unfamiliar.

Mr. Kuvetli insisted on paying for the coffee; Mr. Kuvetli insisted on paying the fare back to the wharf. By a quarter to five they were on board again. An hour later Graham stood on deck watching the pilot's boat chugging back towards the greying land. The Frenchman, Mathis, who was leaning on the rail a few feet away, turned his head.

"Well, that's *that!* Two more days and we shall be in Genoa. Did you enjoy your excursion ashore this afternoon, Monsieur?"

"Oh, yes, thank you. It was . . ."

But he never finished telling Monsieur Mathis what it was. A man had come out of the saloon door some yards away and was standing blinking at the setting sun which streamed across the sea towards them.

"Ah, yes," said Mathis. "We have acquired another passenger. He arrived while you were ashore this afternoon. I expect that he is a Greek."

Graham did not, could not, answer. He knew that the man standing there with the golden light of the sun on his face was not a Greek. He knew, too, that beneath the dark grey raincoat the man wore there was a crumpled brown suit with lumpy padded shoulders; that below the high-crowned soft hat and above the pale, doughy features with the self-conscious mouth was thinning curly hair. He knew that this man's name was Banat.

CHAPTER SIX

GRAHAM STOOD THERE motionless. His body was tingling as if some violent mechanical shock had been transmitted to it through his heels. He heard Mathis' voice a long way away, asking him what the matter was.

He said: "I don't feel well. Will you excuse me, please?"

He saw apprehension flicker over the Frenchman's face and thought: "He thinks I'm going to be sick." But he did not wait for Mathis to say anything. He turned and, without looking again at the man by the saloon door, walked to the door at the other end of the deck and went below to his cabin.

He locked the door when he got inside. He was shaking from head to foot. He sat down on the bunk and tried to pull himself together. He told himself: "There's no need to get worried. There's a way out of this. You've got to think."

Somehow Banat had discovered that he was on the *Sestri Levante*. It could not have been very difficult. An inquiry made at the Wagon-Lit and shipping company offices would have been enough. The man had then taken a ticket for Sofia, left the train when it crossed the Greek frontier, and taken another train via Salonika to Athens.

He pulled Kopeikin's telegram out of his pocket and stared at it. "All well!" The fools! The bloody fools! He'd distrusted this ship business from the start. He ought to have relied on his instinct and insisted on seeing the British Consul. If it had not been for that conceited imbecile Haki . . . But now he was caught like a rat in a trap. Banat wouldn't miss twice. My God, no! The man was a professional murderer. He would have his reputation to consider—to say nothing of his fee.

A curious but vaguely familiar feeling began to steal over him: a feeling that was dimly associated with the smell of antiseptics and the singing of a kettle. With a sudden rush of horror, he remembered. It had happened years ago. They had been trying out an experimental fourteen-inch gun on the proving ground. The second time they fired it, it had burst. There had been something wrong with the breech mechanism. It had killed two men outright and badly injured a third. This third man had looked like a great clot of blood lying there on the concrete. But the clot of blood had screamed: screamed steadily until the ambulance had come and a doctor had used a hypodermic. It had been a thin, high, inhuman sound; just like the singing of a kettle. The doctor had said that the man was unconscious even though he was screaming. Before they had examined the remains of the gun, the concrete had been swabbed down with a solution of Lysol. He hadn't eaten any lunch. In the afternoon it had begun to rain. He . . .

He realised suddenly that he was swearing. The words were dropping from his lips in a steady stream: a meaningless succession of obscenities. He stood up quickly. He was losing his head. Something had got to be done; and done quickly. If he could get off the ship . . .

He wrenched the cabin door open and went out into the alley-way. The Purser was the man to see first. The Purser's office was on the same deck. He went straight to it.

The door of the office was ajar and the Purser, a tall, middle-aged Italian with the stump of a cigar in his mouth, was sitting in his shirt-sleeves before a typewriter and a stack of copies of Bills of Lading. He was copying details of the Bills on to the ruled sheet in the typewriter. He looked up with a frown as Graham knocked. He was busy.

"*Signore?*"

"Do you speak English?"

"No, *Signore.*"

"French?"

"Yes. What is it you wish?"

"I want to see the Captain at once."

"For what reason, Monsieur?"

"It is absolutely necessary that I am put ashore immediately."

The Purser put his cigar down and turned in his swivel chair.

"My French is not very good," he said calmly. "Do you mind repeating . . . ?"

"I want to be put ashore."

"Monsieur Graham, is it?"

"Yes."

"I regret, Monsieur Graham. It is too late. The pilot boat has gone. You should have . . ."

"I know. But it is absolutely necessary that I go ashore now. No, I am not mad. I realise that under ordinary circumstances it would be out of the question. But the circumstances are exceptional. I am ready to pay for the loss of time and the inconvenience caused."

The Purser looked bewildered. "But why? Are you ill?"

"No, I . . ." He stopped and could have bitten his tongue off. There was no doctor aboard and the threat of some infectious disease might have been sufficient. But it was too late now. "If you will arrange for me to see the Captain at once, I will explain why. I can assure you that my reasons are good ones."

"I am afraid," said the Purser stiffly, "that it is out of the question. You do not understand . . ."

"All I am asking," interrupted Graham desperately, "is that you put back a short way and ask for a pilot boat. I am willing and able to pay."

The Purser smiled in an exasperated way. "This is a ship, Monsieur, not a taxi. We carry cargo and run to a schedule. You are not ill and . . ."

"I have already said that my reasons are excellent. If you will allow me to see the Captain . . ."

"It is quite useless to argue, Monsieur. I do not doubt your willingness or ability to pay the cost of a boat from the harbour. Unfortunately that is not the important thing. You say that you are not ill but that you have reasons. As you can only have thought of those reasons within the last ten minutes, you must not be angry if I say that they cannot be of very grave importance. Let me assure you, Monsieur, that nothing but proved and evident reasons of life and death will suffice to stop any ship for the convenience of one passenger. Naturally, if you can give me any such reasons I will place them before the Captain immediately. If not, then I am afraid your reasons must wait until we get to Genoa."

"I assure you . . ."

The Purser smiled sorrowfully. "I do not question the good faith of your assurances, Monsieur, but I regret to say that we need more than assurances."

"Very well," snapped Graham, "since you insist on details I will tell you. I have just found that there is a man on this ship who is here for the express purpose of murdering me."

The Purser's face went blank. "Indeed, Monsieur?"

"Yes, I . . ." Something in the man's eyes stopped him. "I suppose you've decided that I'm either mad or drunk," he concluded.

"Not at all, Monsieur." But what he was thinking was as plain as a pikestaff. He was thinking that Graham was just another of the poor lunatics with whom his work sometimes brought him in contact. They were a nuisance, because they wasted time. But he was tolerant. It was useless to be angry with a lunatic. Besides, dealing with them always seemed to emphasize his own sanity and intelligence: the sanity and intelligence which, had the owners been less short sighted, would long ago have taken him to a seat on the board of directors. And they made good stories to tell his friends when he got home. "Imagine, Beppo! There was this Englishman, looking sane but really mad. He thought that someone was trying to murder him! Imagine! It is the whisky, you know. I said to him . . ." But meanwhile he would have to be humoured, to be dealt with tactfully. "Not at all, Monsieur," he repeated.

Graham began to lose control of his temper. "You asked me for my reasons. I am giving them to you."

"And I am listening carefully, Monsieur."

"There is someone on this ship who is here to murder me."

"And his name, Monsieur?"

"Banat. B-A-N-A-T. He is a Roumanian. He . . ."

"One moment, Monsieur." The Purser got a sheet of paper out of a drawer and ran a pencil down the names on it with ostentatious care. Then he looked up. "There is no one of that name or nationality on the ship, Monsieur."

"I was about to tell you, when you interrupted me, that the man is travelling on a false passport."

"Then, please . . ."

"He is the passenger who came aboard this afternoon."

The Purser looked at the paper again. "Cabin number nine. That is Monsieur Mavrodopoulos. He is a Greek business man."

"That may be what his passport says. His real name is Banat and he is a Roumanian."

The Purser remained polite with obvious difficulty. "Have you any proof of that, Monsieur?"

"If you radio Colonel Haki of the Turkish police at Istanbul, he will confirm what I say."

"This is an Italian ship, Monsieur. We are not in Turkish territorial waters. We can refer such a matter only to the Italian police. In any case, we carry wireless only for navigational purposes. This is not the *Rex* or the *Conte di Savoia*, you understand. This matter must be left until we reach Genoa. The police there will deal with your accusation concerning the passport."

"I don't care a damn about his passport," said Graham violently. "I'm telling you that the man intends to kill me."

"And why?"

"Because he has been paid to do so; that is why. Now do you understand?"

The Purser got to his feet. He had been tolerant. Now the time had come to be firm. "No, Monsieur, I do *not* understand."

"Then if you cannot understand, let me speak to the Captain."

"That will not be necessary, Monsieur. I understand enough." He looked Graham in the eyes. "In my opinion there are two *charitable* explanations of this matter. Either you have mistaken this Monsieur Mavrodopoulos for someone else, or you have had a bad dream. If it is the former, I advise you not to repeat your mistake to anyone else. I am discreet, but if Monsieur Mavrodopoulos should hear of it he might regard it as a reflection upon his honour. If it is the second, I suggest that you lie down in your cabin for a while. And remember that nobody is going to murder you on this ship. There are too many people about."

"But don't you see . . . ?" shouted Graham.

"I see," said the Purser grimly, "that there is another less charitable explanation of this matter. You may have invented this story simply because for some private reason you wish to be put ashore. If that is true, I am sorry. It is a ridiculous story. In any case, the ship stops at Genoa and not before. And now, if you will excuse me, I have work to do."

"I demand to see the Captain."

"If you will close the door as you leave," said the Purser happily.

Almost sick with anger and fear, Graham went back to his cabin.

He lit a cigarette and tried to think reasonably. He should have gone straight to the Captain. He could still go straight to the Captain. For a moment he considered doing so. If he . . . But it would be useless and unnecessarily humiliating. The Captain, even if he could get to him and make him understand, would probably receive his story with even less sympathy. And he would still have no proof that what he said was true. Even if he could persuade the Captain that there was some truth in what he was saying, that he was not, in fact, suffering from some form of delusional insanity, the answer would be the same: "Nobody is going to murder you on this ship. There are too many people about."

Too many people about! They did not know Banat. The man who had walked into a police official's house in broad daylight, shot the official and his wife and then calmly walked out again, was not going to be unnerved so easily. Passengers had disappeared from ships in mid-ocean before. Sometimes their bodies had been washed ashore, and sometimes they hadn't. Sometimes the disappearances had been explained, and sometimes they hadn't. What would there be to connect this disappearance of an English engineer (who had behaved very queerly) from a ship at sea with Mr.

Mavrodopoulos, a Greek business man? Nothing. And even if the body of the English engineer were washed ashore before the fish had rendered it unidentifiable and it were found that he had been killed before he had entered the water, who was going to prove that Mr. Mavrodopoulos—if by that time there were anything left of Mr. Mavrodopoulos but the ashes of his passport—had been responsible for the killing? Nobody.

He thought of the telegram he had sent in Athens that afternoon. "Home Monday," he had said. Home Monday! He looked at his unbandaged hand and moved the fingers of it. By Monday they could be dead and beginning to decompose with the rest of the entity which called itself Graham. Stephanie would be upset, but she'd get over it quickly. She was resilient and sensible. But there wouldn't be much money for her. She'd have to sell the house. He should have taken out more insurance. If only he'd known. But of course it was just because you *didn't* know, that there *were* such things as insurance companies. Still, he could do nothing now but hope that it would be over quickly, that it wouldn't be painful.

He shivered and began to swear again. Then he pulled himself up sharply. He'd *got* to think of some way out. And not only for his own sake and Stephanie's. There was the job he had to do. "It is in the interests of your country's enemies that when the snow melts and the rain ceases, Turkish naval strength shall be exactly what it is now. They will do anything to see that it is so." Anything! Behind Banat was the German agent in Sofia and behind him was Germany and the Nazis. Yes, he'd *got* to think of some way out. If other Englishmen could die for their country, surely he could manage to stay alive for it. Then another of Colonel Haki's statements came back to him. "You have advantages over the soldier. You have only to defend yourself. You do not have to go into the open. You may run away without being a coward."

Well he couldn't run away now; but the rest of it was true enough. He didn't have to go out into the open. He could stay here in the cabin; have his meals here; keep the door locked. He could defend himself, too, if need be. Yes, by God! He had Kopeikin's revolver.

He had put it among the clothes in his suit-case. Now, thanking his stars that he had not refused to take it, he got it out and weighed it in his hand.

For Graham a gun was a series of mathematical expressions resolved in such a way as to enable one man, by touching a button, to project an armour-piercing shell so that it hit a target several miles away plumb in the middle. It was a piece of machinery no more and no less significant than a vacuum cleaner or a bacon slicer. It had no nationality and no loyalties. It was neither awe-inspiring nor symbolic of anything except the owner's ability to pay for it. His interest in the men who had to fire the products of his skill as in the men who had to suffer their fire (and, thanks to his employers' tireless internationalism, the same sets of men often had to do both) had always been detached. To him who knew what even one four-inch shell could accomplish in the way of destruction, it seemed that they should be—could only be—nerveless cyphers. That they were not was an evergreen source of astonishment to him. His attitude towards them was as uncomprehending as that of the stoker of a crematorium towards the solemnity of the grave.

But this revolver was different. It wasn't impersonal. There was a relationship between it and the human body. It had, perhaps, an effective range of twenty-five yards or less. That meant that you could see the face of the man at whom you fired it both before and after you fired it. You could see and hear his agony. You couldn't think of honour and glory with a revolver in your hand, but only of killing and being killed. There was no machine to serve. Life and death were there in your hand in the shape of an elementary arrangement of springs and levers and a few grammes of lead and cordite.

He had never handled a revolver in his life before. He examined it carefully. Stamped above the trigger guard was "Made in U.S.A." and the name of an American typewriter manufacturer. There were two small sliding bosses on the other side. One was the safety catch. The other, when moved, released the breech which dropped sideways and showed that there were cartridges in all six chambers. It was beautifully made. He took the cartridges out and pulled the trigger once or twice experimentally. It was not easy with his bandaged hand, but it could be done. He put the cartridges back.

He felt better now. Banat might be a professional killer, but he was as susceptible to bullets as any other man. And *he* had to make the first move. One had to look at things from his point of view. He'd failed in Istanbul and he'd had to catch up with the victim again. He'd managed to get aboard the boat on which the victim was travelling. But did that really help him very much? What he had done in Roumania as a member of the Iron Guard was beside the point now. A man could afford to be bold when he was protected by an army of thugs and an intimidated judge. It was true that passengers were sometimes lost off ships at sea; but those ships were big liners, not two thousand ton cargo boats. It really would be very difficult to kill a man on a boat of that size without anyone discovering that you had done so. You might be able to do it; that is if you could get your victim alone on deck at night. You could knife him and push him over the side. But you would have to get him there first, and there was more than a chance that you would be seen from the bridge. Or heard: a knifed man might make a lot of noise before he reached the water. And if you cut his throat there would be a lot of blood left behind to be accounted for. Besides, that was always assuming that you could use a knife so skilfully. Banat was a gunman, not a cut-throat. That confounded Purser was right. There were too many people about for anyone to murder him on the ship. As long as he was careful he would be all right. The real danger would begin when he got off the ship at Genoa.

Obviously the thing for him to do there would be to go straight to the British Consul, explain all the circumstances, and secure police protection as far as the frontier. Yes, that was it. He had one priceless advantage over the enemy. *Banat did not know that he was identified.* He would be assuming that the victim was unsuspecting, that he could bide his time, that he could do his work between Genoa and the French frontier. By the time he discovered his mistake it would be too late for him to do anything about rectifying it. The only thing now was to see that he did not discover the mistake too soon.

Supposing, for instance, that Banat had noticed his hasty retreat from the deck. His blood ran cold at the idea. But no, the man had not been looking. The supposition showed, though, how careful he had to be. It was out of the question for him to skulk in his cabin for the rest of the trip. That would arouse immediate suspicion. He would have to look as unsuspecting as he could and yet take care not to expose himself to any sort of attack. He must make sure that if he were not in his cabin with the door locked, he was with or near one of the other passengers. He must even be amiable to "Monsieur Mavrodopoulos."

He unbuttoned his jacket and put the revolver in his hip pocket. It bulged absurdly and uncomfortably. He took the wallet out of his breast pocket and put the revolver there. That was uncomfortable, too, and the shape of it could be seen from the outside. Banat must not see that he was armed. The revolver could stay in the cabin.

He put it back in his suit-case and stood up, bracing himself. He'd go straight up to the saloon and have a drink now. If Banat were there, so much the better. A drink would help to ease the strain of the first encounter. He knew that it would be a strain. He had to face a man who had tried once to kill him and who was going to try again, and behave as if he had never seen or heard of him before. His stomach was already responding to the prospect. But he had to keep calm. His life, he told himself, might depend on his behaving normally. And the longer he hung about thinking it over, the less normal he would be. Better get it over with now.

He lit a cigarette, opened the cabin door and went straight upstairs to the saloon.

Banat was not there. He could have laughed aloud with relief. Josette and José were there with drinks in front of them, listening to Mathis.

"And so," he was saying vehemently, "it goes on. The big newspapers of the Right are owned by those whose interest it is to see that France spends her wealth on arms and that the ordinary people do not understand too much of what goes on behind the scenes. I am glad to be going back to France because it is my country. But do not ask me to love those who have my country in the palms of their hands. Ah, no!"

His wife was listening with tight-lipped disapproval. José was openly yawning. Josette was nodding sympathetically but her face lit up with relief when she saw Graham. "And where has our Englishman been?" she said immediately. "Mr. Kuvetli has told everyone what a magnificent time you both had."

"I've been in my cabin recovering from the afternoon's excitements."

Mathis did not look very pleased at the interruption but said agreeably enough: "I was afraid that you were ill, Monsieur. Are you better now?"

"Oh yes, thanks."

"You have been ill?" demanded Josette.

"I felt tired."

"It is the ventilation," said Madame Mathis promptly. "I myself have felt a nausea and a headache since I got on the ship. We should complain. But"—she made a derogatory gesture in the direction of her husband—"as long as he is comfortable all is well."

Mathis grinned. "Bah! It is seasickness."

"You are ridiculous. If I am sick it is of you."

José made a loud plopping noise with his tongue and leaned back in his chair, his closed eyes and tightened lips calling upon Heaven to deliver him from domesticity.

Graham ordered a whisky.

"Whisky?" José sat up whistling astonishment. "The Englishman drinks whisky!" he announced and then, pursing his lips and screwing up his face to express congenital aristocratic idiocy, added: "Some viskee, pliz, ol' bhoy!" He looked round, grinning, for applause.

"That is his idea of an Englishman," Josette explained. "He is very stupid."

"Oh I don't think so," said Graham; "he has never been to England. A great many English people who have never been to Spain are under the impression that all Spaniards smell of garlic."

Mathis giggled.

José half rose in his chair. "Do you intend to be insulting?" he demanded.

"Not at all. I was merely pointing out that these misconceptions exist. You, for instance, do not smell of garlic at all."

José subsided into his chair again. "I am glad to hear you say so," he said ominously. "If I thought . . ."

"Ah! Be silent!" Josette broke in. "You make yourself look a fool."

To Graham's relief the subject was disposed of by the entrance of Mr. Kuvetli. He was beaming happily.

"I come," he said to Graham, "to ask you to have drink with me."

"That's very good of you but I've just ordered a drink. Supposing you have one with me."

"Most kind. I will take vermouth, please." He sat down. "You have seen we have new passenger?"

"Yes, Monsieur Mathis pointed him out to me." He turned to the steward bringing him his whisky and ordered Mr. Kuvetli's vermouth.

"He is Greek gentleman. Name of Mavrodopoulos. He is business man."

"What business is he in?" Graham found, to his relief, that he could talk of Monsieur Mavrodopoulos quite calmly.

"That I do not know."

"That I do not care," said Josette. "I have just seen him. Ugh!"

"What's the matter with him?"

"She likes only men who look clean and simple," said José vindictively. "This Greek looks dirty. He would probably smell dirty too, but he uses a cheap perfume." He kissed his fingers to the air. "*Nuit de Petits Gars! Numero soixante-neuf! Cinq francs la bouteille.*"

Madame Mathis' face froze.

"You are disgusting, José," said Josette. "Besides, your own perfume cost only fifty francs a bottle. It is filthy. And you must not say such things. You will offend Madame here who is not used to your jokes."

But Madame Mathis had already taken offence. "It is disgraceful," she said angrily, "that such things should be said when there are women present. With men alone it would not be polite."

"Ah yes!" said Mathis. "My wife and I are not hypocrites but there are some things that should not be said." He looked as if he were pleased to be able, for once, to side with his wife. Her surprise was almost pathetic. They proceeded to make the most of the occasion.

She said: "Monsieur Gallindo should apologize."

"I must insist," said Mathis, "that you apologize to my wife."

José stared at them in angry astonishment. "Apologize? What for?"

"He will apologize," said Josette. She turned to him and broke into Spanish. "Apologize, you dirty fool. Do you want trouble? Don't you see he's showing off to the woman? He would break you in pieces."

José shrugged. "Very well." He looked insolently at the Mathises. "I apologize. What for, I do not know, but I apologize."

"My wife accepts the apology," said Mathis stiffly. "It is not gracious but it is accepted."

"An officer says," remarked Mr. Kuvetli tactfully, "that we shall not be able to see Messina because it will be dark."

But this elephantine change of subject was unnecessary for at that moment Banat came through the door from the promenade deck.

He stood there for an instant looking at them, his raincoat hanging open, his hat in his hand, like a man who has strayed into a picture gallery out of the rain. His white face was drawn from lack of sleep, there were circles under the small deep-set eyes, the full lips were twisted slightly as if he had a headache.

Graham's heart drummed sickeningly at the base of his skull. This was the executioner. The hand with the hat in it was the hand which had fired the shots which had grazed his own hand, now outstretched to pick up a glass of whisky. This was the man who had killed men for as little as five thousand francs and his expenses.

He felt the blood leaving his face. He had only glanced quickly at the man but the whole picture of him was in his mind; the whole picture from the dusty tan shoes to the new tie with the filthy soft collar and the tired, frowsty, stupid face. He drank some of his whisky and saw that Mr. Kuvetli was bestowing his smile on the newcomer. The others were staring blankly.

Banat walked slowly over to the bar.

"Bon soir, Monsieur," said Mr. Kuvetli.

"Bon soir." It was grunted almost inaudibly as if he were anxious not to commit himself to accepting something he did not want. He reached the bar and murmured something to the steward.

He had passed close to Madame Mathis and Graham saw her frown. Then he himself caught the smell of scent. It was attar of roses and very strong. He remembered Colonel Haki's question as to whether he had noticed any perfume in his room at the Adler-Palace after the attacks. Here was the explanation. The man reeked of scent. The smell of it would stay with the things he touched.

"Are you going far, Monsieur?" said Mr. Kuvetli.

The man eyed him. "No. Genoa."

"It is a beautiful city."

Banat turned without answering to the drink the steward had poured out for him. He had not once looked at Graham.

"You are not looking well," said Josette severely. "I do not think you are sincere when you say that you are only tired."

"You are tired?" said Mr. Kuvetli in French. "Ah, it is my fault. Always with ancient monuments it is necessary to walk." He seemed to have given Banat up as a bad job.

"Oh, I enjoyed the walk."

"It is the ventilation," Madame Mathis repeated stubbornly.

"There *is*," conceded her husband, "a certain stuffiness." He addressed himself very pointedly to exclude José from his audience. "But what can one expect for so little money?"

"So little!" exclaimed José. "That is very good. It is quite expensive enough for me. I am not a millionaire.

Mathis flushed angrily. "There are more expensive ways of travelling from Istanbul to Genoa."

"There is always a more expensive way of doing anything," retorted José.

Josette said quickly: "My husband always exaggerates."

"Travelling is very expensive to-day," pronounced Mr. Kuvetli.

"But . . ."

The argument rambled on, pointless and stupid; a mask for the antagonism between José and the Mathises. Graham listened with half his mind. He knew that sooner or later Banat must look at him and he wanted to see that look. Not that it would tell him anything that he did not already know, but he wanted to see it just the same. He could look at Mathis and yet see Banat out of the corner of his eye. Banat raised the glass of brandy to his lips and drank some of it; then, as he put the glass down, he looked directly at Graham.

Graham leaned back in his chair.

". . . but," Mathis was saying, "compare the service one receives. On the train there is a *couchette* in a compartment with others. One sleeps—perhaps. There is waiting at Belgrade for the coaches from Bucharest and at Trieste for the coaches from Budapest. There are passport examinations in the middle of the night and terrible food in the day. There is the noise and there is the dust and soot. I cannot conceive . . ."

Graham drained his glass. Banat was inspecting him: secretly, as the hangman inspects the man whom he is to execute the following morning; mentally weighing him, looking at his neck, calculating the drop.

"Travelling is very expensive to-day," said Mr. Kuvetli again.

At that moment the dinner gong sounded. Banat put his glass down and went out of the room. The Mathises followed. Graham saw that Josette was looking at him curiously. He got to his feet. There was a smell of food coming from the kitchen. The Italian woman and her son came in and sat down at the table. The thought of food made him feel ill.

"You are sure you feel well?" said Josette as they went to the dinner tables. "You do not look it."

"Quite sure." He cast about desperately for something else to say and uttered the first words that came into his head: "Madame Mathis is right. The ventilation is not good. Perhaps we could walk on deck after dinner is over."

She raised her eyebrows. "Ah, now I know that you cannot be well! You are polite. But very well, I will go with you."

He smiled fatuously, went on to his table, and exchanged reserved greetings with the two Italians. It was not until he sat down that he noticed that an extra place had been laid beside them.

His first impulse was to get up and walk out. The fact that Banat was on the ship was bad enough: to have to eat at the same table would be intolerable. But everything depended upon his behaving normally. He would *have* to stay. He must try and think of Banat as Monsieur Mavrodopoulos, a Greek business man, whom he had never seen or heard of before. He must . . .

Haller came in and sat down beside him. "Good evening, Mr. Graham. And did you enjoy Athens this afternoon?"

"Yes, thanks. Mr. Kuvetli was suitably impressed."

"Ah, yes, of course. You were doing duty as a guide. You must be feeling tired."

"To tell you the truth, my courage failed me. I hired a car. The chauffeur did the guiding. As Mr. Kuvetli speaks fluent Greek, the whole thing went off quite satisfactorily."

"He speaks Greek and yet he has never been to Athens?"

"It appears that he was born in Smyrna. Apart from that, I regret to say, I discovered nothing. My own private opinion is that he is a bore."

"That is disappointing. I had hopes . . . However, it cannot be helped. To tell you the truth, I wished afterwards that I had come with you. You went up to the Parthenon, of course."

"Yes."

Haller smiled apologetically. "When you reach my age you sometimes think of the approach of death. I thought this afternoon how much I would have liked to have seen the Parthenon just once more. I doubt if I shall have another opportunity of doing so. I used to spend hours standing in the shade by the Propylæa looking at it and trying to understand the men who built it. I was young then and did not know how difficult it is for Western man to understand the dream-heavy classical soul. They are so far apart. The god of superlative shape has been replaced by the god of superlative force and between the two conceptions there is all space. The destiny idea symbolised by the Doric columns is incomprehensible to the children of

Faust. For us . . ." He broke off. "Excuse me. I see that we have another
passenger. I suppose that he is to sit here."

Graham forced himself to look up.

Banat had come in and was standing looking at the tables. The steward,
carrying plates of soup, appeared behind him and motioned him towards
the place next to the Italian woman. Banat approached, looked round the
table, and sat down. He nodded to them, smiling slightly.

"Mavrodopoulos," he said. "*Je parle français un petit peu.*"

His voice was toneless and husky and he spoke with a slight lisp. The
smell of attar of roses came across the table.

Graham nodded distantly. Now that the moment had come he felt quite
calm.

Haller's look of strangled disgust was almost funny. He said pompously:
"Haller. Beside you are Signora and Signor Beronelli. This is Monsieur Graham."

Banat nodded to them again and said: "I have travelled a long way to-day.
From Salonika."

Graham made an effort. "I should have thought," he said, "that it would
have been easier to go to Genoa by train from Salonika." He felt oddly breathless as he said it and his voice sounded strange in his own ears.

There was a bowl of raisins in the centre of the table and Banat put some in
his mouth before replying. "I don't like trains," he said shortly. He looked
at Haller. "You are a German, Monsieur?"

Haller frowned. "I am."

"It is a good country, Germany." He turned his attention to Signora
Beronelli. "Italy is good, too." He took some more raisins.

The woman smiled and inclined her head. The boy looked angry.

"And what," said Graham, "do you think about England?"

The small tired eyes stared into his coldly. "I have never seen England."
The eyes wandered away round the table. "When I was last in Rome," he
said, "I saw a magnificent parade of the Italian army with guns and armoured
cars and aeroplanes." He swallowed his raisins. "The aeroplanes were a great
sight and made one think of God."

"And why should they do that, Monsieur?" demanded Haller. Evidently
he did not like Monsieur Mavrodopoulos.

"They made one think of God. That is all I know. You feel it in the
stomach. A thunderstorm makes one think of God, too. But these aeroplanes were better than a storm. They shook the air like paper."

Watching the full self-conscious lips enunciating these absurdities, Graham wondered if an English jury, trying the man for murder, would find
him insane. Probably not: he killed for money; and the Law did not think
that a man who killed for money was insane. And yet he *was* insane. His was
the insanity of the sub-conscious mind running naked, of the "throw back,"
of the mind which could discover the majesty of God in thunder and lightning, the roar of bombing planes, or the firing of a five hundred pound
shell; the awe-inspired insanity of the primæval swamp. Killing, for this

man, *could* be a business. Once, no doubt, he had been surprised that people should be prepared to pay so handsomely for the doing of something they could do so easily for themselves. But, of course, he would have ended by concluding, with other successful business men, that he was cleverer than his fellows. His mental approach to the business of killing would be that of the lavatory attendant to the business of attending to his lavatories or of the stockbroker towards the business of taking his commission: purely practical.

"Are you going to Rome now?" said Haller politely. It was the heavy politeness of an old man with a young fool.

"I go to Genoa," said Banat.

"I understand," said Graham, "that the thing to see at Genoa is the cemetery."

Banat spat out a raisin seed. "That is so? Why?" Obviously, that sort of remark was not going to disconcert him.

"It is supposed to be very large, very well arranged, and planted with very fine cypresses."

"Perhaps I shall go."

The waiter brought soup. Haller turned rather ostentatiously to Graham and began once more to talk about the Parthenon. It seemed that he liked arranging his thoughts aloud. The resultant monologue demanded practically nothing of the listener but an occasional nod. From the Parthenon he wandered to pre-Hellenic remains, the Aryan hero tales, and the Vedic religion. Graham ate mechanically, listened, and watched Banat. The man put his food in his mouth as if he enjoyed it. Then, as he chewed, he would look round the room like a dog over a plate of scraps. There was something pathetic about him. He was—Graham realised it with a shock—pathetic in the way that a monkey, in its likeness to man, could be pathetic. He was not insane. He was an animal and dangerous.

The meal came to an end. Haller, as usual, went to his wife. Thankful for the opportunity, Graham left at the same time, got his overcoat, and went out on deck.

The wind had dropped and the roll of the ship was long and slow. She was making good speed and the water sliding along her plates was hissing and bubbling as if they were red hot. It was a cold, clear night.

The smell of attar of roses was at the back of his throat and in his nostrils. He drew the fresh unscented air into his lungs with conscious pleasure. He was, he told himself, over the first hurdle. He had sat face to face with Banat and talked to him without giving himself away. The man could not possibly suspect that he was known and understood. The rest of it would be easy. He had only to keep his head.

There was a step behind him and he swung round quickly, his nerves jumping.

It was Josette. She came towards him smiling. "Ah! So this is your politeness. You ask me to walk with you, but you do not wait for me. I have to find you. You are very bad."

"I'm sorry. It was so stuffy in the saloon that . . ."

"It is not at all stuffy in the saloon, as you know perfectly well." She linked her arm in his. "Now we will walk and you shall tell me what is *really* the matter."

He looked at her quickly. "What is *really* the matter! What do you mean?"

She became the *grande dame*. "So you are not going to tell me. You will not tell me how you came to be on this ship. You will not tell me what has happened to-day to make you so nervous."

"Nervous! But . . ."

"Yes, Monsieur Graham, nervous!" She abandoned the *grande dame* with a shrug. "I am sorry but I have seen people who are afraid before. They do not look at all like people who are tired or people who feel faint in a stuffy room. They have a special look about them. Their faces look very small and grey round the mouth and they cannot keep their hands still." They had reached the stairs to the boat deck. She turned and looked at him. "Shall we go up?"

He nodded. He would have nodded if she had suggested that they jump overboard. He could think of only one thing. If *she* knew a frightened man when she saw one, then so did Banat. And if Banat had noticed. . . . But he couldn't have noticed. He couldn't. He . . .

They were on the boat deck now and she took his arm again.

"It is a very nice night," she said. "I am glad that we can walk like this. I was afraid this morning that I had annoyed you. I did not really wish to go to Athens. That officer who thinks he is so nice asked me to go with him but I did not. But I would have gone if you had asked me. I do not say that to flatter you. I tell you the truth."

"It's very kind of you," he muttered.

She mimicked him. " 'It's very kind of you.' Ah, you are so solemn. It is as if you did not like me."

He managed to smile. "Oh, I like you, all right."

"But you do not trust me? I understand. You see me dancing in Le Jockey Cabaret and you say, because you are so experienced: 'Ah! I must be careful of this lady.' Eh? But I am a friend. You are so silly."

"Yes, I am silly."

"But you *do* like me?"

"Yes, I like you." A stupid, fantastic suggestion was taking root in his mind.

"Then you must trust me, also."

"Yes, I must." It was absurd, of course. He couldn't trust her. Her motives were as transparent as the day. He couldn't trust anybody. He was alone; damnably alone. If he had someone to talk to about it, it wouldn't be so bad. Now supposing Banat had seen that he was nervous and concluded that he was on his guard. Had he or hadn't he seen? She could tell him that.

"What are you thinking about?"

"To-morrow." She said that she was a friend. If there was one thing he needed now, it was, God knew, a friend. Any friend. Someone to talk to, to discuss it with. Nobody knew about it but him. If anything happened to him there would be nobody to accuse Banat. He would go scot free to collect his wages. She was right. It was stupid to distrust her simply because she danced in night places. After all, Kopeikin had liked her and he was no fool about women.

They had reached the corner below the bridge structure. She stopped as he had known she would.

"If we stay here," she said, "I shall get cold. It will be better if we go on walking round and round and round the deck."

"I thought you wanted to ask me questions."

"I have told you I am not inquisitive."

"So you did. Do you remember that yesterday evening I told you that I came on this ship to avoid someone who was trying to shoot me and that this"—he held up his right hand—"was a bullet wound?"

"Yes. I remember. It was a bad joke."

"A very bad joke. Unfortunately, it happened to be true."

It was out now. He could not see her face but he heard her draw in her breath sharply and felt her fingers dig into his arm.

"You are lying to me."

"I'm afraid not."

"But you are an engineer," she said accusingly. "You said so. What have you done that someone should wish to kill you?"

"I have done nothing." He hesitated. "I just happen to be on important business. Some business competitors don't want me to return to England."

"Now you are lying."

"Yes, I am lying, but not very much. I *am* on important business and there *are* some people who do not want me to get back to England. They employed men to kill me while I was in Gallipoli but the Turkish police arrested these men before they could try. Then they employed a professional killer to do the job. When I got back to my hotel after I left Le Jockey Cabaret the other night, he was waiting for me. He shot at me and missed everything except my hand."

She was breathing quickly. "It is atrocious! A bestiality! Does Kopeikin know of it?"

"Yes. It was partly his idea that I should travel on this boat."

"But who are these people?"

"I only know of one. His name is Moeller and he lives in Sofia. The Turkish police told me that he is a German agent."

"The *salop!* But he cannot touch you now."

"Unfortunately he can. While I was ashore with Kuvetli this afternoon, another passenger came aboard."

"The little man who smells? Mavrodopoulos? But. . . ."

"His real name is Banat and he is the professional killer who shot at me in Istanbul."

"But how do you know?" she demanded breathlessly.

"He was at Le Jockey Cabaret watching me. He had followed me there to see that I was out of the way before he broke into my room at the hotel.

It was dark in the room when he shot at me, but the police showed me his photograph later and I identified him."

She was silent for a moment. Then she said slowly: "It is not very nice. That little man is a dirty type."

"No, it is not very nice."

"You must go to the Captain."

"Thanks. I've tried to see the Captain once. I got as far as the Purser. He thinks I'm either crazy, drunk, or lying."

"What are you going to do?"

"Nothing for the moment. He doesn't know that I know who he is. I think that he will wait until we get to Genoa before he tries again. When we get there I shall go to the British Consul and ask him to advise the police."

"But I think he *does* know that you suspect him. When we were in the *salone* before dinner and the Frenchman was talking about trains, this man was watching you. Mr. Kuvetli was watching you also. You looked so curious, you see."

His stomach turned over. "You mean, I suppose, that I looked frightened to death. I was frightened. I admit it. Why shouldn't I? I am not used to people trying to kill me." His voice had risen. He felt himself shaking with a sort of hysterical anger.

She gripped his arm again. "Ssh! You must not speak so loudly." And then: "Does it matter so much that he knows?"

"If he knows, it means that he will have to act before we get to Genoa."

"On this little ship? He would not dare." She paused. "José has a revolver in his box. I will try to get it for you."

"I've got a revolver."

"Where?"

"It's in my suitcase. It shows in my pocket. I did not want him to see that I knew I was in danger."

"If you carry the revolver you will be in no danger. Let him see it. If a dog sees that you are nervous, he will bite you. With types like that you must show that you are dangerous and then they are afraid." She took his other arm. "Ah, you do not need to worry. You will get to Genoa and you will go to the British Consul. You can ignore this dirty beast with the perfume. By the time you get to Paris you will have forgotten him."

"If I get to Paris."

"You are impossible. Why should you not get to Paris?"

"You think I'm a fool."

"I think perhaps you are tired. Your wound . . ."

"It was only a graze."

"Ah, but it is not the size of the wound. It is the shock."

He wanted suddenly to laugh. It was true what she was saying. He hadn't really got over that hellish night with Kopeikin and Haki. His nerves were on edge. He was worrying unnecessarily. He said: "When we get to Paris, Josette, I shall give you the best dinner it is possible to buy."

She came close to him. "I don't want you to give me anything, *chéri*. I want you to like me. You *do* like me?"

"Of course I like you. I told you so."

"Yes, you told me so."

His left hand touched the belt on her coat. Her body moved suddenly pressing against his. The next moment his arms were round her and he was kissing her.

When his arms grew tired, she leaned back, half against him, half against the rail.

"Do you feel better, *chéri?*"

"Yes, I feel better."

"Then I will have a cigarette."

He gave her the cigarette and she looked at him across the light of the match. "Are you thinking of this lady in England who is your wife?"

"No."

"But you *will* think of her?"

"If you keep talking about her I shall have to think about her."

"I see. For you I am part of the journey from Istanbul to London. Like Mr. Kuvetli."

"Not quite like Mr. Kuvetli. I shan't kiss Mr. Kuvetli if I can help it."

"What do you think about me?"

"I think that you're very attractive. I like your hair and your eyes and the scent you use."

"That is very nice. Shall I tell you something, *chéri?*"

"What?"

She began to speak very softly. "This boat is very small; the cabins are very small; the walls are very thin; and there are people everywhere."

"Yes?"

"Paris is very large and there are nice hotels there with big rooms and thick walls. One need not see anyone one does not wish to see. And do you know, *chéri,* that if one is making a journey from Istanbul to London and one arrives in Paris, it is sometimes necessary to wait a week before continuing the journey?"

"That's a long time."

"It is because of the war, you see. There are always difficulties. People have to wait days and days for permission to leave France. There is a special stamp that must be put in your passport, and they will not let you on the train to England until you have that stamp. You have to go to the Préfecture for it and there is a great deal of *chi-chi.* You have to stay in Paris until the old women in the Préfecture can find time to deal with your application."

"Very annoying."

She sighed. "We could pass that week or ten days very nicely. I do not mean at the Hotel des Belges. That is a dirty place. But there is the Ritz Hotel and the Lancaster Hotel and the Georges Cinque. . . ." She paused and he knew that he was expected to say something.

He said it. "And the Crillon and the Meurice."

She squeezed his arm. "You are very nice. But you understand me? An apartment is cheaper, but for so little time that is impossible. One cannot enjoy oneself in a cheap hotel. All the same I do not like extravagance. There are nice hotels for less than it costs at the Ritz or the Georges Cinque and one has more money to spend on eating and dancing at nice places. Even in war time there are nice places." The burning end of her cigarette made an impatient gesture. "But I must not talk about money. You will make the old women at the Préfecture give you your permit too soon and then I shall be disappointed."

He said: "You know, Josette, I shall begin in a minute to think that you are really serious."

"And you think that I am not?" She was indignant.

"I'm quite sure of it."

She burst out laughing. "You can be rude very politely. I shall tell José that. It will amuse him."

"I don't think I want to amuse José. Shall we go down?"

"Ah, you are angry! You think that I have been making a fool of you."

"Not a bit."

"Then kiss me."

Some moments later she said softly: "I like you very much. I would not mind very much a room for fifty francs a day. But the Hotel des Belges is terrible. I do not want to go back there. You are not angry with me?"

"No, I am not angry with you." Her body was soft and warm and infinitely yielding. She had made him feel as if Banat and the rest of the journey really did not matter. He felt both grateful to and sorry for her. He made up his mind that, when he got to Paris, he would buy her a handbag and slip a thousand franc note in it before he gave it to her. He said: "It's all right. You needn't go back to the Hotel des Belges."

When at last they went down to the saloon it was after ten. José and Mr. Kuvetli were there playing cards.

José was playing with thin-lipped concentration and took no notice of them; but Mr. Kuvetli looked up. His smile was sickly.

"Madame," he said ruefully, "your husband plays cards very well."

"He has had a lot of practice."

"Ah, yes, I am sure." He played a card. José slapped another one on top of it triumphantly. Mr. Kuvetli's face fell.

"It is my game," said José and gathered up some money from the table. "You have lost eighty-four lire. If we had been playing for lire instead of centesimi I should have won eight thousand four hundred lire. That would be interesting. Shall we play another game?"

"I think that I will go to bed now," said Mr. Kuvetli hurriedly. "Good night, Messieurs-dame." He went.

José sucked his teeth as if the game had left an unpleasant taste in his mouth. "Everyone goes to bed early on this filthy boat," he said. "It is very boring." He looked up at Graham. "Do you want to play?"

"I'm sorry to say that I must go to bed, too."

José shrugged. "Very well. Good-bye." He glanced at Josette and began to deal two hands. "I will play a game with you."

She looked at Graham and smiled hopelessly. "If I do not he will be disagreeable. Good night, Monsieur."

Graham smiled and said good night. He was not unrelieved.

He got to his cabin feeling a good deal more cheerful than he had felt when he had left it earlier in the evening.

How sensible she was! And how stupid he'd been! With men like Banat it was dangerous to be subtle. If a dog saw that you were nervous, he bit you. From now on he would carry the revolver. What was more, he would use it if Banat tried any funny business. You had to meet force with force.

He bent down to pull his suit-case from under the bunk. He was going to get the revolver out then and there.

Suddenly he stopped. For an instant his nostrils had caught the sweet cloying smell of attar of roses.

The smell had been faint, almost imperceptible, and he could not detect it again. For a moment he remained motionless, telling himself that he must have imagined it. Then panic seized him.

With shaking fingers he tore at the latches on the suit-case and flung back the lid.

The revolver was gone.

CHAPTER SEVEN

HE UNDRESSED SLOWLY, got into his bunk and lay there staring at the cracks in the asbestos round a steam pipe which crossed the ceiling. He could taste Josette's lipstick in his mouth. The taste was all that was left to remind him of the self-assurance with which he had returned to the cabin; the self-assurance which had been swept away by fear welling up into his mind like blood from a severed artery; fear that clotted, paralysing thought. Only his senses seemed alive.

On the other side of the partition, Mathis finished brushing his teeth and there was a lot of grunting and creaking as he clambered into the upper berth. At last he lay back with a sigh.

"Another day!"

"So much the better. Is the porthole open?"

"Unmistakably. There is a very disagreeable current of air on my back."

"We do not want to be ill like the Englishman."

"That was nothing to do with the air. It was seasickness. He would not admit it because it would not be correct for an Englishman to be seasick.

The English like to think that they are all great sailors. He is *drôle* but I like him."

"That is because he listens to your nonsense. He is polite—too polite. He and that German greet each other now as if they were friends. *That* is not correct. If this Gallindo . . ."

"Oh, we have talked enough about him."

"Signora Beronelli said that he knocked against her on the stairs and went on without apologising."

"He is a filthy type."

There was a silence. Then:

"Robert!"

"I am nearly asleep."

"You remember that I said that the husband of Signora Beronelli was killed in the earthquake?"

"What about it?"

"I talked to her this evening. It is a terrible story. It was not the earthquake that killed him. He was shot."

"Why?"

"She does not wish everyone to know. You must say nothing of it."

"Well?"

"It was during the first earthquake. After the great shocks were over they went back to their house from the fields in which they had taken refuge. The house was in ruins. There was part of one wall standing and he made a shelter against it with some boards. They found some food that had been in the house but the tanks had been broken and there was no water. He left her with the boy, their son, and went to look for water. Some friends who had a house near theirs were away in Istanbul. That house, too, had fallen, but he went among the ruins to find the water tanks. He found them and one of them had not been broken. He had nothing to take the water back in so he searched for a jug or a tin. He found a jug. It was of silver and had been partly crushed by the falling stones. After the earthquake, soldiers had been sent to patrol the streets to prevent looting, of which there was a great deal because valuable things were lying everywhere in the ruins. As he was standing there trying to straighten the jug, a soldier arrested him. Signora Beronelli knew nothing of this and when he did not come back she and her son went to look for him. But there was such chaos that she could do nothing. The next day she heard that he had been shot. Is that not a terrible tragedy?"

"Yes, it is a tragedy. Such things happen."

"If the good God had killed him in the earthquake she could bear it more easily. But for him to be shot . . . ! She is very brave. She does not blame the soldiers. With so much chaos they cannot be blamed. It was the Will of the good God."

"He is a comedian. I have noticed it before."

"Do not blaspheme."

"It is *you* who blaspheme. You talk of the good God as if He were a waiter with a fly-swatter. He hits at the flies and kills some. But one escapes. Ah, *le salaud!* The waiter hits again and the fly is paste with the others. The good God is not like that. He does not make earthquakes and tragedies. He is of the mind."

"You are insupportable. Have you no pity for the poor woman?"

"Yes, I pity her. But will it help her if we hold another burial service? Will it help her if I stay awake arguing instead of going to sleep as I wish? She told you this because she likes to talk of it. Poor soul! It eases her mind to become the heroine of a tragedy. The fact becomes less real. But if there is no audience, there is no tragedy. If she tells me, I, too, will be a good audience. Tears will come into my eyes. But you are not the heroine. Go to sleep."

"You are a beast without imagination."

"Beasts must sleep. Good night, *chérie!*"

"Camel!"

There was no answer. After a moment or two he sighed heavily and turned over in his bunk. Soon he began gently to snore.

For a time Graham lay awake listening to the rush of the sea outside and the steady throb of the engines. A waiter with a fly-swatter! In Berlin there was a man whom he had never seen and whose name he did not know, who had condemned him to death; in Sofia there was a man named Moeller who had been instructed to carry out the sentence; and here, a few yards away in cabin number nine, was the executioner with a nine millimetre calibre self-loading pistol, ready, now that he had disarmed the condemned man, to do his work and collect his money. The whole thing was as impersonal, as dispassionate, as justice itself. To attempt to defeat it seemed as futile as to argue with the hangman on the scaffold.

He tried to think of Stephanie and found that he could not. The things of which she was a part, his house, his friends, had ceased to exist. He was a man alone, transported into a strange land with death for its frontiers: alone but for the one person to whom he could speak of its terrors. She was sanity. She was reality. He needed her. Stephanie he did not need. She was a face and a voice dimly remembered with the other faces and voices of a world he had once known.

His mind wandered away into an uneasy doze. Then he dreamed that he was falling down a precipice and awoke with a start. He switched on the light and picked up one of the books he had bought that afternoon. It was a detective story. He read a few pages and then put it down. He was not going to be able to read himself to sleep with news of "neat, slightly bleeding" holes in the right temples of corpses lying "grotesquely twisted in the final agony of death."

He got out of his bunk, wrapped himself in a blanket, and sat down to smoke a cigarette. He would, he decided, spend the rest of the night like that: sitting and smoking cigarettes. Lying prone increased his sense of helplessness. If only he had a revolver.

It seemed to him as he sat there that the having or not having of a revolver was really as important to a man as the having or not having of sight. That he should have survived for so many years without one could only be due to chance. Without a revolver a man was as defenceless as a tethered goat in a jungle. What an incredible fool he had been to leave the thing in his suit-case! If only . . .

And then he remembered something Josette had said:

"José has a revolver in his box. I will try to get it for you."

He drew a deep breath. He was saved. José had a revolver. Josette would get it for him. All would be well. She would probably be on deck by ten. He would wait until he was sure of finding her there, tell her what had happened, and ask her to get the revolver there and then. With luck he would have it in his pocket within half an hour or so of his leaving his cabin. He would be able to sit down to luncheon with the thing bulging in his pocket. Banat would get a surprise. Thank goodness for José's suspicious nature!

He yawned and put out his cigarette. It would be stupid to sit there all night: stupid, uncomfortable, and dull. He felt sleepy, too. He put the blanket back on the bunk and lay down once more. Within five minutes he was asleep.

When he again awoke, a crescent of sunlight slanting through the port-hole was rising and falling on the white paint of the bulkhead. He lay there watching it until he had to get up to unlock the door for the steward bringing his coffee. It was nine o'clock. He drank the coffee slowly, smoked a cigarette, and had a hot sea water bath. By the time he was dressed it was close on ten o'clock. He put on his coat and left the cabin.

The alley-way on to which the cabins opened was only just wide enough for two persons to pass. It formed three sides of a square, the fourth side of which was taken up by the stairs to the saloon and shelter deck and two small spaces in which stood a pair of dusty palms in earthenware tubs. He was within a yard or two of the end of the alley-way when he came face to face with Banat.

The man had turned into the alley-way from the space at the foot of the stairs, and by taking a pace backwards he could have given Graham room to pass; but he made no attempt to do so. When he saw Graham, he stopped. Then, very slowly, he put his hands in his pockets and leaned against the steel bulkhead. Graham could either turn round and go back the way he had come or stay where he was. His heart pounding at his ribs, he stayed where he was.

Banat nodded. "Good morning, Monsieur. It is very fine weather to-day, eh?"

"Very fine."

"For you, an Englishman, it must be very agreeable to see the sun." He had shaved and his pasty jowl gleamed with unrinsed soap. The smell of attar of roses came from him in waves.

"Most agreeable. Excuse me." He went to push by to the stairs.

Banat moved, as if by accident, blocking the way. "It is so narrow! One person must give way to the other, eh?"

"Just so. Do you want to go by?"

Banat shook his head. "No. There is no hurry. I was so anxious to ask you, Monsieur, about your hand. I noticed it last night. What is the matter with it?"

Graham met the small, dangerous eyes staring insolently into his. Banat knew that he was unarmed and was trying to unnerve him as well. And he was succeeding. Graham had a sudden desire to smash his knuckles into the pale, stupid face. He controlled himself with an effort.

"It is a small wound," he said calmly. And then his pent up feelings got the better of him. "A bullet wound, to be exact," he added. "Some dirty little thief took a shot at me in Istanbul. He was either a bad shot or frightened. He missed."

The small eyes did not flicker but an ugly little smile twisted the mouth. Banat said slowly: "A dirty little thief, eh? You must look after yourself carefully. You must be ready to shoot back next time."

"I shall shoot back. There is not the slightest doubt of that."

The smile widened. "You carry a pistol, then?"

"Naturally. And now, if you will excuse me . . ." He walked forward intending to shoulder the other man out of the way if he did not move. But Banat moved. He was grinning now. "Be very careful, Monsieur," he said, and laughed.

Graham had reached the foot of the stairs. He paused and looked back. "I don't think it will be necessary," he said deliberately. "These scum don't risk their skins with an armed man." He used the word *excrément*.

The grin faded from Banat's face. Without replying he turned and went on to his cabin.

By the time Graham reached the deck, reaction had set in. His legs seemed to have gone to jelly and he was sweating. The unexpectedness of the encounter had helped and, all things considered, he had not come out of it too badly. He'd put up a bluff. Banat might conceivably be wondering if, after all, he had a second revolver. But bluff wasn't going to go very far now. The gloves were off. His bluff might be called. Now, whatever happened, he *must* get José's revolver.

He walked quickly round the shelter deck. Haller was there with his wife on his arm, walking slowly. He said good morning; but Graham did not want to talk to anyone but the girl. She was not on the shelter deck. He went on up to the boat deck.

She was there, but talking to the young officer. The Mathises and Mr. Kuvetli were a few yards away. Out of the corner of his eye he saw them look at him expectantly but he pretended not to have seen them and walked over to Josette.

She greeted him with a smile and a meaning look intended to convey that she was bored with her companion. The young Italian scowled a good morning and made to take up the conversation where Graham had interrupted it.

But Graham was in no mood for courtesies. "You must excuse me, Monsieur," he said in French; "I have a message for Madame from her husband."

The officer nodded and stood aside politely.

Graham raised his eyebrows. "It is a *private* message, Monsieur."

The officer flushed angrily and looked at Josette. She nodded to him in a kindly way and said something to him in Italian. He flashed his teeth at her, scowled once more at Graham and stalked on.

She giggled. "You were really very unkind to that poor boy. He was getting on so nicely. Could you think of nothing better than a message from José?"

"I said the first thing that came into my head. I had to speak to you."

She nodded approvingly. "That is very nice." She looked at him slyly. "I was afraid that you would spend the night being angry with yourself because of last night. But you must not look so solemn. Madame Mathis is very interested in us."

"I'm feeling solemn. Something has happened."

The smile faded from her lips. "Something serious?"

"Something serious. I . . ."

She glanced over his shoulder. "It will be better if we walk up and down and look as if we are talking about the sea and the sun. Otherwise they will be gossiping. I do not care what people say, you understand. But it would be embarrassing."

"Very well." And then, as they began to walk: "When I got back to my cabin last night I found that my revolver had been stolen from my suit-case."

She stopped. "This is true?"

"Quite true."

She began to walk again. "It may have been the steward."

"No. Banat had been in my cabin. I could smell that scent of his."

She was silent for a moment. Then: "Have you told anyone?"

"It's no use my making a complaint. The revolver will be at the bottom of the sea by now. I have no proof that Banat took it. Besides, they wouldn't listen to me after the scene I made with the Purser yesterday."

"What are you going to do?"

"Ask you to do something for me."

She looked at him quickly. "What?"

"You said last night that José had a revolver and that you might be able to get it for me."

"You are serious?"

"Never more so in all my life."

She bit her lip. "But what am I to say to José if he finds that it is gone?"

"Will he find out?"

"He may do."

He began to get angry. "It was, I think, your idea that you should get it for me."

"It is so necessary that you should have a revolver? There is nothing that he can do."

"It was also your idea that I should carry a revolver."

She looked sullen. "I was frightened by what you said about this man. But that was because it was dark. Now that it is daytime it is different."

She smiled suddenly. "Ah, my friend, do not be so serious. Think of the nice time we will have in Paris together. This man is not going to make any trouble."

"I'm afraid he is." He told her about his encounter by the stairs, and added: "Besides, why did he steal my revolver if he doesn't intend to make trouble?"

She hesitated. Then she said slowly: "Very well, I will try."

"Now?"

"Yes, if you wish. It is in his box in the cabin. He is in the *salone* reading. Do you want to wait here for me?"

"No, I'll wait on the deck below. I don't want to have to talk to these people here just now."

They went down and stood for a moment by the rail at the foot of the companionway.

"I'll stay here." He pressed her hand. "My dear Josette, I can't tell you how grateful I am to you for this."

She smiled as if at a small boy to whom she had promised sweets. "You shall tell me that in Paris."

He watched her go and then turned to lean against the rail. She could not be more than five minutes. He stared for a time at the long, curling bow wave streaming out and away to meet the transverse wave from the stern and be broken by it into froth. He looked at his watch. Three minutes. Someone clattered down the companionway.

"Good morning, Mr. Graham. You feel all right to-day, eh?" It was Mr. Kuvetli.

Graham turned his head. "Yes, thanks."

"Monsieur and Madame Mathis are hopeful to play some bridge this afternoon. Do you play?"

"Yes, I play." He was not, he knew, being very gracious but he was terrified lest Mr. Kuvetli should attach himself to him.

"Then perhaps we make party of four, eh?"

"By all means."

"I do not play well. Is very difficult game."

"Yes." Out of the corner of his eye he saw Josette step through the door from the landing on to the deck.

Mr. Kuvetli's eyes flickered in her direction. He leered. "This afternoon then, Mr. Graham."

"I shall look forward to it."

Mr. Kuvetli went. Josette came up to him.

"What was he saying?"

"He was asking me to play bridge." Something in her face set his heart going like a trip hammer. "You've got it?" he said quickly.

She shook her head. "The box was locked. He has the keys."

He felt the sweat prickling out all over his body. He stared at her trying to think of something to say.

"Why do you look at me like that?" she exclaimed angrily. "I cannot help it if he keeps the box locked."

"No, you cannot help it." He knew now that she had not intended to get the revolver. She couldn't be blamed. He couldn't expect her to steal for him. He had asked too much of her. But he had been banking on that revolver of José's. Now, in God's name, what was he going to do?

She rested her hand on his arm. "You are angry with me?"

He shook his head. "Why should I be angry? I should have had the sense to keep my own revolver in my pocket. It's just that I was relying on your getting it. It's my own fault. But, as I told you, I'm not used to this sort of thing."

She laughed. "Ah, you need not worry; I can tell you something. This man does not carry a gun."

"What! How do you know?"

"He was going up the stairs in front of me when I came back just now. His clothes are tight and creased. If he carried a revolver I would have seen the shape of it in his pocket."

"You are sure of this?"

"Of course. I would not tell you if . . ."

"But a *small* gun . . ." He stopped. A nine millimetre self-loading pistol would *not* be a small gun. It would weigh about two pounds and would be correspondingly bulky. It would not be the sort of thing a man would carry about in his pocket if he could leave it in a cabin. If . . .

She was watching his face. "What is it?"

"He'll have left his gun in his cabin," he said slowly.

She looked him in the eyes. "I could see that he does not go to his cabin for a long time."

"How?"

"José will do it."

"José?"

"Be calm. I will not have to tell José anything about you. José will play cards with him this evening."

"Banat would play cards. He is a gambler. But will José ask him?"

"I shall tell José that I saw this man open a wallet with a lot of money in it. José will see that he plays cards. You do not know José."

"You're sure you can do it?"

She squeezed his arm. "Of course. I do not like you to be worried. If you take his gun then you will have nothing at all to fear, eh?"

"No, I shall have nothing at all to fear." He said it almost wonderingly. It seemed so simple. Why hadn't he thought of it before? Ah, but he had not known before that the man did not carry his gun. Take the man's gun away from him and he couldn't shoot. That was logical. And if he couldn't shoot there was nothing to fear. That was logical too. *The essence of all good strategy is simplicity.*

He turned to her. "When can you do this?"

"This evening would be best. José does not like so much to play cards in the afternoon."

"How soon this evening?"

"You must not be impatient. It will be some time after the meal." She hesitated. "It will be better if we are not seen together this afternoon. You do not want him to suspect that we are friends."

"I can play bridge with Kuvetli and the Mathises this afternoon. But how shall I know if it is all right?"

"I will find a way to let you know." She leaned against him. "You are sure that you are not angry with me about José's revolver?"

"Of course I'm not."

"There is no one looking. Kiss me."

"Banking!" Mathis was saying. "What is it but usury? Bankers are money lenders, usurers. But because they lend other people's money or money that does not exist, they have a pretty name. They are still usurers. Once, usury was a mortal sin and an abomination, and to be a usurer was to be a criminal for whom there was a prison cell. To-day the usurers are the gods of the earth and the only mortal sin is to be poor."

"There are so many poor people," said Mr. Kuvetli profoundly. "It is terrible!"

Mathis shrugged impatiently. "There will be more before this war is finished. You may depend upon it. It will be a good thing to be a soldier. Soldiers, at least, will be given food."

"Always," said Madame Mathis, "he talks nonsense. Always, always. But when we get back to France it will be different. His friends will not listen so politely. Banking! What does he know about banking?"

"Ha! That is what the banker likes. Banking is a mystery! It is too difficult for ordinary men to understand." He laughed derisively. "If you make two and two equal five you *must* have a lot of mystery." He turned aggressively to Graham. "The international bankers are the real war criminals. Others do the killing but they sit, calm and collected, in their offices and make money."

"I'm afraid," said Graham, feeling that he ought to say something, "that the only international banker I know is a very harassed man with a duodenal ulcer. He is far from calm. On the contrary, he complains bitterly."

"Precisely," said Mathis triumphantly. "It is the System! I can tell you . . ."

He went on to tell them. Graham picked up his fourth whisky and soda. He had been playing bridge with the Mathises and Mr. Kuvetli for most of the afternoon and he was tired of them. He had seen Josette only once during that time. She had paused by the card-table and nodded to him. He had taken the nod to mean that José had risen to the news that Banat had money in his pocket and that sometime that evening it would be safe to go to Banat's cabin.

The prospect cheered and terrified him alternately. At one moment the plan seemed foolproof. He would go into the cabin, take the gun, return to his own cabin, drop the gun out of the porthole and return to the saloon with a tremendous weight lifted from his shoulders. The next moment, however, doubts would begin to creep in. It was *too* simple. Banat might be insane but he was no fool. A man who earned his living in the way Banat earned his and who yet managed to stay alive and free was not going to be taken in so easily. Supposing he should guess what his victim had in mind, leave José in the middle of the game, and go to his cabin! Supposing he had bribed the steward to keep an eye on his cabin on the grounds that it contained valuables! Supposing . . . ! But what was the alternative? Was he to wait passively while Banat chose the moment to kill him? It was all very well for Haki to talk about a marked man having only to defend himself; but what had he to defend himself with? When the enemy was as close as Banat was, the best defence was attack. Yes, that was it! Anything was better than just waiting. And the plan might well succeed. It was the simple plans of attack that *did* succeed. It would never occur to a man of Banat's conceit to suspect that two could play at the game of stealing guns, that the helpless rabbit might bite back. He'd soon find out his mistake.

Josette and José came in with Banat. José appeared to be making himself amiable.

". . . it is only necessary," Mathis was concluding, "to say one word— Briey! When you have said that you have said all."

Graham drained his glass. "Quite so. Will you all have another drink?"

The Mathises, looking startled, declined sharply; but Mr. Kuvetli nodded happily.

"Thank you, Mr. Graham. I will."

Mathis stood up, frowning. "It is time that we got ready for dinner. Please excuse us."

They went. Mr. Kuvetli moved his chair over.

"That was very sudden," said Graham. "What's the matter with them?"

"I think," said Mr. Kuvetli carefully, "that they thought you are making joke of them."

"Why on earth should they think that?"

Mr. Kuvetli looked sideways. "You ask them to have to drink three times in five minutes. You ask them once. They say no. You ask them again. They say no again. You ask again. They do not understand English hospitality."

"I see. I'm afraid that I was thinking of something else. I must apologise."

"Please!" Mr. Kuvetli was overcome. "It is not necessary to apologise for hospitality. But"—he glanced hesitantly at the clock—"it is now nearly time for dinner. You allow me later to have this drink you so kindly offer?"

"Yes, of course."

"And you will excuse me please, now?"

"By all means."

When Mr. Kuvetli had gone, Graham stood up. Yes, he'd had just one drink too many on an empty stomach. He went out on deck.

The starlit sky was hung with small smoky clouds. In the distance were the lights of the Italian coast. He stood there for a moment letting the icy wind sting his face. In a minute or two the gong would sound for dinner. He dreaded the approaching meal as a sick man dreads the approach of the surgeon with a probe. He would sit, as he had sat at luncheon, listening to Haller's monologues and to the Beronellis whispering behind their misery, forcing food down his throat to his unwilling stomach, conscious all the time of the man opposite to him—of why he was there and of what he stood for.

He turned round and leaned against a stanchion. With his back to the deck he found himself constantly looking over his shoulder to make sure that he was alone. He felt more at ease with no deck space behind him.

Through one of the saloon portholes he could see Banat with Josette and José. They sat like details in a Hogarth group; José tight-lipped and intent, Josette smiling, Banat saying something that brought his lips forward. The air in there was grey with tobacco smoke and the hard light from the un-shaded lamps flattened their features. There was about them all the squalor of a flashlight photograph taken in a bar.

Someone turned the corner at the end of the deck and came towards him. The figure reached the light and he saw that it was Haller. The old man stopped.

"Good evening, Mr. Graham. You look as if you are really enjoying the air. I, as you see, need a scarf and a coat before I can face it."

"It's stuffy inside."

"Yes. I saw you this afternoon very gallantly playing bridge."

"You don't like bridge?"

"One's tastes change." He stared out at the lights. "To see the land from a ship or to see a ship from the land. I used to like both. Now I dislike both. When a man reaches my age he grows, I think, to resent subconsciously the movement of everything except the respiratory muscles which keep him alive. Movement is change and for an old man change means death."

"And the immortal soul?"

Haller sniffed. "Even that which we commonly regard as immortal dies sooner or later. One day the last Titian and the last Beethoven quartet will cease to exist. The canvas and the printed notes may remain if they are carefully preserved but the works themselves will have died with the last eye and ear accessible to their messages. As for the immortal soul, that is an eternal truth and the eternal truths die with the men to whom they were necessary. The eternal truths of the Ptolemaic system were as necessary to the mediæval theologians as were the eternal truths of Kepler to the theo-logians of the Reformation and the eternal truths of Darwin to the nine-teenth century materialists. The statement of an eternal truth is a prayer to lay a ghost—the ghost of primitive man defending himself against what Spengler calls the 'dark almightiness.'" He turned his head suddenly as the door of the saloon opened.

It was Josette standing there looking uncertainly from one to the other of them. At that moment the gong began to sound for dinner.

"Excuse me," said Haller; "I must see my wife before dinner. She is still unwell."

"Of course," said Graham hurriedly.

Josette came over to him as Haller went.

"What did he want, that old man?" she whispered.

"He was talking about life and death."

"Ugh! I do not like him. He makes me shudder. But I must not stay. I came only to tell you that it is all right."

"When are they going to play?"

"After dinner." She squeezed his arm. "He is horrible, this man Banat. I would not do this for anyone except you, *chéri.*"

"You know I am grateful, Josette. I shall make it up to you."

"Ah, stupid!" She smiled at him fondly. "You must not be so serious."

He hesitated. "Are you sure that you can keep him there?"

"You need not worry. I will keep him. But come back to the *salone* when you have been to the cabin so that I shall know that you have finished. It is understood, *chéri?*"

"Yes, it is understood."

It was after nine o'clock and, for the past half hour, Graham had been sitting near the door of the saloon pretending to read a book.

For the hundredth time his eyes wandered to the opposite corner of the room where Banat was talking to Josette and José. His heart began suddenly to beat faster. José had a deck of cards in his hand. He was grinning at something Banat had said. Then they sat down at the card-table. Josette looked across the room.

Graham waited a moment. Then, when he saw them cutting for the deal, he got slowly to his feet and walked out.

He stood on the landing for a moment, bracing himself for what he had to do. Now that the moment had come he felt better. Two minutes—three at the most—and it would be over. He would have the gun and he would be safe. He had only to keep his head.

He went down the stairs. Cabin number nine was beyond his and in the middle section of the alley-way. There was no one about when he reached the palms. He walked on.

He had decided that any sort of stealth was out of the question. He must walk straight to the cabin, open the door and go in without hesitation. If the worst came to the worst and he was seen as he went in by the steward or anyone else, he could protest that he had thought that number nine was an empty cabin and that he was merely satisfying a curiosity to see what the other cabins were like.

But nobody appeared. He reached the door of number nine, paused for barely a second and then, opening the door softly, went in. A moment later he had shut the door behind him and put up the catch. If, for any reason, the steward should try to get in, he would assume that Banat was there when he found the door fastened.

He looked round. The porthole was closed and the air reeked of attar of roses. It was a two-berth cabin and looked strangely bare. Apart from the scent, there were only two indications that the cabin was occupied: the grey raincoat hanging with the soft hat behind the door and a battered composition suit-case under the lower berth.

He ran his hands over the raincoat. There was nothing in the pockets and he turned his attention to the suit-case.

It was unlocked. He pulled it out and threw back the lid.

The thing was crammed with filthy shirts and underwear. There were, besides, some brightly-coloured silk handkerchiefs, a pair of black shoes without laces, a scent spray and a small jar of ointment. The gun was not there.

He shut the case, pushed it back and opened the washing cabinet-cum-wardrobe. The wardrobe part contained nothing but a pair of dirty socks. On the shelf by the tooth-glass was a grey washcloth, a safety razor, a cake of soap and a bottle of scent with a ground glass stopper.

He was getting worried. He had been so sure that the gun would be there. If what Josette had said were true it *must* be there somewhere.

He looked round for other hiding places. There were the mattresses. He ran his hands along the springs beneath them. Nothing. There was the waste compartment below the washing cabinet. Again nothing. He glanced at his watch. He had been there four minutes. He looked round again desperately. It *must* be in there. But he had looked everywhere. He returned feverishly to the suit-case.

Two minutes later he slowly straightened his back. He knew now that the gun was not in the cabin, that the simple plan had been too simple, that nothing was changed. For a second or two he stood there helplessly, putting off the moment when he must finally admit his failure by leaving the cabin. Then the sound of footsteps in the alley-way nearby jarred him into activity.

The footsteps paused. There was the clank of a bucket being put down. Then the footsteps receded. He eased back the door catch and opened the door. The alley-way was empty. A second later he was walking back the way he had come.

He had reached the foot of the stairs before he allowed himself to think. Then he hesitated. He had told Josette that he would go back to the saloon. But that meant seeing Banat. He must have time to steady his nerves. He turned and walked back to his cabin.

He opened the door, took one step forward, and then stopped dead.

Sitting on the bunk with his legs crossed and a book resting on his knee was Haller.

He was wearing a pair of horn-rimmed reading glasses. He removed them very deliberately and looked up. "I've been waiting for you, Mr. Graham," he said cheerfully.

Graham found his tongue. "I don't . . ." he began.

Haller's other hand came from under the book. In it was a large self-loading pistol.

He held it up. "I think," he said, "that this is what you have been looking for, isn't it?"

GRAHAM LOOKED from the gun to the face of the man who was holding it: the long upper lip, the pale blue eyes, the loose yellowish skin.

"I don't understand," he said, and put out his hand to receive the gun. "How . . . ?" he began and then stopped abruptly. The gun was pointing at him and Haller's forefinger was on the trigger.

Haller shook his head. "No, Mr. Graham. I think I shall keep it. I came for a little talk with you. Supposing you sit down here on the bed and turn sideways so that we can face one another."

Graham strove to conceal the deadly sickness that was stealing over him. He felt that he must be going mad. Amid the flood of questions pouring through his mind there was only one small patch of dry land: Colonel Haki had examined the credentials of all the passengers who had embarked at Istanbul and reported that none of them had booked for the journey less than three days prior to the sailing and that they were all harmless. He clung to it desperately.

"I don't understand," he repeated.

"Of course you don't. If you will sit down I will explain."

"I'll stand."

"Ah, yes. I see. Moral support derived from physical discomfort. Remain standing by all means if it pleases you to do so." He spoke with crisp condescension. This was a new Haller, a slightly younger man. He examined the pistol as if he were seeing it for the first time. "You know, Mr. Graham," he went on thoughtfully, "poor Mavrodopoulos was really very upset by his failure in Istanbul. He is not, as you have probably gathered, very intelligent and, like all stupid people, he blames others for his own mistakes. He complains that you moved." He shrugged tolerantly. "Naturally you moved. He could hardly expect you to stand still while he corrected his aim. I told him so. But he was still angry with you, so when he came aboard I insisted on taking care of his pistol for him. He is young, and these Roumanians are so hotheaded. I did not want anything premature to happen."

"I wonder," said Graham, "if your name happens to be Moeller."

"Dear me!" He raised his eyebrows. "I had no idea that you were so well informed. Colonel Haki must have been in a very talkative mood. Did he know that I was in Istanbul?"

Graham reddened. "I don't think so."

Moeller chuckled. "I thought not. Haki is a clever man. I have a great respect for him. But he is human and, therefore, fallible. Yes, after that fiasco in Gallipoli I thought it advisable to attend to things myself. And then, when everything had been arranged, you were inconsiderate enough to move and spoil Mavrodopoulos' shooting. But I bear you no ill will, Mr. Graham. I was irritated at the time, of course. Mavrodopoulos . . ."

"Banat is easier to say."

"Thank you. As I was saying, Banat's failure made more work for me. But now my irritation has passed. Indeed, I am quite enjoying the trip. I like myself as an archæologist. I was a little nervous at first, but as soon as I saw that I had succeeded in boring you I knew that all was well." He held up the book he had been reading. "If you would like a record of my little speeches I can recommend this. It is entitled 'The Sumerian Pantheon' and is by Fritz Haller. His qualifications are given on the title page: ten years with the German Institute in Athens, the period at Oxford, the degrees: it is all here. He seems to be an ardent disciple of Spengler. He quotes the Master a great deal. There is a nostalgic little preface which was most helpful and you will find the piece about eternal truths on page three hundred and forty-one. Naturally I paraphrased a little here and there to suit my own mood. And I drew freely on some of the longer footnotes. You see, the effect I wanted to create was that of an erudite but loveable old bore. I think you will agree that I did well."

"So there *is* a Haller?"

Moeller pursed his lips. "Ah, yes. I was sorry to inconvenience him and his wife, but there was no other way. When I found that you were to leave on this boat I decided that it would be helpful if I travelled with you. Obviously I could not have booked a passage at the last moment without attracting Colonel Haki's attention; I therefore took over Haller's tickets and passport. He and his wife were not pleased. But they are good Germans, and when it was made plain to them that their country's interests must come before their own convenience, they gave no more trouble. In a few days their passport will be returned to them with their own photographs restored to it. My only embarrassment has been the Armenian lady who is doing duty for Frau Professor Haller. She speaks very little German and is virtually a half-wit. I have been forced to keep her out of the way. I had no time to make better arrangements, you see. As it was, the man who found her for me had quite a lot of trouble convincing her that she wasn't being carried off to an Italian *bordello*. Female vanity is sometimes extraordinary." He produced a cigarette-case. "I hope you don't mind my telling you all these little things, Mr. Graham. It's just that I want to be frank with you. I think that an atmosphere of frankness is essential to any business discussion."

"Business?"

"Just so. Now do please sit down and smoke. It will do you good." He held out the cigarette-case. "Your nerves have been a little jumpy to-day, haven't they?"

"Say what you want to say and get out!"

Moeller chuckled. "Yes, certainly a little jumpy!" He looked suddenly solemn. "It is my fault, I'm afraid. You see, Mr. Graham, I could have had this little talk with you before, but I wanted to make sure that you would be in a receptive frame of mind."

Graham leaned against the door. "I think that the best way I can describe my state of mind at the moment is to tell you that I have been seriously considering kicking you in the teeth. I could have done so from here before you could have used your gun."

Moeller raised his eyebrows. "And yet you didn't do it? Was it the thought of my white hairs that stopped you, or was it your fear of the consequences?" He paused. "No answer? You won't mind if I draw my own conclusions, will you?" He settled himself a little more comfortably. "The instinct for self-preservation is a wonderful thing. It is so easy for people to be heroic about laying down their lives for the sake of principles when they do not expect to be called upon to do so. When, however, the smell of danger is in their nostrils they are more practical. They see alternatives not in terms of honour or dishonour, but in terms of greater or lesser evils. I wonder if I could persuade you to see my point of view."

Graham was silent. He was trying to fight down the panic which had seized him. He knew that if he opened his mouth he would shout abuse until his throat ached.

Moeller was fitting a cigarette into a short amber holder as if he had time to waste. Obviously he had not expected any answer to his question. He had the self-contained air of a man who is early for an important appointment. When he finished with the cigarette-holder he looked up. "I like you, Mr. Graham," he said. "I was, I have admitted, irritated when Banat made such a fool of himself in Istanbul. But now that I know you I am glad that he did so. You behaved gracefully over that awkwardness at the dinner-table the night we sailed. You listened politely to my carefully memorised recitations. You are a clever engineer, and yet you are not aggressive. I should not like to think of your being killed—murdered—by any employee of mine." He lit his cigarette. "And yet, the demands made upon us by our life's needs are so uncompromising. I am compelled to be offensive. I must tell you that, as things stand at present, you will be dead within a few minutes of your landing at Genoa on Saturday morning."

Graham had himself in hand now. He said: "I'm sorry to hear that."

Moeller nodded approval. "I am glad to see you take it so calmly. If I were in your place I should be very frightened. But then, of course"—the pale blue eyes narrowed suddenly—"I should know that there was no possible chance of my escaping. Banat, in spite of his lapse in Istanbul, is a formidable young man. And when I consider the fact that ready waiting for me in Genoa there would be reinforcements consisting of several other men quite as experienced as Banat, I should realise that there was not the remotest chance of my being able to reach any sort of sanctuary before the end came. I should be left with only one hope—that they did their work so efficiently that I should know very little about it."

"What do you mean by 'as things stand at present'?"

Moeller smiled triumphantly. "Ah! I am so glad. You have gone straight

to the heart of the matter. I mean, Mr. Graham, that you need not necessarily die. There is an alternative."

"I see. A lesser evil." But his heart leaped in spite of himself.

"Scarcely an evil," Moeller objected. "An alternative and by no means an
unpleasant one." He settled himself more comfortably. "I have already said
that I liked you, Mr. Graham. Let me add that I dislike the prospect of
violence quite as whole-heartedly as you do. I am lily-livered. I admit it
freely. I will go out of my way to avoid seeing the results of an automobile
accident. So, you see, if there is any way of settling this matter without
bloodshed I should be prejudiced in favour of it. And if you are still uncertain of my personal goodwill towards you, let me put the question in
another and harder light. The killing would have to be hurried, would consequently subject the killers to additional risks and would, therefore, be
expensive. Don't misunderstand me, please. I shall spare no expense if it is
necessary. But, naturally enough, I hope it won't be necessary. I can assure
you that no one, with the possible exception of yourself, will be more delighted than I am if we can dispose of this whole thing in a friendly way as
between business men. I hope you will at least believe that I am sincere in
that."

Graham began to get angry. "I don't care a damn whether you're sincere
or not."

Moeller looked crestfallen. "No, I suppose you don't. I was forgetting that
you have been under some nervous strain. You are naturally interested only
in getting home safely to England. That may be possible. It just depends
on how calmly and logically you can approach the situation. It is necessary,
as you must have gathered, that the completion of the work you are doing
should be delayed. Now, if you die before you get back to England, somebody else will be sent to Turkey to do your work over again. I understand
that the work as a whole would thus be delayed for six weeks. I also understand that that delay would be sufficient for the purposes of those interested.
You might, might you not, conclude from that that the simplest way of dealing with the matter would be to kidnap you in Genoa and keep you under
lock and key for the requisite six weeks and then release you, eh?"

"You might."

Moeller shook his head. "But you would be wrong. You would disappear.
Your employers and, no doubt, the Turkish Government would make inquiries about you. The Italian police would be informed. The British Foreign
Office would address bombastic demands for information to the Italian Government. The Italian Government, conscious that its neutrality was being
compromised, would bestir itself. I might find myself in serious difficulties,
especially when you were released and could tell your story. It would be most
inconvenient for me to be wanted by the Italian police. You see what I
mean?"

"Yes, I see."

"The straightforward course is to kill you. There is, however, a third possibility." He paused and then said: "You are a very fortunate man, Mr. Graham."

"What does *that* mean?"

"In times of peace only the fanatical nationalist demands that a man should surrender himself body and soul to the government of the country in which he was born. Yet, in war time, when men are being killed and there is emotion in the air, even an intelligent man may be so far carried away as to talk of his 'duty to his country.' You are fortunate because you happen to be in a business which sees these heroics for what they are: the emotional excesses of the stupid and brutish. 'Love of country!' There's a curious phrase. Love of a particular patch of earth? Scarcely. Put a German down in a field in Northern France, tell him that it is Hanover, and he cannot contradict you. Love of fellow-countrymen? Surely not. A man will like some of them and dislike others. Love of the country's culture? The men who know most of their countries' cultures are usually the most intelligent and the least patriotic. Love of the country's government? But governments are usually disliked by the people they govern. Love of country, we see, is merely a sloppy mysticism based on ignorance and fear. It has its uses, of course. When a ruling class wishes a people to do something which that people does not want to do, it appeals to patriotism. And, of course, one of the things that people most dislike is allowing themselves to be killed. But I must apologise. These are old arguments and I am sure you are familiar with them."

"Yes, I'm familiar with them."

"I am so relieved. I should not like to think that I had been wrong in judging you to be a man of intelligence. And it makes what I have to say so much easier."

"Well, what *have* you got to say?"

Moeller stubbed his cigarette out. "The third possibility, Mr. Graham, is that you might be induced to retire from business for six weeks of your own free will—that you should take a holiday."

"Are you mad?"

Moeller smiled. "I see your difficulty, believe me. If you simply go into hiding for six weeks, it may be rather awkward to explain matters when you return home. I understand. Hysterical fools might say that in choosing to remain alive instead of choosing to be killed by our friend Banat you did something shameful. The facts that the work would have been delayed in any case and that you were of more use to your country and its allies alive than dead would be ignored. Patriots, in common with other mystics, dislike logical argument. It would be necessary to practise a small deception. Let me tell you how it could be arranged."

"You're wasting your time."

Moeller took no notice. "There are some things, Mr. Graham, which not even patriots can control. One of those things is illness. You have come from Turkey where, thanks to earthquakes and floods, there have been several outbreaks of typhus. What could be more likely than that the moment you get ashore at Genoa a mild attack of typhus should develop? And what then?

Well, of course, you will be taken immediately to a private clinic and the doctor there will, at your request, write to your wife and employers in England. Of course, there will be the inevitable delays of war. By the time anyone can get to see you, the crisis will have passed and you will be convalescent: convalescent but much too weak to work or travel. But in six weeks' time you will have recovered sufficiently to do both. All will be well again. How does that appeal to you, Mr. Graham? To me it seems the only solution satisfactory to both of us."

"I see. You don't have the bother of shooting me. I'm out of the way for the requisite six weeks and can't tell tales afterwards without showing myself up. Is that it?"

"That's a very crude way of putting it; but you are quite right. That *is* it. How do you like the idea? Personally I should find the prospect of six weeks' absolute peace and quiet in the place I have in mind very attractive. It is quite near Santa Margherita, overlooking the sea and surrounded by pines. But then, I am old. You might fret."

He hesitated. "Of course," he went on slowly, "if you liked the idea, it might be possible to arrange for Señora Gallindo to share your six weeks' holiday."

Graham reddened. "What on earth do you mean?"

Moeller shrugged. "Come now, Mr. Graham! I am not short-sighted. If the suggestion really offends you, I apologise humbly. If not . . . I need hardly say that you would be the only patients there. The medical staff, which would consist of myself, Banat, and another man, apart from the servants, would be unobtrusive unless you were receiving visitors from England. However, that could be discussed later. Now what do you think?"

Graham steeled himself to make an effort. He said with deliberate ease: "I think you're bluffing. Hasn't it occurred to you that I may not be such a fool as you think? I shall, of course, repeat this conversation to the Captain. There will be police inquiries when we reach Genoa. My papers are perfectly genuine. Yours are not. Nor are Banat's. I have nothing to hide. You have plenty to hide. So has Banat. You're relying on my fear of being killed forcing me to agree to this scheme of yours. It won't. It won't keep my mouth shut either. I admit that I have been badly scared. I have had a very unpleasant twenty-four hours. I suppose that's your way of inducing a receptive frame of mind. Well, it doesn't work with me. I'm worried all right; I should be a fool if I weren't; but I'm not worried out of my senses. You're bluffing, Moeller. That's what I think. Now you can get out."

Moeller did not move. He said, as if he were a surgeon musing over some not entirely unforeseen complication: "Yes, I was afraid you might misunderstand me. A pity." He looked up. "And to whom are you going to take your story in the first place, Mr. Graham? The Purser? The third officer was telling me about your curious behaviour over poor Monsieur Mavrodopoulos. Apparently you have been making wild allegations to the effect that he is a criminal named Banat who wants to kill you. The ship's officers, including the Captain, seem to have enjoyed the joke very much. But even the

best of jokes becomes tiresome if it is told too often. There would be a certain
unreality about the story that I, too, was a criminal who wanted to kill you.
Isn't there a medical name for that sort of delusion? Come now, Mr. Graham! You tell me that you are not a fool. Please do not behave like one. Do
you think that I should have approached you in this way if I had thought
that you might be able to embarrass me in the way you suggest? I hope not.
You are no less foolish when you interpret my reluctance to have you killed
as weakness. You may prefer lying dead in a gutter with a bullet in your
back to spending six weeks in a villa on the Ligurian Riviera: that is your
affair. But please do not deceive yourself: those *are* the inevitable alternatives."

Graham smiled grimly. "And the little homily on patriotism is to still any
qualms I might have about accepting the inevitable. I see. Well, I'm sorry,
but it doesn't work. I still think you're bluffing. You've bluffed very well. I
admit that. You had me worried. I really thought for a moment that I had to
choose between possible death and sinking my pride—just like the hero in a
melodrama. My real choice was, of course, between using my common sense
and letting my stomach do my thinking for me. Well, Mr. Moeller, if that's
all you have to say . . ."

Moeller got slowly to his feet. "Yes, Mr. Graham," he said calmly, "that
is all I have to say." He seemed to hesitate. Then, very deliberately, he sat
down again. "No, Mr. Graham, I have changed my mind. There *is* something
else that I should say. It is just possible that on thinking this thing over
calmly you may decide that you have been silly and that I may not be as
clumsy as you now seem to think. Frankly, I don't expect you to do so. You
are pathetically sure of yourself. But in case your stomach should after all
take control, I think I should issue a warning."

"Against what?"

Moeller smiled. "One of the many things you don't seem to know is that
Colonel Haki considered it advisable to install one of his agents on board to
watch over you. I tried hard to interest you in him yesterday, but was unsuccessful. Ihsan Kuvetli is unprepossessing, I agree; but he has the reputation
of being a clever little man. If he had not been a patriot, he would have been
rich."

"Are you trying to tell me that Kuvetli is a Turkish agent?"

"I am indeed, Mr. Graham!" The pale blue eyes narrowed. "The reason
why I approached you this evening instead of to-morrow evening is because
I wanted to see you before he made himself known to you. He did not, I
think, find out who I was until to-day. He searched my cabin this evening.
I think that he must have heard me talking to Banat; the partitions between
the cabins are absurdly thin. In any case, I thought it likely that, realizing
the danger you were in, he would decide that the time had come to approach
you. You see, Mr. Graham, with his experience, he is not likely to make the
mistake that you are making. However, he has his duty to do and I have no
doubt that he will have evolved some laborious plan for getting you to France
in safety. What I want to warn you against is telling him of this suggestion

I have made to you. You see, if you should after all come round to my way of thinking, it would be embarrassing for both of us if an agent of the Turkish Government knew of our little deception. We could scarcely expect him to keep silent. You see what I mean, Mr. Graham? If you let Kuvetli into the secret you will destroy the only chance of returning to England alive that remains to you." He smiled faintly. "It's a solemn thought, isn't it?" He got up again and went to the door. "That was all I wanted to say. Good night, Mr. Graham."

Graham watched the door close and then sat down on the bunk. The blood was beating through his head as if he had been running. The time for bluffing was over. He should be deciding what he was going to do. He had to think calmly and clearly.

But he could not think calmly and clearly. He was confused. He became conscious of the vibration and movement of the ship and wondered if he had imagined what had just happened. But there was the depression in the bunk where Moeller had been sitting and the cabin was filled with the smoke from his cigarette. It was Haller who was the creature of imagination.

He was conscious now more of humiliation than of fear. He had become almost used to the tight sensation in his chest, the quick hammering of his heart, the dragging at his stomach, the crawling of his spine which were his body's responses to his predicament. In a queer, horrible way it had been stimulating. He had felt that he was pitting his wits against those of an enemy—a dangerous enemy but an intellectual inferior—with a chance of winning. Now he knew that he had been doing nothing of the kind. The enemy had been laughing up their sleeves at him. It had never even occurred to him to suspect "Haller." He had just sat there politely listening to extracts from a book. Heavens, what a fool the man must think him! He and Banat between them had seen through him as if he were made of glass. Not even his wretched little passages with Josette had escaped their notice. Probably they had seen him kissing her. And as a final measure of their contempt for him, it had been Moeller who had informed him that Mr. Kuvetli was a Turkish agent charged with his protection. Kuvetli! It was funny. Josette would be amused.

He remembered suddenly that he had promised to return to the saloon. She would be getting anxious. And the cabin was stifling. He could think better if he had some air. He got up and put on his overcoat.

José and Banat were still playing cards; José with a peculiar intentness as if he suspected Banat of cheating; Banat coolly and deliberately. Josette was leaning back in her chair smoking. Graham realised with a shock that he had left the room less than half an hour previously. It was amazing what could happen to your mind in so short a time; how the whole atmosphere of a place could change. He found himself noticing things about the saloon which he had not noticed before: a brass plate with the name of the builders of the ship engraved on it, a stain on the carpet, some old magazines stacked in a corner.

He stood there for a moment staring at the brass plate. The Mathises and the Italians were sitting there reading and did not look up. He looked past them and saw Josette turning her head back to watch the game. She had seen him. He went across to the farther door and out on to the shelter deck.

She would follow him soon to find out if he had been successful. He walked slowly along the deck wondering what he would say to her, whether or not to tell her about Moeller and his "alternative." Yes, he would tell her. She would tell him that he was all right, that Moeller was bluffing. But supposing Moeller *weren't* bluffing! "They will do anything to see that it is so. *Anything*, Mr. Graham! Do you understand?" Haki had not talked about bluffing. The wound under the grimy bandage on his hand did not feel like bluffing. And if Moeller wasn't bluffing, what was he, Graham, going to do?

He stopped and stared out at the lights on the coast. They were nearer now; near enough for him to see the movement of the boat in relation to them. It was incredible that this should be happening to him. Impossible! Perhaps, after all, he had been badly wounded in Istanbul and it was all a fantasy born of anæsthesia. Perhaps he would become conscious again soon to find himself in a hospital bed. But the teak rail, wet with dew, on which his hand rested was real enough. He gripped it in sudden anger at his own stupidity. He should be thinking, cudgelling his brains, making plans, deciding; doing something instead of standing there mooning. Moeller had left him over five minutes ago and here he was still trying to escape from his senses into a fairyland of hospitals and anæsthetics. What was he going to do about Kuvetli? Should he approach him or wait to be approached? What . . . ?

There were quick footsteps on the deck behind him. It was Josette, her fur coat thrown over her shoulders, her face pale and anxious in the dingy glare of the deck light. She seized his arm. "What has happened? Why were you so long?"

"There was no gun there."

"But there must be. Something has happened. When you walked into the *salone* just now you looked as if you had seen a ghost or were going to be sick. What is it, *chéri?*"

"There was no gun there," he repeated. "I searched carefully."

"You were not seen?"

"No, I wasn't seen."

She sighed with relief. "I was afraid when I saw your face . . ." She broke off. "But don't you see? It is all right. He does not carry a gun. There is no gun in his cabin. He has not got a gun." She laughed. "Perhaps he has pawned it. Ah, do not look so serious, *chéri*. He may get a gun in Genoa, but then it will be too late. Nothing can happen to you. You will be all right." She put on a woebegone expression. "I am the one who is in trouble now."

"You?"

"Your smelly little friend plays cards very well. He is winning money from José. José does not like that. He will have to cheat and cheating puts him in a bad temper. He says that it is bad for his nerves. Really it is that he likes to win because he is a better player." She paused and added suddenly: "Please wait!"

They had reached the end of the deck. She stopped and faced him. "What is the matter, *chéri?* You are not listening to what I am saying. You are thinking of something else." She pouted. "Ah, I know. It is your wife. Now that there is no danger you think of her again."

"No."

"You are sure?"

"Yes, I am sure." He knew now that he did not want to tell her about Moeller. He wanted her to talk to him believing that there was no longer any danger, that nothing could happen to him, that he could walk down the gangway at Genoa without fear. Afraid to create his own illusion, he could live in one of her making. He managed to smile. "You mustn't take any notice of me, Josette. I'm tired. You know, it's a very tiring business searching other people's cabins."

Immediately she was all sympathy. "*Mon pauvre chéri.* It is my fault, not yours. I forget how unpleasant things have been for you. Would you like us to go back to the *salone* and have a little drink?"

He would have done almost anything for a drink but go back to the saloon where he could see Banat. "No. Tell me what we shall do first when we arrive in Paris."

She looked at him quickly, smiling. "If we do not walk we shall get cold." She wriggled into her coat and linked her arm in his. "So we are going to Paris together?"

"Of course! I thought it was all arranged."

"Oh yes, but"—she pressed his arm against her side—"I did not think that you were serious. You see," she went on carefully, "so many men like to talk about what will happen, but they do not always like to remember what they have said. It is not that they do not mean what they say but that they do not always feel the same. You understand me, *chéri?*"

"Yes, I understand."

"I want you to understand," she went on, "because it is very important to me. I am a dancer and must think of my career also." She turned to him impulsively. "But you will think that I am selfish and I would not like you to think that. It is just that I like you very much and do not wish you to do anything simply because you have made a promise. As long as you understand that, it is all right. We will not talk about it." She snapped her fingers. "Look! When we get to Paris we will go straight to a hotel which I know of near the St. Philippe du Roule Metro. It is very modern and respectable and if you wish we can have a bathroom. It is not expensive. Then we will have champagne cocktails at the Ritz bar. They are only nine francs. While we have those drinks we can decide where to eat. I am very tired of Turkish foods and the sight of ravioli makes me ill. We must have good French food." She paused and added hesitantly, "I have never been to the Tour d'Argent."

"You shall."

"You mean it? I shall eat until I am as fat as a pig. After that we will begin."

"Begin?"

"There are some little places that are still open late in spite of the police. I will introduce you to a great friend of mine. She was the *sous-maquecée* of the Moulin Galant when Le Boulanger had it and before the gangsters came. You understand *sous-maquecée?*"

"No."

She laughed. "It is very bad of me. I will explain to you another time. But you will like Suzie. She saved a lot of money and now she is very respectable. She had a place in the rue de Liège which was better than Le Jockey Cabaret in Istanbul. She had to close it when the war came but she has opened another place in an impasse off the rue Pigalle and those who are her friends can go there. She has a great many friends and so she is making money again. She is quite old and the police do not trouble her. She shrugs her shoulders at them. Just because there is this filthy war there is no reason why we should all be miserable. I have other friends in Paris, too. You will like them when I introduce you. When they know that you are my friend they will be polite. They are very polite and nice when you are introduced by someone who is known in the quarter."

She went on talking about them. Most of them were women (Lucette, Dolly, Sonia, Claudette, Berthe) but there were one or two men (Jojo, Ventura) who were foreigners and had not been mobilised. She spoke of them vaguely but with an enthusiasm half defensive, half real. They might not be rich as Americans understood being rich, but they were people of the world. Each was remarkable in some particular. One was "very intelligent," another had a friend in the Ministry of the Interior, another was going to buy a villa at San Tropez and invite all his friends there for the summer. All were "amusing" and very useful if one wanted "anything special." She did not say what she meant by "anything special" and Graham did not ask her. He did not object to the picture she was painting. The prospect of sitting in the Café Graf buying drinks for *bizness* men and women from the places up the hill seemed to him at that moment infinitely attractive. He would be safe and free; himself again; able to think his own thoughts, to smile without stretching his nerves to breaking point when he did so. It must happen. It was absurd that he should be killed. Moeller was right about one thing at least. He would be more use to his country alive than dead.

Considerably more! Even if the Turkish contract were delayed for six weeks it would still have to be fulfilled. If he were alive at the end of the six weeks he would be able to go on with it; perhaps he might even make up for some of the lost time. He was, after all, the company's chief designer and it would be difficult to replace him in war time. He had been truthful enough when he had told Haki that there were dozens of other men with his qualifications; but he had not thought it necessary to bolster up Haki's argument by explaining that those dozens were made up of Americans, Frenchmen, Germans, Japanese and Czechs as well as Englishmen. Surely the sensible course would be the safe one. He was an engineer, not a professional secret agent. Presumably, a secret agent would have been equal to dealing with men like Moeller and Banat. He, Graham, was not. It was not for him to decide whether or not Moeller was bluffing. His business was to stay alive. Six weeks on the Ligurian Riviera could not do him any harm. It meant lying, of course: lying to Stephanie and to their friends, to his managing director and to the representatives of the Turkish Government. He couldn't tell them the truth. They would think that he ought to have risked his life. It was the sort of thing people did think when they were safe and snug in their arm-chairs. But if he lied, would they believe him? The people at home would; but what about Haki? Haki would smell a rat and ask questions. And Kuvetli? Moeller would have to do something about putting him off. It would be a tricky business; but Moeller would arrange things. Moeller was used to that sort of thing. Moeller. . . .

He stopped with a jerk. For God's sake, what was he thinking? He must be out of his senses! Moeller was an enemy agent. What he, Graham, had been turning over in his mind was nothing less than treason. And yet. . . . And yet what? He knew suddenly that something had snapped in his mind. The idea of doing a deal with an enemy agent was no longer unthinkable. He could consider Moeller's suggestion on its merits, coolly and calmly. He was becoming demoralised. He could no longer trust himself.

Josette was shaking his arm. "What is it, *chéri?* What is the matter?"

"I've just remembered something," he muttered.

"Ah!" she said angrily, "that is not at all polite. I ask you if you wish to go on walking. You take no notice. I ask you again and you stop as if you were ill. You have not been listening to what I was saying."

He pulled himself together. "Oh yes, I've been listening, but something you said reminded me that if I am to stop in Paris I shall have to write several important business letters so that I can post them immediately when I get there." He added with a fair assumption of jauntiness: "I don't want to work while I am in Paris."

"If it is not these *salauds* who tried to kill you, it is business," she grumbled. But she was apparently mollified.

"I apologise, Josette. It shan't happen again. Are you sure you are warm? You wouldn't like a drink?" He wanted to get away now. He knew what he must do and was impatient to do it before he could begin to think.

But she took his arm again. "No, it is all right. I am not angry and I am not cold. If we go up on the top deck you can kiss me to show that we are friends again. Soon I must go back to José. I said that I would only be a few minutes."

Half an hour later he went down to his cabin, took off his coat and went to look for the steward. He found him busy with a mop and bucket in the lavatories.

"Signore?"

"I promised to lend Signor Kuvetli a book. What is the number of his cabin?"

"Three, signore."

Graham walked back to cabin number three and stood for a moment hesitating. Perhaps he should think again before he did anything decisive, anything for which he might be sorry later. Perhaps it would be better if he left it until the morning. Perhaps . . .

He set his teeth, raised his hand and knocked on the door.

CHAPTER NINE

MR. KUVETLI opened the door.

He was wearing an old red wool dressing gown over a flannel night-shirt and his fringe of grey hair stood out from the sides of his head in ringlets. He had a book in his hand and looked as if he had been lying in his bunk reading. He stared at Graham blankly for a moment, then his smile returned.

"Mr. Graham! Is very good to see you. What can I do, please?"

At the sight of him, Graham's heart sank. It was to this grubby little man with a stupid smile that he was proposing to commit his safety. But it was too late to turn back now. He said: "I wonder if I could have a talk with you, Mr. Kuvetli."

Mr. Kuvetli blinked a little shiftily. "Talk? Oh, yes. Come in, please."

Graham stepped into the cabin. It was as small as his own and very stuffy.

Mr. Kuvetli smoothed out the blankets on his bunk. "Please take seat."

Graham sat down and opened his mouth to speak, but Mr. Kuvetli forestalled him.

"Cigarette, please, Mr. Graham?"

"Thank you." He took a cigarette. "I had a visit from Herr Professor Haller earlier this evening," he added; and then, remembering that the bulkheads were thin, glanced at them.

Mr. Kuvetli struck a match and held it out. "Herr Professor Haller is very interesting man, eh?" He lit Graham's cigarette and his own and blew the match out. "Cabins on both sides empty," he remarked.

"Then . . ."

"Please," interrupted Mr. Kuvetli, "will you allow me to speak French? My English is not very good, eh? Your French is very good. We understand better each."

"By all means."

"Now, then, we can talk easily." Mr. Kuvetli sat down beside him on the bunk. "Monsieur Graham, I was going to introduce myself to you to-morrow. Now, Monsieur Moeller has saved me the trouble, I think. You know that I am not a tobacco merchant, eh?"

"According to Moeller you are a Turkish agent acting under Colonel Haki's orders. Is that so?"

"Yes, that is so. I will be truthful. I am surprised that you have not discovered me before this. When the Frenchman asked me what firm I belonged to I had to say Pazar and Co., because I had given that name to you. Unfortunately, the firm of Pazar and Co. does not exist. Naturally he was puzzled. I was able to prevent him from asking more questions then, but I expected him to discuss it with you later." The smile had gone and with it the bright-eyed stupidity which, for Graham, had been the tobacco merchant. In its place was a firm determined mouth, and a pair of steady brown eyes which surveyed him with something very like good-humoured contempt.

"He did not discuss it."

"And you did not suspect that I was avoiding his questions?" He shrugged. "One always takes unnecessary precautions. People are so much more trusting than one supposes."

"Why should I suspect?" Graham demanded irritably. "What I cannot understand is why you did not approach me as soon as you knew that Banat was on the ship. I suppose," he added spitefully, "that you *do* know that Banat is on the ship?"

"Yes, I know," said Mr. Kuvetli airily. "I did not approach you for three reasons." He held up podgy fingers. "Colonel Haki instructed me in the first place that your attitude to his efforts to protect you were unsympathetic and that unless it became necessary I would do better to remain unknown to you. Secondly, Colonel Haki has a low opinion of your ability to conceal your feelings and considered that if I wished to keep my true identity secret I had better not tell you of it."

Graham was scarlet. "And what about the third reason?"

"Thirdly," continued Mr. Kuvetli serenely, "I wished to see what Banat and Moeller would do. You tell me that Moeller has talked to you. Excellent. I would like to hear what he had to say."

Graham was angry now. "Before I waste my time doing that," he said coldly, "supposing you show me your credentials. So far I have only Moeller's word and your own that you *are* a Turkish agent. I've already made some silly mistakes on this trip. I don't intend to make any more."

To his surprise, Mr. Kuvetli grinned. "I am pleased to see that you are in such excellent spirits, Monsieur Graham. I was getting a little worried about you this evening. In this sort of situation, whisky does more harm to the nerves than good. Excuse me, please." He turned to his jacket hanging on the hook behind the door and produced from the pocket of it a letter which he handed to Graham. "That was given to me by Colonel Haki to give to you. I think you will find it satisfactory."

Graham looked at it. It was an ordinary letter of introduction written in French on notepaper embossed with the title and address of the Turkish Ministry of the Interior. It was addressed to him personally and signed "Zia Haki." He put it in his pocket. "Yes, Monsieur Kuvetli, it is quite satisfactory. I must apologise for doubting your word."

"It was correct of you to do so," said Mr. Kuvetli primly. "And now, Monsieur, tell me about Moeller. I am afraid Banat's appearance on the ship must have been a shock to you. I felt guilty about keeping you ashore in Athens. But it was for the best. As to Moeller . . ."

Graham looked at him quickly. "Wait a minute! Do you mean to say that you knew Banat was coming aboard? Do you mean that you hung about in Athens asking all those fool questions solely in order to prevent my finding out before we sailed that Banat was on board?"

Mr. Kuvetli looked sheepish. "It was necessary. You must see . . ."

"Of all the damned . . . !" began Graham violently.

"One moment, please," said Mr. Kuvetli sharply. "I have said that it was necessary. At Çanakkale I received a telegram from Colonel Haki saying that Banat had left Turkey, that it was possible that he might try to join the ship at the Piræus and . . ."

"You knew that! And yet . . ."

"Please, Monsieur! I will continue. Colonel Haki added that I was to keep you here on the ship. That was intelligent. On the ship nothing could happen to you. Banat might have been going to the Piræus for the purpose of frightening you on to the land, where very unpleasant things could happen to you. Wait, please! I went to Athens with you partly to see that you were not attacked while you were ashore and partly so that if Banat did join the ship, you would not see him until we had sailed."

"But why, in the name of goodness, didn't Colonel Haki arrest Banat or at least delay him until it was too late for him to reach the ship?"

"Because Banat would certainly have been replaced. We know all about Banat. A strange Monsieur Mavrodopoulos would have been a new problem."

"But you say that Banat's, or, rather, Moeller's idea might have been to scare me off the boat. Banat could not know that I knew him?"

"You told Colonel Haki that Banat was pointed out to you in Le Jockey Cabaret. Banat was watching you then. He would probably know that you had noticed him. He is not an amateur. You see Colonel Haki's point of view? If they were hoping to drive you on to the land and kill you there, it would be better for them to attempt to do so and fail than for the attempt to be frustrated in time for them to make other arrangements. As it happens, however," he went on cheerfully, "their intention was not to drive you on to the land and my precautions were wasted. Banat did join the ship, but he stayed in his cabin until the pilot had been taken off."

"Precisely!" snarled Graham. "I could have gone ashore, taken a train and been safe in Paris by now."

Mr. Kuvetli considered the criticism for a moment and then slowly shook his head. "I do not think so. You have forgotten Monsieur Moeller. I do not think that he and Banat would have stayed on the boat very long if you had not returned by sailing time."

Graham laughed shortly. "Did you know that then?"

Mr. Kuvetli contemplated dirty fingernails. "I will be very honest, Monsieur Graham. I did not know it. I knew *of* Monsieur Moeller, of course. I was, through an intermediary, once offered a large sum of money to work for him. I had seen a photograph of him. But photographs are mostly useless. I did not recognise him. The fact that he came aboard at Istanbul prevented my suspecting him. Banat's behaviour made me think that I had overlooked something, and when I saw him talking to the Herr Professor I made some inquiries."

"He says that you searched his cabin."

"I did. I found letters addressed to him in Sofia."

"There has," said Graham bitterly, "been quite a lot of cabin searching. Last night Banat stole my revolver from my suit-case. This evening I went to his cabin and tried to find his gun, the gun he used on me in Istanbul. It was not there. When I returned to my cabin, Moeller was there with Banat's gun."

Mr. Kuvetli had been listening gloomily. "If," he now said, "you will please tell me what Moeller had to say we shall both get to sleep much sooner."

Graham smiled. "You know, Kuvetli, I have had several surprises on this ship. You are the first pleasant one." And then the smile faded. "Moeller came to tell me that unless I agree to delay my return to England for six weeks I shall be murdered within five minutes of my landing in Genoa. He says that apart from Banat, he has other men waiting in Genoa to do the killing."

Mr. Kuvetli did not seem surprised. "And where does he suggest that you should spend the six weeks?"

"In a villa near Santa Margherita. The idea is that I should be certified by a doctor as suffering from typhus and that I should stay in this villa as if it were a clinic. Moeller and Banat would be the medical staff if anyone should come out from England to see me. He proposes, you see, to involve me in the deception so that I cannot tell tales afterwards."

Mr. Kuvetli raised his eyebrows. "And how was I concerned?"

Graham told him.

"And, believing Monsieur Moeller, you decided to ignore his advice and tell me about his suggestion?" Mr. Kuvetli beamed approvingly. "That was very courageous of you, Monsieur."

Graham reddened. "Do you think that I might have agreed?"

Mr. Kuvetli misunderstood. "I think nothing," he said hastily. "But"—he hesitated—"when a person's life is in danger he is not always quite normal. He may do things which he would not do in the ordinary way. He cannot be blamed."

Graham smiled. "I will be frank with you. I came to you now instead of in the morning so that there could be no chance of my thinking things over and deciding to take his advice after all."

"What is important is," said Mr. Kuvetli quietly, "that you *have* in fact come to me. Did you tell him that you were going to do so?"

"No. I told him that I thought he was bluffing."

"And *do* you think that he was?"

"I don't know."

Mr. Kuvetli scratched his armpits thoughtfully. "There are so many things to be considered. And it depends on what you mean by saying that he is bluffing. If you mean that he could not or would not kill you, I think you are wrong. He could and would."

"But how? I have a Consul. What is to prevent my getting into a taxi at the dock and going straight to the Consulate? I could arrange for some sort of protection there."

Mr. Kuvetli lit another cigarette. "Do you know where the British Consulate-General in Genoa is?"

"The taxi-driver would know."

"I can tell you myself. It is at the corner of the Via Ippolito d'Aste. This ship docks at the Ponte San Giorgio in the Vittorio Emanuele basin, several kilometres away from your Consulate. I have travelled this way before and so I know what I am saying. Genoa is a great port. I doubt, Monsieur Graham, whether you would complete one of those kilometres. They will be waiting for you with a car. When you took the taxi they would follow you as far as the Via Francia, then force the taxi on to the pavement and shoot you as you sit there."

"I could telephone to the Consul from the dock."

"Certainly you could. But you would have to go through the Customs shed first. You would then have to wait for the Consul to arrive. *Wait*, Monsieur! Do you understand what that means? Let us suppose that you were to reach the Consul by telephone immediately and convince him that your case was urgent. You would still have to wait at least half an hour for him. Let me tell you that your chances of surviving that half-hour would not be lessened if you spent it drinking prussic acid. To kill an unarmed, unguarded man is never difficult. Among the sheds on the quay it would be simplicity itself. No, I do not think Moeller is bluffing when he says that he can kill you."

"But what about this proposal? He seemed very eager to persuade me to agree."

Mr. Kuvetli fingered the back of his head. "There could be several explanations of that. For instance, it is possible that his intention is to kill you in any case and that he wishes to do so with as little trouble as possible. One cannot deny that it would be easier to kill you on the road to Santa Margherita than on the waterfront at Genoa."

"That's a pleasing idea."

"I am inclined to think that it is the correct one." Mr. Kuvetli frowned. "You see, this proposal of his looks very simple—you are taken ill, there is a forged medical certificate, you get better, you go home. *Voilà!* It is done. But think now of the actuality. You are an Englishman in a hurry to get to England. You land in Genoa. What would you do normally? Take the train for Paris, without a doubt. But what is it necessary to do now? You must, for some mysterious reason, remain in Genoa long enough to discover that you have typhus. Also you must not do what anyone else would do in those circumstances—you must not go to a hospital. You must instead go to a private clinic near Santa Margherita. Is it possible that it would not be thought in England that your behaviour was curious? I think not. Furthermore, typhus is a disease which must be notified to the authorities. That could not be done in this case because there would be no typhus and the medical authorities would soon discover the fact. And supposing your friends discover that your case has not been notified. They might. You are of some importance. The British Consul might be asked to investigate. And then what? No, I cannot see Monsieur Moeller taking such absurd risks. Why should he? It would be easier to kill you."

"He says that he does not like having people killed if he can help it."

Mr. Kuvetli giggled. "He must think you very stupid indeed. Did he tell you what he would do about my presence here?"

"No."

"I am not surprised. For that plan to succeed as he explained it to you, there would be only one thing he could do—kill me. And even when he had killed me I should still embarrass him. Colonel Haki would see to that. I am afraid that Monsieur's proposal is not very honest."

"It sounded convincing. I may say that he was prepared to allow Señora Gallindo to make up the party if I liked to take her along."

Mr. Kuvetli leered: a scurfy faun in a flannel night-shirt. "And did you tell Señora Gallindo that?"

Graham flushed. "She knows nothing of Moeller. I told her about Banat. I'm afraid I gave myself away last night when Banat came into the saloon. She asked me what was wrong and I told her. Anyway," he added defensively but none too truthfully, "I needed her help. It was she who arranged to keep Banat occupied while I searched his cabin."

"By arranging for the good José to play cards with him? Quite so. As to the suggestion that she should accompany you, I think that, if you had accepted it, it would have been withdrawn. It would, no doubt, be explained that difficulties had arisen. Does José know of this business?"

"No. I don't think that she would tell him. She's trustworthy, I think," he added with as much nonchalance as he could muster.

"No woman is trustworthy," gloated Mr. Kuvetli. "But I do not begrudge you your amusements, Monsieur Graham." He moistened his upper lip with the tip of his tongue and grinned. "Señora Gallindo is very attractive."

Graham checked the retort that rose to his lips. "Very," he said tersely. "Meanwhile we have reached the conclusion that I shall be killed if I accept Moeller's proposal and killed if I don't." And then he lost control of himself. "For God's sake, Kuvetli," he burst out in English, "do you think it's pleasant for me to sit here listening to you telling me how easy it would be for these lice to kill me! What am I going to *do?*"

Mr. Kuvetli patted his knee consolingly. "My dear friend, I understand perfectly. I was merely showing you that it would be impossible for you to land in the ordinary way."

"But what other way *can* I land? I'm not invisible."

"I will tell you," said Mr. Kuvetli complacently. "It is very simple. You see, although this ship does not actually reach the quayside for the landing of passengers until nine o'clock on Saturday morning, she arrives off Genoa in the early hours, at about four o'clock. Night pilotage is expensive; accordingly, although she takes on a pilot as soon as it begins to get light, she does not move in until sunrise. The pilot boat . . ."

"If you're suggesting that I leave by the pilot boat, it's impossible."

"For you, yes. For me, no. I am privileged. I have a diplomatic *laisser passer*." He patted his jacket pocket. "By eight o'clock I can be at the Turkish Consulate. Arrangements can then be made for getting you away safely and taking you to the airport. The international train service is not as good as it used to be, and the Paris train does not leave until two o'clock in the afternoon. It is better that you do not remain so long in Genoa. We will charter a plane to take you to Paris immediately."

Graham's heart began to beat faster. An extraordinary feeling of lightness and ease came over him. He wanted to laugh. He said stolidly: "It sounds all right."

"It will be all right, but precautions must be taken to see that it is so. If Monsieur Moeller suspects that there is a chance of your escaping, something unpleasant will happen. Listen carefully, please." He scratched his chest and then held up a forefinger. "First; you must go to Monsieur Moeller tomorrow and tell him that you agree to his suggestion that you should stay in Santa Margherita."

"What!"

"It is the best way to keep him quiet. I leave you to choose your own opportunity. But I will suggest the following: it is possible that he will approach you again, and so perhaps it will be best if you give him time to do so. Wait until late in the evening. If he has not approached you by then, go to him. Do not appear to be too ingenuous, but agree to do what he wants. When you have done that, go to your cabin, lock the door, and remain there. Do not leave your cabin under any circumstances until eight o'clock the following morning. It might be dangerous.

"Now comes the important part of your instructions. At eight o'clock in the morning you must be ready with your baggage. Call the steward, tip him, and tell him to put your baggage in the Customs shed. There must be no mistake at this point. What you have to do is to remain on the ship until I come to tell you that the preparations have been made and that it is safe for you to land. There are difficulties. If you remain in your cabin the steward will make you go ashore with the rest, including Monsieur Moeller and Banat. If you go on deck, the same thing will happen. You must see that you are not forced to go ashore before it is safe for you to do so."

"But how?"

"I am explaining that. What you must do is to leave your cabin and then, taking care that nobody sees you, to go into the nearest unoccupied cabin. You have cabin number five. Go into cabin number four. That is the next cabin to this. Wait there. You will be quite safe. You will have tipped the steward. If he thinks of you again at all it will be to assume that you have gone ashore. If he is asked about you he will certainly not look in unoccupied cabins. Monsieur Moeller and Banat will naturally be looking for you. You will have agreed to go with them. But they will have to go ashore to wait. By that time we shall be there and able to act."

"Act?"

Mr. Kuvetli smiled grimly. "We shall have two men for every one of theirs. I do not think that they will try to stop us. Are you quite clear about what you have to do?"

"Quite clear."

"There is a small matter. Monsieur Moeller will ask you if I have made myself known to you. You will, of course, say yes. He will ask you what I said. You will tell him that I offered to escort you to Paris myself and that when you insisted on going to the British Consul, I threatened you."

"Threatened me!"

"Yes." Mr. Kuvetli was still smiling, but his eyes had narrowed a little. "If your attitude towards me had been different it might have been necessary for me to threaten you."

"What with?" Graham demanded spitefully. "Death? That would have been absurd, wouldn't it?"

Mr. Kuvetli smiled steadily. "No, Monsieur Graham, not death but with the accusation that you had accepted bribes from an enemy agent to sabotage Turkish naval preparations. You see, Monsieur Graham, it is just as important for me that you return to England without delay as it is for Monsieur Moeller that you should not return."

Graham stared at him. "I see. And this is a gentle reminder that the threat still stands if I should allow myself to be persuaded that Moeller's proposal is, after all, acceptable. Is that it?"

His tone was deliberately offensive. Mr. Kuvetli drew himself up. "I am a Turk, Monsieur Graham," he said with dignity, "and I love my country. I fought with the Gazi for Turkey's freedom. Can you imagine that I would let one man endanger the great work we have done? I am ready to give my life for Turkey. Is it strange that I should not hesitate to do less unpleasant things?"

He had struck an attitude. He was ridiculous and yet, for the very reason that his words were at so odd a variance with his appearance, impressive. Graham was disarmed. He grinned. "Not at all strange. You need have no fears. I shall do exactly what you have told me to do. But supposing he wants to know when our meeting took place?"

"You will tell the truth. It is just possible that you were seen to come to my cabin. You can say that I asked you to do so, that I left a note in your cabin. Remember, too, that we must not be seen in private conversation after this. It will be better if we do not have any sort of conversation. In any case there is nothing more to be said. Everything is arranged. There is only one other matter to be considered—Señora Gallindo."

"What about her?"

"She has part of your confidence. What is her attitude?"

"She thinks that everything is all right now." He reddened. "I said that I would travel with her to Paris."

"And after?"

"She believes that I shall spend some time with her there."

"You did not, of course, intend to do so." He had the air of a schoolmaster dealing with a difficult pupil.

Graham hesitated. "No, I suppose I didn't," he said slowly. "To tell you the truth, it has been pleasant to talk of going to Paris. When you're expecting to be killed . . ."

"But now that you are not expecting to be killed it is different, eh?"

"Yes, it's different." Yet was it so different? He was not quite sure.

Mr. Kuvetli stroked his chin. "On the other hand it would be dangerous to tell her that you have changed your mind," he reflected. "She might be indiscreet—or angry, perhaps. Say nothing to her. If she discusses Paris, everything is as it was before. You can explain that you have business to do in Genoa after the ship docks and say that you will meet her on the train. That will prevent her looking for you before she goes ashore. It is understood?"

"Yes. It is understood."

"She is pretty," Mr. Kuvetli went on thoughtfully. "It is a pity that your business is so urgent. However, perhaps you could return to Paris when you have finished your work." He smiled: the schoolmaster promising a sweet for good behaviour.

"I suppose I could. Is there anything else?"

Mr. Kuvetli looked up at him slyly. "No. That is all. Except that I must ask you to continue to look as *distrait* as you have been looking since we left the Piræus. It would be a pity if Monsieur Moeller should suspect anything from your manner."

"My manner? Oh, yes, I see." He stood up and was surprised to find that his knees felt quite weak. He said: "I've often wondered what a condemned man feels like when they tell him that he has been reprieved. Now I know."

Mr. Kuvetli smiled patronisingly. "You feel very well, eh?"

Graham shook his head. "No, Mr. Kuvetli, I don't feel very well. I feel very sick and very tired and I can't stop thinking that there must be a mistake."

"A mistake! There is no mistake. You need not worry. All will be well. Go to bed now, my friend, and in the morning you will feel better. A mistake!"

Mr. Kuvetli laughed.

CHAPTER TEN

AS MR. KUVETLI had prophesied, Graham did feel better in the morning. Sitting up in his bunk drinking his coffee, he felt curiously free and competent. The disease from which he had been suffering was cured. He was himself again: well and normal. He had been a fool to worry at all. He ought to have known that everything would be all right. War or no war, men like him weren't shot in the street. That sort of thing just didn't happen. Only the adolescent minds of the Moellers and the Banats could entertain such possibilities. He had no misgivings. Even his hand was better. In the night the bandage had slipped, taking with it the bloody dressing which had been sticking to the wound. He was able to replace it with a piece of lint and two short strips of adhesive plaster. The change, he felt, was symbolic. Not even the knowledge that in the day before him he had some highly disagreeable things to do, could depress him.

The first thing he had to consider was, of course, his attitude towards Moeller. As Mr. Kuvetli had pointed out, it was possible that the man would wait until the evening before making any attempt to find out if the line he had put out the previous evening had caught the fish. That meant that he, Graham, would have to sit through two meals with Moeller and Banat without giving himself away. That, certainly, would not be pleasant. He wondered whether it might not be safer to approach Moeller at once. It would, after all, be far more convincing if the victim made the first move. Or would it be less convincing? Should the fish still be struggling on the hook when the line was reeled in? Evidently Mr. Kuvetli thought that it should. Very well. Mr. Kuvetli's instructions should be followed exactly. The questions of how he was going to behave at lunch and dinner could be left to settle themselves when those times came. As for the actual interview with Moeller, he had ideas about making that convincing. Moeller should not have things all his own way. Rather to his surprise, he found that it was the thought of what he had to do about Josette which worried him most.

He was, he told himself, treating her shabbily. She had been kind to him in her way. Indeed, she could not have been kinder. It was no excuse to say that she had behaved badly over that business of José's revolver. It had been unfair of him to ask her to steal for him: José was, after all, her partner. It would not even be possible now for him to give her that handbag with a thousand-franc note in it, unless he left it for her on his way through Paris, and it was always possible that she would not go to the Hotel des Belges. It was no good protesting that she was out for what she could get. She had made no secret of the fact and he had tacitly accepted it. He was treating her shabbily, he told himself again. It was an attempt to rationalise his feelings about her and it was strangely unsuccessful. He was perplexed.

He did not see her until just before lunch, and then she was with José.

It was a wretched day. The sky was overcast and there was an icy northeast wind with a hint of snow in it. He had spent most of the morning in a corner of the saloon reading some old copies of L'Illustration he found there. Mr. Kuvetli had seen and looked through him. He had spoken to no one except the Beronellis, who had given him a defensive "buon giorno," and the Mathises, who had returned his greeting with a frigid bow. He had thought it necessary to explain to the Mathises that his rudeness of the previous evening had been unintentional and due to his feeling ill at the time. The explanation had been accepted by them with some embarrassment and it had occurred to him that they might have preferred a silent feud to an apology. The man had been particularly confused as if he were finding himself in some way ridiculous. They had soon decided that they must go for a walk on deck. Through the porthole Graham had seen them a few minutes later walking with Mr. Kuvetli. The only other person on deck that morning had been Moeller's Armenian demonstrating pathetically, for there was a heavy swell, that her dislike of the sea was no mere figment of her "husband's" imagination. Soon after twelve Graham had collected his hat and coat from his cabin and gone out for the stroll which he had decided should precede the drinking of a large whisky and soda.

He was on his way back to the saloon when he encountered Josette and José.

José stopped with an oath and clutched at his curly soft hat which the wind was trying to snatch from his head.

Josette met Graham's eyes and smiled significantly. "José is angry again. Last night he played cards and lost. It was the little Greek, Mavrodopoulos. The attar of roses was too strong for the California Poppy."

"He is no Greek," said José sourly. "He has the accent of a goat as well as the smell. If he is a Greek I will . . ." He said what he would do.

"But he can play cards, *mon cher caïd.*"

"He stopped playing too soon," said José. "You need not worry. I have not finished with him."

"Perhaps he has finished with you."

"He must be a very good player," Graham put in tactfully.

José eyed him distastefully. "And what do you know about it?"

"Nothing," retorted Graham coldly. "For all I know it may be simply that you are a very bad player."

"You would like to play perhaps?"

"I don't think so. Cards bore me."

José sneered. "Ah, yes! There are better things to do, eh?" He sucked his teeth loudly.

"When he is bad-tempered," Josette explained, "he cannot be polite. There is nothing to be done with him. He does not care what people think."

José pursed up his mouth into an expression of saccharine sweetness. " 'He does not care what people think,' " he repeated in a high, derisive falsetto. Then his face relaxed. "What do I care what they think?" he demanded.

"You are ridiculous," said Josette.

"If they do not like it they can stay in the lavabos," José declared aggressively.

"It would be a small price to pay," murmured Graham.

Josette giggled. José scowled. "I do not understand."

Graham did not see that there was anything to be gained by explaining. He ignored José and said in English: "I was just going to have a drink. Will you come?"

She looked doubtful. "Do you wish to buy José a drink also?"

"Must I?"

"I cannot get rid of him."

José was glowering at them suspiciously. "It is not wise to insult me," he said.

"No one is insulting you, imbecile. Monsieur here asks us to have drinks. Do you want a drink?"

He belched. "I do not care who I drink with if we can get off this filthy deck."

"He is so polite," said Josette.

They had finished their drinks when the gong sounded. Graham soon found that he had been wise to leave the question of his attitude towards Moeller to answer itself. It was "Haller" who appeared in answer to the gong; a Haller who greeted Graham as if nothing had happened and who embarked almost immediately on a long account of the manifestations of An, the Sumerian sky god. Only once did he show himself to be aware of any change in his relationship with Graham. Soon after he began talking, Banat entered and sat down. Moeller paused and glanced across the table at him. Banat stared back sullenly. Moeller turned deliberately to Graham.

"Monsieur Mavrodopoulos," he remarked, "looks as if he has been frustrated in some way, as if he has been told that he may not be able to do something that he wishes to do very badly. Don't you think so, Mr. Graham? I wonder if he is going to be disappointed."

Graham looked up from his plate to meet a level stare. There was no mistaking the question in the pale blue eyes. He knew that Banat, too, was watching him. He said slowly: "It would be a pleasure to disappoint Monsieur Mavrodopoulos."

Moeller smiled and the smile reached his eyes. "So it would. Now let me see. What was I saying? Ah, yes . . ."

That was all; but Graham went on with his meal, knowing that one at least of the day's problems was solved. He would not have to approach Moeller: Moeller would approach him.

But Moeller was evidently in no hurry to do so. The afternoon dragged intolerably. Mr. Kuvetli had said that they were not to have any sort of conversation and Graham deemed it advisable to plead a headache when Mathis suggested a rubber of bridge. His refusal affected the Frenchman peculiarly. There was a troubled reluctance about his acceptance of it, and he looked as if he had been about to say something important and then thought better of it. There was in his eyes the same look of unhappy confusion that Graham had seen in the morning. But Graham wondered about it only for a few seconds. He was not greatly interested in the Mathises.

Moeller, Banat, Josette and José had gone to their cabins immediately after lunch. Signora Beronelli had been induced to make the fourth with the Mathises and Mr. Kuvetli and appeared to be enjoying herself. Her son sat by her watching her jealously. Graham returned in desperation to the magazines. Towards five o'clock, however, the bridge four showed signs of disintegrating and, to avoid being drawn into a conversation with Mr. Kuvetli, Graham went out on deck.

The sun, obscured since the day before, was pouring a red glow through a thinning of the clouds just above the horizon. To the east the long, low strip of coast which had been visible earlier was already enveloped in a slate grey dusk and the lights of a town had begun to twinkle. The clouds were moving quickly as for the gathering of a storm and heavy drops of rain began to slant in on to the deck. He moved backwards out of the rain and found Mathis at his elbow. The Frenchman nodded.

"Was it a good game?" Graham asked.

"Quite good. Madame Beronelli and I lost. She is enthusiastic, but inefficient."

"Then, except for the enthusiasm, my absence made no difference."

Mathis smiled a little nervously. "I hope that your headache is better."

"Much better, thank you."

It had begun to rain in earnest now. Mathis stared out gloomily into the gathering darkness. "Filthy!" he commented.

"Yes."

There was a pause. Then:

"I was afraid," said Mathis suddenly, "that you did not wish to play with us. I could not blame you if such were the case. This morning you were good enough to make an apology. The true apology was due from me to you."

He was not looking at Graham. "I am quite sure . . ." Graham began to mumble, but Mathis went on as if he were addressing the seagulls following the ship. "I do not always remember," he said bitterly, "that what to some people is good or bad is to others simply boring. My wife has led me to put too much faith in the power of words."

"I'm afraid I don't understand."

Mathis turned his head and smiled wryly. "Do you know the word *encotillonné?*"

"No."

"A man who is governed by his wife is *encotillonné.*"

"In English we say 'hen-pecked.' "

"Ah, yes?" Obviously he did not care what was said in English. "I must tell you a joke about it. Once I was *encotillonné.* Oh, but very badly! Does that surprise you?"

"It does." Graham saw that the man was dramatising himself, and was curious.

"My wife used to have a very great temper. She still has it, I think, but now I do not see it. But for the first ten years of our marriage it was terrible. I had a small business. Trade was very bad and I became bankrupt. It was not my fault, but she always pretended that it was. Has your wife a bad temper, Monsieur?"

"No. Very good."

"You are lucky. For years I lived in misery. And then one day I made a great discovery. There was a socialist meeting in our town and I went to it. I was, you must understand, a Royalist. My family had no money, but they had a title which they would have liked to use without their neighbours sniggering. I was of my family. I went to this meeting because I was curious. The speaker was good, and he spoke about Briey. That interested me because I had been at Verdun. A week later we were with some friends in the café and I repeated what I had heard. My wife laughed in a curious way. Then when I got home I made my great discovery. I found that my wife was a snob and

more stupid than I had dreamed. She said that I had humiliated her by saying such things as if I believed them. All her friends were respectable people.
I must not speak as if I were a workman. She cried. I knew then that I was
free. I had a weapon that I could use against her. I used it. If she displeased
me I became a socialist. To the smug little tradesmen whose wives were her
friends I would preach the abolition of profit and the family. I bought books
and pamphlets to make my arguments more damaging. My wife became very
docile. She would cook things that I liked so that I would not disgrace her."
He paused.

"You mean that you don't believe all these things you say about Briey and
banking and capitalism?" demanded Graham.

Mathis smiled faintly. "That is the joke about which I told you. For a time
I was free. I could command my wife and I became more fond of her. I was a
manager in a big factory. And then a terrible thing happened. I found that I
had begun to believe these things I said. The books I read showed me that I
had found a truth. I, a Royalist by instinct, became a socialist by conviction.
Worse, I became a socialist martyr. There was a strike in the factory and I, a
manager, supported the strikers. I did not belong to a union. Naturally! And
so I was dismissed. It was ridiculous." He shrugged. "So here I am! I have become a man in my home at the price of becoming a bore outside it. It is funny,
is it not?"

Graham smiled. He had decided that he liked Monsieur Mathis. He said:
"It would be funny if it were wholly true. But I can assure you that it was not
because I was bored that I did not listen to you last night."

"You are very polite," began Mathis dubiously; "but . . ."

"Oh, there is no question of politeness. You see, I work for an armaments
manufacturer, and so I have been more than interested in what you have had
to say. On some points I find myself in agreement with you."

A change came over the Frenchman's face. He flushed slightly; a small delighted smile hovered round his lips; for the first time Graham saw the tense
frown relax. "On which points do you *not* agree?" he demanded eagerly.

At that moment Graham realised that, whatever else had happened to him
on the *Sestri Levante*, he had made at least one friend.

They were still arguing when Josette came out on deck. Unwillingly, Mathis
interrupted what he was saying to acknowledge her presence.

"*Madame.*"

She wrinkled her nose at them. "What are you discussing? It must be very
important that you have to stand in the rain to talk about it."

"We were talking politics."

"No, no!" said Mathis quickly. "Not politics, economics! Politics are the
effect. We were talking about causes. But you are right. This rain is filthy.
If you will excuse me, please, I will see what has happened to my wife."
He winked at Graham. "If she suspects that I am making propaganda she
will not be able to sleep to-night."

With a smile and a nod he went. Josette looked after him. "He is nice,
that man. Why does he marry such a woman?"

"He is very fond of her."

"In the way that you are fond of me?"

"Perhaps not. Would you rather we went in?"

"No. I came out for some air. It will not be so wet round on the other side of the deck."

They began to walk round to the other side. It was dark now and the deck lights had been put on.

She took his arm. "Do you realise that to-day we have not really seen each other until now? No! Of course you do not realise it! You have been amusing yourself with politics. It does not matter that I am worried."

"Worried? What about?"

"This man who wants to kill you, imbecile! You do not tell me what you are going to do at Genoa."

He shrugged. "I've taken your advice. I'm not troubling about him."

"But you will go to the British Consul?"

"Yes." The moment had come when he must do some really steady lying. "I shall go straight there. Afterwards I shall have to see one or two people on business. The train does not leave until two o'clock in the afternoon, so I think that I shall have time. We can meet on the train."

She sighed. "So much business! But I shall see you for lunch, eh?"

"I'm afraid it's unlikely. If we did arrange to meet I might not be able to keep the appointment. It'll be best if we meet on the train."

She turned her head a little sharply. "You are telling me the truth? You are not saying this because you have changed your mind?"

"My dear Josette!" He had opened his mouth to explain again that he had business to attend to, but had stopped himself in time. He must not protest too much.

She pressed his arm. "I did not mean to be disagreeable, *chéri*. It is only that I wish to be sure. We will meet at the train if you wish it. We can have a drink together at Torino. We reach there at four and stop for half an hour. It is because of the coaches from Milano. There are some nice places to drink in Torino. After the ship here it will be wonderful."

"It'll be splendid. What about José?"

"Ah, it does not matter about him. Let him drink by himself. After the way he was rude to you this morning, I do not care what José does. Tell me about the letters you are writing. Are they all finished?"

"I shall finish them this evening."

"And after that, no more work?"

"After that, no more work." He felt that he could not stand much more of this. He said: "You'll get cold if we stay out here much longer. Shall we go inside?"

She stopped and withdrew her arm from his so that he could kiss her. Her back was taut as she strained her body against his. Seconds later she drew away from him, laughing. "I must remember," she said, "not to say 'whisky-soda,' but 'whisky and soda' now. That is very important, eh?"

"Very important."

She squeezed his arm. "You are nice. I like you very much, *chéri.*"

They began to walk back towards the saloon. He was grateful for the dimness of the lights.

He did not have long to wait for Moeller. The German agent had been in the habit of leaving the table and going to his cabin as soon as a meal was finished. Tonight, however, Banat was the first to go, evidently by arrangement; and the monologue continued until the Beronellis had followed him. It was an account of comparisons made between the Sumero-Babylonian liturgies and the ritual forms of certain Mesopotamian fertility cults and it was with unmistakable triumph that he at last brought it to an end. "You must admit, Mr. Graham," he added, lowering his voice, "that I have done extremely well to remember so much. Naturally, I made a few mistakes, and a good deal was lost, I have no doubt, in my translation. The author would probably fail to recognize it. But to the uninitiated I should say it would be most convincing."

"I have been wondering why you have taken so much trouble. You might have been talking Chinese for all the Beronellis knew or cared."

Moeller looked pained. "I was not talking for the Beronellis, but for my own private satisfaction. How stupid it is to say that the memory fails with the approach of old age. Would you think that I am sixty-six?"

"I'm not interested in your age."

"No, of course not. Perhaps we could have a private talk. I suggest that we take a walk together on deck. It is raining, but a little rain will not hurt us."

"My coat is on the chair over there."

"Then I will meet you on the top deck in a few minutes' time."

Graham was waiting at the head of the companionway when Moeller came up. They moved into the lee of one of the lifeboats.

Moeller came straight to the point.

"I gather that you have seen Kuvetli."

"I have," said Graham grimly.

"Well?"

"I have decided to take your advice."

"At Kuvetli's suggestion?"

This, Graham reflected, was not going to be as easy as he had thought. He answered: "At my own. I was not impressed by him. Frankly, I was amazed. That the Turkish Government should have put such a fool of a man on the job seems to me incredible."

"What makes you think he is a fool?"

"He seems to think that you are making some attempt to bribe me and that I am inclined to accept the money. He threatened to expose me to the British Government. When I suggested that I might be in some personal danger he seemed to think that I was trying to trick him in some stupid way. If that's your idea of a clever man, I'm sorry for you."

"Perhaps he is not used to dealing with the English brand of self-esteem," Moeller retorted acidly. "When did this meeting take place?"

"Last night, soon after I saw you."

"And did he mention me by name?"

"Yes. He warned me against you."

"And how did you treat the warning?"

"I said that I would report his behavior to Colonel Haki. He did not, I must say, seem to care. But if I had any idea of securing his protection, I gave it up. I don't trust him. Besides, I don't see why I should risk my life for people who treat me as if I were some sort of criminal."

He paused. He could not see Moeller's face in the darkness but he felt that the man was satisfied.

"And so you've decided to accept my suggestion?"

"Yes, I have. But," Graham went on, "before we go any farther, there are one or two things I want to get clear."

"Well?"

"In the first place, there is this man Kuvetli. He's a fool, as I've said, but he'll have to be put off the scent somehow."

"You need have no fears." Graham thought he detected a note of contempt in the smooth heavy voice. "Kuvetli will cause no trouble. It will be easy to give him the slip in Genoa. The next thing he will hear of you is that you are suffering from typhus. He will be unable to prove anything to the contrary."

Graham was relieved. Obviously, Moeller thought him a fool. He said doubtfully: "Yes, I see. That's all right, but what about this typhus? If I'm going to be taken ill I've got to be taken ill properly. If I were really taken ill I should probably be on the train when it happened."

Moeller sighed. "I see that you've been thinking very seriously, Mr. Graham. Let me explain. If you were really infected with typhus you would already be feeling unwell. There is an incubation period of a week or ten days. You would not, of course, know what was the matter with you. By to-morrow you would be feeling worse. It would be logical for you to shrink from spending the night in a train. You would probably go to a hotel for the night. Then, in the morning, when your temperature began to rise and the characteristics of the disease became apparent, you would be removed to a clinic."

"Then we shall go to a hotel to-morrow?"

"Exactly. There will be a car waiting for us. But I advise you to leave the arrangements to me, Mr. Graham. Remember, I am just as interested as you are in seeing that nobody's suspicions are aroused."

Graham affected to ponder this. "All right then," he said at last. "I'll leave it to you. I don't want to be fussy, but you can understand that I don't want to have any trouble when I get home."

There was a silence and for a moment he thought that he had overacted. Then Moeller said slowly: "You have no reason to worry. We shall be waiting for you outside the Customs shed. As long as you do not attempt to do anything foolish—you might, for example, decide to change your mind about

your holiday—everything will go smoothly. I can assure you that you will
have no trouble when you get home."

"As long as that's understood."

"Is there anything else you want to say?"

"No. Good night."

"Good night, Mr. Graham. Until to-morrow."

Graham waited until Moeller had reached the deck below. Then he drew
a deep breath. It was over. He was safe. All he had to do now was to go to
his cabin, get a good night's sleep and wait for Mr. Kuvetli in cabin number
four. He felt suddenly very tired. His body was aching as if he had been
working too hard. He made his way down to his cabin. It was as he passed
the landing door of the saloon that he saw Josette.

She was sitting on one of the *banquettes* watching José and Banat playing
cards. Her hands were on the edge of the seat and she was leaning forward,
her lips parted slightly, her hair falling across her cheeks. There was something about the pose that reminded him of the moment, years ago it seemed,
when he had followed Kopeikin into her dressing-room at Le Jockey Cabaret.
He half expected her to raise her head and turn towards him, smiling.

He realized suddenly that he was seeing her for the last time, that before
another day had passed he would be for her merely a disagreeable memory,
someone who had treated her badly. The realization was sharp and strangely
painful. He told himself that he was being absurd, that it had always been
impossible for him to stay with her in Paris and that he had known it all
along. Why should the leave-taking trouble him now? And yet it did trouble
him. A phrase came into his head: "to part is to die a little." He knew suddenly that it was not Josette of whom he was taking his leave, but of something of himself. In the back streets of his mind a door was slowly closing
for the last time. She had complained that for him she was just a part of
the journey from Istanbul to London. There was more to it than that. She
was part of the world beyond the door: the world into which he had stepped
when Banat had fired those three shots at him in the Adler-Palace: the
world in which you recognised the ape beneath the velvet. Now he was on
his way back to his own world; to his house and his car and the friendly,
agreeable woman he called his wife. It would be exactly the same as when
he had left it. Nothing would be changed in that world; nothing, except himself.

He went on down to his cabin.

He slept fitfully. Once he awoke with a start, believing that someone was
opening the door of his cabin. Then he remembered that the door was
bolted and concluded that he had been dreaming. When next he awoke, the
engines had stopped and the ship was no longer rolling. He switched on the
light and saw that the time was a quarter past four. They had arrived at
the entrance to Genoa harbour. After a while he heard the chugging of a
small boat and a fainter clatter from the deck above. There were voices too.

He tried to distinguish Mr. Kuvetli's among them, but they were too muffled. He dozed.

He had told the steward to bring coffee at seven. Towards six, however, he decided that it was useless to try to sleep any more. He was already dressed when the steward arrived.

He drank his coffee, put the remainder of his things in his case and sat down to wait. Mr. Kuvetli had told him to go into the empty cabin at eight o'clock. He had promised himself that he would obey Mr. Kuvetli's instructions to the letter. He listened to the Mathises arguing over their packing.

At about a quarter to eight the ship began to move in. Another five minutes and he rang for the steward. By five to eight the steward had been, received with barely concealed surprise fifty lire, and gone, taking the suit-case with him. Graham waited another minute and then opened the door.

The alley-way was empty. He walked along slowly to number four, stopped as if he had forgotten something, and half turned. The coast was still clear. He opened the door, stepped quickly into the cabin, shut the door, and turned round.

The next moment he almost fainted.

Lying across the floor with his legs under the lower berth and his head covered with blood, was Mr. Kuvetli.

CHAPTER ELEVEN

MOST OF THE BLEEDING seemed to have been caused by a scalp wound on the back of the head; but there was another wound, which had bled comparatively little and which looked as if it had been made with a knife, low on the left side of the neck. The movements of the ship had sent the slowly congealing blood trickling to and fro in a madman's scrawl across the linoleum. The face was the colour of dirty clay. Mr. Kuvetli was clearly dead.

Graham clenched his teeth to prevent himself retching and held on to the washing cabinet for support. His first thought was that he must not be sick, that he must pull himself together before he called for help. He did not realise immediately the implications of what had happened. So that he should not look down again he had kept his eyes fixed on the porthole and it was the sight of the funnel of a ship lying beyond a long concrete jetty that reminded him that they were going into harbour. In less than an hour the gangways would be down. And Mr. Kuvetli had not reached the Turkish Consulate.

The shock of the realisation brought him to his senses. He looked down.

It was Banat's work without a doubt. The little Turk had probably been stunned in his own cabin or in the alley-way outside it, dragged out of sight into this, the nearest empty cabin, and butchered while he was still insensible. Moeller had decided to dispose of a possible threat to the smooth working of his arrangements for dealing with the principal victim. Graham remembered the noise which had awakened him in the night. It might have come from the next cabin. "Do not leave your cabin under any circumstances until eight o'clock the following morning. It might be dangerous." Mr. Kuvetli had failed to take his own advice and it *had* been dangerous. He had declared himself ready to die for his country and he had so died. There he was, his chubby fists clenched pitifully, his fringe of grey hair matted with his blood and the mouth which had smiled so much half open and inanimate.

Someone walked along the alley-way outside and Graham jerked his head up. The sound and the movement seemed to clear his brain. He began to think quickly and coolly.

The way the blood had congealed showed that Mr. Kuvetli must have been killed before the ship had stopped. Long before! Before he had made his request for permission to leave by the pilot boat. If he had made the request, a thorough search for him would have been made when the boat came alongside and he would have been found. He had not yet been found. He was not travelling with an ordinary passport but with a diplomatic *laisser passer* and so had not had to surrender his papers to the Purser. That meant that unless the Purser checked off the passenger list with the passport control officer at Genoa—and Graham knew from past experience that they did not always bother to do that at Italian ports—the fact that Mr. Kuvetli did not land would not be noticed. Moeller and Banat had probably counted on the fact. And if the dead man's baggage had been packed, the steward would put it in the Customs shed with the rest and assume that its owner was lying low to avoid having to give a tip. It might be hours, days even, before the body were discovered if he, Graham, did not call anyone.

His lips tightened. He became conscious of a slow cold rage mounting in his brain, stifling his sense of self-preservation. If he did call someone he could accuse Moeller and Banat; but would he be able to bring the crime home to them? His accusation by itself would carry no weight. It might well be suggested that the accusation was a ruse to conceal his own guilt. The Purser, for one, would be glad to support that theory. The fact that the two accused were travelling with false passports could, no doubt, be proved, but that alone would take time. In any case, the Italian police would be amply justified in refusing him permission to leave for England. Mr. Kuvetli had died in trying to make it possible for him to reach England safely and in time to fulfil a contract. That Mr. Kuvetli's dead body should become the very means of preventing the fulfilment of that contract was stupid and grotesque; but if he, Graham, wanted to be sure of saving his own skin, that was what must happen. It was strangely unthinkable. For him, standing there above the dead body of the man whom Moeller had described as a patriot, there seemed to be only one thing of importance in the world—that Mr. Kuvetli's death should be neither stupid nor grotesque, that it should be useless only to the men who had murdered him.

But if he were not going to raise the alarm and wait for the police, what was he going to do?

Supposing Moeller had planned this. Supposing he or Banat had overheard Mr. Kuvetli's instructions to him and, believing that he was sufficiently intimidated to do anything to save himself, had thought of this way of delaying his return. Or they might be preparing to "discover" him with the body and so incriminate him. But no: both those suppositions were absurd. If they had known of Mr. Kuvetli's plan they would have let the Turk go ashore by the pilot boat. It would have been his, Graham's, body that would have been found and the finder would have been Mr. Kuvetli. Obviously, then, Moeller could neither know of the plan nor suspect that the murder would be discovered. An hour from now he would be standing with Banat and the gunmen who were to meet him, waiting for the victim to walk unsuspectingly . . .

But the victim would not be unsuspecting. There was a very slender chance . . .

He turned and, grasping the handle of the door, began to turn it gently. He knew that if he thought twice about what he had decided to do he would change his mind. He must commit himself before he had time to think.

He opened the door a fraction of an inch. There was no one in the alley-way. A moment later, he was out of the cabin and the door of it was shut behind him. He hesitated barely a second. He knew that he must keep moving. Five steps brought him to cabin number three. He went in.

Mr. Kuvetli's luggage consisted of one old-fashioned valise. It was standing strapped up in the middle of the floor, and perched on one of the straps was a twenty lire piece. Graham picked up the coin and held it to his nose. The smell of attar of roses was quite distinct. He looked in the wardrobe and behind the door for Mr. Kuvetli's overcoat and hat, failed to find them, and concluded that they had been disposed of through the porthole. Banat had thought of everything.

He put the valise up on the berth and opened it. Most of the things on top had obviously been stuffed in anyhow by Banat, but lower down the packing had been done very neatly. The only thing of any interest to Graham, however, was a box of pistol ammunition. Of the pistol which fired them there was no sign.

Graham put the ammunition in his pocket and shut the valise again. He was undecided as to what he should do with it. Banat had obviously counted on its being taken to the Customs shed by the steward, who would pocket the twenty lire and forget about Mr. Kuvetli. That would be all right from Banat's point of view. By the time the people in the Customs shed started asking questions about an unclaimed valise, Monsieur Mavrodopoulos would be nonexistent. Graham, however, had every intention of remaining in existence if he could possibly do so. Moreover, he intended—with the same proviso—to use his passport to cross the Italian frontier into France. The moment Mr. Kuvetli's body was found the rest of the passengers would be sought for questioning by the police. There was only one thing for it: Mr. Kuvetli's valise would have to be hidden.

He opened the washing cabinet, put the twenty lire piece on the corner by the bowl, and went to the door. The coast was still clear. He opened the door, picked up the valise, and lugged it along the alley-way to cabin number four. Another second or two and he was inside with the door shut again.

He was sweating now. He wiped his hands and forehead on his handkerchief and then remembered that his fingerprints would be on the hard leather handle of the valise as well as on the door handle and washing cabinet. He went over these objects with his handkerchief and then turned his attention to the body.

Obviously the gun was not in the hip pocket. He went down on one knee beside the body. He felt himself beginning to retch again and took a deep breath. Then he leaned across, gripped the right shoulder with one hand and the right side of the trousers with the other and pulled. The body rolled on to its side. One foot slid over the other and kicked the floor. Graham stood up quickly. In a moment or two, however, he had himself in hand sufficiently to bend down and pull the jacket open. There was a leather holster under the left arm but the gun was not in it.

He was not unduly disappointed. The possession of the gun would have made him feel better but he had not been counting on finding it. A gun was valuable. Banat would naturally take it. Graham felt in the jacket pocket. It was empty. Banat had evidently taken Mr. Kuvetli's money and *laisser passer* as well.

He got up. There was nothing more to be done there. He put on a glove, cautiously let himself out and walked along to cabin number six. He knocked. There was a quick movement from within and Madame Mathis opened the door.

The frown with which she had prepared to meet the steward faded when she saw Graham. She gave him a startled "good morning."

"Good morning, Madame. May I speak to your husband for a moment?"

Mathis poked his head over her shoulder. "Hullo! Good morning! Are you ready so soon?"

"Can I speak to you for a moment?"

"Of course!" He came out in his shirt sleeves and grinning cheerfully. "I am important only to myself. I am easy to approach."

"Would you mind coming into my cabin for a moment?"

Mathis glanced at him curiously. "You look very serious, my friend. Yes, of course I will come." He turned to his wife. "I will be back in a minute, *chérie.*"

Inside the cabin, Graham shut the door, bolted it and turned to meet Mathis's puzzled frown.

"I need your help," he said in a low voice. "No, I don't want to borrow money. I want you to take a message for me."

"If it is possible, of course."

"It will be necessary to talk very quietly," Graham went on. "I do not want to alarm your wife unnecessarily and the partitions are very thin."

Fortunately, Mathis missed the full implications of this statement. He nodded. "I am listening."

"I told you that I was employed by an armaments manufacturer. It is true. But in a sense I am also, at the moment, in the joint services of the British and Turkish Governments. When I get off this ship this morning, an attempt is going to be made by German agents to kill me."

"This is true?" He was incredulous and suspicious.

"I am afraid it is. It would not amuse me to invent it."

"Excuse me, I . . ."

"That's all right. What I want you to do is to go to the Turkish Consulate in Genoa, ask for the Consul and give him a message from me. Will you do that?"

Mathis stared hard at him for a moment. Then he nodded. "Very well. I will do it. What is the message?"

"I should like to impress upon you first that this is a highly confidential message. Is that understood?"

"I can keep my mouth shut when I choose."

"I know I can rely on you. Will you write the message down? Here is a pencil and some paper. You would not be able to read my writing. Are you ready?"

"Yes."

"This is it: 'Inform Colonel Haki, Istanbul, that agent I.K. is dead, but do not inform the police. I am forced to accompany German agents, Moeller and Banat, travelling with passports of Fritz Haller and Mavrodopoulos. I . . .'"

Mathis's jaw dropped and he let out an exclamation. "Is it possible!"

"Unfortunately, it is."

"Then it was not seasickness that you had!"

"No. Shall I go on with the message?"

Mathis swallowed. "Yes. Yes. I did not realise. . . . Please."

"'I shall attempt to escape and reach you, but in the event of my death please inform British Consul that these men are responsible.'" It was, he felt, melodramatic; but it was no more than he wished to say. He felt sorry for Mathis.

The Frenchman was staring at him with horror in his eyes. "Is it not possible," he whispered. "Why . . . ?"

"I should like to explain but I am afraid that I can't. The point is, will you deliver the message for me?"

"Of course. But is there nothing else that I can do? These German agents —why can you not have them arrested?"

"For various reasons. The best way you can help me is to take this message for me."

The Frenchman stuck out his jaw aggressively. "It is ridiculous!" he burst out and then lowered his voice to a fierce whisper. "Discretion is necessary. I understand that. You are of the British secret service. One does not confide these things but I am not a fool. Very well! Why do we not together shoot down these filthy Bosches and escape? I have my revolver and together. . . ."

Graham jumped. "Did you say that you had a revolver—here?"

Mathis looked defiant. "Certainly I have a revolver. Why not? In Turkey . . ."

Graham seized his arm. "Then you can do something more to help me."

Mathis scowled impatiently. "What is that?"

"Let me buy your revolver from you."

"You mean you are unarmed?"

"My own revolver was stolen. How much will you take for yours?"

"But. . . ."

"It will be more use to me than to you."

Mathis drew himself up. "I will not sell it to you."

"But. . . ."

"I will give it to you. Here. . . ." He pulled a small nickel-plated revolver out of his hip pocket and thrust it in Graham's hand. "No, please. It is nothing. I would like to do more."

Graham thanked his stars for the impulse which had led him to apologize to the Mathises the previous day. "You have done more than enough."

"Nothing! It is loaded, see? Here is the safety catch. There is a light pull on the trigger. You do not have to be a Hercules. Keep your arm straight when you fire . . . but I do not have to tell you."

"I am grateful, Mathis. And you will go to the Turkish Consul as soon as you land."

"It is understood." He held out his hand. "I wish you luck, my friend," he said with emotion. "If you are sure that there is nothing else that I can do. . . ."

"I am sure."

A moment later Mathis had gone. Graham waited. He heard the Frenchman go into the next cabin and Madame Mathis's sharp voice.

"Well?"

"So you cannot mind your own business, eh? He is broke and I have lent him two hundred francs."

"Imbecile! You will not touch it again."

"You think not? Let me tell you he has given me a cheque."

"I detest cheques."

"I am not drunk. It is on an Istanbul bank. As soon as we arrive I shall go to the Turkish Consulate and see that the cheque is a good one."

"A lot they will know—or care!"

"Enough! I know what I am doing. Are you ready? No! Then . . ."

Graham breathed a sigh of relief and examined the revolver. It was smaller than Kopeikin's and of Belgian manufacture. He worked the safety catch and fingered the trigger. It was a handy little weapon and looked as if it had been carefully used. He looked about him for a place to put it. It must not be visible from the outside yet he must be able to get at it quickly. He decided eventually on his top left hand waistcoat pocket. The barrel, breach and half the trigger guard just fitted in. When he buttoned his jacket the butt was hidden while the lapels set in a way that concealed the bulge. What was more, he could, by touching his tie, bring his fingers within two inches of the butt. He was ready.

He dropped Mr. Kuvetli's box of ammunition through the porthole and went up on deck.

They were in the harbour now and moving across to the west side. Towards the sea the sky was clear but a mist hung over the heights above the town, obscuring the sun and making the white amphitheatrical mass of buildings seem cold and desolate.

The only other preson on deck was Banat. He was standing gazing out at the shipping with the absorbed interest of a small boy. It was difficult to realise that, at some moment in the last ten hours, this pale creature had come out of cabin number four with a knife which he had just driven into Mr. Kuvetli's neck; that in his pocket at that moment were Mr. Kuvetli's papers, Mr. Kuvetli's money and Mr. Kuvetli's pistol; that he intended to commit within the next few hours yet another murder. His very insignificance was horrible. It lent a false air of normality to the situation. Had Graham not been so acutely alive to the danger he was in, he would have been tempted to believe that the memory of what he had seen in cabin number four was the memory not of a real experience, but of something conceived in a dream.

He was no longer conscious of any fear. His body was tingling in a curious way; he was short of breath, and every now and again a wave of nausea would rise up from the pit of his stomach; but his brain seemed to have lost touch with his body. His thoughts arranged themselves with a quick efficiency that surprised him. He knew that short of abandoning all hope of reaching England in time to fulfil the Turkish contract by the specified date, his only chance of getting out of Italy alive lay in his beating Moeller at Moeller's own game. Mr. Kuvetli had made it clear that Moeller's "alternative" was a trick devised with the sole object of transferring the scene of the killing to a less public place than a main street of Genoa. In other words, he was to be "taken for a ride." In a very short time now, Moeller, Banat and some others would be waiting with a car outside the Customs shed ready, if necessary, to shoot him down there and then. If, however, he were considerate enough to step into the car they would take him away to some quiet place on the Santa Margherita road and shoot him there. There was just one weak spot in their plan. They thought that if he were to get into the car he would do so believing that he was to be driven to a hotel in order to make an elaborate show of falling ill. They were mistaken; and in their being mistaken they presented him with the beginnings of a way out. If he acted quickly and boldly he might be able to get through.

They would not, he reasoned, be likely to tell him as soon as he got in the car what they were going to do. The fiction about the hotel and the clinic near Santa Margherita would be maintained until the last moment. From their point of view, it would be much easier to drive through the narrow streets of Genoa with a man who thought he was going to have six weeks' holiday than with a man who had to be forcibly prevented from attracting the attention of passers-by. They would be inclined to humour him. They might even let him register at a hotel. In any case, it was unlikely that the car would go right through the city without being held up once by the traffic. His chances of escape lay in his being able to take them by surprise. Let him once get free in a crowded street, and they would have great difficulty in catching him. His objective, then, would be the Turkish Consulate. He had chosen the Turkish Consulate rather than his own, for the simple reason that with the Turks he would have to do less explaining. A reference to Colonel Haki would simplify matters considerably.

The ship was approaching the berth now, and men were standing on the quay ready to catch the lines. Banat had not seen him, but now Josette and José came out on deck. He moved quickly round to the other side. Josette was the last person he wanted to talk to at that moment. She might suggest that they share a taxi to the centre of the city. He would have to explain why he was leaving the quay in a private car with Moeller and Banat. There might be all sorts of other difficulties. At that moment he came face to face with Moeller.

The old man nodded affably. "Good morning, Mr. Graham. I was hoping to see you. It will be pleasant to get ashore again, won't it?"

"I hope so."

Moeller's expression changed slightly. "Are you ready?"

"Quite." He looked concerned. "I haven't seen Kuvetli this morning. I hope everything is going to be all right."

Moeller's eyes did not flicker. "You need not worry, Mr. Graham." Then he smiled tolerantly. "As I told you last night, you can safely leave everything to me. Kuvetli will not worry us. If necessary," he went on blandly, "I shall use force."

"I hope that won't be necessary."

"And so do I, Mr. Graham! So do I!" He lowered his voice confidentially. "But while we are on the subject of the use of force, may I suggest that you are not in too much of a hurry to land? You see, should you happen to land before Banat and I have time to explain the new situation to those who are waiting, an accident might happen. You are so obviously an Englishman. They would have no difficulty in identifying you."

"I had already thought of that."

"Splendid! I am so glad that you are entering into the spirit of the arrangements." He turned his head. "Ah, we are alongside. I shall see you again in a few minutes, then." His eyes narrowed. "You won't make me feel that my confidence has been misplaced, will you, Mr. Graham?"

"I shall be there."

"I am sure that I can count on you."

Graham went into the deserted saloon. Through one of the portholes he could see that a section of the deck had been roped off. The Mathises and the Beronellis had already joined Josette, José and Banat and, as he watched, Moeller came up with his "wife." Josette was looking round as if she were expecting someone, and Graham guessed that his absence was puzzling her. It was going to be difficult to avoid an encounter with her. She might even wait for him in the Customs shed. He would have to forestall that.

He waited until the gangway had been hoisted into position and the passengers, headed by the Mathises, were beginning to troop down it, then went out and brought up the rear of the procession immediately behind Josette. She half turned her head and saw him.

"Ah! I have been wondering where you were. What have you been doing?"

"Packing."

"So long! But you are here now. I thought that perhaps we could drive together and leave our luggage in the *consigne* at the station. It will save a taxi."

"I'm afraid I shall keep you waiting. I have some things to declare. Besides, I must go to the Consulate first. I think that we had better keep to our arrangement to meet at the train."

She sighed. "You are so difficult. Very well, we will meet at the train. But do not be late."

"I won't."

"And be careful of the little *salop* with the perfume."

"The police will take care of him."

They had reached the passport control at the entrance to the Customs shed and José, who had walked on ahead, was waiting as if the seconds were costing him money. She pressed Graham's hand hurriedly. "*Alors, chéri! A tout à l'heure.*"

Graham got his passport and slowly followed them through to the Customs shed. There was only one Customs officer. As Graham approached he disposed of Josette and José, and turned to the Beronellis' mountainous bundles. To his relief, Graham had to wait. While he was waiting he opened his case and transferred some papers that he needed to his pocket; but several more minutes passed before he was able to show his transit *visa*, have his suit-case chalked and give it to a porter. By the time he had made his way through the group of mourning relatives which had surrounded the Beronellis, Josette and José had gone.

Then he saw Moeller and Banat.

They were standing beside a big American sedan drawn up beyond the taxis. There were two other men on the far side of the car: one was tall and thin and wore a mackintosh and a workman's cap, the other was a very dark heavy-jowled man with a grey belted ulster and a soft hat which he wore without a dent in it. A fifth and younger man sat at the wheel of the car.

His heart thumping, Graham beckoned to the porter, who was making for the taxis, and walked towards them.

Moeller nodded as he came up. "Good! Your luggage? Ah, yes." He nodded to the tall man, who came round, took the case from the porter, and put it in the luggage boot at the back.

Graham tipped the porter and got in the car. Moeller followed him and sat beside him. The tall man got in beside the driver. Banat and the man in the ulster sat on the pull-down seats facing Graham and Moeller. Banat's face was expressionless. The man in the ulster avoided Graham's eyes and looked out of the window.

The car started. Almost immediately, Banat took out his pistol and snapped the safety catch.

Graham turned to Moeller. "Is that necessary?" he demanded. "I'm not going to escape."

Moeller shrugged. "As you please." He said something to Banat who grinned, snapped the safety catch again and put the gun back in his pocket.

The car swung into the cobbled road leading to the dock gates.

"Which hotel are we going to?" Graham inquired.

Moeller turned his head slightly. "I have not yet made up my mind. We can leave that question until later. We shall drive out to Santa Margherita first."

"But . . ."

"There are not 'buts.' I am making the arrangements." He did not bother to turn his head this time.

"What about Kuvetli?"

"He left by the pilot boat early this morning."

"Then what's happened to him?"

"He is probably writing a report to Colonel Haki. I advise you to forget about him."

Graham was silent. He had asked about Mr. Kuvetli with the sole object of concealing the fact that he was badly frightened. He had been in the car less than two minutes, and already the odds against him had lengthened considerably.

The car bumped over the cobbles to the dock gates, and Graham braced himself for the sharp right turn that would take them towards the town and the Santa Margherita road. The next moment he lurched sideways in his seat as the car swerved to the left. Banat whipped out his gun.

Graham slowly regained his position. "I'm sorry," he said. "I thought we turned right for Santa Margherita."

There was no reply. He sat back in his corner trying to keep his face expressionless. He had assumed quite unwarrantably that it would be through Genoa itself, and on to the Santa Margherita road that he would be taken for his "ride." All his hopes had been based on the assumption. He had taken too much for granted.

He glanced at Moeller. The German agent was sitting back with his eyes closed: an old man whose work for the day was done. The rest of the day was Banat's. Graham knew that the small deep-set eyes were feeling for his, and that the long-suffering mouth was grinning. Banat was going to enjoy his work. The other man was still looking out of the window. He had not uttered a sound.

They reached a fork and turned to the right along a secondary road with a direction sign for Novi-Torimo. They were going north. The road was straight and lined with dusty plane trees. Beyond the trees there were rows of grim-looking houses and a factory or two. Soon, however, the road began to rise and twist, and the houses and factories were left behind. They were getting into the country.

Graham knew that unless some wholly unexpected way of escape presented itself, his chances of surviving the next hour were now practically non-existent. Presently the car would stop. Then he would be taken out and shot as methodically and efficiently as if he had been condemned by a court martial. The blood was thundering in his head, and his breathing was quick and shallow. He tried to breathe slowly and deeply, but the muscles in his chest seemed incapable of making the effort. He went on trying. He knew that if he surrendered himself to fear now, if he let himself go, he would be lost, whatever happened. He must not be frightened. Death, he told himself, would not be so bad. A moment of astonishment, and it would be over. He had to die sooner or later, and a bullet through the base of the skull now would be better than months of illness when he was old. Forty years was not a bad lifetime to have lived. There were many young men in Europe at that moment who would regard the attainment of such an age as an enviable achievement. To suppose that the lopping off of thirty years or so from a normal span of life was a disaster was to pretend to an importance which no man possessed. Living wasn't even so very pleasant. Mostly it was a matter of getting from the cradle to the grave with the least possible discomfort; of satisfying the body's needs, and of slowing down the process of its decay. Why make such a fuss about abandoning so dreary a business? Why, indeed! And yet you did make a fuss . . .

He became conscious of the revolver pressing against his chest. Supposing they decided to search him! But no, they wouldn't do that. They'd taken one revolver from him, and another from Mr. Kuvetli. They would scarcely suspect that there was a third. There were five other men in the car, and four of them at least were armed. He had six rounds in the revolver. He might be able to fire two of them before he himself were hit. If he waited until Banat's attention had wandered he might get off three or even four of them. If he were going to be killed, he'd see that the killing was as expensive as possible. He got a cigarette out of his pocket and then, putting his hand inside his jacket as if he were looking for a match, snicked off the safety catch. For a moment he considered drawing the revolver there and then, and trusting to luck and the driver's swerving to survive Banat's first shot; but the gun in Banat's hand was steady. Besides, there was always a chance that something unexpected might happen to create a better opportunity. For instance, the driver might take a corner too fast and wreck the car.

But the car purred steadily on. The windows were tightly shut, and Banat's attar of roses began to scent the air inside. The man in the ulster was becoming drowsy. Once or twice he yawned. Then, obviously to give himself something to do, he brought out a heavy German pistol and examined the magazine. As he replaced it, his dull pouched eyes rested for a moment on Graham. He looked away again indifferently, like a passenger in a train with the stranger opposite to him.

They had been driving for about twenty-five minutes. They passed through a small straggling village with a single fly-blown-looking café with a petrol pump outside it, and two or three shops, and began to climb. Graham was vaguely aware that the fields and farmlands which had flanked the road till then were giving way to clumps of trees and uncultivatable slopes, and guessed that they were getting into the hills to the north of Genoa and west of the railway pass above Pontedecimo. Suddenly the car swung left down a small side road between trees, and began to crawl in low gear up a long twisting hill cut in the side of a wooded slope.

There was a movement by his side. He turned quickly, the blood rushing up into his head, and met Moeller's eyes.

Moeller nodded. "Yes, Mr. Graham, this is just about as far as you are going."

"But the hotel . . . ?" Graham began to stammer.

The pale eyes did not flicker. "I am afraid, Mr. Graham, that you must be very simple. Or can it be that you think that I am simple?" He shrugged. "No doubt it is unimportant. But I have a request to make. As you have already caused me so much trouble, discomfort and expense, would it be asking too much of you to suggest that you do not cause me any more? When we stop and you are asked to get out, please do so without argument or physical protest. If you cannot consider your own dignity at such a time, please think of the cushions of the car."

He turned abruptly and nodded to the man in the ulster who tapped on the window behind him. The car jerked to a standstill, and the man in the ulster half rose and put his hand down on the latch which opened the door beside him. At the same moment Moeller said something to Banat. Banat grinned.

In that second Graham acted. His last wretched little bluff had been called. They were going to kill him, and did not care whether he knew it or not. They were anxious only that his blood should not soil the cushions he was sitting on. A sudden blind fury seized him. His self-control, racked out until every nerve in his body was quivering, suddenly went. Before he knew what he was doing, he had pulled out Mathis's revolver and fired it full in Banat's face.

Even as the din of the shot thudded through his head, he saw something horrible happen to the face. Then he flung himself forward.

The man in the ulster had the door open about an inch when Graham's weight hit him. He lost his balance, and hurtled backwards through the door. A fraction of a second later he hit the road with Graham on top of him.

Half stunned by the impact, Graham rolled clear and scrambled for cover behind the car. It could, he knew, last only a second or two now. The man in the ulster was knocked out; but the other two, shouting at the tops of their voices, had their doors open, and Moeller would not be long in picking up Banat's gun. He might be able to get in one more shot. Moeller, perhaps . . .

At that moment chance took a hand. Graham realised that he was crouching only a foot or so away from the car's tank, and with some wild notion of hindering the pursuit should he succeed in getting clear, he raised the revolver and fired again.

The muzzle of the revolver had been practically touching the tank when he pulled the trigger, and the sheet of flame which roared up sent him staggering back out of cover. Shots crashed out, and a bullet whipped by his head. Panic seized him. He turned and dashed for the trees, and the slope shelving away from the edge of the road. He heard two more shots, then something struck him violently in the back, and a sheet of light flashed between his eyes and his brain.

He could not have been unconscious for more than a minute. When he came to he was lying face downwards on the surface of dead pine needles on the slope below the level of the road.

Dagger-like pains were shooting through his head. For a moment or two he did not try to move. Then he opened his eyes again and his gaze, wandering inch by inch away from him, encountered Mathis's revolver. Instinctively he stretched out his hand to take it. His body throbbed agonisingly, but his fingers gripped the revolver. He waited for a second or two. Then, very slowly, he drew his knees up under him, raised himself on his hands and began to crawl back to the road.

The blast of the exploding tank had scattered fragments of ripped panelling and smouldering leather all over the road. Lying on his side amid this wreckage was the man in the workman's cap. The mackintosh down his left side hung in charred shreds. What was left of the car itself was a mass of shimmering incandescence, and the steel skeleton buckling like paper in the terrific heat was only just visible. Farther up the road the driver was standing with his hands to his face, swaying as if he were drunk. The sickening stench of burning flesh hung in the air. There was no sign of Moeller.

Graham crawled back down the slope for a few yards, got painfully to his feet and stumbled away, down through the trees towards the lower road.

CHAPTER TWELVE

IT WAS AFTER MIDDAY before he reached the café in the village and a telephone. By the time a car from the Turkish Consulate arrived, he had had a wash and fortified himself with brandy.

The Consul was a lean, business-like man, who spoke English as if he had been to England. He listened intently to what Graham had to say before he said much himself. When Graham had finished, however, the Consul squirted some more soda water into his vermouth, leaned back in his chair and whistled through his teeth.

"Is that all?" he inquired.

"Isn't it enough?"

"More than enough." The Consul grinned apologetically. "I will tell you,

Mr. Graham, that when I received your message this morning, I telegraphed immediately to Colonel Haki, reporting that you were very likely dead. Allow me to congratulate you."

"Thank you. I was lucky." He spoke automatically. There seemed to be something strangely fatuous about congratulations on being alive. He said: "Kuvetli told me the other night that he had fought for the Gazi and that he was ready to give his life for Turkey. You don't, somehow, expect people who say that sort of thing to be taken up on it so quickly."

"That is true. It is very sad," said the Consul. He was obviously itching to get to business. "Meanwhile," he continued adroitly, "we must see that no time is lost. Every minute increases the danger of his body being found before you are out of the country. The authorities are not very well disposed towards us at the moment, and if he were found before you had left, I doubt if we could prevent your being detained for at least some days."

"What about the car?"

"We can leave the driver to explain that. If, as you say, your suit-case was destroyed in the fire, there is nothing to connect you with the accident. Are you feeling well enough to travel?"

"Yes. I'm bruised a bit and I still feel damnably shaky, but I'll get over that."

"Good. Then, all things considered, it will be as well if you travel immediately."

"Kuvetli said something about a 'plane."

"A 'plane? Ah! May I see your passport, please?"

Graham handed it over. The Consul flicked over the pages, shut the passport with a snap and returned it. "Your transit visa," he said, "specifies that you are entering Italy at Genoa and leaving it at Bardonecchia. If you are particularly anxious to go by air we can get the visa amended, but that will take an hour or so. Also you will have to return to Genoa. Also, in case Kuvetli is found within the next few hours, it is better not to bring yourself to the notice of the police with a change of arrangements." He glanced at his watch. "There is a train to Paris which leaves Genoa at two o'clock. It stops at Asti soon after three. I recommend that you get on it there. I can drive you to Asti in my car."

"I think some food would do me good."

"My dear Mr. Graham! How stupid of me! Some food. Of course! We can stop at Novi. You will be my guest. And if there is any champagne to be had we shall have it. There is nothing like champagne when one is depressed."

Graham felt suddenly a little light-headed. He laughed.

The Consul raised his eyebrows.

"I'm sorry," Graham apologised. "You must excuse me. You see, it is rather funny. I had an appointment to meet someone on the two o'clock train. She'll be rather surprised to see me."

He became conscious of someone shaking his arm and opened his eyes.

"Bardonecchia, signore. Your passport, please."

He looked up at the wagon-lit attendant bending over him and realised that he had been asleep since the train had left Asti. In the doorway, partly silhouetted against the gathering darkness outside, were two men in the uniform of the Italian railway police.

He sat up with a jerk, fumbling in his pocket. "My passport? Yes, of course."

One of the men looked at the passport, nodded and dabbed at it with a rubber stamp.

"*Grazie, signore.* Have you any Italian bank-notes?"

"No."

Graham put his passport back in his pocket, the attendant switched the light off again, and the door closed. That was that.

He yawned miserably. He was stiff and shivering. He stood up to put his overcoat on and saw that the station was deep in snow. He had been a fool to go to sleep like that. It would be unpleasant to arrive home with pneumonia. But he was past the Italian passport control. He turned the heating on and sat down to smoke a cigarette. It must have been that heavy lunch and the wine. It . . . And then he remembered suddenly that he had done nothing about Josette. Mathis would be on the train, too.

The train started with a jerk and began to rumble on towards Modane.

He rang the bell and the attendant came.

"Signore?"

"Is there going to be a restaurant car when we get over the frontier?"

"No, signore." He shrugged. "The war."

Graham gave him some money. "I want a bottle of beer and some sandwiches. Can you get them at Modane?"

The attendant looked at the money. "Easily, signore."

"Where are the third-class coaches?"

"In the front of the train, signore."

The attendant went. Graham smoked his cigarette and decided to wait until the train had left Modane before he went in search of Josette.

The stop at Modane seemed interminable. At last, however, the French passport officials finished their work and the train began to move again.

Graham went out into the corridor.

Except for the dim blue safety lights, the train was in darkness now. He made his way slowly towards the third-class coaches. There were only two of them, and he had no difficulty in finding Josette and José. They were in a compartment by themselves.

She turned her head as he slid the door open and peered at him uncertainly. Then, as he moved forward into the blue glow from the ceiling of the compartment, she started up with a cry.

"But what has happened?" she demanded. "Where have you been? We waited, José and I, until the last moment, but you did not come as you had promised. We waited. José will tell you how we waited. Tell me what happened."

"I missed the train at Genoa. I had a long drive to catch it up."

"You drove to Bardonecchia! It is not possible!"

"No. To Asti."

There was a silence. They had been speaking in French. Now José gave a short laugh and, sitting back in his corner, began to pick his teeth with his thumbnail.

Josette dropped the cigarette she had been smoking on to the floor and trod on it. "You got on the train at Asti," she remarked lightly, "and you wait until now before you come to see me? It is very polite." She paused and then added slowly: "But you will not keep me waiting like that in Paris, will you, *chéri?*"

He hesitated.

"Will you, *chéri?*" There was an edge to her voice now.

He said: "I'd like to talk to you alone, Josette."

She stared at him. Her face in that dim, ghastly light was expressionless. Then she moved towards the door. "I think," she said, "that it will be better if you have a little talk with José."

"José? What's José got to do with it? You're the person I want to talk to."

"No, *chéri.* You have a little talk with José. I am not very good at business. I do not like it. You understand?"

"Not in the least." He was speaking the truth.

"No? José will explain. I will come back in a minute. You talk to José now, *chéri.*"

"But . . ."

She stepped into the corridor and slid the door to behind her. He went to open it again.

"She will come back," said José; "why don't you sit down and wait?"

Graham sat down slowly. He was puzzled. Still picking his teeth, José glanced across the compartment. "You don't understand, eh?"

"I don't even know what I'm supposed to understand."

José peered at his thumbnail, licked it, and went to work again on an eye tooth. "You like Josette, eh?"

"Of course. But . . ."

"She is very pretty, but she has no sense. She is a woman. She does not understand business. That is why I, her husband, always look after the business. We are partners. Do you understand that?"

"It's simple enough. What about it?"

"I have an interest in Josette. That is all."

Graham considered him for a moment. He was beginning to understand only too well. He said: "Say exactly what you mean, will you?"

With the air of making a decision, José abandoned his teeth and twisted on his seat so that he was facing Graham. "You are a business man, eh?" he said briskly. "You do not expect something for nothing. Very well. I am her manager and I do not give anything for nothing. You want to amuse yourself in Paris, eh? Josette is a very nice girl and very amusing for a gentleman. She is a nice dancer, too. Together we earn at least two thousand francs a week in a nice place. Two thousand francs a week. That is something, eh?"

Memories were flooding into Graham's mind: of the Arab girl, Maria, saying, "She has many lovers"; of Kopeikin saying, "José? He does well for himself"; of Josette herself saying of José that he was jealous of her only when she neglected business for pleasure; of innumerable little phrases and attitudes. "Well?" he said coldly.

José shrugged. "If you are amusing yourself, we cannot earn our two thousand francs a week by dancing. So, you see, we must get it from somewhere else." In the semi-darkness, Graham could see a small smile twist the black line of José's mouth. "Two thousand francs a week. It is reasonable, eh?"

It was the voice of the philosopher of the apes in velvet. *"Mon cher caïd"* was justifying his existence. Graham nodded. "Quite reasonable."

"Then we can settle it now, eh?" José went on briskly. "You are experienced, eh? You know that it is the custom." He grinned and then quoted: *"'Chéri, avant que je t'aime t'oublieras pas mon petit cadeau.'"*

"I see. And who do I pay? You or Josette?"

"You can pay it to Josette if you like, but that would not be very *chic*, eh? I will see you once a week." He leaned forward and patted Graham's knee. "It is serious, eh? You will be a good boy? If you were, for example, to begin now. . . ."

Graham stood up. He was surprised at his own calmness. "I think," he said, "that I should like to give the money to Josette herself."

"You don't trust me, eh?"

"Of course I trust you. Will you find Josette?"

José hesitated, then, with a shrug, got up and went out into the corridor. A moment later he returned with Josette. She was smiling a little nervously.

"You have finished talking to José, *chéri?*"

Graham nodded pleasantly. "Yes. But, as I told you, it was you I really wanted to talk to. I wanted to explain that I shall have to go straight back to England after all."

She stared at him blankly for a moment; then he saw her lips drawing in viciously over her teeth. She turned suddenly on José.

"You dirty Spanish fool!" She almost spat the words at him. "What do you think I keep you for? Your dancing?"

José's eyes glittered dangerously. He slid the door to behind him. "Now," he said, "we will see. You shall not speak to me so or I shall break your teeth."

"Salaud! I shall speak to you as I like." She was standing quite still, but her right hand moved an inch or two. Something glittered faintly. She had slipped the diamanté bracelet she was wearing over her knuckles.

Graham had seen enough violence for one day. He said quickly: "Just a moment. José is not to blame. He explained matters very tactfully and politely. I came, as I said, to tell you that I have to go straight back to England. I was also going to ask you to accept a small present. It was this." He drew out his wallet, produced a tenpound note, and held it near the light.

She glanced at the note and then stared at him sullenly. "Well?"

"José made it clear that two thousand francs was the amount I owed. This note is only worth just over seventeen hundred and fifty. So, I am adding another two hundred and fifty francs." He took the French notes out of his wallet, folded them up in the larger note and held them out.

She snatched them from him. "And what do you expect to get for this?" she demanded spitefully.

"Nothing. It's been pleasant being able to talk to you." He slid the door open. "Good-bye, Josette."

She shrugged her shoulders, stuffed the money into the pocket of her fur coat and sat down again in her corner. "Good-bye. It is not my fault if you are stupid."

José laughed. "If you should think of changing your mind, Monsieur," he began mincingly, "we . . ."

Graham shut the door and walked away along the corridor. His one desire was to get back to his own compartment. He did not notice Mathis until he had almost bumped into him.

The Frenchman drew back to let him pass. Then, with a gasp, he leaned forward.

"Monsieur Graham! Is it possible?"

"I was looking for you," said Graham.

"My dear friend. I am so glad. I was wondering. . . . I was afraid. . . ."

"I caught the train at Asti." He pulled the revolver from his pocket. "I wanted to return this to you with my thanks. I'm afraid that I haven't had time to clean it. It has been fired twice."

"Twice!" Mathis's eyes widened. "You killed them both?"

"One of them. The other died in a road accident."

"A road accident!" Mathis chuckled. "That is a new way to kill them!" He looked at the revolver affectionately. "Perhaps I will not clean it. Perhaps I will keep it as it is as a souvenir." He glanced up. "It was all right, that message I delivered?"

"Quite all right, and thank you again." He hesitated. "There's no restaurant car on the train. I have some sandwiches in my compartment. If you and your wife would like to join me. . . ."

"You are kind, but no thank you. We get off at Aix. It will not be long now. My family lives there. It will be strange to see them after so long. They . . ."

The door of the compartment behind him opened and Madame Mathis peered into the corridor. "Ah, there you are!" She recognised Graham and nodded disapprovingly.

"What is it, chérie?"

"The window. You open it, and go out to smoke. I am left to freeze."

"Then you may shut it, chérie."

"Imbecile! It is too stiff."

Mathis sighed wearily and held out his hand. "Good-bye, my friend. I shall be discreet. You may depend upon it."

"Discreet?" demanded Madame Mathis suspiciously. "What is there to be discreet about?"

"Ah, you may ask!" He winked at Graham. "Monsieur and I have made a plot to blow up the Bank of France, seize the Chamber of Deputies, shoot the two hundred families and set up a Communist government."

She looked round apprehensively. "You should not say such things, even for a joke."

"A joke!" He scowled at her malevolently. "You will see if it is a joke or not when we drag these capitalist reptiles from their great houses and cut them to pieces with machine-guns."

"Robert! If someone should hear you say such things . . ."

"Let them hear!"

"I only asked you to shut the window, Robert. If it had not been so stiff I would have done it myself. I . . ."

The door closed behind them.

Graham stood for a moment looking out of the window at the distant searchlights: grey smudges moving restlessly among the clouds low down on the horizon. It was not, he reflected, unlike the skyline that he could see from his bedroom window when there were German planes about over the North Sea.

He turned and made his way back to his beer and sandwiches.